KU-287-744

CONDENSED BOOKS

With the exception of actual personages identified
as such, the characters and incidents in the fictional
selections in this volume are entirely the product of
the authors' imaginations and have no relation
to any person or event in real life.

THE READER'S DIGEST ASSOCIATION LIMITED
Berkeley Square House, London W1X 6AB

THE READER'S DIGEST ASSOCIATION
SOUTH AFRICA (PTY) LTD
Reader's Digest House, 130 Strand Street, Cape Town

Printed by BPCC Petty Ltd, Leeds
Bound by BPCC Hazell Books Ltd, Aylesbury

Original cover design by Jeffery Matthews FSIAD

For information as to ownership
of copyright in the material in this book see last page

CONDENSED BOOKS

DEATH ROLL
Sam Llewellyn

MICHAEL JOSEPH

THE EVENING NEWS
Arthur Hailey

DOUBLEDAY UK IN ASSOCIATION WITH SOUVENIR PRESS

THE FLIGHT OF THE SWAN
Elizabeth Webster

SOUVENIR PRESS

TIEBREAKER
Jack M. Bickham

ROBERT HALE

CONTENTS

DEATH ROLL

Sam Llewellyn

Martin Devereux has two loves: yacht racing, and the boatyard he runs with his elderly partner Henry. But someone is out to get him.

While mysterious accidents threaten his business Martin finds he is no longer in demand as a helmsman, and when Henry disappears his fears deepen. It takes a voyage to the Mediterranean to open Martin's eyes to a world of corruption where innocent lives are forfeit. Fighting to stay afloat in more ways than one, Martin must trust no one and risk all.

THE EVENING NEWS

Arthur Hailey

From the bestselling author of *Airport* and *Strong Medicine* comes this explosive novel set in the high-powered world of television news.

Here are the front-line men and women who risk their lives to film a story; the executives who mastermind the broadcasts; the celebrated CBA newsreader Crawford Sloane and top correspondent Harry Partridge. These two men pride themselves on their impartial reporting, until the day they are forced to take starring roles in their own desperate drama.

THE FLIGHT OF THE SWAN

Elizabeth Webster

For Laurie Collins, life's promises have turned sour. The charming man she married nine years ago is now a drunk and a frustrated failure. She and the family live in fear of his violent rages.

Then one day Laurie sees three dazzling white swans flying overhead. She suddenly remembers that beyond the mean London street where she lives, there is a world of nature, of beauty, of freedom. And she knows that she must find it, for herself and for her two small children.

page 267

TIEBREAKER

Jack M. Bickham

Danisa Lechova is the shining young star of Yugoslav tennis, dedicated, brilliant, and tirelessly trained by her devoted coach. But this beautiful girl is a wavering citizen of the Eastern bloc, wanted by both the KGB and the CIA, and jealously guarded by her ambitious family.

When American tennis champion and part-time agent Brad Smith is sent to Belgrade to help Danisa defect, he finds himself in very deep water. Not least because he's falling in love with his blue-eyed assignment . . .

page 391

DEATH ROLL

A CONDENSATION OF THE BOOK BY

Sam Llewellyn

TITLE PAGE BY GEOFF HUNT
STORY ILLUSTRATIONS BY ROGER TOWERS

My heart walloped in my chest. I turned, and saw four eyes. Two of them belonged to the stocky, grey-haired man who was standing on the end of the jetty. The other two were in the end of the barrels of the twelve-bore shotgun he was pointing at my face . . .

This was the unexpected welcome which greeted Martin Devereux when he returned, after a disastrous America's Cup trial in Australia, to what he hoped would be the peace and quiet of his English boatyard.

For Martin it is the shock start to an accelerating roller coaster of violence and terror that sweeps him away from his home and business, down to the corrupt, moneyed coasts and criminals of the Costa del Crime.

1

The voice in my ear shouted, 'Tack now!'

It sounded thin and tinny, because it was coming two thousand vertical feet to the VHF receiver in the pocket of my shorts.

'Wait,' I said into the throat mike that left my hands free for the yacht's leather-covered wheel.

Silence fell, except for the rattle of the helicopter carrying Geoffrey Lampson, our sailing coach, in the blue Australian sky above, and the whoosh and plunge of the big aluminium hull. I enjoyed it. There are few silences when you are working up a twelve-metre to the point where it's good enough to sail in the elimination races for the America's Cup.

Astern and to starboard, across two hundred feet of glittering blue sea, the claret-red bow of our sister ship *Castor* sliced into a blue wave and kicked water back at her foredeckman, wrestling the head of a sail into the groove of the forestay. The foredeckman was called Bill Rogers and the sun was glinting off the sweat on his face. He did not look well; before the race he had told me he had flu. But the men who run the Constellation Challenge do not see flu as a reason for staying ashore.

'Wait,' I said again. I could feel the tension coming off the men; ten of them, sweating under the Sydney sun in the aluminium hull. A twelve-metre is not the ballerina of the sea that yachting journalists would like you to believe: it has more in common with a tank, twenty-five tons of metal, hugely overpowered, built for battle. I squinted up into the bright sky. The helicopter was flying backwards. Geoffrey Lampson would be red with fury, because far below on the wrinkled shield of the water the pawns were not doing as they were told.

'*Pollux*,' squawked Lampson in my ear. 'Tack now!'

I looked astern. *Castor*'s foredeck was a billowing mass of sail. Bill Rogers was battering it down. He looked sluggish, off balance. *Now*.

'Go!' I said, and spun the wheel.

Pollux's nose turned through the wind. The aluminium boom clanked across, the genoa slid smoothly round the front of the mast, and a spatter of spray sailed aft as she leaned again, to starboard this time, and shot across *Castor*'s bows. Rogers flung himself flat on the deck as *Castor* turned after us and her genoa swept across the foredeck above him.

'Good,' squawked Lampson, claiming the credit for my timing. 'Worked very well, Martin. Keep her on that tack.'

I was sweating with heat, tension and anger at the chittering from the mechanical insect hovering above me. 'Tack again,' I said.

The winches jingled and we were back on starboard.

The gap of water between the boats was three hundred feet now. Paul Welsh, *Castor*'s helmsman, was shouting. He sounded nervous, which was fine. We had won the start, and now, inch by inch, we were moving away.

Castor and *Pollux* were owned by the Constellation Challenge. For six weeks we had been practising against each other, out here in the blue Tasman Sea. And for six weeks, I had been getting more and more depressed. To put together a challenge for the America's Cup you need a lot of money, managers who know how to organise a couple of boats, and people who sail the boats fast. In a good syndicate, making the boat go is the object of the exercise, and there will be no nasty tricks.

But the Constellation Challenge was being run by Lord Honiton, a pillar of the very exclusive Pall Mall Yacht Club. Honiton ran an international management consultancy and a medium-sized property empire, and nasty tricks were as essential to him as oxygen. He had appointed Geoffrey Lampson as coach, and Lampson had gone out and hired the crews. I had been doubtful about joining up, but invitations to helm a potential Cup challenger do not land on the mat every day. I had been regretting my decision ever since.

In the boat astern, Paul Welsh was squinting up at his sails. He was going to have a try at tacking away.

'Tacking,' I said, and wound the big leather-bound wheel.

We tacked simultaneously. I saw Paul's black eyebrows meet in a scowl. We were old adversaries, and he hated losing—particularly to me.

A puff of wind got under the sail stacked on *Castor*'s foredeck. It jumped and billowed. Paul shouted, 'Kill that,' his voice raw and angry.

Bill Rogers went up to the deck after it. I could see that he was groggy, travelling at half speed.

'Tacking!' shouted Paul.

Myself, I would have waited till Bill had done his stuff. But Paul was completely ruthless when it came to winning. The foot of her genoa swept across the foredeck. Bill just stared, not even beginning to move. The sail caught him flat in the stomach and swept him into the sea.

'Man overboard!' I yelled at Paul.

But the towering pyramid of *Castor*'s sailcloth came on. Paul must have assumed that Bill had dropped flat and let the sail go over his back.

'Nobody heard,' said someone.

The pursuit boats were a good half-mile astern. The sea off Sydney is very big, and there are sharks in it.

'Let's go,' I said. 'Go about, quick!'

The deck surged under my feet as I wound the wheel hard over. We went round with a flap and roar of sails, and our foredeckman said, 'I see him!' I caught a glimpse of a black head bobbing on the crest of a wave.

Then I heard the hail. I turned. What I saw was Paul's bow, a sharp red blade tearing down an ink-blue slope of water, straight at *Pollux*'s mid-section. I spun the wheel. The gibbering in my ear was climbing the octave. Lampson was screaming about the rules of racing, which forbade me tacking across an opponent's bow unless I had clear water. But when a man has fallen overboard, race rules yield to common sense.

I roared again, 'Man overboard!'

Castor's bow came on. *Pollux* was turning hard, but even so the sharp claret-coloured bow caught her on her transom stern with a crunch and a clang. The deck lurched under my feet, flinging me onto the mainsheet-man. The yachts wallowed together, *Castor*'s nose buried in *Pollux*'s tail. Metal grated on metal with a long, wrenching groan. For a second I thought: It's all right, it's not the rudder, it's not a vital spot.

Then I saw the runner, the rigging that runs from close to the boat's stern to halfway up the mast. It has a big block at its bottom which you use to tension the runner and support the mast. The stay is under four tons of load. As *Castor*'s bow wrenched out of the gash it had cleft in our stern, the block moved.

I shouted, 'Look out!' just as the block tore out of its mounting. Something walloped my right forearm, hard. The mast, unflexing, flung the block at the sky like bait on the end of a fishing line. Then the middle of the mast flexed forwards. I heard a voice shouting about easing sheets, taking the genoa's load off the mast, and realised it was my own.

Too late. There was a heavy *crack*, and the top fifty feet of the mast bulged forward and collapsed. Sails tore and our hull became heavy and sluggish in the water. Shouting started. There was a big pain in my right forearm. I found I was bending forward over it. I wanted to put my head on the cool metal deck, but I could see Bill in the blue water thirty feet downwind. He was jerking his head around nervously, looking for sharks. With my good hand I yanked a horseshoe life belt out of a recess in the deck and tossed it at him. I did not see if he caught it. The pain in my arm was growing. The radio was screaming in my ear. I yelled, 'Shut up,' and tossed the whole rig clumsily overboard. Four crewmen were helping Bill up over the side. They were having an easy job of it, because *Pollux*'s freeboard had become, very low. I thought with a jolt, She's sinking.

Castor came alongside. My crew scrambled over. I waited till last, partly because that is what captains are supposed to do, but also because by now I was having trouble moving. My right hand was hurting so much that I needed my left to hold it still. So they leaned over and grabbed the back of my shirt and dragged me aboard. Paul Welsh was looking at me, his tanned forehead creased over his movie star's nose.

'What the *hell*, Martin?' he said. 'You tacked in my water. You didn't have to do that. The pursuit boat would have picked him up.'

He was establishing his alibi, but my arm hurt too much for me to argue. I held it tenderly and looked overboard at *Pollux*.

One of the pursuit boats was coming to take her in tow. But I could tell from the way the white bubbles splattered out of the jagged hole in her back end that it was going to be too late. Soon she would slide away like a porpoise into the deep, and half a million pounds' worth of boat would fall slowly towards the bottom of the Tasman Sea.

THE HOSPITAL WAS CLEAN and cool, full of little palm trees and reporters shouting questions about sunk boats, and was this another of Martin Devereux's displays of aggression? I kept my mouth shut in case I threw up all over them. They clustered round the door of the room where the doctor was. The doctor shut it in their faces and did nasty things under bright lights. Then he told me I was very lucky. Something had hit my radius and ulna a hell of a whack, three inches above the wrist; both bones were broken, but the wrist joint was unaffected. I looked at the plaster and the fingers sticking out of the end, numb with local anaesthetic, and said yes. I did not feel very lucky. All I wanted to do was go home and lie down until my arm had lost its sense of outrage.

The Constellation Challenge looked after its helmsmen well, believing (as Honiton put it) in separating the officers from the ratings. It had rented me an apartment in the top back of a big wooden house in Rushcutters Bay, with a big window in the living room, and a balcony. The glass was cool on my forehead. The view was of blue water and bluish gum trees, with heavy suburban houses crouching in the greenery.

12

But I was tired of its foreignness. I wanted to see the grey sky of Marshcote, my home on the south coast of England. Back there the pubs would be noisy, full of the smell of salt and wet jerseys and smoke. My business partner Henry and his wife Mary would be stumping round the boatyard, swearing at the rain which would undoubtedly be drifting across the marshes and pocking the water in the marina basin.

But this was Sydney, and there was going to be hell to pay.

I went into the bathroom and glowered at myself in the mirror. I have got a big, roundish face, blue eyes and a large nose. My chin sticks out, which is part of the reason people think I am aggressive. My hair is fairish brown, and needed cutting. The sun had got at my nose, which was peeling. Otherwise, I was greenish-grey. By no means a pretty picture.

I struggled out of my clothes and into the shower, holding my plaster up and out of the water, which helped the throbbing, but not much. Then I got dry and went into the bedroom and lay down on the bed. After a bit, the arm grew so bad that I ate the hospital painkillers and became drowsy. The telephone rang by the bed. The voice at the other end did not bother with hellos. 'Devereux,' it said, 'where were you?'

'I've been to hospital,' I said. 'I've broken my arm.'

'Ah,' said Honiton. 'Sorry to hear that.' His voice was warm as Alaska. 'Have you got a minute? We want to debrief.'

'I'm on my way,' I said, and hung up.

I got a taxi. The Challenge office was tacked onto the sheds by the inner harbour. It contained two palm trees, three desks, six telephones, and this evening it also contained some powerful people.

There was Geoffrey Lampson, his heavy red jowls hanging over his white collar. There was Georgie Honiton, tanned and spruce in a blazer, smiling his urbane smile as he chatted with plump Mr Morton from the Constellation Bank, the Challenge's main sponsors. And there was Paul, who had brought two trimmers and a tactician. They all sailed with him when he was match racing, and presumably came in for a share of his prize money, so he could count on their loyalty. I began to feel uneasy.

Paul grinned at me. I grinned back, shoving the ugly banging in my arm to the back of my mind. He had very little to grin about. The ramming had been his fault.

'Patched you up, eh?' said Honiton, his eyes on my cast. 'So we're all here,' he went on. 'Good evening, everyone. Perhaps you'd like to start, Geoffrey?'

Lampson's thick red hands lay like cuts of meat on the desk. 'All right,' he said. 'Martin, sorry you hurt yourself. But I might as well tell you straight. I was giving you instructions from the chopper. You ignored them. You tacked slap across Paul's bow.'

'In order to pick up Bill Rogers. He'd gone overboard.' I kept my voice calm and level.

'We know,' said Geoffrey, breathing heavily. 'We have eyes. There were support boats. They would have pulled him out.' His voice was gaining momentum. 'But instead, you put your boat about a length in front of Paul—'

'Four lengths,' I said. 'Easily.'

'That is not what Paul says,' said Geoffrey. 'That's not what I saw.' I stared at him. He was lying. Why?

The explanation swam up through the painkillers. A helmsman with a broken arm was out of action for at least a fortnight. And if that helmsman was reckoned by Honiton to be dangerously independent, who better to parade in front of the sponsors as the man who had sunk their investment?

I said, 'You know damned well that is not true. The pursuit boats were half a mile astern. There are sharks in that sea. Paul didn't alter course, so it was a fair assumption he hadn't seen Bill. I was obliged to go back for him, and Paul was obliged to keep clear of me.'

Honiton's jaw thrust forward. 'Paul maintains that you tacked in his water immediately before the collision.'

'I'm afraid the guys in the crew will back me up,' said Paul, with a boyish flash of his white teeth.

'Not Bill,' I said.

'Ah,' said Paul. 'But he was overboard, wasn't he?'

I looked at him, and at Geoffrey and Honiton, and knew there was nothing else I could say. They had put the dotted line round my neck, and written CUT HERE.

I said, 'You left Bill for the support boat because you were well behind, and I was slowing down for him. And when you saw you could foul me too, you came in to ram. You sank *Pollux*, and now you're trying to stick me with it.' There was a deep, deadly silence.

'I think you'd better withdraw that,' said Honiton.

I felt sick. 'That's enough of this rubbish. I am resigning, as of now.'

Their faces became stiff—not with surprise, I realised; they were holding their breath, hoping I would not unsay what I had just said and make them do their own dirty work.

Honiton said, 'You are not behaving very well, Martin. In fact, I shall make it my business to tell those whose job it is to know, how you have conducted yourself.'

'I may get over it,' I said. Then I walked out of the room through the reporters yelling questions, and put my throbbing arm into a taxi. I was going home. To England.

14

NEXT DAY, ON THE MORNING PLANE to London, the stewardess brought the papers round. The front page of the *Sydney Herald* summed it up neatly. DEV SINKS BOAT, BREAKS ARM, WALKS OUT, it said. The story was full of conventional regrets from Honiton. It would have been full of quotes from me, too, if I had spoken to anybody last night.

Instead, it gave a quick and mostly accurate résumé of my life. It pointed out that I was among the top sixteen match racers in the world, and among the three most outspoken. It wondered whether what it called my notorious propensity for plain speaking had led to my resignation.

I threw the paper away, eased my bad arm in its sling, and looked out of the window at the coast of New South Wales, down there in the April dawn.

It looked as if Martin Devereux had better settle down to being a junior partner in the South Creek Boatyard, and forget about match racing for a year or so. I pulled Mary's week-old letter out of my briefcase, and read it for the tenth time.

Hope it's all going well, the letter said. *We've been having non-stop gales, as you can imagine*. I could. I had grown up with Mary and Henry, in their red-brick house by the harbour where the wind howled across the marshes. *Henry is working too hard. Everybody wants fitting-out and they all want it done by Easter, and Henry's damned if he's going to let any of them down*. I could imagine that, too. Henry was strongly attached to the notion that a gentleman's word is his bond.

Actually, I'm getting worried about the old chap. We're losing a lot of customers, and I'm afraid it's because he's getting too old for it. There was a terrible pile-up this last gale, two boats written off. The insurance premiums are up through the roof. I folded the letter and shoved it back into the briefcase. Henry was getting old, all right; he was seventy-one. I took one of the hospital's painkillers, and settled back. By the sound of things, there was going to be much to do at South Creek and very little time for match racing.

2

Twenty-six hours after take-off from Sydney, I got off at Marshcote Junction, at 5.12 am. The station yard was dark and wet with a thin rain that tasted of the sea. My arm was aching and my jet lag was screaming for coffee, but there was no coffee in Marshcote at five in the morning. There were no taxis either. I hoisted my bag onto my good shoulder and walked through the soaking streets towards the creek.

South Creek Boats is a mile and a half to the southeast of Marshcote.

Down to the bank of the creek, turn left, and follow the track over three rickety wooden bridges across gullies in the marshes. The wind slammed rain into my face but as I slogged across the flats I was grinning, because I was nearly home.

The sky was grey now, and over to the right was the long, dark rampart of the sea wall. Ahead, silhouetted against the dawn, was a huddle of buildings, with beyond them a clump of masts. South Creek.

There are few trees in Marshcote, and most of them are at South Creek. It also possesses the highest ground for miles, in the form of a bank of gravel which rises some twenty feet above the marshes. Some time in the seventeenth century someone built a red-brick house on the rise. Then at the turn of this century an enterprising ship repairer bought a steam dredger and deepened the natural basin where South Creek entered the sea. Henry MacFarlane had bought the house on his return from the war, and in 1948 had built three long, low, corrugated-iron sheds beside the basin.

As I leaned into the wind for the last quarter-mile, I got a sudden whiff of diesel exhaust. Straining my eyes into the murk, I saw a car, a boxy four-wheel-drive affair, heading slowly back down the road that ran along the causeway towards Marshcote. Five minutes later I was in the car park by the side of the basin where eighty people kept their yachts at pontoons Henry had laid. Overhead, a couple of herring gulls whipped sideways through the wind. At the pontoons in the basin, the masts stood in orderly rows.

One of the masts moved.

It was over on the outside jetty, a tall mast, and it carried no sail. There was no sound of an engine. It was gathering speed, sliding behind the other masts, behaving like the mast of a boat adrift.

I dropped my bag and started to run along the jetty.

The mast was moving straight downwind. It belonged to a Moody Grenadier, a fat cruising yacht with a big deckhouse that caught as much wind as a medium-size sail. There were no lights, and nobody on board.

My feet slammed on the duckboards of the pontoon. The Moody was bearing down on a Seadog ketch, moored at the end. There was going to be a crunch that would cost someone a lot of money.

I heaved myself over the Seadog's lifelines and ran along the narrow side-deck. The Moody was ten feet away, and closing fast.

A careful owner had left fenders down the side of the Seadog. I untied a big one clumsily, left-handed, and dangled it over the stern. The Moody hit the fender with the side of its cockpit. The fender squashed like a marshmallow, but did not burst. The Moody hung for a moment, then began to scrape past with a horrible grating sound. I saw a mooring

16

line hanging overboard, grabbed the boat hook out of its clips on the Seadog's coachroof, and twitched the line out of the water. Then I hauled the line in and wrapped it round the Seadog's after mooring cleat.

The mooring line tautened. The Seadog lurched outwards on its warps as the bigger boat tried to tow it into open water. But the Moody stopped, six feet out there in the water off the end of the pontoon, held like a great pendulum by a single line. It looked as if I had saved the Moody's owner an expensive rebuild.

A voice from the jetty said, 'All right, you bastard.'

My heart walloped in my chest. I turned, and saw four eyes. Two of them belonged to the stocky, grey-haired man who was standing on the end of the jetty. The other two were in the end of the barrels of the twelve-bore shotgun he was pointing at my face.

'Good morning,' I said.

'Good Lord,' said Henry MacFarlane, lowering the gun. 'What the hell are you doing here?'

I said, 'Some idiot forgot to tie a boat up.'

Henry's grizzled head moved on his thick neck. His eyes rested on the Moody. 'Lucky you came,' he said.

In the growing light, he looked as if he had been carved from stone. He had always been like that: hard as granite. But there was a sag to the flesh of his jaw that had not been there last time I had seen him.

'Let's put her away,' I said.

'Couple of our boat men'll do that,' he said. 'When they come in to work.'

We made the Moody fast alongside the Seadog. Then we walked back along the jetty and round to the Moody's empty berth. The rings for her mooring lines were empty.

'Didn't break,' said Henry, contemplating the rings. 'Weren't cut. Came untied.'

I said, 'There was a car leaving as I arrived.'

He looked across at me. 'Probably the milkman. Let's get some breakfast.'

The kitchen felt hot as a blast furnace after the raw wind outside. It was a bare room, with six wooden chairs, an enamel-topped table and a catalogue from a firm of winchmakers on the wall. Henry put the tin coffeepot on the Rayburn and said, 'Mary's not up. What the hell have you been doing to your arm?'

It was typical of him that with a hundred and fifty thousand pounds' worth of boat recently adrift in his marina, he should be more interested in my arm. I told him what had happened in Australia.

Then I said, 'Who is coming in here and setting boats adrift?'

'I don't know,' he said. 'I don't know.'

He took a cigarette out of his gunmetal case and lit it. He said, 'I'll take you round later. See what you think.' He got up too quickly and poured out the coffee before it was brewed. I realised that Mary was not the only one who was worried about whether he could cope any more.

He slammed the thick white mug down in front of me and stumped over to the fridge. 'Milk. Where is the blasted stuff?'

'The milkman doesn't come till eight,' said a voice from the door. It was Mary, in a blue dressing gown and sheepskin slippers.

Hugging Mary was like hugging a full-grown oak.

'Jolly nice to see you,' she said. Her face was as weather-beaten as Henry's, her eyes blue and humorous. There were lines round them I did not remember. She got a cup of coffee and sucked down a mouthful, then set about frying some bacon.

We talked about who had done what to whom in the town. I knew Mary better than I knew anyone else in the world. She was a big, determined woman who said exactly what she thought, and had little time for anyone who did not do likewise. Henry nodded and grinned from time to time. But mostly he kept his eyes on his cup.

The South Creek morning started up. Half a dozen men in overalls came in, said good morning, and left. There was Tony Fulton, the yard foreman, a large, indispensable man with an adolescent's grin and huge shoulders. When I was not around he did most of the serious work, and ran the yard's charter fleet of eight 25-foot cruising yachts. Then there was Dick Hammer, small and dark, who was in charge of the moorings; the mechanic, the fitter, and a couple of dogsbodies. When Henry told him the Moody had gone adrift, Hammer went out to check the lines.

'Come on,' said Henry, when he had eaten. 'Let's go and look round.'

We trudged round the fuel dock, the sheds and the pontoons. Then we walked to the corner of the car park where the chocked yachts stood.

'What's this?' I said.

In the corner, two of the charter boats were lying on their sides, or what was left of their sides. They looked as if they had been attacked with road drills.

'Pretty horrible, eh?' said Henry grimly. 'We'd chocked 'em up for the winter. Storm of wind. They came off their chocks. Down into the water, bump, bump, bump.'

We went to the edge and looked over. There were still bits of Fibreglass among the jagged boulders, like shreds of meat in a lion's teeth.

'Write-offs,' he said. 'Insurance man not pleased.'

It had turned into a grey, dingy morning. The office was full of the smoke of the men's first roll-ups. The telephone was ringing. Henry got

18

involved. I went back to the house. Mary smiled with genuine pleasure when she saw me.

'So,' she said. 'Are you back for long?'

It would not be encouraging to tell her that Honiton was doing his best to blight my sailing career. 'I thought there'd be work to do here.'

'Oh, *yes*,' she said. I could hear the relief in her voice. 'That would be wonderful.'

I said, 'Henry showed me the boats that went over in the gale. You don't often get a northerly that strong.'

'It wasn't a northerly,' said Mary.

'What?' I said. I did not understand. The boats had been on the northern lip of the basin; a southerly would have blown them inland, not into the water.

'The gale,' she said. 'It was blowing from the south.'

Her head went down onto her hands, and tears started to run between her big red fingers.

I had known Mary since she had taken me over when I had been eleven. But I had never seen her cry before. I stood beside her and patted her wide, solid back with my good hand, and felt inadequate. I said, 'What's going on?'

'You know Henry,' she said. 'He won't tell me.'

As senior partner Henry owned the land and took the big decisions. As junior partner I came and went as I pleased, organised the year's work, and helped when racing permitted. It was usually a good arrangement.

'It's all getting out of control,' she said. 'I don't know what the hell he's up to. You know what he's like.'

I knew. Henry believed in fighting his own battles.

'He'd talk to you,' she said. 'Would you try?'

'Of course,' I said.

The door slammed open. 'Come on,' said Henry. 'Let's go and haul the pots, if you're not too disabled.'

'Of course not,' I said. Jet lag and broken limbs must not stand in the way of the central tenet of Henry's life: *the lobster pots must be hauled*.

His square face cracked in a big yellow grin. 'Good boy,' he said. 'Bloody nice to have you back.'

OUT IN THE CREEK, the last of the ebb tugged at the keel of *Hellcat*, Henry's potting boat, as we headed for the deep water of the estuary. We motored in silence, except for the heavy chug of the diesel and the cry of the gulls.

'Bit slow compared to what you're used to,' Henry said.

'Quieter,' I said.

A flock of black-and-white Brent geese planed over the seagrass beds of the mudflats. It was always like this out here, where the sandbars spread white fingers under the pale green water and the waves thundered on the margins of the land. It had been like this the first time I had come here, a few days before my twelfth birthday. My father had died three months previously; my mother had left him long before. Tappamore, our grey Georgian Irish ruin, had succumbed to ivy and creditors. And I had been a small, aggressive boy with a suitcase and a letter addressed to Henry in my father's writing.

Henry had told me about the letter afterwards. They had met in the war, and become friends. My father had formed such an admiration for Henry that he had decided that Henry would be the best person to look after a twelve-year-old, education paid for, pending his entry into the adult world. To pay for my keep there was ten thousand pounds, which Henry had invested in South Creek on my behalf.

The estuary widened on either side. Oystercatchers glided over the beaches. We jinked round the breakers on the end of the bar at the estuary's mouth and were shot by the ebb into the open sea.

Henry's pots were set at the base of the cliffs of Oar Head. I brought the boat up to the yellow buoy with MacF stencilled on it. He caught it on the boat hook, looped the tail-line on the winch, and began to haul.

There were six pots on the first string. They contained no lobsters at all. I rebaited with stinking mackerel, and we moved on to the next buoy.

We caught two lobsters. Baiting one-handed was tricky, and I was getting tired. So I was relieved when the last-but-one pot glimmered from the black depths as I stooped to the bait bin.

'Ah, ye brute!' cried Henry, behind me.

I turned. There was a huge lobster in his hand, waving blue claws the size of a child's boxing gloves.

'Seven pounds if he's an ounce!' said Henry. He snapped elastic bands onto the claws and laid the lobster reverently in the fish box. As he re-shot the pots, he sang *Hearts of Oak*, loudly. When the last one had gone, I brought the bows round.

I knew Henry's moods. This was one of his triumphant phases, in which he would talk. I said, 'Who's been knocking over your boats?'

He gazed up at the sun. 'Sea Horse Land,' he said. 'Property company from London.'

I stared at him. '*What?*'

'Bloke came down a couple of months ago,' said Henry. 'Horrible little creep in a shiny suit. Left me his card. Offered to buy the whole place. I told him to go to hell.' He bent down behind the coaming to light a cigarette from the gunmetal case. 'He rang the next week. I said the same

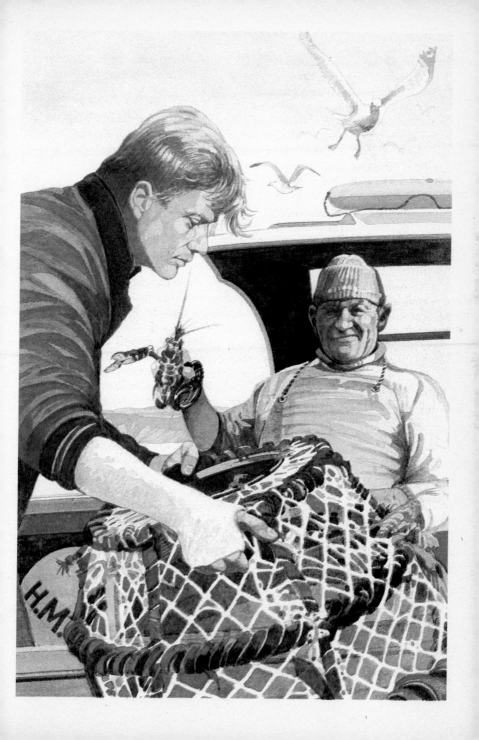

thing. Then he asked about my insurance—wondered if I had enough.'

'I see. But property companies don't go round wrecking businesses.'

'This one does,' said Henry.

'Did you tell the police?'

'Of course I did. I told them I thought those yachts didn't fall, they were pushed. They came and had a look and told me it was maybe the wind.' Smoke veiled his face and whipped across the blue bight of the bay. 'The wind was in the wrong direction.'

I said, 'What are you going to do about it?'

Henry's eye rested on the seven-pound lobster in the box.

'I've got a bit of a scheme,' he said.

'What sort of scheme?'

'A scheme,' said Henry, and I knew that what we had here was a Henry resolved to show the world he was not losing his grip. It was on the tip of my tongue to remind him that I was his partner, and that Mary was his wife. But I knew that unless he was ready to talk, a nudge from the junior partner would only deepen the silence. So I cranked up the throttle a notch and we chugged in silence back to South Creek.

THAT NIGHT I SLEPT in Point House, a small cottage that sits on a grassy knoll in the dunes a mile from South Creek. I had bought it ten years ago for less than the price of a secondhand car. The living room has two pictures of Brent geese on the walls, a flagstone floor, and a wood stove in the corner. It is a place far removed from twelve-metre yachts and the gloss of Sydney.

I woke early, made double-strength coffee, then went outside, fired up my old grey Land-Rover, and drove to the yard. The office was empty. The clock on the wall said 7.40. I sat down at Henry's desk and looked through his address book. There were business cards stuck in next to the names and telephone numbers. The one I was looking for carried a stylised picture of a sailing boat and a palm tree. SEA HORSE LAND, it said. In the bottom left-hand corner, it said *Terence Raistrick*, and a telephone number. There was no address.

I picked up the telephone and dialled a London number. The voice on the other end sounded sleepy.

'Harry?' I said.

'Oh, God,' said the voice. 'What do you want, at this hour?'

Harry Chase and I had been at school together. He was a crime reporter on the *Guardian*. He got preferential holiday rates from South Creek Charter, and we had dinner together in London sometimes.

I told him I wanted to know about Sea Horse Land.

'Never heard of it,' he said. 'Is there a story?'

'Couldn't say, yet.' I read him the telephone number on the card. 'Can you get me an address for that?'

'Car phone.'

'Then how about an owner and an owner's address?'

He groaned. 'Must I?'

'Going boating this summer?'

'Call you later,' he said, and put the phone down.

For the next hour, the phone rang. Mostly it was owners, fussing about their boats. Then at nine o'clock, I picked it up and heard a smooth, confident voice.

'Martin?' it said. 'Jack Archer here. Ringing for the Pulteney Yacht Club.'

'Yes,' I said. Jack Archer was a small, pink man, a director of Padmore and Bayliss, Britain's biggest production boatbuilder. Recently he had got on to the committee of the Pulteney Yacht Club, a smart new outfit seventy miles down the coast. He was clever and ambitious, and I was pretty sure I knew what he wanted.

'The Iceberg Cup,' he said. 'I . . . that is, we at the Club . . . would very much like you to sail.'

The Iceberg Cup was a recent invention, and by no means one of your top match-racing events. In fact, it was distinctly second-rate. I said, 'I'm not sure I'm fit.'

'Broken arm, I heard,' said Archer. Archer heard everything. He would certainly have heard about my row with Honiton.

'What are we sailing?' I said.

'Bayliss 34s,' he said. 'It's on Tuesday week.'

I reflected. Archer was asking a newsworthy, if shaky, skipper to compete in a second-rate event, in boats his company produced. It all added up to publicity for him.

'Seven and a half grand for the winner,' said Archer.

The boatyard could do with seven and a half grand, and I could do with a race to sail. 'All right,' I said. 'Thanks. I'd like to.'

'Great,' said Archer, full of enthusiasm. '*Great.*'

I called Charlie Agutter and asked if he could organise a crew at short notice. Charlie was a friend from the days when we had both sailed in the British Captain's Cup team. Also, he had designed the Bayliss 34, so he would be a useful man to have aboard. Charlie said he could.

As I rang off, Tony stuck his head round the door, looking for Henry. I said, 'Hang about a minute.' He sat down. He was big enough to dwarf his chair.

'Tony,' I said. 'What's going on?'

'You saw them boats,' he said. 'The ones that went over the edge.

23

Then there was the diesel. Somebody let water into the diesel-holding tank. Bloody awful mess, seven hundred gallons spoilt. And there's been a lot of little things. That boat you caught this morning. It's not the first. There was two last week slipped their lines. One of 'em's up on the hard with a hole in its bow.'

'And you reckon someone's doing it?'

His leathery face was impassive. 'We tie good knots, we keep water out of diesel, and we don't bung expensive boats onto the stones for fun.'

That was true. During the five years he had been yard foreman, the yard's efficiency had brought the customers in droves.

'Have you seen anything? Anyone hanging round the yard?'

He shrugged. 'There's a lot of ways in. Short of hiring Securicor, there's not a lot you can do. Particularly when you're Henry's age.'

The office door opened. A thin man with a grey moustache came in. ''Scuse me, gents,' he said. 'Come to look at a Baltic ketch called *Aldebaran*.' He pulled a packet of Rothmans from the pocket of his suede jacket, lit one.

I said, 'What part of *Aldebaran* do you want to look at?'

'The lot,' he said. 'My card.' The card said MATES & BUSHELL—*Surveyors—Sheerness*.

'Who's asked for a survey?' I said.

'Bloke called Paul Welsh,' said the thin man. 'For a client. 'E rung me from Australia.'

I sat there, until I realised that my mouth was hanging open.

'I'll pop into my overalls,' said the surveyor. 'Can you get 'er on the hoist?'

'What the hell has Paul Welsh got to do with this?' I asked.

Tony's wide brown forehead creased with worry. 'You ought to hear it from Henry,' he said. 'I've got to see to the boat.'

I went over to the house to find Henry. He was sitting at the partner's desk in his office. 'A surveyor's come to look at *Aldebaran*,' I said. 'He said Paul Welsh had sent him.'

'Ah,' said Henry. 'Yes. That makes sense.' He rubbed his jaw. 'Look, Martin. We've been very short of money. You know I used to run a sort of brokerage here. Well, Paul Welsh wrote to me six weeks ago, made me an offer for the goodwill. I took it. I knew you wouldn't like it, but we needed the money. So I sold it to him.'

I stood and looked at him. His eyes had a pleading expression that did not belong there. He had done what was best according to his lights.

'Fifty thousand quid,' he said. 'That's what he paid. And if he can sell *Aldebaran* before she falls to bits, that'll be more money. Let's have a look at that surveyor.'

24

It was no good asking him why Paul Welsh would want a brokerage as small as South Creek. Henry was not the kind of man to worry about secret motives. But I was. Paul was rich, but he did not go round laying out fifty thousands in simple charity. There was more to it than that.

I followed Henry along the breakwater to where *Aldebaran*'s rotten white hull hung dripping in the travel hoist. The surveyor was walking round with a bradawl, digging at planks. 'Nice boat,' he said.

Henry gave him the kind of smile he would have given a madman. I returned to the office.

At quarter past twelve, Harry Chase rang.

'Your number,' he said, 'belongs to a company called Sea Horse Land.'

'I know.'

'Registered in the Isle of Man. Directors, a bank manager and a solicitor, the usual. Nothing else traceable. Except an address where the phone company sends the bills. Which is, Twenty-two, Upper Tier, Waterfront, Southampton.'

3

I found Tony sitting in his usual corner in the Burnett Arms, sipping a pint and talking to a crab fisherman.

I said, 'We're off to Southampton.'

'What for?' he said.

'Visiting Sea Horse Land. I want to ask them some questions about people who untie other people's boats and put water in other people's fuel.'

His glass stopped halfway to his lips. 'You sure?' he said.

'I'm not sure about anything,' I said, 'so we'd better start now.'

He stared at me for a moment, then sighed. 'Waste of time,' he said. 'There's a yardful of boats to fit out.'

'We'll take your car,' I said.

We drove more or less in silence to Southampton.

Waterfront was one of those new developments that property developers put up in an attempt to make money by bringing maritime glamour to derelict reaches of Southampton Water. A shopping arcade overlooked a marina gap-toothed with empty berths, and Upper Tier was a gallery of offices that ran round inside the arcade. Number 22 was between a travel agent and a yacht broker. It had a plate-glass front, a model of a marina, and a girl sitting at a green desk. Behind her was a door.

'Can I help you?' she asked. Her voice was American.

'Looking for Mr Raistrick,' I said. 'Of Sea Horse Land.'

'Have you an appointment?' she enquired. She was pretty, with grey-green eyes and short blonde hair.

'No,' I said. 'It concerns South Creek Boatyard.'

The grey-green eyes sharpened suddenly. 'Who shall I say is calling?'

I told her. She pressed a button on her desk, and said, 'Mr Devereux and Mr Fulton of South Creek Boats to see you, Mr Raistrick.'

There was no answer. Somewhere behind the back wall of the office, an outer door slammed. 'I'm sorry,' said the girl, 'Mr Raistrick doesn't appear to be—'

I took two steps forward and pulled the door open. The girl said, 'Hey!' But by that time, I was already in the back office.

The outside walls were all glass. Beyond the glass, a catwalk ran along the outside of the building. There was a door onto the catwalk. It was open, because a dark-haired man had run out, his feet hammering on the steel deck. He turned his head and I caught a glimpse of a white, suety face with a heavy black moustache.

It is not easy to run when you have a heavy cast on your arm. 'Tony!' I yelled. 'Catch him!'

Tony began to run. He was fast. They disappeared down a spiral staircase that dived off the end of the catwalk and into a Victorian shot tower at the corner of the building. I followed them.

Inside the shot tower the spiral staircase descended into shadow. My footsteps rang in the central well. Down below, somebody groaned.

Out in the car park, a starter motor whinnied and rubber squealed. Three turns down the stairway, a dark shape was hanging through the banisters.

I ran down. It was Tony, one side of his pale face covered with blood. He said, 'Little bastard tripped me.' I helped him to his feet and back up the stairs.

The girl was waiting outside, looking shocked and white. We went into the inner office and she brought some water and we cleaned Tony up. He had a ragged cut above his eye. When she went down to the lavatory to empty the bowl, I followed her.

I said, 'I want a home number for Mr Raistrick.'

As we walked back to the office she said, 'He didn't give me his home number. I've only worked here a week.' She wrote a London number on a piece of paper. 'I guess I won't be working here much longer. This is a company Mr Raistrick used to call a lot. I know he took instructions from them. They might be able to help you with your problem. Maybe it would be best if you didn't say I gave you the number.'

I gave her the South Creek number. I said, 'Perhaps you could call if Mr Raistrick comes back.'

26

She smiled. Her colour had returned, and it was an attractive smile, but it did not give anything away.

I fetched Tony from the inner office and we headed back to South Creek. Tony's eye was swelling and he lapsed into sullen silence.

We stopped at a call box and I rang the number the girl had given me. A woman's voice said, 'Marine Investments.'

I said, 'I'd like to speak to one of the directors.'

'What is it concerning?'

I hesitated. If I gave the wrong answer, I would be fobbed off. But there was a right answer. I said, 'I'd like to discuss the sale of the South Creek Boatyard.'

'Who shall I say is calling?' I gave her my name. There was a pause, and then a man's voice came on the line.

'Hello?' it said. 'And what can we do for you, this afternoon?' The voice was rich and plummy.

'Who's that?' I said.

'James,' said the voice. 'Your cousin James.'

I stood there for a moment with my brain whirring. James de Groot was my second cousin, and a director of dozens of companies.

'Well?' he said. 'What do you want?'

I said, 'You have been dealing with an Isle of Man company called Sea Horse Land.'

'Have I?' he said warily.

It was beginning to add up. I said, 'It wouldn't surprise me if it was you who told your friends at Sea Horse Land about a nice bit of beachfront called South Creek, ripe for development. You can tell them from me that it isn't for sale. You can also tell them that there are laws against extortion and damage to private property. I will be giving your name and the name of your friend Terence Raistrick to the police tomorrow.'

'I think you will have difficulty proving these allegations,' said James, 'if that is what they are.'

'I'll manage,' I said. 'Tell your friends.' I put the telephone down, and got back into the car.

I could not face Mary or Henry, so after Tony had dropped me off I drove straight to Point House, walked out onto the flats and watched a chequered flock of Brent geese feeding on the seagrass. Harry Chase occasionally passed on rumours that the Fraud Squad were taking an interest in James, but it was faintly puzzling; the Sea Horse Land campaign against South Creek was more violent than his usual style.

I turned away from the geese, and walked back through the dunes to the house. After this afternoon Cousin James would be going back to good clean fraud. Peace had broken out.

SOMEONE WAS HAMMERING. I opened an eye. There was shouting mixed with the hammering.

'All right!' I yelled, and stumbled out of bed and opened the door.

It was Tony Fulton. There was a long plaster over his eye, and he looked pale and haggard.

'What time is it?' I said.

'Nine. And you'd better come,' he said. 'Henry's gone.'

'Gone?' I said.

'He went out to haul his pots round about six. He came back on the tide, brought the pots home. Mary says he packed a case before he went. I've got to get back. They're going mad down there.'

I pulled on a pair of jeans, a jersey and a pair of Docksiders, fumbling with my bad hand. The sun was up and the marsh smelt green as I walked across the dunes to the house. Mary was in the garden, on her hands and knees, grubbing the year's first grass from between the paving stones with the broken blade of a table knife. She hated weeding, but when things went badly wrong she was subject to sudden orgies of it, as if by tidying up the garden she could tidy up her life.

'Oh,' she said. 'Hello.' She did not look up.

'I hear Henry's gone,' I said.

'That's right.' Her voice was clipped. 'Nothing to worry about. He's done it before.' That was true: this was not the first time he had left me to look after her—not that she needed any looking after.

'It's all right,' I said. 'I've been to talk to some people, there won't be any more accidents. Tony and I can run things.'

She looked up. Her hair was hanging across her face in grey ropes, and her blue eyes had a stunned look. 'It's not the yard,' she said. 'It's him. He's not young any more. He's got a weak heart.'

'He'll be all right,' I said. And because I had cleared things up with James, I was confident I was telling the truth.

IT WAS A HARD WEEK. The Iceberg Cup started on the following Tuesday, and there was no word from Henry. On the Saturday morning, Tony came in. He sat down, rolled himself a cigarette, and fired it up.

'Well?' I said.

'That surveyor,' he said. 'The one who looked at *Aldebaran*. He's turned in a good report.'

'He must be blind,' I said.

'Boat's sold,' said Tony. 'And she's off to the Med as soon as the new owners can fix it. That's what matters.'

I nodded. It was very good news indeed, for Henry and Mary. It was less good news for the purchaser, but that was the surveyor's problem.

'I'll buy us a drink later,' I said.

He grinned at me, then went out, leaving on the table the newspaper he brought up from Marshcote every morning. I turned to the back pages, as usual, to check who had done what in the world of fast boats.

The story was in the top right-hand corner. CONSTELLATION PULLS OUT, it said. The story was simple enough. The burden of it was that Martin Devereux, a helmsman whose aggressive instincts had got the better of his common sense, had sunk half a million pounds' worth of twelve-metre, damaged another and resigned. The sponsors had lost the will to continue, and the syndicate had fallen apart.

I read it twice. That was enough. Then the telephone rang.

'Good morning, good morning,' said Jack Archer's voice on the other end, brisk as a faceful of wave. 'All right for Tuesday? Arm and everything?'

'In plaster, but fine,' I said, and waited: Jack Archer was a busy man, unlikely to waste telephone time enquiring about my health.

'Read the papers?' said Archer. 'Yes. Just thought I'd tell you that we're expanding the numbers of boats racing. OK?'

'Fine,' I said. There was not much else I could say. 'Who else?'

'Jacques LeBreton,' he said. 'And Paul Welsh. He's free, now. And I can also tell you that you are going to be entered for the Marbella.'

'The Marbella,' I said. A Mediterranean race, and one of the best.

'That's right,' said Archer. 'Six weeks away, of course. Honiton's on the committee, but they're inviting you. Plenty of time.'

I took two deep breaths. 'Archer, you are a crafty little devil.'

'I know,' said Archer. 'The sponsors are very pleased. Wonderful needle match, you and Paul. Devereux wrecks Welsh's chances. Not that Welsh had a hope. Everyone's doing a story. Reporters will ring. Make it good, would you?'

'Naturally,' I said, and rang off.

Archer was right about the reporters. The telephones did not stop for the rest of the morning. I told them that I was greatly looking forward to the Iceberg Cup, implied that I loved Paul Welsh like a brother, and made plans to spend a long lunchtime in the Burnett Arms to wash the taste of the lies out of my mouth.

I was on my way to the door when it opened, and Mary came in. She looked better than she had for a week. 'Look at that,' she said, and tossed a postcard on the desk.

It had a picture of a punk with a Mohican haircut. On the other side was the address, a Gatwick postmark, and a message in Henry's neat handwriting: *Off to Spain. Taking pills. All love, H.*

'So he's all right,' she said. 'Silly old fool. Why won't he tell me before he goes? I could do with a bit of sun myself. Goodness, it's a relief.'

I put my arm round her shoulders, happy that Henry had thought to end her worries. But he had told me in the boat that he had got a scheme. That did not sound like a holiday. I had an uneasy feeling that Henry was sending cards just to keep Mary happy. And if that was the case, it was possible I knew less about what was going on than I thought.

4

Pulteney is one of your great British fishing villages, only slightly spoiled by progress. It has a good horseshoe-shaped harbour, with grey stone quays and a lifeboat station. It is a better place to run a boatyard than Marshcote, because the steep streets of little stone houses where the fishermen used to live are now inhabited by rich people who love yachts and gin and tonic. And the warehouses fronting the quay now house not fish and nets, but yacht brokers and chandlers, and Charlie Agutter.

Charlie Agutter was about thirty-five, a thin man with dark hair that stuck out in spikes like a sea urchin's spines. In his time, he had been a very good helmsman. Nowadays, he was a sought-after tactician, and one of the best yacht designers in the world.

I dug him out of his office, and we walked onto the quay. It was early in the year for Pulteney, a grey day, with a force-five westerly knocking off the tops of a dirty-looking sea outside the harbour mouth. The flags on the mast of the Yacht Club stood out stiff as boards.

'We're meeting the rest of the crew in the pub,' he said.

I looked at the Yacht Club with dislike. 'Good,' I said. We went into The Mermaid, at the other end of the quay. Three big men were waiting for us in the bar. The biggest was Scotto Scott, a New Zealander who looked after Charlie's boats. Then there were Noddy and Slicer, mastman and foredeckman respectively. I ordered them lagers, and we chatted. After lunch, I wrapped waterproof tape round my cast and we went down to Spearman's yard. They had the race boats over in the berths on the outer pontoon. Jack Archer was waiting by the boats, pink and dapper in blazer and grey flannel trousers. He came forward and distributed plump, dry handshakes. 'Good to see you. Glad you could come.' He winked. 'Welsh isn't here yet.'

The boats lined up at the pontoon were long and flat and sharp. We let go the lines and motored away from the dock. A TV cameraman filmed us past the breakwater and into the river.

'Nice boat,' I said. Charlie nodded. He had designed the 34 to be fast and agile. The banks of the Poult fell away on either side. The boat

30

heeled and the tiller came alive. I turned off the engine. In sudden silence, we soared into the open sea.

It had all gone now: Cousin James, Paul and Honiton, Henry and his postcard. What was left was the rudder's bite, the lift of the cockpit sole underfoot and the flutter of the telltales. Match races are sailed one against one, in identical boats. In most other forms of racing, skippers can modify their boats to get an edge over the opposition. In match racing, there are no technical advantages. You win if you get your boat going as fast as it will go, so we took the Bayliss, and we worked on it. We did sail changes till Noddy and Slicer poured sweat. We took it out into the big seas and watched what happened when you jammed its nose into a head sea and set its stern to a following sea. We poked and pried and tinkered, took the boat's performance apart, looked at it through a microscope and put it together again. Charlie noted it all down on a clipboard. We came up the river at low water on a dead run, motored in, and spent the next two hours going through Charlie's checklist. When we had finished it was half past five, getting dark. We walked down the breakwaters together, in a clump, talking. Our day had brought the team together, and made us confident, expecting to win.

THEY MADE THE DRAW that night. The heats were sailed all against all, nine races per boat. The four skippers with the highest scores were to go through to the semifinals. We won all our heats but one, when the clew pulled out of the jib. We beat Paul by two minutes, about which he was not happy. We were at the top of the points, and he was equal second.

On Wednesday night there was a bunfight in the Yacht Club, and they drew for which semifinalist would race against which. Archer rummaged in the hat and came up smiling the smile of a fulfilled publicist.

'First semifinal,' he said. 'Welsh against . . . Devereux.'

There was a rustle in the room. Heads ducked to whisper, and two or three reporters sidled away to the telephones. It looked as if the sponsors were going to get their money's worth.

Next morning, the forecast said southwesterlies force five to six. The cobbles of Quay Street were shiny with rain, and the wind dashed it in our faces hard enough to make us squint. It was a lot of wind for match racing. On the quay, we looked up at the Yacht Club's mast for the flag that would mean racing had been abandoned. But there was only the blue ensign and the sponsor's house flag, crackling in the breeze.

The race boats had been brought round from the marina and were moored in rafts of two alongside the quay. As we went down the ladder and into the cockpit, a gust moaned in the shrouds. Two boats down, Paul Welsh was lounging in the back of his cockpit, dressed in dove-grey and white wet gear. The water in the harbour was black and restless.

'Rough,' said Charlie.

'We're off,' I said.

We peeled away from the wall and the sails were up by the time we hit the entrance. A gust whizzed across the water, laying the boat far over. Water came green down the lee deck, and the stanchions trailed white plumes of spray.

Astern, the triangle of Paul's sails moved behind the quays. White spray broke over his bow as he hit the first of the waves outside the harbour. My mouth was dry. I had a cup of tea from the Thermos, but it made no difference.

The VHF yammered. The committee ordered two reefs in the mainsail. We took in the reefs. The boat felt more comfortable now, less inclined to stand on its ear when the gusts came tearing in from the southwest.

Charlie sat huddled over his watch, the red hood of his oilskins hiding his face. 'Two minutes to first gun,' he said.

There are two guns in a match race. The first is eight minutes before the start. It signals that the competitors can enter the start area, the funnel whose mouth is the start line, and that hostilities can commence. Most match races are won or lost at the start. The idea is that by hard manoeuvring you can get ahead of your competitor, and into a position where you can frustrate his intentions all the way round the course.

I watched Paul's white sails dip as a gust caught him. The first gun went. Cautiously, I edged into the starting area. He hung back, waiting, his sails rattling. Getting in among the opposition on a day like this was asking for trouble. So we stayed apart, head-to-wind, the boats pitching in the short, nasty chop.

'Three minutes,' said Charlie.

'Sheets,' I said.

The winches jingled. The sails came in, became hard white wings. The boat picked up speed, bore off the wind onto the right-hand side of the course. We went out in a wide loop, tacked, and came back very fast, heading for the right-hand end of the line.

'He's going left,' said Charlie.

I kept half an eye on Paul. The bow chopped at the waves, the impacts booming in the hollows of the hull. On the starboard bow, the big inflatable buoy marking the right-hand end of the start line bore down.

'Ten,' said Charlie. 'Nine. Eight.'

The buoy was fifty yards away. The boat heeled as a gust battered the sails down at the jumping grey sea.

'One. Zero,' said Charlie.

Over the committee boat, the wind ripped grey smoke from the barrel of the starting gun. The bow smashed a wave to white spume. We hammered out onto the course. Paul was level now, on the other tack.

'He's coming,' said Charlie.

Out of the corner of my eye I could see Paul bearing away, picking up the speed off the wind that would shoot him under our stern and give him the momentum to round up onto our starboard bow. The sound of his passage over the waves was a hard rattle, and white water spewed from his lee rail. He was a long way off the wind, his nose pointing far astern.

'Tacking,' I said quietly.

Our boat heaved on a wave, the boom clacked over, and we were on the port tack. Paul's face was dark with anger. He had gone so far off the wind to build up speed that he had lost ground. Now, we were between him and the windward mark, covering him tight, and there was nothing he could do about it.

We led him up to the windward mark, and rounded the buoy clean as a whistle. On the first downwind leg, he trailed us by a hundred yards of hard grey waves.

'Got him,' said Scotto.

I did not answer. I was concentrating. No race is finished until you get the gun. 'Gybing,' I said, and leaned on the tiller.

We passed the buoy on starboard, and moved up onto the windward leg. 'Leaving him for dead,' said Noddy.

I sailed hard up to the windward mark. Spray lashed back over the deck. He's right, I thought; it's not a race, it's a procession.

Then I saw the patch of weed. It was long, and it stretched fifty yards from side to side, a slab of water where the ripples were smoothed to an oily gloss. My arm moved before my mind gave it conscious orders, heaving the tiller towards me. But by that time we were in the middle of the patch.

Charlie said, 'Boatspeed's down.'

The boat felt sluggish in the water. When I glanced over my shoulder, I could see Paul's bow, growing. 'Weed on the rudder,' I said.

We did everything we could think of. We sailed backwards, prodded with oars and boat hooks. The weed stayed put. We trailed in a full five minutes after Paul.

Scotto went overboard into the freezing water, and pulled handfuls of slim brown fronds off the rudder. We drank tea, and I watched Paul. Two more races, I thought. Two more races, and I can win both of them.

But there was something wrong. I told myself the weed had been mere bad luck; but there was a bad, sick feeling in my stomach. Paul had the South Creek brokerage, and he had the luck.

For the second race we reached out beyond the left-hand end of the line. We were clear of weed, going well, and I was plotting the track that would get us a start where the puffs were now coming that would lift us onto the windward mark.

Charlie said, 'One minute.'

We hard-tacked from one reach onto the opposite reach, 180 degrees. The boom came over with a bang. Now the forestay was lined up on the left-hand buoy of the start line, and beyond it, Paul Welsh. We were hurtling together, us on port tack, Paul on starboard, parallel with the line. The spray came down the deck like buckets of pebbles.

'Gun,' said Charlie.

There was too much wind to hear the gun's thump. The buoy whipped past to port. I kept waiting for the calm to come, the icy lens that would make everything clear, so I knew what the other man was going to do before he did it.

It did not come.

'I'm going down to starboard,' I said. We had to bear off downwind, accelerate, tack onto his tail. Water came across the deck, splattered my face. I could hear the *boom* of Paul's hull as it bounced onto a wave.

'Now.'

I pulled the tiller. The nose swung downwind. Paul was coming level now. As we went down, I saw his boom coming in at eye level. I hauled the tiller. But my boat came upright on the front of a wave. We were in the trough, and he was on the crest. The alloy tube of his boom whacked into the taut wire of our port shroud. He began to shout. He had a right to. He had been the right-of-way boat. I had collided with him.

They were all shouting now. Our shroud slid down to the end of the boom. I set my teeth, and pressed my broken arm against my chest, waiting for the crash. It did not come. Instead Paul's boat was away, sliding astern. Sweat was running down my body. I looked up.

The shroud should have been a tight line from the masthead, over the tip of the spreader, and into the chainplate. Instead, it had a slack curve that flopped in the wind.

'It's off the spreader!' yelled Noddy.

'Screw that,' said Scotto.

Below, the VHF said, 'Protest upheld. Devereux disqualified. Second race to Welsh.'

'Now he tells us,' I said. And we began to clear up the mess.

BACK IN THE HARBOUR Paul was on the quay, flashing his teeth and looking cool and dashing. He had a right to. I had gone out for the second race nervous as a kitten, expecting to be attacked. I had got what

34

I had expected, and reacted too fast, and it had lost us the semifinal.

I dodged the journalists, went back to Charlie's house and had a shower. There was a reception in the Yacht Club. I was strongly inclined not to go. We sat in his living room sipping whisky. He said, 'You'd better go and be a diplomat, Devereux.'

I was about to argue. But there is no sense in arguing when you know the other man is right.

At the Yacht Club a public-relations man was talking into a microphone. But I was not looking at him, I was looking at a girl with dark eyebrows and short blonde hair. The girl who had sat behind the receptionist's desk in the office in the Waterfront building. And she was looking at me.

I started to elbow through the crowd. The speaker was praising the sporting spirit. The girl's eyes were grey-green. She said, 'I hoped you would be here. I'll meet you outside.'

Outside, beams of late sun were gilding the puddles in the worn granite of the quay. She was wearing a white silk shirt and a tailored jacket with brass buttons and an RNLI badge on her lapel. She looked very proper. We stepped over the mooring lines of a couple of trawlers and in at the door of The Mermaid.

I bought drinks. We sat down. I said, 'I didn't expect to meet you again. What's your name?'

She said, 'Helen Gallagher. I came looking for you. I wanted to ask you some questions.'

'Go ahead.'

'Why did you come to Southampton?' she asked.

'Because your Mr Raistrick had made an offer for South Creek, a boatyard in which I have a share,' I said. 'And when we refused it, accidents started to happen. But then I called the number you gave me, and I've stopped the trouble.'

Her grey-green eyes were sceptical. She said, 'How much do you know about Sea Horse Land?'

There was something about this woman that did not add up. I had very little reason to trust her, but it was difficult not to. I said, 'I know the guy who runs the company whose number you gave me. He likes to make money, but he doesn't want to go to jail. I've spoken to him. He's stopped.'

She nodded, finished her drink, and stood up.

'Is that all?' I said.

'That's all. I'll go back by myself, OK?'

I drank another half-pint. Our interview had left a peculiar taste in my mouth. She had come all the way to Pulteney simply to ask me a couple of not very important questions. I was pretty sure that she had not been interested in the facts about Sea Horse Land, but in finding out what I knew. I had the distinct impression that I was being checked up on.

5

The feeling of curiosity was still with me when I woke the next morning. I went straight down to the office and rang James. He did not sound pleased to hear me.

'I want to know your exact relationship with Sea Horse Land,' I said.

'Mind your own damn business,' he said. He paused. 'Sea Horse is finished,' he went on. 'It got out of control. There may still be a certain amount of activity in Spain, but I really couldn't say.'

I said, 'Where's Raistrick?'

He said, 'I have no idea.' I could believe that. 'And if I were you, I shouldn't go asking a lot of stupid questions.'

I said, 'I need to know what's left of Sea Horse Land in Spain. Names and addresses.'

He cleared his throat. 'Don't know any,' he said.

I said, 'You know my friend Harry Chase, the journalist. Do you want him to start asking?'

'He can ask,' said James. 'But I can't tell him what I don't know.'

I said, 'Wait and see,' and hung up, and stared at the chart of the basin drawing-pinned to the wall. If James was not knuckling under to threats of journalists, either he had nothing to tell, or he was very frightened.

Whichever was the case, Henry was in Spain, and on his own. And so, here in England, was Mary, who had looked after me from the age of twelve. Now she needed looking after herself. I decided not to go out to Point House. I'd lunch with her and stay the night.

Paul won the Iceberg Trophy that day. When Charlie Agutter rang me with the news I told him to pass on my congratulations. There was still the Marbella Cup.

That night, I lay in the familiar night sounds of South Creek and dozed. Outside the wind was blowing, the sea thundering on the beach beyond the sea wall.

Suddenly I was fully awake. My room was immediately over Henry's office. Above the racket outside, I could hear another noise, a cautious slithering and knocking that came up through the floor and into the bedroom.

I swung my feet out of bed onto the cold floorboards and pulled on my trousers and a jersey. Then I opened the door and started downstairs.

36

There was a faint stripe of yellow coming from under Henry's study door.

I was halfway down the stairs. My right foot came down, feeling its way along the skirting board to the next step, close to the wall to prevent the creak. Slowly, I shifted my weight.

The stair creaked like a full-rigged ship taking a squall. The light in the office went out.

I covered the rest of the stairs in one jump, twisted the door handle and barged in. I got a fleeting impression of black, with a square of lighter grey which was the window. Then something collided with my head, and my ears rang as I crashed down into a pile of box files.

A shape crossed to the window: wide shoulders, a thick body struggling with the sash. I came to my feet just as the man at the window got the sash up. He lurched outwards and there was a distinct crackle as he fell into the flowerbed. I went after him feet first, and landed on something that must have been a body, because it grunted and rolled away. The blood was pounding in my ears. I could see him now, a dark, bulky shape crawling out of a tangle of vegetation.

'Stop right there,' I yelled. 'You're nicked.' He did not stop. I lowered my head and went in at him. We grappled for a moment against the wall of the house, and I tried to get my foot behind his ankles to throw him. But his body was wide and thick, and the plaster cast made it impossible to lock my hands behind him. He wrenched free, caught hold of my cast and slammed it against the corner of the wall.

My stomach heaved, and the thudding in my ears became a roaring. There was something wrong with my knees. I sank down onto the wet grass and folded over my arm.

From above, Mary's voice said, 'Who's that?' and a light came on.

The man's footsteps thumped across the lawn. I tried to go after him, but my knees were still not working and by the time I was at the low brick wall that separated the garden from the yard, a starter was whinnying out in the car park. I watched the headlights as the wheels juddered across the grit and settled for the road inland. It had a high, boxy silhouette. It was too far away for me to see the number plate. The exhaust smelt of diesel.

I staggered back into the house, hugging my right arm to my body as if it was a baby.

Mary said, 'What the hell's going on?'

'Burglars,' I said. She looked pale, still half-asleep. 'I don't think they got anything. Ring the police. Tell them it's a four-wheel-drive car, Toyota Land Cruiser type.'

The study floor was knee-deep in papers and box files. Mary pawed at them, not knowing where to start, and I stood and looked at the open window and thought of overweight burglars who would have the instinct to try to smash the plaster cast of a man with a broken arm. Suddenly my stomach heaved. I went into the garden and was sick.

The policemen came. There was Sergeant Hone from Marshcote, and three CID men from Exeter. They had not picked up the car. It could be anywhere by now, they said, being as how it was four-wheel drive.

I nodded, and thought of the high, boxy car with the diesel exhaust I had seen leaving the morning I had arrived from Australia. They asked if anything was missing, and Mary told him their guess was as good as hers. Then I described the man, which was no help.

When the police had gone, Mary said, 'It seems odd. Somebody comes in the dead of night, rummages about, doesn't pinch anything.'

It was light, now. I went out to the office to sign some letters. When Tony Fulton arrived for his Saturday morning in the yard, I called him in. 'We need a man on the gate,' I said. 'All night. Every night.'

He stared at me.

'With a radio,' I said. 'I'll have the other end in Point House.'

'They won't like it,' he said.

'They'll have to put up with it,' I said.

Tony shrugged his enormous shoulders. 'If you say so,' he said.

I worked until the sun was a big orange ball dropping behind the masts in the basin. Then I went out into the car park. Tony was there. 'Dick's on duty,' he said. 'Got two copies of *Penthouse*, half a gallon of tea, an ounce of Old Holborn and the radio. No one'll get past him.'

'Thanks.' I climbed into the Land-Rover, waved to Dick, and headed for Point House.

I was tired. I heated up a steak and kidney pie and ate it. When I had washed up I banked the fire, tested the VHF receiver, and turned up the volume so I would hear Dick if he tried to make contact in the night.

Then I sat and stared at my chessboard. But the pieces kept assuming new formations in my mind: James and Helen and Raistrick, and the burglar prowling round South Creek. I could see the yard in miniature, the basin with the pontoons, the corrugated-iron sheds, the red-brick house on its bank of gravel. Then the focus changed, became shadowy . . .

A log crashed on the fire. My head jerked up. Slowly, I got out of the chair and made my way up the narrow stairs.

WHEN I OPENED MY EYES it was still dark. The moon was coming in at the window, printing silver squares across the white bedspread. My watch said 4.38. I lay for a few seconds, listening to the moan of the wind, trying to work out what had woken me.

Then the voice came again. 'Martin!' it shouted. There was fear in it. More than fear: panic. I went to the window.

The glade in the dunes lay flat and grey under the moon. A car was parked at the far end, its headlights skewed at the sky. Across the glade was running a big, lumpy figure in a long, flapping robe. Mary.

I pulled on my trousers, jersey and boots and ran downstairs as she came through the front door. Her hair was wild, her blue dressing gown covered in sand, and her face was streaked with tears. 'Damn pontoon!' she panted. 'My car's stuck. Come on.'

We ran outside. I started the Land-Rover.

'Pontoon's adrift,' she said, and then said no more, because she was too busy hanging on to her seat as I flung the Land-Rover at the bumps.

As we came across the marsh and down to the basin, I could see that there was something wrong by the way the masts stuck up against the paling of the eastern sky. Normally, they stood in orderly ranks. Now, there was an ugly bunch of them down by the car park.

We roared round the basin. I jumped down, shouted, 'Where's Dick?'

'Haven't seen him,' she said. 'I've rung Tony.'

I ran to the edge of the basin. The masts were like a pine wood after a gale. The pontoon, a heavy wood and galvanised-iron float fifty foot long, had come all the way across the harbour on the wind. The boats that were moored to it bow-on had preceded it. The whole mess had hit the concrete boulders, and now it sat there, rocking. The noise was horrible: the noise of the dock grinding half a million pounds' worth of boats to glass dust.

I looked around for Dick's boat, but it was not in its usual place by the fuel dock. I ran back to the Land-Rover, grabbed a torch and played its beam over black water and splintered Fibreglass.

'What can I do?' asked Mary tremulously.

I said, 'Put some clothes on.'

The yellow disc of torchlight settled on the outside of the dock. Dick's boat was there, long and black. I went down the wall, climbed over the shattered transom of a big Westerly and onto the dock. Dick's boat was not moored: it was just sitting there, held on its fenders by the pressure of the wind.

I jumped in, steadying myself on the engine cover. 'Dick!' I shouted. No reply.

The engine was still warm. I hit the starter button, and the 120-horsepower diesel started with a heavy chug. I got one of the long warps out of the locker and bent an end of the warp to a ringbolt at each end of the pontoon. Then I made fast the middle of the warp to the samson post on the stern, kicked the gear lever *ahead*, and eased the throttle forward.

39

The engine roared. As the bridle tightened the boat became the apex of a triangle with the pontoon as its base. Foam churned silver under the stern. Ropes groaned. Astern, the masts shifted uneasily as the weight of the pontoon came off them. Very slowly, I hauled the pontoon out into the open water. The boats came after, hanging from their warps like battered peapods.

There were lights on the shore now. A squat vehicle drove out on the far breakwater: the winch truck.

'Got a cable,' said Tony's voice from the stern. 'It's on the winch. Bend it on.' He passed me the eye of a heavy wire hawser. I tied the loop of the bridle onto the eye, knocked the knot off the samson post, and got out of the way so the winch could take the strain. Soon the winch was roaring and the mass of the pontoon was moving back across the basin.

I tied up the boat and ran round to join Tony at the winch truck. The light was growing. The hawser was stretching bar-tight across the water to the scarred hulks that had once been five elegant yachts.

'Lucky you caught it,' Tony said. There were hollows under his eyes. 'Could've been a lot worse.'

'Have you seen Dick?' I asked.

'No. Probably asleep in the shed.'

The light had grown enough to reveal figures on the far side of the basin. There were two yard hands, and Mary. The yard hands were prodding with a boat hook around the water's edge.

Cold prickled under my jersey. I ran round the outside of the basin. Mary was standing on the wall, looking down. 'Oh, no,' she was saying. 'Oh, no.'

Dick Hammer was at the bottom of the wall, where the men had pulled him out of the water. In the early dawn he looked perfectly white. He was dead. He must have been under water for an hour or more.

We pulled him up to the top of the wall. The police arrived, and the ambulance. A policewoman took Mary inside and made her tea.

I went and looked at the first mooring point of the pontoon. It should have been secured by heavy galvanised chain to iron rings on ringbolts set four feet into the concrete of the breakwater. In the light of my torch, the chain hung straight down into the harbour. The galvanising had rust flecks, but no more than normal.

'That chain was new this season,' said Tony. He pulled up the end that was dangling in the water. 'Must have been a dodgy link.'

'Two dodgy links,' I said. 'One for each end of the pontoon.'

Tony looked at me steadily.

'Somebody cut those links,' I said. Poor Dick, I was thinking. Poor bloke, with his *Penthouse* and his sandwiches and his tea.

DIVERS WENT DOWN. They found the remains of two links. One looked as if it had been ground away, little by little. The other looked as if it had twisted and snapped as one end of the pontoon blew downwind.

'Frankly,' said Detective Sergeant Hone, 'it looks like a problem of maintenance.'

'Or sabotage,' I said.

Hone said, 'We'll have to wait for the inquest. Meanwhile, I wonder if we could have a little chat in the office?'

We had a little chat. I told him that it looked to me as if South Creek had been subjected to a continuous campaign of sabotage. He nodded tiredly. 'I've been making enquiries,' he said. 'I hear that South Creek's got a bit of a reputation for disasters.'

'That's the rumour,' I said. 'It's not the truth. A company called Sea Horse Land is trying to buy the yard cheap. They're wrecking boats to drive the customers away.'

'So you say,' said Hone. He sighed, and his eyes strayed out of the window. 'But just suppose you were wrong,' he said. 'Just suppose the yard was being run by . . . untidy minds. I understand you're away a lot. And Commander MacFarlane is . . . well, he's not as young as he used to be.'

He got up. 'Now, if you don't mind, I'll have a word with your men.' The notices on the wall fluttered as he went out through the door.

The telephone rang. I picked it up. The line sounded hollow and distant. A voice said, through a storm of crackles, 'Hello? Who's that?'

It was a dreadful line. But it was unmistakably the voice of Henry MacFarlane.

'Henry,' I said. 'Thank God you rang.'

'Is anyone hurt?' he said.

'Dick. Dead—drowned.'

There was a silence. Then he said, 'Poor Dick. Poor Dick.'

I said, 'How did you know?'

'Someone out here,' he said.

'Where are you?'

'Spain.' Even through the crackles on the line, he sounded distracted. 'Now look here. It's taking longer than I thought. There are some things you've got to do. For a start, keep an eye on that chap Paul Welsh.'

I had been up most of the night. My head was numb. 'Why?'

'Never mind why. Don't let the bastard out of your sight.' The line crackled. '. . . *Aldebaran.*'

'What about *Aldebaran*?'

'Find out who's bringing her out to Marbella. Come with the boat. I'm going to need help.'

41

I said, 'Henry, what's going on?'

'No time to chatter,' said Henry. 'You're sailing in the Marbella Cup, aren't you? So you can come out in *Aldebaran*. Now. The next thing. Haul the pots.' I got the impression that he was trying not to be overheard. 'And take it to the bank. It's bloody important. Got to go. All love to Mary. Tell her I'm taking the pills. Poor old Dick. Look here, I'll get in touch later.'

'Where are you?' I said. 'Take what to the bank?'

But the line had gone dead.

I sat and wondered what was taking longer than he thought, and how on earth Henry had known what had happened at South Creek. Then I went over to the house to see Mary.

She was in the garden, weeding. I said, 'Henry rang. He's still in Spain. He's taking his pills. He sent his love.'

Her face lit up for a moment. 'Well,' she said. 'That's something.'

'He had to get off the line,' I said. 'Otherwise I would have put him through.'

She shrugged. Blast you, Henry, I thought. Why didn't you ring her instead of me?

'Did you tell him about Dick?' she asked.

'He already knew,'

She frowned. 'How?'

'He didn't say.'

She stood up, easing her back, hands on knees. 'Let's go in. I want a drink.'

She poured herself three fingers of whisky into a glass. I told her exactly what Henry had said. 'So,' she said, when I had finished, 'he wants you to haul the pots. He's raving. He hauled them before he left. Better have a look.' She squeezed my hand and smiled, her pale blue eyes blurred with a mixture of whisky and tears.

We walked across the yard to the jetty. Henry's pots were stacked neatly against the black corrugated-iron end of the shed.

'How many did he set?' I said.

'Forty-eight,' she said. 'Just him and that little winch on *Hellcat*. Every damn day. At his age.'

I looked at the stack. Eight rows, stacked six high—

There were only seven rows.

I said, 'It's six short.'

'Is it?' she said.

'He said "Haul the pots",' I said. 'Where would he drop them?'

'The Eel Hole,' she said. 'He always put a string in there because nobody else ever did. No lobsters there, of course. Just congers.' She put a hand on my arm. 'I'm feeling a bit feeble,' she said. 'I'm going to go and lie down.'

I watched her go, her shoulders bowed, as if she was carrying a heavy weight, and I thought: Whatever you are up to, Henry, it had better be worth this. Then I went down to *Hellcat*, started the engine and cast off.

A dozen or so other men's pot buoys bobbed in the water under Oar Head. I shoved the tiller to port, and swept round the dogleg between the two fences of rock that guarded the Eel Hole.

Inside the ring of rocks was a quarter of an acre of clear green water, in the middle of which was a yellow pot buoy with MacF stencilled on it. I pushed the boat hook under it, caught the tail-rope, looped it onto the winch and began to haul.

The first two pots came up empty. My pulse was hammering now, and not only because of the exertion of hauling with one and a half hands. The third pot had a big conger in it. I tipped it overboard and kept hauling.

The fourth pot was empty. So was the fifth.

As the sixth came up through the clear water, I could see a shape, squat and square, in the curved wicker.

I heaved the pot aboard, put my left hand in the hole, and drew out the watertight enamel cash box that Henry had carefully fitted in before slinging it into the sea. Then I pushed the tiller hard over and headed for the exit.

THE CASH BOX SAT on the study desk. Henry liked things about him that were solid: you could have shot this one through the *Ark Royal* without denting anything but the *Ark Royal*.

Mary said, 'So that's what it was. He used to keep it on the shelf by the window.' She shook her head. 'But why did he take so much trouble to hide it?'

I said, 'He wants it taken to the bank.'

'The bank's shut,' said Mary. 'It's Sunday.'

We stood and looked at it. Mary said, 'If we knew what was inside, we might know what the old fool was up to. We ought to take it out of his hands.' Her voice was weary. 'I'm tired of him swanning off like this.' She paused. 'Perhaps that's what your burglar wanted.' She walked over to the desk. 'So where's the key?'

There were whole boxes of keys in Henry's desk. None of them fitted the cash box.

'Hacksaw,' she said.

I took out my knife, scratched the side. The paint came off, but the metal remained unscored. 'Casehardened,' I said.

'What about one of those welding torch things?'

'If what's inside is paper, it'll burn it up.'

'So how do we do it?'

'Take it to a locksmith tomorrow.'

'Blast,' she said. 'I want to know.' She paused. 'And I don't want it in the house overnight.'

I said, 'I'll take it to Point House.'

She gave me a suitcase to put it in. I lugged it out to the Land-Rover, dumped it in the passenger seat.

The car park was full. It always filled up on a good day in spring, and down in the basin owners were cleaning up their boats. I ducked into the big shed before anyone could catch me. It was cool and dim in there, with the soothing dinosaur shapes of chocked boats. There was a telephone extension in the corner. I picked up the receiver and dialled Paul Welsh's number.

'Hello,' he said, in his smooth Etonian voice.

I said, 'Who's delivering *Aldebaran* to Marbella?'

'Is it any business of yours?' The voice was still smooth, but now cold and hostile.

'Yes,' I said. 'It's Henry's boat until it's paid for, and he's asked me to check up for him.'

'Very well,' said Paul. 'I'm delivering her myself.'

'Yourself?' I said. It was as surprising as if he had suddenly told me he was giving up racing and joining the Merchant Navy. 'What's wrong with a professional deliverer?'

'Insurance problems.'

'They won't accept your surveyor's report?'

He said, 'All you have to know is that I am being paid for this boat in Marbella, and I am delivering her on my own responsibility.'

'Ah,' I said. I was beginning to understand Henry's worries. The purchaser was going to hand over the money on the quay at Marbella—a shrewd move, if Paul had twisted the surveyor's arm to give a glowing report. If *Aldebaran* did not survive the delivery trip, the purchaser would save his money, and Henry would lose his.

I sighed. 'Got a crew yet?' I said.

'I'll take a couple of guys from the yard.'

'Which yard?'

'South Creek, of course.'

I said, as mildly as I could, 'I'm afraid I can only let you have one.'

'Well then,' he said, 'that'll have to do. Who is it?'

'Me,' I said.

'Now wait a minute.'

'As crew,' I said. 'And owner's representative.'

There was a long pause. Finally, he said, 'Well, why not?'

I said 'Goodbye, skipper,' and walked out to the Land-Rover.

One of the sliding windows on the driver's side was open. I unlocked the door, climbed in. The suitcase was still on the passenger seat. Leaning over, I felt its weight. Suddenly, I was sweating. It was easy to lift onto my knee: too easy. I flicked the catch.

The suitcase was empty. The cash box had gone.

The car park was emptying out. I ran down to the office. Tony was drinking tea. I said, 'Did you see anyone near the Land-Rover?'

He said, 'The whole bloody place has been crawling all day.'

I ran back to the house. Mary was sitting in the garden, reading the *Spectator*. I said to her, 'The box. It's gone.'

'Gone?' she said. Her eyes were pale and haunted. She stared at South Creek, her home for forty years, where people had started to wreck boats and steal things. Then she began to cry.

I felt like crying myself.

6

Aldebaran was a seventy-foot ketch, built for the Baltic timber trade back in the 1920s. She had two masts, gaff-rigged. Forward of the mizzen was a brassbound wheel in the cockpit, with a companionway to the saloon. The saloon itself was panelled with wormy pine. The settees had worn, buttoned-leather upholstery. Smells eddied like fog belowdecks: bilge water, spilt paraffin. Her engine was an antique Perkins, and her steering gear was operated by a system of chains and pulleys that clanked like the family ghost.

From a distance, she was a vision. Close up, she was a bad dream.

The best the yard had been able to do by way of a refit was to install two heavy-duty electric bilge pumps and a petrol generator to run them. Then we had bolted a couple of big winches to the deck to give us control over her vast sail area and ponderous spars, and crossed our fingers.

On the morning of the sixth day after my telephone call to Paul, I had bacon and eggs and coffee with Mary. We had heard no more from Henry. She put her hand on my arm. 'Bring him home,' she said.

We got up, and walked round the basin to the pontoon. With a shiny new life raft lashed in its canister under the mizzen boom, *Aldebaran* looked almost purposeful.

Paul arrived in a taxi and told two of the yard hands to help stow gear. There were better things for the yard hands to be doing, but I kept my mouth shut. It would be good practice for the weeks ahead. Mary helped, too, and I noticed that Paul stayed out of her way.

At noon, I started the diesel and came up on deck. Mary kissed me goodbye, and walked down the gangplank slowly and stiffly, like an old woman.

Paul was at the wheel, lean and immaculate in guernsey and sharply pressed canvas trousers. 'Cast off fore and aft,' he shouted. 'Get 'em in, get 'em in!' Tony winked across the widening gap of dirty water, and tossed me the line.

I coiled the lines down. Mary was waving. *Aldebaran*'s nose eased out of her berth. There was a rush of white water under her counter as Paul put the helm hard over to kick her stern round. Then her long bowsprit was easing out between the breakwaters, and the diesel drove her fat sides down the creek towards the glitter of the sun on the southern horizon. The figures on the breakwater shrank, and South Creek's masts vanished in the great sweep of marsh and sky.

'Sail, please,' said Paul.

I went forward, got the main halyard on the winch, and ground up the main. It was hard work. Then I pulled up the jib and the foresail. My arm had come out of plaster at the beginning of the week, and it was not back to full strength. I was sweating as I went aft to the mizzen.

When the mizzen was up, Paul stopped the engine. *Aldebaran*'s sails bulged like dirty white wings, and the wake made a white line on the blue water.

The weather forecast said winds southerly, four to five. There was a depression heading north three hundred miles west of Ireland, which meant that we should have a comfortable close reach down to Ushant, by which time we would be in a new weather system. After that, we had to tiptoe across the Bay of Biscay and round down the Portuguese Trades. Then it was a matter of taking our chance through the Straits of Gibraltar and on to Marbella. It was about 1,100 miles—two weeks with a fair wind, and any time you liked without. To start the Marbella Cup, we had to get there in three.

Over the weather-grey teak rail on the starboard quarter, Oar Head was sinking into the sea. I went and sat with my back to the nice new life raft and let the April sun shine on my face, and listened to the creak and boom of a big wooden ship in a long, even sea. I had sailed wooden boats out of South Creek ever since I was thirteen. In theory, I should have been pleased to get back to the wooden boat. In practice, what I felt was apprehensive.

The first few days went smoothly enough. We fell into a sort of routine, Paul and I: six hours on, six hours off. *Aldebaran* plugged

46

doggedly south-southwest, demanding little attention. All we had to do was listen to the weather forecast, run the generator for three hours a day to charge the batteries that ran the autopilot and the rest of the electronics, keep the bilges pumped dry, and try to stay civil. At the end of my watches, I cooked spaghetti or stew for both of us. At the end of Paul's, he ate corned beef sandwiches, without offering me any.

We were a week out, a hundred miles off the northwestern corner of Spain, when the trouble began. I turned in at midnight, caught the shipping forecast: westerly, five to six. When I woke up for the early watch, the ship's motion had changed. Gone was the long, smooth corkscrew, steadied by the press of the wind in the sails. Now the motion was edgier, a sharp pitching, with from time to time a heavy *crunch* as the bow dug in.

I rolled out of my sleeping-bag and into my boots, and stumbled forward into the dark cavern of the hold to start the generator. The pumps whined, labouring heavily; pressed as hard as this, her seams were working, and she was taking water. Then I pulled on oilskin trousers and coat, and went on deck.

Before I went below, the moon had been shining on waves as smooth and black as whales' backs. Now they were the colour of slate in the bleak morning light, and the westerly wind tearing at *Aldebaran*'s old shrouds ripped off their crests and drooled trails of dirty scum into their troughs. Paul was at the wheel. He turned his head and nodded at me. There were exhausted hollows under his eyes. I was tired myself. Even in fair weather, seventy feet is a lot of boat to sail with just two men.

'Autopilot won't hold her,' he said.

'She wants a reef,' I said. 'She's not a racing boat.'

He turned abruptly. 'I want to get there,' he said.

The wail of the rigging became a shriek. The deck tilted steeply underfoot. Paul struggled with the wheel, to stop her paying off. I grabbed a spoke and heaved. Slowly her nose came up. Below, the bilge pumps screamed, chewing air as the water ran far over to leeward.

'It's going to get worse,' I said. 'Shall we take the main off?'

He looked at the main, then at me. 'Better safe than sorry,' he said, with irony.

I did not tell him that nobody was getting any points for looking like a hero. Instead, I clipped my safety harness to the jackstay running along the deck, and took the main off. It was hard work, winches or no winches. Without Paul's help, it took half an hour.

When I had finished, *Aldebaran* was moving more easily. The sky was bleak and hazy, the sun surrounded by a dirty halo. Down in the saloon, the radio crackled. *Warnings of gales in Sole, Biscay, Finisterre.* We were

bang in the middle of Finisterre. *Westerly severe gale force nine imminent, veering northwesterly later.*

I went below, leaving her to the autopilot. Paul had made his usual single corned beef sandwich, and was eating it. He said, 'We're in for a blow.'

'I heard the forecast. So what do you want to do?' I said.

'Go for shelter.'

I said, 'We won't get a landfall till night. By that time it'll be blowing force eight, nine maybe. You'll be running ahead of a gale onto a lee shore.'

He said, 'I'm not riding it out in this bloody thing.' His voice was a little too high and a little too fast.

'Think about it.'

His heavy black brows came together over his nose. He wanted to hit me, but he knew enough to know I was right.

'So let's shorten sail again,' I said, as soothingly as I could. 'Then we can get some kip.'

On deck, the wind hit us like a cold hammer. A gust ripped across the sea and screamed in the rigging. I struggled aft and put three reefs into the mizzen. The sail was so old it felt as soft as chamois leather.

'Foresail!' I shouted.

There was no question of him staying at the wheel this time. I unsheeted the outer jib, and the mizzen pulled her head to wind, the bowsprit drawing huge pictures in the sky. We groped our way along the boom to the foredeck, clung there. The tack of the outer jib was secured to an outhaul at the end of the bowsprit. I slackened the halyard. Paul shuffled forward, uncleated the outhaul, and hauled.

The tack was meant to come towards him as he pulled it. It did not move. 'Jammed!' he yelled.

Aldebaran was on a crest. Below the spar, a fifteen-foot cliff of sea had opened out. As she dived into the trough, her bow chopped into the green water until the cliff was a hill rolling up and away, and the bowsprit was digging white spray out of its side.

He clipped his harness onto the outhaul block and began to work his way out along the bowsprit to the snarl-up. He got there. His shoulders jerked as he wrenched at the jam. And then I saw the wave.

From the base of the mast, I saw Paul perched eight feet out on the spar, and beyond him a huge grey wall that growled and muttered as it bore down. As the bow lurched up the impossibly steep face of the wave, the crest curled over and began a fast, roaring slide. I flung myself forward, grabbed his lifeline, and heaved until I could grasp his hood. Then the wave hit.

It crashed aboard like a runaway bulldozer. My legs went up and my head went down, and something slammed into my face so I opened my mouth to shout, and there was only water to breathe. There was a wrenching jerk at my upper chest. Lifeline, I thought. My legs were fluttering like flags in the rush of water. Gone, I thought. We've gone.

But the water in front of my eyes was lightening. I could breathe again. The roar of the wave faded aft. My right hand was still clamped on something. Paul's hood. It was still attached to his jacket, and he was still inside the jacket. I shouted, 'Are you all right?'

He moved. He turned his head. His face was yellowish. I looked at the end of the bowsprit. The tangle had gone. So had the sail.

'Help me,' I said. 'Storm jib. Help me.'

He did not move. So I opened the sail-locker hatch and wrestled out the storm jib. By the time I had finished wrenching its big bronze hands onto the forestay, he had gone below.

I sheeted the storm jib to windward, scuttled aft and lashed the helm. *Aldebaran* turned her nose off the wind and lay hove-to, taking the waves under her starboard bow. That was all I could do for the moment.

I went below. Paul was asleep, wet gear and all, on the leeward settee. Shock, I thought. I put a blanket over him. I was not feeling too terrific myself. I filled the generator with petrol and ran the pumps for a while. Then I wedged myself in a corner and waited.

The wind rose steadily, and the seas with it. Sunset happened somewhere behind a roof of cloud. I lit the cabin oil lamp. It swung violently on its gimbals, hurling shadows across the stained panelling.

At nine o'clock Paul was still wedged in his bunk. I had stood his watch for him. Now I wanted to lie down and sleep. I took a fix of our position on the Decca, went over and shook him by the shoulder. His eyes opened immediately. 'Your watch,' I said. 'We're hove to, fifty miles west of Vigo. Wind, force eight to nine.'

He lay there staring at me. It was a disconcerting stare. I knew what it meant. He was listening. I had been listening, too.

Every time the boat's nose came off a wave, it banged as if someone was hitting it with a sledgehammer. Years of sailing boats made of Fibreglass and aluminium made you forget the creaking and groaning a wooden hull makes as it moves. But it was not the creaking that was the worry. It was the heavy slosh of water in the bilges.

I said, 'I'm starting up the pumps again. Then I'm turning in.'

In the hold, my torch's beam picked up a thin sheen of water on the sides. At the downhill edge of the deck's planks, a strip of black water sluiced to and fro. Under her planks, there would be two or three feet of the stuff.

I went over to the generator and fired it up. Then I switched on the pumps. When I came back into the saloon, Paul was still lying on his bunk. He said, 'I'm ill. I hit my head.'

I was too tired for theatricals. I said, 'I thought you were in charge round here.'

His head snapped up, and he smiled at me. 'You make a very good delivery skipper,' he said. 'It's just about your mark.'

My heart was beating slow and steady, driving the anger round my exhausted body. I said, 'So what's a big shot like you doing buying a two-bit brokerage, then?'

'I have my reasons,' he said. His smile was gaining in confidence. 'But they'd be a bit complicated for you.'

It had been a long week, and a long watch, and I was not going to be polite any more. 'Oh, I understand, all right,' I said. 'I understand you cheated me and a lot of other guys off the Constellation Challenge. So let's try something simple for a change.' I was standing over him. 'How much did you pay for the brokerage?'

'Fifty thousand pounds.'

'I'll bet you your brokerage I sail you under the water in the Marbella Cup.'

Fifty thousand pounds was a drop in the bucket for him. For me to raise it would mean mortgaging everything I possessed. There was a silence. My stomach was in a tight knot. Devereux had opened his big mouth, and now he was going to have to sail his way out of it.

Paul's smile had gone now. 'Why not?' he said. 'And when I win, you and those two pensioners can push off and get a council flat.'

I grinned at him. 'Your watch,' I said.

'Get stuffed,' he said.

Suddenly the deck rose, then fell away like a lift with the cable cut. Outside there was a roar like a train passing close by.

Then I heard a new noise. It sounded like an avalanche, a rumbling of heavy objects falling down a slope. It was coming from the hold. It was the sound of the ballast shifting.

I could hear Paul shouting even over the sound of the storm. He was lying on the cabin sole, clutching his head. I stepped over him and ran into the hold.

Normally, it was a long, empty room with a wooden floor and walls. The ballast lived under the floor planking, held down by a net of cables bolted to the ribs. In the dim yellow light that was all the batteries could provide, it was a battlefield of smashed floorboards, sloping steeply down to the right. A lot of the cables must have broken, allowing the heavy ballast to punch through and tumble down to the starboard side.

Aldebaran was listing heavily, and a lake of black water slopped across the floor to starboard. I went back into the saloon. I said, 'Put some petrol in the generator. We're really going to need it for the pumps.'

Paul looked at me as if he did not understand. He was so frightened he could no longer think. He had to be told what to do. I explained to him slowly. He did what he was told.

I started the pumps. Then I began to clear away the broken decking. That took half an hour. By the time I had finished, the lake of black water was receding, sloshing evilly through the piled lumps of old iron. I braced myself against the bucking of the sides and began to heave the ballast uphill.

It was horrible work. The iron was mostly railway line, and the lengths lay hugger-mugger in the curve of the hull, like a nightmare version of the children's game where you have to move one stick without disturbing the rest of the pile. It was a tribute to *Aldebaran*'s will to live that they had not gone straight through her side.

By the time I had done ten, my hands were bleeding and fiery with salt and dirt. Half a ton down, I thought. Only another nine and a half tons to go. I set my teeth and went back for the next one.

I bent, fished in the inky waters. My hands met something square and smooth. I pulled it out. It was a cold-cast ballast pig, a mixture of resins and lead.

I lugged it up to the keelson, lowered it, went back. There were more of the cold-cast blocks. Someone at the yard must have taken them out of one of the wrecks and dropped them in. I felt pathetically grateful. They did not rip the hands like the iron, and they weighed a lot less.

52

At first, anyway. But by the time I had made fifty trips, I was wandering in a haze of pain. I kept falling down. My ears were buzzing, and I knew that I could not go on.

I staggered aft to the saloon and ate a whole tin of corned beef, straight out of the can. Paul had made himself a meticulous bed inside his lee cloth and was lying in it face down.

The food made me cold and sleepy. The generator thrummed drowsily from the hold. The angle of the lamp on the bulkhead was not so acute as it had been. The chronometer said 0412 hours. Six hours since the ballast had gone. The barometer was low, but steady.

I went on deck.

The cloud had split into flying islands that raced by in a deep gulf of stars. Overhead the three-quarter moon hung, unbearably bright after the dim yellow of the cabin. It shed an evil glow over the ragged edges of the clouds and licked at the great mountains of water cruising down on the port bow, turning the spray at their crests to glittering snow. It was a landscape out of hell.

Shivering, I worked my way down the deck to check the jib. Spray drenched me. When I went below again the saloon seemed warm and cosy. I sat down again and lay back. It was like lying in a bunk in a runaway roller coaster, but it was the most comfortable place I had ever been.

I went to sleep.

When I woke, I did the rounds as Henry had taught me: check position (by dead reckoning as well as Decca), check glass, check weather, check ship. Then, and only then, I put the kettle on. Henry had always insisted: ship first, crew second. Paul was still huddled in his bunk. His eyes followed me balefully.

'Breakfast?' I said.

'No.' He had been drinking. His breath reeked of whisky.

I said, 'You'd better sober up. There'll be plenty to do.'

'Listen to teacher.'

I put a saucepan on the stove, tipped in baked beans, a tin of stew and a glob of chilli sauce. When it started to bubble, I put it into two bowls.

Paul wrinkled his nose. 'Disgusting,' he said.

It was time for the weather. I turned on the radio, scribbled down the gale warnings that rippled drearily out: '. . . *Finisterre westerly severe gale force nine veering northwest imminent, increasing storm force ten later.*'

Paul said, 'Force ten. It's going to blow force ten. In this thing.' He got up, lurched, hung on to the grabrail above his bunk as *Aldebaran* took a wave and rolled far to starboard. 'Listen,' he said. 'We've got to do something. She could go any minute.'

I said, 'What do you suggest?'

'Mayday,' he said. 'Let's send a mayday.' His face was flushed now, enthusiastic. 'It makes sense, right?'

He was smiling now, like a used-car salesman.

'Look,' I said. 'This boat belongs to Henry, and we are delivering it. And I am not going to sit here and watch you send maydays because you've got the bloody wind up.' I stood up. 'Go and stick your head in a bucket and sober up, and then we'll get this thing to Spain.'

I went on deck. It was still grey waves high as houses, and wind screaming in the rigging till your head got sore. But the clouds were higher now, the streaks of blue more frequent. I began to feel a thread of hope. Depressions had been known to change direction, and weather forecasts to be wrong.

Aldebaran was in remarkably good shape, despite her twenty-degree list. The pumps were howling below, and streams of water were pouring from their hoses. As I ducked back down the companionway, Paul was sitting in front of the VHF radio, his face white and set. His fingers were clumsy on the dial. He picked up the mike, thumbed the TRANSMIT button. 'Mayday, mayday, mayday,' he said. 'This is—'

It was all he had time for. Before he could finish I had dragged him out of the seat and the microphone clattered away on the end of its lead.

He hit me in the stomach, hard. I doubled up. It must have taken me half a minute to get my breath back. I scrambled clumsily up the companionway. Paul was on deck aft of the cockpit, struggling one-handed with the lashings of the life raft.

'No!' I shouted. 'You stupid bastard!'

He turned on me the face of a man in a nightmare. 'Stay away!' he yelled. 'You're so keen on your bloody boat, you can go down with it!'

He pulled out a knife and slashed wildly at the life raft's lashings. One of them parted. I hesitated for a second. He was drunk and crazy. The sea was like the inside of a giant washing machine. If he went into the raft he would drown for sure.

So I jumped at him.

My jump missed, but it threw him off balance. His hands went out to grab the life raft's cradle. I saw his knife go flying to the end of its lanyard; and something else. Something that froze me in my tracks.

It was the thing that had been occupying his left hand while he sawed at the lashings with his right. It was the cash box I found in Henry's lobster pots; the cash box someone had stolen out of my Land-Rover in the South Creek car park. It slid away down the slope of the deck, checked for a moment on the shallow bulwark, tripped, and disappeared over the side of the boat.

54

A wave thundered down, came cracking in over the bowsprit. The world went green and white. And when it came back to its right colours, there was no life raft. Three hundred feet downwind, it wheeled, slithering in the spray on the upslope of a wave. Then it flicked over the crest, and was gone. Paul looked after it for a long time. Then he pushed his knife back into its sheath.

I said, 'Where did you get that box?'

His eyes were terrified. He said in a croaking whisper, 'Raistrick.'

I was too tired even to think about it. I took the knife off him. Then I said, 'We are going to move the rest of the ballast. This time you're going to help me.'

In the dirty grey glimmer from the skylight we moved three tons of iron ballast and cold-cast slabs from the starboard side to the centre line, and nailed planks over them to hold them down. By that time it was three in the afternoon. Paul moved like a man in a trance, his face white and expressionless.

The gusts became less frequent as the evening drew on, and the waves stopped breaking. By seven o'clock it was blowing force three, and I was struggling with the brassbound spokes of the wheel as we reached eastwards over a huge green groundswell, moving steadily in on the rugged coast of Spain. And at six o'clock next morning, Paul picked a big mooring buoy under the castle at Bayona.

I gave one look back at the way we had come, where the twenty-foot groundswell was smashing itself on the Islas Cices at the entrance to the Ria de Vigo. Then I took off my oilskins for the first time in four days and lay down in the white shambles of the mainsail in the hot Spanish sun, and went to sleep.

7

It was evening when I woke up. There was a dirty blue launch alongside, fendered with car tyres. The man aboard had a huge black moustache, and I could understand enough of his Spanish to work out that he was the harbourmaster.

An hour later we had cleared customs and were alongside a neat stone quay. I was sitting on the deck sipping San Miguel out of the bottle and watching the sardine fleet coming in over a blue sea when Paul came on deck. He was wearing a clean shirt and a pair of white duck trousers with a sharp crease. I had been thinking about the cash box. He had not mentioned it since it had gone overboard, and he did not seem worried that I had seen it. So I had to assume that he did not know that it had been stolen. But he knew it was important, or he would not have tried to jump into the life raft with it in a force eight gale.

'Going ashore?' I said.

He nodded.

I said, as innocently as I could, 'Why was that box so important? The one that went overboard? Who was it for?'

Paul grinned at me. 'If you must know, it was for Georgie Honiton.'

I stared up at him, and tried to imagine a set of circumstances under which Lord Honiton would arrange a midnight burglary, then a daylight theft, in order to secure somebody else's property. It was not conceivable. Unless whatever was in the box actually belonged to Honiton, and Henry had been keeping it away from him. Or unless Honiton was an associate of my cousin James or his Spanish partners.

'What was in it?' I said.

He shrugged. 'He asked me to bring it. That was all.' He stared at me for a moment, then he said, 'You've got no idea, have you?' He stepped ashore and walked away across the quay.

I watched the gulls above me in the blue sky. The cash box was under a lot of water, and the cash box was the only evidence. But I wanted an explanation, and I could not see that when we got to Marbella there would be anything to prevent me from asking for one. If Lord Honiton was on the race committee he would certainly be there.

SIX DAYS LATER, at dawn, the ruby and emerald flash of Tarifa came out of the sea on the port bow. As the light grew I could see the town through glasses, its grey rocks white with bursting spray. We moved on into thickening shipping, between the jagged ranges of the Rif to the south and Gibraltar ahead and to the north. The sky was hazed with heat, the sea ahead a white-hot dazzle in the morning sun. Slowly *Aldebaran* toiled into the Mediterranean.

It was not an abrupt transition. The clean winds and the boisterous blue of the Atlantic hung on for some miles beyond the Pillars of Hercules. The sierras rose to the north, dun and hazy in the hot breeze. As the Rock went hull-down, the shoreline began to lose its dark fur of pines and to sprout a pox of glaring white concrete. After Estepona the sierras rose steeply, and at their feet the buildings jostled for space, spreading into the foothills and onto the grey beaches.

Seven hours out of Gibraltar, Marbella was coming up on the port bow. I gazed at the yellowish vapour hanging over the tangled buildings ashore. There was no wind; the sails flopped, and the braying of cars' horns drifted across the scum on the glassy blue water. The smog stank of money to burn.

56

We had to take the sails down. Paul said, 'I am greatly looking forward to destroying you in the Marbella Cup. I presume the bet stands?'

I said, 'The bet stands. You'd better get in some practice.'

He shrugged and went below. I heard him talking on the radio, getting a telephone number ashore, laughing a false laugh. He came up as *Aldebaran* slid between the breakwaters into the glassy, diesel-slicked waters of Puerto Banús.

We tied up at the *dique* by the control tower. The customs came aboard, glum men in olive-drab uniforms. They made us take them down into the hold, and shook their heads over the pumps and the engine, which sat there weeping black oil.

One of them, a crumpled fellow with a big stomach trying to get out of his shirt, made drinking movements with his thumb. 'You have whisky?' he said.

I led them up to the saloon and showed them our spirit store, which amounted to a dozen tins of Foster's and a half-full bottle of whisky. They looked at them, and nodded. I wondered if I was supposed to offer them some.

Heavy footsteps sounded on deck. The hatchway darkened. A voice roared, 'Anyone home?'

Paul looked nervous. He said, 'Deke! Here!'

A man came down the companion steps. His shoulders were wide enough to blot out most of the light. He was about fifty, with a short fuzz of tightly curled grey hair. His face was big, with the reddish-brown tan of a northern skin that has lived for years in the sun. His cheeks were long and flat, like a boxer's, below pale-lashed blue eyes.

'This is Martin Devereux,' Paul said. 'Martin, this is Deke Kellner, *Aldebaran*'s new owner.'

'Yeah,' said Kellner. He sat down on one of the settees, took in the customs men, and said, 'Paco. Pepe. How's it going, eh?'

The customs men simpered. Kellner yanked two beers out of the locker and handed them one each. 'My new boat,' he said. His voice was hoarse South London. 'Nice, eh?' The customs men smiled weakly, and nodded. Kellner was a hard man to disagree with. 'Let's all 'ave a drink.' We all ripped the tops off beers. 'Good 'ealth,' said Kellner.

We finished the beers. Kellner said, 'Let's get 'er over to the yard, then, and up out of the water.' We all stood up. I am six foot tall; he was half a head taller.

'Fanks, Paco, Pepe.' He watched the customs men jump onto the quay. 'T'riffic blokes,' he said.

I cast off the lines. *Aldebaran* moved across the filthy water between gleaming lines of yachts, and into the slot in the quay. The slings were already in the water. 'You don't waste any time,' I said.

Kellner laughed enormously, as if what I had said was really funny. 'Nah,' he said. 'Nah, we don't waste any time at all. The surveyor suggested there might be a bit of work needed doin'.'

We jumped onto the dock. The hoist motor whined. *Aldebaran* soared into the air, streaming water like the rose of a watering can. 'You little *beauty*,' said Deke. 'Right. Me an' Paul's got a little meeting at my house. I want to give 'im a cheque. But there's a party later. 'Bout ten. See you there?'

I said, 'See you there.'

Aldebaran settled on the concrete hardstanding. Small, dark men swarmed round her with timbers and chocks.

I shouldered my bag and went through the gates in the chain link fence and into the sweltering crush of holidaymakers on the quay. There were taxis outside so I climbed into one, and gave the driver the name of the hotel the race organisers had booked. There was a lot to do.

THE WALK FROM THE TAXI to the revolving door of the Hotel El Gordo plastered my sweat with street dust. My room was air-conditioned to resemble a refrigerator paved with Moorish tiles. I showered, dried myself, pulled on dark blue canvas trousers and a dark blue cotton shirt, and picked up the telephone. My fingers were stiff with hauling *Aldebaran*'s ropes, so it took three tries to dial the Marbella Club.

I asked for Lord Honiton. 'Lor' 'Oniton is away,' said the perfect-servant voice on the other end. The voice told me Honiton would be returning tomorrow evening. I made an appointment and hung up.

I rang South Creek. Mary answered. She sounded pleased to hear my voice.

'We're here,' I said, making it sound cheerful. 'Cheque follows. Any news from Henry?'

'A card,' she said. 'Posted a week ago from Madrid. Said it was hot.'

'That's not much help.'

'Better than nothing. Tony's looking after things here.' She paused. 'Look out for him.'

'Of course,' I said, trying to fill my voice with confidence. We rang off.

I dialled the apartment number that Charlie Agutter had given me. He and the boys had come on ahead by road. He answered.

'I'm here,' I said.

'Terrific,' he said. 'Come and have dinner.'

'Got to go to a party,' I said. 'Deke Kellner.'

'Got a nightclub, hasn't he?' said Charlie. 'Keep your hand on your wallet, if I might make so bold as to suggest.'

'I was going to,' I said. 'Practice tomorrow, ten?'

Rather than sit under the air conditioner and freeze to death, I thought I might as well go for a walk and get a feel of dry land. So I went downstairs and got a taxi to ferry me through the dustclouds, and climbed out a mile short of the address Deke had given me.

It was nine o'clock, and the air was cool. The road had a curve to it, with white villas peering through the dark green orange trees. After three weeks of the flat chlorine smell of the sea it was good to sniff the woodsmoke of barbecues and the heavy scent of jasmine floating out of the gardens.

After twenty minutes the road forked sharply to the left. The right-hand fork petered out in an area of rough grass, planted with olives. The grey-green leaves of the olives whispered in the breeze that came in from the sea. Somewhere nearby, a dog started to bark. I turned regretfully away from the olive grove, and walked towards Deke Kellner's house, whose high white wall bordered it on the left.

The coloured tiles let into the white stucco of the gatepost said NUESTRA CASA, our house. There was an entry-phone above the name. I pushed the bell and gave my name.

Kellner's voice on the other end had a background of noise and laughter. 'Come in,' he said. 'Don't push the gates, they're automatic.'

I stood in front of the heavy black wrought iron. The lock buzzed and clicked, and the gates swung back with a hiss of hydraulics. They looked as if they had come off a bank vault.

The gates hissed to behind me. I was in a garden: geraniums, hibiscus, the ubiquitous orange trees. Ahead, the drive serpentined between clumps of oleanders. Above the leaves, segments of red-tiled roof and turret-like white chimneys showed. Underfoot, the turf was green and well watered.

As I walked forward a sound started inside the wall: a curious, scratchy panting. It was getting closer, and it raised the hairs on the nape of my neck.

I began to walk quickly towards the house. The evening had turned cool, but I found I was sweating again. Calm down, I thought, you're on your way to a party.

The noise appeared round the corner. It came from a matched pair of Doberman pinschers, trotting on tiptoe, two barracudas on legs. They stopped fifteen feet away, one forty-five degrees to my right, the other forty-five degrees to my left, so I could not concentrate on both of them at once. Someone had taught them to do that.

My heart was beating too fast. I slid my hand to my pocket, looking for my knife. But I was off *Aldebaran*, wearing my party clothes, and I am

59

not used to going to parties where it is a good idea to carry a knife.

The noise had changed. It was continuous, now; a revolting hissing gurgle, from deep in their throats. Their black lips were pulled back from their white teeth. The panting was what they did instead of barking, I realised. This gurgling was what they did instead of growling.

'Hey!' I shouted. 'Somebody!'

There was silence. The front of the house was high and white, with a streak of bougainvillea. I could hear voices, a woman's laugh. This is ridiculous, I thought. You're going to get eaten alive sixty feet away from a cocktail party. How had the other guests survived?

We stood there, the Dobermans and me, at the three corners of an invisible triangle.

Then I heard a car's engine, and the hiss of the gate. The engine accelerated. Out of the corner of my eye I could see the car, a green SEAT. I waved as hard as I dared, to attract the driver's attention. The engine slowed. Without looking round I said, 'Open the passenger door, please.' The dogs' gurgle almost drowned the engine. The door's latch clicked at my back.

I turned and ran.

It was ten yards to the car. The first dog got me when I had run eight of them. I jerked my arm up, and smashed my forearm into its throat at the place where the jaw joins the neck. It made a nasty coughing noise and went down onto the ground. Its friend had to swerve to avoid it, as I wrenched open the passenger door, piled in and slammed it behind me.

The Doberman took off ten feet away from the door. For a split second, I was looking straight into its brown eyes. Then it hit the window.

I turned to the driver, checked, stared at the short blonde hair, aquiline nose, black eyebrows. She had had her hair cut. Last time I had seen her, she had been pale. Now, she was the colour of heather honey. Helen Gallagher. She was grinning at me.

'When you come to Deke's house, you come in a car,' she said. 'You OK?'

'Fine,' I said. 'I'm glad you arrived.'

'Me, too,' she said. 'I hate to see a good man chewed.'

I sat back in my seat, and concentrated on getting my breath back. 'How come they make that horrible noise?' I said.

'Deke had them de-barked,' she said. 'Strike silent, strike sure.'

She drove through a second pair of gates, parked alongside a group of Mercedes and BMWs. It occurred to me that she knew a lot about Deke Kellner.

'One thing,' she said. 'It would be good if we didn't know each other.'

She got out of the car before I could ask her why.

I followed her into the house. She was wearing a black dress, very short. Her legs were brown, and on her feet she wore red shoes with very high heels. The effect was striking, but puzzling. There was a touch of the floozy about it that did not match the Helen Gallagher I remembered from England.

But I had no time to wonder about it, because she had led the way confidently past a big, flat-faced man in a dinner jacket, up some marble steps and into the roar of voices.

'Who's that?' I asked, pointing at the man in the dinner jacket.

'They call him Jacky Damage,' she said. Then the party was upon us.

Deke Kellner walked through the throng. He was wearing an open-necked white Mexican shirt, and two gold medallions and a shark's tooth dangled in his grizzled chest hair.

'Helen!' he said, and swept her to his chest. Then he looked at me. 'Come together, did you?'

'She rescued me,' I said. I told him about the dogs. He laughed until I thought he was going to choke.

'How about a drinkette?' said Helen. Something had happened to her voice, it had lost its cultured East Coast accent and acquired a croak that went with the too-high heels and the too-tight dress.

'Yeah,' said Deke. He grabbed a bottle of champagne and two glasses from a table, and poured us some. 'So the bloody dogs 'ad a go,' he said. 'That'll teach you to go for walks in 'ot countries.' He laughed again, his eyes twinkling in their mesh of jolly wrinkles.

'I hope the dogs are all right,' I said, insincerely.

'We get them in packets of twenty,' he said.

I decided to play naive. 'Why do you need all this security, if you don't mind me asking?'

'Can't be too careful,' said Deke. 'Funny place, round 'ere. Lot of riffraff. Can't count on the protection of the constabulary.' He started to laugh again. He had been drinking, I decided. 'So you and young Paulie's going to sail in this race,' he said.

'That's right. Do you follow match racing?'

'Nah,' said Deke. 'But some of us put up a few quid for this Marbella Cup. Any excuse for a party.' He laughed his automatic bark of a laugh. 'I like a sail, though.'

'What are you going to do with *Aldebaran*?'

'Mend 'er up a bit,' said Deke. 'She's a nice boat. Sound boat.'

I nodded. If Deke thought *Aldebaran* was sound, Paul must have done a very good sales job on him.

I decided to change the subject. 'What do you do?' I asked.

61

'This an' that,' he said. 'Got the club. Various business interests.' He might as well have put up a placard with NO COMMENT on it.

'Is that right?' I said. 'Well, here's to *Aldebaran*, and her new owner.'

Deke raised his glass. Helen giggled and raised hers, and we drank. Deke said, 'Lissen. I got to go and see a bloke. I'll introduce you.' He swept me round the room and rattled off half-a-dozen names in quick succession. They were mostly English, the sort of brown, smooth people you meet at expensive golf clubs. The men had unnecessarily hard handshakes and silk cravats, and the women had too much jewellery and the reptilian skin that comes from long exposure to the sun. We spoke about the Marbella Cup. They were not much interested in the racing, but they were greatly fascinated by the size of the prizes. And all of them were drinking champagne from glasses the size of bird baths.

As they got drunker, they talked about property. All of them seemed to be buying and selling bits of land to each other. Apparently sites were changing hands for upwards of a million pounds. Honiton the property baron was certainly sitting where the action was.

The party roared on. Steaks appeared. The colour of the wine changed to red, and someone started playing the piano. A man with smooth olive skin and black hair greying at the temples over long, wiry sideburns, stood beside the accompanist and sang *Smoke gets in your eyes*.

'That's Jake Schwartz,' said the woman beside me. 'He's singing down the club. He's got a lovely voice.'

'What club?' I said.

'The Red House,' she said. 'Deke's club.'

'I must drop in,' I said.

'Yeah,' she said. 'Ol' Jakie's got a lovely voice.'

But I was not watching him, I was watching Helen, who was sitting with her chin on her long brown hands, gazing at Schwartz with adoration. There are some things I cannot stomach even in a good cause, so I wandered out of the big room with the piano, past the sober, incurious eyes of Jacky Damage.

Under an archway off the landing outside was a sort of picture gallery. Most of the pictures were crudely painted rubbish, except for one, a portrait of a craggy old woman, glaring out at a world from which she would take no nonsense of any kind. It was the face of a female edition of Deke. It had to be his mother.

I turned to go back to the big room. Then I heard voices on the landing. One of them was Deke Kellner's. The other was Paul's.

'It was blowing a gale,' Paul said loudly. 'I couldn't help it. Honestly. I did my best—'

'But it wasn't good enough, was it?' Kellner's voice was quiet and reasonable. 'You've put me to a lot of extra trouble, Paulie. It's very upsetting.' He raised his voice. 'Jacky!' he called. I stepped behind a brass vase of dyed papyrus plumes as Jacky Damage padded past the archway. 'Jacky. Mr Welsh was just leaving.'

There was an odd noise, halfway between a grunt and a moan. Then there was a dull tumbling, as of a body falling, and laughter. Deke Kellner's laugh, loud and hearty. I ran onto the landing.

Kellner was standing at the top of the flight of marble stairs, leaning against the black wrought-iron balustrading. Paul Welsh was lying at the bottom of the stairs. As I watched, he got to his hands and knees. Blood was flowing from his Greek god's nose.

'Fell down the stairs,' said Deke. 'You was probably looking for the little boys' room, am I right?'

I went down the stairs, took Paul's arm and helped him up. Deke smiled, and shook his head like a kindly uncle. 'God bless you, Martin. You're a good man.'

The lavatory was done out in brown tiles. Paul splashed his face with water, and I gave him some lavatory paper for his nose. One of the cubicle doors opened and a man came out. He had a silly grin on his face and small eyes too bright to be natural. He was tucking a rolled-up 5,000-peseta note into the breast pocket of his blue-and-white seersucker jacket. The sort of rolled-up note one sniffs cocaïne through. 'Evenin', all,' he said cheerily.

I nodded to him. He banged into me with his shoulder. 'Oops,' he said. 'Sorry, sorry. No harm done.' He brushed me down.

'I'm fine,' I said curtly.

'Ah,' he said. 'Sorry for being alive.' Giggling, he lurched out of the room.

Paul's nose had stopped bleeding. I said, 'Why did he throw you downstairs?'

He opened his mouth to answer, snapped it shut again. 'What the hell are you talking about?' he said. 'I slipped.' Holding a pad of lavatory paper to his face, he left the room.

I followed him. The piano was still thumping and they were all singing along with Jakie. Helen was standing beside the singer, her bare brown arm round his shoulders.

Suddenly I felt tired, and sober, and depressed. I had a taxi number in my wallet. I put my hand in my pocket.

The wallet had gone.

At first, I thought I had dropped it, so I retraced my steps to the top of the stairs, then on into the lavatory.

One of the cubicle doors was shut. There were sniffing noises coming from inside. The wallet was nowhere to be seen. Hell, I thought: it must be out in that horrible garden, with the dogs.

The cubicle door opened, and the man with too-bright eyes came out again. Suddenly I remembered the pat and fumble of his hands as they had dusted off my jacket.

I said, 'Give me my wallet back.'

'No,' he said. 'Not me.' His hands came up, slowly at first, then quick. I jerked my head aside. The fingers that were meant to go in my eyes gouged my forehead. My head hit the wall.

I heard the door slam, the flap of his espadrilles on the marble stairs. A car's engine started with a roar, and tyres screamed on the drive.

I washed the cut on my forehead and walked back to the room. Helen was by the piano, with a glass of orange juice in front of her. I said, 'Somebody's just picked my pocket.' I felt a bloody idiot. I had never had my pocket picked before.

She turned towards me. 'Do you know who did it?'

I described the man with the hands.

'Squeal,' she said. 'His name is Squeal. He runs the Bar Bric-a-Brac, in downtown Marbella. I guess if you ask him nicely, he might give you back whatever he took off you, unless he's sold it to buy nose candy.'

Jake Schwartz materialised alongside us in a cloud of heavy aftershave. 'Am I ever *hoarse!*' he said, in a disc-jockey's drawl, and drank deeply from Helen's glass.

'Hey, hey!' said Deke's voice. 'Everybody 'aving a good time?'

'Sure,' said Schwartz. '*Terrific.* But I have to work, right? I'm due at the Red House and I'd better get moving.'

'I'll follow in my car,' said Helen.

'Can I get a ride through the pets?' I said.

Deke laughed. Schwartz said, 'Terrific. Suits me.'

I said, 'I'll go with Helen. She's already saved my life once.'

That went down well. Deke said, 'All right, then. Ta-rar for now.'

From the car park, Helen waved coquettishly up at the balcony, bottom stuck out as she posed. I got into the passenger seat. She slammed the door. The gates opened. As we went down the drive the dogs were waiting boredly on the smooth green lawn. They knew there was no future in biting cars. The second set of gates opened.

I looked at her. She was looking straight ahead, her determined chin in profile against the big white villas by the road. I said, 'First Southampton. Then Pulteney. Now here. What's your angle?'

'A girl's gotta eat.'

I said, 'How is hanging around with a lot of small-time hoods helping you eat?'

64

We had come to the main road. Her head snapped round. 'Two things,' she said. She sounded Ivy League again, and furious. 'Don't ever make the mistake of thinking that Deke Kellner is small time. And don't ever tell me what I should do.' She paused. Suddenly she leaned over towards me, and I felt the faintly sticky touch of her lips on my cheek. 'Don't get hurt,' she said. 'Now, get out of here.'

And the next thing I knew I was standing in the hot night under the hazy stars, and her tail lights were dwindling under the palm trees down the wide road towards Marbella. It would have been a long walk home, if I had not had a 1,000 peseta note in my trouser pocket for a taxi.

8

The crew meeting next morning was at the Club Deportivo marina in Marbella, at ten.

At ten to ten I was on the breakwater that flings an arm round the marina. The sea breeze was just getting up, and it set my heart thumping with pleasurable anticipation as I walked towards the eight tall, slim masts at the end of the quay. Practice today, the first heats tomorrow.

They were already working on the boat when I got to the end of the breakwater. Charlie Agutter looked tired, as usual. The rest of our crew, Scotto and Noddy and Slicer, looked large and brown and hot.

We cast off the lines, and I backed the boat out of its berth and motored past the white ends of the breakwater and into the dazzling blue Mediterranean. The sails went up. I turned off the engine and pulled the nose off the wind. In the new quiet, the cockpit came suddenly alive underfoot, and the chuckle of the wake became a tiny roar at the tail of the long, sloping transom. After the wallowings of *Aldebaran*, it was pure pleasure.

'Trouble with sailing in Marbella,' said Charlie, squinting up at the long, smooth curve of the mainsail. 'Not enough wind.'

'Boat doesn't mind,' I said.

'She's not too bad,' said Charlie, pulling the long peak of his cap down over his eyes. He was a man acutely afflicted by modesty.

There was so little wind that a lot of cruiser racers would have been dead in the water. But the Bayliss 34 flew wings of brilliant Dacron and caught the zephyrs, and the little roar of water under her transom never slackened.

Under the boom, the white palaces of Marbella sprawled in the trees behind their dirty grey beaches. There were other sails on the water, little white triangles twisting and turning on the glittering blue, practising.

65

Scotto said, 'There's Fournier. And Paul Welsh.'

Fournier was a Frenchman, a charmer off the water and a Great White Shark on it. He was going to be a problem.

'Paul,' I said. I saw again the crumpled figure at the bottom of the marble stairs. The white palaces were suddenly sinister. Honiton was in there somewhere, presumably fretting over a tin box that had never arrived. And Henry, up to nobody knew what. 'We'll murder the bastard,' I said.

'Yeah,' said Scotto, and grinned.

By twelve o'clock we were settling down into a nice, easy rhythm. The sun was directly overhead; even in our hats we were dried and salted like peanuts.

Charlie said, 'Let's go in, get some lunch.'

We headed for the shimmering line of the shore, and I banged the boat alongside. I was so absorbed in what we were doing that I nearly forgot Squeal. I walked straight from the marina up through the dust of the town to find the Bar Bric-a-Brac.

The blind on the dirty plate-glass window was up, and when I pushed the door it swung inwards. On the left-hand side was a long mahogany bar with nobody behind it. Above the bar was a wrought-iron rack from which hung a line of pewter tankards. On the walls were dozens of narrow shelves, full of cuckoo clocks, jam jars, old bottles, candlesticks, presents from holiday resorts in England.

A blonde girl came out of a door at the back. When she had given me a San Miguel, I said, 'Where's Squeal?'

'In bed over at his place,' she said. 'He 'ad a late night.' Her accent was Stepney. 'But he usually pops round to get his heart started, about now.'

She picked some knitting out of the corner by the icebox and went to sit as far away from me as she could. I sipped at my beer.

The door opened and Squeal came in. He was wearing a dirty beige linen suit, and he did not look at all well. He hoisted himself onto a stool and said, 'Give us a vodka, dear.' He did not even look at me.

The blonde brought him a tumbler of vodka mixed with a little tomato juice, and a big dollop of Tabasco. He lifted it to his lips with both hands, and took a couple of gulps. She gave him a napkin to dry his streaming eyes, and said, 'You got a visitor.'

He turned round to look at me. Last night, with the glitter of cocaine in his eyes, he had had a sort of presence. Today, he looked like a rodent with a very bad hangover. There was no recognition in his face. 'And what can we do you for?' he said.

'You can give me my wallet back,' I said, and stepped off my stool so that I was between him and the door.

66

'What wallet?' he said.

'The wallet you took out of my pocket at Deke Kellner's party,' I said.

The hangover round his eyes got worse. 'I don't know what you're talking about,' he said, and picked up his drink.

I kept my voice nice and casual. 'All I want is the wallet back.' I thought about Deke, the solid presence of the man, and decided to take a little gamble. 'Otherwise I'll ask Deke to get it back for me.'

It worked. His eyes shifted away as if they were looking for the emergency exit. Deke was clearly someone to be frightened of.

'Think about it,' I said. 'Old Deke might be a little upset about your thieving off his guests.'

He looked at the dirty tiles under the legs of his stool, then at the girl. Neither of them seemed to be much help. Then he gulped the last of his drink, and dived his left hand into the pocket of his jacket. 'I never nicked no wallet,' he said. 'I found one on the ground, though. I meant to 'and it in to Deke, but . . . well, you know 'ow it goes. I forgot. Is that yours?' He held it out towards me. It was mine. I took it.

'I do believe it is,' I said. 'Pity about the money.' Twenty thousand pesetas in cash was missing from the inside compartment.

'Money?' he said. 'I never saw no money in it.'

'Of course you didn't,' I said. I tucked the wallet away. 'Well, you've done me a big favour. Have another drink?'

He pretended to wonder whether he should or not, and finally gave in gracefully. We drank to each other. 'Nice bar you've got here,' I said. 'Are you not going back to England, then?'

He shook his head at his glass. 'Nah,' he said. 'Few problems up there, know what I mean?'

I thought I did. 'Trouble with the officers?'

He nodded, looking at me sideways across his long nose.

'And old Deke is in the same boat,' I said.

I knew as soon as I had said it that I had gone too far. Squeal had spent too much time in too many interview rooms not to recognise a leading question when he saw one.

His eyes became suddenly wary. 'Deke,' he said, 'is a very 'ard man. And he would not like me to discuss what I may or may not know about him.' He stood up, suddenly, his face twisted with anger. 'So push off,' he said. 'Go on, 'op it!'

I stood up. He stood up. But he had underestimated the effect of the vodka on his legs. He took a step backwards, tripped over the stool, and crashed into the narrow shelves on the wall behind him. They collapsed in a cloud of dust, sending a shower of bric-a-brac onto the tiles. I pushed it aside with my feet, heading for the door.

Then, halfway to the door, I stopped.

One of the objects off the shelves was a slim box made of grey metal, curved so it would fit comfortably into a pocket. I knew that box. I stooped and picked it up. The inscription on the lid said *To H.M., from the crew of HMS* Rutland, *1942*. The box was a gunmetal cigarette case, and the last time I had seen it, six weeks ago, it had been the property of Henry MacFarlane.

I held the box in my hand, turning it over and over. I had admired it as a child; later, I had counted it part of Henry's stubborn eccentricity that he should use a cigarette case at all, let alone one made of gunmetal.

Behind me, Squeal said, 'Go on! Push off, before I call the cops!'

I turned round and walked towards him. His mouth fell open, and his skinny body shrank as if someone had let the air out of him. My hand went out, and grabbed the front of his suit. I walked him backwards across the bar to the far wall.

I held the gunmetal cigarette case in front of his little yellow eyeballs. 'Tell me,' I said, 'where, *exactly*, did you come across this?'

His eyes closed. 'Can't remember,' he said.

I picked him up and shoved him against the wall. His skull made an ugly knocking sound on the stucco. 'That case belongs to a good friend of mine,' I said. 'I am going to keep banging you against the wall until you tell me where you found it.' I banged him again.

'Police,' gasped Squeal. 'Mona, police.'

I looked over my shoulder. Mona was still knitting. 'She knows what you ought to do,' I said. 'So do it.'

'Let me go, and I'll tell you,' he said.

I dropped him. It was a pleasure not to be close enough to smell him.

'I was doing a little job for a property company,' he said.

'Name of the property company?'

'Morris Holdings.' He simpered. 'I 'ad to go and deliver some stuff to a geezer. Some papers. I seen that little box lying on a table. I thought it looked like it would, you know, fit the decor. So I nicked it.'

'Very nice,' I said. 'Who was this geezer?'

'Bloke called Neville,' he said. 'Major Neville.'

'Where does he live?'

Squeal's yellow incisors showed under his sharp upper lip. 'He *did* live down Guadalmina,' he said. 'But he probably don't live there no more, because of the papers I served on him. They was something to do with him getting out of the house.'

'How long ago was this?' I asked.

'Three weeks.'

'Write down the address,' I said. He wrote it down. I paid for the drinks and left a small tip for Mona. She did not thank me.

I went to the bank, then hired a car and headed for Guadalmina. Someone had built a lot of villas down there. But the road eventually became a track, and the neat gardens of oleander and orange petered out into a large area of burnt scrub. To the left, an iron gate under a big almond tree led through a wall. There was a long, low house in there, walls painted white, green shutters, red-tiled roof.

A lizard skittered from under my feet as I opened the gate. It was a wonderfully quiet place. I walked to the front door and banged the knocker. The sound echoed in the house with the peculiar ring of tiled floors. There were no footsteps, no voices. I knocked again, walked round. Doors and shutters were locked tight.

A voice behind me said, '*Hola!*' When I turned, an old man was standing there. His scrawny brown shoulders stuck out of a filthy singlet, and on his head was a straw hat.

I asked him where I could find Señor Neville. He launched into a torrent of Andalusian Spanish. He seemed to be saying that they had left three weeks previously. I asked when they would be coming back. '*No,*' he said. '*Casa vendida*. The house is sold.'

I asked him where the Nevilles were now.

'*Banús,*' he said, gesturing to the east. '*Banús.*'

I watched him thoughtfully. It was reasonable to suppose that Henry had come to Spain on business connected with whatever had been in the cash box. According to Paul, the cash box had been destined for Honiton, who had made a lot of money in property. And here was a house which Henry had visited and which had recently been sold.

I gave the old man two hundred pesetas. Then I went off to Puerto Banús, into the harbourmaster's office in the Moorish tower at the southwestern corner of the basin, and asked for the Nevilles.

The man in the office looked bored, and said, 'Motor cruiser, *Shearwater*. Down the far end,' and waved a limp hand beyond the floating palaces, across to the far jetties where the boats were smaller and scruffier.

Shearwater was a twenty-eight-foot wooden motorboat. She was kept well: the gangplank that came over her stern shone as if it had been dipped in varnish, and the green awning over the cockpit had been ironed. I knocked on the rail, and called, 'Anyone home?'

A woman's head came out of the companionway. The hair was grey, the face that of an elderly and aristocratic parrot. 'Good morning,' she said, without visible enthusiasm.

'Mrs Neville?' I said. 'Have you got a minute for a chat?'

'What about?'

'About Henry MacFarlane.'

She frowned. Her sharp eyes ran me up and down, checking my Admiral's Cup T-shirt, navy-blue shorts, deck shoes. It was a combination scruffy enough to add up to respectability. She said, 'You'd better come aboard.'

The cabin was panelled with mahogany. A man was sitting at the table. He had a thin brown face and a clipped white moustache, and the backs of his hands were covered with liver spots. He had on a cream shirt and a silk cravat.

The woman said, 'This young man thinks we know someone called Henry MacFarlane.'

The man's eyes were old and watery, and suspicious. 'Does he?' he said.

I said, 'I understand a man served some papers on you, three weeks ago. While he was in your house he stole a cigarette case that belonged to Henry MacFarlane.'

'Are you some sort of policeman?' he said.

'No,' I said. 'Henry MacFarlane is by way of being my stepfather.'

'What's your name?' I told him. 'Sailor?' he said. 'Read about you in the papers.'

'Yes. Henry and I are partners in a boatyard.'

'Ah,' said the major. 'Yes. I think I ought to tell you. MacFarlane came to see us. Said he was chasing a company that was trying to diddle him. Someone had told him we were dealing with the same company.'

'Sea Horse Land,' I said.

'Those terrible people,' said Mrs Neville.

'He asked us not to tell anyone he'd come to see us. He said it would be dangerous.'

'We believed him,' said Mrs Neville. 'After what had happened to us.'

I took a deep breath. Henry, you old brute, I thought. Off to Marbella to play detective. But how did you know where to come, and where the hell are you now?

'How long ago was this?'

'Three weeks. Two and a half. Three days after we got notice to quit.'

'Have you seen him since?'

'Said he was off to Madrid,' said the major. 'Actually, we've been a bit busy, since.'

'You sold your house,' I said. 'I went there, looking for you. It's very rude of me to be so inquisitive. But would you mind telling me what happened?'

'*La Residencia*,' Major Neville said. 'Bought it years ago. Just after the war. Came back to live here ten years ago. Well, I mean, whole place'd changed, but luckily I'd bought the farm when it was nothing but goats. So there we stayed. Jolly nice place.'

'A lovely place,' said his wife. 'Terribly peaceful.'

'Anyway,' said the major, 'About four months ago, chap came to the door and said he wanted to buy the house. I suppose it must have got pretty valuable.' I thought of Deke's bronzed guests, discussing million-pound building sites. 'Never occurred to me to check. This chap was a bit persistent. Spaniard, he was. Menendez. I told him to go away. He went, easy enough. That night, the woods caught fire.'

'The woods?'

'Pine trees. Scrub. That sort of thing. Well, there it was, burned to a cinder. Lucky it didn't get the house. And then who should pop up but Menendez again. Said he was sorry about the woods, accidents would happen. Said we really should consider going somewhere . . . nicer.' He snorted. 'Well, I told him off pretty sharpish, I can tell you. And off he went.'

'And then it all started to happen,' said his wife. Her face was pink and animated. 'The orange trees died. Somebody put battery acid on the roots. There were graffiti all over everything. Someone put a dead pig in the well. We had our own water, you know. And then—' She screwed up her face, as if she did not even want to think about what happened next.

'We had a dog,' said the major. 'A black labrador. Winston. I suppose you get silly about dogs. We never had any children. Anyway, we came down to breakfast one morning, and there was poor old Winston.'

'Poor old Winston,' said his wife.

'In the middle of the dining-room table. Somebody had cut his head off. Actually we never found the head. So we went out and buried him in the garden. We were getting pretty stubborn by then. So they changed tactics. There's a land register in Madrid. When we bought the house, nobody ever paid any attention to it. So we never registered. This Sea Horse Land lot went to the descendants of the chap I bought it off, got a *factura* off him—'

I said, 'What's a *factura*?'

'Bill of sale,' said the major. 'Sworn in front of a lawyer. They bribed the chap, got a crooked lawyer, took it to Madrid, got the register changed. And that was us gone.' There was a silence. 'Actually it wasn't as much of a wrench as we'd thought. We'd come to hate the place, you see. Everything was going to hell. I suppose they'll build houses all over it, or turn it into a nightclub.'

His eyes were far away. 'We've decided to give up. Go back to UK. I expect we'll get by.'

The wife said, 'Yes.' She turned her face to me. 'We really liked Henry

MacFarlane,' she said. 'I do hope you find him.'

I left them in the wreckage of their lives. It was time for my appointment with Lord Honiton.

THE MARBELLA CLUB was a village of white stucco cottages peering through heavy swags of jasmine and geraniums. I negotiated the glare of the evening sun off half a dozen Rolls-Royces, and made my way to the door of the Honiton residence.

Honiton was sitting under a white umbrella on the terrace, a glass of what looked like gin and tonic on the table. He was wearing a blue blazer, Pall Mall Yacht Club tie, and white trousers. When he looked up, his crafty amber eyes were hostile, but he smiled.

'Well?' he said. 'What can I do for you?'

He did not offer me a chair. I pulled one up anyway. I said, 'You have made a lot of money out of property.'

He frowned. 'I was under the impression you wished to see me on race business.'

I said, 'There are some things we should discuss first. An object was stolen from the South Creek Boatyard. That object turned up in the possession of Paul Welsh. When I asked him what he was doing with it he said he was delivering it to you. What I want to know is, what is someone like you doing receiving stolen goods?'

There was a long silence. Finally, Honiton said, 'This is an extraordinary allegation.'

I felt like a bull in a china shop. But I charged on anyway, going on guesswork. 'You are a business associate of James de Groot,' I said. 'And through James you are linked to a company called Sea Horse Land, which has been operating a sabotage campaign against a business in which I am a partner—'

'Stop,' said Honiton. 'I fear you have been misled. I have no connection with Sea Horse Land. Eleven months ago, I resigned my directorship.'

So I had hit upon the truth. 'Why?' I asked.

'I did not like some of the . . . business methods . . . of the other directors,' he said.

I shrugged. I knew about the business methods of Sea Horse Land. I said, 'So why would Paul Welsh say he was acting on your behalf?'

He swirled his glass, jingling the ice-cubes. 'That,' he said, 'is the most puzzling aspect of the affair. I can only assume that he . . . wished to divert suspicion from someone else.'

'Friendly of him,' I said.

Honiton's eyelids were heavy with the cynical wisdom of his class.

72

'There are certain pressures none of us can resist,' he said. 'Paul is a very promising young man. I don't propose to hold this slip against him.'

I nodded. 'So what was the pressure?' I said.

He got up. 'I am telling you this for Paul's sake,' he said. 'Not because I give a damn what happens to you. Sea Horse has another director. His name is Deke Kellner.'

'Deke Kellner,' I said.

Honiton said, 'I expect you will be wanting to get along. I shall watch you race with interest.'

I stood up. I was thinking of Paul, talking to Kellner, terrified because he had lost the box. And later, his nose pouring blood at the bottom of the marble staircase. He had lied to me in Bayona because he had been scared out of his wits. And James had been scared out of his wits, in England. Both of them had been scared by the idea of admitting they had dealings with this Kellner. And Henry, who was seventy-one years old, was out gunning for him.

'Thank you,' I said. 'That is very interesting.'

Then I went back to the hotel and had dinner. I wondered what I should be doing, besides going to bed early and thinking about winning tomorrow's heats. The answer was not hard to come by. I should be keeping a careful eye on Deke Kellner, not to mention Helen Gallagher.

I went and had a couple of drinks in a bar. Then I drove to the long, low building under the palms by the coast road that was the Red House.

It was coming up to midnight. As I went up the steps and under the thatched portico, my legs told me that I had been on the move since early in the morning, and that they would like eight hours' sleep at my earliest convenience. I told them to shut up and went into the club.

It was like most nightclubs: a dance floor, with tiers of tables alongside and a stage at the far end. I went and got a beer from the operative behind the thatched bar. There was enough light for the customers to be able to stare at each other. I recognised a tennis hero, a couple of footballers and a millionaire songwriter. And then I saw a mop of blonde hair at a table in the half-dark near the stage: Helen. There were two men with her; one of them, by his hulking shoulders and frizzy grey hair, was Deke. The other was Paul Welsh.

The house lights went down. A spotlight caught a man in a glittering dinner jacket as he trotted across the dance floor and onto the stage. It was Jake. His teeth were shiny between his long black sideboards. The band started to play, and he started to sing, *It's not unusual*.

I strolled across the floor, climbed up the steps to their table and sat down. I greeted Deke first; he was the sort of person who would expect that. Then I nodded to Paul, and turned to Helen.

She was watching me vacantly, head on one side. 'Terrible singer,' I said, and grinned at her.

'I think he's terrific,' said Paul. I could see in the gloom the whites of his eyes flicking towards Deke, to see if Deke approved.

''E's bloody terrible,' said Deke, and laughed so loud that the singing faltered. He banged me on the knee. 'You're a good boy, Martin,' he said. ' 'Ave a drink, eh?'

I had another beer. The singing stopped, eventually, and the discotheque started to bang. Jake came and sat down with us. Helen snuggled up to him. I kept my eyes off her.

Deke said, 'You was fantastic, Jake. Wasn't he, Martin?' He winked at me, so Jake could see.

I was not in the mood for sitting around bitching at nightclub singers. I said to Helen, 'Shall we have a dance?'

Helen patted Jake on the shoulder and kissed his cheek, then led the way onto the floor with the exaggerated swing of the hips that went with her talking-to-Deke voice.

They were playing a Tammy Wynette song. She hung on to me, and we danced close together for a few bars. Her body was firm and pliant.

I said, 'What the hell are you doing here?'

She said, 'Merging with the landscape.'

'Have you seen an old guy called MacFarlane? Grey-haired English man. Sunburned. Smokes.'

'Not that I know of,' she said. 'Easy with the questions.'

'There are things I wish to know,' I said.

I felt her crisp blonde hair brush my cheek. 'You want to be very careful what you do,' she said, 'because people will be watching you.'

We danced a moment in silence. 'Like who?' I said.

'Like our genial host,' she said. 'He watches people very, very hard. He watches me, which is why I am making out I am deeply in love with that creep Jake. You want to give him something to watch.'

We had pivoted. Deke's hair was a red aureole under the spot. His eyes were on us.

'What are you doing here?' I said again.

'If I tell you, you will get us both hurt,' she said. 'So I won't tell you.' She reached up her hand, and I felt the light pressure of her nails at the nape of my neck. 'Like I said last night,' she said. 'Don't get hurt.'

'Nor you,' I said. Our hands clasped, briefly.

'*Ow!*' she shrieked. 'Good *grief!* My foot!' She started to hobble off the floor. When I tried to take her arm, she batted me away. It was a great performance. I could feel the blood rising to my face. Deke's laugh rang down from the table.

I sat and grinned like an idiot while Helen claimed that I had feet bigger than a New York cop, and that her toes were jelly. Deke listened with half an ear, watching the dancers. After a while he got up and said to me, 'I'm giving a party tomorrow night. All you boating people. Celebrate that Marbella Cup. Bring your crew. Paul'll bring 'is, and we'll try and get a few more of 'em organised. Get stuck into the ol' rum drinks. Ta-ra for now.'

I watched the four of them disappear into the crowd, laughing. It was late, and I was exhausted.

9

Next morning I felt as if I had slept in a microwave oven. I crawled out of bed, wrapped up against the air conditioning, and looked at myself in the bathroom mirror. Same old face, redder than usual, dark circles under the eyes. I had a quick breakfast of coffee, hard bread and butter, climbed into the car I'd hired the previous day, and headed back to Marbella harbour.

In front of the Club Deportivo there was a TV van and a few photographers. Flashguns went off in my face as I hurried up the steps and into the big, crowded room on the ground floor. There were three men on the platform at the end. Two of them I did not recognise. The third was Lord Honiton.

He flicked his amber eyes at me. 'Now we're all here, I shall explain the rules,' he said in his cold, dry voice. 'For the benefit of the press as much as the skippers.'

He explained. It was the same set-up as the Iceberg Cup. Two marks, a mile apart, one directly upwind of the other; the start halfway up the windward leg; a gun eight minutes before the start gun. The course was twice round the circuit, except in the semifinals and finals, which would be decided on the best of three single-circuit races. The umpires were in powerboats astern. In the event of a protest, they would decide on the spot who had been in the wrong, and instruct him via the radio of the appropriate penalty, which for minor infringements would be a time-wasting 720-degree turn on the spot. There were to be heats during the first day, all against all. The top four point scorers would then move on to the semifinals, and the winners of the best-of-three semifinals would sail the finals.

I saw Paul near the front of the crowd. He was frowning at his clipboard. It was good to see him and Honiton in the same room. It produced a healthy burn of anger in the pit of my belly, a clarity of vision. Winning was a job that had to be done, and barring accidents we were going to do it.

After the briefing I pushed through the crowds and down towards the taped-off area at the end of the quay. Charlie and the crew were waiting.

I jumped into the cockpit. 'Who have we got first?'

'Gilchrist.'

Gilchrist was an Australian offshore racer. He was a good helmsman, but he was new to the one-on-one aggression of match racing. We sailed out into the blue morning a little ahead of him, waltzed across the starting line a hundred yards ahead of him, and led him in procession all the way round.

The rhythm stayed with us. The next start was against Gulbransson, a Swede. We went into the middle of the starting area and stole his wind while he tried to sail backwards out of our shadow. Next one along, we edged Richie Barrett over the line ten seconds before the gun, compelling him to go back and recross, which put us a minute in the lead.

We had lunch on the water, and sailed four races that afternoon. We won all of them.

When I stepped onto the quay, a journalist came up to me and said, 'Congratulations.' He was young, with brown wavy hair. 'I've never seen anyone sail like that before.'

I grinned at him. 'How's Paul Welsh doing?'

He shrugged. 'OK, I guess. He won his. But not like you.'

I said, 'Keep watching,' and went down the quay to my car.

I pulled up the road past the pavement cafés on the seafront. The Bar Bric-a-Brac was open, but the sight of it depressed me. It reminded me of the Nevilles, and Henry's cigarette case, and the missing cash box.

Then I jabbed my foot on the brake pedal, and the car squealed to a halt.

Major Neville had said that Henry had visited them a couple of days *after* Squeal had served the papers on them. So how could Squeal have found Henry's cigarette case at the Nevilles? Someone was lying, and I was ready to bet it was not Major Neville.

I turned the car round in its tracks and drove back to the Bric-a-Brac.

The blonde woman was behind the bar, knitting. Her puffy black eyes were suspicious.

I said, 'Where's Squeal?'

'Out,' she said.

'Where does he live?'

She shrugged. I pulled a 5,000-peseta note out and put it on the bar. 'Address', I said.

I covered the note till she said, 'Edificio Granada. 6038.'

When my hand came off the money she whipped it away and smirked, as if she was being very clever. 'But 'e ain't there. 'E's gone to a party.'

'Where?' I said.

'Mr Kellner's,' she said, with a sort of reverence.

Back at the hotel, there were twenty telephone messages. Everyone liked the way we had sailed that day. I dialled London. The voice on the other end said, '*Guardian*.'

'Newsroom,' I said. 'Harry Chase.'

When they put me through, I said, 'Have you heard of a Deke Kellner?'

'Kellner,' he said, his voice heavy with Tom Thumb cigars. 'Nah. Why?'

I told him I was in Spain, and described Deke.

'Costa del Crime, eh? I'll ask around.'

I thanked him, and hung up.

For Deke's party I changed into black trousers, clean deck shoes, navy-blue shirt and seersucker jacket. I put a knife and a little torch into my trousers pocket; if I got a chance to look round at Nuestra Casa, I wanted to be equipped. Then I headed for the Shark Club at Puerto Banús, where I had arranged to meet the crew.

Charlie was sitting at a table with Scotto. I ordered a beer.

Charlie said, 'What time are we supposed to be at this party?'

'We've got an hour.'

'Let's have a look at that ketch you brought over.'

We paid the bill and walked along the waterfront, past the shops selling snakeskin bikini bottoms. *Aldebaran* was chocked in the far corner of the yard, towards the sea.

'Jeez,' said Scotto. 'What a heap.'

For all his eagerness when we first arrived, Deke did not seem to have touched her since. Her hull was a peeling barrel against the sky. There was a ladder propped against her on the seaward side. I went up it and across her gaping deck seams.

I was wrong; someone had been at her. Her main hatch was open, the bottom of the hold had been torn up, and some of the ballast had been removed.

'*Oiga!*'

I looked over the side. A small man in blue overalls was coming towards me. He was wearing a security firm's badge and shaking his head. I told him I had sailed the boat to Marbella, and he told me I was lucky to be alive. Then he escorted us to the yard gate.

'You're telling me this Deke bought that thing off a photograph?' said Charlie. I nodded. 'And it passed a survey?' We walked on. 'Strikes me,' said Charlie, 'that your friend Paul Welsh maybe had a word with the surveyor.'

'I reckon he bribed the bastard,' said Scotto. 'If I was this Deke bloke I'd kick his backside all over Spain.'

I did not say anything. I had no views at all on what Paul had or had not been up to.

Night was falling. The lights came on suddenly. We had another drink. After half an hour, we set out for Deke's party.

'Struth,' said Scotto, 'someone's been spending a few bob.'

From the gate, I could see cars parked in front of the heavy front door. The dogs must be locked up for the evening.

I stopped the car. 'Take her in,' I said. 'I'm going for a walk.'

The air was warm. I went out of the gate. I wanted to see the lie of the land outside the walls.

A little breeze ruffled the trees in the olive grove. I liked the olive grove. It and the Nevilles' house were the only two places I had seen on this coast that had any trace of wildness. The olive grove was land, not real estate. At its end, Deke's garden wall curved round the top of a low, scrubby cliff above a beach. I scrambled down onto the beach. The sea murmured; the wall ran on to the left, with a door in its centre. Steps led to the door. I tried the handle. It was locked.

Beyond the door, the wall met the neighbour's fence. It was reinforced with prickly pears, and I did not fancy climbing through it. I went back the way I had come, following the wall through the olive grove.

It was rough underfoot, hard to negotiate in the growing dusk. I kept my eyes on my feet. Halfway along, something pale caught my eye at the base of the wall. I stopped, picked it up, shone my torch on it.

It was a little brown plastic bottle, with a white label on it. It said: *One three times a day or as required. Commander H. MacFarlane.* The bottle was empty. I slipped it into my pocket with a hand that shook. Above me, a red-tiled roof ran down to the top of the wall. Garden sheds. Deke's garden sheds. Slowly, I walked back in through the heavy iron gates. The floodlights were on in the garden. The orange trees threw no shadows, and there were no hiding places.

The heavy oak front door swung open. Beside it stood Jacky Damage, like a lethal butler.

There was a roar of voices from the marble stairs. I walked up past the paintings and the dyed papyrus plumes. Charlie and Scotto were by the bar. Deke came towards us, wearing his usual white shirt and carrying a bottle of champagne.

I introduced him to Charlie and Scotto. I could feel the bulge of the pill bottle in my pocket. Charlie said, 'So that's your ketch in the yard?'

'Yeah,' said Deke, grinning. 'What d'you reckon?'

'Needs a bit of work,' said Charlie. 'Are you going to do it here?'

'Haven't decided,' said Deke, with a big smile. 'Somewhere or other.' His eyes roamed the crowd. 'You seen Paulie?'

I shook my head.

He winked. 'No,' he said. 'No. Probably reckons he needs his beauty sleep, after the way you sailed today.' He laughed, and punched me on the arm, and moved off into the crowd.

Scotto watched him go. 'Must be insane,' he said. 'Why the hell did he make you bring it all the way out here when he could have had it mended in England for half the money?'

When I had first heard *Aldebaran* had been sold, I had jumped to the conclusion that the purchaser was either an enthusiast or very stupid. Deke was neither of these things, and it was hardly credible that he should have used the boat merely as a vehicle for Paul and his tin box.

'Very hard to say,' I said.

At that moment I caught a glimpse of a tan shoulder and a head of greasy, thinning hair on the other side of the balcony. I went after it.

I caught up with Squeal at the head of the stairs. His face was yellowish and sallow. It went paler when he saw me. His eyes were snapping; he had been at the white goods already. 'What do you want?' he said.

'Where did you find that cigarette case?'

'Keep quiet,' he said in a terrified hiss. 'I told you. Nevilles.'

'Try again,' I said, more loudly.

'Jesus,' he said. 'It was here.'

'Over the wall,' I said. 'In the olive grove.'

'How did you know?' His face was white as paper. This time, I knew he was not lying.

I said, 'Where is the man it belongs to?'

He was not listening any more. He was looking over my shoulder, and his face was an even more terrible colour. Then he turned and ran down the stairs. The front door slammed, and he was gone.

I turned. Jacky Damage was standing behind me. He smiled, a wide smile that stretched the skin of his stony face like rubber.

' 'Scuse me,' he said, and went down the stairs at a horribly agile run.

I went out onto a balcony beyond the bar, to get some good, deep breaths of the clean night air. Henry had been in the olive grove. He had dropped his cigarette case and an empty pill bottle. What had he been doing there? I looked across the garden. Over against the wall there was a long white shed. There was a barred area in the middle, the kennels. At the far end there was something that might have been a garage. This end, there was a door and a shuttered window.

Of course, I thought. It was not necessary for Henry to have dropped his pill bottle in the orchard. He could have thrown it over the wall, from inside, perhaps as a signal.

My mouth was suddenly dry. I was inside the walls. The dogs were locked up. I had to look those sheds over.

'Cor,' said Scotto. He was leaning over the rail beside me. There was a blue swimming pool down there in the lawn, the trees and shrubs around it heavily floodlit, draped with fairy lights. But Scotto was not admiring the fairy lights. What he was admiring were the three girls in the swimming pool. They were very pretty girls, and they did not have any clothes on.

Beyond the pool I could see Helen Gallagher. She was wearing red stilettos, a pair of satin boxer's shorts, and a singlet that said JOE BUGNER TRAINING CAMP. There was a gold slave bracelet on her left ankle.

I walked back down the steps and out to the pool. The girls were still swimming. I watched them for a couple of minutes, fixing a grin to my face. Nobody seemed to be taking any interest in me, so I stumbled away into the bushes. Stumbling was good camouflage, by this time of the evening.

Once in the bushes, I pulled off my pale-blue jacket and hung it in the branches. My heart was beating too fast. The bushes thickened towards the little hut at the end of the pool. I crept away from the noise and the floodlights, and pulled myself over the wooden palisade of the pool enclosure.

The cicadas yelled in the bushes, and the party roared on the balcony and round the pool. But the garden was horribly silent. I could hear my own breathing, and the thump of my feet on the grass.

I got into the dead ground at the back of the pool hut. There was the high, white wall, with the door to the beach. The wall curved round to the right, towards the huddle of sheds and the garage. Anyone walking there would stand out against it like a lump of coal on a wedding dress. I took a deep breath, bent double to keep as much of me as possible against the black shadow of the herbage, and made for the sheds.

It was a horrible feeling. I walked slowly, expecting at any moment to hear the yells that would stop me in my tracks. But there were no yells, only the roar of the party, and the rustle of the sea beyond the wall and the olive grove next door.

I was against the end gable of the sheds where it stuck out at right angles from the garden wall. There was a shadow in the angle, and I crouched in its shelter, waiting for my heart to slow. The house was a sculpture of white sugar with red tiles, clad in a nimbus of floodlights.

There were three sheds, joined end-to-end. I ran up to the far end, past the kennels. The dogs stirred in their sleeping quarters. The end shed was a garage, with a silver Mercedes in it. If Henry was here, he was in the shed at the other end.

So I moved very cautiously back the way I had come. In the middle shed, a breathy rasping started. The dogs were barking. I opened the end door and slid inside.

It smelt like a garden shed. The disc of light from my torch travelled over lawnmowers, rakes, a shelf of weedkiller bottles. A gecko scuttled down the wall. It was all pure and innocent.

There was a connecting door on the inside far wall of the shed. I said, 'Henry.' There was no reply. I pushed it open, stepped over a pile of old flowerpots and went in. The light ran over hanks of string, packets of seeds, an old wheelbarrow. In the corner was a pile of what might have been potting compost. Everything in the shed looked grey and dusty. But the compost was warm, chocolatey brown, as if it had just been emptied there. I picked up a bamboo cane that was leaning against the wall, and dug it into the pile. An inch under the surface, it met a solid obstruction.

Bending, I brushed away the brown dust. There was a silver-grey surface underneath, metallic yet not metallic. I got hold of a corner, and pulled. I had to use both hands; it must have weighed fifty pounds. I held the torch in my mouth, and looked at it.

I had seen this slab before, or plenty of slabs exactly like it. Last time had been in the hold of *Aldebaran* in the gale. It was cold-cast ballast, a mixture of resins and lead that you mix up and cast to whatever shape you require. And I remembered looking down through *Aldebaran*'s main hatch earlier this evening, seeing the planking torn up in her hold.

There were more in the pile. I covered them up quickly, picked up the one I had found first and went back into the first shed. I wanted to examine the slab at my leisure and privately.

Very cautiously, I put my head round the outside door. I switched off the torch, pocketed it. Then I picked up the slab, tucked it under my chin, and flung it at the top of the wall like a shot-putter. It was heavy. It hit the stucco a foot below the top, bounced back, and landed with a dull thump on the lawn. The rasping from the kennels grew stronger.

My arm was aching fiercely where I had broken it. I knew I was not going to be able to throw the slab over without help. I went back into the shed. There was an old table in the corner, stacked high with flowerpots. I pulled them off, struggled outside with the table and pushed it against the wall. I climbed up onto the table. The line of shadow from the shed fell diagonally across the white surface of the wall. My head and shoulders would be showing above it, making a perfect silhoutte for anyone who was watching. I heaved the slab, up and out, heard the *thump* as it hit the ground on the far side, and waited for the shout from the house.

There was no shout. But somewhere in the house a bell was ringing, on and on.

I got down from the table, heaved it into the shed, and started to creep back round the swimming pool. Then, from behind me, there was the kind of buzz an entry-phone makes when someone opens the door by remote control, and a gurgling.

The dogs were out.

They trotted onto the grass, their bodies monochrome phantoms among the floodlit trees. I caught one glimpse of them out of the corner of my eye. Then I began to run for the pool palisade.

This time, I did not care who saw me. I wanted to get far away from those teeth, and I hit the palisade like a train running into the buffers, pulled myself up and got a foot hooked over the edge. The first dog ran up the wall as if it was flat ground. Its teeth clashed by my right shoulder. I felt the rip of cloth. It fell back. My body rolled over the fence, and went down the other side with a bang that knocked the breath out of me.

There was shouting now. Through the bushes, the swimming pool shone sapphire blue. I could hear bodies crashing through the shrubbery. I grovelled my way across the dead leaves under the bushes away from the palisade. My clothes, I thought. They're filthy, they'll give me away.

I knew what I had to do. I ran through the last of the bushes and dived into the cool water of the pool. When I came up, people were shrieking, 'He's got his clothes on!'

The crashing in the bushes had stopped. Deke came out and strutted up to the edge of the pool. The light made a bright aureole of his grey, curly hair. I could not see his face. 'You've torn your shirt,' he said.

I looked down. 'So I have,' I said.

'You want to be more carefuller,' said Deke. He spun on his heel and walked away.

I stood in the middle of the pool while the swimmers splashed and giggled around me. I felt cold. But that was not why I was shivering.

Dripping, I collected Charlie and Scotto. It was after midnight, time to go. We got into the car. Both sets of gates had to be opened for us now, and the Dobermans trotted from bush to bush, heads pointed.

Outside the outer gate, I cut the lights and turned into the olive grove. The car bounced across the rutted ground until we were opposite the rise of the shed roofs. The ballast slab gleamed dull grey in the dry grass close to where I had found the pill bottle. I heaved it into the boot, turned the car round and drove back to the road.

Charlie said, 'What is this?'

'Ballast from *Aldebaran*,' I said. 'I think I have just discovered why Kellner bought the boat.'

'Why?'

I said, 'Tell you in the morning.' Fact was, I wasn't yet quite sure. I dropped them at their apartment and drove into the town.

Squeal's little yellow eyes had watched a lot of what went on at Deke's house. I wanted to find out exactly how much.

The lights were on at the Bric-a-Brac. They were dim, but bright enough to show that there were five tourists sitting at the bar. Mona was in her corner by the icebox, brown fingers moving over her knitting. No Squeal.

I started the car and headed uptown. Away from the front, the only signs of life were a couple of taxis; one of the taxi drivers directed me to the Edificio Granada. I left the car a block away and walked. It was a tall white block of a building. Washing hung in the dark, empty walkways. Far away, a radio was playing flamenco and a dog was barking.

I went up to the sixth floor. Thirty-eight was dark, the front door closed. My heart sank.

I pushed. My hand caught ragged wood. Peering in the dim light, I saw that someone had dug away the rabbet with a chisel, so they could get at the lock. It was a Yale lock. Its tongue was exposed.

Pulling out my knife, I dug the point of the blade into the brass tongue and pulled it back.

The door swung quietly open.

The stink was revolting: old grease, stale tobacco, dirty clothes. And there was silence, the silence you get when there is nobody in.

My hand went to the light switch by the door, flicked it down. Nothing happened. There were some matches in the litter on the kitchen table, *cerillas*, little waxy sticks that burn with a big, clear flame. The first one cast huge shadows on the greasy ceiling. I went through a door and into the living room.

It was empty, except for two chairs and a coffee table. I flicked the light switch. That one did not work either. Fuse, I thought, and lit another match. The bedroom was empty. The bathroom door was ajar. I pushed it open, and went in. Then I took one big breath, and my heart started banging as if it was trying to hammer its way out between my ribs.

Squeal was in the bath, watching me. His eyes were wide open. His face was twisted into a horrible caricature of a grin. But the eyes were not seeing me. They would never see anything again. Because the cable from the shaver socket, the unfused Spanish shaver socket, ran to the big radio that sat on Squeal's scrawny belly in the bath, with the water halfway up it. Now I knew why the lights would not turn on.

The match burned my fingers. I lit another, and put my finger on Squeal's shoulder. It was cool, but not cold.

I ran out of the apartment, slammed the door behind me, and pounded up the street to my car.

When I got back to the hotel I double-locked the door of my room, slid the ballast slab under the bed and my wet clothes onto the floor. Then I went into the bathroom and turned on the shower.

Someone knocked on the door.

I stopped dead, with my hand on the shower tap. Squeal would have arrived home, panting. When the knock sounded at the door, he had not answered. After that, the smash and rip of the chisel . . . I found my hand shaking so badly I had to grip the shower tap to stop it.

'It's Helen Gallagher,' said a voice.

I wrapped a towel round my waist and started for the door.

She was alone. She had taken her shoes off, and was carrying them in her hand. She looked defenceless and very pretty. 'Come in,' I said.

She came in. She said, 'Do you have a drink?'

I gave her some whisky in a toothmug.

She sat down in an armchair and threw her shoes across the room. 'Oh, that feels good,' she said. 'Listen, I have to hurry.' I poured myself some whisky and sat down on the bed.

She said, 'I didn't want to disturb you.' She made an impatient movement of her hand. 'But I found this,' she said, and passed me a piece of paper.

It was crumpled, as if it had come out of a wastepaper basket. There was a lot of typing on it, in legal Spanish. It looked like a bill of sale, referring to a piece of land.

But it was not the text that caught my attention. It was the area below the typewriting. There was the signature of a lawyer, and of a purchaser, all neat and correct. Except that the vendor had not signed. Instead, he had written in black ink NO SALE, and dated it, and I knew the writing. It was loose and straggling; but it was unmistakably Henry MacFarlane's. And the name typed in for the vendor was his also.

I looked at the date. It was dated this morning.

I said, 'My God.'

She said, 'I found it in the wastebasket in Deke's room. That MacFarlane was the guy you were looking for, right?'

I stared at her. 'Today,' I said. 'He was with Deke today.'

'I guess so,' she said, and looked at her watch. 'I pulled it out of the wastebasket this evening.'

'So where is he?' I said.

'Who knows?' Her face suddenly looked thin and worried. 'But don't ask. Don't do anything at all, right now. Martin, you're in trouble. Deke's angry.'

I did not want to think about me being in trouble. I began remembering Squeal's face leering at me out of the bath. I said, 'Someone killed Squeal tonight.'

Her face was very still. She said, 'Jesus.' Then, 'He saw you running across the grass at his house with the dogs after you. I was watching.' She paused. 'He was laughing. He said, "Better luck next time." '

I said, 'I'm going to get him first.'

She said, 'If you knew Deke as well as I do, you wouldn't be saying things like that. So far he's been playing with you. Now he'll kill you.'

'I'm going to get him first,' I repeated.

She said, 'What are you trying to do?'

I told her about Henry MacFarlane, and Mary, and South Creek. When I had finished she sat and said nothing. I thought, You bloody fool, you don't know anything about her. The bill of sale could be bait.

I said, 'What are you?'

She said, 'I'm an actress. I came halfway round the world to do a job. See that certain people get what's coming to them. And in the middle of it all I meet this guy who's tearing round like a bull in a china shop, trying to get himself killed. And he's after the same thing as I am.'

'Which is?'

She got up. 'Listen to me. Stay in crowds. Don't go to the cops, because you never know who he is paying off. I'll see what I can find out about your friend Henry. Come to the Red House car park at two tomorrow morning, and follow me home. Now I have to go.'

I said, 'What were you doing in Deke's wastepaper basket?'

She said, 'It's a hobby of mine. I'll tell you tomorrow.'

She came close to me. Her arms went round my neck, and she kissed me hard. I kissed her back. Then she took a deep breath, and wriggled her toes into the red high-heeled shoes. 'See you tomorrow,' she said.

The door closed, and the clack of her heels faded down the marble corridor.

When she had gone, I looked at my watch. It said 1.00 am. I poured myself more whisky, and sat in the armchair, and tried to work out why Henry would be refusing to sign bills of sale, and to stop my thoughts latching on to Squeal.

Helen's scent was on my mouth. Whisky drowned it. The first time I had seen her in Spain she had tried to warn me off. The second time, she had taken me into her confidence. And now she was dangling carrots inscribed by Henry MacFarlane, and asking me to follow her God knows where, at an hour of the night when fatal accidents were easy to arrange.

86

She practically lived in Deke's pocket. If you wanted a perfect set-up, she was it.

I finished the whisky and climbed into bed. When I closed my eyes, I knew that I was going to be waiting in the Red House car park tomorrow night at 2.00 am.

10

First thing when I woke, I rang Mary. As I dialled, I tried not to let myself think that if Helen was right about Deke, this could be the last time I would be speaking to her.

She sounded cheerful. 'Read the paper,' she said. '*The Times* says you are inspired.'

'I've got some news about Henry.'

'What?' Her voice was suddenly tense.

Keep it light, I told myself. 'Nothing much,' I said. 'Just someone who's seen him around, yesterday.'

'Is he all right?'

'By the sound of it,' I said. I did not like the scrawling quality of his usually precise handwriting. But the 'NO SALE' was authentically Henry. 'Did he ever talk about property in Spain?'

'No,' she said. 'Never. At least . . .'

'Yes?'

'He used to go there birdwatching. D'you remember? Until about five years ago, with his friend Sam Ethridge. Every spring, when he should have been painting boats. Then Sam died, and he didn't go any more.' I had a vague memory of Henry packing a Panama hat and field glasses, and heading for destinations unknown accompanied by a grey-haired man with a large moustache. But Henry had always been off somewhere, so it had made no specific impression. 'Why do you ask?'

'I've got an idea he's selling some land.'

'Oh,' she said. 'I hope he's not making deals.'

'No,' I said. 'I don't think he is.'

'So he can't do too much damage.'

I made a soothing noise. She said goodbye, and wished me luck in the semifinals. And I went out into the heat and glare of the morning, carrying the ballast slab in a sack. At a hardware store in San Pedro de Alcantara I bought a lump hammer and a chisel, and then I drove round to Charlie's apartment. I arranged the slab on Charlie's kitchen floor, put the chisel on it, and split it in half, and then in quarters.

'Do you have to?' said Scotto, making faces at his first cup of coffee.

Charlie said, 'I suppose it beats ripping up telephone books. Now he's going to break the quarters into—'

He never finished. Because in the middle of the flat surface of one of the breaks was a rumpled polythene bag. I cut away the plastic film with my knife. 'Look what our Deke keeps in his potting shed,' I said.

On the palm of my hand, the morning sun was shining on two little stones. They seemed to drink in its rays through the facets cut into their sides and then pour them out again dyed blood-red, so that the white ceiling of the room swam with motes of ruby-coloured light.

'Struth,' said Scotto.

We chopped the slabs up into dust. There were five more rubies. And a lot more slabs in Deke's potting shed.

I said, 'You were asking why Deke didn't have that ketch done up in England.'

Charlie nodded. 'Hardly worthwhile,' he said. 'She only had to make the one trip. Well, strike me pink.'

Scotto said, 'Who loaded them up?'

'He had his own special surveyor,' I said. 'Paul looked after the repairs. He hired his own men.'

'Go to the cops,' said Scotto. 'Now.'

I said, 'Not yet.'

Helen had said that Deke had friends in the police. I wanted to wait until after two o'clock in the Red House car park before I made any moves against him. All the same, I had to make an excuse.

'This bloke's into everything,' I said. 'Jewels, extortion, you name it. If the police move in, things are going to get confused. He'll go to ground. And nothing will stick. *Aldebaran*'s not the only boat in Spain with cold-cast ballast.'

Charlie was still looking at the jewels. 'Enterprising chap, your friend Deke,' he said. 'Wonder where he got them from.'

I picked up the telephone, dialled the *Guardian* in England, got Harry Chase. Amazingly, he was already in his office.

'Oh, there you are,' said Harry. 'Your friend Deke Kellner sounds a bit unsuitable.'

'In what way?'

'Family man, southeast London style. Cousins everywhere. Armed robber, wanted for questioning in connection with the Walstein robbery.'

I had never heard of the Walstein robbery. I told him so.

'Blimey,' he said. 'Don't you read the papers? It was five years ago. He had some mate who worked there who knew when the shipments came in. So one day, Mr Walstein is looking through a box of sparklers at his office in Hatton Garden, and Deke comes in with a couple of family

88

friends. They all had sawn-off shotguns. Deke scooped up the jewels, about three million quids' worth, and left after breaking Walstein's fingers. He was laughing, my friend said. Out loud.'

'He's got a wonderful sense of humour,' I said.

'And then he turned up in Spain,' said Harry. 'Nobody knew how. He just popped up one day, passport stamped, resident's permit, the lot.'

I said, 'Why would anyone want to bring jewels to Spain?'

'Córdoba,' said Harry. 'Jewellery capital of the Mediterranean. Sell your gold, launder your stones, recut the Crown Jewels if you want them to. Listen, have we got something in the way of a story here?'

'You will be the first to know,' I said, and hung up.

We put the jewels in a safe deposit. Then we spent the morning practising, and the afternoon racing.

When we came ashore that evening, Paul had sailed seven, won six. We had sailed seven, won seven. The draw for the semifinals was in the Club Deportivo. Honiton's lips compressed in a thin smile as he unfolded the slips of paper. 'Welsh against Gibson,' he said. 'Devereux against Fournier.'

I carefully stayed with the crew all evening. We went to a brightly lit restaurant, and drank beer in a brightly lit bar, places with no dark corners where an accident could happen. At 1.45 I left the bright places and drove to the car park of the Red House.

FAIRY LIGHTS LOOPED in the branches of the trees made an avenue to the entrance. People were spilling out onto the grit, laughing and leaning on each other. Cars began to move away. Then two people came down the steps: a man, long-legged, in glittering trousers, and a slim woman with a short skirt and blonde hair. Jake and Helen. She reached out an arm and touched him on the shoulder; he blew her a kiss, and they walked to their respective cars.

I set my teeth and followed her out of the car park and left onto the main Marbella road. There were hundreds of headlights. Any one of them could mask the cold eyes of Deke or Jacky Damage.

Helen left the main road and drove through a private estate of villas set well back from the road, separated by stretches of scrub and umbrella pine. There was a pair of headlights in my rearview mirror.

The headlights turned off to the left. I found I was breathing too fast. Then Helen turned down a track. A small white house gleamed in the headlights, set among trees. Her car stopped. I parked alongside and got out, slowly. The feet would come out in hard, deadly thumps, running. I stood with my back to the car, waiting for it to happen. But there were only the cicadas in the warm night, and the howl of a distant motorbike.

'Come in,' she said.

Suddenly everything was warm and ordinary. There was sand under-foot, and pine needles. Inside there were white walls with pictures of bulls, and red terracotta floors. I began to relax.

She opened the door of a big room and said, 'I'll be right down. There's beer on the shelf.'

I sat and half-waited for Jacky Damage to come in at the door with a sawn-off shotgun. He did not come. Instead, Helen came, wearing a black towelling dressing gown that looked very good against her short blonde hair.

She sat down on the sofa and said, 'I was at the house all day. I didn't see or hear your friend Henry MacFarlane. I'm sorry.'

'That's fine,' I said, to cover my intense disappointment. Then I said, 'Do you know who Deke Kellner really is?'

She laughed, without humour. Then she went to a cupboard and pulled out a big red scrapbook. She sat opposite me, tossed it in my lap. I opened it.

The first page held a glossy American real estate brochure. QUAGUE LANDING, it said. EXCLUSIVE SPACE FOR YOU—AND YOUR DREAMS. There was the usual picture of boats, an artificial harbour, houses with steep-pitched roofs. On the next page, the newspaper stories began. TWO DIE IN BARN FIRE, said the first one. The rest were variations on the same theme, clipped from papers ranging from the Boston *Globe* to the Quague *Examiner*. The story said that Jack Walton, a retired Harvard professor, and his wife Una had died in the blazing ruins of their hay barn during haymaking. The theory was that the grass had been too wet when stacked, and that the bales had spontaneously ignited. Jack and his wife had been shifting the bales at the time of the fire, and had been unable to escape. After their deaths the Walton farm, landing included, had been sold to a property company.

I did not have to read the company's name to know that it was called Sea Horse Land.

'Who were the Waltons?' I said.

'My parents,' said Helen. 'My parents never made hay out of wet grass. They burned them alive in the barn. First they found the landing. Then they made rumours that Jack and Una were having money problems. Then they drew up a bill of sale, and forged Jack's signature. Then they killed them before they could get their lawyers on to it. But nobody believed that, except me.'

'I believe it,' I said. I was thinking of the things that had happened at South Creek. 'But how did you get this far?'

'I took a look at Sea Horse,' she said. 'It's registered in the Isle of

Man. They wouldn't talk to me there. So I changed my name and hung about and made good friends with a guy in the Southampton office.' She looked at me with her steady grey-green eyes. 'And he gave me James de Groot's address and, well, I got to meet James. I got to be good friends with him too. And he gave me the Southampton job.'

'I am not at all surprised,' I said. My own relationship with James could wait till later.

'James is a director of Sea Horse Land, did you know that? Deke thinks he has class, so he's useful. He lines up the deals. He doesn't ask too many questions about the way Deke . . . negotiates.'

'What about Paul Welsh?'

'Paul Welsh is an errand boy,' she said. 'He thinks it's cute to hang out with bad guys. I guess Deke has him around because he likes to see him wriggle.' She paused.

I said, 'How do you know about this?'

She said, 'I work in the front office here now. He thinks I'm too dumb to be a problem. So I get leads, and I follow them. And when something lands in the wastebasket, I copy it. It's not evidence. But he has plenty of friends in the police, anyway. He'll be hard to catch, in Spain.'

'But can't he be extradited?'

'He moves around,' she said matter-of-factly. 'All over. He trades passports, you name it, it's no problem. But next time he's out of the country, I find out where he's going, and I tell the police, and they take him.'

I said, 'How long can you keep this up?'

She smiled. It was a fierce smile. 'Won't be long. He's going to England any day now.'

'How do you know?'

'Your friend Paul is helping him get out. His mother's ill.'

I said, 'How's he going, and when?'

'You'd have to ask Paul,' she said. 'His mother lives in a place called Sheerness. She won't leave the country. She's very sick, dying. They're a close family, the Kellners.'

I remembered the dreadful old lady under the archway at Nuestra Casa. I said, 'How long have you been . . . collecting evidence?'

'Three months,' she said. 'Three . . . goddamn . . . months.' Tears ran down her face.

I went to sit beside her. I put my arm round her. I said, 'Don't worry. Not tonight, anyway.'

She put her head against my chest. Her body was stiff in my arms. Then she relaxed, and pulled her head away, and said, 'OK. No worrying.' She sat up and dried her eyes.

The telephone rang.

'Leave it,' I said. 'It's three in the morning.'

'Uh-uh.' She shook her head. 'It'll be Jake. He needs his hand held.' She picked up the receiver. 'Yeah,' she said. 'Jake. Poor honey. Poor Jake.' The receiver jabbered in her ear. Then she said. '*What?*'

The voice on the other end was high and agitated. She said, 'Poor honey. Relax, baby. It's over now. You go back to the apartment and take one of your pills.'

The jabbering faded. She put the telephone down. She said, 'The dogs got out at Deke's.' Her voice sounded strained. 'There was some guy in the garden. An old British guy. Jake said he shouted a lot.'

I sat up fast. 'Did the dogs get him?'

'I don't think so. Jake said he couldn't watch.' Her voice was level, telling me because she had to, not because she wanted to.

'What did they do with him?'

'Jake said they put him in with the dogs.'

'No,' I said. I stood frozen with horror. Why would they want Henry eaten alive? Then I knew. Once again, I could see the label on the pill bottle gleaming in the dry grass of the olive grove behind the dogs' run. You bloody fool, I said to myself. He's been there all along. In a room leading off that cage.

'They'll kill you,' she said. 'You'll never get him out.'

'I'll be back.'

She stood in the door as I started the car. The light from inside shone through her hair in a golden halo. I pulled out onto the main road and headed east.

Down at the Club Deportivo, a pair of green-clad policemen were leaning on their bikes and watching the young element falling down the steps of the discotheque. I ran down the quay to the jetty, fumbling in my pocket for the key. I needed a ladder to get over Kellner's wall, and bolt-cutters to get into the cage. The bolt-cutters were in the starboard locker. Back up the quay again, I climbed into the car and drove towards the road, looking for building sites.

There was no shortage. I found one down a side street, with a site hut. I unlocked it with the bolt-cutters, pulled out a short ladder and a pile of old sacks. I jammed the ladder in at the back window of the car, tossed the sacks into the driver's seat and got in after them.

There were no lights in the road down to Deke's house. I drove the car all the way into the olive grove. When I turned off the engine, the only sounds were the cicadas and the rattle of leaves and the plunge of the sea on the beach. I pulled the ladder out of the window, leaned it against the wall where the shed roof stopped, and started to climb.

THE FLOODLIT LAWNS SPREAD out like a pool of poisonous water below. I laid two sacks over the broken glass set into the top of the wall, sat on them, and let the ladder down the other side. To my left, the rasp of the dogs began. I went down the ladder.

The kennels had a sort of barred porch. Inside the bars, the dark forms of the Dobermans moved quickly to and fro, like sharks in a tank. As I came closer they began flinging themselves against the bars. Their teeth shone in the floodlights.

My palms were slippery with sweat. I knew where I had to go.

'Good dogs,' I said. *'Good dogs.'* They hurled themselves at the bars.

The porch gate was in the centre. It closed with a simple spring latch. The bars were vertical, with a horizontal brace halfway up. I breathed deeply. Then I opened the door, standing behind it.

The dogs came out, so fast that their paws skidded on the grass as they turned back to tear me into pieces. But by then I had my foot on the horizontal and was pushing up and over. The dogs bounced up, snapping at my legs. I went over the top and landed on the concrete with a thump, my hand on the bars, pulling the gate shut behind me with a metallic crash that seemed loud enough to wake the dead.

Then I stumbled back and leaned against the wall to get my breath.

Across the grey lawn, the big white house was dark and quiet. The Dobermans raved throatily through the bars. I turned my back on them, and examined the wall.

There was a door in it, which led to a little room that smelt of dog. I closed the door, and turned on my torch. The beam played over bare cement walls, and another door. This one had a padlocked bolt. The bolt-cutter went through the padlock like cheese. I pulled back the bolt, and the door swung open.

The room had cement walls and a concrete floor. On the floor stood a galvanised bucket and a hard chair. There was something in the corner that might have been a pile of rags. I went down on my knees beside it.

The pile of rags moved. It said, 'Push off.' The voice was blurred and indistinct. But it was unquestionably the voice of Henry MacFarlane.

I said, 'Henry. It's Martin.'

There was a groan, and the sound of stirring. Then he said, 'By God. It's you.'

I said, 'Come on. Let's get you out of here.'

'Not easy.'

The torch beam caught his face.

When I had last seen him, it had been square and solid as a rock. Now it was a mass of pouches and hollows. His breathing was loud and hoarse.

'Hands,' he said.

I pointed the torch. His fingers were thick and blackened, because someone had trussed his wrists together with wire, and looped a chain round the wire, and padlocked the chain to a bolt in the wall.

I could not speak. The bolt-cutters sliced through the chain, and I cut the wire from his hands as gently as I could.

He struggled. 'Help me up,' he said.

I helped him sit up. The effort made his breathing thick and stertorous. 'Can you walk?'

'Just.'

He was in no state to run away from dogs. I shone the beam of the torch round the walls. There were no windows.

Then I remembered. 'The pill bottle,' I said. 'How did you get it out?'

He was bent over his hands. The returning circulation must have made them agonisingly painful. 'Roof,' he said. 'Stood on a chair. Shoved 'em out under the eaves with bucket bottom.'

I pulled the chair up against the end wall, stood on it. Pole rafters supported heavy clay tiles. I was taller than Henry, but my fingertips only just touched the rafters. Taking a deep breath, I bent my knees and jumped. My left hand caught one of the battens supporting the tiles. I groped with my right hand, ramming the fingers between tile and rafter. The fingers found a purchase, tightened. I walked my feet up the wall until I was hanging from the rafters like a sloth, found a lodging for my left foot, hung a moment to catch my breath. Then I got my right one in among the tiles, and kicked.

They gave, then fell back into place.

My fingers were cramping, and the tendons of my forearm felt like red-hot wires. I kicked again.

There was a long scraping slither, and a crash. The night air flowed in through a hole the size of three tiles. I kicked the battens away, shoved a leg through, and wriggled my body out onto the roof.

'Getting a ladder,' I said, into the dark hole. Henry was coughing.

I went along the roof to the wall and pulled up the ladder. A couple of tiles skidded underfoot, bursting like bombs on the stony soil of the olive grove. The dogs set up a harsh, breathy roaring on the lawn. I fed the ladder through the dark hole and went down.

Henry was still sitting on the floor. I said, 'Come on.'

He looked up at me. 'Ticker,' he said. 'Can't.'

'Yes, you bloody well can,' I said. 'Get up.' I grabbed his wrists, and pulled. His skin felt loose, like the skin of an invalid. 'Now get onto the ladder,' I said.

He half fell against it. I held him upright. The torch clattered to the floor and went out. I left it.

94

'Climb,' I said.

There was a silence. 'Can't move,' he said.

I bent down, and put my head between his legs, as if I was giving a child a lift on my shoulders. 'Hang on with your hands if you can,' I said. Then I took his weight, and started to climb.

He was surprisingly light. As he came out of the hole in the roof I felt him flop sideways. I pushed through, into the grey half-light of the dawn. The sound of his breathing almost blotted out the sound of the dogs.

A yellow oblong showed through the trees. Someone had switched a light on in the house.

I said, 'Sorry about this.' I grasped his left wrist and pushed his body off the wall. He groaned as the weight came on his arm. I lowered him the last three feet. Then I jumped after him, dragged him to the car, bundled him into the passenger seat. Someone was shouting on the other side of the wall. I heard a starter motor cough in the garage as I twisted the key. My own engine started first time. The back wheels spun in a cloud of dust. We bounced towards the gate.

It opened and the wing of a car came past the gatepost. A Mercedes. I floored the accelerator, and we hit with a huge, metallic *bang*. The Mercedes slewed away, and the black serpent of the road wound clear in the half-light. I looked quickly round. Water was spewing into the Mercedes' headlights, doubtless coming from the radiator. They stayed immobile in the gateway. My own car was wobbling, but did not seem to be vitally injured. The needle came round to 140 kph, and I kept it there.

There were no lights in the rearview mirror as we turned onto the main road. Henry stirred. His face was a bad, ashy white. 'We'll get you to a hospital,' I said. Not in Marbella, though. Accidents could happen in Marbella. 'In Malaga. Can you last out?'

He struggled in his seat, fighting for breath. We were entering the outskirts of the town. I pulled over, helped him upright, fastened his seat belt and got back on the road. His colour improved a little. He said, 'There's no parking in the olive grove.'

'Quiet,' I said. 'Save your breath.' He's raving I thought.

'No parking in the olive grove next door to bloody Kellner,' he said. 'You know why?' I shook my head. ''S my olive grove.'

'The olive grove next to his house belongs to you?'

'Bought it in nineteen forty-seven,' said Henry. 'Like old Neville. Except I registered mine, in Madrid. Used to go birdwatching there.'

I looked round. He was watching me, and his eyes glittered with the old, sly Henry sparkle. 'Kellner tried to get it,' he said. 'Last five beachfront acres for miles. Worth millions. Don't need millions.' The words came out slowly and painfully, with many pauses for breath. 'I

95

went to see the bastard, to negotiate. Didn't want it built on. Argued. Went away for a few days. He asked me back. Tried to get me to sign it away. All that stuff at South Creek was to persuade me.'

'You rang up,' I said. 'After Dick died.'

He nodded. The effort seemed to tire him. 'They told me about that,' he said. 'It was Paul Welsh that kept 'em in touch. They said he knew where that box was . . .'

The road was empty except for a couple of beer trucks heading for Torremolinos.

'But he didn't,' said Henry. 'My fault Paul got it. Should have left it in the pots. But I panicked. Told you to take it to the bank. Bloody fool.'

'What was in it?'

'*Factura*. Bill of sale. Once he had that, he could burn it, put his lawyers on to it, make a new one, change the register, nobody the wiser. Dropped it overboard, I hear.'

'Yes.'

'By this time the bastard had locked me up. Said he'd kill me. Had a new *factura* drawn up. Put it in front of me. All legal. I wouldn't sign.'

'I saw it,' I said. 'No sale.'

He laughed, a slow wheezing laugh.

The sun was up. Ahead and to the left, an airliner was roaring into the morning air over the Malaga Coca-Cola plant.

'Beautiful place, that olive grove,' said Henry. 'Lovely birds.' He lapsed into silence. Then he said, 'You racing today?'

'Semifinals,' I said. 'If I get through, I could be racing Paul.'

'Beat the bastard,' said Henry. 'Hammer the little swine.'

He lay back, panting. I said, 'Henry. I want you to rest and get better. Then we will get together. And what you know will put Deke Kellner in prison for twenty-five years.'

'Fine,' he said. 'Fine.'

We turned into the gates of the hospital. I jumped out, ran in and explained to the receptionist. They brought a stretcher. As Henry went through the doors, he said, 'Race. And look after yourself.'

I hesitated. My eyes stung with tears. It was typical of Henry to use up precious breath for my sake.

I got back into the car, and headed for Marbella.

IT WAS SEVEN O'CLOCK when I got back. The town was clean and silent, except for the whisper of the jacaranda leaves in the square. I parked outside Charlie's apartment and rang the bell. There was nobody in the street, but it was a nasty, naked feeling, waiting for him to answer.

When he let me in, I told him what had happened. Then I lay down on

96

the sofa and went to sleep. When I woke at one o'clock, refreshed, we had coffee and omelettes in a cafeteria. Then we went down to the Puerto Deportivo.

As we motored the yacht out of the marina, the wind that had been blowing the leaves in the olive grove last night was still coming in off the sea. It was a solid, heavy breeze, and the forecast said it was going to stay that way, due south veering southwesterly later.

Fournier was already on the water. He was a fair-haired man, with a blond beard. He waved when he saw us.

Up in the starting area there were a dozen or so spectator boats.

'There's Deke,' said Charlie, pointing at a big yellow Sunseeker with black tiger stripes.

I did not look. All my attention was on the white triangle of Fournier's sails, rocking-horsing over the indigo waves a hundred yards to windward. I could see the sweat shining on his forehead.

'One minute,' said Charlie.

I took off my white peaked cap and rearranged it. I was sweating too, but not the way Fournier was. There is a kind of radar you have to have, in match racing. It tells you how the other guy feels about his boat, about you. Today, it told me that Fournier was on the defensive.

Which suited me fine.

'Here we go,' said Charlie. The gun thumped.

'Tacking,' I said, and moved the tiller over.

The boom clacked across, and the lee rail pulled a long, roaring gurgle out of the sea.

'He's tacked,' said Charlie.

Fournier's crew were ready, but their nerves put them maybe half a second behind, and during that half-second we had the nose in front, and our sails were taking the edge off their wind, and they were stuck.

'Tack now,' I said, and we were away on the right-hand side of the course, waiting for Fournier where we had to be to catch the windshift.

'Murdered him,' said Noddy.

'Too easy,' I said. 'He was nervous. He won't be so easy next time.'

Charlie and the boys worked well. The spinnaker popped out like a huge orange at the windward mark, and we flew round. The windshift did not materialise, but that was no problem; morale is everything, and Fournier's had taken a hammering at the start. So we came over the line a full thirty seconds ahead of him.

But there was no backslapping. There were more races to sail.

Fournier's grin was not so convincing at the start of the second race. We sailed him out of the water, and crossed the line ten boat lengths ahead. And that was that.

97

'You're in tomorrow's final,' said Charlie. 'Nice work.'

The radio crackled below. Scotto put his head out of the companion hatch. 'Paul Welsh won his,' he said.

Beat the bastard, Henry had said. I grinned at Scotto. I was truly delighted.

In the clubhouse I sipped a beer and grinned at journalists. After twenty minutes I and my crew trooped outside onto the steps, and flashbulbs popped. Then we went into the car park, to collect our cars and head for the showers. I peeled off the bunch for the twenty-yard walk to my car.

There are trees outside the Club Deportivo. Dusk was coming on, and their leaves were black against the sky. A green SEAT was parked under the trees at the far side, where I had parked my car. As I took the keys out of my pocket, Helen Gallagher leaned out of the SEAT's window. She said, 'They—'

I did not hear the rest because at that moment something collided with the base of my skull. A jagged star of pain exploded in my head, and I pitched forward. A car had drawn up behind me. Someone opened the back door, and as I fell into the dark inside, something hit me again, same place, and I thought, with a deep misery, Helen, you bitch, you were stringing me along. Then there was a laugh, long and loud. Deke's laugh. But the laugh was moving further and further away.

IT WAS COLD: so cold that I was shivering. The pain arrived in the back of my neck and behind my eyes. There was a noise of some kind. Sluggishly, I worked out what it was. Water, slamming against a hull. The sound of a boat under way. An engine. There were footsteps. 'Let's do it here,' said a voice.

I still did not understand what was going on. But down in my scrambled brains, some part of me knew. I found I was shuddering like a stunned fish. Hands grabbed my arm.

'Christ,' said a second voice. ''E's bloody 'eavy.'

I said, 'What is this?' But all that came out was a croak.

''E's awake,' said the first voice.

'Not for long,' said the second. I knew that one. It belonged to Jacky Damage. I felt myself being dragged along, legs trailing. My head did not like being upright. It throbbed evilly.

There was a light breeze blowing. I could see lifelines, a tiller, white Fibreglass under the moonlight. We were aboard a cruising boat, sailing on a broad reach, kept there by the autopilot nudging at the tiller.

The breeze felt cool on my hot forehead. It became easier to think. Out there in the night, motoring parallel to the boat, was a big motor yacht. Sailing yacht and motor yacht carving parallel wakes on the black sea under the moon.

'Go on, then,' said Jacky Damage. 'Get up on the edge.' My knees were against the seat in the cockpit. Something banged into my skull where it met my neck. Agony exploded in my head, and I tried to shout. No sound came out. I went forward, hands out to brace myself against the fall.

The hands did not work, because I was not falling onto anything hard. Arms outstretched, I went smash into black, salty water.

11

I went in with my mouth open. Water poured in, and I choked. I could feel myself rolling, and for a moment I did not know which way up I was. But my head broke water, and I got rid of the bitter mouthful. *Get organised*, I told myself. The pain in my head was very nasty; the water was cool, but it did not seem to be helping. *Get organised!*

I heard the sudden thunder of engines in the night. A disc of light appeared, a little sun throwing off dazzling white rays. Searchlight, I thought. Down, down. They'll run you down. So I struggled down again, into the cold black. I could hear the rapid ticking of propellers in the water. Holding my breath made my head worse. I did not want to be seen on top of the water, but I could not stay down any longer. I let myself come up, gasped air.

The searchlight went out. The engines faded. The moon gleamed palely in the sky. The sea was black and huge. It heaved with a long, slow lift of swell. To my left I could see red and green sidelights, a white stern light, the pale loom of a sail in the moonlight. It was the cruiser from which I had been thrown overboard, sailing away on autopilot towards the coast of Africa. Must have slipped overboard, they would say of me when the boat came ashore. Sad, very sad.

Suddenly the sea felt very cold.

Far away to my right, a frieze of orange and white lights was strung along the horizon, the lights of the coast. But they were too widely spaced to be the lights of Marbella. My numb brain gnawed at the problem. Where was I?

A wave bigger than the rest rolled under me. From its crest, I saw that along the base of the lights, the individual points coalesced into a glowing mass. The lights over there were scattered among the mountains above Marbella; if the glowing mass of the town itself was visible only from a big wave that would put me more than ten miles offshore. Ten miles is a long, long way to swim in the middle of the night, even if you are fit.

I blinked at the lights, and tried to tell myself that I could swim ashore easily, if I took my time. Then I saw Deke's calculating eyes. He would have done his homework. I would no more be able to swim to Marbella than cross the Atlantic on roller skates.

I trod water, and spat out salt, and concentrated on keeping my breathing slow. Panic would be no good. But I thought of the tiredness: the aching limbs, the slow sink into the water. And the struggle against choking, far away, where no one would hear.

Somewhere at the back of my mind, a tiny voice said: Why string it out? It's better to let go; close your eyes, float down into the dark, away from the agony in your head . . .

My head broke the surface. I shouted, '*No!*' The sound was pathetic in the dark heave of the water. I kicked off my trousers, and pulled my shirt over my head. Then, turning my face to the lights, I began to swim.

It was easy swimming at first, but soon my shoulders started to hurt, and the pain spread up into the bruised patch at the base of my skull and over into my eyes. My legs were stiff, too. I rolled onto my back and rested, looking up at the sky. It was deep black, set with billions of heavy yellow stars that did not give a damn. Sod you, I thought, I'll show you, and I rolled onto my stomach again, and began to kick for the lights.

I breathed water again, choked, and felt my arms becoming slower and slower. I rested again. It was getting harder to float, so I rolled back. Soon the arms would stop, and that would be that. Squinting at the dazzle of lights on the horizon, I struggled on.

One of the lights moved.

Car, I thought. Late-night driver. Lucky bastard.

The light moved again, out of the bright patch that had hidden it, and across a less brilliant patch. I felt my heart speed up, breathed a faceful of spray. There were three lights. The lowest was red; a ship showing her port side. Above it was a white light, with directly above it another red. And I knew what they meant as well as if I had the nautical almanac open in the water in front of me: *a vessel fishing, other than trawling*.

It could not be more than half a mile away, that vessel fishing other than trawling. Clenching my teeth, I began to plod heavily towards it. *Stay there*, I yelled in my mind. *Stay there!*

My arms were numb; they moved like the paddles of an old, old steamer. The boat was only two hundred yards away now. I could see its side like a black wall, the figures of men moving in the working lights on her main deck. I stopped in the water, raised a hand, shouted. But there is a lot of noise on the deck of a fishing boat, and my voice sank into the racket like a stone into deep mud.

I was a mere hundred yards away now. A man was standing looking up
at a machine on deck. He had his back to me. I yelled, thrashed the
water. He did not turn. I'll get close, I said to myself, planning. Then I'll
yell again. My shoulders were on fire, my back like red-hot iron bars.
The man was so close I could see the sleeves of his T-shirt fluttering in the
breeze. The engine noise sounded lower. White water churned under the
counter. Slowly at first, then gathering speed, the fishing boat began to
move ahead.

I was too late. I went mad, or as mad as you can go when your arms are
dropping off your shoulders and your legs no longer function. I moved
the last twenty yards to the ship's side, felt the kick of the propeller's
wash spin over me. Then I was watching the tall black stern move into

the darkness and treading water, watching salvation fade into the dark.

Something bashed my arm. I jumped away from it, thinking, Shark, creature of blackness. It brushed me again. I put my hand out to push it away, and felt a smooth, round object. A net float.

My hand closed on rope. The rope was moving. It tried to pull my arms out of their sockets. I hung on, buried in water, my legs tangled in the meshes, as the net went through the sea and walloped me against the lovely steel plating of the fishing boat's side. I was shouting as I went up the side. Someone heard the shouting as I came over the rail, and stopped the big steel roller that was winding in the net. I saw three stocky men who had not shaved, staring, with their mouths open.

'*Buenas noches*,' I said.

Then everything went hazy. I have a vague memory of being led to a bunk that smelt of rotten fish and wine and black tobacco, and looking at my fingers, which were as wrinkled as a washerwoman's. Then I must have passed out. The next thing I knew, someone was shaking me by the shoulder. It was one of the fishermen, grinning and shoving a cup of coffee at me. My head hurt, and the muscles in my shoulders felt as if they were all mixed up with broken glass, but I managed to choke down some of the coffee, which was heavily laced with brandy. The fisherman gave me a pair of overalls, much too small. He showed me his watch, an elaborate Japanese object. It said five past ten. I went on deck.

Marbella was white-hot under the morning sun, and the smell of the harbour was acrid in my nostrils. I went and shook hands with the whole crew. They looked mystified, but seemed pleased I was alive. Then I hobbled down the gangplank and collared a taxi to the marina. I was bulging out of the overalls, but since it was Marbella nobody looked twice, and I had more important things on my mind than clothes. Helen, I thought. Helen had set me up.

But what was even more important than Helen was the race.

Down at the end of the breakwater, the sails were already up. The taxi driver followed me out there through the crowds. Charlie looked up from the cockpit and said, 'Where the hell have you been?'

I climbed stiffly down. Charlie paid the driver, and Scotto lent me a pair of shorts. 'Sorry,' I said. 'Got held up.'

'You're not supposed to be alive,' said Charlie. 'They found a boat sixty miles off of here at six this morning, autopilot alarm going, nobody on board. Someone said you'd been seen going out to her earlier.'

I said, 'Who said that?'

Charlie shrugged. 'Rumour.'

Somebody else had heard the rumour. Down the dock, Paul Welsh was putting elastic bands on his spinnaker. Or had been; because now he was staring across at me as if he had seen a ghost.

I called, 'Morning, Paul. You ready?'

He grinned, a weak grin that hardly stretched his face.

Charlie said, 'What's wrong with him?'

I said, 'His friend Kellner got Jacky Damage to take me out on your missing boat. They banged me on the head and threw me overboard.' I pointed out at the blue sheet of the sea.

Charlie looked at the sea, then at me. 'Overboard?' He frowned at me. 'Are you sure you're fit to sail?'

I looked across at Paul. His fingers were fumbling as he taped up a rigging screw. I said, 'I've never felt better in my life.'

THE SPECTATOR BOATS CAME OUT with us, black against the glitter of the sun; Honiton and the men with the notebooks and lenses. Best of three races, one circuit per race, winner takes all.

'Gun,' said Charlie.

Eight minutes to the start. I went into the area fast, stayed in the middle. Paul squeezed up to leeward, trying to grab the advantage. The dogfight began, the looping and weaving. Suddenly I could feel the certainty radiating out of me like light. Get ready, you bastard, I thought. Get ready.

'One minute,' said Charlie.

Paul was sitting on our rail as we went down for the left-hand buoy of the starting line. I could hear the wakes roaring between the plastic hulls. The buoy was dead ahead, in the slice of blue between the forestay and the shroud. Any more to port, and I would be outside, forced to go round again. We were spot-on, our noses dead level, racing down for the line with perhaps a foot between us. I wiped sweat off my forehead with my sleeve, said, 'Sheet.' I saw Charlie lick his lips as Scotto eased the mainsheet. He was counting the seconds: fifteen, fourteen, thirteen. He looked worried. We were going for the line at a horrible pace.

But easing the sheet slowed us, and Paul's bow inched ahead. He seemed to shoot out in front as we slowed, bounding forward as the buoy came up ten yards ahead.

'Nine, eight, seven,' said Charlie. *'The bastard's over early.'*

Paul's bow had crossed the line a good six seconds before the gun. I could hear him screaming at his mainsheet man.

'Protest!' we roared.

He was so close that I could hear his VHF crackle as the umpires told him to do his penalty turn, right round in the water. We crossed the line bang on the gun. Next time I looked, he had got round, and tacked out for the right-hand side. When we crossed tacks he was a long way back.

We held him all the way up the windward mark: our spinnaker popped out nice and easy, and we headed down for the buoy with the wind on the backs of our necks. Paul got round two hundred yards behind. We were a minute and a half ahead at the finishing gun.

We sat and drank orange juice while we waited for the next race. The other semifinalists went by. I should have been watching them. But I was sitting on the cockpit bench because I was not sure my knees would support me.

'You look terrible,' said Scotto.

'You should see the other guy,' I said.

He nodded and loped away onto the foredeck to see to the spinnaker. Charlie said, 'Couple of minutes to the next gun.'

'Let's get it over,' I said. Best of three. One more would be enough.

The trimmers sheeted home. The breeze snapped the sails into their tight, gleaming curves, and I pointed the nose at the left-hand end of the line. Over to starboard, beyond the umpire's inflatable boat, I could see the taut white triangle of Paul's sail as he headed for his end of the line.

'Minute to gun,' said Charlie.

'Let it all go,' I said.

The sails, unsheeted, roared as the wind caught them both sides and made them flutter like flags. Ahead, the two bottle-shaped buoys of the start line sat one on top of the other, like the sights of a rifle. On the far side of the sights, Paul's boat was heeling gently, spilling wind, a little white moustache in the ink-coloured water under the bow.

'Thirty seconds,' said Charlie.

'Go,' I said.

The winches roared. The sails became hard white wings, and the wake hissed like a snake where the rudder cut the water. The buoy flashed past a second after the gun. We started three-quarters of a boat's length ahead on the port tack. Three-quarters of a boat's length is not far, but it is far enough, because on the windward leg it meant that we were not only between Paul and the buoy, but polluting the wind in his sails with our dirty air.

'Watch him,' said Charlie, between his teeth.

I was watching. When you are behind, sailing to windward in a two-boat race, your only chance is to break away from the leader's cover, and go off on your own. The only way the leader can lose the race is to relax his cover, or make a cock-up. We did not relax our cover.

The sweat was pouring down my face as the bottle of the windward mark grew in the haze beyond the shrouds. My shoulder muscles felt as if they had been tied in knots, and my head was throbbing in the molten glow of the sun off the water.

104

'He's keeping up well,' said Charlie.

He was. The certainty I had felt at the start had slipped. The marker bottle grew; I could hear the waves slapping against it over the hiss of our progress and the bubble of the umpire's launch. 'Snappy with that kite,' I said. Noddy and Slicer, foredeckman and mastman, nodded. Being snappy with spinnakers was how they earned their living. Gently, I began to bear away for the buoy in a long, smooth acceleration curve. There was the dark frost of a gust on the water ahead. Sun and sea swam in my eyes. The nose came round. The kite went up, Noddy's arms moving with the urgency of a boxer on the punchbag. I was sailing too fast. The puff hit as we were halfway round, and the sail swung to starboard. The bottle rushed up, three feet away. And as we passed, the big bulge of nylon sail swung sideways and brushed against the top.

'*Jesus!*'

We held our breath. We did not have to hold it long.

'Protest!' roared the voice astern.

The VHF began to crackle. I did not wait to be told that we had touched the buoy and were therefore liable to re-sound it. I slammed the tiller over. Noddy let the kite fly. We were round again in twenty seconds. But a boat sailing at eight knots can go a fair distance in twenty seconds. As we came off the buoy and the spinnaker sheet came in, Paul's boat was eighty yards down the track, kite up and drawing, and we were nowhere.

Charlie said, evenly, 'He's got a long way to go.'

I steadied my breathing. He was right. Gradually, the fat half-moon of his transom grew. But it was very late; we had a lot of catching up to do.

He came round the buoy and hauled in his sheets just as we came down on it. I saw his face under the boom. When he saw me looking, he raised a hand from his tiller and put up the middle finger and jabbed it in the air towards us.

'Very sporting,' I said. Then I hauled the tiller towards me and in came the spinnaker, and the winches roared as we dug the lee rail in and galloped up on his tail.

But he had us covered, and there was nothing we could do. I split away for the far end of the line, but he got the gun ten seconds ahead of us.

We were level: one race all.

We sat there and did not say anything for a while. I wanted to put my head down on the seat and go to sleep for a couple of weeks. But that would not have been good for morale. So I started to think about Paul instead. He knew I was better than him. Rather than lose, he would sail foul. He had done it in Australia, and he would do it again. So I sipped orange juice and squinted across to where he and his crew were sitting in their cockpit, heads close together. One race: fifty thousand quid and the Marbella Cup.

'Watch him,' I said. 'He'll get nasty now.'

They all nodded: Charlie, dark and thin, Scotto, large and blond, and Noddy and Slicer, bullet heads on necks that ran straight to their shoulders. They could get nasty, too.

'Three minutes,' said Charlie.

We moved along to the end of the line. Overhead, two helicopters clattered. Television boats hovered outside the start area, closing in tight as we began our run down. The breeze was hot, pouring over the sea from the south. Mixed with the smell of sea was a hint of dust: Africa.

We were at the right-hand end of the line this time, coming in on starboard tack. A puff of smoke floated off the committee boat, followed by the little *thud* of the one-minute gun. The breeze was freshening. Ahead, Paul was bearing down on wings of spray. I had right of way. There was twenty yards between us when I eased the tiller towards me. As our nose bore away, Paul luffed violently, jamming his nose into the wind to avoid the collision that would have disqualified him. I heard him bellowing over the roar of unsheeted sails, and permitted myself a very small grin. Confident men did not bellow.

Our boat had picked up now, rattling across the waves on a reach as I bore away, then came up and crashed through the wind as we came onto Paul's tail. We shot up to starboard of Paul, let go the sheets, and sat there. As long as we did not fall off the wind and collide with him, we were safe. I looked across. He was ten feet away. His face was dark with anger. A gust was rolling its shadow across the water on our starboard bow. We both pointed up, the tall silver wands of our masts leaning in parallel, ours to windward of his, as the wind wailed in the shrouds. I saw the man on Paul's genoa move his hand, stealthily.

Scotto had seen it too. His hand moved like a snake, released our genoa sheet. Our genoa spilt wind, and the mast bounced upright. So did Paul's, but a moment later, scything through the place where ours had been a second before. If our masts had touched, it would have been deemed that I had rammed Paul, the right-of-way boat. At best, it would have been a 720-degree turn for us. At worst, it would have been disqualification.

'Tack!' I yelled.

'Forty-five seconds to start,' said Charlie.

We came onto port and moved away to the right. Sweat was pouring down my body.

Charlie said, 'Seven . . . six . . . five . . .'

I bore away, picking up speed as the starting line buoy came closer.

106

'Zero,' said Charlie.

The gun sounded, and the buoy hissed past two seconds later. Looking down the line, I saw the other buoy still obscured by Paul's white hull. We were ahead, by maybe a second.

'Tack now,' I said.

And over we went onto starboard, with right of way, heading back into the middle of the course.

I was concentrating on judging where that white pyramid of sails coming towards us on port was going to arrive when we crossed tacks. It was the crucial moment in the race, that crossing of tacks. Whoever was ahead then stood an excellent chance of staying there.

As he came closer, I could feel the grin beginning.

We passed a length and a half forward of his nose, and tacked to cover. They were all shouting at each other now.

He tacked again, to escape our wind shadow. We tacked again, to stay between him and the mark. The game of cat-and-mouse began.

The next five minutes was an edgy clatter of tack and counter-tack. By the time we were on the buoy at the end of the course, we had increased our lead to three lengths.

The buoy came up on the starboard bow. This time, we were far enough ahead to save hoisting the spinnaker until we were well round.

'Go,' I croaked.

Noddy began to haul. The yellow nylon soared aloft. It stopped half-way. Noddy gave two jerks at the halyard. 'Stuck,' he said. My stomach turned over. Scotto was already on his feet, pounding along the coach-roof to the mast. He squinted up against the glare. I glanced over my shoulder. Ten yards away, Paul's yellow bubble of nylon was bearing down on us.

'Got it!' shouted Scotto. The spinnaker went all the way up, wobbled and filled. But while we had been wrestling with the halyard, Paul had gone through, and now he was a good two boat lengths clear in front.

I took a deep breath, and let it out. My head was pounding. I moved the tiller, aiming the shadow of the spinnaker at the black curly hair on the back of Paul's neck. We began to gain ground. 'You're holding him,' said Charlie.

Paul gybed, drew away. I concentrated on trying to creep over to port, where the puffs were coming from. Inch by inch, we began to move up again. I saw his main flutter in my dirty wind before he gybed. We gybed. He gybed again. All that existed was heat, and the men on his foredeck, and the crash of the boom. We went round the buoy at the opposite end of the course on starboard, hardening up as we rounded. And there he was, sitting on our wind, our nose level with his stern.

'Here we go,' I said.

They all looked at me. Their eyes were sceptical.

'Tacking,' I said.

We whistled away from under his stern. I watched Paul. He looked at us, then at the finish line, three hundred yards away but straight into the wind. Then he tacked. His crew made a sound. It was a low groan, because the genoa hitched on the mast on its way over, and as he came round and settled on port, we were dead level, sailing under him.

We went through the water six inches apart, hard on the wind, heeled at precisely the same angle. He'll tack away, I thought. And I knew I did not have the strength to make another tack.

I looked at Scotto, and I said, 'Sheet.'

Then I shoved the tiller away from me.

Scotto eased the genoa. The boat came suddenly onto an even keel. There was a harsh clatter of metal in the sky. Paul's mast, heeled over our decks, had collided with ours.

Paul turned away. It had been my right of way. Thank you for the idea, I thought. He went through a penalty pirouette. We left him for dead, sailed over the line sedate as a flotilla cruiser. The gun banged.

I sat down on the cockpit seat, and let my head fall into my hands.

'You did it!' roared Charlie. 'You did it!'

I nodded. I beat the bastard, I thought. I beat the bastard.

12

Honiton was on the quay, standing to attention in his blazer, his Pall Mall Yacht Club tie flapping in the breeze. He walked up to me.

'Congratulations,' he said. 'I shall be recommending that you be invited to compete in the Senator's Cup.' The words sounded strained.

I thanked him and walked on past, pushing my way through the crowds on the quay. Helen, I was thinking. Now Helen can explain.

My hired car was under the trees, where I had left it twenty-four hours ago. I climbed in and screamed away between the glaring white hotels, out onto the main road. Horns blared at me as I roared across the east-bound lane. I turned off. Sand was blowing as I stumbled out of the car and up to the front door of Helen's house.

The door was open, swinging in the wind. I walked straight in, and into the living room.

There were books all over the floor, the pictures off the wall. The telephone receiver was dangling at the end of its cord. I opened the cupboard where she had kept the scrapbook. The scrapbook was gone.

I ran through the rooms shouting her name. There was smashed china, broken pictures. Upstairs, the bathroom was a shambles. The cabinet above the washbasin was closed. It was the only closed door in the house. I opened it.

The inside of the door was covered in red smears. For a moment I thought it was blood. But it was lipstick, and the smears were writing. *Mart Gone Eng Dekes mom ask Paul.*

I remembered her face the last time I had seen it, in her car under the trees. She had not been trying to set me up. She had been trying to warn me.

Deke's mother was dying in Sheerness. But if Deke went openly to England, Deke would get arrested. So he would not be climbing onto a scheduled flight with Helen on his arm. He had been through her house and found her dossier. Now she was his hostage, insurance for him against people like me.

I drove back to the hotel, and rang Paul's number. He had already left. I would have to catch him in England. I got myself the first seat out, on an Iberia flight in four hours' time. Then I drove to Malaga, and went to the hospital.

Henry looked very old. There was a drip in his arm and oxygen cylinders by his bedside. He said, 'Mary's coming out. She's taking me home.'

I would have liked to see her myself, but there was still a long way to go. I said that was good, and patted his hand. Mary was safety, and someone to look after him. That was what he needed now. I sat with him a while in the antiseptic hush, soaking up the distant hiss of doors, the birdsong of women's laughter. As I got up to leave, he said, 'You beat Welsh?'

'Yes.' I hesitated. 'We had a side bet,' I said. 'He doesn't own the brokerage any more.'

Henry stared at me, his eyes suddenly clear. 'Cheeky young devil,' he said. 'You may not be my son, but you bloody well behave like it.'

I left him, and plunged into the crowds at Malaga airport.

IT WAS SEVEN O'CLOCK by the time I extricated myself from Heathrow. The aeroplane had given me time to work out where I was going, and I had an hour's sleep. The cool English air made me feel stronger and clearer-headed.

I rented a car from the Hertz desk, and drove across to the M3. On the outskirts of Basingstoke I stopped at a garage and bought a motorcycle security chain complete with padlock. Then I drove on into the green country round Winchester.

At seven thirty I turned in between the tall brick gate pillars of Philby Grange, residence of Paul Welsh. It was the kind of house stockbrokers built in the 1930s after they had seen Hampton Court, with timbered gables, barley-sugar chimneys and an eruption of dormer windows.

Paul's BMW was on the gravel in front. I came to a crunching halt by the front steps. It was quiet in the house except for distant watery noises. I walked quickly through to the back of the house. The noises grew louder. There was an indoor swimming pool at the Grange, which was where the noise was coming from: a huge iron conservatory, with green tiles and indoor plants.

Paul had been swimming in the pool. He was drying himself by the edge. He looked round sharply when he heard my footsteps, and wrapped his towel round his waist. 'What do you want?' he said.

I said, 'A chat.' I kept on walking, right up to him. He decided not to give way. That was his mistake. As I took the last step, I pulled my arm back and hit him, as hard as I could, in the solar plexus.

He made a revolting noise and leaned forward, all the way. I gave him my knee in his face. He rocked back. There were heavy white wrought-iron chairs under a potted palm. I jerked one over, shoved it behind his knees. He sat down, hard. I took out of my jacket the chain I had bought at the garage. Quickly I looped it round his waist, under the chair's arms and round the back, and clicked the padlock shut.

He had recovered enough to glare at me. 'Let me go,' he said.

'Paul, I want to know about Deke.'

He said. 'You know as much about Deke as I do.'

I said, 'I found Henry MacFarlane half dead in a shed at Deke's. He told me that you organised the sabotage at South Creek. I want to know all about it.'

He looked at my face. He started to talk. 'It was James,' he said. 'I met him with James, in Spain. James said he had this bloke who wanted to make deals on beachfront land, for marina development. It was respectable, too. Honiton was with them. So I went in with them.' He shivered. 'I'm cold,' he said.

'Keep talking,' I said.

'So we did some deals,' he said. 'Straightforward deals. Then he asked me to keep an eye out for some sites in England. I knew of South Creek so I told him about it. I said Henry'd never sell any of the land. Deke just laughed and said no problem. And things started to happen at South Creek. You know about them.' He paused, ran his tongue round his lips.

'Why did you buy the brokerage?'

'Investment,' he said. 'When MacFarlane sold, Sea Horse would have had to buy the goodwill off me.'

'So you had them coming and going.'

'Quite.'

'What about Raistrick?' I said.

'He was nobody. An errand boy. He got things done.'

'And you did things too, didn't you, Paul?' I said. 'You set the pontoon adrift.'

'No,' said Paul, shaking his head violently. 'Not me. I was at a dinner party in Norfolk that night. You can check.' He was almost whimpering.

'So who gave you the cash box?'

'Raistrick,' said Paul. 'There was a message from Deke. He wanted it delivered.'

I watched. 'Did you know what was in *Aldebaran*'s cargo?'

'There wasn't any,' he said.

'Yes, there was,' I said. And I told him about the jewels.

His jaw hung slackly. He said, 'You're joking.'

I said, 'If you want to find out who is joking, you can go and look in my safe deposit in the Banco de Bilbao in Marbella. Now, Deke is on his way to England, and I want to know how he is arriving. When and where.'

'Would he tell me?' said Paul.

'Yes,' I said.

'Never,' said Paul.

I went round behind him, until he could not see me. I gripped the back of the chair and flung it sideways. He went over with a crash. There was a crack as his head hit the tiles. I went down beside him, grabbed his left hand, which was uppermost, and jammed the wrist over the hard iron angle between the chair's arm and the back. He screamed.

'Tell me,' I said. 'Tell me.'

His voice was high and quick. 'His mother's ill. He's got a boat at Le Tréport. A pilot cutter. He'll be coming up the Horse Channel to the Medway tomorrow.'

'Is Helen Gallagher with him?'

'Yes.'

'That's all right, then,' I said. 'Thank you for your kind assistance.'

I dropped the keys to the padlock into the pool, pulled him a safe distance away from the edge and left him there, keeled over on his horrible green tiles, naked in the white iron chair.

IT WAS DARK OUTSIDE. The hire car's lights made a yellow tube in the darkness. I arrived at South Creek at ten o'clock. The gate was shut. A man in a black uniform with silver buttons and a peaked cap walked round to the car window, leading an Alsatian. I told him who I was. 'Mrs MacFarlane's left for Spain,' he said.

I went in search of Tony Fulton, our yard foreman. His house was dark, so I drove down the long red-brick streets of Marshcote to the Burnett Arms. He was leaning on the end of the bar, reassuringly large and brown, a full pint in front of him, talking to a couple of fishermen. When he saw me, he got me a pint. I had a pie, too.

'Bloody terrible about Henry,' he said. 'Heart, is it?'

'He's OK now.' I did not want to explain. I said, 'I want you to come up to the North Foreland. We'll charter a boat. I've got a job on.'

'Racing?' said Tony.

'Just a day out on the water.'

'One of our charter boats is up Ramsgate,' he said. 'Bloke got seasick. He left today. What's the job?'

'Tidying up something that happened in Spain.'

He sipped his pint. 'You got that *Aldebaran* there all right, then,' he said. 'Get on with Paul?'

'Bit iffy,' I said. 'He's got some nasty friends.'

'Wouldn't be surprised,' said Tony.

I finished my drink. 'I'm off,' I said. 'You coming?'

'I'll follow on,' said Tony. 'See you there in the morning. Nine o'clock OK? Boat's in Ramsgate marina. *Opal*.'

I got into the car, told my eyes to stay open, and headed for Ramsgate.

Opal was a twenty-nine-foot Sadler. Her seasick charterer had left her jammed into a visitor's berth in the inner harbour. I climbed aboard, let myself in with the spare keys and tumbled into the settee berth in the saloon. I was exhausted. But every time I shut my eyes I saw a pilot cutter crabbing cross-Channel in the westerly, with Deke at the tiller. And I wondered what Deke would do with Helen once he didn't need her as an insurance policy any more.

I thrashed around on the bunk until the light came. Then I went up into the town and got a cup of tea and a bacon sandwich. It was a pink and grey dawn; the forecast said westerlies, light, with fog patches.

I went back to the Sadler and cleaned her up. I was swabbing her decks when Tony came down the pontoon.

'Bastard of a drive,' he said, tossing his bag onto the deck. His fair hair hung lank and greasy, and there was a day's stubble on his big chin. The boat rocked as he heaved himself aboard. I started the engine and cast off the lines. Tony reversed off the berth, pivoted the boat with a kick of engine against rudder.

'Where to?' he said, as we motored through the lock gates into the outer harbour.

'North,' I said, and cranked out the roller genoa all the way.

We ghosted into the grey Channel seas, making for the mouth of the

112

Medway. Over to port, the clutter of buildings round the North Foreland light came up above the low white cliffs. The tide was ebbing hard; it was low at two.

'What's it all about?' said Tony.

'We're meeting someone,' I said. 'He's going up the estuary on the tide. He'll be using the Horse Channel.'

I had not allowed myself to think what would happen if he did not turn up. The tide runs fast through the banks and shallow channels of the Thames estuary. It was three hours to low water. If Deke didn't go in on the flood tide he wouldn't go in at all.

Tony said, 'Who is this bloke?'

'Guy who was giving us trouble at South Creek.'

'Ah,' said Tony. 'So why didn't you call the law?'

'He's got somebody with him,' I said. 'He'll hurt her if he sees anything like the law. We've got to be discreet.'

'Discreet,' said Tony. 'Yeah.'

Two hours went by. We were an hour off low tide. Down to the west, the shore was splattered with Margate. We were anchored now. I was smoking Tony's roll-ups in the Sadler's plastic cockpit.

At four o'clock, Tony said, 'They've missed the tide. I reckon we push off 'ome.'

'No,' I said, not because I thought he was wrong, but because I did not want to give up. 'He may be on the next tide.'

'So?' said Tony. 'It'll be black as your hat. You'll never see him.'

An hour passed. The sun was sinking, the tide coming in fast.

'We've had it,' I said.

'Thank God for that,' said Tony. 'Can we go 'ome now?'

The horizon was a clean curve under a sky of high cloud and patches of blue. Down to the southwest, a couple of yachts were heading in for Dover. Three container ships plugged along in the shipping lane to seaward. And suddenly, far to the south, a whisker cut the smooth blue line. I focused the binoculars on it. In the disc of the glasses, it became a gaff peak and the top halves of two foresails.

'Got him,' I said. He was late, but he could still just about make it to Sheerness.

The sun sank behind the land. The clouds over in the west turned gold and red; the Calais hovercraft from Ebbsfleet whined astern. And the gaff peak came up out of the darkening sea and grew a dark hull with a pram dinghy lashed bottom-up to the cabin top.

There was one head in the cockpit. Helen would be below. She had to be below.

We turned our nose north and started motoring back up the Downs.

113

We kept three miles ahead of them, our nose pointed as if we were heading for Ramsgate. The sky darkened. The cutter astern turned on her navigation lights. Very carefully and very gently, we followed her from in front towards the bulge of the North Foreland. We were catching the first of the ebb. When it was full dark, I turned off the running lights.

Tony said, 'What are you going to do?'

'Let him go by,' I said. 'Follow him all the way home. Nail him as he goes ashore.'

The red-and-white flash of the North Foreland came abeam at ten-thirty. Tony was chomping Spam sandwiches. I was eating nothing at all. The black sea was full of lights: to port, the sodium glare and neon of the towns, and to starboard, the red and green jewels of big traffic moving in and out of the estuary. He was three-quarters of a mile in front as we rounded the headland.

There was a different smell round there. It was not the clean, salty smell of the Channel, but the smell of all the muck that had come down the Thames, flushing the south of England. Lights blinked ahead. The first of them was quick-flashing white, the SE Margate light at the entrance to the South Channel, with beyond it the Gore Channel.

The tide was still ebbing. The buoys stretched ahead, winking. Deke's port light started fading away northward. It left the white flash of the SE Margate buoy to port. 'What's 'e playing at?' said Tony.

The chart was spread on the seat. I flicked a shaded torch at it. The main channel runs along the north coast of Kent, cut off from the estuary by a long sandbank, inside which there is another channel, slender and difficult, shoaling to a mere foot of water at spring tides. It is, understandably, a quiet place: a useful back door to the Horse Channel if you did not want anyone to see you coming.

We crept after them. We were moving very, very slowly. I was getting jumpy. All round us banks of sand would be rising, invisible in the black. To the north, the only thing that was not black was the pinpoint of light. If we lost it, I lost Helen.

'Take her,' I said to Tony. I went below. My stomach felt like a walnut: it needed feeding. But as I was looking in the food locker a voice spoke from the companion hatch.

'Put your hands on your head,' it said. 'Get up slowly, and come up here.'

A pair of hands appeared in the hatchway. They were holding a thick, blunt gun. They belonged to Tony Fulton.

'Move,' said his voice. 'Or I'll blow you all over the cabin.'

I put my hands on my head. As I did so, I caught sight of my watch. An hour to low water.

'Up,' said Tony.

I went out of the cabin and into the cockpit. He was a black shadow standing by the tiller, steering with his hip, the gun a dark bar in his hands. Tony? I said to myself, and tried to feel surprised. But I could only feel numb.

'How long have you been at South Creek?' I said. 'Five years, is it?'

'That's right,' said Tony.

'Ever since the Walstein robbery,' I said.

'Very clever,' said Tony.

The numbness was fading. In its place came fear. I could see the chart in my mind. Must keep him talking, I thought. Must stay alive.

'And you were doing a bit of moonlighting,' I said. 'What was on those charter boats you ran? A few more sparklers in the ballast?'

'Maybe,' said Tony.

'And *Aldebaran* took the last of it. Because old Deke was converting the Walstein jewels into property, a nice little earner for your retirement. But you're armed robbers, you and Deke, and you couldn't help using your old techniques when it came to negotiation deals. Pity about Dick.'

'That was an accident,' said Tony. 'He seen me. I had to.'

'I suppose it was you that stole the cash box. And you got Raistrick to clout you one in Southampton.' I sighed, theatrically. 'You've been a bloody nuisance, Tony.'

I saw the silhouette of his head nod. 'Yeah,' he said. 'I reckon I have.'

'What seems odd to me,' I said, 'is that you had all those jewels, if you wanted them. There was old Deke, living the life of Riley in Spain. And there was you, putting antifouling on boats at South Creek. Why?'

'I didn't want to get involved,' said Tony. 'I was going straight.'

'So why did you do it?'

He said, 'I done it because me old Mum told me to.'

I did not understand. 'But why?' I said. 'You liked Henry and Mary. We got on. Five years is a long time. So why stick with a bastard like Deke?'

' 'E's my brother,' said Tony in a hard, flat voice. 'You're all right, I'll give you that. But 'e's my brother, and now I'm taking him to see our old Mum before she passes on. And that's different.'

I looked down, remembering the portrait of the old woman in the house near Marbella. I knew I was going to die unless I did something, now. But I could not think of anything to do.

The deck under my foot hesitated, moved forward, tripped again. The keel had touched bottom.

I took one step up onto the cockpit seat, and jumped over the side. As I went there was a huge explosion, the night turned bright red, and

something very hot seared my right ear. Then I hit the water.

It was freezing cold, with a flat, foul taste. I stayed under for as long as I could, cringing away from the blast of the gun. The tide was ebbing hard; as I came up, the pale semicircle of *Opal*'s transom moved. He had got her off the bottom. And over to the right was the red running light of the pilot cutter.

I felt sick. It was not the taste of the water; it was the feeling of struggling in the great black emptiness again, in a flume that wanted to fling me out into the straits of Dover, suck me down, and turn me into fish food. While Helen was up there, half a mile away, ten feet from that red light . . .

I started to swim for the light.

Of course, I made no headway against the ebb. But as I swam, the current made me crab outwards until I was dead astern of the light. I could see the chart in my mind. *Not that far now.*

The red light vanished behind its baffle. There was a white stern light now, and the dull green shine of a starboard light on the black water. And as I saw the green, I grinned in the darkness. I had been right.

The lights should have been in line. They were not. The white was perceptibly higher than the green. The pilot cutter was firmly aground, and canting over to starboard. So I swam until my shoulder muscles were on fire, and the muscles of my belly ached, towards the darkness to the right of that canted line of lights.

When I had been swimming for five minutes, I let my legs sink. My feet hit something under the water. Hard sand. The bottom.

I stood there for a moment, with the water shoving past my chest. The lights were a quarter of a mile away. The channel here was no more than four hundred yards wide, bordered by unmarked banks. Deke had got it wrong. He was stuck for at least two hours.

Out in the channel, I heard a splash and a roar of anchor chain. Tony in *Opal*. There were more splashings, the whirr of an outboard. Tony was coming to have a chat with his brother. I bent my knees, bringing my nose down to the water. The whirring travelled across to the pilot cutter, stopped.

Very cautiously, I started to walk up the tide towards the lights. At first it was hard going. The water was chest-deep, and running at more than a knot. But soon the water shallowed to waist-deep, then knee-deep, then ankle-deep. Then I was on dry land.

I crouched on the sand and wondered what the hell to do next. Four hundred yards away there was a dull glow from the cutter's cabin windows. There was none from the companion hatch. Tony and Deke were below. Helen was below.

The air smelt raw and wet. The lights were growing halos. Fog. I set my teeth to stop them chattering, and began to walk quietly along the sandbank towards the pilot cutter. The cabin lights were soft yellow squares. Forward of the square cabin windows were two round portholes, serving the forepeak. I waded into the black water, moving gently so as not to make a disturbance, towards the black hulk of the grounded cutter. The inflatable dinghy from *Opal* bobbed astern. The water deepened again.

When I was up to my waist, the cutter loomed high above me, her rail tilted down towards the water. Aft, the main hatch from the cockpit to the cabin was closed. Forward of the cabin top and the mast, I could dimly see another hatch. It would lead to the forepeak.

I stood still, holding my breath. A murmur of voices came from the main cabin, and music: the James Last orchestra. I waded very carefully round to the bows.

The rail was a couple of feet above the water. I grasped it with both hands, pulled myself up like a man getting out of a swimming pool. It seemed to make a noise like Niagara Falls. I hung there, waiting for the main hatch to burst open. The voices kept up their murmur. James Last rattled on. Deke laughed, his empty, horrible laugh. Nothing happened.

Very quietly, I crawled up the deck to the forward hatch, ran my fingers round its edge. They found a hasp, secured only by a shackle.

I twisted the shackle pin. It gave, unscrewed. Slowly, I worked it round until it came free. Cautiously, I wriggled my fingers under the rim of the hatch. James Last ground to a halt. The next track started. I waited for the noise to get going and lifted the hatch.

Light streamed out. I whispered, 'Don't make a sound.' Down there in the dazzle, a voice said gently, 'Martin?' Helen's voice.

My eyes were getting accustomed to the light. She was pale, and her yellow-blonde hair was wild. She stared at me for a moment as if she was trying to make herself believe what she was seeing. I whispered, 'Come out.'

I laid the hatch-cover back on the deck, stretched my right arm down. The bones of her wrist were slender as a bird's in my grasp. When I strightened, she came up the hatch without touching the sides.

I said, 'Wait until you can see. Then go over the side, get aft, and untie the dinghy. Take it away.'

There was the tiniest of splashes as Helen went overboard. Down in the cabin, Deke laughed. Laugh on, I thought. I'll bottle you up and hand you over to the law. The whole package.

I closed the hatch and reshackled it. Then I padded aft. The cockpit was a large one, full of dark, bulky objects. Very gently, I laid my hand on the companion hatch. It was a two-part hatch, with a slider on top, and louvred doors below. My fingers crept across the top sill of the door, found what they were looking for: three rings, one for each door, one on the hatch slider. Slip a pin through there, and nobody got out.

One of the voices below coughed. The music stopped, and there was a stirring. The hatch slammed back under my hands. The doors opened. A blaze of yellow lamplight poured into the foggy air. I jumped back to the far end of the cockpit. The head in the yellow hatchway was Deke's.

He said, '*Hello*,' in a nasty, quiet voice. His shoulders came out of the hatch. From the cabin behind, Tony was shouting a question.

I groped with my right hand and found something. A can, with a handle. I got a purchase on the can, and heaved it at Deke's head.

Suddenly the fog was full of the reek of spilt petrol. Deke roared and fell back down the hatch. I scrambled to my feet, found the rail, and tumbled over the edge into three feet of water.

'My eyes!' Deke screamed. 'My eyes!'

I splashed round to the stern. There was a dark torpedo shape on the water. The tender. I lunged at it. My fingers hit smooth neoprene, skidded, and caught a bight of rope. An outboard roared next to my ear. I shouted, 'He's got a gun!'

The cutter lay in a nimbus of light. There was a human figure standing on her side, black in silhouette, huge against the light. There was something in its hands that roared and spat a long tongue of flame. The tender jumped in the water.

I shouted, 'Swerve!'

'It won't steer,' shouted Helen.

The tube under my arm was shrinking. I yelled, 'Get down!' There were bubbles in the water by my head. The outboard went under, and stopped.

Helen screamed, 'It's sinking!'

'It won't sink,' I said. 'Get in the water.' She splashed in. I wrapped my free arm round her.

A second tongue of flame blasted into the night. I flinched. The shot went wide. But the flame of the gun did not go away. It spread, backwards.

Suddenly the pool of yellow light in the cutter's cockpit was very bright, with a bluish tinge, and there was a huge *whoomph* and a breath of air hot enough to burn my wet face. The mast and the rigging of the cutter were brilliantly lit. Then there was an explosion; a real explosion this time, with a shock wave that pounded my kidneys. And the flames changed colour to dirty orange, and black smoke rolled low over the silky water, pressed down by the fog.

The inflatable had two compartments. Only one of them was punctured. I unscrewed the engine, let it loose. The oars were still in the bottom. I climbed into the flooded boat, gave one oar to Helen, and took the other myself. Helen was shuddering with cold and shock.

'Paddle,' I said harshly.

It took half an hour to get alongside *Opal*. She was aground, but the tide had turned and was flowing in strongly.

I climbed aboard, and pulled Helen in. She put her arms round me. Tears were running down her face. The stink of burning passed over us. In the cockpit, we pressed our bodies together to pull warmth one to the other, in the presence of the death glaring on the fog-wreathed sandbank.

Helen said, 'It's getting light.' It was true. The fog was greying overhead. In the pale glimmer of the dawn I could see lines of exhaustion bitten into her face.

I said, 'Put some dry clothes on.' She went below. I followed her, called Channel 16, emergency.

When we came back on deck, the fog had lifted. The Kentish Flats stretched miles away to the Isle of Sheppey. Helen took my hand. *Opal* stirred to the tide, bumped and floated. I pulled up the anchor, and we turned the bow for the far pencil-line of the land.

SAM LLEWELLYN

Sam Llewellyn was born on Tresco in the Isles of Scilly where his mother's family had settled 'when it was a lawless spot in the 1830s'. The son of a bishop the young Llewellyn was brought up in north Norfolk. He has never lost his love of the sea, learning to sail 'the hard way' at the age of eight. Boats have always been part of his life.

Then, between leaving school and going up to Oxford University, Llewellyn took a job running a small night club in Marbella, 'which then really was just a small fishing village'. Even in those days, he remembers, part of the Spanish coast was becoming a haven for the kind of shady characters now associated with the 'Costa del Crime', and this early encounter with people 'like Deke Kellner' was not forgotten.

After Oxford, Llewellyn worked as a publishing editor in England and Canada, managing also to sail extensively on the Canadian Great Lakes, in yachts built for the Round Britain race and the Whitbread round-the-world race. Already the author of several books, in 1987 he received wide critical acclaim for his first sailing thriller, *Dead Reckoning*, which was followed by *Great Circle* (a Condensed Books selection). But it was Llewellyn's memories of Marbella that were to provide the inspiration for his latest book, *Death Roll*. Going back to revisit his old haunts confirmed his earlier impressions, almost too convincingly. 'It was fascinating, not to say a bit frightening,' he wryly admits. 'I suspect that there are certain places in southern Spain I shall have to avoid for some time to come.'

Having lived for some years in Ireland, Llewellyn now spends the winter writing in his medieval house in Herefordshire where he lives with his Canadian wife and their two young children. In the summer he divides his time between research, writing and—of course—sailing.

THE
EVENING NEWS

A CONDENSATION OF THE BOOK BY

ARTHUR HAILEY

ILLUSTRATED BY:

D Gonzalez

The CBA National Evening News is an
institution; its chief newsreader, Crawford
Sloane, a national star. Polished and self-
assured, the handsome anchorman seems to
have everything: a devoted family, wealth
and fame, and the support of his talented
colleagues—including Harry Partridge, an
old friend since their days as Vietnam war
correspondents. But Sloane's world falls
apart when his wife Jessica becomes a pawn
in a terrorist's deadly game, where power is
all and life is cheap. And when Sloane turns
to Partridge for help, Harry must face not
only deadly danger but the ghost of his old
love for Jessica.

A nail-biting drama, bristling with the
authenticity that is the trademark of this
supreme storyteller.

PART ONE   CHAPTER 1

At CBA Television News headquarters in New York, the initial report of a stricken Airbus A300, on fire and approaching Dallas–Fort Worth Airport, came only minutes before the network's first feed of the National Evening News.

It was six twenty-one pm Eastern daylight time when CBA's bureau chief at Dallas told a producer on the New York Horseshoe through a speakerphone, 'We're expecting a big aircraft crash at DFW any moment. There's been a midair collision—a small plane and an Airbus with a full passenger load. The small plane went down. The Airbus is on fire and trying to make it in. The police and ambulance radios are going wild.'

'Jeez! What's our chance of getting pictures?' another Horseshoe producer asked.

The Horseshoe, an outsize desk with seating for twelve people, was where the network's flagship news broadcast was planned and nurtured, from early each weekday morning until the last second of air time every night. Over at rival CBS they called it the Fishbowl, at ABC the Rim, at NBC the Desk. But whatever name was used, the meaning was the same.

Here, reputedly, were the network's best brains when it came to making judgments and decisions about news: executive producer, anchorman, senior producers, director, editors, writers, graphics chief, and their ranking aides. There were also half a dozen computer terminals, wire news service printers, a phalanx of state-of-the-art telephones, and TV monitors on which could be called up instantly anything from unedited tape, to a prepared news segment ready for broadcast, to competitors' transmissions.

The Horseshoe was on the third floor of the CBA News building in a central open area, with offices for senior staff members on one side. Presiding at the head of the often frenzied Horseshoe was Chuck Insen, executive producer. Lean and peppery, he was a veteran newsman at the age of fifty-two, and elderly by TV standards, though he showed no sign of diminished energy even after four years in a job that often burned people out in two. Chuck Insen could be curt and often was; he never suffered fools or small talk. Under the pressures of his job there just wasn't time.

At this moment—it was a Wednesday in mid-September—pressures were at maximum intensity. Since early morning, the line-up of subjects for the National Evening News had been reviewed, debated, amended and decided. Correspondents and producers around the world had contributed ideas and received instructions. In the process the day's news had been whittled down to eight reports averaging two minutes each, plus two voice-overs and four tell stories. A voice-over was the anchorman speaking over pictures, a tell story, the anchorman without pictures; for both, the average was twenty seconds.

Now, suddenly, because of the breaking story from Dallas, it had become necessary to reshape the entire news line-up. Though no one knew how much more information would come in or if pictures would be available, at least one item had to be dropped, others shortened and the sequence of stories changed. The broadcast would start while rearrangement was continuing. It often happened that way.

'We'll go with Dallas at the top.' The crisp order came from Insen. 'Crawf will do a tell story. Do we have wire copy yet?'

'AP just in. I have it.' The answer was from Crawford Sloane, the anchorman. He was reading an Associated Press bulletin handed to him moments earlier. Sloane, whose familiar craggy features, grey-flecked hair, jutting jaw and authoritative yet reassuring manner were watched by some seventeen million people every weeknight, was in his usual privileged seat on the executive producer's right. He, too, was a news veteran and had climbed the promotion ladder steadily after exposure as a CBA correspondent in Vietnam. Now, after three years in the nightly anchor slot, he was a national institution, one of the media elite.

In a few minutes Sloane would leave for the broadcast studio one floor below. Meanwhile, for his tell story he would draw on what had already come from Dallas, plus some additional facts in the AP report. He would compose it himself. Not every anchor wrote his own material, but Sloane liked to do it when possible. Right now he had to do it fast.

Insen's raised voice could be heard again: the executive producer was telling one of his three senior producers, 'Kill Saudi Arabia. Take ten seconds out of Nicaragua . . .'

126

Sloane manoeuvred his swivel chair backwards to confront a computer keyboard. Concentrating, mentally shutting out the commotion around him, he tapped out the opening sentences of tonight's broadcast:

From Dallas-Fort Worth, word is just in on what may be a tragedy in the making. Minutes ago there was a midair collision between two passenger planes over the town of Gainesville, Texas, north of Dallas. One was a heavily loaded Airbus of Muskegon Airlines. The other plane—a small one, it's believed—went down. There is no word on its fate or of casualties. The Airbus is still in the air, but on fire as its pilots attempt to reach Dallas–Fort Worth Airport for a landing. On the ground, firefighters and ambulance crews are standing by . . .

Sloane added a sentence telling viewers to stay tuned for further developments, then hit a key for print-out. Over at Teleprompter they would get a print-out, too, so that by the time he reached the broadcast studio the story would be ready for him to read from the prompter screen.

As Sloane headed for the stairs, Insen was demanding of a senior producer, 'Dammit, what about pictures from DFW?'

'Chuck, it doesn't look good.' The producer, a phone cradled in his shoulder, was talking to the national editor. 'The burning airplane is nearing the airport but our camera crew is twenty miles away. They won't make it in time.'

Insen swore in frustration.

He had a philosophy about those millions out there who watched the evening news. What they wanted, he believed, were the answers to three questions: Is the world safe? Are my home and family safe? Did anything interesting happen today? Above all else, Insen tried to ensure that the news each evening supplied those answers.

Right now he was tight-lipped and unsmiling. The key question was: Will there or won't there be a story soon, with pictures, from DFW?

IF MEDALS WERE AWARDED for dangerous service in the field of television, Ernie LaSalle, the national editor, would have had a chest full. A small, energetic man of only twenty-nine, he had served with distinction as a CBA field producer in Lebanon, Iran, Angola, Nicaragua and other messy places. Nowadays LaSalle viewed the domestic American scene, which could be equally messy at times, from a comfortable chair in a glass-panelled office overlooking the main newsroom.

LaSalle was neatly bearded and carefully dressed. As national editor his responsibilities were large. He was one of two senior functionaries in the newsroom; the other was the foreign editor. Both had newsroom desks which they occupied when any particular story became hot.

The newsroom was one floor below the Horseshoe, and so was the broadcast studio, which used the bustling newsroom as its visual backdrop. Viewers had the illusion that the anchorman was in, and part of, the newsroom. But in fact there was thick soundproof glass between the two, so that no newsroom noises intruded. A control room, where a director put the technical components together, was in the news building basement.

It was now seven minutes since the Dallas bureau chief had reported the wounded Airbus approaching DFW. LaSalle slammed down one phone and picked up another, at the same time reading a computer screen on which a new AP report had appeared. He would continue to cover the story, simultaneously keeping the Horseshoe advised of developments.

From his newsroom desk LaSalle could see the usual prebroadcast action in the brightly lit studio as Crawford Sloane came in. The time was six twenty-eight pm, two minutes before first-feed air.

As SLOANE SLIPPED into the anchor- desk chair, facing the centre camera of three, a make-up girl moved in. Sloane had had make-up applied ten minutes ago, but since then he had been sweating. Now the girl mopped his forehead, dabbed on powder, ran a comb through his hair and applied a touch of hair spray.

Sloane murmured, 'Thanks, Nina,' then glanced over his papers, checking that the opening words of his tell story on top corresponded with those displayed in large letters on the Teleprompter in front of him, from which he would read while appearing to look directly at viewers. The papers, which newsreaders were often seen to shuffle, were a precaution, for use only if the Teleprompter failed.

The studio floor manager called out loudly, 'One minute!'

IN THE NEWSROOM, Ernie LaSalle suddenly sat up straight, smiling broadly as he listened on the phone to the Dallas bureau.

LaSalle picked up a red reporting telephone connecting him, through amplified speakers, to every section of the news operation. 'National desk. LaSalle. Good news. We now have immediate coverage at DFW Airport. Partridge, Abrams and Van Canh are onto the story and running. Abrams just reported to the Dallas bureau. More: a mobile satellite van has abandoned another assignment and is en route to DFW, expected soonest. We expect pictures in time for the first-feed news.'

A muffled cheer drifted down the open stairway from the Horseshoe above. Crawford Sloane, in the studio, swung round and gave LaSalle a cheerful thumbs up.

An aide put a paper in front of the national editor, who glanced at it, then continued on the speakerphone, 'Also from Abrams this report about the passengers . . . '

When LaSalle finished reading it struck him that everything that had come from Dallas in the past few minutes was totally professional. But that was not surprising, since the team of Abrams, Partridge and Van Canh was one of the crack combinations of CBA News. Rita Abrams, once a correspondent and now a senior field producer, was noted for her quick assessment of situations and resourcefulness in getting stories back. Harry Partridge was one of the best correspondents in the business. He normally specialised in war stories and, like Crawford Sloane, had reported from Vietnam, but he could be relied on to do an exceptional job in any situation. And cameraman Minh Van Canh, a Vietnamese who was now an American citizen, was noted for his fine pictures, sometimes shot in dangerous situations with disregard for his own safety.

By now it was a minute past the half-hour and the National Evening News had begun. Reaching for a control beside his desk, LaSalle turned up the audio of an overhead monitor and heard Crawford Sloane doing the top-of-the-news tell story about DFW. On camera, a hand slipped a paper in front of him—the report LaSalle had just dictated. Glancing down and ad-libbing, Sloane incorporated it into his prepared text. It was the kind of thing the anchorman did superbly.

UPSTAIRS AT THE HORSESHOE the mood had changed. Now, though pressure and urgency remained, there was cheerful optimism that the Dallas situation was well in hand. Chuck Insen and others were huddled, watching monitors, arguing, making decisions, squeezing out seconds, doing still more cutting and rearranging to leave the needed space. There was a sense of everyone doing what they did best—coping in a time-confined, emergency situation

Swift exchanges, jargon-loaded, flowed back and forth.

'This piece is picture-poor.'

'Make that copy shorter, pithy.'

'The last fifteen seconds of that piece is deadly. Drop it.'

'First segment just finished. Have gone to commercial. We're forty seconds heavy.'

'Take out that sequence. It does nothing.'

An observer unfamiliar with the scene might wonder: Are these people human? Don't they care? Have they no feeling of involvement, not an ounce of grief? Have any of them spared a thought for the nearly three hundred terrified souls on that aeroplane who may shortly die?

And someone knowledgeable about news would answer, Yes, they will care, maybe right after the broadcast. Or, when some have reached home, the horror of it all will touch them, and depending on how it all turns out, a few may weep. At this moment, though, no one has the time. These are news people. Their job is to record the passing parade, the bad with the good, and to do it swiftly, efficiently and plainly.

FOR THE GROUP of four journalists at Dallas–Fort Worth Airport, the day had begun in predawn darkness, when they had left El Salvador and flown to Mexico City; then they had travelled on to DFW.

The four were Harry Partridge, Rita Abrams, Minh Van Canh, and Ken O'Hara, the CBA crew's sound man. All were weary from two months of rough and dangerous living while reporting on several nasty wars in Latin America. Now, in a bar in Terminal 2E, they were awaiting flight connections to differing destinations.

Partridge, a tall and lanky figure, had an untidy shock of fair hair that made him look boyish, despite his forty-odd years and the fact that his hair was greying. At this moment he was relaxed and expecting to leave, a few minutes from now, on an American Airlines flight to Toronto. He had ahead of him three weeks of sorely needed rest.

Rita Abrams's connecting flight would be to Minneapolis–St. Paul, from where she was headed for a holiday on a friend's farm in Minnesota. A tough woman who was as demanding of herself as of those she worked with, she had a weekend rendezvous planned there with a married senior CBA official, a piece of information she was keeping to herself. Minh Van Canh and Ken O'Hara were going home to New York. Minh was a quiet, sturdy figure, not much more than five foot tall, with wide brown eyes that looked out impassively from his dark, pockmarked face. The trio of Partridge, Rita and Minh was a frequent working combination. On their most recent trip O'Hara had been with them as sound recordist, for the first time. He was young, pale and pencil-thin. Around them lay all their cameras and equipment, on which the CBA logo was prominent.

Rita was forty-three, and six years ago was still appearing on camera as a news correspondent, though far less often than when she was younger and more glamorous. Everyone knew it was unfair that men were allowed to continue facing the camera as they grew older, whereas women were shunted aside. A few women had tried to beat the system, but Rita, instead of starting a fight she couldn't win, had switched to producing, and had been triumphantly successful. Along the way she'd had some tough foreign assignments. Now she was sent automatically—along with Harry—to where the fighting was fiercest and the living hardest.

Partridge became aware of some activity nearby. Two of the airport's Department of Public Safety, DPS, officers had walked into the bar casually, but had suddenly become attentive. They were listening to an

130

announcement over their walkie-talkies. He caught the words, 'Midair collision . . . approaching runway one-seven left . . . all DPS personnel report . . . ' Abruptly, hurrying, the officers left.

The others in the group had heard too. Rita jumped up. 'I'll find out what's happening.' She left the bar hurriedly, and Van Canh and O'Hara began to gather their cameras and sound gear.

One of the DPS officers was still in sight. Rita caught up with him. 'I'm from CBA News.' She showed her network press card. 'What's going on?'

The officer hesitated. 'You're supposed to call the Public Information Office—'

Rita said impatiently, 'I'll do that later. It's urgent, isn't it? Tell me.'

'Muskegon Airlines is in trouble. One of their Airbuses had a midair. It's coming in on fire. We're on Alert Two, which means all the emergency stuff is rolling, heading hard for runway one-seven left.' His voice was serious. 'Looks pretty bad.'

'I want my camera crew out there. Now and fast.' Rita pointed to the officer's walkie-talkie. 'Can you call Public Information on that?'

'I could.'

'Do it. *Please!*'

Her persuasion worked. The officer called and explained her request, but Rita gestured to the walkie-talkie. 'Let me speak.'

The DPS officer pressed a transmit button and held the radio out. She spoke urgently into the mike: 'We're network. We'll do any paperwork you want afterwards. But please, *please,* get us to the scene now.'

'Stand by.' A pause, then a new voice with crisp authority. 'OK, get to gate nineteen, fast. Look for a station wagon with flashing lights. I'm on my way to you.'

Rita squeezed the officer's arm. 'Thanks, pal!'

She hurried back to Partridge and the others. Briskly, she related what she had learned. 'This could be big. Go out on the airfield. I'll do some phoning, then I'll find you.' She glanced at her watch: five twenty pm, six twenty in New York. 'If we're fast we can make the first feed.'

Partridge nodded, accepting Rita's orders. Officially, a field producer like Rita Abrams was in charge of an entire crew, including the correspondent. However, in the case of a 'big-foot' senior correspondent like Harry Partridge, the official pecking order sometimes got turned round, with the correspondent taking charge. But when Partridge and Rita worked together, neither gave a damn about status. They simply wanted to send back the best reports they could produce.

While Rita hurried to a payphone, Partridge, Minh and O'Hara moved quickly towards gate 19, looking for an exit to the air-traffic ramp below. Near the gate was a doorway marked RESTRICTED AREA, and beneath that, EMERGENCY EXIT ONLY—ALARM WILL SOUND.

Without hesitation Partridge pushed through, the others following. As they clattered down a stairway, an alarm bell sounded behind them. They ignored it and emerged onto the ramp.

The ramp was crowded with aircraft and airline vehicles. Suddenly a station wagon appeared, travelling fast, with roof lights flashing. Its tyres screeched as it halted at gate 19.

Minh opened a door and jumped inside. The others piled in after him. The driver, a slim young black man, pulled swiftly away. Without looking back he said, 'Hiya, guys! I'm Vernon—Public Info.'

Partridge introduced himself and the others.

From the ramp area, they crossed two taxiways and travelled east on a parallel access road. Two runways were on their right. Alongside the further one, emergency vehicles were assembling.

RITA ABRAMS, IN THE TERMINAL, was talking on a payphone to CBA's Dallas bureau. The bureau chief, she had discovered, had been trying to get a local CBA crew to the scene. He learned with delight of the presence of Rita and the others.

She told him to advise New York, then asked, 'What's our satellite feed situation?'

'Good. A mobile satellite van is on the way from Arlington.'

The news excited her. Arlington was only thirteen miles away. There was now a good possibility of getting a story and pictures to New York via satellite in time for the first-feed National Evening News.

THE STATION WAGON carrying the CBA trio was nearing runway 17L. It halted on a taxiway from where the incoming aircraft's approach and landing would be seen. 'This will be the on-site command post,' Vernon said to them.

Emergency vehicles were converging. From the airport's firefighting force were four mammoth Oshkosh M15 foam vehicles, an aerial ladder truck and two smaller Rapid Intervention Vehicles. Half a dozen police cruisers disgorged officers who pulled out silver fire suits and climbed into them. Ambulances from nearby communities were streaming into the airport and assembling nearby.

Partridge had been the first to jump from the station wagon and was already scribbling notes. Minh Van Canh had clambered to the car's roof and now, standing, his camera ready, was scanning the sky to the north. Behind him was Ken O'Hara, trailing wires and a sound recorder.

Almost at once the stricken inbound flight was visible, about five miles out, with heavy black smoke behind it. Van Canh raised his camera, holding it steady, one eye tight against the viewfinder.

In the viewfinder the shape of the approaching Airbus was becoming clearer. Also clearer was a halo of bright flame on the right side. To Minh, it seemed amazing that the entire plane had not yet been engulfed.

Inside the station wagon, Vernon had switched on an aviation band radio. The calm voice of an air traffic controller could be heard speaking to the Airbus pilots. 'You are slightly below glide path . . . drifting left of centre line . . . Now on glide path, on centre line . . . '

The pilots were clearly having trouble holding altitude and an even course. At moments the plane's nose veered away; then, as if from urgent efforts in the cockpit, it swung back towards the runway. Those on the ground were asking themselves: Would the Airbus make it all the way in?

Van Canh, fondling a zoom lens, had his camera running. The Airbus was over the airport boundary. . . Then it was closer in, barely a quarter mile from the runway. But the fire was growing more intense, and two of the four right-side tyres of the landing gear were burning. There was a flash as a tyre exploded.

Now the burning Airbus was over the runway, its landing speed 150 mph. As it passed the waiting emergency vehicles, they swung onto the runway, following at top speed. The plane's landing gear made contact with the ground and another tyre exploded, then another. Suddenly all the right-hand tyres disintegrated; the wheels were down to their rims. Simultaneously there was a banshee screech of metal, a shower of sparks, and a cloud of cement dust in the air. Somehow, miraculously, the pilots managed to hold the Airbus on the runway. And as it stopped, the fire flared up.

The fire trucks closed in, pumping foam within seconds. Gigantic whorls of it piled up like mountains of shaving cream.

On the plane, the two forward doors were opening, escape slides tumbling out. On the left side, away from the fire, a mid-fuselage door was open. Some passengers were already coming down the chutes. But at the rear, neither of the two escape doors had so far opened.

Through the three open doors smoke was pouring out of the plane. Passengers emerged coughing and gasping for air.

Firemen from the RIVs had swiftly rigged ladders to the unopened rear doors. As the doors were opened manually from outside, more smoke poured out. The firemen hurried inside, intent on extinguishing any interior fire and helping passengers to leave.

The outward flow of passengers slowed noticeably. Harry Partridge made a quick estimate that nearly two hundred people had emerged, of the 297 reportedly aboard. Firemen began to carry out some who appeared badly burned—among them two women flight attendants.

Minh Van Canh continued to videotape the action around him, aware that he was the only cameraman on the scene and that in his camera he had something unique. Probably not since the Hindenberg airship disaster had a major air crash been recorded in such detail, while it happened.

Ambulances had arrived at the on-site command post. Within minutes the crash victims would be on their way to area hospitals. With the arrival of a helicopter bringing doctors and nurses, the command post was becoming an improvised field hospital.

The flight deck crew now emerged from the Airbus, pointedly declining help. The captain, a grizzled four-striper, already knowing of the many dead, was openly crying. Minh held the captain's grief-stricken face in close-up. It proved to be the final shot as Rita's voice called, 'Hurry, guys! Bring what you've got. We're feeding to New York by satellite.'

Rita had arrived on a Public Information shuttle bus. In the distance, the mobile satellite van could be seen. Its folding satellite dish was being opened and aimed skywards.

Minh lowered his camera. Two other TV crews had arrived on the same shuttle bus as Rita, along with print-press reporters and photographers. They and others would carry the story on. But only Minh had the real thing, the crash exclusive pictures. And he knew with inward pride that today and in days to come, his pictures would be seen around the world and become a piece of history.

ON THE WAY to the satellite van Partridge began drafting the words he would speak. Rita told him, 'As soon as you're ready, cut a soundtrack, do a closing stand-up. Meanwhile, I'll feed quick and dirty to New York.'

As Partridge nodded acknowledgment, Rita glanced at her watch: five forty-three pm, six forty-three in New York. For the first-feed National Evening News, there was barely fifteen minutes left of broadcast time.

Partridge continued to write, mouthing words silently. Minh handed two tape cassettes to Rita, then put a fresh cassette in the camera, ready for Partridge's audio track and stand-up close.

Inside the satellite van, in a small control room, a technician was aligning the van's uplink transmitter with a satellite more than twenty-two thousand miles above them. Whatever they transmitted would go on the satellite, then instantly by downlink to New York to be rerecorded.

Rita expertly ran Minh's tapes through an editing machine, viewing them on a TV monitor. Not surprisingly, she thought, the pictures were superb. On normal assignments, a producer and videotape editor together would select portions of the tapes. Then, over the soundtrack of a correspondent's comments, they would put all components together as a fully edited piece. But today there wasn't time. So, making fast decisions,

Rita chose several of the most dramatic scenes, which the technician transmitted as they were—in TV jargon, quick and dirty.

Outside the satellite van, Partridge completed his script and, after conferring briefly with Minh and O'Hara, recorded a soundtrack. Allowing for the anchorman's introduction in New York, he began:

'Pilots in a long-ago war called it comin' in on a wing and a prayer. There was a song with that name . . . It's unlikely anyone will write a song about today. The Muskegon Airlines Airbus was sixty miles out from Dallas–Fort Worth . . . having come from Chicago with a near-full passenger load . . . when the midair collision happened . . . '

The best news writing, as this correspondent knew, was not in neat sentences and paragraphs. Fragments of sentences worked better. Facts must be taut, verbs strong and active; a script should crackle. Finally, by manner and intonation the correspondent should convey a meaning, too: he or she had to be an excellent reporter, and an actor as well.

Partridge concluded with a stand-up—himself, head and shoulders, speaking directly to the camera. Behind him, activity was continuing around the wrecked Airbus.

'There is more of this story to come . . . tragic details, the toll of dead and injured. But what is clear, even now, is that collision dangers are multiplying . . . on the airways, in our crowded skies . . . Harry Partridge, CBA News, Dallas-Fort Worth.'

The cassette, with the narration and stand-up, was passed to Rita inside the van. Trusting Partridge, knowing him too well to waste precious time checking, she ordered it transmitted to New York.

THE CBA NEWS HEADQUARTERS building in New York was a plain and unimpressive eight-storey brownstone on the east side of upper Manhattan. Formerly a furniture factory, only the shell of its original structure now remained, the interior having been remodelled to house a sultan's fortune in electronic wizardry. And here, two floors below street level, was a vital department with a prosaic name—the One-inch Tape Room.

All reports from CBA crews around the world came in to the One-inch Tape Room. From there, too, all taped recordings of finished news went out to viewers. Endemic to the One-inch Tape Room were enormous pressures, taut nerves, instant decision-making and urgent commands, especially just before and during broadcasts of the National Evening News. At such times, to the uninitiated, the scene gave an impression of disorganised bedlam, but in fact the operation functioned smoothly and quickly. Mistakes could be disastrous. They rarely happened.

Half a dozen sophisticated reel-to-reel tape machines, using one-inch magnetic tape and built into consoles with TV monitors above, dominated the activity. At each console sat a skilled operator receiving, editing and transmitting tapes swiftly, according to instructions.

An hour or so before National Evening News broadcast time, a senior producer moved down five floors from the Horseshoe to preside over the One-inch Tape Room. There, shouting instructions while semaphoring with his arms, he viewed incoming material for that night's news, ordered further editing if necessary, and kept the Horseshoe informed of which expected items were now in-house and how they looked.

The senior producer most often in charge was Will Kazazis, Brooklyn-born of an excitable Greek family. Despite this inherited trait, he never lost control. It was Kazazis who received Rita Abrams's satellite transmission from DFW—first Minh Van Canh's pictures sent quick and dirty, then Harry Partridge's audio track and stand-up tape.

The time was six forty-eight—ten minutes of news remaining. A commercial break had just begun. Kazazis told the operator who had taken the feed, 'Slap it together fast. Use all of Partridge's track. Put the best pictures over it. Now move, move, move!'

Through an aide, Kazazis had already let the Horseshoe know that the Dallas tape was coming in. Now, by phone, Chuck Insen, who was in the broadcast control room, demanded, 'How is it?'

Kazazis told the executive producer, 'Fantastic! Beautiful!'

Knowing there wasn't time to view the piece himself, Insen ordered, 'We go after this commercial. Stand by.'

With less than a minute to go, the tape operator was continuing to edit, hurriedly combining pictures, commentary and sound.

INSEN'S COMMAND WAS REPEATED to the anchorman and a writer seated near him. A lead-in was already prepared by the writer and passed to Crawford Sloane, who skimmed it, quickly changed a word or two, and nodded thanks. A moment later the anchor's Teleprompter switched over to the DFW story. In the broadcast studio as the commercial break neared its conclusion, the floor manager called, 'Ten seconds ... five ... four ... ' At a hand signal, Sloane began:

'Earlier in this broadcast we reported a midair collision near Dallas between a Muskegon Airlines Airbus and a private plane. The private plane crashed. There are no survivors. The Airbus, on fire, crash-landed at Dallas–Fort Worth Airport a few minutes ago, and there are heavy casualties. On the scene is CBA News correspondent Harry Partridge, who has just filed this report.'

Only seconds before, the frantic editing in the One-inch Tape Room had been completed. Now, on millions of TV sets across much of the United States and Canada, a dramatic picture of an approaching, burning Airbus filled the screen, and Partridge's voice began. The exclusive report and pictures had made the first-feed National Evening News.

There would be a second feed immediately after the first. There always was, and it would be broadcast in the East by affiliated stations that did not take the first feed, widely in the Midwest, and most Western stations would record the second feed for broadcast later.

The Partridge report from DFW would, of course, lead the second feed. CBA's while-it-happened pictures were a world exclusive and would be repeated many times in the days to follow.

CHAPTER 2

It was seven forty pm when Crawford Sloane, driving a Buick Somerset, left the garage at headquarters. A few minutes later, as he turned onto Fifty-ninth Street heading east towards the FDR Drive, he thought about the broadcast just concluded and about Harry Partridge.

For Partridge, Sloane recognised, the reporting job from Dallas had been one more solid performance in an outstanding professional career. Through DFW's airport paging system Sloane had been able to reach Partridge by phone and congratulate him and his crew. From an anchorman that kind of thing was expected. Where Partridge was concerned, though, the conversation had a touch of awkwardness.

Within the car, in a moment of silent, private honesty, Sloane asked himself: How do I feel about Harry Partridge? The answer, with equal honesty, came back: He makes me feel insecure.

The two of them had known each other for more than twenty years, the same length of time each had been with CBA News. Yet they were opposites in personality.

Sloane was precise, fastidious in dress and speech. He could be slightly distant with people he did not know well, though in any human contact there was almost nothing his sharp mind missed.

Partridge, by contrast, was casual in behaviour, his appearance rumpled; he favoured old tweed jackets and had an easygoing manner which made people feel comfortable. Sometimes he gave the impression of not caring much about anything, but only because he had learned early, as a journalist, that he could discover more by concealing his keen intelligence.

They had differences in background too. Crawford Sloane, from a middle-class Cleveland family, had done his early television training in that city. Harry Partridge, Canadian-born, had served his TV news apprenticeship with the Canadian Broadcasting Corporation, and before that had worked as an announcer-newscaster-weatherman for small stations in Alberta, where his father was a farmer.

Sloane had a degree from Columbia University. Partridge hadn't even finished high school, but in the working world of news, his *de facto* education expanded rapidly.

For a long time at CBA their careers were parallel; as a result, they came to be looked on as competitors. In late 1967 the network sent them both to Vietnam, supposedly to work as a team. Sloane, though, viewed the war as a golden opportunity to advance his own career: even then he had the anchor desk in his sights. One essential, he knew, was to appear on the evening news as often as possible. Therefore, soon after arriving in Saigon, he decided not to stray too far from Pentagon East—headquarters of the Military Assistance Command for Vietnam, outside Saigon.

Harry Partridge had remarked, 'Crawf, you'll never get to understand this war by attending the Saigon Follies or hanging around the Caravelle.' The first was the name the press corps gave to military briefings, the second, a hotel which was a popular watering hole with the press, senior military and US embassy civilians.

'If you're talking about risks,' Sloane had answered huffily, 'I'm willing to take as many as you are.'

'Forget risks. I'm talking about coverage in depth.'

No one could ever say about his time in Vietnam that Sloane didn't work hard. And he also took risks. But he was seldom away more than twenty-four hours and was usually available in Saigon for military and diplomatic briefings.

His shrewd ploy worked. He had always been impressive on camera and was even more so in Vietnam. He became a favourite with the New York producers, was frequently on the evening news, and built up a following.

Harry Partridge, on the other hand, sought out deeper stories which required longer investigation and took him, with a cameraman, to distant parts of Vietnam. Some of his reports contradicted official military statements in Saigon; others confirmed them. It was that second kind of reporting—fairness to the US military—that separated him and a handful of others from the majority of Vietnam correspondents. An example was Partridge's report that US forces during the enemy's Tet offensive were doing much better than they were being given credit for. The media proclaimed Tet as a smashing Communist victory, a claim that calmer research two decades later showed to be untrue.

Partridge's excursions into areas of heavy fighting usually kept him away from Saigon for a week, sometimes longer. Once, when he went underground into Cambodia, he was out of touch for nearly a month. Every time, though, he returned with a strong story, and after the war some were still remembered for their insights.

Unfortunately, because his reports were less frequent than Crawford Sloane's, Partridge didn't get noticed as much.

Something else in Vietnam affected the future of Partridge and Sloane: Jessica Castillo.

CRAWFORD SLOANE SWUNG ónto the northbound ramp of the FDR Drive alongside the East River. He accelerated. His home in Larchmont, New York, north of Long Island Sound, was half an hour away.

Behind him, a blue Ford Tempo increased its speed also.

Sloane was relaxed, as he usually was at this time of day. And as his thoughts drifted they returned to Jessica who, in Saigon, had been Harry Partridge's girlfriend. In the end she had married Crawford Sloane.

In those days, she had been twenty-six, slim, with long brown hair, a lively mind and, on occasion, a sharp tongue. She took no nonsense from the journalists with whom she dealt as a junior information officer at the United States Information Service.

Members of the press went to the agency sometimes more than they needed, bringing queries that might allow them time with Jessica. She played along with the attention, but when Sloane first knew her, Harry Partridge was firmly number one in her affections.

Even now, Sloane thought, there were areas of that early relationship between Partridge and Jessica of which he knew nothing, things he had never asked about and now would never know. But he would never stop wondering about those times.

JESSICA CASTILLO AND HARRY PARTRIDGE were drawn to each other the first time they met—even though the meeting was antagonistic. Partridge had gone to USIS seeking information that he knew existed but which had been refused him by the US military. It concerned the widespread drug addiction of American troops in Vietnam.

Partridge had seen plenty of evidence of heroin addiction during his travels, and the New York Horseshoe had given him a green light to pursue the story. But when he entered Jessica's office and broached the subject, she clammed up tight. 'I can't talk about that.'

Her attitude offended him and he said accusingly, 'You mean you *won't* talk? This problem needs a public airing so something can be done, lady. So other green kids coming out here can be warned and maybe saved. You call yourself an information officer. I call you a concealment officer.'

Jessica flushed. Unused to being talked to that way, she glared at him angrily. Then, noticeably, the anger diminished, and she asked quietly, 'What is it you want to know?'

Partridge moderated his tone to match hers. 'Statistics mostly. I know someone has them, that records have been kept, surveys taken.'

'Do you know Rex Talbot?'

'Yes.' Talbot was a young American vice-consul at the embassy on Thong Nhut Street, a few blocks away.

'I suggest you ask him about the reports he has on file. There's no need for him to know I sent you. You could let him think you know . . . '

He finished the sentence. '. . . a little more than I really do. It's an old journalist's trick.'

'The kind of trick you just tried to use on me.'

Partridge smiled. 'You're not as soulless as I thought. How about exploring this subject some more over dinner tonight?'

To her own surprise, Jessica accepted.

Later they discovered how much they enjoyed each other's company, and it turned out to be the first of many such meetings. They dined often together at the Caravelle, strolling afterwards in the hotel garden, an oasis of quiet amid the discord of Saigon. Their relationship endured many separations, and inevitably a moment came when desire overwhelmed them both. Partridge was surprised that it was Jessica's first experience; deeply moved when she told him, 'Oh, I love you so!' He would remember that time as one of those rare and magic moments when all problems and concerns—Vietnam, the war's ugliness, future uncertainties—seemed far away; all that mattered was the present and themselves. Long after, he could never remember if he had told her that he truly loved her, but knew he did and always would.

In any other time and place they might have married quickly. Jessica wanted to be married; she also wanted children. But Partridge, for reasons he afterwards regretted, held back. In Canada he had had one failed marriage and knew that the marriages of TV newsmen were often disastrous. TV news correspondents, could be away from home two hundred days a year or more, were unused to family responsibilities, and encountered temptations on the road that few could permanently resist. Coupled with that there was Vietnam. Partridge's life was at risk each time he left Saigon, and though luck had been with him so far, the odds were against that luck enduring. So it wasn't fair, he reasoned, to burden Jessica with the likelihood of heartbreak later on.

He confided some of this to her early one morning after they had spent the night together. Jessica was shocked by what she perceived as a puerile cop-out by a man to whom she had already given her heart and body. She told him coldly that their relationship was at an end.

140

Partridge left Saigon a few hours later, and was away a month.

Crawford Sloane had met Jessica several times while she was in Harry's company, and saw her occasionally in the USIS offices when his work took him there. He was strongly attracted to her and longed to know her better, but recognising she was Partridge's girl he had never asked her for a date. Now, hearing that she and Partridge had split up, he promptly asked her to dine with him. She agreed, and they went on seeing each other. Two weeks later, Sloane proposed marriage.

Jessica, taken by surprise, asked for time to think. Her love for Harry had been passionate and all-consuming, and she still loved him, she was sure of that. If he had come back and asked her to marry him, she would probably have said yes. But, clearly, Harry wasn't going to ask.

On the other hand, there was Crawf. Jessica felt a strong affection for him. He was kind and gentle, loving, intelligent. And he possessed a stability that Harry, while an exciting person, sometimes lacked. For a lifetime, which was more important—excitement or stability? After weighing everything as best she could, Jessica accepted Sloane's proposal.

Sloane was ecstatically happy. They were married at once, in the US embassy, by an army chaplain. Partridge did not learn of the marriage until his return to Saigon, and only then did he realise, with overpowering sadness, how much he had lost.

If Jessica shared some of Partridge's regrets, she kept it to herself and put them behind her. She had made her choice and was determined to be a good wife, which she was. Now—incredibly, it seemed—Jessica's and Crawford's silver wedding anniversary was less than five years distant.

AT THE WHEEL of the Buick Somerset, Sloane was at the midpoint in his journey home. The same Ford Tempo that had followed him from CBA News headquarters was still behind.

It was not surprising that he had failed to notice the other car, either tonight or during the past several weeks when it had followed him. Its driver—a young, thin-lipped, cold-eyed Colombian, code name Carlos, was an expert at stalking any quarry.

Carlos, who had entered the United States two months ago on a forged passport, shared this stealthy surveillance with six others—five men and a woman. Like Carlos, the others were identified only by fictitious first names. Until their present task began, they had been unknown to one another. Only Miguel, the leader, who tonight was several miles away, was aware of their real identities.

In the fast-moving expressway traffic Carlos allowed three other cars to move up between himself and Sloane. Beside Carlos another man noted the time and made an entry in a log. This was Julio—swarthy and bad-tempered, with an ugly facial scar from a knifing. Behind them, in the back seat, was a mobile cellular phone, one of six that linked vehicles with a hidden temporary headquarters.

As the Buick entered the streets of Larchmont, the Ford Tempo followed discreetly, stopping well short of the Sloane house, which was located on Park Avenue, facing Long Island Sound. The house, befitting someone with Sloane's substantial income, was large and imposing. Sloane used a remote control in the car to open the door of a three-car garage, and drove in, closing the door behind him.

SLOANE COULD HEAR VOICES as he walked through the corridor between the garage and the house. He opened a door to the hallway and heard Jessica call out from the living room, 'Is that you, Crawf?'

He made the standard response. 'If it isn't, you're in trouble.'

Her melodious laugh came back. 'Be with you in a minute!'

He heard a clink of glasses and knew that Jessica was mixing martinis, her nightly homecoming ritual to help him unwind.

'Hi, Dad!' the Sloanes' eleven-year-old son, Nicholas, shouted from the stairway. Nicky was tall for his age and slim, with curly brown hair. His intelligent eyes lit up as he ran to hug his father.

Sloane returned the embrace. It was the kind of greeting he appreciated, and he had Jessica to thank for that. Almost from the time Nicky was born, she had taught him that love should be expressed in tactile ways. Jessica would have none of Crawf's built-in reserve. 'When you're married, darling, barriers come down. It's why we were "joined together". Remember those words? So for the rest of our lives you and I are going to say to each other exactly what we feel—and show it, too.'

But with other people his reserve lived on. Sloane couldn't remember when he had last hugged his own father, uncertain how old Angus—stiff, even rigid, in his personal behaviour—might react.

'Hello, darling!' Jessica appeared wearing a soft green dress, a colour he always liked. They embraced warmly, then went into the living room.

Sloane asked his son, 'How's the music world?'

'Great, Dad. I'm practising Gershwin.'

Neither Sloane nor Jessica could remember exactly how old Nicky had been when he began to exhibit an interest in music, but it was in his very early years, and now music was his dominant interest. He played often on their grand piano, and took lessons from a former concert pianist who lived nearby. A few weeks ago the tutor had told Jessica, 'Your son already has a mastery of music unusual for his age. Later he may follow one of several paths—as a performer or composer. Music will, I predict, be the mainstream of his life.'

142

Jessica glanced at her watch. 'Nicky, it's getting late.'

'Ah, Mom, let me stay up! Tomorrow's a school holiday.'

'And your day will be as full as any other. The answer is no.' Jessica was the family disciplinarian, and after affectionate good-nights, Nicky left. Soon after, they could hear him playing a portable electronic keyboard in his bedroom.

In the softly lit living room Jessica returned to the martinis she had been mixing. Watching her, Sloane thought, How lucky can you get? It was a feeling he often had about Jessica and the way she looked after more than twenty years of marriage. She no longer wore her hair long and didn't bother to conceal streaks of grey. There were also lines round her eyes. But her figure was slim and shapely, and he still felt proud to enter a room with her beside him.

As she handed him a glass she commented, 'A rough day?'

'It was. You saw the airplane story on the news?'

'Yes. Those poor passengers—what a terrible way to die! They just had to sit there, waiting.'

'What did you think of Harry?'

'He was good.'

'He was better than good. He did it like that.' Sloane snapped his fingers. 'We beat the pants off the other networks.' The martini had relaxed him, as it always did.

'You're feeling good tonight,' Jessica said, 'and you have another reason to.' She handed him an envelope, already opened since she handled most of their private business. 'It's a letter from your publisher and a royalty statement.' As Sloane read the papers, his face was lit by a smile.

Crawford Sloane's book, *The Camera and the Truth,* had been published several months earlier. In terms of sales, it got off to a slow start. But as the weeks passed, certain comments in it gained attention in general news columns—the best publicity a book can have.

In a chapter about terrorism Sloane had written bluntly:

No politician anywhere has the guts to say it, but hostages, including American hostages, should be regarded as expendable.

The only way to deal with terrorists is by counterterrorism, which means whenever possible seeking out and covertly destroying them—the only language they understand. It includes not striking bargains with terrorists or paying ransom, directly or indirectly, ever!

We who live in the United States will not remain free from terrorism in our own back yard much longer. But neither are we prepared for this pervasive, ruthless kind of warfare.

Sloane put aside the impressive royalty account.

'You deserve what's happened, and I'm proud of you,' Jessica said. 'Especially because it isn't like you to take chances on being controversial.' She paused. 'Oh, your father phoned. He's arriving early tomorrow and would like to stay a week.'

Sloane grimaced. 'That's pretty soon after the last time.'

'He's lonely and he's getting old. Maybe if you're that way some day, you'll have a favourite daughter-in-law you'll want to be with.'

They both laughed, knowing how fond Angus was of Jessica and vice versa. In some ways the two were closer than the father and son. Since the death of Crawford's mother several years before, Angus Sloane had been living alone in Florida.

'I enjoy having him around,' Jessica said. 'So does Nicky.'

'OK then, that's fine.'

Talk between Sloane and Jessica continued over dinner, always a favourite time. Sloane said thoughtfully, 'I know what you meant, that it isn't like me to venture out on a limb. I guess, in my life, I haven't taken chances as often as I might. But I felt strongly about some things in the book. Still do.'

'The terrorism part?'

He nodded. 'Since the book was written I've done some thinking about how terrorism could affect you and me. It's why I've taken some special precautions you ought to know about.'

While Jessica regarded him curiously, he went on. 'Have you ever thought that someone like me could be kidnapped, become a hostage?'

'I have when you've been overseas.'

He shook his head. 'It could happen here. Like some others in television, I work in a goldfish bowl. If terrorists begin operating in the US—and I believe they soon will—people like me will be attractive bait because anything we do, or is done for us, gets noticed in a big way.'

'What about families? Could they be targets too?'

He shook his head. 'That's highly unlikely. Terrorists would be after a name. Someone everybody knows.'

Jessica said uneasily, 'You spoke of precautions. What kind?'

'The kind that would be effective *after* I'd been taken hostage.'

'I don't like this conversation,' Jessica said. 'You're making me nervous. And what good are precautions after it happens?'

'Before it happens,' he said, 'I have to trust the network to provide security protection. But afterwards, I wouldn't want any ransom to be paid by the network or anyone else. So I've made a solemn declaration— it's all in legal form—to that effect. After that declaration was made public, I'd like to think you wouldn't go some other route.'

144

Jessica protested. 'You'd rob me of the right to make a decision!'

He said gently, 'No, dearest. I'd relieve you of a terrible responsibility.'

'But supposing the network were willing to pay a ransom?'

'I doubt if they would go against my wishes, which are on record.'

'You said the network is giving you some kind of security protection. It's the first I've heard of it. Just what kind?'

'When there are telephoned threats, or screwball letters which sound a certain way, or a rumour of some kind of possible attack—it happens at all networks and especially to anchor people—then private security men are called in. They hang around the CBA News building, wherever I'm working, doing whatever security people are supposed to do.'

'You've never told me,' Jessica said. There was an edge to her voice, though it was not clear whether she was angry or just anxious.

Sloane told his wife, 'When someone is kidnapped, nowadays it's a certainty they will be compelled to make videotape recordings. Those recordings are sometimes played on television. If there's a prearrangement of signals, a hostage has a good chance of getting a message back.'

'If this weren't so serious, it would sound like a spy novel!' Jessica said. 'So what kind of signals have you arranged?'

'Licking my lips, which is something anyone might do, would mean, I am doing this against my will. Do not believe anything I am saying. Scratching or touching my right ear lobe would mean, My captors are well organised and strongly armed. Touching my left ear lobe would mean, Security here is sometimes lax. An attack from outside might succeed. There are some others, but we'll leave it for now. I don't want all this to distress you.'

'Well, it does distress me,' Jessica said. She wondered: *Could* it happen? *Could* Crawf be kidnapped and spirited away? It seemed unbelievable, but almost every day unbelievable things happened. She said thoughtfully, 'I do wonder why you haven't taken that security course we talked about.'

This was an antiterrorism course intended to prepare people for just the possibility Sloane had raised—how to behave as a victim in a hostage situation. Also taught was unarmed self-defence—something Jessica had urged her husband to learn.

'Finding time for that course is the problem,' Sloane said. 'Speaking of that, are you still taking CQB lessons?'

CQB was shorthand for close quarters battle, a specialised version of unarmed combat. That was something else Jessica had wanted Crawford to do, but when he simply couldn't find time she took the lessons herself.

'I'm not taking them regularly any more,' she answered. 'Though I do an hour every month or two to keep refreshed.'

Sloane nodded. 'Good.'

That night, still troubled by what had passed between them, Jessica found it difficult to sleep.

Outside, the occupants of the Ford Tempo watched as one by one the lights in the house went off. Then they made a report by cellular phone and, ending that day's vigil, drove away.

SHORTLY AFTER SIX THIRTY AM the surveillance of the house resumed. A Chevrolet Celebrity was being used this morning, and slouched down in the car's front seats were the Colombians, Carlos and Julio.

At seven thirty an unforeseen event occurred when a taxi arrived at the Sloane house. From it an elderly man emerged, carrying a suitcase. He went into the house and remained there. The newcomer's unexpected presence prompted a call to the watchers' temporary headquarters some twenty miles away.

Their efficient communications and ample transport typified an operation on which expense had not been spared. The organisers were associates of Colombia's Medellín cartel, a coalition of vicious, criminal, fabulously wealthy drug lords. In the present instance, while operating under cover in the United States, Medellín was working not for itself but for the Peruvian Maoist terrorist organisation *Sendero Luminoso,* or 'Shining Path'. Recently in Peru, Sendero Luminoso had grown more powerful, while the official government became increasingly inept and weak. Drug money contributed heavily to Sendero finances.

Now, in the surveillance Chevrolet, the two Colombian hoodlums were searching through a collection of Polaroid photos.

Julio, on the telephone, spoke in code phrases. 'A blue package has arrived. Delivery number two. The package is in storage. We cannot trace the order.' Translated: A man has arrived by taxi. He has gone into the house. We do not know who he is.

The sharp-edged voice of Miguel, the project's leader, snapped back, 'What is the docket number?' Translated: What age is he?

Julio looked to Carlos for help. '*Un viejo.* How old?'

'Tell him, docket seventy-five.'

Julio did, producing another terse question. 'Is anything special about the blue package?'

Abandoning code, Julio lapsed into plain language. 'He carried a suitcase in. Looks like he plans to stay.'

IN HACKENSACK, NEW JERSEY, in a dilapidated rented house, the man whose code name was Miguel silently cursed Julio's carelessness. Those idiots he was forced to work with! He had warned all of them, over and over, that on radiophones anyone could be listening. *Estúpidos!* The

146

success of their mission, plus their lives and freedom, were at stake.

Miguel himself had always been obsessively cautious. It was why he had never been arrested, even though he was on 'most wanted' lists of police forces in North and South America and some in Europe too, including Interpol. Still in his late thirties, he was physically unremarkable; anyone passing him on a street might think he was a bank clerk. This ordinariness had been Miguel's great good fortune, as was the fact that he did not radiate authority. His power of command remained hidden except to those on whom he exercised it, and then it was unmistakable.

Although Colombian, Miguel could also appear American. In the late 1960s and early 70s he had attended the University of California at Berkeley, majoring in English and learning to speak it without an accent. In those days he was using his real name, Ulises Rodríguez.

Miguel's father, a well-to-do Bogotá neurosurgeon, hoped his only son would follow him into medicine. Instead, as the 1970s neared, the son foresaw opportunities for himself in Colombia, a country that was changing from a prosperous democracy to a lawless, rich mobsters' haven, ruled through dictatorship, savagery and fear.

After Berkeley, back home in Colombia, Miguel flirted with the developing alliance of mad-dog drug lords. He had a pilot's licence and made several flights conveying coca paste from Peru to Colombia for processing into cocaine. Then came the infamous Medellín drug cartel with its brutal murders. Miguel participated in all the major killings and many minor ones, and had long since lost count of the corpses in his wake. Killing did not trouble him at all. He became a gun-for-hire terrorist who was, because of his icy calm and efficiency, constantly in demand.

It was this life of danger, risk and action which had brought him, on a fake passport, to the US a month and a half ago.

In New York, Miguel had gone immediately to 'Little Colombia'—a sizable Colombian community in Jackson Heights, Queens. A thriving narcotics centre, it was one of New York's most dangerous high-crime areas. There, in a safe house arranged by a Medellín cartel agent, Miguel began his planning, drew on money made secretly available, and assembled the small force he would lead. That force's seven members, including Miguel, had been selected in Bogotá.

Julio, at this moment on surveillance duty, and Socorro, the only woman in the group, were Colombians. Both had been sent to the United States by Medellín several years before, their only instructions to establish themselves and wait until their services were needed. That time had now arrived.

Julio was a communications specialist. Socorro, during her waiting period, had trained and qualified as a nursing aide. She had an additional affiliation. Through friends in Peru she had become a member of the revolutionary Sendero Luminoso.

The other Colombians in the group were Rafael, Luís and Carlos. Rafael, heavily built, was a mechanic and general handyman. Luís had been chosen for his driving skill—he was expert at eluding pursuit. Carlos was young, quick-witted and had organised the surveillance of the past four weeks. All three spoke English fluently.

The final member was an American, code-named Baudelio. Miguel mistrusted him totally, yet Baudelio's knowledge and skills were essential to the mission's success.

Now, in Hackensack, at the group's temporary operating centre, Miguel considered his response to the surveillance report he'd received from Larchmont. Before leaving Bogotá, Miguel had received a dossier on the Sloane family. Crawford Sloane had a father who fitted the description of the new arrival. Well, if the old man had come to visit his son, it constituted a nuisance but nothing more. The father would almost certainly have to be killed later that day.

Depressing the telephone transmitter, Miguel ordered, 'Take no action about the blue package. Report new billing only.' New billing meant: if the situation changes.

'Roger,' Julio acknowledged curtly.

Replacing the cellular phone, Miguel glanced at his watch. Almost seven forty-five am. In two hours all seven members of his group would be in place and ready for action. Everything that was to follow had been carefully planned, precautions taken. There could be no postponement. Outside the United States, other movements, dovetailing with their own, were already in motion.

CHAPTER 3

Angus Sloane put down his coffee cup and patted his silver-grey moustache with a napkin. 'No better breakfast,' he declared, 'has been served this morning in all of New York State.'

'And none with higher cholesterol either,' his son said from behind an open *New York Times*, across the table. 'Don't you know all those fried eggs are bad for your heart?'

'Who's counting?' Jessica said. 'Besides, you can afford the eggs, Crawf. Angus, would you like another?'

'No thank you, my dear.' The old man, sprightly and cherubic—he had just turned seventy-three—smiled benevolently at Jessica and gave a contented sigh.

148

They were all seated in the bright and cheerful breakfast annexe, where Jessica had prepared for Angus his favourite bacon and eggs. He had arrived a half-hour earlier, embracing his daughter-in-law and grandson warmly and shaking hands more formally with Crawford.

'About my heart and eggs,' Angus said, 'I figure if my ticker's lasted this long, I shouldn't worry about cholesterol. My heart and I have been in some tight spots and come through them. I could tell you about a few during my war. That's World War Two to you, Nicky.'

'Weren't you on the first B-17 bombing raid to Schweinfurt, Dad?' Sloane asked.

'Yes,' he said, and then, to Nicholas, 'That was deep in Germany, Nicky. At the time, not a nice place to go.' The old man's face was creased with pain. He went on, his voice quavering, 'At Schweinfurt we lost fifty B-17s. There were ten in a crew. That's five hundred fliers lost that single day. They were good men. So many good men. So many of my friends . . . '

'Gramps,' Nicky said. He had been listening intently. 'When you were in the war, were you frightened very much?'

'Frightened? I was terrified! But let me tell you, Nicky, there's nothing wrong with being scared. It can happen to the best. What counts is hanging on, somehow staying in control.'

'I hear you, Gramps.'

Sloane glanced at his watch. It was time to leave. He rose from the breakfast table, put on his suit jacket and said goodbye to Jessica and Nicky. Then, looking at the frail figure of his father, he suddenly had a pang of conscience for what he had failed to understand sooner. He moved close to Angus, put his arms round him and kissed him on both cheeks.

The old man seemed flustered. 'Hey, hey! What's all this?'

Looking him directly in the eye, Crawford said, 'I love you, you old coot.'

At the doorway he glanced back. On Angus's face was a seraphic smile.

WHEN THE SURVEILLANCE DUO of Carlos and Julio saw Crawford Sloane leave his home, they reported immediately by code to Miguel.

By now, Miguel had left the Hackensack operating centre and with others, in a Nissan van, was crossing the George Washington Bridge from New Jersey to New York. He issued, also in code, the order that prearranged plans were now in effect. He reasoned confidently that what they were about to do was the totally unexpected.

AT ABOUT THE SAME TIME that Crawford Sloane left his Larchmont home to drive to CBA News headquarters, Harry Partridge woke in Port Credit, near Toronto. He had travelled the night before on a delayed flight from Dallas and had slept deeply. He spent the first few moments of the new day taking in familiar landmarks of his apartment's bedroom.

The nomadic nature of his work meant that Partridge got to the apartment for only a few brief periods each year. And even though he stored his few possessions here, the apartment was not registered in his name. The official tenant was Vivien Williams, who lived here permanently. Every month, from wherever in the world Partridge happened to be, he sent Vivien a cheque for the rent, and in return she lived there and kept it as his haven. The arrangement—which had other conveniences, including occasional lovemaking—suited them both.

Vivien was a nurse who worked in the Queensway Hospital nearby. She was in her mid-forties, with angular, strong features and straight black hair, now streaked with grey. Warm, easygoing and generous, she had been widowed before Partridge knew her and had one child, a daughter in Vancouver. Partridge was fond of Vivien, though not in love with her and aware he never would be. He suspected that she was in love with him but accepted the relationship they had.

Vivien came into the bedroom, carrying a tray with morning tea. While he sipped it, she regarded him quizzically. His face showed lines of strain and tiredness; his unruly shock of fair hair was in need of trimming.

Aware of her appraisal, Partridge asked, 'What's the verdict?'

Vivien shook her head in mock despair. 'Just look at you! I send you off healthy and fit. Two and a half months later you come back looking tired, pale and underfed.'

'I know, Viv.' He grimaced. 'It's the life I lead.' Then, with a smile, 'So here I am, a mess as usual. What can you do for me?'

She said, with a mixture of affection and firmness, 'First, I'll give you a good, healthy breakfast. I'll bring it to you in bed. After that I'm going to trim your hair. Later, I'm taking you for a sauna and massage—I've already made the appointment.'

Partridge lay back and threw up his hands. 'I love it!'

Vivien went on, 'Tomorrow I figured you'll want to see your old cronies at CBC—you usually do. But in the evening I have tickets for an all-Mozart concert in Toronto. You can let the music wash over you. I know you like that. Apart from all that, you'll rest or do whatever you want to.'

Partridge felt a surge of gratitude for Vivien. She was rock-solid, a refuge. He asked, 'Don't you have to work?'

'I've arranged to take some vacation, starting today.'

He told her, 'Viv, you're one in a million.'

When Vivien had gone and he could hear her preparing breakfast, Partridge's thoughts returned to yesterday.

150

There had been that congratulatory call—they had paged him for it in the DFW terminal—from Crawford Sloane. Crawf had sounded awkward, as he often did when they talked. There were times when Partridge wanted to say, 'Look, Crawf, if you think I have any grudge against you—about Jessica or your job or *anything,* forget it!' But he knew that kind of remark would strain their relationship even more.

Inevitably, when thinking in a personal way about Sloane, there was always the memory of Jessica, though it was never more than memory because there was nothing between them now, not even occasional communication, and they seldom met socially. Nor had Partridge ever blamed Sloane for his loss of Jessica, having recognised that his own foolish judgment was the cause. When he could have married her, Partridge decided not to, so Sloane simply stepped in, proving himself the wiser of the two, with a better sense of values at that time . . .

Vivien reappeared, bringing breakfast in stages: freshly squeezed orange juice, thick hot porridge with brown sugar and milk, followed by poached eggs on wholewheat toast, strong black coffee, the beans freshly ground, and finally more toast and Alberta honey. He knew he would enjoy it all and was grateful once more to Vivien for her thoughtfulness.

JESSICA WENT SHOPPING every Thursday morning and she intended to follow her usual routine that day. When Angus learned this he volunteered to accompany her, and Nicky, who had a school holiday, asked to go too so that he could be with his grandfather.

The three of them left the house in Jessica's Volvo station wagon shortly before eleven am. It was a beautiful morning, the trees rich with autumn colours and sunlight glistening off Long Island Sound.

The Sloanes' daily maid, Florence, was in the house and watched the trio leave from a window. She also saw a car, parked across the street, start up and follow in the same direction as the Volvo. She gave no thought to the second vehicle.

Jessica's first stop was the Grand Union supermarket in the central business area of Larchmont. She parked in the store's car park and then, accompanied by Angus and Nicky, went inside.

The Colombians, Julio and Carlos, had trailed the station wagon. Carlos, who had reported the departure from the house, now made another cellular phone call, announcing that 'the three packages are in container number one.'

This time Julio was driving. Following Miguel's instructions, Carlos left the Chevrolet Celebrity and moved on foot to a position near the store. When he was in place, Julio drove the Chevy away to the safe seclusion of the Hackensack operating centre.

THE PHONE MESSAGES reached Miguel in the Nissan van, parked near Larchmont's railway station. With him were Luís, Rafael and Baudelio, though all four were out of sight because of dark, thin plastic sheets covering the van's windows. Luís was at the wheel.

When they heard that three people had left the house, Rafael exclaimed, '*Ay!* That means the *viejo*'s come along.'

Miguel was still considering the complication of the third person. Their long-standing plan had involved only the Sloane woman and the boy. All along, they—not the newsman Crawford Sloane—had been the Sendero Luminoso/Medellín objective. The two were to be seized and held as hostages for as yet unspecified demands.

When Carlos's second message came, indicating that all three were inside the supermarket, Miguel nodded to Luís. 'Roll!'

The next stop, just a few blocks away, would be the store parking lot.

While they were moving, Miguel turned to look at Baudelio, the American in the Medellín group, who continued to be a source of worry.

Baudelio was in his mid-fifties but looked older. Gaunt, lantern-jawed, with sallow skin and a droopy grey moustache, he looked like a walking ghost. He had once been a doctor, a specialist in anaesthesiology practising in Boston, and a drunk. When left to his own devices, he was still a drunk. But he was no longer a doctor; his licence to practise had been revoked.

With no future in the United States, he had decided to go to Colombia, a place where he could use his considerable medical skills without arousing any questions. By reading medical journals, he managed to stay up-to-date in his specialty. All this background had been made known to Miguel, with a warning that while this assignment lasted, Baudelio was to be forbidden any alcohol. Also Miguel decided not to trust him with a firearm. Thus he was the only one in the group not armed.

The Grand Union supermarket was now directly ahead. Carlos saw the Nissan passenger van arrive. The parking lot was not crowded and the Nissan entered a conveniently vacant slot alongside Jessica's Volvo. When Carlos had observed this, he turned into the store.

JESSICA GESTURED to her partly filled shopping trolley and told Angus, 'If there's something you especially like, just drop it in.'

Nicky said, 'Gramps likes caviar.'

'I should have remembered,' Jessica said. 'Let's get some.' They moved to the gourmet section, Angus inspecting prices.

It was at that moment that Jessica noticed a young man, slightly built and well dressed, approaching a woman shopper nearby. He appeared to ask a question. The woman shook her head. Mildly curious, Jessica watched the young man as he approached her.

'Excuse me, ma'am,' Carlos said. 'I'm trying to locate someone.' Jessica noticed a Spanish accent, though that was not unusual in New York. She also thought the speaker had cold eyes. 'A Mrs Crawford Sloane.'

Jessica was startled. 'Oh? I'm Mrs Sloane.'

'Ma'am, I have some bad news.' Carlos's expression was serious. 'Your husband has been in an accident. He's badly injured. The ambulance took him to Doctors Hospital in Manhattan. I was sent to take you there. Your maid said you'd be here.'

Jessica gasped and turned deathly pale. Nicky, who had heard only the last few words, looked stunned. Angus was the first to recover and take charge. 'Jessie, let's go.'

'It's Dad, isn't it?' Nicky said.

Jessica put her arm round Nicky. 'Yes, dear. We're going to him now.' Still dazed by the shattering news, they went quickly with the young man towards the store's main door. Angus followed. Something was bothering him; just what, he wasn't sure.

Outside in the car park, Carlos led the other two towards the Nissan van. Both doors on the side nearer the Volvo were open.

Carlos said, 'We'll go in this vehicle, ma'am. It will be . . . '

'No, no!' Jessica, tense and anxious, was groping in her bag for her car keys. 'I'll take my car. I know where Doctors Hospital—'

Carlos interposed himself between the Volvo and Jessica. Grasping her arm, he said, 'Ma'am, we'd rather you—'

Jessica tried to withdraw her arm, but Carlos held her more firmly and pushed her forward. She said indignantly, 'Stop that! What is this?'

A few feet behind, Angus now realised what had been troubling him. The strange young man had said, 'The ambulance took him to Doctors Hospital.' *But Doctors Hospital didn't take emergencies.* Last year Angus had visited a patient there and had got to know the hospital well. *Emergencies were sent to New York Hospital, a few blocks south . . .*

So the young man was lying! Angus shouted, 'Jessica, don't go! Nicky, run! Get—'

The sentence was never finished. A pistol butt crashed down on Angus's

154

head, and he fell to the ground unconscious. Luís had jumped out of the driver's seat and attacked him from behind. In almost the same motion, Luís grabbed Nicholas.

Jessica began screaming. 'Help! Someone . . . please help!'

The burly Rafael, who had joined Carlos in seizing Jessica, now clamped a massive hand across her mouth and flung her inside the van. Then, jumping in himself, he continued to hold her as she struggled. From a medical bag Baudelio produced a gauze pad soaked in ethyl chloride. He slapped the pad over Jessica's nose and mouth and held it there. Instantly her eyes closed, her body sagged and she became unconscious. Nicholas, struggling too, was hauled inside and given the same treatment.

The ex-doctor knew the effect of ethyl chloride would last only five minutes. Working quickly, he used scissors to cut the sleeve of Jessica's dress, and injected a strong sedative into her upper arm. He gave the boy a similar injection.

Miguel, meanwhile, had dragged the unconscious Angus over to the van. To Miguel's amazement, no one appeared to have witnessed what had happened. He ordered Rafael, 'Help me get him in.'

It was accomplished in seconds. Then, as he entered the van himself, Miguel saw he had been wrong. An elderly woman, white-haired and leaning on a stick, was watching from some twenty yards away. She appeared uncertain and puzzled.

As Luís moved the van forward, Miguel called in a cheerful voice, 'Don't be alarmed. It's just part of a film we're making.'

He saw relief on the woman's face. Then they left the parking lot and, soon after, Larchmont. Within five minutes they were on the New England Thruway, heading south and moving fast.

CHAPTER 4

Priscilla Rhea had been a schoolteacher in Larchmont and had pounded into several generations of local youngsters the fundamentals of square roots and quadratic equations. She had also urged them to have a sense of civic responsibility and never to shirk their obvious duty. But all of that was prior to her retirement fifteen years earlier, before age and illness had slowed her body, then her mind.

Nevertheless, she was exercising her thought processes now. Her natural anxiety at seeing three people taken into a van, apparently against their will, was relieved by the shout that it was all part of a film show. That made sense. Film and television crews seemed to be everywhere nowadays, photographing against real backgrounds. But then, the moment the van had gone Priscilla looked around for the cameras and film crew, and for the life of her she couldn't find any.

The sensible thing, she told herself, was to do her bit of shopping at Grand Union and mind her own business. Just the same, there was her lifelong credo of not shirking responsibility. She walked slowly, using her stick, over to the still empty parking slot next to Jessica's station wagon. Her attention was caught by small pools of liquid on the ground. Curiously, she leaned down to touch it. Seconds later she looked with horror at her fingers. They were covered in what was unmistakably blood.

OFFICER JENSEN from the Larchmont Police Department stood by his patrol car outside the Grand Union and listened sceptically to what Priscilla Rhea had to say. She remembered details—the colour of the van, a light tan, and the fact that it had dark windows. No, she had not noticed a registration number, but when she told him about some splotches on the parking lot that looked like blood, his interest began to mount. He walked over to inspect. By this time most of the liquid had dried, though there was enough that was moist to reveal it as red to the touch.

Hurrying back to where he had left Priscilla, he found her talking to several people who were curious about what was going on.

One man volunteered, 'Officer, I was inside and saw four people leave in a hurry—two men, a woman and a boy.'

'I saw them too,' a woman said. 'That was Mrs Sloane, the TV anchorman's wife. She often shops here. When she left she looked like something bad had happened.'

The officer asked, 'Did anyone see a van, colour light tan?'

'Yes, I saw that,' the first man said. 'It pulled into the lot as I was walking to the store. It was a Nissan passenger van with New Jersey plates. Oh, one other thing. It had dark windows.'

'Hold it!' the officer said, addressing the growing crowd. 'Any of you who have information, please stay.' He jumped into the white police cruiser and grabbed the radio mike. 'Car four two three to headquarters. Possible kidnap at Grand Union parking lot. Request help.'

Sirens from other cruisers were soon heard responding to the request.

SOME EIGHT MILES AWAY, the Nissan van was about to leave the New England Thruway and enter a maze of streets in the New York City borough of the Bronx. Both Luís and Miguel had been looking behind for signs of any pursuit. There were none.

Just the same, Miguel urged Luís, 'Move it!'

Baudelio had several times checked the vital signs of their two sedated captives, and all appeared to be well. The old man was now stirring, slight

156

moans escaping him. Anticipating possible trouble, Baudelio prepared another hypodermic of sedative and injected it.

Rafael now produced three brown blankets and he and Carlos, with Baudelio watching, wrapped the prisoners in them. Sufficient blanket was left folded at the top so it could be turned back to cover the face when the three were removed from the van. Carlos tied each rolled bundle with cord round the middle.

Conner Street, in the Bronx, which they had reached, was desolate, grey and depressing. Luís turned right into a deserted industrial area and halted the van. As he did, a truck from the opposite side of the street pulled across and stopped ahead of the Nissan. The truck was a white GMC with a painted sign, 'Superbread', on either side.

There was no such product as Superbread. The truck was one of six vehicles obtained by Miguel. Like all his other vehicles, it had been repainted several times. Today the truck was being driven by the woman, Socorro, who jumped out and went round to open the rear doors. At the same time the door of the van was opened and the bundles, their faces covered, were quickly transferred to the GMC truck.

Miguel and Luís were busy removing identifying features from the Nissan van. Miguel peeled off the dark, thin plastic sheets from the windows while Luís replaced the van's New Jersey plates with New York ones. Luís then took over the wheel of the GMC truck, which now contained the unconscious Jessica, Nicholas and Angus, as well as Miguel, Rafael, Baudelio and Socorro. After a swift U-turn they headed back to the thruway and, within less than ten minutes after leaving it, were back on it in the new vehicle, continuing south.

Carlos, now driving the empty Nissan van, also made a U-turn. He, too, made for the Interstate, but heading north.

After three miles he left the Thruway, then continued north on secondary roads as far as White Plains. There he drove to a public parking garage adjoining an indoor shopping complex—Center City Mall.

Parking on the third level, Carlos moved with apparent casualness through his next activities. From a locker in the van's interior he withdrew a Styrofoam container. It contained a formidable quantity of plastic explosive, plus a small detonator unit with a release pin, two lengths of pliant wire and a roll of adhesive tape. He taped the explosive and detonator out of sight behind the front seats, then ran wires from the release pin to the inside handles of each front door. Getting out of the side door, he carefully locked all doors. Now, opening either front door would pull the release pin from the detonator.

Carlos left the parking garage through the shopping mall, then used public transport to Hackensack, where he would rejoin the others.

157

BERT FISHER LIVED and worked in a tiny apartment in Larchmont. He was sixty-eight and a widower. His business cards described him as a news reporter, though in the parlance of journalism he was really a stringer.

Like other stringers, Bert was the local representative of several news organisations, some of which paid him a small retainer. He submitted information or written copy and got paid for what was used. Though age had slowed him a little journalism was still in his blood, and he kept several scanner radios switched on so as to hear communications of local police, fire departments and other public services.

That was how Bert heard Officer Jensen's transmission alerting Larchmont police headquarters to a possible kidnap. At the word kidnap, Bert sat up straight and reached for copy paper to make notes.

By the time the transmission finished, Bert knew he needed to call New York City television station WCBA.

AT WCBA-TV AN ASSISTANT news director took Bert Fisher's call. A wholly owned affiliate of the CBA network, WCBA was a local station serving the New York area. In a bustling, noise-filled newsroom the assistant news director listened while Bert Fisher described the police radio message, and his intention to go to the Larchmont scene.

'All right, Fisher, get going!'

Hanging up, the assistant news director walked over to the newsroom desk where the station's woman news director presided, and told her about the call.

After hearing him out, she confirmed his decision. But afterwards a thought occurred to her. She picked up a telephone that connected her directly to CBA network news and spoke to Ernie LaSalle, the national editor. Repeating what she had just heard, she added, 'I know Larchmont is where Crawford Sloane lives. So I thought you'd want to tell him.'

'Thanks,' LaSalle said. 'Call if there's anything more.'

When he hung up, Ernie LaSalle momentarily weighed the information. On instinct and impulse he picked up the red reporting phone.

'National desk. LaSalle. We are advised that at Larchmont, New York, the local police radio reports a possible kidnapping. No other details. Our friends at WCBA are following up and will inform us.'

As always, the national editor's words were carried throughout the CBA News headquarters. One floor above the newsroom, senior producers at the Horseshoe paused to listen. One of them, pointing to Crawford Sloane, who could be seen through the closed glass door of his private office, observed, 'If there's a kidnapping let's be thankful it's someone else in Larchmont. Unless that's Crawf's double in there.' The others laughed.

158

Sloane heard LaSalle's announcement through his desk speaker. His interest quickened at the mention of Larchmont. Curious about more information, he headed for the newsroom.

AFTER TELEPHONING WCBA-TV, Bert Fisher hurried out of his apartment, to his battered twenty-year-old Volkswagen beetle. He kept a scanner radio in the car and set it to the Larchmont police frequency as he headed downtown to the Grand Union. Partway there some more radio exchanges caused him to change direction.

'Car four twenty-three to headquarters. Proceeding to house of possible victims of incident. Address, sixty-six Park Avenue. Request a detective.'

'Headquarters to four twenty-three. Ten four.'

A brief pause, then, 'Headquarters to car four twenty-six. Proceed urgently to Sixty-six Park Avenue. Investigate officer's report, car four twenty-three.'

Clearly, the action was heating up. Now, heading for Park Avenue, Bert felt excited about that address—66. He wasn't sure, but if the house belonged to the person he thought it did, this was really a big story.

OFFICER JENSEN had just entered the driveway of 66 Park Avenue when a second police car pulled in behind. Detective Ed York, an old-timer on the force, stepped out. York and Jensen conferred briefly, then walked to the house together. The policemen identified themselves to Florence, the Sloanes' daily maid, and, surprised, she let them in.

'There's a possibility,' York informed her, 'that something may have happened to Mrs Sloane.' He began asking questions which Florence answered, her concern mounting.

Yes, she had been in the house when Mrs Sloane, Nicky and Mr Sloane's father left to go shopping. That was about eleven o'clock. Mr Sloane had left for work just before Florence arrived, which was 9.30. No, there had been nothing unusual when Mrs Sloane and the others drove away. Except—well . . .'

'What do you mean by "Except—well"?' the detective asked.

'Well, when they were leaving, I saw a car parked on the other side of the street. When Mrs Sloane drove away, all of a sudden the car went the same way she did. I didn't think about it at the time.'

'Can you describe the car?' Jensen said.

'It was dark brown, I think. Sort of medium size.'

'Did you recognise the make?'

Florence shook her head. 'They all look the same to me.'

The detective and Jensen returned outside. As they did, two more police cruisers arrived. One brought a uniformed sergeant and the other the

Larchmont chief of police. The chief was tall and rangy, with a deceptively low-key manner. After a hasty conference, the chief asked Detective York, 'You think this is for real? A kidnap?'

'At this moment,' York said, 'everything points that way.'

The chief mused. 'If it *is* a kidnap and they cross a state line, it becomes the FBI's jurisdiction. That's the Lindbergh law.' He added, 'I'm calling in the FBI now.'

He returned to his car and picked up the radio mike. A minute or two later, rejoining the others, the chief ordered York to go back to the house and stay inside. The sergeant and Jensen were instructed to remain on duty outside.

Knowing that Larchmont's most famous resident was involved, the chief said sourly, 'Soon there'll be more people here than flies round a garbage truck. Let no one past the front gate except the FBI. When the press get here, direct them to headquarters.'

At that moment they heard the sound of a noisy car approaching. Their heads turned. It was a battered Volkswagen beetle, and the chief said glumly, 'Here's the first.'

BERT FISHER STOPPED HIS VW at the kerb and climbed out, then hurried forward. 'Chief, can you make a statement?'

'A statement about what?'

'Oh, come on, Chief! I've heard all the radio buzz, including your instruction just now to call in the FBI.' Bert looked round him, realising his hunch was right. 'This is Crawford Sloane's home. And is it Mrs Sloane who's been kidnapped?'

The chief hesitated, then said, 'Well, if you heard all the messages, you'll know we aren't certain of anything yet. But yes, we do think Mrs Sloane may have been abducted, along with the Sloanes' son Nicholas and Mr Sloane's father.'

Bert knew this was the most important story of his life. 'Do you have any idea who might have done this?' he asked.

'No. Oh, just one thing. Mr Sloane has not been informed and we're trying to get in touch with him. So before you start sounding off, for God's sake give us time to do that.'

The chief turned away and Bert dived for his VW. Despite the chief's caveat, he had no intention of waiting for anything. As he turned out of Park Avenue, he saw another car turning in and recognised the local stringer for WNBC-TV. So the competition was on to the story. Now, if he was to stay ahead, he had to move fast. Not far away, on Boston Post Road, he found a payphone. As he punched out the numbers of WCBA-TV, his hand was trembling uncontrollably.

AT ELEVEN TWENTY AM in the pressure-driven newsroom of WCBA-TV, tension was rising as it always did during the hour preceding the local New York station's News at Noon. Today, especially, there was a heavy budget of news with several developing stories competing for the lead position. Amid a scene of near bedlam, Bert Fisher's phone call was routed to the same assistant news director as before.On hearing who was calling, the assistant snapped, 'We're swamped here. Make it quick!'

Bert did. The young newsman said incredulously, 'You're sure?'

'I have confirmation from the chief of police.' Bert added proudly, 'He gave me an exclusive statement.'

The assistant was already on his feet, shouting urgently to the news director, 'Line four!' He told an assignment editor beside him, 'We need a camera crew in Larchmont fast.'

The woman news director listened to Bert Fisher, making notes of the essentials. 'Stay on the line,' she told him. Then, to a writer at a desk nearby, 'Take line four. It's Fisher, Larchmont. Get everything he has, then write it as our noon lead.'

She picked up a telephone connecting her to the network. Ernie LaSalle answered and she told him, 'The kidnap in Larchmont is confirmed. Half an hour ago unknown persons violently seized Crawford's wife, his son, and his father.'

'Good God!' The national editor's shock and incredulity came down the line. 'Has Crawf been told?'

'I don't think so.'

'Are the police involved?'

'Very much so, and they've called in the FBI.' She added, 'We've heard that WNBC is on to the story, though a bit behind us. Look, we'll go with this at noon, and I'm considering breaking into programming now. But I thought, since this is family—'

LaSalle snapped, 'Don't do a damn thing. The brass will be in on this. And if anybody breaks it, we will.'

Taking seconds only, Ernie LaSalle debated his options. One was to take time to contact Crawford Sloane and gently convey to him the frightening information. A second was to pick up the red reporting phone and announce to the entire news division the kidnapping of the Sloane family, after which urgent action to make an on-air report would undoubtedly begin. The third was to issue an order to interrupt network programming with a special bulletin. In LaSalle's judgment the news just received was not only pre-eminent but of immense public interest.

He opted for the second choice. Influencing his decision was the knowledge that another New York station, WNBC-TV—owned by NBC network—was on the scene. There wasn't time for humane niceties. I'm sorry as hell to do this to you, Crawf, LaSalle thought, and picked up the red reporting phone.

'National desk. LaSalle. The earlier reported kidnapping at Larchmont, New York, has been confirmed by the local chief of police. The reported victims are Mrs Crawford Sloane, young Nicholas Sloane and'—despite his resolve and professionalism, LaSalle found his voice breaking —'and Crawford's father, who were violently seized and driven away by unknown persons. WCBA has reliable on-scene coverage. National desk recommends taking network air immediately.'

Horror and consternation swept through the news division like a tidal wave. Everyone stopped working. Many looked at each other, asking silently: Did I really hear that?

Senior staffers at the Horseshoe were equally appalled, though their shock lasted only moments. After it, out of habit and discipline, they were galvanised into action. Chuck Insen, as senior producer in the building, left his office on the run for the broadcast control room, four floors below.

Impatiently awaiting an elevator, his mind overflowed with sympathy for Sloane. He must have heard the hot-line call. Which raised a crucial question. When urgent breaking news was deemed significant enough to interrupt programming, it was the evening news anchorman—in CBA's case, Crawford Sloane—who faced the cameras. But there was absolutely no way Sloane could be expected to handle this sudden, harrowing news about his own family.

At that moment an elevator arrived and the business correspondent of CBA News, Don Kettering, prepared to step out. Kettering, middle-aged with a thin moustache, looked like a well-to-do businessman himself. Before he could leave the elevator Insen shoved him back inside.

Insen said. 'You heard the speakerphone just now?'

'Yes, I'm damn sorry. I was going to tell Crawf—'

'Where you're going,' Insen said, 'is on the air. Get to the flash studio and take the hot seat. Crawf can't do this.'

Kettering, a quick thinker and an experienced general reporter, nodded. 'Do I get some briefing?'

'We'll give you all we have. You'll get a minute to do a quick study, then ad-lib. More will be fed to you as it comes in.'

'Right.'

As Insen left the elevator, Kettering pressed a button which would take him up to the broadcast floor.

Elsewhere, other activity was in high gear. In the newsroom the northeast assignment editor was rounding up two network camera crews and correspondents. They were to proceed posthaste to Larchmont and obtain pictures of the kidnap scene as well as interview the police and any

162

witnesses. A mobile transmitting van would follow.

In a small research department adjoining the Horseshoe, half a dozen people were hastily assembling the few known facts about Crawford Sloane's family—few because Jessica had always insisted on privacy for herself and Nicholas. Main research, though, had acquired a photograph of Jessica, which was coming through on a fax machine, a graphics editor waiting to convert it to a slide. Printing out from another computer was the war record of Angus Sloane. There would be a photo of him, too.

A research assistant grabbed all the available material and ran down a flight of stairs to the flash-facility studio where Don Kettering had just arrived. Right behind, a messenger from the national desk brought a print-out of Bert Fisher's report, received from WCBA-TV. Kettering sat down at the studio's central desk and immersed himself in reading. Around him technicians were arriving, lights coming on. Someone clipped a microphone onto Kettering's jacket. A cameraman framed Kettering in his lens.

The flash facility was the smallest studio in the building, no bigger than a modest living room. It had a single camera and could be activated and ready in moments.

Meanwhile, in the darkened control room where Chuck Insen was now established, a woman director slid into her seat facing a bank of TV monitors, an assistant beside her. Operators and technicians were taking their places, a stream of orders flowing.

'Stand by, camera one. Mike check.'

'Bill, this will be a live announcement. "We interrupt this programming" open, and "resume programming" close. OK?'

'OK. Got it.'

'Do we have a script yet?'

'Negative. Don may go ad lib.'

'Bring the video up ten units. OK. Got it.'

'Camera one, let's see Kettering.'

More monitors were coming alight, among them one from the flash facility. The face of Don Kettering filled the screen.

The director's assistant was telling network master control, 'We expect to break into the network with a bulletin. Please stand by.'

The director enquired, 'Is the special slide ready?'

A voice responded, 'Here it is.'

On another monitor, bright red letters filled the screen:

CBA NEWS SPECIAL BULLETIN

'Hold it there.' The director turned in her chair to speak to Insen. 'Chuck, we're ready as we'll ever be. Do we go or not?'

The executive producer told her, 'I'm finding out now.' He was talking to the news division president who was in the main newsroom where Crawford Sloane was pleading for delay.

WHEN THE SHATTERING NATIONAL desk announcement began, Crawford Sloane was on his way to the newsroom. He stopped at the head of a stairway to listen; then, scarcely believing what he had heard, he stood dazed and in a state of shock.

His trance was interrupted by a Horseshoe secretary who came running after him, calling, 'Mr Sloane! The police want to talk to you urgently.'

He followed the woman back and took the call in his office.

'Mr Sloane, this is Detective York. I'm at your home and have some unfortunate—'

'I just heard. Tell me what you know.'

'Actually, sir, it's very little.' Detective York recited the known facts. Then he added, 'I've been asked to tell you there's concern about your own safety. You'll receive police protection.'

Sloane's mind was whirling. Consumed with anxiety, he asked, 'Is there any idea who might have done this?'

'No, sir. It all happened suddenly. We're in the dark.'

'Do many people know about this—what's happened?'

'As far as I know, not many.' The detective added, 'The longer we can keep it that way, the better, because . . . '

Sloane scarcely heard. Interrupting the detective, he raced for the stairs and descended them swiftly. Ahead he could see the towering figure of the CBA news president in hasty conference with several others round the national desk.

Leslie Chippingham, a thirty-year veteran of TV news, was six foot four and weighed a trim two hundred and five pounds. His face was more rugged than handsome, the eyes bright blue and the hair a forest of tight curls, now mostly grey. He was saying, 'Then I guess we should go with what we have.'

Sloane broke into the circle. 'No, no, no! Les, don't go with it! We need more time. Publicity could harm my family.'

LaSalle said, 'Crawf, we know what you're going through. But this is a big story, and others have it. WNBC—'

Sloane shook his head. 'I still say no!' He faced the news president directly. 'Les, I beg of you—delay!'

There was an embarrassed silence. Everyone knew that in other circumstances Sloane would be the first to urge going ahead. But no one had the heart to say, Crawf, you're not thinking coherently.

Chippingham glanced at the newsroom clock: eleven fifty-four.

164

LaSalle had taken over Insen's phone call. Now he reported, 'Chuck says everyone's set to go. Are we breaking into the network or not?'

Chippingham said, 'I'm still deciding.' He debated: should they wait until noon? On monitors overhead he could see the national feeds of all networks. On CBA a popular soap opera was in progress; commercials would follow. Cutting in now would be costly. Would another six minutes make much difference?

At that moment, several newsroom computers emitted a beep. On screens a bright 'B' appeared—the signal for an urgent press wire bulletin. Someone called out, 'AP has the story.'

On the national desk another phone rang. LaSalle answered, listened, then said quietly, 'Thank you for telling us.' Hanging up, he informed the news president, 'NBC called as a courtesy. They're going with the story on the hour.'

The time was fifteen seconds short of 11.55.

Making a decision, Chippingham said, 'We go now!' Then, to LaSalle, 'Tell Chuck to break the network.'

IN THE CBA NEWS HEADQUARTERS building, two floors below street level in a small, plain room, a pair of technicians sat facing complex switching systems with a galaxy of coloured lights and dials, computer terminals and television monitors. Two sides of the room were glass.

This was network master control, technical command post for the entire CBA national network. Through here all network programming flowed: entertainment, news, sports, documentaries, presidents' addresses, prerecordings and national commercials. Surprisingly, for all its importance as an electronic pulse centre, master control's appearance was uninspiring.

At master control, each day of broadcasting advanced according to a meticulous plan. Principally, execution of the plan was by computer, with the two technicians overseeing it—and occasionally interceding when unexpected events required regular programming to be interrupted.

An interruption was occurring now.

Moments earlier, on a direct line from the news division control room, Chuck Insen had instructed, 'We have a news special. It's for the full network. We're taking air—*now!*'

As he spoke, the slide 'CBA News Special Bulletin', fed from the news control room, came up on a master control monitor.

The master control operator who received the call knew the command 'now' meant exactly that: no delay, no holding. So, moving a switch, the operator cut the commercial being broadcast, thereby costing CBA some twenty-five thousand dollars in revenue. With another switch he put the 'Special Bulletin' slide on the network video feed. Instantly, the words appeared on the screens of more than twelve million television sets.

Seconds later an announcer's voice was heard: 'We interrupt our regular programming to bring you a special report from CBA News. From New York, here is correspondent Don Kettering.'

In the news control room, the director ordered, 'Cue Don!'

Across the nation the face of CBA's business correspondent filled television screens.

His voice and expression serious, Kettering began, 'Police in Larch mont, New York, have reported the apparent kidnapping of the wife, young son and father of CBA News anchorman Crawford Sloane. . .'

The time was 11.56 am. Beating its competitors, CBA News had broken the story first.

PART TWO   CHAPTER 5

The aftereffects of CBA's special bulletin announcing the Sloane family kidnap were instantaneous and widespread.

NBC News, whose courteous gesture of informing CBA had robbed it of a possible lead, followed with its own bulletin barely a minute later—ahead of its original plan to break the story at noon.

CBS, ABC and CNN, alerted by wire service-reports, were all on the air with the news in minutes. So were independent TV stations across the country. Radio stations were even faster to spread the story.

Shortly after the initial bulletins, the press and other media reporters reached Larchmont and interviewed—as an observer put it—'almost every breathing body in sight'. The ex-schoolteacher, Priscilla Rhea, proved to be the favourite interviewee, with the police chief a close second.

A startling new development emerged when several people living near the Sloanes came forward with information that the Sloane house had been under observation for perhaps a month. A succession of vehicles had been seen near the house for long periods, the occupants remaining inside. The interviewers asked the obvious question: Why had no one reported the apparent surveillance to the police?

In each case the answer was the same: it had been assumed that security protection was being provided for the famous Mr Sloane, and why would neighbours interfere with that? Now, belatedly, information about the various vehicles was being sought by police.

Overseas media, too, were showing keen interest in the kidnap story. While the face and voice of Crawford Sloane were not as familiar to foreigners as to North Americans, the involvement of a major TV personality seemed of international consequence in itself. This reaction was proof that the modern network anchorman had become a special breed, ranking in public idolisation with kings and queens, film and rock stars, popes, presidents and princes.

CRAWFORD SLOANE'S MIND was a turmoil of emotions. He moved through the next several hours in a daze.

What troubled him greatly was the memory of his conversation the preceding evening with Jessica. It was he who had brought up the possibility of kidnap but, as he now thought guiltily, his own selfishness and self-importance had made him assume that only he could be a victim. Jessica had even asked, 'What about families? Could they be targets too?' But he had dismissed the idea, not believing it could happen.

Sloane fretted impatiently, wanting to take some action yet knowing there was little he could do. Another reason for staying put was the arrival of three FBI field agents, who began a flurry of activity centred round him. They demanded of CBA that the entire building be secured immediately, then phoned the New York City Police Department to discuss police protection for him. Having been assured that everything possible would be done, they questioned him at length.

'Mr Sloane, is there anything you have reported on the news which could have caused special antagonism on the part of someone?' asked Special Agent Otis Havelock, senior in the trio.

Sloane said ruefully, 'Once a day, at least.'

The FBI man nodded. 'Two of my colleagues will view tapes of your broadcasts for the past two years, to see if ideas suggest themselves. How about antagonistic mail?'

'I never see it. People in network news are shielded from it.'

Havelock's eyebrows went up as Sloane continued, 'Everything we broadcast generates a phenomenal amount of mail. Reading all those letters would take too much time. Then we'd probably want to respond, which would take more time still. Management also believes that we're better able to keep our sense of perspective and fairness if protected from individual reactions to the news.' Sloane shrugged. 'Some may disagree, but that's the way it is.'

'So what happens to the mail?'

'It's handled by a department called Audience Services. All letters are answered and anything judged important is sent to Mr Chippingham, the news division president.'

Havelock made a note. 'We'll go through that, too.'

During a pause, Chuck Insen knocked on Sloane's office door.

The executive producer said, 'If I can interrupt—Crawf, we all want to do the best we can—for you, for Jessica, Nicky . . . '

Sloane acknowledged, 'Yes, I know.'

'We feel you shouldn't do the news tonight. For one thing, it will be heavily *about* you. For another, what we're wondering is if you'd feel up to being interviewed—live?'

Sloane considered, then said thoughtfully, 'Do you think I should?'

'Now that the story's out,' Insen said, 'I think the wider attention it gets, the better. There's always a chance that someone watching might come through with information.'

'Then I'll do it.'

Insen nodded, then continued, 'The other networks and the press want to interview you. How do you feel about a press conference?'

Sloane gestured helplessly, then conceded, 'All right.'

Insen asked, 'When you're through here, Crawf, can you join Les and me in my office? We'd like your views about some other plans.'

Havelock interjected, 'As much as possible, I'd like Mr Sloane to stay in his office and be close to this telephone.'

'I'll be close to it anyway,' Sloane assured him.

LESLIE CHIPPINGHAM was already seated in Insen's office when Sloane and Insen joined him. He had just telephoned Rita Abrams in Minnesota with the unhappy news that their planned lovers' weekend would have to be abandoned. There was no way, he explained, that in the midst of this breaking story he could leave New York.

Rita, while disappointed, understood. People in TV news were used to having their lives disrupted, even their illicit affairs.

Now Chippingham said, 'Chuck, spell it out for Crawf.'

'The fact is,' Insen said, looking at Sloane directly, 'we do not have confidence in government agencies' ability to handle this situation. Now, I don't want to depress you, but we all remember how long it took the FBI to find Patty Hearst—more than a year and a half. And there's something else.' From his desk he produced a copy of Sloane's book, *The Camera and the Truth*, and opened it at a marked page.

'You wrote, yourself, Crawf, "We who live in the United States will not remain free from terrorism in our own back yard much longer. But neither are we prepared for this pervasive, ruthless kind of warfare." ' Insen closed the book. 'Les and I agree with that. Totally.'

A shocked silence followed. At length Sloane said, 'Do you seriously think that *terrorists*—'

'At this point,' Chippingham put in, 'we've no idea who the people are or what they want. We believe that we ourselves—an experienced news

168

organisation accustomed to investigative reporting—have a better than average chance of discovering where your family has been taken.'

For the first time that day, Sloane's spirits rose.

Chippingham continued, 'So we've decided to set up our own CBA News investigative task force. Our effort will be nationwide at first, then, if necessary, worldwide. We'll use all our resources plus investigative techniques that have worked in the past. As for people, we'll throw in the best talent we have, starting now.'

Sloane felt a surge of gratitude. He started to say, 'Les, Chuck—'

Insen stopped him. 'There's one thing we want to ask you at this point, Crawf. The task force needs to be headed by an experienced correspondent or producer, someone in whom you have confidence. Is there anyone you'd like to name?'

Crawford Sloane hesitated for the briefest moment, weighing his personal feelings against what was at stake. Then he said firmly, 'I want Harry Partridge.'

THE MEDELLÍN GROUP OF KIDNAPPERS, like foxes returning to a hidden burrow, had gone to ground in their temporary headquarters, the rented property south of Hackensack, New Jersey. It was a collection of old decaying structures—a main house and three outbuildings—which had been unused for several years until Miguel, not wishing to reveal that the place would be used for little more than a month, signed a one-year lease, with full payment in advance.

The property was ideal in numerous ways. The large house could accommodate all seven members of the gang, and the outbuildings made it possible to keep six vehicles out of sight. No other houses were close by, and privacy was aided by surrounding trees. A further advantage was that Teterboro Airport was not much more than a mile away. Teterboro, used mainly by private aircraft, figured largely in the kidnappers' plans.

The three prisoners, still drugged and unconscious, had been carried to a large room on the first floor of the main house. Two hospital cots with restraining side rails stood in the centre of the room. Jessica was on one; the boy, Nicholas, on the other. Their arms and legs were secured by straps—a precaution in case they regained consciousness. Alongside the two cots was a narrow metal bed that had been hastily brought in to accommodate Angus. His limbs were secured with lengths of rope.

The ex-doctor, Baudelio, was working around the three recumbent forms. On a table covered with a green cotton cloth he had laid out instruments, intravenous stands and drug packages. Assisting him was the woman, Socorro.

With raven-dark hair twisted into a bun behind her head, Socorro had a

169

slim, lithe body, olive skin, and features that might have been beautiful had she not worn a permanently sour expression. She seldom spoke and never revealed what went on in her mind. For these reasons Miguel had mentally labelled Socorro 'the inscrutable one'. While he had no reason to mistrust her, he occasionally wondered if her long exposure to the American scene had diluted her Colombian and Peruvian loyalties.

From a tilted-back chair on the far side of the room, Miguel said to Baudelio, 'Tell me what it is you are doing.'

Midazolam, the sedative I administered, will very soon wear off. When it does, I shall begin injections of propofol, a longer-acting drug, more suitable for what is ahead. Propofol is a tricky drug to use.'

Miguel asked, 'Are you sure you can handle it?'

'If you have doubts,' Baudelio said sarcastically, 'you are free to get someone else.' When Miguel failed to answer, he went on, 'Because these people will be unconscious when we transport them, we must be certain there is no vomiting and aspiration into the lungs. Therefore, while we are waiting there will be a period of enforced starvation. In two days' time we shall be ready to put them into those.' Baudelio gestured behind him.

Propped upright against the wall were two open funeral caskets, solidly constructed. One was smaller than the other. The caskets reminded Baudelio of a question. Pointing to Angus Sloane, he asked, 'Do you want him prepared, or not? If we take him, we'd need another . . . '

Miguel said irritably, 'I do not need to be told that.'

If there had been some way to do so, Miguel would have asked his superiors. But to telephone would leave the record of a call. Miguel had been emphatic with everyone that the cellular phones were solely for vehicle-to-vehicle or vehicle-to-headquarters use. Positively no calls were to be made to other numbers.

Therefore, the decision was his alone. Obtaining an extra casket also meant taking additional risks. Was it worth it?

Miguel reasoned that it was. He told Baudelio, 'Yes, the old man goes.'

Baudelio nodded. Despite his outward assurance, he was nervous around Miguel today because, the night before, he had committed what he now recognised as a serious breach of security. While Baudelio was alone, in a moment of profound loneliness and dejection, he had used one of the cellular phones to call Peru. It was a woman he had spoken to, his slatternly living companion and only friend, whom he sorely missed.

It was because of Baudelio's continuing anxiety about that call that he was slow to react when, unexpectedly, a crisis confronted him.

Jessica, during the struggle outside the supermarket, had had only a minute or two to grasp what was happening before blackness supervened and she fell into deep unconsciousness.

But now, without knowing how long it had lasted, she was reviving, her memory returning. She became aware, faintly at first, of sounds around her, of voices. Then, as more moments passed, the voices became clearer, the awful memory of events at Larchmont sharpened.

Jessica's eyes opened. At first she could not understand why her arms and legs wouldn't move. Then she saw that they were constricted by a strap and realised she was on what looked like a hospital bed.

She turned her head slightly and froze in horror at what she saw. Nicky was on another bed, imprisoned like herself. Beyond him Angus, too, was tied down with ropes. And then—Oh, no! Oh, God!—she glimpsed the two open funeral caskets, one smaller than the other.

At once she began to scream and struggle wildly. Somehow, in her demented terror, she managed to get her left arm free.

Hearing the screams, the three conspirators, who had been looking elsewhere, swung towards her. By then Jessica had seen them all. She reached out with her left hand, trying desperately to find something to use as a weapon to protect herself. The table of instruments was beside her and she seized what felt like a kitchen paring knife. It was a scalpel.

With Socorro's help, Baudelio tried to refasten Jessica's free arm. But Jessica was faster. In her desperation she reached out with the scalpel, managing to gash Baudelio's face, then Socorro's hand. Thin red lines appeared on both, then blood gushed out.

Miguel, hurrying forward, hit Jessica savagely with his fist. He retrieved the scalpel, then helped Baudelio to restrap Jessica's arm. Defeated and helpless, she broke down in tears.

Nicky's sedation was also wearing off. Becoming aware of the shouting, and of his mother nearby, he, too, began screaming. But despite his struggles, he couldn't free himself from the straps. Angus, who had been sedated last, did not stir.

By now the noise and confusion were overwhelming, but both Baudelio and Socorro needed treatment for their wounds. Socorro put an adhesive dressing on her cut hand. She then taped gauze pads over Baudelio's face. Nodding an acknowledgment, he pointed to the assembled equipment and murmured, 'Help me.'

Socorro tightened the strap above Jessica's left elbow. Then Baudelio inserted a hypodermic needle into a vein and injected the propofol he had prepared earlier. Jessica, watching and screaming, fought against the drug's effect until her eyes closed and once more she was unconscious.

Baudelio and Socorro moved on to Nicky and repeated the process. Then, before he could regain consciousness and cause trouble, Angus was also given propofol.

Miguel had been glowering at Baudelio. Now he stormed at him, 'You incompetent idiot! You could have ruined everything!'

'I know.' Despite the gauze pads, blood was streaming down Baudelio's face. 'I made an error. It will not happen again.'

His face flushed with anger, Miguel stalked out.

AT ABOUT ELEVEN FIFTY AM, in the apartment at Port Credit, Harry Partridge had switched the TV to a Buffalo, New York, station—a CBA affiliate. Vivien had gone out until midafternoon.

Partridge hoped to learn from the noon news the latest developments following yesterday's airline disaster. Consequently, when programming was interrupted by the CBA News Special Bulletin, Partridge was watching.

He was as shocked as everyone else. As he watched Don Kettering's face on the screen and heard the continuing report, he felt, more than anything, a personal concern for Jessica. And mixed with this emotion was a sense of comradeship and pity for Crawford Sloane.

Partridge also knew that his vacation, which had scarcely begun, was already over. It was no surprise to receive a phone call some minutes later, asking him to come to headquarters in New York. What did surprise him was that it was from Crawford Sloane.

Sloane's voice was barely under control. 'I desperately need you, Harry,' he said. 'Les and Chuck are setting up a special unit; it will work on two levels—daily reports on air, and deep investigation. They asked me who I wanted in charge. I told them there's only one choice—you.'

In all the years they had known each other, Partridge realised they had never been closer than at this moment. He responded, 'Hang in there, Crawf. I'll be on the next flight.'

'Thank you, Harry. Anyone you especially want with you?'

'Yes. Find Rita Abrams, wherever she is—in Minnesota some where—and bring her in. The same for Minh Van Canh.' Thinking quickly, Partridge added, 'And I want Teddy Cooper.'

Teddy Cooper was CBA's bureau researcher in London, twenty-five years old and a cheerful cockney. He was also, in Partridge's opinion, a near genius at turning ordinary research into shrewd detective work.

'You've got him,' Sloane replied. 'He'll be on the next Concorde out of England.'

After they hung up, Partridge resumed his own preparations. Even before Sloane's call he had begun packing the suitcase that only an hour earlier he had unpacked.

He telephoned Air Canada, making a reservation on a flight leaving Toronto at two forty-five pm. It was due into New York's La Guardia at four o'clock. Next he called for a taxi to collect him in twenty minutes.

172

After his packing was finished, Partridge scribbled a goodbye note to Vivien. He knew she would be disappointed at his abrupt departure, as he was himself. Along with the note he left a generous cheque to pay for some improvements to the apartment.

As he looked round for a place to leave the note, the intercom sounded from the lobby below. The taxi he'd ordered had arrived.

The last things he saw as he left were the tickets for the next day's Mozart concert, lying on the sideboard. He reflected sadly that those—as well as other unused tickets and invitations in the past—represented, more than anything else, the uncertain pattern of a TV newsman's life.

THE AIR CANADA FLIGHT out of Toronto had a light passenger load, and Partridge had a three-seat section to himself. While en route to New York, he sipped a vodka and tonic and allowed his thoughts to drift.

He considered, on a personal level, Jessica and himself.

Over the years since Vietnam, he had grown accustomed to regarding her as belonging only in the past, as someone he had once loved but who was no longer relevant to him and in any case far beyond his reach. To an extent, Partridge realised, his thinking had been an act of self-discipline, a safeguard against feeling sorry for himself, self-pity being something he abhorred. But now, because Jessica was in danger, he admitted to himself that he cared as much about her as he ever had. *Face it, you're still in love with her.* And not with some shadowy memory but with a real, living, vital person. Whatever his role was to be in searching for Jessica, Harry Partridge knew that his love for her would drive and sustain him, even though he would hold that love secretly within himself.

He dragged himself back to the present shortly before the flight landed in New York. He was first off the plane and strode quickly through the terminal. With only hand baggage, he was able to take a taxi to CBA News headquarters without delay.

As he headed for Chuck Insen's office, a senior producer at the Horseshoe called, 'Hi, Harry! Chuck's at a press conference that's been arranged for Crawf. The whole thing's being taped.'

Then, as Partridge walked towards the Horseshoe, the producer added, 'Oh, in case no one's told you, you'll be anchoring the news tonight.'

THE PRESS CONFERENCE was well attended by print, television and radio reporters, along with camera and sound crews. It was held in another CBA building, a block away from headquarters. On a sound stage, folding chairs had been hastily set up; all were occupied, with many participants standing.

Crawford Sloane began with a brief statement. He expressed his shock

173

and anxiety, then appealed to the news media and the public for any information which might help disclose where his wife, son and father had been taken, and by whom.

Twice during his statement he had to pause to control emotion in his voice. Each time there was a sympathetic silence. Then he announced he would answer questions.

At first the questioning was also sympathetic. Inevitably, though, the press corps weighed in with tougher queries. An Associated Press woman reporter asked, 'Do you think it's possible that your family has been seized by terrorists?'

Sloane shook his head. 'It's too early even to think about that.'

The AP woman objected. 'You're ducking the question. Is it *possible?*'

Sloane conceded, 'I suppose it's possible.'

A grey-haired CNN correspondent held up a copy of Sloane's book. 'Do you continue to believe, as you wrote here, that "hostages should be regarded as expendable", and are you still opposed to paying ransom—as you put it, "directly or indirectly, ever"?'

Sloane had anticipated the question. 'I don't believe anyone as emotionally involved as I am can be objective about that.'

The CNN man persisted. 'I'll put it another way: Do you regret having written those words?'

'At this moment,' Sloane said, 'I find myself wishing they weren't being quoted against me.' Despite his discomfort, he acknowledged mentally that at plenty of press conferences in the past he had played hardball as an interrogator himself.

An offbeat query came from a *Newsday* reporter: 'I've heard that your son Nicholas is a talented musician and might become a concert pianist one day. Is that true?'

Sloane knew that in other circumstances Jessica would object to the question as an intrusion. At this moment, though, he didn't see how he could avoid answering it. 'Our son does love music, always has. As to his being a concert pianist, or anything else, only time will tell.'

At length, when the questions seemed to be winding down, the session ended. Sloane was immediately surrounded by well-wishers.

THAT EVENING IN THE HIDEAWAY in Hackensack, Miguel watched a portable television, switching between news programmes. The Sloane family kidnapping was the top item, though there were no reports of new leads. Watching CBA's National Evening News, Miguel was amused to see that Crawford Sloane was not in his usual anchor position; the substitute was someone named Partridge. Sloane, however, was interviewed on air and shown at a press conference.

Something of interest coming out of it was the description of the Sloane brat as a possible concert pianist. Without any clear notion of how he might use it, Miguel tucked the nugget of information away.

Early the next morning, Miguel informed Luís that at eleven o'clock the two of them would be driving into Manhattan in the hearse. The hearse was the group's sixth vehicle, a secondhand Cadillac in good condition; it had stayed out of sight at the Hackensack house.

With Luís driving, they took a circuitous route from Hackensack, changing direction several times to be sure they were not followed. They entered the Lincoln Tunnel and emerged in Manhattan at eleven forty-five am.

Both Miguel and Luís were wearing dark suits, appropriate to their presence in a hearse. Miguel told Luís, 'We go now to the funeral place—the same one as before. You remember?'

Luís nodded and turned towards the Queensboro Bridge, which led to the New York City borough of Queens.

CHAPTER 6

At times when news was quiet, a network news organisation is like a slumbering giant. It operates at considerably less than a hundred per cent utilisation, and a substantial number of its talented people have what is referred to in the trade as downtime—meaning they are not actively at work. Which was why, when this major news event occurred, there were experienced hands who could be grabbed and fired up.

On Friday morning, one day after the Sloane family kidnapping, the firing-up process had begun, as the special task force headed by Harry Partridge, with Rita Abrams as senior producer, assembled in CBA News headquarters.

Wasting no time, Harry asked, 'Any new developments?'

'Zilch on the kidnap,' Rita answered. 'But there's a mob scene outside Crawf's house.'

The two were in the task force conference room. 'These days everyone wants to touch the hem of an anchorman,' Rita continued. 'Now that they've learned his address, Crawf's fans are pouring into Larchmont by the thousand. The police are having trouble coping.'

'We have a camera crew on site?'

'Sure have. They camped out all night. I've told them to stay in place until Crawf leaves for work.'

Partridge nodded his approval. 'You know we've been given pretty much a blank cheque where talent is concerned?'

175

'So I was told. I've asked for three producers to begin with—Norman Jaeger, Iris Everly and Karl Owens.'

'Great choices.' Partridge knew them well. They were among the best in CBA News. 'What I'd like,' he said, 'is to have a meeting as soon as possible with everyone who'll be working with us. We can begin work on a spot for tonight's news.'

'I'll set it up for ten o'clock,' Rita said.

'IN ALL THE YEARS I've lived here,' the Larchmont police sergeant said, 'I've never seen anything like it.'

He was speaking with FBI Special Agent Havelock, who had emerged from the Sloane house a few minutes earlier to survey the throng of spectators outside.

The crowd had been growing in size since dawn and now packed the sidewalks in front of the house. In some places they had spilled onto the road, where police officers were trying, not too successfully, to control the people and keep passing cars moving. Otis Havelock was concerned that Sloane, who was inside getting ready for work, might be mobbed on his way out.

Clustered by the front gate were television crews and other reporters. As Havelock appeared, TV cameras swung towards him amid a roar of shouted questions.

'Have you heard from the kidnappers?'

'How's Sloane holding up?'

'Can we talk to Crawford?'

'Who are you?'

In response Havelock waved his hands dismissively.

Beyond the press group, the crowd appeared orderly, though the appearance of Havelock had increased the buzz of conversation.

The FBI man said to the police sergeant, 'Any idea where these people are from?'

'I asked a few,' the sergeant said. 'They mostly drove in from outside Larchmont. I guess it's seeing all that excitement on TV and wanting a glimpse of Mr Sloane. The streets around are full of cars.'

Havelock returned to the house. Inside, he told Crawford Sloane, who looked tired and gaunt, 'When we leave, it will be in two unmarked FBI

cars. I want you in the second. We'll drive away fast.'

In the end, Crawford Sloane entered the FBI car so quickly that it was observed by only a few people in the crowd outside.

THE RESEARCHER FROM CBA'S London bureau, Teddy Cooper, had been flown in as promised, that morning. He came directly to the task force offices, and reported to Harry and Rita. The three went to the conference room where the group meeting was assembling. On the way in, they met Crawford Sloane who had arrived a few minutes earlier.

Cooper, a wiry slip of a man, radiated energy and confidence. His brown lank hair, worn long, made him seem even younger than his twenty-five years. Though a born-and-bred Londoner, he had been in the United States several times before and was familiar with New York.

Partridge said to him, 'You'll be in charge of research here, with two assistants.'

The assistant researchers, a young man and woman borrowed from another CBA project, were already in the conference room. While waiting for the meeting to begin, Partridge introduced them to Cooper and the trio began discussing a Sequence of Events board already occupying an entire wall of the room. A standard procedure in task force reporting, it would record every known detail about the kidnapping, in proper sequence. On another wall was a second large board, headed Miscell-aneous. This would contain incidental intelligence, some of it speculation or rumour.

The boards' purpose was twofold: first, to apprise everyone of available information; second, to focus progress reviews and brainstorming sessions which often provoked new ideas.

At ten o'clock, Rita Abrams opened the meeting. She was seated at the head of a long table, Harry Partridge beside her. Leslie Chippingham arrived and took his place at the table, too. As he caught Rita's eye they exchanged discreet smiles.

Crawford Sloane seated himself at the far end. He did not expect to contribute to the discussion at this point and had confided to Partridge, 'I feel helpless right now, like a loose nut.'

Also at the table were the three producers Rita had recruited. Norman Jaeger, the oldest, was a CBA veteran. Soft-spoken, imaginative and scholarly, he was a producer for the network's highly acclaimed magazine programme, 'Behind the Headlines'. Next to Jaeger was Iris Everly, petite, in her mid-twenties, and a brightly shining star on the news production scene. Karl Owens, the third producer, was a workhorse who had gained his reputation through tireless investigative work. Others present were cameraman Minh Van Canh, a staff writer and a secretary.

178

'We all know why we're here,' Rita said, opening the meeting in a businesslike tone. 'First, I'll talk about organisation. After that, Harry will direct how we should march editorially.'

Rita paused from her businesslike tone and looked down the table at Crawford Sloane. 'Crawf, I want to tell you, very simply and from all of us—for your sake, your family's, and our own because we care—we're going to do our *damnedest!'*

From the others there was a sympathetic murmur.

Sloane managed to utter, 'Thank you,' his voice choked.

'From here in,' Rita went on, 'we shall operate on two levels—the long-term project and the daily breaking story. Norm,' she continued, addressing the oldest producer, 'you're to be in charge of long term.'

'Right.'

'Iris, you'll do the day by day, starting with a spot for the news tonight.'

Iris Everly said crisply, 'Got it.'

To the third producer, Owens, Rita said, 'Karl, you'll move between the two project sides as needed.' Her attention turned to Cooper. 'Teddy, you'll go to Larchmont.'

Cooper looked up with a grin. 'Yes, ma'am. I'll dig around and make like the famed Sherlock H.'

'After this meeting,' Rita advised him, 'Minh will go to Larchmont, heading two fresh camera crews. You'll go with him, Teddy, and meet Bert Fisher who's a stringer for our local affiliate station. He was first to break the story yesterday.'

Minh Van Canh, his square face impassive as usual, nodded.

'For now, that takes care of the nuts and bolts,' Rita said. 'More important, there's editorial direction. Harry, over to you.'

'Our first objective,' Partridge began, 'is to find out more about the kidnappers. Who are they? Where are they from? What are they aiming for? Of course, very soon they may tell us that themselves; however, we won't wait for that to happen. Somewhere, the kidnappers have left traces. Everybody leaves traces. The trick is to locate some.' He said to Jaeger, 'Concentrating on that will be your job, Norman.'

Jaeger nodded.

'Iris, about our spot for tonight's news. Do you have a framework?'

'If there's no fresh dramatic news like communication from the kidnappers, we may go to the mob scene this morning outside Crawf's house. Then, as this is the first full day since the event, I'd like a recap of yesterday.'

'What about reactions?' Jaeger asked. 'Like, in Washington.'

Partridge answered, 'A short bite only, from the President, I think. Maybe some citizen interviews if we have time.'

'But nothing from Capitol Hill?'

'Maybe tomorrow,' Partridge said. 'Maybe never. Everyone on the Hill will want to get in on the act.'

After another fifteen minutes of discussion Rita tapped the table. 'That'll do,' she announced. 'The talking is over. The real work begins.'

BACK IN HIS OFFICE, Harry Partridge began the procedure known to all journalists as working the phones.

Open in front of him was his private Blue Book—a catalogue of people he knew worldwide who had been useful to him and vice versa. The news business was full of debits and credits; at times like this, credits were called in. Luckily, most people were flattered to be sought after by TV news.

Partridge's list of those he would call today included contacts in the Justice Department, White House, State Department, CIA, Immigration, Congress, several foreign embassies, New York's Police Department, Mexico's Judicial Police, and a lawyer with organised-crime clients.

The ensuing phone conversations were mostly low-key and began, 'Hi, this is Harry Partridge. We haven't been in touch for a while.' The personal mode continued with enquiries about wives, husbands, children—Partridge kept notes of those names too—then eased into the current scene. 'I'm working on the Sloane kidnapping. I wonder if you've heard any rumbles, or have ideas of your own . . . Will you ask around and call me back?'

It was standard practice, at times tedious and always requiring patience. Sometimes it produced results, occasionally delayed ones, often none. From today's telephoning nothing specific emerged, though the most interesting conversation was with the organised-crime lawyer.

A year ago the man's daughter, on a college trip to Venezuela, had been present at a drug orgy in which two students had died. Partridge, covering the story, had decided not to use the girl's name or picture in his report.

Today, after listening to Partridge's casual opener, the lawyer responded bluntly, 'I owe you. But I haven't heard anything. Sometimes, my clients get to hear about things. I'll do some discreet asking around and if I find out anything I'll call you.'

At the end of an hour, when he had covered half the names on the list, Partridge took a break and went to the conference room to pour himself coffee. Returning, he did what almost everyone in TV news did daily: went through *The New York Times* and Washington *Post*. It always surprised visitors to TV news centres to see how many copies of those newspapers there were around. The fact was, despite TV's own news achievements, a subtle ingrained attitude persisted that nothing was really news until printed in the *Times* or *Post*.

Then the strong voice of Chuck Insen broke into Partridge's reading.

'I bring tonight's line-up, Harry,' the executive producer said, entering the office. 'We've planned a split-anchor news. You're to be half the horse.'

'Rear end or front?'

Insen smiled faintly. 'Which of us ever knows? Anyway, from tonight on,. you'll anchor anything to do with the kidnap, which—unless the President gets shot before air time—will be our lead again. Crawf will anchor the rest of the news, as usual; we're damned if a bunch of thugs, whoever they are, are going to dictate how life goes on at CBA.'

'Fine with me,' Partridge said. 'I presume it is with Crawf.'

'Frankly, it was Crawf's idea. Like any king, he feels insecure if off his throne too long, and staying invisible would achieve nothing. Oh, another thing—right at the end of the news Crawf will say a few spontaneous words thanking those who've sent messages about his family.'

'Spontaneous words?'

'Of course. We have three writers toiling over them now.'

ALMOST A MONTH AGO, Miguel had bought funeral caskets for transporting his two intended kidnap victims to Peru from Godoy's, a small, shabby funeral home in Astoria.

Alberto Godoy was obese, bald, with nicotine-stained fingers and bloated features. Miguel's meeting with him had begun in his tiny, cluttered office.

'I have elderly parents who wish certain planning for their eventual . . . er, passing.' Miguel continued with his concocted story as Godoy listened with a mixture of boredom and disbelief. At the end, his only question was, 'How will you pay?'

'Cash.'

Godoy became a shade more friendly. 'This way.'

In the basement Miguel had found two caskets that were suitable, one of average size, the other smaller. He paid $5,500 total for them, then took them to the safe house for later transfer to Hackensack.

Now, almost a month later, he returned to Alberto Godoy's establishment in search of one more casket.

Miguel instructed Luís to park their hearse a block from the Godoy Funeral Home. He then walked to the home, where a woman receptionist directed Miguel to the proprietor's office.

The fat man regarded Miguel warily. 'You again. What do you want?'

'I've been asked to do a favour for an elderly friend. He's seen the caskets I bought for my parents, and asked if I would pick up another, for him. To be paid for as before.'

181

Godoy peered at Miguel with shifty eyes. 'Mister, I run a business here. What I want to know is, am I setting myself up for trouble?'

'There'll be no trouble. Not if you cooperate.' Miguel let his own voice take on menace, and it had an effect.

'All right, you got it,' Godoy said. 'But since last time the price has gone up. For that same adult model, four thousand.'

Without speaking, Miguel opened his wallet and began counting out the money. Then he told Godoy, 'I have transport outside. Get the casket to your loading dock.'

At the dock, Godoy was surprised to see a hearse appear. The two previous caskets, he remembered, had been taken away in a truck. Still suspicious of his visitor, Godoy wrote down the hearse's licence number as the car drove away, though not really knowing why. Back in his office, he pushed the piece of paper into a drawer.

Godoy smiled as he put the four thousand dollars in an office safe, then he decided to do what he often did—go to a nearby bar for a drink.

A short time later, mellowed by three whiskies, he related to a group of cronies how some punk had bought two caskets and put them—so he said—in his parents' home, ready for the old folks to croak, and then come back for another casket, all of it like he was buying chairs or saucepans. As the others roared with laughter, Godoy further confided that he'd charged the dumb punk three times the regular price.

At the bar was a former Colombian who wrote a column for an obscure Spanish-language weekly published in Queens. On the back of an envelope, the man wrote the gist of Godoy's story. It would make a good item, he thought, for next week's column.

AT CBA NEWS it had been a frantic day, especially for the Sloane kidnap task force. The story had been allotted five and a half minutes of the national evening news, an extraordinary duration in a business where fifteen-second segments were fiercely fought over. As a result, almost the entire effort of the task force was devoted to that day's production.

With Harry Partridge anchoring the opening portion of the news, the evening broadcast began:

'After thirty-six hours of agonised waiting there is still no fresh news about the family of CBA anchorman Crawford Sloane, whose wife, young son and father were kidnapped yesterday morning in Larchmont, New York. The whereabouts of Mrs Jessica Sloane, eleven-year-old Nicholas, and Mr Angus Sloane remain unknown . . .'

As each name was mentioned, a still photo appeared on the screen, over Partridge's shoulder.

'Also unknown are the identities or objectives of the kidnappers. While the FBI, now in charge of the investigation, is withholding comment, privately FBI officials admit no progress has been made. Since yesterday an outpouring of concern and anger has come from the highest levels . . . '

The broadcast continued with a statement from the President that 'such evil' had no place in America. It was followed by equally strong comments from a black steelworker in Pittsburgh and a white housewife in Topeka.

Then the scene shifted to Larchmont, where viewers were shown the melee outside the Sloane house that morning. In an interview the elderly former schoolteacher, Priscilla Rhea, described yet again the struggle in the car park. Minh Van Canh used his camera creatively, going in for an extreme close-up of Miss Rhea's face. It showed every wrinkle in sharp relief, but also brought out her intelligence and sturdy character. She said of the kidnappers, 'They were brutal men, beasts, savages.'

Next, the Larchmont police chief confirmed that there had been no breakthrough in the case and the kidnappers had not been heard from. A final statement in the special news segment was made by CBA's corporate president, Margot Lloyd-Mason.

CBA HAD BEEN THE LAST of the major broadcast networks to fall victim to what was known in the business as 'the invasion of the Philistines'. That was, the takeover of the networks by industrial conglomerates whose insistence on constantly enlarging profits outweighed their sense of privilege and public duty.

Nine months ago the network had been swallowed by a corporate giant with worldwide holdings, Globanic Industries Inc. Like General Electric, which had earlier acquired NBC, Globanic was a major defence contractor. The transformation of CBA began with the arrival of Margot Lloyd-Mason as the network's corporate president and chief executive officer. Known to be efficient, ruthless and ambitious, she was already a vice-president of Globanic. It was rumoured that her move to CBA was a trial run for the eventual chairmanship of the parent company.

Leslie Chippingham had first encountered his new chief when, a few days after her arrival, he received a peremptory message through a secretary to go at once to 'Stonehenge', the network's name for CBA's Third Avenue headquarters. He went in a chauffeur-driven limousine.

Margot Lloyd-Mason was tall, with upswept blonde hair, a high-cheekboned face and shrewdly appraising eyes. She wore an elegant taupe Chanel suit with a paler-toned silk blouse. Chippingham found her attractive but formidable, her manner and cool.

'You may use my first name,' she told the news president, making it sound like an order. Then, without wasting time, she got down to business. 'You came here in a chauffeured limo.'

Chippingham was startled. 'Yes, I did.' The car and driver were one of the perks of his job, but the experience of being spied on—which had obviously happened—was new and unsettling.

'In future, use a taxi. I do. So can you. And something else. The news division's budget is to be cut by twenty per cent immediately. You'll receive a memo from me tomorrow, and I shall expect a report within a week on how economies have been made.'

Chippingham was too dazed for more than a polite leave-taking. He knew that from now on his job as news president was going to be monumentally more difficult.

The matter of budget cutting was an area where all networks were vulnerable and everyone knew it, including Leslie Chippingham. The news divisions in particular had become fat, overstaffed and ripe for pruning.

When it happened at CBA News—the result of the demanded economies—more than two hundred people lost their jobs. The firings produced cries of outrage from those left jobless, and the print press had a bonanza. That had all taken place many months before the kidnap.

IT HAD BEEN LESLIE Chippingham's idea to include Margot Lloyd-Mason in the evening's special broadcast. Yesterday, soon after breaking into the network with the bulletin, Chippingham had reported to Margot by telephone, and did so again in the morning. Her reaction had, on the whole, been sympathetic, and she had telephoned Crawford Sloane expressing hope that his family would be recovered quickly.

While speaking with the news president, though, she added two caveats.

'Part of the reason something like this happens is that networks have misguidedly let anchor people become larger than life, so the public thinks of them as something extra special, almost gods.' She did not elaborate on how a network could control public concepts, even if it wished to, and for his part Chippingham saw no point in arguing the obvious.

The other proviso concerned the kidnap task force.

'I don't want you going wild about spending money,' Margot Lloyd-Mason asserted. 'You should be able to do whatever is necessary within the existing news budget.'

Chippingham said, 'Margot, I'll remind you that our ratings for the National Evening News shot up last night and I expect that to continue while this crisis lasts.'

'Which merely goes to show,' she answered coolly, 'that unfortunate events can be turned to profit.'

184

While involving the corporate president in the evening's broadcast seemed appropriate, Chippingham also hoped it might soften her attitude towards some special expenditures that, in his view, would be needed.

On air, Margot spoke with authority, using words scripted for her but with revisions of her own: 'I am speaking for all the people of this network and our parent company, Globanic Industries, when I declare that our total resources are available in the search for the missing members of the Sloane family. We deplore what has happened, and we hope to see our friend and colleague, Crawford Sloane, united with his wife, son and father in the shortest possible time.'

CHAPTER 7

The lack of progress after a frantic first day for the task force did not surprise Harry Partridge. He knew it took members of any new team at least a day to orientate themselves. Just the same, it was imperative they formulate more plans.

'Let's have a working dinner,' he said to Rita during the afternoon.

She arranged for the six principals in the task force— Partridge, Rita, Jaeger, Iris, Owens, Cooper—to meet for Chinese food immediately after the National Evening News. Rita chose Shun Lee West, on West Sixty-fifth, near Lincoln Center, a favourite with TV news folk.

Their table was in a quiet corner at the rear of the restaurant. Near the end of the soup course Partridge addressed Cooper. The young Englishman had spent most of the day in Larchmont, talking to everyone who had any knowledge of the kidnapping. 'Teddy, let's hear your impressions so far.'

Cooper opened a well-worn exercise book. 'OK, impressions first. Number one: it was a pro job all the way. The punks who planned it knew their business and didn't leave evidence behind. Number two: they had loadsa money.'

Norman Jaeger asked, 'How do you know?'

'Hopin' you'd ask.' Cooper grinned as he looked round the table. 'You've heard about the neighbours who now say they saw cars, and once or twice trucks, outside the Sloane house? Well, five people have reported that since yesterday; today I talked to four of them. They all said they saw those cars on and off for three weeks, maybe a month. And they described a regular fleet—all this year's models, eight different colours. So I asked myself, Did the gang have eight different cars?'

'They could have,' Iris Everly said, 'if they were hired.'

Cooper shook his head. 'Not the professional bunch we're tackling. I think they probably had three cars and repainted them, say once a week, hoping to lessen the chances of being noticed. Only thing was, in the repainting they made a stupid mistake.'

While they were talking fresh dishes had appeared—sautéed shrimp with peppers, fried prawns, snow peas, fried rice. There was a pause to enjoy the hot food, then Cooper continued, addressing Partridge.

'This afternoon, your stringer, Bert Fisher, phoned some car dealers for me. He learned that some of the colours people saw aren't available for those models. For instance, a Larchmont neighbour said he saw a yellow Ford Tempo, but there's no such colour made. Same with a blue Plymouth Reliant. The mob we're looking for did the repaint jobs themselves.'

Partridge said doubtfully, 'That's a pretty big supposition.'

'But is it?' Rita asked. 'These people practically ran a fleet of vehicles— at least five we know of. Wherever they kept them would have to be sizable. So isn't it likely it would be big enough to include a paint shop?'

'An operating headquarters, you mean,' Jaeger said. He turned to Teddy. 'Isn't that what you're talking about?'

'Yep.' Cooper beamed. 'Sure am.'

The group ate thoughtfully, concentrating on what had just been said.

'An operating centre,' Rita mused. 'Where?'

'Number one, it would have to be well clear of Larchmont,' Cooper said. 'Staying anywhere in the area would be dangerous. But, number two, it shouldn't be too far. The snatchers would know that in minutes, maybe, there'd be an alarm and police all over would be looking for them. Therefore they'd have calculated how much time they had. Guessing, I'd say, half an hour.'

Owens said slowly, 'Translating that to miles, if I'm reading you right, and remembering the area—I'd say twenty-five.'

'Just what I figured.' Cooper produced a New York area map and opened it. Taking Larchmont as the centre, he drew a circle with his finger. 'I reckon the headquarters is somewhere inside here.'

The kidnappers and their victims, he believed, were at that operating centre now, the gang members lying low until the initial searching eased up. Then the gang and prisoners would move to some more distant location, perhaps in the United States, possibly elsewhere.

But Owens pointed out, 'That's an enormous area you're talking about, densely populated, and there's no way of searching it effectively, even with an army.' He added, needling Cooper, 'That is, unless you have another brilliant idea.'

'Not right now,' Cooper answered. 'I need a good night's shuteye first.'

They ended the discussion there, and though the next day was Saturday, Partridge summoned a task force meeting for ten am.

186

SLEEP DID NOT COME easily to Partridge that night. Too much had happened in the preceding thirty-six hours. His mind was full, a kaleido-scope of events, ideas, responsibilities, all of them intertwined with thoughts of Jessica, the past, the present . . . memories revived.

Where was she now? Was Teddy right about a twenty-five-mile radius? Was there a chance that somehow he, Harry, like a knight in shining armour, could successfully lead a crusade to find and free his former love?

Cut the whimsy! Save thoughts about Jessica and the others for tomorrow.

In a New York hotel room, slowly, sadly, the image of Jessica faded. At last, exhausted, Harry Partridge slept.

IN THE HACKENSACK BASE Miguel received a message by telephone at seven thirty am on Saturday. Alert and waiting, he picked up the handset on the first ring and answered, *'Sí?'*

The caller then challenged him with a prearranged code word, *'Tiempo?'* to which Miguel responded, *'Relámpago.'*

Miguel's answer to the query 'Weather?' had been 'Lightning'. It conveyed: 'We are ready to go. State place and time.'

The crucial message followed: *'Sombrero,* twenty hundred.'

Sombrero was Teterboro Airport, less than a mile away. The words twenty hundred indicated the time—eight pm—when the kidnappers and their victims would board a Colombia-registered Learjet 55LR. The LR signified Long Range. It would fly them first to Opa-locka Airport, Florida, and then directly to Peru.

The caller was a diplomat attached to the Colombian consulate general in New York. A Sendero Luminoso sympathiser, he had been a conduit for messages since Miguel's arrival in the United States a month ago.

After receiving the call, Miguel informed the others. Those to travel on the Learjet, with the kidnap victims, were Miguel, Baudelio, Socorro and Rafael. Julio would remain in the United States, becoming, once more, a Medellín cartel sleeping agent. Carlos and Luís would leave separately for Colombia within the next few days.

Julio, Carlos and Luís, though, had a last duty after the Learjet had gone: to abandon the remaining vehicles.

Miguel told Rafael first. The burly handyman-mechanic, who was in the outbuilding they used as a paint shop, grunted and nodded, seeming more interested in the GMC 'Superbread' truck, which had been trans-formed to a black one with the name 'Serene Funeral Homes' in discreet gold lettering on both sides.

Miguel pointed to the truck's New Jersey licence plates. 'These are new?'

Rafael nodded. 'From the last set. Ain't been used yet, an' I switched the others.' Now all five remaining vehicles had licence plates not seen during the surveillance.

Miguel went outside. Within a cluster of trees, Julio and Luís were digging a deep hole in which to bury the cellular phones and some medical equipment which Baudelio would leave behind. He told them of the plans, then found Carlos, in another outbuilding, burning surveillance records of the Sloane house in an iron stove. When Miguel told him about the evening departure, he seemed relieved.

A small pile of Carlos's clothing was beside the stove. Miguel, Carlos and Baudelio would all wear dark suits during the departure, when they would pose as mourners, using a carefully designed cover story. Everything else would be left behind.

Miguel pointed to the clothes. 'Don't burn those—too much smoke. Take everything out of the pockets and remove any labels. Then bury the rest.' He gestured towards Julio and Luís.

After leaving Carlos, Miguel sought out Baudelio. He found him with Socorro in the large room where the captives were held, which by this time resembled a hospital ward. Baudelio, the right side of his face covered with dressings, looked like a patient himself, but he was continuing with preparations for departure and after Miguel informed him of the seven forty pm departure time, he acknowledged, 'We will be ready.'

The former doctor confirmed that the three captives would be deeply unconscious during the time they would spend in the sealed caskets. Also, the enforced starvation period for all three—which would be fifty-six hours in all—was satisfactory.

Miguel paused, looking down at the three bodies. They appeared peaceful, their faces untroubled. The woman had a certain beauty, he thought. The man looked dignified, like an old soldier at rest. The boy seemed frail, his face thin, which didn't matter as long as he was alive on arrival in Peru. All three were pale, with only a little colour in their cheeks, but were breathing evenly. Satisfied, Miguel turned away.

The funeral caskets were horizontal, on trestles, a series of tiny vent holes drilled into each. Baudelio explained that soda lime granules would also be spread inside, to absorb carbon dioxide from exhaled breath. 'There'll be an oxygen cylinder, controllable from outside,' he went on. 'And as a precaution I'll catheterise all three of them.'

Socorro had been watching, her face inscrutable as always, as Miguel examined the caskets. As part of the planned tableau, she would be a grieving mourner.

He asked her, 'When we need it, can you cry?'

Baudelio interjected, 'I will place a grain of pepper beneath her lower eyelids. Same for mine. Our tears will be copious.'

188

Despite earlier misgivings, Miguel felt satisfied that Baudelio knew what he was doing. Socorro too. Now it was simply a question of waiting through the day.

AT CBA NEWS HEADQUARTERS on Saturday morning the special task force meeting had assembled at ten am. Seated at the head of the conference table, Partridge had opened the discussion when a speakerphone broke in—an announcement from the main newsroom:

'Assignment desk. Richardson. This bulletin just in from UPI :

'White Plains, New York—A passenger van, believed to be the vehicle used in Thursday's kidnap of the Crawford Sloane family, exploded violently a few minutes ago. At least three persons are dead, many others injured. Police were on their way to inspect the van when the explosion occurred in a parking building adjoining Center City shopping mall. It happened as many weekend shoppers were arriving in their cars.'

Even as the bulletin was continuing, chairs were being pushed back, people scrambling to their feet. Partridge was first out of the conference room, hurrying to the newsroom, with Rita Abrams close behind.

Saturday morning in the main CBA newsroom was eerily quiet, with barely a third of the desks occupied. Today's assignment manager, Orv Richardson, was covering for the national desk as well when he saw Harry Partridge and Rita Abrams burst into the newsroom and hurry his way.

While Partridge skimmed the UPI bulletin and read a follow-up story feeding in on a computer monitor, Rita told Richardson, 'We should go on air immediately. Who has authority?'

'I have a number.' He quickly tapped out digits for a CBA News vice president at home. When the man answered, Richardson explained the situation and asked for authorisation to take the air with a special bulletin. The vice-president shot back, 'You have it. Go!'

What followed was a near replay of Thursday's intrusion into the network, though with a different cast. Partridge was in the flash-facility studio, occupying the correspondent's hot seat, Rita was acting executive producer, and in the control room a different director appeared.

CBA was on air within four minutes of receiving the UPI bulletin. There was no time to write a script. Partridge simply memorised the contents of the wire reports and ad-libbed.

The special broadcast was over in two minutes. There were the bare facts only, few details, and no on-scene pictures. A fuller report, Partridge promised viewers, would be aired later on CBA's Saturday National Evening News.

As soon as the red camera lights went out in the flash studio, Partridge phoned Rita in the control room. 'I'm going to White Plains,' he told her. 'Will you set it up?'

'I have already. A camera crew is on the way. Iris, Teddy Cooper and I are going as well. Iris will produce a piece for tonight. There's a car and driver waiting.'

DURING THE PRECEDING NIGHT an alert security guard in the Center City Mall parking building had noted the presence of a Nissan passenger van with New York plates. He wondered if it could be the one being sought in connection with the Sloane family kidnapping. He wrote a query to that effect in his report, and the maintenance supervisor, reading it next morning, promptly called the White Plains Police Department, who ordered a patrol car to investigate. The time, according to police records, was nine fifty am.

The maintenance supervisor, however, did not wait for the police arrival. Instead he went to the Nissan van, taking along a large bunch of car keys he had accumulated over the years. Quite quickly he found a key that fitted the van and opened the driver's door. It was his final act in the few remaining seconds of his life.

With a roar someone later described as 'like fifty thunderstorms', the Nissan van disintegrated in an intense, engulfing ball of flame. So did a substantial part of the building and several cars nearby. The Center City Mall itself sustained structural damage, and in the mall and beyond, windows and glass doors were shattered. Other debris descended on adjoining streets, traffic and people.

The shock effect was total. When the initial roar subsided, the screams began, followed by incoherent shouts and curses, hysterical pleas for help and, soon after, sirens approaching from all directions.

In the end it seemed extraordinary that the human toll was no greater than it was.

One thing became self-evident. The Nissan van had indeed been used by the kidnappers two days earlier. The proximity to Larchmont and the fact that the van was booby-trapped both pointed to that conclusion. So did the owner's name, address and insurance data which, when checked against motor vehicle records, were quickly discovered to be phoney.

One other conclusion was expressed by the White Plains police chief at the explosion scene. He told reporters grimly, 'This was clearly the work of hardened terrorists.'

When asked if, extending that reasoning, it was foreign terrorists who had abducted the Sloane family trio, the chief answered, 'That didn't happen on my turf, but I would think so.'

190

'LET'S MAKE THAT FOREIGN terrorist theory our main focus for this evening's news,' Harry Partridge told Rita and Iris Everly when he heard about the police chief's comment.

The CBA contingent had arrived a few minutes ago in two vehicles—the camera crew aboard a Jeep Wagoneer; Partridge, Rita, Iris and Teddy Cooper in a car driven by a network courier—both having covered the twenty-five miles from mid-Manhattan in a sizzling thirty minutes. News people gathered at the scene and a growing crowd of spectators was being herded behind police barriers. Minh Van Canh and sound man Ken O'Hara were already getting videotape of the wrecked building, the injured who continued to be removed, and of piles of twisted burning vehicles. They had also joined an impromptu press conference in time to tape the police chief's statement.

After assessing the situation, Partridge summoned Minh and O'Hara and began conducting on-camera interviews with some of those involved in rescue efforts as well as witnesses to the explosion. It was work that could have been performed by the camera crew alone or with a producer. But it gave Partridge a sense of involvement, of *touching* the story directly for the first time.

Touching an ongoing news story was psychologically essential to a correspondent. Partridge had been working on the Sloane family kidnap for some forty-two hours, but until now without direct contact with any of its elements. At moments he had felt caged, with only a desk, a telephone and a computer monitor connecting him to the reality outside. Going to White Plains fulfilled a need.

It also raised some questions: now that a terrorist connection was virtually confirmed, were any civilised resources capable of tracking and outwitting so evil an enemy? And even if the answer happened to be yes, wasn't it an empty conceit to believe that an unarmed news-reporting cadre like CBA News could succeed where police, governments, intelligence and military so often failed?

Partridge wondered, Should I advise for pragmatic reasons the abandonment of active engagement by CBA, advocate our return to a standard role of news observing or, failing that, at least pass on responsibility to someone else? At the same time, he realised that they had never had a story quite like this before, with so much depending not just on what they reported but on what they could do.

PARTRIDGE, RITA AND TEDDY Cooper rode back to Manhattan together—at a pace considerably less frantic than their drive out. Cooper, whose decision to go to White Plains had been made at the last moment, appeared preoccupied. Partridge and Rita, too, at first seemed disinclined to talk. While they had witnessed, many times, the effects of terrorism overseas, to observe its invasion of American suburbia was traumatic.

'So who the hell are they?' Partridge pounded a fist into his palm. 'That's what we must concentrate on. Who?'

Rita answered, 'It's natural to think first of the Middle East—Iran, Lebanon, Libya . . . the religious line-up: Hezbollah, Amal, Shiites, Islamic Jihad, PLO, you name it.'

Partridge nodded. 'They may want to make an impression here.' He looked at Cooper. 'Any other thoughts?'

'Maybe you should be looking south, Harry.'

'Latin America,' Rita said. 'It makes sense. Nicaragua's the most likely, Honduras or Mexico possibilities, even Colombia.'

They continued to theorise but reached no conclusion. Partridge said to Teddy, 'What's at work in that convoluted mind of yours?'

Cooper considered, and began, 'I'm guessing that the kidnappers have left this country. And taken Mr S's family. What happened this morning was like a signature. To let us know the kind of people they are, how rough they play. It's a reminder for later on.'

Rita asked, 'If you're right, where does that leave us?'

'It leaves us having to decide if we want to make a big, expensive effort to find their hideaway, if it's going to be empty when we get there. Harry said yesterday: Everybody leaves traces.'

Their car was nearing Manhattan. 'Last night,' Partridge reminded Cooper, 'you told us you'd try for an idea to locate the gang's headquarters. Is that "big, expensive effort" part of it?'

'It would be. It would also be a long shot. Let's figure what kind of a place the mob would need, to park at least five vehicles, set up a paint shop, provide quarters for four people, probably more. Well, it would most likely be one of three things—a small disused factory, an empty warehouse, or a big house with outbuildings. But whichever it was, it would need to be somewhere isolated, lonely.'

'The trouble is,' Partridge objected, 'even in our twenty-five-mile radius from Larchmont there could be thousands of places like that.'

'I said it would be a long shot, but there might just be a way. Start by chewing this over: when those snatchers got here, they'd most likely pick a general area. After that, they'd do what anyone else would—study the classifieds in every newspaper, regional and local, inside that twenty-five-mile radius. OK, what we should do is look for ads for the kinds of buildings we just talked about—especially any ad that ran for a while, then suddenly stopped.'

Rita gasped. 'Have you any idea how many papers, dailies and weeklies, and how many people . . . ?'

192

Cooper shrugged. 'No, not exactly, except it's a hell of a lot. But what we'd do is hire people—bright young kids—to look through them all. And it has to be done fast, before the trail gets cold.'

Partridge announced his judgment. 'I salute you for an original idea, Teddy, but I think what you'd be trying to do is impossible. The amount of help you'd need would cost a fortune. Either way,' Partridge added, 'we can't make a decision here. Les Chippingham will do that.'

THE TWO-AND-A-HALF-MINUTE SPOT produced by Iris Everly for the Saturday National Evening News was dramatic, shocking and video-rich. At White Plains, Minh Van Canh had, as always, employed his camera creatively. Iris, back at CBA News headquarters and working with a videotape editor, had fashioned a small masterpiece of news theatre.

The spot began with the pile of burning cars, then cut to the injured being carried out. Partridge had recorded an audio track, over which pictures of the devastation were superimposed, which began, 'Today any remaining doubt that the kidnappers of the Crawford Sloane family are full-fledged terrorists was savagely dispelled. . . . '

The polished end result required hours of painstaking editing, a facet of TV news seldom understood by viewers. Partridge also recorded a final stand-up for the piece, facing a camera on the street outside the CBA News building. Since returning from White Plains, he had agonised about what he would say. Some of the words he had considered using would, Partridge knew, bring anguish to Crawf. So should he soften them, or be the hard-nosed newsman with a single standard—objectivity? In the end, the decision simply happened:

'The events in White Plains today—a monstrous tragedy for that city's innocent victims—is also the worst of news for my friend and colleague, Crawford Sloane. It means that his wife, young son and father are in the hands of savage, merciless, unknown outlaws.

'The nature and timing of the crime at White Plains also raise a question many are now asking: Have the kidnap victims been removed from the United States and conveyed to some distant place, wherever that may be? Harry Partridge, CBA News, New York.'

CHAPTER 8

The kidnappers and their victims were almost ready to steal out of the country. From the Hackensack hideaway, Julio would drive the hearse to Teterboro Airport, Luís the 'Serene Funeral Homes' truck. Both vehicles were loaded and ready. The hearse contained a single casket in which Jessica lay, under deep sedation. Angus and Nicky, also unconscious and in closed caskets, were in the truck.

Strangely, the sight of the caskets subdued the conspirators, as if the roles they had rehearsed in their minds and were about to act out had somehow become easier to assume.

As the moment to leave approached, Socorro had appeared in a black linen dress with matching jacket. Her hair was tucked under a black cloche and she wore gold earrings and a thin gold necklace. She was crying copiously, the result of Baudelio's prescription of a grain of pepper beneath each lower eyelid.

Rafael, Miguel and Baudelio, each wearing a dark suit and tie, looked suitably cast as mourners. If questions were asked, Rafael and Socorro would pose as brother and sister of a dead Colombian woman, killed in a fiery auto accident while visiting the US. Her remains were being flown home for burial with those of her young son who—so the story went—was also killed in the accident. The third 'body', Angus, would be described as an older relative who had been travelling with the other two.

Baudelio would be a member of the bereaved family, Miguel a close family friend. A critical feature of the story was that all three bodies were so badly burned as to be unrecognisable. Miguel counted on that to deter any opening of the caskets.

Elaborate documentation corroborated the cover story—fake death certificates, and new passports for Miguel, Rafael, Socorro and Baudelio, all obtained through one of Miguel's Little Colombia contacts.

In the courtyard of the Hackensack house, Miguel checked his watch. Seven forty pm. He climbed into the front seat of the hearse and told Julio tersely, 'Go!'

Dusk had settled in as they headed for Teterboro.

TETERBORO WAS A BUSY AIRPORT used exclusively by private planes. Along the northwest perimeter were the headquarters of several companies which provided operating services for all aircraft. Each company had a private entrance to the airport and handled its own security.

Of Teterboro's service companies, the largest was Brunswick Aviation, the one which the incoming Learjet 55LR from Colombia would use.

Approaching the brightly lit Brunswick building, the hearse was blocked by a gate. Beside it stood a uniformed security man. Next to him a tall, balding man in civilian clothes was peering at the oncoming hearse. A police detective? Miguel felt a tightening of his gut. The second man stepped forward with authority. Luís lowered his window and the man asked, 'Do you have an unusual shipment for Señor Pizarro?'

194

A wave of relief swept over Miguel. It was a coded question, pre-arranged. He used an answering code: 'The consignment is ready for transfer and all papers are in order.'

The newcomer nodded. 'I'm your pilot. Name's Underhill.' His accent was American. 'Let's get going.' As he went round to the passenger side, Underhill motioned to the guard and the gate swung open. Clearly, there was to be no security check.

It was a squeeze with four on the hearse's front seat, but they managed to close the door. The pilot directed Luís as they moved onto a taxi strip between blue lights. The GMC truck was behind.

Several aircraft loomed ahead. The pilot pointed to the largest, a Learjet 55LR. From its shadows a figure emerged.

Underhill said tersely, 'Faulkner. Copilot.'

On the Learjet's left side a clamshell door was open, the lower half filled by steps. The copilot had gone inside and lights were coming on. Luís manoeuvred the back of the hearse close to the Lear's steps for unloading. The truck had stopped and Julio, Rafael and Baudelio jumped down.

At the Learjet doorway, Underhill said to Miguel, 'I don't want to know anything about you or your business. We're providing a contract charter flight. Nothing else.'

Miguel nodded. He knew both pilots would earn golden pay for this journey tonight.

With the copilot supervising, the first casket, containing Jessica, was transferred from the hearse to the jet. Inside, the right-side seats had been removed and straps provided to hold the caskets in place.

By the time the first casket was loaded, the hearse had been moved away and the truck backed in. The other two caskets followed speedily, after which Miguel, Baudelio, Socorro and Rafael boarded and the clamshell door was closed. As Miguel seated himself and looked through a window, the lights of the two vehicles were already receding. The radio crackled as tower clearance was asked for and received.

Moments later the Learjet taxied and took off, climbing swiftly through the darkness and heading south for Florida.

IT WAS NOT UNTIL AFTER the first-feed Saturday National Evening News that the special task force meeting resumed at CBA News headquarters. By then it was seven ten pm.

Seated once more at the head of the conference room table, Harry Partridge surveyed the others—Rita, Norman Jaeger, Iris Everly, Karl Owens, Teddy Cooper. Most looked tired. The room itself was messy, with waste containers overflowing, dirty coffee cups abounding, and discarded newspapers littering the floor.

The Sequence of Events and Miscellaneous boards had been added to considerably. The most recent contribution was a summary of this morning's White Plains havoc. But there was still nothing conclusive about the kidnappers' identities or their victims' whereabouts.

'Reports, anyone?' Partridge asked.

Jaeger raised a hand, then spoke in his quiet, scholarly fashion. 'For most of today I've been telephoning Europe and the Middle East—our bureau chiefs, correspondents, stringers, fixers—asking about terrorist activity. Have any terrorists disappeared from sight recently? If they have, is it possible they could be in the United States? And so on.'

Jaeger paused, shuffling notes. 'There are some rumours and rumbles. No proof, though.' He threw up his hands. 'All these hoodlums are like slippery shadows.'

Leslie Chippingham entered the conference room, followed a moment later by Crawford Sloane. Partridge observed Sloane and thought the anchorman looked ghastly, even more pale and gaunt than yesterday, though it was not surprising with the growing strain. As the meeting fell silent, the news president urged, 'Carry on, please.'

Partridge thanked Norm Jaeger, then turned to Karl Owens. 'I know you've been enquiring southwards, Karl. Any results?'

'Nothing positive. I've talked with the same kind of contacts as Norm—mine in the major Latin American cities. Nothing fits a group movement of the kind we're looking for. I did stumble on one thing from Colombia, about a guy called Ulises Rodríguez.'

'A particularly nasty terrorist,' Rita said. 'I've heard him referred to as the Abu Nidal of Latin America.'

'He's all of that,' Owens agreed, 'and he's also believed to have been involved in several Colombian kidnappings. Three months ago Rodríguez simply disappeared. Those who should know are convinced he's active somewhere. But wherever he is, he's stayed successfully out of sight.'

'This gets interesting,' Rita said. 'Is there anything more?'

Owens nodded. 'Rodríguez studied English at Berkeley and speaks it with an American accent. I called our San Francisco bureau and asked to have someone sent over to Berkeley to do some checking. They sent Fiona Gowan who happens to be a Berkeley graduate. Fiona got lucky, and—if you'll believe it—located an English Department faculty member who actually remembers Rodríguez from the class of seventy-two.'

Rita sighed. 'We believe it.' The others round the table were listening intently. Her tone said: *Get on with the story!*

'Rodríguez was a loner, had no close friends. Also, it seems, he was camera-shy. Eventually it got to be a joke, so a classmate who was a pretty good artist did a charcoal sketch of Rodríguez without his knowing. He made a dozen copies which he doled out to his friends.'

'Those copies . . . ' Partridge began.

'We're on to it, Harry.' Owens smiled. 'Just before this meeting Fiona called me to say she's located one of the copy sketches and will have it to us by tomorrow.'

There was an approving murmur round the table. 'Nice staff work,' Chippingham said.

'We should keep a sense of proportion,' Owens pointed out. 'It's only a guess that Rodríguez is involved with our kidnap.'

'What we can do is show the picture around Larchmont and ask if anyone remembers seeing him,' Partridge said. 'Anything else?'

'Washington bureau checked in,' Rita said. 'The FBI has nothing new. Their forensic people are working on what was left of the Nissan van at White Plains, but they're not hopeful. They're depending on the kidnappers making contact.'

Partridge looked down the table at Sloane. 'I'm sorry, Crawf, but that seems to be all we have.'

Rita reminded him, 'Except for Teddy's idea.'

Partridge nodded to the young Englishman, and Cooper brightened as attention focused on him. 'It's a possible way to find out where the snatchers had their hide-out.'

Cooper repeated the proposal made to Partridge and Rita earlier that day, to examine classified ads appearing over the past three months in newspapers within twenty-five miles of Larchmont. Objective: to match the kind of property he visualised as the kidnappers' headquarters. He ended, 'It's a long shot, I admit.'

'I wouldn't even put it that high,' Chippingham said, frowning. 'How many people would we need for the detail work?'

Rita said, 'I estimate sixty people with some supervision.'

Chippingham turned to Partridge. 'Harry, are you seriously recommending this?'

Partridge hesitated. This morning during the drive back from White Plains, he had mentally labelled Teddy's notion a harebrained scheme. Now he felt that taking a stand was a good idea, even with a long shot.

'Yes, Les,' he said. 'In my opinion we ought to try it.'

Chippingham was unhappy with the answer. Margot Lloyd-Mason's edict echoed in his mind: *'I don't want you going wild spending money.'*

'Harry, I'm going to veto that one,' Chippingham said. 'I simply don't think it has enough potential to justify the effort.'

Jaeger began, 'I would have thought, Les . . . '

Before he could finish, Crawford Sloane said sharply, 'Les, aren't you really saying you won't spend the money?'

'That's a factor; you know it always is.'

Sloane said icily, 'Then I have a question and I'd like an answer. Has Margot Lloyd-Mason put on a spending freeze?'

Chippingham said uneasily, 'We've discussed budget, that's all. For anything worthwhile, I'll simply call Stonehenge . . . '

Sloane stormed, 'And what *I'll* call is a press conference—to tell the world that while my family is suffering in some hellhole, this wealthy network is haggling over pennies . . . '

The others round the table were equally indignant.

Norman Jaeger was the first to speak. He said quietly, 'Harry thinks we should give Teddy's idea a chance. So do I.'

Karl Owens joined him. 'Me too.'

'Add me to the list,' stated Iris Everly.

Rita, a touch reluctantly, caring about Chippingham, said, 'I guess you'd better count me in.'

'OK, OK, let's cut the histrionics,' Chippingham said. He knew that either way he was the loser, and silently cursed Margot. 'Maybe I was wrong. Crawf, we'll go ahead.' But he wouldn't, Chippingham decided, ask for Margot's approval; he knew too well what her response would be. He would authorise the expense and take his chances.

Rita, practical as always and seeking to defuse the scene, said, 'If we're moving on this, we can't afford to lose time. We should have researchers working by Monday. So where do we begin?'

'We'll call in Uncle Arthur,' Chippingham said. 'I'll speak to him at home tonight and have him here tomorrow to begin recruiting.'

Crawford Sloane brightened. 'A good idea.'

With tensions eased, Partridge said, 'Les, there's something I think needs saying. At the best of times I wouldn't want your job. But especially right now, I'm certain that none of us here could juggle the priorities and people that you're having to—at least, not any better.'

Chippingham looked at Partridge gratefully and nodded.

WITH THE GRACE OF A GULL the Learjet 55LR descended through the night towards two parallel strands of lights, marking runway one-eight of Opa-locka Airport. Beyond the airport were the myriad lights of Greater Miami. The time was just after eleven pm.

In the passenger cabin Miguel turned to Baudelio who, a few feet away, was monitoring the three caskets. Baudelio nodded, indicating all was well, and Miguel considered a potential problem.

His own and the Medellín cartel's intelligence about the rules and habits of US Customs was the reason Opa-locka had been chosen as the airport of departure. Like Teterboro, Florida's Opa-locka was used by private aircraft only. Because of incoming flights from overseas, it had a small US Customs office. Usually no more than two officers were on duty, and then only until seven pm. The present Learjet journey had been scheduled on the assumption that by this late hour customs would be closed.

But there was still the chance of occasional checks. Miguel knew that specific papers were required for each body. With careful foresight he had obtained all the documents; they were forgeries, but good ones. Yet the rules were that a casket must be opened, its contents inspected by a Customs officer. Miguel felt himself tense as the Learjet landed smoothly and taxied in to Hangar One.

OPA-LOCKA AIRPORT, though busy, had few buildings, and the area's overall dry flatness conveyed the impression of a desert.

Amid that desert, Hangar One was an oasis. It was an attractive, modern building, only part of which was a hangar. The whole comprised a luxury passenger terminal. Similar facilities existed for pilots, plus a comprehensive flight planning area. It was in that area that Customs Inspector Wally Amsler approached the Learjet pilot, who was studying weather data.

'Good evening, Captain. You're scheduled out for Bogotá.'

The pilot, Underhill, looked up. 'That's right.'

In fact, the Learjet's destination was a dirt landing strip in the Peruvian Andes and the flight there would be nonstop. But Underhill's instructions specified that his departure data should show Bogotá.

'If you don't mind,' Amsler said politely, 'I'd like to inspect your ship and your people aboard.'

Underhill did mind, but knew it would do no good to say so. He only hoped that his oddball quartet of passengers could satisfy this customs guy sufficiently to have him clear the plane. He was uneasy about his own involvement with whatever was going on.

There was something unusual, possibly illegal, about those caskets, Denis Underhill suspected. Not for a moment did he believe the story told to him at the time the charter was arranged about accident victims and a grieving family. However, remembering that his pay for the flight would be munificent, he decided to use the accident victims' yarn now, thereby putting himself on the record whatever else might happen.

'It's a sad situation,' he told the customs man, and went on to describe the tale he had been told.

He and Amsler walked from the Hangar One main building to the Learjet, parked nearby. The Lear's door was open and Underhill preceded Inspector Amsler up the steps into the cabin. He announced, 'Lady and gentlemen, we have a friendly visit from United States Customs.'

199

AFTER THE LEARJET LANDED, Miguel had talked seriously to the other three group members. He had warned them of the possibility of a customs inspection and that they must be prepared to play their rehearsed roles. There was clearly some anxiety, but all indicated they were ready. Socorro slipped a grain of pepper beneath each lower eyelid, and almost at once her eyes filled with tears. Miguel made it clear that he would be the principal spokesman. Consequently, it was not a total shock when Underhill made his announcement and a customs officer appeared.

'Good evening, folks.' Amsler looked around, taking in the caskets and the passengers—three seated, Miguel standing.

'Good evening, officer.' Miguel was holding a sheaf of documents and four passports. He proffered the passports first.

Amsler accepted them but didn't look down. Instead he asked, 'Where are you going and what is the purpose of this flight?'

'This is a tragic journey, officer, and a once happy family is now overwhelmed with grief.'

'And you, sir. What is your name?'

'I am Pedro Palacios, a close friend of the bereaved family.' Miguel was using a new alias for which he had a matching Colombian passport. He added, 'My friends have asked me to speak for them because they are not proficient in English.'

Amsler looked at Miguel's passport and, glancing up, compared the photo with his face. 'You speak good English, señor.'

Miguel answered with assurance, 'Part of my education was at Berkeley. I love this country dearly.'

Opening the remaining passports, Amsler compared the photos in them with the other three people, then, nodding, he returned to Miguel. 'Tell me about those.' Amsler gestured to the caskets.

Miguel let his voice become choked. 'There was a terrible accident. This lady's sister, her sister's young son, an older gentleman also of the family, were on vacation in America. In Philadelphia a truck, out of control, crossed the turnpike at great speed . . . It struck the family's car, killing everyone. A fire burned . . . the bodies . . . *My god, the bodies!'*

At the mention of bodies, Socorro wailed and sobbed. Rafael had his head down in his hands, his shoulders shaking.

Miguel thrust the remaining documents forward. 'It is all here. Please, officer, I ask you—read for yourself.'

Amsler took the papers and leafed through them. The death certificates appeared to be in order; so did the body disposition permits and the entry permissions for Colombia. He read the words 'bodies burned . . . mutilated beyond recognition', and his stomach turned at the thought of what he had to do next.

By law the caskets had to be opened. He told Miguel, 'I'm truly sorry, but regulations require that the caskets be opened for inspection.'

It was what Miguel had most feared. 'Oh, please, officer. I beg of you! There has been so much anguish, so much pain.'

Amsler told Miguel, 'I did not write the regulations. I suggest the caskets be taken to somewhere private. Your pilot can arrange it.'

Miguel knew he could not allow it. His hand slipped under his coat. He felt the Makarov 9mm pistol and slid off the safety. Glancing at Rafael, he saw the big man nod.

Placing himself between the customs man and the door, he tightened his fingers on the gun. This was the moment. *Now!*

In that instant, a voice spoke. 'Echo one-seven-two. Sector.'

It startled everyone except Amsler, used to hearing the walkie-talkie he carried on his belt. He lifted the radio to his lips. 'Sector, this is Echo one-seven-two.'

'Echo one-seven-two,' the voice rasped back, 'Lima two-six-eight requests you terminate present assignment and contact him immediately by land line.'

Amsler transmitted the acknowledgment. He had received an emergency order he could not disobey. Lima 268 was the code number of his sector boss for the Miami area. He had to get to a phone fast.

'I have been summoned away, Señor Palacios,' he said. 'Therefore I will clear your flight now and you may leave.'

Amsler was unaware of the suddenly lowered tension and relief.

A short time later the Learjet 55LR, clear of United States airspace and on course for Sion, Peru, climbed into the night.

CHAPTER 9

In CBA News, Arthur Nalesworth—urbane, dignified, and nowadays known to everyone as Uncle Arthur—had, in his younger years, been a very big wheel. During three decades at the network he had worked his way up to be executive vice president of the entire news division. Then his luck had changed and, like many before and since, he was shunted to the sidelines at the age of fifty-six. He was given the choice of early retirement or a minor, make-work post.

Most people faced with those alternatives chose retirement, out of pride. Arthur Nalesworth, who was not consumed by self-importance, chose to keep a job—any job.

Unexpectedly, Uncle Arthur found his own job. It involved young people, candidates for jobs.

CBA executives had always found it a nuisance when asked by a succession of people—friends, relatives, business contacts—'Will you help my son/daughter/godchild/pupil/protégé get a job in television news?' But not any more. Arthur Nalesworth saved his colleagues all that trouble. Now a CBA big shot could say, 'Certainly I'll help. We have a special vice-president to deal with bright young people. Tell your candidate to call this number for an interview.'

The interview was always given, because Arthur Nalesworth interviewed *everybody*. And gradually certain young people employed at his urging moved quickly and successfully into the news department's mainstream.

Thus, on a Sunday morning in the third week of September, Uncle Arthur arrived at CBA News to play his part in the search for Jessica, Nicholas and Angus Sloane. He came to the task force conference room where Partridge, Rita and Teddy Cooper were on hand to greet him. Now in his mid-sixties, he had a kindly face and a full head of silver hair.

He listened while Cooper described the attempts to identify the kidnappers and outlined his idea of searching through real estate ads in an attempt to locate the kidnappers' headquarters.

Partridge added, 'At the moment, Arthur, it's the best we have.'

'My experience,' Arthur replied, 'is that when you have nothing whatever to proceed on, long shots are the way to go.'

Cooper then accompanied Uncle Arthur to his small office where the older man spread files and index cards around until they covered the surface of his desk. Next, he began telephoning— each call sounding as if a familiar friend were on the line.

He worked patiently through his files. By the end of the day Uncle Arthur made known that sixty of his 'brightest and best' would be reporting to CBA News for duty on Monday morning.

EARLY ON SUNDAY the Learjet 55LR entered airspace over San Martin Province in the sparsely populated Selva, or jungle, region of Peru. On the dimly lit flight deck both pilots craned forward, their eyes searching the darkness. Not far ahead were high mountain ranges. The local time was four fifteen am.

The copilot, Faulkner, was first to see the ground beacon. The white light flashed three times, then went out, but not before Faulkner, who was at the controls, had put the aircraft into a turn.

Captain Underhill was busy with a radio, using a special frequency and a prearranged call sign. A reply shot back with permission to land. The same beacon light came on again and continued to flash. Moments later three flares sprang into view along the hard-dirt strip.

'I'll take us in,' Underhill said, and assumed the controls. He made a pass over the area. He knew they would need every foot of ground available, knew too there were trees and heavy foliage on both sides of the landing strip. Once satisfied, he began an approach pattern.

Their two bright landing lights sliced the darkness ahead. Now the strip was barely fifty feet distant. This was it! They touched the rough, uneven ground with a bump. Reverse thrust . . . brakes! The end of the strip was disconcertingly close, but they made it—with nothing to spare.

The Learjet's engines fell silent and Faulkner left his seat to open the door. In sudden contrast to the controlled temperature inside, the outside air was suffocatingly hot and humid.

The waiting force on the ground comprised eight men. Even in the darkness it was possible to see that all were sturdy peasant types, stockily built. The youngest-looking of the eight stepped forward, identified himself as Gustavo, and declared his willingness to accept Miguel's orders. Then he turned to Socorro with a bow of respect—because of her affiliation with Sendero Luminoso.

Miguel told Gustavo to have his men unload the caskets. Meanwhile Captain Underhill, who had just emerged from the aircraft, found himself looking into the barrels of six Kalashnikov rifles. Four of the Peruvians entered the plane, and one by one the caskets were unloaded and carried into the small hut. Baudelio and Socorro followed inside.

AN HOUR AND A HALF had passed since the Learjet's landing. During the intervening time the jet had been refuelled and Underhill was now looking for Miguel to inform him of their departure.

The hut door was partially closed and, hearing voices inside, the pilot pushed it open. The next instant he stopped—shocked and horrified at what he saw. Seated on the dirt floor were three figures, their backs to the wall, heads lolling, comatose but certainly alive. Two of the caskets—now open and empty—had been placed on either side of the trio to help prop them up. A single oil lantern illuminated the scene.

Underhill knew immediately who the three were. He listened daily to radio news and read newspapers. It was impossible not to know about the kidnapped family of the famous US anchorman.

Icy fear crept over Denis Underhill. Flying Latin American charters he had skirted the borderlines of crime before. But he had never, ever before been involved in anything as utterly felonious as this.

It was at that moment that a figure moved quickly towards him from the far side of the hut. It was Miguel. With a Makarov 9mm pistol in his hand, he motioned, 'Out!'

Underhill moved outside, ahead of Miguel. There, Miguel said menacingly, 'You just *thought* you saw something. You didn't, after all.'

Underhill responded hastily, 'That's right. Didn't see a damn thing.'

Miguel was calculating swiftly. If he killed one pilot he would have to kill both, which would mean the Learjet could not be flown out, for the time being—a complication he could do without. 'Get the airplane out of here,' he snarled, 'and afterwards keep your mouth shut. If you don't, I promise that wherever you are you'll be found and killed. Is that clear?'

Trembling with relief, Underhill nodded. 'It's clear.' Then he turned and walked back to the airstrip.

AFTER LESS THAN THREE FULL DAYS of investigation an important success had been achieved by the CBA News special task force.

In Larchmont, New York, an infamous Colombian terrorist, Ulises Rodríguez, had been positively identified as one of the kidnappers of the Sloane family trio. And perhaps the leader of the kidnap gang.

On Sunday morning, as promised, a copy of the charcoal sketch of Rodríguez, drawn twenty years earlier by a fellow student at Berkeley, had arrived at CBA News headquarters. At this point CBA had the information exclusively.

Late on Sunday four task force members—Harry, Rita, Karl Owens and Iris Everly—discussed the breakthrough. Owens urged that it be included in Monday's edition of the National Evening News. When Partridge hesitated, Owens argued forcefully.

'Look, Harry, no one has this yet: we're ahead of the pack. If we hold off, word about Rodríguez may get out and we'll lose our exclusive.'

'I know,' Partridge said. 'I'd like to go with it. But there are reasons to wait. I'll make a decision tomorrow.'

With that, the others had to be content .

One decision Partridge made privately was that Crawford Sloane must be informed. Crawf, he reasoned, was suffering such mental agony that any forward step would come as a relief. Late as it was—nearing ten pm—Partridge decided to visit Sloane himself.

He ordered a CBA car and driver to meet him at the news building's main entrance.

'I'm grateful you came out, Harry,' Crawford Sloane said, after Partridge had made his report. 'Will you go on air with this tomorrow?'

'I'm not sure.' Partridge added, 'I want to sleep on it.'

The two newsmen were having drinks in the living room where, only four evenings earlier, Sloane thought sadly, he had sat with Jessica and Nicholas after his own return from work.

'Whatever you decide,' Sloane said, 'I'll back your judgment. Either way, do you have enough reason to take off for Colombia?'

Partridge shook his head. 'Not yet, because Rodríguez is a gun-for-hire.

He's operated all over Latin America, Europe too. So I need to know more—specifically, where this operation is based. Tomorrow I'll work the phones again.'

As Partridge was leaving, Sloane put a hand on his shoulder. 'Harry, my friend,' he said, his voice emotional, 'I've come to believe that the only chance I have of getting Jessica, Nicky and my dad back is through you. There have been times when you and I weren't the closest companions, and for that, I'm sorry. But apart from that, I want you to know that most of what I have and care about in this world is riding on you.'

Partridge tried to reply, but couldn't. Instead he nodded, touched Sloane on the shoulder, too, and said, 'Good night.'

PART THREE   CHAPTER 10

Jessica was trying desperately to hold on to awareness, to keep her mind functioning and to understand what was going on around her. Mostly, she was not succeeding. She would have moments of clarity in which she could see other people and feel pain. Then abruptly everything would ebb away, becoming a swirling mist in which she could grasp nothing.

Now, once more, awareness had swirled in. There was a man leaning over her . . . *Wait!* She had seen him before—she had slashed his face with a knife because *he had done something to Nicky!* Wild anger sent adrenalin pumping, brought back movement to her limbs. She reached up, and her nails raked his bandaged face.

With a cry, Baudelio leaped back. He put a hand to his cheek; it came away red with blood. That damn woman had messed up his face again! Enraged, he leaned forward and hit her, hard.

An instant later he regretted having done it. He had wanted to see how far all three captives were advanced in consciousness—up to this point they had come out of sedation satisfactorily. But they should all be given water soon; he would attend to that.

Socorro appeared beside him and he told her to fetch some water. She nodded and went out into the damp jungle. Miguel, who had just entered the hut, called after her, 'And find something to tie their hands.'

Turning to Baudelio, Miguel ordered, 'Get the prisoners ready. First we go by truck. After that, everyone will walk.'

Jessica, now only feigning unconsciousness, heard it all. In hitting her, Baudelio had actually done her a favour. The jolt had brought her borderline awareness suddenly into focus. Everything was coming back:

the Grand Union supermarket . . . then in the parking lot, the brutal seizure of herself, Nicky and . . .

Nicky! Had he been harmed? Where was he now? And Angus. Oh, poor Angus! Barely opening her eyes, she shifted to see whether Nicky was with her. *Oh, thank God!* He was right alongside. His eyes were opening and closing; he was yawning. Angus was beyond Nicky, eyes closed, but she could see that he was breathing. Where were they? Jessica's quick glimpses of this place had shown her a small semidarkened room, windowless and lit by an oil lantern. She was seated on what felt like a dirt floor and it was incredibly hot and sticky, which puzzled her. Voices interrupted.

'The woman is faking,' Miguel said.

'I know,' Baudelio replied. 'She's fully conscious.'

Jessica lifted her head. She recognised both men looking down at her—the one whose face she had cut, the other whom she had caught sight of briefly in the van. Her voice was raspy, but she managed to say, 'You'll be sorry for this.'

'Silence!' Miguel said. He extended his right foot and shoved it into Jessica's ribs. 'On your feet! We have places to go.'

The kick made her wince. Then from beside her she heard Nicky stir and say, 'What's happened? Where are we?'

It was Angus who answered softly, 'It looks to me, old son, as if we've been kidnapped by some pretty nasty people. But keep your cool. Be strong! Your dad'll find us.'

Jessica felt a hand on her arm and heard Nicky's voice say gently, 'Mom, are you OK?'

Miguel shouted, 'All of you! Keep silent!' He turned to Baudelio. 'Get them ready to go.'

Socorro had returned, carrying a water jug and some rope.

'They should have water first,' Baudelio said. He added with a hint of petulance, 'That is, if you want them kept alive.'

'First tie their hands behind their backs,' Miguel ordered. 'I want no more trouble.' Scowling, he left the hut.

PHYSICALLY, JESSICA FELT BETTER for the water. Before leaving the hut, Nicky and Angus had been given water, too, by a sour-faced woman whom Jessica also remembered seeing briefly before—she believed during her initial struggle with the man she had labelled Cutface.

Trying to appeal as one woman to another, Jessica whispered between mouthfuls, fed to her from a tin cup, 'Thank you for the water. Please! Will you tell me where we are, and why?'

The woman hissed, 'You heard the order. *Silencio!* Speak again and you will go without water for a day.'

206

After that, Jessica stayed silent. She, Nicky and Angus had been moved through dense woodland to the back portion of an open truck, along with a miscellaneous cargo of boxes and sacks. Then half a dozen motley-dressed men carrying guns had boarded also, followed by Cutface. The tailgate was raised and the truck began to move, bouncing unevenly over rough ground.

The heat was even more intense than in the hut. So where were they? Seeking clues, Jessica began listening to snatches of speech between the men with the guns, and recognised the language as Spanish.

Her thoughts were distracted by the sight of Nicky. Since the truck had begun to move, he had had trouble keeping his body upright and, because of his tied hands, had slid down so that with every bump his head was hitting the floor. Frantic, she now saw one of the gun-toting men take notice of Nicky's plight. The man moved Nicky back against a sack, his feet touching a box so that he wouldn't slip again. Jessica tried to thank the man with her eyes and a half-smile. In return he gave the slightest of nods. The man mumbled some words that Nicky, having recently begun Spanish lessons at school, seemed to understand. As the journey contin ued, there were two more exchanges between the man and the boy.

After about twenty minutes the truck stopped and Jessica, Nicky and Angus were shoved and lifted off it. Miguel came round from the front and announced curtly, 'From here we walk.' Gustavo and two other armed men led the way through thick foliage over a barely discernible trail. Though the trees overhead provided shade, the incredible heat persisted amid a constant buzz of insects.

At one point Nicky said in a low voice, 'This leads to a river, Mom. Then we're going in a boat, the man on the truck said.'

Soon after that, Jessica heard Angus murmur, 'I'm proud of you, Nicky. You're being very brave.'

She was relieved that the old man was coping. At the next opportunity she said, 'I've been wondering about rescue, trying to guess where we are.'

Nicky supplied the answer. 'The man told me, Mom. We're in Peru.'

IT WAS NINE THIRTY AM on Monday. Within the past half-hour sixty bright young men and women had reported for temporary work at CBA News. All were now assembled on the sound stage of the CBA auxiliary building. Among the group was a young black man named Jonathan Mony. 'You may want to use Jonathan as a supervisor,' Uncle Arthur told Teddy Cooper, adding, 'He's a Columbia Journalism grad who's been working as a waiter because he needs the money.'

Mony had the build and agility of a professional basketball player. His features were finely cut, with compelling, confident eyes. His first question to Cooper after introducing himself was, 'May I help you set this up?'

Cooper, who liked Mony instantly, responded, 'Sure,' and within minutes Mony was showing fresh arrivals to seats and explaining the forms to them.

That had been forty minutes ago. Now Teddy Cooper was concluding his introductory remarks. 'So, before leaving here you'll be assigned to local newspaper offices or libraries where you will read issues published during the past three months. Not just reading, though, but Sherlock Holmesing for clues to lead us to those body snatchers. You need not come back here at the end of each day, but you must report by telephone—and call immediately if you find anything important.'

There was a hum of conversation, which quickly quietened as Cooper continued. 'As well as looking for the kind of buildings I've described, I want you to be alert for anything unusual. Just possibly the kidnappers have left a trace behind. So look hard and look intelligently. You were hired because we think you're smart, so prove us right.'

ON ARRIVAL AT CBA NEWS that morning, Harry Partridge had telephoned his lawyer contact, whose clients were from organised crime.

The response was less than cordial. 'I'm sure none of the people I represent were involved with the kidnapping. When you and I talked, I told you I would find out what I could. But I have to tread carefully.'

Inwardly sighing, Partridge said, 'I understand.'

The lawyer's voice moderated. 'Give me a few more days. And don't call me; I'll call you.'

Hanging up, Partridge reflected that while contacts could be useful, you didn't necessarily have to like them.

Earlier that morning he had reached a decision on whether or not to reveal on the National Evening News that a known Colombian terrorist, Ulises Rodríguez, had been linked conclusively to the Sloane family kidnap. His decision was to withhold the information for the time being. If the only lead were broadcast, Rodríguez could hear of it and be driven further under cover, which would considerably lessen the chances of discovering the Sloanes. Partridge also told himself, We should remember that this news thing we do is not some holy grail. When reporting endangers life and liberty, news has to take second place.

Because of its importance Partridge told Les Chippingham and Chuck Insen of his decision. Both men agreed to trust his judgment, and Partridge settled down to resume telephoning.

Unlike last week, when his calls had been mainly to US sources, today he tried to reach contacts in Colombia and countries immediately adjoining it, including Peru. Another difference was having the positive

Rodríguez lead, which translated into a double-barrelled question: Do you know of a terrorist named Ulises Rodríguez? If so, have you any idea what he's reputed to be doing?

Responses to the first part of the question were almost entirely yes, and to the second, no. An interesting point, though, emerged from a conversation with a Colombian friend, a radio news reporter in Bogotá.

'Wherever he is,' the broadcaster said, 'I'd almost guarantee it isn't this country. He's a Colombian after all, and he's too well known to be here for long without word getting around.'

Then there was Peru. Partridge had made a call to that country that left him wondering. It was to another old acquaintance, Manuel Seminario, owner-editor of the weekly magazine *Escena,* published in Lima. After Partridge announced his reason for calling, Seminario had exclaimed, 'My God! I should have realised you'd be involved. That kidnapping is a terrible thing. We'll have a full-page piece in this week's issue. Is there anything new we should include?'

'There *is* something new,' Partridge said. 'But for now we're keeping it under wraps, so I'd appreciate this being off the record. We believe Ulises Rodríguez is involved.'

There was a silence before Seminario said softly, 'You are speaking of bad company, Harry. That man is suspected of masterminding kidnappings, skulking in and out of Peru from Colombia for employment by others here. It is the way our criminal-revolutionary elements, such as Sendero Luminoso, work. As you know, in Peru nowadays kidnapping is almost a way of life.'

'I did know that,' Partridge said. 'Have you heard any talk of Rodríguez being in Peru, or recently working for anyone there?'

'Well . . . no.'

'Did I sense some hesitation?'

'Not about Rodríguez. Everything here, on what I call the criminal-revolutionary front, has been strangely quiet for several weeks. I have seen the signs before and it often means something big is about to happen. Usually unpleasant.'

Seminario's voice changed tempo, became businesslike. 'My dear Harry, it has been a pleasure talking to you. Do come to see me soon in Lima—a standing invitation.'

Through the day the words kept coming back to Partridge: 'It often means something big is about to happen.'

COINCIDENTALLY, ON THE SAME DAY, Peru was discussed at an ultra-private, top-echelon meeting of CBA network's corporate owners, Globanic Industries Inc. The meeting was a twice-yearly, three-day, policy workshop chaired by the conglomerate's chairman and chief executive officer, Theodore Elliott. Attendance was confined to other CEOs—those of Globanic's nine subsidiaries, all major companies themselves.

The meeting took place at the Fordly Cay Club near Nassau in the Bahamas, one of the world's most exclusive clubs whose facilities included a yacht harbour, a golf course, tennis courts and white-sand beaches.

The first morning session was held in a small, comfortable library, where the deep rattan chairs were upholstered in beige leather. Theo Elliott, appropriately dressed in white slacks and a light blue polo shirt, was tall, lean and broad-shouldered, with a strong jaw and a full head of white hair. The hair was a reminder that in two years' time the chairman would reach retirement age and be succeeded by one of the others present.

There were three strong candidates, of whom Margot Lloyd-Mason was one. Margot was conscious of this as she reported on CBA. Speaking precisely, she disclosed that since Globanic's acquisition of CBA, strict financial controls had been introduced. As a result, third-quarter profits would be up twenty-two per cent over the year before.

'That's a fair beginning,' Theodore Elliott commented, 'though we'll expect even better in future.

Margot had dressed carefully today, not wanting to appear too feminine, yet not wishing to lose the advantage of her sex. At first she'd considered wearing a tailored suit, as she often did in her office at Stonehenge. In the end, being in the semitropics, she wore beige linen slacks and a cotton sweater in a soft peach shade. The outfit emphasised her well-proportioned body, a judgment confirmed by lingering glances from some of the men.

Continuing her report, Margot mentioned the recent kidnapping of the Crawford Sloane family.

The chairman of International Forest Products, a hard-driving businessman from Oregon, interjected, 'That's too bad, and we all hope they catch those people. Just the same, your network's getting a lot of attention from it.'

'So much attention,' Margot informed him, 'that our National Evening News ratings have soared almost three points within the past five days, which means an additional six million viewers and puts us strongly in front as number one. It's also raised the rating of our daily game show immediately after the news. And the same is true of our prime-time shows. The sponsors are all delighted.' She added, 'Networks know from experience that if viewers tune in to the evening news the odds are they will stay with that network for the next ninety minutes, sometimes more.'

'So it's an ill wind . . . as the old saying goes,' the Forest Products chief said, smiling.

Margot smiled back. 'Since we're here in private I'll agree, though please don't quote me.'

Late in the morning it was the turn of 'Fossie' Xenos, chairman of Globanic Financial Services, to address his fellow CEOs. A second-generation Greek-American, Fossie retained a boyish manner, appearing much younger than his forty-one years. Since taking over Globanic Financial, he had created sparkling profits for the company, plus a dynamic reputation for himself. Margot Lloyd-Mason viewed him as her most formidable rival for the conglomerate chairmanship.

Today Fossie Xenos reported on a secret project expected to produce a multibillion-dollar bonanza for Globanic. It involved so-called debt-to-equity swaps and a gigantic real estate investment fund, both relating to Peru, with Globanic working closely with that country's government. Currently, Peru had more than sixteen billion dollars of foreign debt on which it had defaulted, and the international financial community would lend it no more money. Suffering a desperate economic crisis, the country was anxious to regain reputable status and begin borrowing once more. At the same time, Globanic had quietly bought up four and a half billion dollars of Peru's outstanding debt, paying an average five cents on the dollar.

The government of Peru had been informed they could wipe out that debt by buying it from Globanic for ten cents on the dollar, but with all bookkeeping payments in Peru's own weak currency. Three critical conditions were attached to Globanic's acknowledgment of Peruvian currency. Globanic didn't want cash but instead the debt-to-equity swap, giving it total ownership of two spectacular resort locations now owned by the Peruvian government. Along with those vast amounts of land would go guarantees that Globanic was free to develop the resorts in its own way.

Fossie's report ended with the information that agreement between the Peruvian government and Globanic Financial had been reached a few days earlier, with all of Globanic's demands accepted. As he sat down, the audience applauded.

Theo Elliott, beaming, enquired, 'Questions, anyone?'

Margot spoke up. 'Tell us about Peru's stability, Fossie. Lately there's been an increase in revolutionary activity, not just in the usual Andes areas, but in Lima and elsewhere. Under those circumstances will vacationers want to go there?'

Fossie answered cheerfully, 'All my information is that the revolutionary outlook is short term and that Peru will survive with a solid, law-abiding democracy favourable to expanded tourism.'

'If that's all the questioning,' Theo Elliott pronounced, 'let me just say this: I don't want anything to damage our still delicate relationship with the government of Peru and thereby spoil what could well evolve into the deal of the century.' The chairman rose. 'Now that's understood, let's have lunch.'

CHAPTER 11

Jessica, Nicky and Angus, their hands tied behind them, were still stumbling along the narrow trail hemmed in by dense trees and undergrowth. Some armed men were ahead, others behind, prodding with their rifles to urge the captives on. And it was hot. Incredibly hot. Sweat poured from them all, and Jessica worried desperately about the other two. She herself was suffering an intense headache and nausea.

The ground beneath her feet had become soggy, making it increasingly difficult to walk. Suddenly, behind her, she heard a sharp cry and a thud. Angus had fallen. Gamely, the old man struggled to get up, but failed because of his tied hands. Behind him the men with guns laughed.

From the front of the column, Miguel now appeared, with Socorro and Baudelio behind him. Before anyone could speak, Jessica screamed, 'We know we can't escape, and so do you. Why, then, tie our hands? All we want is to help ourselves, to keep from falling. I beg you, untie us!'

As Miguel hesitated, Socorro told him softly, 'If one of them breaks a leg or arm, or even has a cut, it could become infected. In Nueva Esperanza we'll have no means of dealing with it.'

Beside her, Baudelio said, 'She's right.'

Miguel, with an impatient gesture, snapped an order in Spanish. The man who had helped Nicky in the truck stepped forward. With a knife he cut the rope binding Jessica's wrists. Nicky was next. Angus's bonds were severed too. Amid shouted commands, they again moved forward.

In the past few minutes, Jessica had learned several things. First, their destination was Nueva Esperanza, though the name meant nothing to her. Second, the man who had befriended Nicky was Vicente—she had heard him called by name. Third, the woman who interceded with Miguel, the same one who had struck her in the hut, possessed some medical knowledge. So did Cutface. Possibly one or the other was a doctor.

Moments later, as the column rounded a bend in the trail, a wide river appeared ahead. As they drew nearer, Jessica could see two wooden workboats, each with twin outboard motors, moored close to the riverbank. Prodded by guns, she, Nicky and Angus waded knee-deep through water to board the first boat and, after climbing in, were ordered to sit on the damp bottom boards. Some of the armed men who had been in the truck and on the trail now climbed into the prisoners' boat, and both boats started to move upriver. Jessica noticed that other men, who had been in charge of the boats, were also armed. The chances of getting away, even if there were somewhere to go, seemed nonexistent.

Nicky turned to Jessica. 'Mom, I'm scared.'

Jessica, holding him, admitted, 'Darling, so am I.'

SOME THREE HOURS LATER both boats slowed, their bows turning from the main river into a smaller stream, the banks on either side closing in.

Like everyone else, Jessica, Nicky and Angus were soaked in a deluge of rain shortly before landing.

At Nueva Esperanza, their boat made fast against a wooden jetty, the rain stopped as suddenly as it had begun, but the spirits of all three sank as they saw the awful, forbidding place ahead.

Beyond a rough path from the riverbank was a series of dilapidated houses built partly from old packing cases and rusted corrugated iron. Most were windowless, though two had what appeared to be small shopfronts. Thatched roofs showed disrepair, and some had gaping holes. A muddy path led out of the hamlet between two walls of jungle until it disappeared at the top of a hill.

After being escorted by the armed men up the path, the prisoners were herded into the shack which stood furthest from the river. It took a few moments for their eyes to adjust to the semidarkness. When they did, Jessica screamed in anguish.

'Oh, my God, no! You can't shut us in those! Not in cages, like animals! *Please, no!*'

Set against the far wall were three small partitioned cells made of thin but strong bamboo stalks. Between each cell, wire screening had been nailed so there could be no physical contact between occupants. The door of each cell was fitted with a sliding steel bar and a heavy padlock. Inside was a low wooden bed with a thin soiled mattress and a galvanised pail. The whole place stank.

While Jessica pleaded and protested, she was seized and pushed into the enclosure furthest from the shack's outer door. Then the cell door closed and she heard the padlock click. At the opposite end of the shack, Angus was fighting and arguing too, but he was subdued, thrown in, and the padlock fastened. In the cell next to her own, Jessica heard Nicky sobbing.

TEN DAYS HAD PASSED since the sixty recruits were turned loose by CBA News to make a study of the region's newspapers, searching for a headquarters that the kidnappers might have used.

The FBI, while not saying specifically that it had reached a dead end, had nothing new to report. The CIA, now rumoured to be involved, would make no statement.

Then, on a Wednesday morning, Harry Partridge looked up to see Teddy Cooper in the doorway of his private office and, behind him, Jonathan Mony. Partridge waved them in.

'We may have something, Harry,' Cooper said. He motioned to the young black researcher. 'Go ahead.'

'Yesterday I went to a local newspaper in Astoria, Queens,' Mony began. 'Found nothing. Then, coming out, I saw the office of a Spanish-language weekly called *Semana*. It wasn't on the list, but I went in. I speak Spanish pretty well, and they let me check their latest issue.'

Cooper spread a tabloid-style newspaper on Partridge's desk. 'Here's a column we think will interest you, with Jonathan's translation.'

Partridge glanced at the paper, then read the translation:

You wouldn't think, would you, that some people buy funeral caskets the way you and me pick up cheese at the grocery. Happens, though.

Seems this guy came to Alberto Godoy of Godoy's Funeral Home and bought two caskets off the shelf—one regular, one small—for his old Mom and Dad, the tiny one for Mom. Hey, how's that for a hint to the old folks?

Last week—that's six weeks later—this same guy comes back, wants another casket like before, regular size. He took it away, paid cash, same as he did for the other two. Didn't say who this one was for. Wonder if his wife's been cheating.

Tell you who doesn't care, that's Albert Godoy. Says he's ready and eager for more business of the same kind.

'A few minutes ago we phoned the *Semana* office,' Cooper said. 'Jonathan got lucky. The guy who wrote the column was there. And he said he wrote the piece a week ago last Friday. Which happened to be the day after the kidnap.'

Stay calm, Partridge told himself. *Don't get carried away.*

He looked at the other two. 'Do you think—'

'What I think,' Cooper said, 'is that we may have found how Mrs Sloane and the others were taken out of the country.'

'In caskets? Do you believe they were dead?'

Cooper shook his head. 'Doped. It's been done before.'

'As soon as I can, I'll interview that funeral man, Godoy,' Harry said.

'I'd like to come with you,' said Mony hopefully.

Partridge smiled at the young man. 'I think you've earned it, Jonathan. Let's leave immediately.'

As Cooper left, Partridge picked up a telephone and ordered a network

214

car. On the way out, passing through the main newsroom, he and Mony encountered Don Kettering, CBA's business correspondent, who had gone on the air with the special bulletin when news of the Sloane kidnap first broke.

Now he asked, 'Anything new, Harry?'

Partridge respected Kettering as a first-class reporter. 'Something *has* come up, Don. What are you doing now?'

'Not much. Wall Street's quiet today. Need some help?'

'Could be. Come with us. I'll explain as we go.'

Twenty minutes later Harry Partridge, Don Kettering and Jonathan Mony faced Alberto Godoy in his cluttered funeral-home office in Queens. The undertaker regarded the visitors suspiciously.

'Mr Godoy,' Partridge said, 'as I told your receptionist, we're all from CBA News.'

'You been doin' all them Sloane kidnap bits.'

'Yes, I have, and that's partly why we're here.' Producing his copy of *Semana,* Partridge asked, 'Have you seen this?'

The undertaker's features soured. 'All that's my private business. And if you all don't mind, I've got work to do.'

Don Kettering spoke, leaning forward over the undertaker's desk. 'Listen to me carefully, Godoy. A network like ours has a lot of clout, and if we have to, we'll use it. We need answers to questions fast. And if we don't get honest answers, we'll bring in—here, today—the FBI, the New York police, the sales-tax force and the IRS to talk about those three caskets you sold. So take your choice. You can deal with us or them.'

Godoy licked his lips. 'I'll answer your questions, fellas.'

'Mr Godoy,' Partridge said, 'who was it bought those caskets?'

'He said his name was Novack. I didn't believe him.'

'When I show you a picture, tell me your reaction.' He held out a photocopy of the charcoal sketch of Rodríguez.

Without hesitation Godoy said, 'That's him. That's Novack. Seen him twice. He's older than the picture—'

'Yes, we know.' Partridge felt a surge of satisfaction. During the questions and answers following, he extracted as much from the undertaker as he could. In the end, however, it became clear that Ulises Rodríguez had been careful not to leave a trail behind him.

As Partridge, Kettering and Mony were about to leave, Godoy opened a drawer in his desk in which he kept a supply of cigarettes. He caught sight of a sheet of paper bearing his own handwriting. He had stuffed the paper in more than a week ago and forgotten it until now. He took it out.

'What is it?' Partridge asked sharply.

'I told you he had a Caddy hearse, with another guy driving.' Godoy

215

held out the paper. 'This was the hearse's licence number.'

'Thanks,' Partridge said, 'we'll check this out.' He put the paper in a pocket, though he was not hopeful about the outcome. He remembered that the licence number of the Nissan van in the White Plains explosion had been phoney and led nowhere. Still, any lead had to be pursued.

Partridge now reasoned that most of what they had uncovered would have to go on air within the next few days. There was a limit to how much information could remain dammed up at CBA; though luck had been with them so far, it could change at any moment. Also, they *were* in the news business. Partridge felt his excitement rise at the prospect of reporting progress.

Also, he decided, the time had come to begin his own search of Latin America. He intended to leave for Bogotá, Colombia, as soon as he could get away. Whether or not Ulises Rodríguez was in that country, Colombia was the obvious place to start.

PARTRIDGE DROPPED KETTERING and Mony off, then went to a sporting goods store to buy some heavy socks, a pair of hiking boots and a sturdy torch. He suspected he might need all three quite soon. By the time he returned to CBA, it was midafternoon.

In the task force conference room, Rita waved him over. 'A man's been trying to reach you since this morning. Wouldn't leave his name. I told him you'd be back sooner or later.'

'Thanks. There's something I want to tell you. I've decided to go to Bogotá. I want to be there early tomorrow.'

'And how much do we broadcast, and when?'

'Everything we know, and soon. Exactly when, we'll discuss with Les and Chuck, but starting right now, we'll work all night putting everything together. Call the task force in for a meeting'—Partridge glanced at his watch—'at five o'clock.'

'Yessir!' Rita, enjoying action, smiled.

At the same moment, the phone on her desk rang. After answering, she covered the mouthpiece and told Partridge, 'It's the same man—the one who's been trying to get you all day.'

He took the phone. 'This is Harry Partridge.'

'Don't use my name at any point in this conversation.' The caller's words sounded muffled but Partridge recognised the voice of his contact, the organised-crime lawyer. 'I'm calling from a payphone, so the call's not traceable. And if you ever name me as the source of what I'm about to tell you, I shall swear you're a liar and deny it. When this call ends, my debt to you is paid in full. Understood?'

'Fully understood.'

216

'Some of my clients have Latin American connections, so the information is solid. The people you are looking for were flown out of the United States last Saturday and are now imprisoned in Peru. Got that?'

Partridge answered grimly, 'I have it.' Rita's eyes were fixed on him as he added, 'I need a name. Who's holding them?'

'Goodbye.'

'Wait! I'll speak a name and if I'm right, don't say anything.'

A pause, then, 'Make it fast.'

Partridge took a breath. 'Sendero Luminoso.'

At the other end, silence. Then a click as the caller hung up.

Partridge turned to Rita. 'Cancel what I said about going to Bogotá. Now, it's Lima.'

CHAPTER 12

During those terrible first minutes when Jessica, Nicky and Angus were thrust into their separate cages, and Jessica wept on hearing Nicky sobbing, there was a period of mental dislocation and misery to which they all succumbed.

But not for long. Before ten minutes had passed, Jessica called out softly, 'Nicky, can you hear me?'

A subdued answer came back. 'Yes, Mom.' It was followed by movement as Nicky approached the screen between their cells. In the semidarkness they could just see each other.

Jessica asked, 'Are you OK?'

'I think so.' Nicky's voice quivered, 'I don't like it here.'

'Oh, darling, neither do I. But until we can do something, we have to hold on. Keep reminding yourself that your father, and a lot of other people, are searching for us. Your father knows so many people, there isn't anyone he can't call on for help.' Jessica hoped she sounded reassuring.

As she spoke, a figure moved into view from the shadows beyond the cells. It was one of the gunmen, a heavyset man whom they would later identify as Ramón. He carried a Kalashnikov rifle, and aiming it at Jessica he ordered, *'Silencio!'*

About to protest, Jessica heard Angus advise softly, 'Jessie, don't!' She curbed her impulse and they all fell silent.

It was their first experience with a succession of armed guards, one of whom was always on duty in the hut. As they quickly discovered, the strictness of the guards varied. The most easy-going was Vicente, the man who, on Miguel's orders, had cut the ropes binding their wrists. Apart from motioning them to keep their voices lowered, Vicente allowed them to talk. Ramón was the strictest, permitting no talking at all.

As the first few days passed, a pattern of living took shape. Three times daily, a monotonous diet of unappetising food—principally cassava, rice and noodles—was brought to them. Drinking water was handed in to each cell; occasionally, there were bowls and water with which to wash. Every forty-eight hours, the pails they'd been given were removed and emptied.

Nicky's morale, which was the most important to Jessica, at least remained stable. He also began attempting conversation with the guards. Although his Spanish was rudimentary—he had been taking lessons for only a few months—he managed to gain some information.

From Vicente they learned of the impending departure of 'the doctor' —obviously Cutface—who was 'going home to Lima'. However, 'the nurse' would stay on, and this was clearly the woman, whose name they discovered was Socorro.

At Jessica's suggestion, Nicky asked Vicente if the prisoners were to be allowed outside at all. To this question, Vicente shook his head. Jessica, persisting, asked to have a message passed to Socorro that the prisoners would like to see her.

To their surprise, later that day Socorro came. She stood in the doorway, her slim, lithe body a distinctive silhouette, her nose wrinkling at the all-pervasive smell of the cells.

Without waiting, Jessica spoke. 'Unless we get out of here into some fresh air for a while, we'll all be desperately ill.'

'You have have no right to ask for this,' Socorro snapped.

Jessica slammed back, 'I have a right to care about my son; also my father-in-law who is old and has been treated brutally.'

Socorro shrugged. 'I will try to have more air let in here.' Her lips twitched in the nearest thing to a smile. 'It will be healthier for the guards.'

Next day two men arrived with tools. They cut open several spaces in the walls facing the cells. Immediately, the daytime semidarkness was replaced by light, and there was a welcome flow of air through the building.

But the victory was minor and, as it proved, there were major agonies still to be endured.

SIX DAYS AFTER THE CAPTIVES and their escorts arrived at Nueva Esperanza, Miguel received a series of written orders from Sendero Luminoso. Originating in Ayacucho, they were delivered by a messenger travelling in a truck that took two days to cover five hundred tortuous miles over soggy jungle trails. Several items of specialised equipment were also delivered.

The most important instruction involved making a videotape recording of the woman prisoner. A script was supplied and no deviation from its wording would be permitted. Another instruction confirmed that Baudelio's duties were at an end. He would accompany the messenger back to Ayacucho, from where he would fly to Lima.

Miguel turned his attention to the special recording equipment. It comprised a Sony Camcorder, with cassettes, a tripod, a photoflood kit and a portable generator, gasoline-powered. Suspecting that the woman would be difficult, he chose Gustavo and Ramón to help him with the recording session. Neither was likely to be squeamish, whatever punishment they were asked to inflict.

Soon after daylight the following morning, Miguel, Gustavo and Ramón appeared in the prisoners' hut. All three were carrying equipment which Jessica recognised instantly. Taking his time, Miguel installed the Camcorder on its tripod and arranged the photoflood lights, which he plugged into an extension cable. Moments later the area in front of the three cells was brightly lit, the lights focused on an empty chair which the Camcorder faced.

Miguel walked towards Jessica's cage. He held out three handwritten pages, and his voice was cold and hard. 'This is what you will say, bitch—exactly that and no more.'

Jessica took the pages, read them quickly, then tore them into pieces which she threw through the bamboo bars. 'I won't do it.'

Miguel nodded to Gustavo waiting nearby. 'Get the boy.'

Despite her determination, a shiver of apprehension ran through Jessica as she watched Gustavo open Nicky's cage. He seized Nicky by one arm, twisting it and propelling him outside.

Frantic now, Jessica demanded, 'What are you going to do?'

No one answered. Instead, Ramón brought the guard's chair from the other side of the hut. Gustavo pushed Nicky into it and the two men tied him with rope. Before securing his arms, Gustavo loosened Nicky's shirt, exposing his small chest. Ramón, meanwhile, was lighting a cigarette.

Jessica cried out, 'Wait! Perhaps I was hasty. Please wait!'

Miguel signalled to Ramón, who inhaled, bringing the tip of his cigarette to a glowing red. Then, with a single swift movement, he removed the cigarette and pressed the burning end against Nicky's chest.

For the briefest moment the boy was so surprised that no sound escaped him. Then, as he felt the burning, searing agony, he screamed.

Jessica was screaming too—wildly, incoherently, tearfully pleading for the torture to cease, assuring Miguel she would do whatever he wanted. 'Anything! But stop! Oh, stop!'

From the third cell, Angus was banging against the screen of his cage and shouting too. 'You filthy bastards! You're animals.'

Miguel waited until some of the noise had subsided, then informed

Jessica, 'You will sit in front of the camera and speak. I have written on cards what you are to say. The cards will be held up and you will follow them exactly. Is that understood?'

'Yes,' Jessica said dully, 'it's understood.'

She closed her eyes. To protect Nicky she would concentrate on what had to be done. But then, a sudden thought occurred to her.

At home in Larchmont, the night before the kidnap, Crawf had described signals which a hostage making a video recording could transmit surreptitiously. Crawf had said, 'Licking my lips would mean,"I am doing this against my will. Do not believe anything I am saying." Scratching or touching my right ear lobe, "My captors are well organised and strongly armed." Left ear lobe, "Security here is sometimes lax. An attack from outside might succeed." '

Jessica's cell was opened by Gustavo. Her impulse was to run to Nicky, but Miguel's face was glowering. Guided by Gustavo, she sat in the chair facing the photofloods and Camcorder. The message she would speak was written on two cards which Gustavo now held up. Miguel had moved to the Camcorder. He ordered, 'When I drop my hand, begin.'

The signal came and Jessica spoke, trying to keep her voice even.

'We have all been treated well and fairly. Now that the reason we were taken has been explained to us, we understand why it was necessary. We also have been told how easy it will be for our American friends to ensure our safe return home. To have us released, you must simply follow— quickly and exactly—the instructions which accompany this recording.'

Immediately after the word recording, Jessica moistened her lips with her tongue. She knew she was taking a risk, but the action passed unnoticed, and she felt a thrill of satisfaction as she continued reading from the cards.

'If you do not obey those instructions, you will not see any of us, ever again. We beg of you, do not let that happen . . . '

Meanwhile, she must make a choice, left ear or right? It was true the people here were armed and perhaps well organised, but security *was* lax at times, and often at night their guards fell asleep. Making her decision, Jessica casually scratched her left ear lobe. She spoke the last words.

'We will be waiting, counting on you, desperately hoping you will make the right decision.'

Seconds later, it was over. As Jessica closed her eyes in relief, Miguel switched off the floodlights, a small smile of satisfaction on his face.

FROM THE MOMENT on Wednesday afternoon when Harry Partridge announced his decision to leave for Peru, the CBA News special task force moved feverishly into top gear.

Immediately ahead, to be written and partially recorded overnight, was a report anchored by Partridge which would dominate the National Evening News on Friday, some thirty-six hours after his departure. This would contain all that was known concerning the kidnapping.

Partridge called a task force meeting in the conference room for five o'clock, and it was well attended. Les Chippingham and Crawford Sloane, looking more haggard than ever, were there. Partridge was at the head of the table, with Rita Abrams beside him. Iris Everly arrived several minutes late. Teddy Cooper was present, and Minh Van Canh came in, as did producers Norman Jaeger and Karl Owens.

Partridge began by announcing his intention to leave for Peru early the next morning, and the decision to broadcast everything they knew on Friday evening's news.

Les Chippingham cut in. 'Harry, I think we should go one step further and do the one-hour news special, also on Friday night, covering the whole kidnap sequence at length. You guys sound as if you have plenty to fill an hour.'

'Plenty and more,' Rita Abrams assured him.

From there other decisions flowed. Partridge announced that Minh Van Canh and Ken O'Hara would accompany him to Peru. Rita would remain in New York for overall supervision of the Friday-evening news report and one-hour special. Then, later that night, she would follow Partridge and the others.

Partridge, who had discussed the subject earlier with Chippingham, disclosed that after his own departure, Don Kettering would head the kidnap task force in New York. However, neither the National Evening News report of Friday nor the one-hour special should convey any hint that Partridge had already left for Peru. In fact, if it could be made to appear at some point that he was broadcasting live—though without actually being deceptive—so much the better.

Nothing that would happen through that night and the next two days, Les Chippingham declared, must be discussed, even with others in the news division. The news president continued, 'Let us not do or say *anything* that could release our news prematurely and deprive Harry of the twenty-four hours' lead time he so clearly needs.'

IT WAS A FEW MINUTES before six am when Harry Partridge, Minh Van Canh and Ken O'Hara took off from Teterboro Airport for Lima, Peru. Partridge and the other two had come directly from CBA News headquarters to the airport in a network car. During the busy night of composing and recording his co-anchor introductions, Partridge had managed to slip away for half an hour to his hotel and pack a bag.

221

On the right side of the passenger cabin two facing seats had been lowered to become a bed, with a mattress, sheets and blankets invitingly in place. By the time they were in the air, Partridge was nearly asleep.

Filling his mind, though, was Jessica. No matter what the odds against him, he would find her and bring her back. Somehow, he would save her.

PART FOUR   CHAPTER 13

The contrasts of Lima, Harry Partridge thought, were as stark and grimly apparent as the crises and conflicts, political and economic, which bitterly divided all of Peru. The immense, sprawling capital city displayed both opulent wealth and squalid poverty. Grandiose homes surrounded by manicured gardens adjoined hideous *barriadas,* or slums. Partridge had a sense of some form of insurrection ready to explode.

Partridge, Minh Van Canh and Ken O'Hara arrived in Peru's immense, sprawling capital city soon after one pm. They had been met at the airport by Fernández Pabur, CBA's regular stringer in Peru and—when required—the network's fixer. Fernández was about thirty-five, heavyset and energetic. He whisked them through customs and arranged a suite for Partridge in the elegant five-star Cesar's Hotel in Miraflores, with good rooms for the other two.

Before reaching Peru, Partridge had decided that the only course to follow was to act as a TV news correspondent normally would—meeting known contacts, seeking out new ones, searching for news, travelling where he could, questioning, questioning, and all the while hoping some clue would emerge as to where the captives might be held. After that, of course, would come the greater problem of how to rescue them.

Using the TV correspondent routine, first he visited Victor Velasco, the international manager of Entel Peru, the national telecommunications company with headquarters in downtown Lima. He made arrangements for Entel to be CBA's base for communication with New York, including satellite transmissions. When other US network crews arrived, they would use the same facilities. Partridge discreetly handed over to Velasco a thousand dollars for his trouble. Then he phoned Manuel Seminario from the hotel, asking the *Escena* magazine owner-editor to dinner.

It was now eight fifteen and they were sipping Pisco sours, the popular Peruvian cocktail, at La Pizzeria. Slightly built and dapper, with a neatly trimmed Vandyke beard, Seminario was wearing an elegant Brioni suit. He had with him a slim burgundy leather briefcase.

Partridge reported why he was in Peru. He added, 'I've been hearing that Sendero is increasingly active in Lima.'

'Exceedingly so,' Seminario agreed. 'Their people move around freely, and a recent bombing, which went wrong, was an exception. Most are successful.'

Partridge asked, 'Do you have any advice for me?'

'One thing you must realise is that Sendero Luminoso may already know of your presence here; their spies are everywhere. But even if not, they will learn of it shortly. So, you must have a bodyguard to accompany you, particularly if you go out at night.'

Partridge smiled. 'That seems to have happened already.' Fernández Pabur had insisted on collecting Partridge from the hotel and bringing him here, and he was armed. He waited outside while Harry had dinner.

Seminario asked, 'Are you carrying a gun yourself?'

Partridge shook his head.

'You must. Many of us do.'

When they had finished talking, most other diners were gone and the restaurant was preparing to close. Outside, Fernández was waiting. On the way back to the hotel Partridge asked him, 'Can you get me a gun?'

'Of course. Do you have a preference?'

Partridge considered. The nature of his work had made him knowledgable about guns and he had learned to use them. 'I'd like a nine-millimetre Browning; also a silencer.'

'You will have it tomorrow.'

FRIDAY WAS A DAY of action at CBA, New York.

At six am, on the programme 'Sunrise Journal', a CBA News trailer went out along with the commercials. The trailer was a recorded message spoken on camera by Harry Partridge: 'Tonight . . . on CBA's national evening news . . . an exclusive report of startling new developments in the kidnapping of the Crawford Sloane family. 'And at nine pm Eastern time a one-hour News Special—Network in Peril: The Sloane Kidnap.'

LES CHIPPINGHAM SAW the trailer while having an on-the-run breakfast in his Eighty-second Street apartment. The news president was in a hurry, knowing he must keep Margot Lloyd-Mason informed. He could see his CBA limo and driver already waiting outside. The limousine reminded him of Margot's instruction at their first meeting that he should use taxis instead, an order he had ignored. He must not ignore keeping Margot informed, however, and would call her as soon as he reached the office, since she was likely to have seen the trailer too.

The decision was unnecessary. In his limo, the driver handed him a phone. Margot's voice barked, 'What is all this about developments and why haven't I been told?'

'It happened suddenly. I intended to call you as soon as I got in.'

'John Q. Public has been told. Why should I have to wait?'

'Margot, the public has not been told; they will be, this evening. You, on the other hand, are going to be told as soon as I reach my desk.'

There was a pause, then, 'Do it as soon as you get in.'

Some fifteen minutes later, connected again with the network president and CEO, Chippingham began: 'First, from your point of view the outlook is excellent. We've achieved several exclusive breakthroughs which tonight may give CBA the largest news audience in our history, with matching ratings. Unfortunately, the news about the Sloane family is less than good for Crawf.'

'Where are they?'

'In Peru. Held by Sendero Luminoso.'

'*Peru!* Are you absolutely sure?' Her startled reaction surprised him.

'We've had some of our most experienced people on this, especially Harry Partridge, and what they've discovered is convincing. I've no doubt.'

She said sharply, 'I'd like to talk to Partridge.'

'I'm afraid that isn't possible. He's already in Peru. We expect an update from him for Monday's news.'

'Why are you moving so quickly?'

'This is the news business, Margot. We always work that way.' The question astonished him. So did the hint of nervousness in Margot's voice. It prompted him to say, 'You seem concerned about Peru. Why?'

There was a moment's hesitation before she answered. 'At the moment Globanic Industries has a substantial business arrangement there. A great deal is at stake, and it's essential that our alliance with the Peruvian government remains good.'

'May I point out that CBA News doesn't have an alliance with the Peruvian government—good or bad. We have to report the news the way it is. Also, as soon as our story breaks tonight, everyone else—networks, print press, you name it—will jump on the Peru story too.'

Margot said impatiently, 'CBA *is* Globanic. Globanic has an alliance with Peru; therefore so does CBA. Keep me informed,' she added. 'If there's any change, especially about Peru, I want to know immediately.'

Chippingham heard a click as the connection was severed.

IN HER ELEGANT OFFICE at Stonehenge, Margot Lloyd-Mason pondered. Should she call Theo Elliott, or not? She recalled the Globanic chairman's words about Peru at the Fordly Cay Club meeting: 'I don't want anything

224

to spoil what could evolve into the deal of the century.' In the end, she decided that she must inform him.

To her surprise, he reacted calmly. 'Well, if that Shining Path rabble did the kidnapping, I suppose there's no way it can *not* be reported. But let's not forget that the Peruvian government is in no way involved. Be sure your news people make that clear.'

'I'll see that they do,' Margot said.

'They can go even further,' Theo Elliott continued. 'Clearly the Peruvian government will do everything possible to find the kidnapped Americans—using Peru's military and police. So let's ensure they get proper credit, with upbeat pictures on our news.'

Margot hesitated. 'I'm not sure about going that far, Theo.'

'Then *be* sure!' The chairman's voice rose. 'We own the damn network, don't we? So once in a while let's put that ownership to our advantage. At the same time, remind your news people that this is a competitive, profit-orientated business that pays their fancy salaries, and they are a part of it, like it or not. If they don't like it they can get out!'

ON FRIDAY, WHEN THE NEWS broke on the National Evening News first feed at six thirty pm, it was immediately copied and repeated throughout the world, with CBA News acknowledged as the source. At other TV networks, testy inquests were soon held, asking how they had missed out on it. Meanwhile, TV networks hastily revised their second newscast feeds, using swiftly supplied videotape displaying 'Courtesy CBA'.

Amid the media rush, a major new development occurred.

Don Kettering, now heading the CBA kidnap task force, heard about it shortly before ten pm as the one-hour news special was nearing its conclusion. Kettering was still at the anchor desk when Norman Jaeger telephoned during a commercial break. Jaeger was now senior producer since Rita Abrams had left for her flight to Peru an hour ago.

'Don, there's to be a task force session after we've finished.'

'Has something happened, Norm? Something hot?'

'Hot as hell! Les says that over at Stonehenge they've received the kidnappers' demands along with a videotape of Jessica Sloane.'

IT WAS TEN THIRTY PM on Friday. In a private viewing room at CBA News ten people were assembled: Les Chippingham and Crawford Sloane; from the task force, Don Kettering, Norm Jaeger, Karl Owens and Iris Everly; from CBA corporate headquarters at Stonehenge, Margot Lloyd-Mason, Tom Nortandra—an executive vice-president—and Irwin Bracebridge, president of CBA Broadcast Group; and from the FBI, Special Agent Otis Havelock.

Earlier in the evening, a small plain package had been delivered by messenger to Stonehenge, addressed: President, CBA Network. After a routine security check it was sent to Margot Lloyd-Mason's floor where Nortandra, who happened to be working late, received the package and opened it. Realising its importance, he telephoned Margot at dinner.

Margot hurried to Stonehenge where she, Nortandra and Bracebridge, who had also been called in, screened the videotape and read an accompanying document. Immediately they arranged a meeting at CBA News headquarters.

Before the meeting, Bracebridge, a former news president himself, took Sloane aside. 'Crawf,' he told him, 'if you prefer to watch the video alone first, we'll understand.'

Sloane had driven in from Larchmont with FBI Agent Havelock. He shook his head. 'Thanks, but I'll see it with all of you.'

It was Don Kettering who called to an operator behind the small audience, 'OK, let's go!'

Lights in the viewing room dimmed. Almost at once a large, elevated TV screen went to black with scattered pinpoints of light, as was usual when running a blank tape without pictures. But sound was on the tape and was transmitted suddenly—a series of piercing screams. The group was transfixed. Sloane sat up straight, exclaiming in a broken voice, 'Oh, God! That's Nicky!'

As abruptly as it had begun, the screaming was cut off.

A moment later a picture appeared—of Jessica's head and shoulders against a plain background. Her face was set and serious, and to those in the group who knew her, she appeared wan and under strain. But her voice was firm and controlled.

She began, 'We have all been treated well and fairly. Now that the reason we were taken has been explained to us, we understand why it was necessary. We also have been told how easy it will be for our American friends to ensure our safe return home. To have us released, you must simply follow—quickly and exactly—the instructions which accompany this recording, but be sure of this . . . '

At the words 'sure of this', there was a sharp intake of breath by Sloane and a muted exclamation. The tape continued.

'. . . If you do not obey these instructions, you will not see any of us, ever again. We beg of you, do not let that happen . . . '

Again a sudden sound from Crawford Sloane—a whispered exclamation, *'There!'*

'We will be waiting, counting on you, desperately hoping you will make the right decision and bring us safely home.'

After Jessica concluded, there was a silence in which her face remained

227

on screen, her features expressionless. Then both sound and picture ended. In the viewing room the lights came on.

'About the screams at the beginning,' Irwin Bracebridge said. 'We think that was patched in from another tape.'

Les Chippingham asked gently, 'Are you certain that that first sound was Nicky, Crawf?'

Sloane said bleakly, 'Positive.' Then he added, 'Jessica gave two signals.'

'What kind of signals?' Chippingham sounded puzzled.

'The first was licking her lips, which means, "I am doing this against my will. Don't believe anything I'm saying."'

'Clever!' Bracebridge said. 'Good for Jessica!' Others nodded approval.

Sloane went on, 'We talked about signals the night before all this happened. I thought that one day I might need them myself. I guess Jessica remembered.'

'Mrs Sloane said something on the tape about instructions,' Iris Everly put in. 'Do we have them?'

Margot Lloyd-Mason answered by nodding to Nortandra. 'You'd better read them aloud.'

The executive vice-president moved under a light. 'The title of this document is, *The Shining Time Has Come.*

' "For Sendero Luminoso the time to advance along the Shining Path has come. We are ready to make ourselves better known and understood. For many years the lying capitalist-imperialist media have ignored or misrepresented the heroic struggle of Sendero Luminoso's people. That will now be changed. It is why capitalist captives have been taken and held as hostages.

'The American CBA television network is hereby ordered to do the following:

'One: Commencing with the second Monday after receipt of this demand, CBA National Evening News will be cancelled for five weekdays—one full week.

'Two: In its place another programme, to be delivered to CBA in five tape cassettes, will be broadcast. The programme's title is, "World Revolution: Sendero Luminoso Shows the Way."

'Three: Neither CBA nor any other agency will attempt to trace the source of the cassettes. Any such attempt will result in immediate execution of one of the three prisoners held in Peru.

'Four: If there is full obedience to these orders, the three prisoners will be released four days after the fifth broadcast. But if the orders are not obeyed, the prisoners will not be seen again." '

228

'There's something else,' Nortandra continued. 'Copies of the tape cassette of Mrs Sloane have been sent to other television networks and to the press.'

A silence followed. Several people glanced at Crawford Sloane, who was slumped in his chair, his face grimly set.

It was Les Chippingham who said finally, 'Well, now we know. All along we've wondered what these people wanted. We'll put out a bulletin at midnight, which gives us an hour to consider how to handle the news and, more important, what our response will be.'

'There is no way that we can accept those ridiculous terms,' Margot declared. 'We will certainly not put our network evening news out of business for one whole week.'

'However, we don't have to say that,' Nortandra pointed out. 'We can say something like, The demands are being carefully considered.'

'I doubt if that would deceive Sendero Luminoso,' Jaeger told him. 'Whatever else they may be, they aren't fools.'

'This calls for finesse, not a blunderbuss approach.'

'Finesse all you want,' Margot snapped, 'but what's involved here is a corporate matter requiring executive decision.'

'*No!* Dammit, no!' The words were shouted. Heads turned. The speaker was Crawford Sloane, no longer seated and dejected, but standing, eyes fiery. 'Keep corporate out of this! I *know* we can't close down CBA News for one week, Mrs Lloyd-Mason. What we *can* do, here at news, is use our skills, our know-how, to play for time. That, and use Harry Partridge, who's the best hope we have—*my* best hope to get my family home.'

Before anyone could react, Bracebridge tried a conciliatory tone. 'A time like this is hard on everyone.' He turned to the network president. 'Margot, I believe that what's been presented is worth considering, remembering that your end decision is understood and accepted.'

Margot hesitated. 'Very well,' she informed Chippingham, 'you may decide a temporary strategic response.'

CHAPTER 14

Throughout the weekend the news about Sendero Luminoso's demands and the videotape of Jessica Sloane stayed prominently in the news. Calls flooded in to CBA requesting some comment from the network. In every case the response was the same: CBA had no comment.

The absence of a CBA reaction, however, did not stop others from expressing opinions. A majority view seemed to be, Don't give in! A surprising number, though, saw no harm in meeting the demands as a price of the prisoners' release, prompting Norm Jaeger to comment in disgust, 'Can't those birdbrains see that by creating a precedent we'd invite every lunatic group in the world to kidnap television people?'

Within CBA, those who knew the story had promised Les Chippingham they'd keep secret the decision not to accept Sendero Luminoso's terms. They appeared to have kept their word. Unfortunately, the only one to break it was Margot Lloyd-Mason who, on Sunday, advised Theodore Elliott of everything that had transpired.

GLOBANIC INDUSTRIES' WORLD HEADQUARTERS occupied a mansion-style office complex some thirty miles outside Manhattan. It was there, at ten am on Monday, that Glen Dawson, a young reporter for the *Baltimore Star*, was waiting to interview Globanic's chief comptroller about palladium, a precious metal currently in the news. Globanic owned mines in Brazil, where labour riots were threatening supplies.

Dawson waited outside the comptroller's office in an inconspicuous corner of an elegant circular lounge. He was sitting there when a door opened and two figures emerged. One was Theodore Elliott, the other was Alden Rhodes, Under Secretary for Economic Affairs. Continuing a conversation begun inside, Rhodes was saying, 'Those threats from the Peru rebels put you in a difficult spot.'

The Globanic chairman nodded. 'In one way, yes. We've made a decision, though it hasn't been announced. What we're *not* going to do is let a bunch of crazy Commies push us around.'

'So CBA won't cancel their evening news?'

'Absolutely not! As for running those Shining Path tapes, not a hope in hell . . . ' The voices faded as they walked on.

Dawson quickly scribbled the exact words he had heard on a note pad, using a magazine as a cover. His pulse was racing. He knew he had exclusive information which countless journalists had been seeking unsuccessfully since Saturday night.

'Mr Dawson,' a receptionist called, 'you may go in now.'

The interview with Globanic's comptroller seemed endless to Dawson; what he had stumbled on seemed a ticket to a more exciting future. At length, pleading a deadline, he made his escape.

He could still make the paper's main afternoon edition.

GLEN DAWSON'S STORY, composed at his computer terminal back at the bureau's office, led the *Baltimore Star*'s main afternoon edition. The banner headline read: 'CBA Says No To Sloane Kidnappers'.

Even before the *Baltimore Star* hit the streets, the wire services had the story, giving credit to the *Star*. Later that evening the *Star* was quoted on

230

all network news broadcasts, including CBA's, where the news was received with near despair.

Next morning in Peru, the media featured the disclosure with special emphasis on Theodore Elliott's 'bunch of crazy Commies' description of Sendero Luminoso.

A RADIO REPORT of Theodore Elliott's rejection of the kidnappers' demands and his low opinion of Sendero Luminoso reached the jungle hamlet of Nueva Esperanza and the terrorist Ulises Rodríguez, alias Miguel. Soon after, a telephone conversation took place between Miguel and a Sendero leader in Ayacucho. They talked in veiled references, though to both men the meaning was understood.

This was that something must be done immediately to prove to the TV network, CBA, that they were dealing with neither fools nor weaklings. Killing one of the hostages was a possibility. Miguel, however, suggested another course of action which—remembering something he had learned while at Hackensack—he believed would be devastating psychologically to those in New York.

This was promptly agreed to, and Miguel began his preparations by sending for Socorro.

JESSICA, NICKY AND ANGUS looked up as a small procession filed into the shack. It consisted of Miguel, Socorro, Gustavo, Ramón and one of the guards. It was now six days since Jessica had made the videotape recording. Nicky's burn was sufficiently healed that he was no longer in pain. Jessica still felt guilty about his suffering, and was determined he would not be hurt again.

Consequently, when Nicky's cell was opened and the terrorists crowded in with him, Jessica cried anxiously, 'What are you doing? I beg of you don't hurt him! He's suffered enough!'

It was Socorro who swung round to face Jessica and shouted, 'Shut up! There's no way you can stop what's going to happen.'

Jessica screamed frantically, 'What *is* happening?' Miguel, she saw, had brought a small wooden table into Nicky's cell while Gustavo and the fourth man were holding Nicky so he couldn't move. Jessica cried again, 'For God's sake, let him go!'

Nicky, already frantic, screamed and struggled. On the other side of Nicky's cell, Angus was banging his screen and shouting.

While the boy continued to squirm, crying pitifully, Gustavo forced Nicky's right index finger on top of the table. Ramón produced a sheath knife, and with a single swift movement the finger was severed at the second joint. Then the men exposed the little finger of the boy's right hand

and, with another chop of Ramón's knife, that finger too was separated from the hand.

Jessica emitted a piercing wail. 'Oh, no! Not fingers! Please let me go to my son. Don't you understand? He plays the piano! It's his life—'

'I know.' Miguel smiled. 'I heard your husband say so on television. When he receives those fingers he'll wish he hadn't.'

Jessica covered her face with her hands, her body racked by sobbing.

By now, Nicky—barely conscious, his features ashen—had fallen back on the narrow bed with agonised moans. As Miguel, Ramón and the fourth man left the cell, taking the table with them, Socorro cleaned Nicky's hand to forestall infection. Then, after covering both wounds with several gauze pads, she securely bandaged the entire hand.

AS THE HOURS PASSED, and darkness advanced, the guard changed. Vicente came on duty and Socorro arrived. She was carrying the water bowl, more gauze pads, a bandage and a kerosene lamp, which she took into Nicky's cell. Gently she sat Nicky upright and began to change the dressing on his hand. Nicky seemed easier, in less pain.

After a while Jessica called out softly, 'Socorro, *please* . . .'

Immediately, Socorro signalled Jessica to be silent.

When the bandaging was done, Socorro left Nicky's cell but didn't lock it. Instead, she came and opened Jessica's, and waved her out. Then Socorro pointed to the open door of Nicky's.

'You must go back before daylight,' Socorro whispered. She nodded in the direction of Vicente. 'He will tell you when.'

Moments later, Jessica was holding Nicky. 'Oh, Mom!' he said. As best they could, they hugged each other. Soon after, Nicky fell asleep.

COMMUNICATION BETWEEN THE CBA Lima contingent and CBA New York was frequent now, with Partridge and Rita being filled in on stateside developments, while Harry continued the tactics he had begun.

At two pm on Tuesday in the task force conference room, Teddy Cooper took a phone call from an excited Jonathan Mony. 'I think we found it.'

'Found what, and where are you?'

'The place the kidnappers used, I'm almost sure. And I'm in Hackensack, New Jersey. There was an ad in the *Bergen Evening Record*—that's the local paper—that seemed to fit what we were looking for, and we followed through.'

One of the young women researchers had discovered the ad, for 'a large house with spacious outbuildings, in a secluded location'. On reading it, she had contacted Mony who now carried a CBA paging device. He had joined her at the newspaper's business office, then visited the property with her. An hour later a CBA car pulled into the Hackensack property, bringing Kettering, Jaeger, Cooper and a two-man camera crew. Mony introduced the young woman researcher, Cokie Vale, a petite redhead.

'The first thing you should see,' Mony told them, 'is on the second floor of the house.' He led the way into the dilapidated main house and up a stairway. Near the head of the stairs he opened a door and stood back while the others filed in.

The room was clean, painted white and with new floor covering. Overhead fluorescent lights two hospital cots, both with side rails and straps. Beside the cots was a narrow metal bed with straps attached.

Kettering said, 'The whole place looks like a first-aid station.'

Jaeger nodded. 'Or set up to handle three doped people, one of them unexpected.'

They moved to an outbuilding. Inside, it was obvious it had been a paint shop. Cans of green and yellow paint—some partially used—remained.

'This is the place,' Jaeger said. 'It has to be.'

Kettering nodded. 'I agree. So let's get to work. We'll use this on the news tonight.'

'There's one more thing,' Mony said.

Cokie Vale led the group to a cluster of trees away from the buildings and explained, 'Somebody's been digging here—not long ago.'

Among the group, eyes shifted back and forth. If something had been buried—what? Kettering said, 'I'd like to take a look.'

'There are some shovels in the furnace room,' Mony told him.

'Get them,' Kettering ordered. 'Let's start digging.'

A short time later it became evident that what they were opening was not a grave, but a repository of items left by the property's recent occupants. Some things were innocuous: clothing, toiletries, newspapers—but others were more significant: medical supplies, maps, tools.

Mony was down in the hole when his foot touched something solid. A moment later he pulled out an object and called, 'Hey, look at this!'

It was a cellular phone in a canvas outer cover. Passing it up to Cooper, Mony said, 'I think there's another underneath.'

Not only was there another, but four more after that. Soon the six were laid out, side by side.

They called the local police, asking them to inform the FBI.

EVEN BEFORE THE NATIONAL EVENING NEWS went on the air, Kettering had telephoned a friend high up in the New York and New Jersey telephone systems, about the cellular phones. Holding a list of numbers compiled by Cooper, Kettering requested the name and address of the person to whom the six telephones were registered, plus a list of all calls made to or from those numbers during the past two months.

'There isn't a lot,' his friend informed him. 'The registered name and address look like a fake. Not that we ever had to send a bill. Right after numbers were issued for those phones, someone made a deposit of three thousand dollars. Less than a third of the money was used and that's because, with one exception, all calls were solely between the six phones and not to other numbers.'

'But you said there was an exception.'

'Yes—on September thirteenth, a direct-dial call to Peru.'

'That's the day before the kidnap. Do you have a number?'

'Of course.'

Moments later, after consulting a notebook, Kettering made another call. When a voice answered, '*Buenas tardes,* Cesar's Hotel,' Kettering requested, 'Mr Partridge, *por favor.*'

HARRY PARTRIDGE, MINH VAN CANH and the sound man, Ken O'Hara, had been joined on Saturday by Rita Abrams and the videotape editor, Bob Watson. Their first combined report was transmitted by satellite from Lima on Monday and led CBA's National News that night.

Partridge's editorial theme had been the drastically deteriorating situation in Peru—economically and in terms of law and order. Sound bites from Manuel Seminario, owner-editor of *Escena,* made those points, supplemented by pictures of an angry mob from the slums, looting a food store and defying police. And Seminario had posed the unanswerable question: 'What is it in us Latin Americans that makes us chronically incapable of stable government?'

Now it was Tuesday night and, in bed after a discouraging day, Partridge was brooding on Peru. The whole country was a paradox—a conflicting mixture of military despotism and free democracy. He had come close to that subject today during an interview with Cesar Acevedo, a lay leader of the Catholic Church. They had met in a private office at the rear of the Archbishop's Palace on the Plaza de Armas, official centre of the city. 'I believe,' Partridge had asked, early in their meeting, 'that from time to time you have to deal with Sendero Luminoso?'

Acevedo smiled. ' "Have to deal" is correct. The Church does not, of course, approve of Sendero.'

The lay leader explained that Sendero Luminoso ordered priests and other church workers out of some areas when antigovernment action was intended, so they could not witness it. If the orders were disobeyed, Sendero would not hesitate to kill.

A sudden thought occurred to Partridge. 'Are there any places, right at this moment, where your people have been told to leave, where Sendero Luminoso doesn't want outside attention?'

'There is one such area. Come! I will show you on the map.' Mounted on a wall was a large map of Peru. Acevedo pointed to a section of San Martin Province, ringed in red. 'Until about three weeks ago we had a large medical team there, performing a vaccination programme. Then Sendero Luminoso, which controls the area, insisted that they leave.

Partridge studied the encircled section; it was depressingly large. He read place names: Tocache, Uchiza, Sion, Nueva Esperanza. Without much hope he wrote them down. Even if the captives were at one of those places, it would do no good to enter the area without knowing which.

Now, in his hotel room, he had a sense of frustration at his lack of progress. And time, he knew, was running out.

Abruptly, the bedside telephone rang.

'Harry?' Partridge recognised Don Kettering's voice. 'Some things have happened that you ought to know about.'

RITA, ALSO IN CESAR'S HOTEL, answered her room phone.

'I've just had a call from New York,' Partridge said. He repeated what Don Kettering had told him about the discovery of the Hackensack house and the cellular phones, adding, 'Don gave me a Lima number that was called. I want to find out whose it is and where.'

'Give it to me,' Rita said. 'I'll try to get that Entel guy, Victor Velasco, and start him working on it. Call you back if there's any news.'

It was not until Wednesday afternoon that the Lima telephone number was identified. 'It is, of course, restricted data,' Velasco explained to Partridge and Rita, who were in CBA's Entel editing booth, working on another news spot for New York.

'I had trouble persuading one of my colleagues to release the information,' Velasco continued, 'but eventually I did.' On a sheet torn from a memo pad were the words: *Calderón, G.*—547 Huancavelica Street, 10F.

'We need Fernández,' Partridge said.

'He's on his way here,' Rita informed him.

The swarthy, energetic stringer-fixer arrived within the next few minutes. Told about the Huancavelica Street address, Fernández nodded briskly. 'I know it. An old apartment building near Avenida Tacna.'

'I want to go there now,' Partridge told him. He turned to Rita. 'I'd like you, Minh and Ken to come along.'

Avenida Tacna was a wide, busy thoroughfare, and Huancavelica Street crossed it at right angles. Number 547 was a large, drab building with peeling paint and chipped masonry. A group of men, standing idly around, watched with unfriendly expressions as Fernández and Partridge stepped out of the station wagon Fernández had hired, leaving Rita, Minh Van Canh and Ken O'Hara to wait with the driver.

Inside the building a smell of dirt and general decay assaulted them. Apartment F was at the end of a gloomy corridor. At Partridge's knock, the door opened two or three inches, halted by an inside chain. Simultaneously a woman's high-pitched voice let loose a tirade in Spanish.

Fernández spoke in reasonable, soothing tones. As he continued the shouting stopped, then the chain was released and the door opened.

The woman standing before them was probably around sixty. Long ago she might have been beautiful, but time and hard living had made her blowsy and coarse, her skin blotchy, her hair unkempt. Her eyes were red and swollen from crying. Fernández walked in and the others followed.

Fernández talked briefly with the woman, then turned to Partridge. 'A few hours ago the man she lived with here was murdered.'

Partridge said in English, 'We are truly sorry to hear of your friend's death. Have you any idea who killed him?'

When Fernández had translated for her, the woman mouthed a stream of words ending with, 'Sendero Luminoso.'

It confirmed what Partridge had feared. The person they had hoped to see—whoever he was—had connections to Sendero, but was now beyond reach. He said to Fernández, 'Tell her I would be grateful if she would answer some questions. Offer her money, if necessary.'

Fernández repeated the request and translated the reply. 'She says yes, if she can. And, by the way, her name is Dolores.'

Partridge continued with Fernández translating. 'Your man friend who was killed—what kind of work did he do?'

'He was a doctor. He put people to sleep.'

'An anaesthetist?'

Dolores shook her head, not understanding. Then she went to a cupboard and produced a file containing papers. She passed them to Partridge and he saw that they were medical diplomas. The first declared that Hartley Harold Gossage, a graduate of Boston University Medical School, was entitled to practise medicine. The second diploma certified that he was a qualified specialist in anaesthetics.

Among the other papers was a letter on the stationery of the Massachusetts Board of Registration in Medicine. It began, 'You are hereby notified that your licence to practise medicine has been revoked for life.'

Partridge put the letter down. A picture was becoming clearer. The man who had lived here was a disbarred American anaesthetist who had some connection with Sendero Luminoso. The kidnap victims had been spirited out of the United States, presumably drugged or sedated at the time. It

236

seemed likely that the former doctor, Gossage, had done the sedating.

With Fernández's help he resumed the questioning of Dolores. 'Why do you believe that Sendero Luminoso murdered your doctor friend?'

'Because he worked for those *bastardos*. And he told me only yesterday he was afraid he knew too much.' A pause, then a recollection. 'Sendero had a name for him—Baudelio.'

'Was he away from Lima recently?'

A vigorous series of nods. 'For a long time. I missed him . . . he phoned me from America,' she added.

Everything was fitting together, Partridge thought. But there was one important question left. He was almost afraid to ask it. 'After Baudelio was in America and before returning here, was he somewhere in Peru?'

Dolores nodded affirmatively. 'Yes. Nueva Esperanza.'

Partridge could scarcely believe what so unexpectedly had come his way. His hands shook as he turned pages in his notebook—to the list of places that Sendero had ordered the Catholic medical teams out of. A name leaped out at him: *Nueva Esperanza*.

HE WAS STILL FIRST and foremost a TV news correspondent, Partridge reminded himself as he went downstairs to discuss with Rita, Minh and O'Hara the video shots they needed—of Dolores, the apartment and the building's exterior. Partridge wanted close-ups, too, of the medical diplomas and the letter striking Gossage/Baudelio off the medical register.

Even though Baudelio's role in the kidnapping was important to the full news story, Partridge knew that revealing it would be a mistake, alerting Sendero to the information his CBA group possessed exclusively. However, he wanted the Baudelio segment prepackaged, ready for use when the time came.

Now Partridge was free to move on to essentials—planning a rescue expedition to Nueva Esperanza as quickly as he could. At the thought of it, his excitement rose, the old addiction to danger stirring within him.

CHAPTER 15

On Thursday morning Crawford Sloane went to CBA News headquarters knowing nothing of the breakthrough in Lima the day before. He arrived slightly later than usual, at ten fifty-five; a young FBI agent named Ivan Ungar accompanied him. The FBI was still guarding against a possible attempt to kidnap him. Sloane took an elevator to the fourth floor and walked to his office adjoining the Horseshoe. He left the door of his office open. Ungar seated himself on a chair outside.

As Sloane hung up his raincoat, he noticed on his desk a white Styrofoam package of the kind used by takeaway restaurants. To his surprise, the package was neatly tied with white string and had 'C. Sloane' written on it. Without much interest, he snipped the string with scissors and eased the package open.

After staring at the contents in dazed disbelief, Crawford Sloane screamed—a tortured, earsplitting scream. Heads shot up among those working nearby. FBI agent Ungar leaped from his chair and raced in, drawing a gun. But Sloane was alone, staring down at the package, his eyes wide and crazed, his face ashen.

Agent Ungar examined the box, saw two human fingers and, swallowing his revulsion, swiftly took charge. He shouted to those crowding into the office, 'Everyone out, please!' Picking up a phone, he pressed the OPERATOR button and demanded, 'Security—fast!' When there was an answer, he rapped out, 'This is FBI Special Agent Ungar. Advise all guards that no one is to leave this building. After that, call the police for help.'

While Ungar was speaking, Sloane collapsed into his chair. The executive producer, Chuck Insen, elbowed his way in through the growing throng and asked, 'What's all this about?'

Recognising him, Ungar gestured to the white box, then instructed, 'Nothing in here must be touched. I suggest you take Mr Sloane somewhere else and lock the door until I come back.'

Insen nodded. He eased the anchorman from the room and took him to his own office, firing orders on the way. He told a secretary, 'Talk to the switchboard; there's a doctor on call—get him here.' To a producer, 'Get Don Kettering up here; we'll need something for the news tonight.'

Inside his office, Insen helped Sloane into a chair. Sloane was leaning forward, his head in his hands. Speaking half to himself, he agonised, 'Those people knew about Nicky playing the piano. And how did they know? *I let it out!* At that press conference after the kidnap.'

Insen said gently, 'I remember that, Crawf. But you were answering a question. In any case, who could have foreseen . . . ' He stopped, knowing that reasoning at this moment would do no good.

THE TEMPORARY BAN on people leaving the building was lifted when everyone inside was identified and their presence accounted for. It seemed likely that the package had been left much earlier, and no one had seen anything unusual.

In the midst of the general gloom another small package was delivered. This one found its way to Margot Lloyd-Mason's Stonehenge office suite early on Thursday afternoon. Inside was a videotape cassette sent by Sendero Luminoso. Margot sent it immediately to the CBA News president, Les Chippingham. He called in Don Kettering and Norman Jaeger, and the trio viewed the tape in Chippingham's office.

All three noted at once the recording's high quality, both technically and in presentation. The opening titles, beginning with *'World Revolution: Sendero Luminoso Shows the Way'*, were superimposed over some of Peru's most breathtaking scenery. The majestic music of Beethoven's Third Symphony, *Eroica,* accompanied the opening.

'They had production people who know their business,' Kettering murmured. 'I'd expected something cruder.'

The extremist message which followed was delivered over scenes of rioting in Lima, of industrial strikes, of the grisly aftermath of attacks on Andes villages by government forces. 'We are the world,' an unseen commentator expounded, 'and the world is ready for revolution.'

What followed was predictable. 'Revolution is justified because of imperialist exploitation of all poor people in the world. . . Sendero is more humane than the superpowers who are willing to destroy mankind with nuclear arsenals . . . '

'If we were running this instead of the evening news,' Chippingham commented, 'the ratings would be in the cellar.'

The tape ended with additional Beethoven, more scenic beauty and a rallying cry from the commentator, 'Long life to Marxism-Leninism-Maoism, our guiding doctrine!'

'All right,' Chippingham said at the end. 'Only the three of us have viewed this tape. I suggest we don't discuss it with anyone.'

The news president glanced at a clock: three fifty-three. 'At four o'clock, Don, break into the network with a bulletin. Say that we've received a tape from the kidnappers, but it's defective. Getting a replacement tape to us is now up to Sendero Luminoso.'

'Right!'

The misinformation issued by CBA News was circulated promptly and widely. Because Peru was one hour behind New York in time, the CBA statement was available in Lima for evening radio and TV news as well as the following day's newspapers.

Also in the day's news was a report of the discovery of Nicky's severed fingers by his distraught father.

In Ayacucho, Sendero leaders noted both reports. As to the second, about a damaged tape, they did not believe it. What was needed, they reasoned, was some more compelling action.

AFTERWARDS, JESSICA REMEMBERED, she had a sense of foreboding as soon as she woke that morning in the half-light of dawn. Over the past three days her earlier confidence that rescue would come had ebbed away, though she had tried to conceal it from Angus and Nicky.

Today was Friday. Yesterday Nicky had been in less pain, but he was silent and brooding, unresponsive to Jessica's attempts to lift him from his deep despair.

With the arrival of full daylight, Jessica heard activity outside and footsteps approaching the prisoners' shack. The first person to enter was Gustavo, leader of the guards, who went directly to Angus's cell and opened it.

Miguel was immediately behind. He was scowling as he, too, moved towards Angus, carrying something Jessica had not seen him with before—an automatic rifle. At the sight of the powerful weapon her heart beat faster. *Oh, no! Not Angus!*

Gustavo had roughly pulled the old man to his feet.

Jessica called out, 'Listen to me! What are you doing? Why?'

Angus turned his head towards her. 'Jessie dear, don't be distressed. There's nothing you can do. These people are barbarians. They don't understand decency or honour . . . ' He straightened his body and squared his shoulders. 'We haven't much time,' he added. 'Both of you—stay strong and keep believing! Remember, Crawford is doing everything he can. Help is coming!'

Tears were streaming down Jessica's face. Her voice choked, she managed to call, 'Dearest Angus! We love you so much!'

'I love you too, Jessie . . . Nicky!' Gustavo was pushing Angus forward, propelling him from the cell.

Then he was outside the shack, beyond their sight. Seconds passed, and the silence was broken by four shots.

OUTSIDE, AT THE EDGE of the jungle, Miguel stood over the dead body of Angus Sloane.

The four shots he fired had killed the old man instantly. Miguel had fulfilled the instructions received from Sendero Luminoso last night. Gustavo would now begin a distasteful chore which was expected of him. Soon a boat from Nueva Esperanza would leave for a nearby jungle airstrip, after which the aeroplane would transport to Lima the result of Gustavo's work.

LATER THAT SAME MORNING, a car skidded to a halt outside the American embassy in Lima. A man carrying a large cardboard box jumped out. He deposited the box outside the embassy's protective railings, then ran back to the car, which sped away.

A US Marine guard sounded an alarm, and a bomb disposal squad was summoned. When the box proved to contain no explosives, it was opened

240

carefully—revealing the severed head of an elderly man. Alongside the head were a wallet containing a US Social Security card, a Florida driver's licence, and other documents belonging to Angus Sloane.

THE PLAN TO ATTEMPT a rescue at Nueva Esperanza was complete. At dawn on Saturday, Partridge and his crew would fly from Lima.

But since learning the prisoners' location, Partridge had fretted impatiently. His first inclination had been to leave at once, but Fernández Pabur's arguments plus his own experience had persuaded him to delay.

'We need at least two days to prepare,' Fernández pointed out.

The 'we' made clear that the resourceful stringer-fixer intended to be part of the expedition. 'You will need me,' he stated simply. 'I have been in the Selva many times. The jungle can be a friend; it can also be an enemy. I know its ways.'

Air transport was their principal concern. On Thursday morning Fernández collected Partridge and Rita and took them to a one-storey office building not far from Lima's airport. They entered a small office, and Fernández introduced his companions to the owner of AeroLibertad, a charter flight service, and its chief pilot, Oswaldo Zileri.

Zileri was in his thirties, with a trim, athletic build. His attitude was businesslike and direct. He told Partridge, 'I understand you intend to pay a surprise visit to Nueva Esperanza. The plane you are chartering is a Cheyenne Two. There will be two pilots and room for seven passengers. How you fill those seven seats is your affair. Now, may we talk money?'

They agreed on a six-thousand-dollar cash deposit, then Zileri led them to a chart table where a large-scale map of San Martin Province was spread open. 'On the outward journey from Lima, I recommend landing here.' With a pencil Zileri indicated a point on the map.

'Isn't that a roadway?'

'Yes, but there is little traffic, often none. At several points like this one it's been widened and resurfaced by drug shippers so that planes can land. From that point a rough trail goes close to Nueva Esperanza.'

Fernández put in, 'I have a good map of the trail.'

'Now, about your return,' Zileri said. 'Fernández and I have discussed this and have a suggested plan.'

Two possible pick-up points existed for the return journey: first, the highway where the initial landing was intended, and second, Sion airstrip, which, after leaving Nueva Esperanza, could be reached by river, plus a three-mile overland journey. The reason for the two alternatives was, as Fernández explained, 'We do not know what will happen at Nueva Esperanza, or which way will be best for us to leave by.'

The plane making the pick-up could easily pass over both places and respond to a signal from the ground. Partridge's group would carry a flare gun with green and red flares. Green would mean, Land normally, everything is clear, red, Land as quickly as possible, we are in danger.

The discussion continued, salient facts emerging and decisions being made. Finally, looking at Partridge directly, the pilot said, 'We shall keep our part of the agreement and do our best for you.'

Back at the hotel, Partridge held a meeting with all the CBA group members to decide who would make the journey. Three definite selections were: Partridge; Minh Van Canh, since some visual record was essential; and Fernández. Allowing for three extra passengers returning, this left a fourth place open. In the end Partridge chose the sound man, Ken O'Hara. Rita would remain in Lima.

SINCE WEDNESDAY, when he had learned that Nueva Esperanza was the target, Partridge had asked himself: should he inform the Peruvian authorities, specifically the antiterrorism police? On Thursday he had even gone for advice to Sergio Hurtado, a radio broadcaster, who had warned him not to seek help from the armed forces and police.

Speaking in mutually agreed confidence, Partridge had informed Sergio of the latest developments and asked if his advice was still the same.

'Absolutely,' Sergio had answered. 'In exactly the kind of situation you are looking at, government forces are notorious for going in with maximum firepower. They wipe out everyone, innocent as well as guilty, and ask questions afterwards.'

Sergio had been fidgeting with a paper on his desk. Now he said, 'Before you came here, had you received any bad news?'

Partridge shook his head.

'Then I'm sorry to give you some, Harry.' Picking up the paper, Sergio passed it across. 'This just came in.'

'This' was a Reuters dispatch about the receipt of Nicholas Sloane's fingers at CBA, and his father's brokenhearted grief.

'Oh, God!' Partridge was overwhelmed by anguish. If only their planned action could have been undertaken sooner! He knew that regrets about his pace of progress would haunt him for a long time.

'Harry,' Sergio was saying, 'there's something else. Isn't your company, CBA, owned by Globanic Industries?'

'Yes, it is.'

The broadcaster slid open a desk drawer and removed several clipped sheets. 'I obtain my information from many sources and it may surprise you that one is Sendero Luminoso. They sent this recently, hoping I would broadcast it.'

Partridge accepted the sheets and began reading.

'As you can see,' Sergio said, 'it purports to be an agreement between Globanic Financial Services and the Peruvian government. Globanic will receive enormous amounts of land, including two major resort locations, for what can only be called a giveaway price. In return, some of Peru's international debt will be reduced. It's an exceedingly rich deal for Globanic, a poor one for Peruvians.'

Partridge waved the pages. 'Can I have a copy?'

'Keep that one. I have another.'

DURING THE NEXT DAY, Friday, the CBA group learned through Peru radio the tragic news of Angus Sloane's death. Partridge was quickly on the scene at the American embassy with Minh Van Canh, and sent a report via satellite for the National Evening News that evening. By that time, too, other network crews and print-press reporters had arrived.

Later, after doing what was needed, he went back to his hotel and spent the evening lying on his bed, awake, lonely and dejected.

Next morning he was up before dawn, his intention being to complete two tasks. One was to compose a simple, handwritten will; the other to draft a telegram. Soon after, on the way to the airport in the station wagon, he asked Rita to witness the will, and left it with her. He also asked her to send the telegram, which was addressed to Oakland, California.

They also discussed the Globanic-Peru agreement. Partridge told Rita, 'When you've read it, let Les Chippingham have this copy. But it has nothing to do with why we're here and I don't plan to use the information.' He smiled. 'I suppose that's the least we can do for Globanic since they butter our bread.'

THE CHEYENNE JI TOOK OFF from Lima in the still, predawn air without incident. Seventy minutes later the plane reached the jungle highway where Partridge, Minh, O'Hara and Fernández were to disembark.

By now there was ample light to see below. The highway was deserted. On either side, miles of jungle stretched like a vast green quilt. Turning briefly from the controls, Oswaldo Zileri called back, 'We're going in. Be ready to get out fast. I don't want to stay on the ground a second longer than necessary.'

Then, with a steep, fast-descending turn, he lined up over the highway, touched down, and stopped after a surprisingly short run. As quickly as they could, the four passengers tumbled out, taking backpacks and equipment. Moments later, the aircraft taxied into position and took off.

'Let's get under cover fast,' Partridge urged the others, and they headed for the jungle trail.

CHAPTER 16

Unknown to Harry Partridge during his crowded day on Friday, a crisis concerning him had erupted in New York.

While breakfasting at home that morning, Margot Lloyd-Mason received a telephone message that Theodore Elliott wished to see her 'immediately' at Globanic's main headquarters. She had no idea why.

When she entered the chairman's office, Elliott demanded, 'Why the hell aren't you keeping better control of your news people in Peru? Last night I received a call from President Castañeda in Lima. He claims everything CBA has been putting out about Peru is negative and damaging. He's mad as hell with your network, and so am I!'

They were both standing. Elliott, glowering, had not asked her to sit down. She asked, 'Is there anything specific, Theo?'

'You're damn right there is!' The Globanic chairman pointed to half a dozen video cassettes on his desk. 'I sent for the tapes of your evening news programmes for this week. They're full of doom and gloom. Nothing saying Peru has a great future ahead, or that it's a wonderful place to go for a vacation, or that those lousy Shining Path rebels will be beaten very soon! I warned you about this, but you obviously weren't listening.'

'Perhaps we can do something to improve what's happening.' Margot was thinking quickly, realising her future in Globanic could be at stake.

'I'll tell you *exactly* what you'll do.' Elliott's voice had become steely. 'I want that meddling reporter—Partridge is his name—brought back on the next plane and fired. I want him out of CBA so that I can call the president of Peru and say, "Look! We threw the troublemaker out. We're sorry we sent him to your country." '

Margot said, 'Theo, I have to point out that Partridge has been with the network a long time and has a good record.'

Elliott permitted himself a sly smile. 'Then give him a gold watch. Just get rid of him, so I can make that phone call on Monday. And Margot?'

'Yes, Theo?'

'Don't think that I'm not aware how you're hoping one day to sit where I am now.' The chairman waved a hand. 'That's all. Call me later today, when the Peru thing is wrapped up.'

IT WAS LATE MORNING when Margot, back in her office at Stonehenge, sent for Leslie Chippingham.

When he appeared, she came speedily to the point. 'I'm giving you an order. The employment of Harry Partridge is to be terminated at once. I want him out of CBA by tomorrow. I'm aware he has a contract, and

244

you'll do whatever we have to under it. Also, he's to be out of Peru, preferably tomorrow, but no later than Sunday.'

Chippingham stared at her. 'You can't be serious!'

Margot told him firmly, 'I *am* serious.'

'The hell with that!' Chippingham's voice was emotional. 'I'm not standing by and seeing one of our best correspondents, who's served CBA well for twenty-odd years, thrown out for no reason. What's Harry done?'

'If you must know, it's a question of his type of coverage.'

'Which is the absolute best! Ask anybody!'

'I don't need to. In any case, not everyone agrees with you.'

Chippingham regarded her suspiciously. 'This is Globanic, isn't it?'

'Be careful!' she warned him. 'I don't plan to do any more explaining, but if my order has not been carried out by the end of the day, I'll appoint someone else acting news president and have them do it.'

He looked at her with a mixture of wonder and hatred.

'But if you decide to stay employed,' Margot went on coldly, 'report to me this afternoon that what I wanted has been done.'

BACK AT CBA NEWS HEADQUARTERS, Chippingham instructed his secretary that he was not to be disturbed. He needed time to think.

He knew he had reached a crisis. If he did as Margot ordered and fired Harry Partridge, he would forfeit his self-respect. He would have done something shameful and unjust to a decent, highly skilled and respected human being, a friend and colleague, merely to satisfy Theodore Elliott's whim. On the other hand, if he didn't do it, someone else would. And Margot would have no trouble finding someone. There were too many ambitious people around CBA News.

So Partridge was going down the drain anyway—at least at CBA. But when word got round that Harry was leaving CBA and was available, he need not be unemployed for fifteen minutes. Other networks would fall over themselves vying for him. But what about a fired and fallen news president? That was a totally different story. Chippingham knew he would not be sought out by other networks. They wanted news presidents who were successes, not someone dismissed in doubtful circumstances.

The prospect was daunting. Unless he did what Margot wanted.

Fifteen minutes later, Chippingham read over a letter which he had typed himself and intended to fax to Lima. It began:

Dear Harry,

It is with great regret that I have to inform you that your employment by CBA News is terminated, effective immediately.

Under the terms of your contract with CBA . . .

About to sign it, Chippingham heard a knock at his office door. Instinctively, he turned the letter face down.

Crawford Sloane entered, holding a press wire print-out. When he spoke, his voice was choked. 'Les,' he said, 'I had to see you. This just came in.'

Chippingham read the print-out. Reuters reported from Lima the tragic death of Angus Sloane.

'Oh, God! Crawf, I'm . . . ' Unable to finish the words, Chippingham shook his head.

Sloane said, 'I can't do the news tonight. I told them outside to—'

'Forget everything, Crawf. We'll take care of it.'

'No! There's something I must do. I want to go to Lima. While there's still a chance for Jessica and Nicky. I must be there.'

Chippingham said doubtfully, 'Are you sure, Crawf ?'

'I'm going, Les,' Sloane said. 'Don't try to stop me. If CBA won't pay for the trip, I will.'

'That won't be necessary,' Chippingham said.

IT WAS LATE THAT AFTERNOON before Chippingham's letter to Partridge was signed and faxed to Entel Peru in Lima, where it would be delivered to the CBA booth in the same building. Chippingham added a note asking for the letter to be placed in an envelope addressed to Mr Harry Partridge and marked 'Personal'.

At six fifteen pm, Chippingham telephoned Margot Lloyd-Mason, who was still in her office. He told her, 'I have done what you asked,' then gave her the news about Sloane's father.

'I heard,' she said, 'and I'm sorry. About the other, you cut it fine and I was beginning to think you wouldn't call. But thank you.'

AWAY FROM THE HIGHWAY where the Cheyenne II had landed, the trek through the jungle was difficult and slow.

The trail—if it could be called that—was often overgrown and frequently disappeared entirely. Partridge and the other three men had to hack a way through dense vegetation, using machetes. Tall trees formed a canopy above their heads under an overcast sky which hinted of rain to come. At lower levels, bamboos, ferns, lianas and parasitic plants were everywhere intertwined.

Fernández's large-scale contour map showed several hills near Nueva Esperanza, one of which might serve as an observation post. From there, hidden by the jungle, they could observe the hamlet. Nueva Esperanza itself was about nine miles from their present position—a formidable distance under these conditions.

One thing that encouraged Partridge was the second message Jessica had conveyed during her videotape recording, as reported by Sloane. Jessica had scratched her left ear lobe to mean: Security here is sometimes lax. An attack from outside might succeed. Soon that information would be put to the test.

It was well into the steamy afternoon when Fernández warned them that Nueva Esperanza might be near. 'We must not be seen,' he said. 'If we hear anyone coming, we must melt into the jungle quickly.'

Soon after that, the going became easier and several other trails crisscrossed their own. After another hour they entered a clearing and, beyond it, could see a shack amid jungle trees.

Fernández inspected the clearing, including the hut, satisfying himself that no one was there. Then he led the others a little way into the jungle again. Halting, he parted a cluster of ferns and motioned them to look. About half a mile away and two hundred feet below were two dozen or so shacks located on a riverbank. A muddy path led from the buildings to a rough wooden jetty where a motley collection of boats was moored.

Partridge said softly, 'I guess we found Nueva Esperanza.'

The sun was already near the horizon, the journey having taken far longer than expected. 'I want to observe as much as possible before dark,' Partridge told the others. 'Minh, bring the other binoculars and join me forward. Fernández and Ken, pick a sentry post and make sure we're not approached from behind.'

Partridge dropped to his belly and wriggled forward, carrying the binoculars he had brought. Minh, beside him, did the same. Moving the binoculars slowly, they studied the scene below.

At the jetty, two men were working on a boat. A woman left one shack, emptied a pail of slops behind it, and returned inside. Garbage littered the area. Viewed overall, Nueva Esperanza appeared to be a jungle slum.

Partridge began studying the buildings individually. Presumably the prisoners were being held in one of them. A full day's observation would be needed and there could be no question of a rescue attempt tonight and departure by air tomorrow morning. He settled down to wait and watch.

As always in the tropics, darkness fell quickly. In the houses a few dim lights had come on. Partridge lowered his binoculars after more than an hour of concentration.

At that moment Minh touched his arm, gesturing towards the huts. Partridge picked up his binoculars and peered again. At once he saw movement in the now dim light—a man walking down the path between two groups of houses. Unlike the others they had seen, this man had a rifle slung over his shoulder.

The man reached a single shack and disappeared inside. For a few minutes nothing happened. Then, from the same shack, a different man emerged and walked away. He, too, was carrying a gun.

Could it be, Partridge wondered excitedly, a changing of the prisoners' guard? And could that shack hold Jessica and Nicky Sloane?

AT PARTRIDGE'S REQUEST, Minh stayed another hour alone at the observation point and later Ken O'Hara relieved him.

'Everyone get as much rest as you can,' Partridge ordered. Earlier, Fernández had rigged hammocks with mosquito netting inside the hut they had found on arrival. 'But we should man the observation point and the sentry post in the clearing all the time,' he went on. 'Which means only two people can sleep at once.' After discussion it was decided they would work two-hour shifts.

Their routine continued the next day. During this time, at the sentry post there had been no alarms. The observation point, however, had produced specific information. There *was* a regular change of an armed person suggesting that prisoners were indeed housed in that building. But the casualness of the changeover, Partridge believed, confirmed the message conveyed by Jessica: Security here is sometimes lax.

Since morning, what appeared to be food in containers had been delivered twice by a woman entering the building. All comings and goings were by boat: no road vehicle was seen. The people being observed were relaxed and did not seem to expect any aggressive incursion from outside.

At dusk, Partridge called the others together and told them, 'We've watched long enough. We go down tonight.'

He told Fernández, 'You'll guide us from here. I want to arrive at that hut at two am. Everyone must be silent all the way.'

Minh asked, 'Is there an order of battle, Harry?'

'I'll enter first,' Partridge answered. 'I'd like you right behind me, Minh, covering my back. Fernández will hang behind, watch the other houses for anyone appearing, but join us if we need help.' He turned to O'Hara. 'Ken, you'll go directly to the jetty. I've decided we'll leave by boat. Jessica and Nicholas may not be up to the journey we had coming here.'

O'Hara said, 'I assume you want me to grab a boat.'

'Yes, and disable some of the others, but no noise!'

A mixture of excitement and apprehension gripped them all.

And for Harry, beyond all other thoughts, was Jessica. Jessica, who was now close at hand, somewhere inside that hut.

BACK IN LIMA on Saturday morning, after watching the Cheyenne II depart, Rita Abrams had twice been taken by surprise.

First a message awaiting her at CBA's Entel Peru booth announced that Crawford Sloane would be in Lima by early morning. She promptly called Cesar's Hotel, where he would be staying, and left a request that he phone. Second, and even more surprising, was the faxed letter from Les Chippingham, sent the previous evening to Harry Partridge. The instruction to place the letter in an envelope marked 'Personal' had clearly not been noticed and it arrived open so that anyone could read it. Rita did, and was incredulous.

Harry had been fired, dismissed by CBA! The more Rita thought about it, the more outrageous it seemed, especially now. She was furious with Chippingham. Meanwhile, there was no way she could tell Partridge, since he was already on his way to Nueva Esperanza.

SLOANE DIDN'T TELEPHONE. After arriving at the hotel and receiving Rita's message, he took a taxi immediately to Entel. His first question to Rita was, 'Where's Harry?'

'In the jungle,' she answered. She took in the extra lines of strain on his face, the anguish in his eyes. Swallowing hard, she described the expedition to Nueva Esperanza, explaining what Harry and the others were trying to do. At length she said, 'Let's go have breakfast. There's a cafeteria in the building.'

Over coffee and croissants, Rita said gently, 'Crawf, we were all shocked and saddened by the news about your father. Harry blamed himself for not moving faster, but we didn't have—'

Sloane stopped her with a gesture. 'Harry's my friend. I'll never blame him for anything—whatever happens. No one could have done more.'

'I agree,' Rita said, 'which is what makes this so unbelievable.' She produced Les Chippingham's faxed letter.

Sloane took the letter, read it twice, then shook his head. 'This is a mistake. It has to be.'

'This is no mistake, Crawf. There must be something behind it. Yesterday at CBA—did anything happen out of the ordinary?'

Sloane considered. 'Well, Les was at Stonehenge.'

A sudden thought struck Rita. 'Could it have been something to do with this?' Opening her bag, she took out the clipped sheets of paper Partridge had given her that morning.

Sloane took the sheets and read them. 'Interesting! A huge debt-to-equity swap between Globanic and the Peruvian government. Really big money! Where did you get this?'

'From Harry.' She explained how Partridge had received the document from a radio commentator, Sergio Hurtado. Rita added, 'Harry didn't plan to use the story. Said it was the least we could do for Globanic which puts butter on our bread.'

'There *could* be a link between this and Harry's firing,' Sloane said thoughtfully. 'I see a possibility.'

'What are you thinking of ?' Rita asked.

'Calling Margot Lloyd-Mason. Let's go upstairs.'

At the CBA Entel Peru booth, he picked up the phone and tapped out the US overseas code and the number of Stonehenge.

An operator told him, 'Mrs Lloyd-Mason is not in her office today.'

'This is Crawford Sloane. Will you give me her home number, please?' He wrote it down as she read it out.

This time, the phone was answered by a male voice that sounded like a butler. Sloane identified himself and asked for Mrs Lloyd-Mason.

He waited several minutes, then Margot's voice said, 'Yes?'

'This is Crawf. I'm calling from Lima.'

'So I was told, Mr Sloane. I'm curious to know why you are calling me at home.'

'Thank you.'

Unusually for someone of his standing, Sloane had never been on a first-name basis with the CBA president, and clearly she intended to keep it that way. He guessed from her tone that he would get nowhere with direct questions. He decided to try a timeworn journalist's trick.

'Mrs Lloyd-Mason, yesterday when you decided that you would fire Harry Partridge, I wonder if you realised how much he's accomplished in the effort to find and free my wife, son and father?'

The reply was explosive. 'Who told you it was my decision?'

He was tempted to answer, You just did! But restraining himself, he said, 'In the TV news business, almost nothing is secret.'

Margot snapped, 'I do not wish to discuss this now.'

'That's a pity,' Sloane said, 'since I thought we might talk about the connection between Harry's firing and that big debt-to-equity swap Globanic is arranging with Peru. Did Harry's honest reporting offend someone with a stake in that deal?'

At the other end of the line there was a long silence. Then, her voice subdued, Margot asked, 'Where did you hear that?'

'Well,' Sloane said, 'the fact is, Harry Partridge learned about it. He's a first-class reporter, you know, one of the best in our business. Anyway, Harry decided not to use the information. His words were, "That's the least I can do for Globanic, which puts butter on our bread." '

Margot didn't respond. He asked, 'Are you wishing, by chance, that you hadn't done what you did to Harry Partridge?'

'No.' The answer seemed disembodied, as if Margot's mind was far away. 'No, I was thinking of other things.'

'Mrs Lloyd-Mason'—Sloane employed the cutting tone he adopted

250

occasionally for repulsive items in the news—'has anyone told you lately that you're a cold-hearted bitch?'

He put down the receiver.

THE AEROLIBERTAD OWNER and pilot, Oswaldo Zileri, had heard of Crawford Sloane and was appropriately respectful. 'I wish you and your friends well, Mr Sloane.'

'Thank you,' Sloane said. He and Rita were in Zileri's modest office near Lima's airport.

'I have heard the sad news about your father.' The pilot shook his head. 'Are you wondering if there might be room for you and Miss Abrams to go on the trip to bring the people back?'

'Yes.'

'It will be OK. You must be here before dawn tomorrow—and the next day, if we go.'

'We will be,' Rita said. She turned to Sloane. 'Harry wasn't optimistic about making a rendezvous the first day after going in. The flight is a precaution, in case they need it.'

CHAPTER 17

It was two ten am in Nueva Esperanza. Jessica had been drifting in and out of sleep, dreaming at times—the dreams becoming nightmares and merging with reality.

Moments earlier, certain she was awake, Jessica had peered through the roughly cut opening facing her cell, and what she thought she saw in the dim light was the face of Harry Partridge. Then the face disappeared. Was she still dreaming?

The face appeared again, rising slowly above the window level, and this time it stayed. *Could it be?* Her heart leaped as she decided: *Yes, it was!*

The face was mouthing something silently. She managed to grasp the words, 'The guard.' Where was the guard?

Vicente had come on duty an hour ago—apparently drunk. Jessica could see him now. He was seated in the guards' chair out of sight of the window. His eyes seemed closed; his automatic rifle was propped against the wall alongside him. Nearby a kerosene lamp hung from a beam.

Carefully Jessica answered Harry by inclining her head towards where Vicente was seated. At once Harry began to form words again. Once more, she understood the message: 'Call him!'

Jessica nodded slightly. Her heart was pounding. It could only mean that the rescue they had hoped for was finally happening.

'Vicente!' she called, then tried again. 'Vicente!'

He stirred; his eyes opened and met Jessica's.

She beckoned him. Vicente stood, started to come towards her, then quickly turned back to collect his rifle. He held it in a businesslike way, she noticed, clearly ready to use it if required.

CROUCHED LOW BENEATH THE WINDOW, Partridge gripped his nine-millimetre Browning pistol, the silencer extending from the barrel. So far tonight everything had gone as planned, but he knew the most crucial part of the action was about to begin.

One thing was working in his favour: Jessica was resourceful, quick to think and understand—exactly as he remembered her.

He listened to her call twice, heard noises from somewhere out of sight, then footsteps as the guard walked over. Now the man faced Jessica. Harry recognised that he was carrying a Kalashnikov automatic rifle. Compared with the Kalashnikov, his own Browning was a peashooter.

The conclusion was inescapable: he would have to get his shot in first, and kill the guard. But there was an obstacle. Jessica was exactly in line with the guard. A shot aimed at him could hit her too.

Partridge *had* to gamble. There was no other choice. Taking a breath, he called out loudly, clearly, 'Jessica, drop to the floor—*now!*'

Instantly the guard spun round, his rifle raised. But Partridge already had the Browning sighted; he squeezed the trigger and fired with a near-silent *pfft*. For an instant the man looked surprised, then fell.

Partridge turned towards the outside doorway, but a swiftly moving shadow was ahead of him. It was Minh Van Canh, who now came forward, his own UZI at the ready. Minh went swiftly to the guard, then confirmed with a nod that the man was dead. Next, Minh moved to Jessica's cell, inspected the padlock and asked, 'Where is the key?'

Jessica was scrambling to her feet. She told him, 'Over where the guard was sitting. Nicky's too.'

In the adjoining cell, Nicky stirred from sleep. He took in the new arrivals—Partridge, approaching and holding the Kalashnikov rifle he had just picked up, and Minh, collecting keys which were hanging from a nail. 'Who are they, Mom?'

'Friends, dear. Very good friends.'

Nicky, still sleepy, brightened. Then, with a flash of recognition, he said, 'You're Mr Partridge.'

Jessica said emotionally, 'Oh, bless you, Harry! Dear Harry!'

Speaking softly, Partridge cautioned, 'We're not out of this yet, and we've a way to go. We all have to move quickly.'

Minh had returned with the keys and was trying them one by one in the padlock of Jessica's cell. Suddenly the lock opened, and Jessica walked out. Within seconds Nicky was free too.

'Help me!' Partridge told Minh. Together they dragged the body of the guard to Nicky's cell and lifted it onto the low wooden bed. Partridge lowered the light in the kerosene lamp so it was merely a glimmer.

'Let's go,' he said.

In his free hand he kept the Kalashnikov. He had also pocketed two spare magazines he found on the guard's body.

Minh was ahead of them at the doorway. He had retrieved his camera from outside and, using a special night lens, was recording their departure with the cells as background. He would have passable pictures, even in this dimmest of lights. At that moment Fernández burst in. 'Coming here—a woman! By herself. I think she's armed.'

Everyone froze where they were. Jessica was to one side of the doorway. Minh faced the opening directly; the others were further back, in shadow. Partridge had the Kalashnikov raised.

Socorro walked in briskly. She was holding a Smith and Wesson revolver, and in the almost nonexistent light at first mistook Minh, who was closest, for the guard. Then, startled, she realised her mistake and, glancing left, saw Jessica. Instantly, she raised her revolver.

Jessica saw the move coming and immediately remembered the close-quarters battle moves from her self-defence classes. With lightning speed, she leaped at Socorro, bracing her left arm and thrusting it forcefully up inside the other woman's right. Socorro's arm flew up and the gun dropped. The entire manoeuvre took barely a second.

Without a pause Jessica thrust two fingers hard under Socorro's chin, impeding her breathing. Simultaneously she placed a leg behind Socorro and pushed, throwing her off-balance. Jessica then turned her and placed her in a tight stranglehold. The next step would be to break her neck.

Gasping, Socorro pleaded in a whisper, 'Let me go . . . I will help you . . go with you to escape . . . I know the way.'

Partridge had come close enough to hear. 'Can you trust her?'

Jessica hesitated, in a moment of compassion. Socorro had disobeyed Miguel's orders, allowing Jessica to join Nicky in his cell. But it was also Socorro who had benn so callous when Nicky's fingers were being cut off.

Shaking her head, Jessica told Partridge, 'No!'

Their eyes met. Harry nodded briefly, and turned away.

Shuddering, Jessica tightened her grip. There was a snapping sound, and the body she was holding slumped. She let it fall.

Encountering no one, the group moved through the darkened hamlet. Fernández, who had been watching the other buildings, eventually caught up with them.

253

At the jetty O'Hara showed them an open wooden workboat about thirty foot long, with twin outboard motors. Two lines secured it.

'Everybody aboard!' Partridge ordered.

Fernández helped Jessica and Nicky into the boat. Minh jumped in last as O'Hara, casting off, used an oar to push out from shore. Fernández grabbed a second oar. Together he and O'Hara rowed towards midstream, and Nueva Esperanza began to fade in the moonlight.

When Partridge considered that the boat was well out of earshot, he told Ken O'Hara to start the engines. They fired immediately, and the boat surged forward. Bright moonlight, reflected on the water, made navigation relatively easy along the river's winding course.

'We aim for the Sion airstrip,' Partridge told the others. 'When we leave the river, we'll have to push hard and fast through the jungle, so get whatever rest you can.'

AS TIME PASSED, Jessica became more composed; her involuntary shaking ceased. She knew she would never have peace of mind about what she had done. But Nicky was safe—at least for the moment—and that was what mattered most. She had been watching him, aware that ever since they left the prison shack he had stayed close to Harry. Now he had settled beside him in the boat; Harry had put his arm round Nicky's shoulders, and the two at this moment seemed as one.

Jessica liked that. She had once loved Harry, in a way she still did, especially now when gratitude and love mingled. It was not strange at all that her son instinctively shared that feeling.

Partridge, too, had been thinking of the past—what he and Jessica had once meant to each other. And even in this short time he could see that all the things he'd most admired—her quick mind, strong spirit, warmth, resourcefulness—were still in place. He asked her now, 'Back there, did you ever give up hope?'

'There were times when I came close to it, but never entirely,' Jessica said. She smiled. 'Of course, if I'd known you were in charge of the rescue, that would have made a difference.'

'We were a team,' he told her. 'Crawf was part of it. He's gone through hell, but then so have you. When we get back, you'll need each other.'

He sensed she knew what he was also saying: though he had returned briefly to her life, he would shortly disappear from it again.

'That's a sweet thought, Harry. And what will you do?'

He shrugged. 'Go on reporting. There'll be other wars.'

'And in between wars?'

To some questions there were no answers. He changed the subject. 'Your Nicky's fine—the kind of boy I'd like to have had.'

254

It could have happened, Jessica thought. For both of us, all those years ago. Then she reached out and put her hand on his.

'Thank you, Harry,' she said. 'Thank you for everything—the past, the present . . . my dearest love.'

MIGUEL FIRED THREE SHOTS into the air, shattering the silence. He knew it was the quickest way to sound an alarm.

It was three fifteen am, precisely forty minutes since the boat containing Partridge and the others had left the jetty.

Barely a minute ago he had discovered Vicente's and Socorro's bodies and realised the prisoners were gone. His anger was savage and explosive. He wanted to bludgeon those responsible for the escape, but he was painfully aware that he deserved a share of the blame. He had never taken seriously the possibility of a rescue attempt; Nueva Esperanza, so deep in Sendero territory, had seemed remote and safe. Miguel thought bitterly that when Sendero Luminoso got word of this, he would pay with his life. His priority was to recapture the prisoners—at any cost!

Now, alerted by his shots, the other guards were running towards him with Gustavo in the lead,.

'You useless morons!' he raged at them. ' Strangers came here while you slept and you ignored them! Find out how they left. There must be traces!'

Gustavo was back within moments. 'They left by the river!'

Miguel hurried to the jetty. He told Gustavo, 'I want the two best boats, with two motors on each. Use everybody! Work fast, fast, fast! Then I want everyone on the dock, with guns and ammunition.'

He decided that whoever engineered the prisoners' release almost certainly came by air. Therefore they would leave the same way. Miguel instructed one armed boatload to go to the nearer jungle strip, a second to Sion. He decided to go with the Sion-destined boat.

A few minutes before four am, both boats were under way. Miguel's boat was substantially faster and pulled ahead soon after leaving the jetty. Gustavo was at the helm.

CHAPTER 18

The Cheyenne II lifted off from Lima Airport at dawn.

Rita was beside Sloane in the aircraft's second row of seats. Ahead of them were the pilot, Oswaldo Zileri, and a young copilot, Felipe Guerra.

Yesterday, Sunday, they had flown over the prearranged points but without result. Sloane had had difficulty distinguishing one from another, so impenetrable did the Selva seem when viewed from above. 'It's like parts of Vietnam,' he told Rita, 'but more tightly knit.'

Today, as dawn changed to daylight, the Cheyenne II began a slow descent towards the Selva and the Upper Huallaga Valley.

PARTRIDGE KNEW he had miscalculated. They were late.

What he had not allowed for in choosing Sion was a problem with their boat, which happened about two hours after leaving Nueva Esperanza. Both outboard motors had been running smoothly when a strident horn abruptly sounded on the port-side motor. Ken O'Hara stopped the engine; as he did, the horn went silent. With the starboard engine alone operating, the boat was moving at a seriously slower speed.

O'Hara examined the engine. 'It's overheated; almost certainly the coolant pump has gone. Even if I had tools . . . ' He let the words trail off.

'Run it,' Partridge said. 'Let's get the most out of it.'

The engine ran for a few minutes, then stopped and would not start again. With the boat's speed reduced by half, the remainder of their river journey, instead of taking an hour, would take two.

In fact, it took two and a quarter hours, and now, shortly before seven am, their landing point was in sight. They would have to cover in an hour the three miles of jungle trail to the Sion airstrip.

'We have to do it,' Partridge said, explaining their problem to Jessica and Nicky. 'It may be exhausting, but there's no time to rest. Fernández will lead. I'll be in the rear.'

Minutes later the keel scraped on a sandy beach and they walked ashore through shallow water. They were about to enter an opening in the jungle wall when Fernández halted, motioning everyone to silence. Cocking his head to one side, he asked Partridge softly, 'Do you hear?'

Partridge thought he could hear a distant murmuring sound.

'Another boat,' Fernández said. 'From the direction we've just come. Still a good distance away, but coming fast.'

Without further delay they moved into the jungle. The trail was not as difficult as the one the rescue team had traversed two days earlier, because it was only slightly overgrown. Just the same, it was treacherous underfoot. Fernández set a fast forced pace.

Partridge wondered how long Jessica and Nicky would last under this gruelling pressure. After a while he decided Jessica would make it; she had the determination and stamina. Nicky, though, showed signs of flagging.

Partridge insisted that the boy and Jessica be up forward, immediately behind Fernández. Assuming the boat they had heard was carrying their pursuers, any assault would come from behind. If that happened, Harry would do his best to fight off the attack while the others carried on. He had already checked his rifle and had the two spare magazines handy.

257

Partridge looked at his watch: seven thirty-five. Remembering the eight o'clock rendezvous with AeroLibertad, he hoped they had covered three-quarters of the way.

Moments later they were forced to stop. Fernández had fallen, his foot trapped in a muddy mess of roots. As Partridge hurried towards him, the man grimaced with pain.

'I appear to have done some damage,' he gasped. 'I am sorry.'

When the foot was free, Fernández was unable to walk without excruciating pain. His ankle was broken, or badly sprained.

'We'll make a litter and carry you,' Partridge said.

Fernández shook his head. 'There is not time, Harry. They are following, and not far away. You must go on, and leave me.'

Jessica told Partridge, 'We *can't* leave him here.'

About to add his own protest, Partridge knew Fernández was right: there could be no other choice than to leave him.

'I need to say something quickly, Harry,' Fernández said. Partridge knelt beside him; Jessica joined them.

'I have a wife and four children,' Fernández continued. 'I would like to think someone will take care of them.'

'You work for CBA,' Partridge said, 'and CBA will do it. I give you my solemn word promise. The childrens' education—everything.'

Fernández nodded, then motioned to an M-16 rifle he had been carrying. 'Take this—you may need it. But I do not intend to be taken alive. I would like a pistol.' Partridge gave him the Browning.

'Oh, Fernández!' Jessica's eyes filled with tears. 'Nicky and I owe you so much.' She leaned over and kissed him.

'Go!' Fernández urged. 'Do not waste more time.'

As Jessica rose, Partridge leaned forward and held Fernández tightly. Rising, he moved away. He did not look back.

WHEN MIGUEL SAW A BOAT beached at the entrance to the jungle, he was glad he had joined the Sion airstrip sortie. He was even more pleased when Ramón, leaping quickly from their own boat to shore, ran to the other boat and announced that their engine had burned out.

As well as Miguel, the Sendero group comprised seven well-armed men. They filed quickly into the jungle.

'WE'RE EARLY,' RITA ABRAMS told the pilot, Zileri, as they approached the Sion airstrip—first point of call on their itinerary. She had just checked her watch: seven fifty-five.

'We'll circle and watch,' he said. 'In any case, this is the least likely place for your friends to be.'

As they had yesterday, all four in the plane—Rita, Sloane, Zileri and the copilot, Felipe—peered down at the short, tree-lined airstrip. Like yesterday, there was no visible activity at all.

ALONG THE JUNGLE TRAIL, Nicky was finding it increasingly difficult to maintain the punishing pace. Jessica and Minh were helping him, each grabbing an arm and partially lifting him over difficult patches. It had been about ten minutes since they left Fernández. Ken O'Hara was now up ahead, leading; Partridge was still in the rear.

Above their heads, the trees appeared to be thinning; also the trail had widened. It was a sign, Partridge hoped, that they were nearing the airstrip. At that moment, from behind, came a short, sharp crack— unmistakably a single shot. It had to be Fernández, Partridge reasoned. The stringer-fixer had provided a final service—a warning that pursuit was close. As if in confirmation, several other shots followed.

Partridge himself was near exhaustion. Through the past fifty hours he had pushed himself to the limit. Mentally meandering, he decided what he wanted most was relief from action. When this adventure ended, he would resume the vacation he had barely started, and simply disappear. And wherever he went, he would take Vivien—the woman who loved him. Jessica had been the past; Vivien could be the future . . .

Suddenly the airstrip was in view. Overhead, an aeroplane was circling—it was a Cheyenne! Ken O'Hara was loading a green cartridge into the flare gun, meaning, Land normally, everything is clear.

With equal suddenness, from behind, came the sound of two more shots, this time much closer.

'Send up a red flare, not a green!' Partridge yelled at O'Hara. Red for: Land as quickly as possible, we are in danger! O'Hara fired a red flare, and then another. The plane had already turned towards them.

'They've seen us!' Partridge said. When he knew which way the plane was going to land, he would pick a position to fight off the pursuers while the others boarded first. The answer quickly became evident. The Cheyenne II was in a tight descending turn; it would land facing away from the jungle trail where the shooting had been coming from.

Partridge told O'Hara, 'Get Jessica and Nicky down by the landing strip fast! When the plane gets to the far end, they'll swing round and taxi back. Did you hear that, Minh?'

'I heard.' Minh, with an eye glued to his camera, was imperturbably taking pictures, as he had at various moments throughout the journey.

Jessica asked anxiously, 'What about you, Harry?'

He told her, 'I'm going to cover you by firing down the trail. As soon as you're aboard, I'll join you. Now, get going!'

O'Hara put an arm round Jessica, who was holding Nicky, and hurried them away.

Partridge could now see several figures in the jungle, advancing on the airstrip, guns pointed. He dropped behind a hillock. Lying on his belly, he rested the Kalashnikov in front of him, the sights directed at the moving figures. He squeezed the trigger and, amid a burst of fire, saw one of the figures fall, the others dive for cover. At the same time he heard the Cheyenne II swoop in low.

'THERE THEY ARE!' Crawford Sloane shouted. 'I see them! It's Jessica and Nicky!' The plane was still on its landing run, travelling fast on an uneven dirt surface. As the end of the short strip loomed nearer, Zileri braked hard and swung the plane round. Then, accelerating both engines, he taxied back down the strip.

The Cheyenne II stopped at the point where Jessica, Nicky and O'Hara were waiting. The copilot, Felipe, had already opened the door. Nicky first, then Jessica and O'Hara climbed aboard, outstretched hands helping to pull them in. Minh appeared and scrambled in behind the others.

As Sloane, Jessica and Nicky hugged each other, O'Hara called out breathlessly, 'Harry's up ahead. We have to get him.'

'I see him,' Zileri said. 'Hold on!' He opened the throttles again and the plane shot forward, taxiing fast.

At the runway's far end he turned the plane again, ready for takeoff. Gunfire was heard through the open doorway.

'Your friend will have to make a run for it.' Zileri's voice was urgent. 'I want to get the hell out of here.'

PARTRIDGE HAD BOTH SEEN and heard the plane; it was about a hundred yards away. He would make it at a fast run, keeping low. First, though, he had to spray fire back into the jungle trail.

Squeezing the trigger, he poured a deadly hail of bullets along both sides of the jungle path. When the magazine had emptied, he dropped the rifle, sprang to his feet and ran.

Partridge was a third of the way to the plane when a bullet struck the back of his right knee. He fell instantly. Terrible pain swept over him, and he knew that he would never reach the plane. There was no time left. Summoning all his strength, he raised himself, waving the Cheyenne forward. All that mattered now was that his intention was clear.

MINH WAS IN THE DOORWAY, shooting pictures. Sloane cried out, 'Harry's hit! He's waving for us to go, but we have to get him!'

Jessica cried out, 'Yes! Oh yes!'

260

'You can't,' Zileri said. 'There isn't time.'

Just then, several bullets hit the plane. Zileri pushed the throttles forward. Felipe secured the door. As air speed built up, Zileri eased back on the control column. The Cheyenne II left the airstrip and climbed.

Jessica and Nicky were holding each other, weeping. Sloane, his eyes closed, could not believe what he had just seen.

Partridge saw the plane go, and tears long held back began to flow. Then more bullets hit him, and he died.

ABOARD THE CHEYENNE II, several minutes passed before anyone felt capable of speech. Crawford Sloane was holding Jessica and Nicky close to him, oblivious to all else.

At length Sloane raised his head and asked Minh Van Canh, 'About Harry . . . did you see anything more?'

Minh nodded sadly. 'I was focused on him. He was hit again, several times. There isn't any doubt.'

It was Rita, the professional with responsibilities, who asked Minh, 'May I see some of your pictures?'

Minh passed his Betacam to Rita. Squinting through the viewfinder, she watched videotape shots of Harry wounded, then falling to the fatal bullets. As she handed the camera back, Rita's eyes were moist.

Sloane asked, 'Did Harry have anybody—a girlfriend?'

'There was—is—someone,' Rita said. 'Her name's Vivien. She lives in Port Credit, outside Toronto.'

'We should call. I'll talk to her if you like.'

'Yes, and when you do, tell her that Harry made a will before he left, and I have it. He told me he was leaving everything to her.'

Reaching into her briefcase, Rita produced a Teletype message received through Entel Peru.

'Before Harry left,' she told the others, 'he asked me to send a cable to a surgeon friend in Oakland, California. It seems he is among the world's ranking experts on injured hands. The cable asked questions about Nicholas. This is the reply.'

She passed the typed sheet to Sloane, who read it aloud:

'HAVE READ INFO YOU SENT, ALSO DETAILS IN NEWSPAPERS ABOUT YOUR YOUNG FRIEND'S HAND. HE SHOULD AND CAN LEARN TO ROTATE HAND DOWNWARD UNTIL WHAT REMAINS OF INDEX AND LITTLE FINGERS COMES IN CONTACT WITH PIANO KEYS. WILL TAKE PATIENCE, PERSEVERANCE. BEING YOUNG HELPS.

TAKE CARE OF YOURSELF HARRY. WARMEST REGARDS.

JACK TUPPER, MD'

There was a silence, then Sloane said, 'I guess there will never be a time when there isn't something we'll have reason to thank Harry for.'

'Fernández, too,' Jessica reminded him. Now she told Crawford and Rita of the promise Harry had made about providing for Fernández's wife and four children.

'If Harry said that,' Sloane said, 'he was speaking for CBA and it's binding, like a legal document.'

'There's one snag,' Rita pointed out. 'It happened after Harry was fired, even though he didn't know it.'

'It makes no difference,' Sloane said. 'Harry's promise will be honoured. I'll see it's put into effect.'

The Cheyenne II droned on, still climbing, gaining altitude to pass over the peaks of the Andes, after which they would descend towards Lima.

Rita noted that the flight would take another forty minutes. What was necessary now, she realised, was to put a report together for the National Evening News tonight. It would be a long, dramatic one and would use most of Minh's best pictures. Crawf would do the narration and stand-ups. He was a professional, like Rita and the rest.

But there must first be a bulletin to say that Nicky and Jessica were safe. When CBA News received it in New York, they would break instantly into network programming. They would send just a few pictures, transmitting quick and dirty—the way they had from Dallas-Fort Worth Airport for the Airbus crash story that she, Harry, Minh and Ken O'Hara had worked on less than a month ago.

Rita tapped Zileri on the shoulder, pointing to the aircraft radio. 'Can you patch a phone call through to New York?'

She scribbled a number and passed it forward. In a surprisingly short time a voice said, 'CBA foreign desk.'

Zeleri passed back a microphone. 'Go ahead,' he told her.

She held the transmit button down. 'This is Rita Abrams. Get me a bird out of Lima for a bulletin at ten thirty Lima time. Make sure the Horseshoe knows.'

A voice replied laconically, 'You got it. Will do.'

'Thanks. Goodbye.' She handed the microphone back.

A script was needed for the bulletin. Rita scribbled a few phrases, then decided Crawf would find the right words. He always did. He would probably ad-lib in part. He was good at that too.

In what was left of the flight, she and Crawf must work together. Unfortunately, it meant pulling him away from the arms of Jessica and Nicky. But he would accept the need and so would they. Like everyone else in the business, they all understood that the news came first.

'Crawf,' Rita said gently, 'you and I have work to do.'

262

ARTHUR HAILEY

When Arthur Hailey brings out a new novel, it is more than just another book: it is a publishing event. *The Evening News* is Hailey's tenth blockbuster in a string of successes including *Hotel, Airport, Wheels,* and *Strong Medicine* (all Condensed Books selections). And, like the others, this one plumbs the depths of a large and complex industry.

Why television news this time? 'I'm a newsaholic,' Hailey explains. 'When I was a boy growing up in Britain, I was fascinated by the news, whether it came in the newspaper my father brought home or on the wireless.' As a television dramatist in Canada in the 1950s, he also gained an insider's understanding of the TV world.

Still, when he began his research for *The Evening News*, he undertook it with the same intensity that has become his trademark. He travelled from network boardrooms to small newsrooms, and spoke to everyone from news executives to studio technicians. He also journeyed twice into the jungles of Peru to seek background on the Sendero Luminoso guerrillas. Peruvian authorities warned him, however, against trying to meet the terrorists. 'It's unlikely I would have lived long enough to write up my research notes,' Hailey comments wryly. In all, his research for the book absorbed him for a year and a half; the writing took two years more.

Now, as Arthur Hailey approaches the age of seventy, he is circumspect about his future plans. He may write a few short novels, he suggests. But for the present he and Sheila, to whom he has been married for thirty-nine years, are content to enjoy their home in Lyford Cay, the Bahamas. 'I won't stop writing,' he says. 'But I won't let my life be taken over for years at a time as those other books demanded. It's a promise I made to my wife,' he adds with a smile. 'And she'll make sure I keep it!'

THE
FLIGHT
OF
THE
SWAN

A CONDENSATION OF THE BOOK BY

ELIZABETH
WEBSTER

ILLUSTRATED BY TED LEWIN

Fly . . . fly . . . free . . .
For Laurie Collins the sound of the swans'
wings spoke an irresistible message. Fly
from a brutal husband. Fly to save her
children. Fly and be free for ever.
But after flight would come new needs.
Because freedom isn't taking off. It's
knowing where to land . . .

PART 1

THE HIDE

The sound came across the sky, high and sweet and strange. Laurie looked up, hugging herself to stop the trembling . . . The shock and fear did not go away, the bruises on her body did not stop hurting, but the rhythmic thrum like distant music was coming nearer, and it seemed to bring with it a kind of peace . . . or maybe reassurance. Out there, it said, high in the sky, is a world of clear air and sunlight. A world of freedom.

She craned her neck to look higher, above the trees of the cramped back gardens, and there—sailing in majestic, steady flight—were three white swans. Their necks were stretched out, pointing towards the glowing west, and their wing-beats were slow and strong and filled with music.

'Free . . . free . . . free . . .' sang the pulsing wings. 'Fly . . . fly . . . fly . . .' they sang, as they passed over, high above her head.

She watched them out of sight. Yes! she thought: Fly, fly, fly! It's all very well for you, you beautiful things, with all the wide sky to sail in. And she stood there shivering in the shabby back yard with its scuffed brown grass and dustbins spilling out along the broken fence.

'Mum?' called Jason from the kitchen door. 'Mum? I've made some tea.'

She drew a long shaky breath. 'Coming,' she said, and went back inside.

'Come on, Mum . . .' Jason's arms were round her, leading her to a chair. 'He's gone out.' He set the cup of tea before her, and awkwardly tried to smooth the long fair hair into place. 'Shall I fetch the sponge for your eye?'

She shook her head. 'It's all right.' But it wasn't all right. Not at all.

267

Especially the matter-of-fact voice of her young son, speaking with the casual acceptance born of many such occasions . . . Shall I fetch the sponge for your eye? . . . Shall I sweep up the broken plates? . . . Shall I find the sticking plaster? . . . Shall I phone the doctor?

She reached out an unsteady hand for the cup.

'I put three sugars in,' said Jason. He did not add 'for shock', but he knew what it was for. Yes, he knew.

The boy's concerned young face was pale with the effort to be some support and comfort. The grey eyes were anxious and too big in his pinched face, and the freckles on his nose seemed to stand out extra strong.

She put an arm round him and hugged him close. 'Don't worry, Jay. I'm fine . . . Where's Midge?'

He gave her an odd look, adult far beyond his eight years. 'She crawled into the broom cupboard and went to sleep. So I left her there—where it was safe. She's still asleep.'

Laurie sighed. A sudden wave of desolation washed over her. What was the use? She was trapped in this squalid little council house, with a man who did nothing but shout and flail at the unjust world with his fists. Who could not find the work he was used to, and could not accept the fact that he was a failure, and who spent most of his time and his money drinking, down at his seedy local. This man took out his own anger and frustration on his exhausted wife, while their small daughter Midge crept into the broom cupboard and cried herself to sleep and her young brother Jason stood by and tried to comfort his frightened mother. It was too much. It was all too much . . .

There was a knock on the door. It was the day for paying the milk bill. When Laurie opened the door, Dave, the neighbourhood milkman, looked compassionately at her. Dave knew what was going on at No 14. 'Everything all right, missus?' he asked.

'Yes, thanks.' She handed over the money with a shaking hand. 'Everything's all right.'

But it wasn't, of course. It wasn't all right at all. Out there, beyond the milk float, was a sunny street and a sky where swans' wings pulsed in radiant flight . . .

'Jay,' she said suddenly, 'get your coat. I'll wake Midge.'

She opened the broom-cupboard door. The child lay curled up on an old ironing blanket. One flushed cheek was resting on the head of an old string mop, and her hair—honey-gold like her mother's—was spread out round her head in limp tangles. One hand clutched her favourite toy, an ancient yellow lion whose velvet coat had worn very thin.

She scooped Midge up, found her coat and pushed her sleepy arms into it. Then she picked up her own coat and handbag and followed Jason into the narrow hall. But as they reached the front door, someone stood in their way.

'Where the hell d'you think you're going?' said Jeff.

Laurie's heart clenched in terror. He was drunk again—drunk and seethingly angry.

'I was . . . taking them for a walk.'

'Oh, you were, were you? Well, you can just walk back in again.' He shoved her back towards the kitchen. 'D'you know what the time is? I suppose it's too much to ask to have a meal ready when I come home.'

'But you're early.'

'*Early?* When I've been down at the Job Centre scouring the ads all day!'

She looked at him. It was clear where he had been most of the day. But it wasn't worth protesting. He had been violent enough at lunchtime, and already fairly drunk then. Now he was violent and very drunk. She shivered.

'Don't put on that martyred look, you cow!' he shouted. 'Get back in there and cook something or I'll—'

Jason's taut young hand slipped into hers. She looked down and saw the warning look in his eyes. Not now, he seemed to be saying. Don't let him start another fight now.

She went back to the kitchen, and began to sling some food together.

But when she put the plate of food in front of Jeff, he stared at it in disgust. 'What's this? Where's the meat?' He pushed it round with his fork.

'I can't afford meat every day. You don't give me enough money.'

He slammed a hand down on the table. 'I give you plenty,' he growled. 'You're just a bloody bad manager.'

'If you didn't spend so much in the pub,' she said, suddenly brave, 'you could have meat every day!'

He picked up the plate of vegetable stew and threw it at her. The hot sticky mess hit the wall and splashed back onto her face. The plate smashed and a piece of jagged china flew up and cut her cheek. Blood and gravy trickled down her face.

Jeff got up and came towards her, toweringly angry. 'I drink,' he said, 'to forget I'm married to a snivelling slut like you—' He slammed her hard against the sink, bruising her backbone against its sharp rim. 'Look at you! You bleeding slag heap! . . . Wash that muck off your face!'

Blindly, she turned to reach for a wet cloth in the sink, and he hit her again. Her head struck the wall, hard, and for a moment she could not see. A singing began in her ears, almost like the flight of the swans.

'And I drink—' he shouted, looming over her '—because I can't get a job, and no one cares a damn what happens to me. D'you know what they offered me today? Tar-spreading on the roads—and I'm a *salesman!*'

She was holding the wet cloth against her face, staring at him out of dilated eyes. Wings were beating in her head, trying to get out . . . Everything was tilting slightly . . .

'Dear God, a *salesman!*' he cried, and began to shake her wildly. 'Dragged down to this!' He swept an arm round at the littered kitchen and the frightened children on the floor, and then brought it back smartly across her face. 'I suppose you think I should spread tar, don't you?'

She did not answer. Tar-spreading didn't seem a particularly degrading occupation. Certainly not worse than drinking yourself silly in the pub, and knocking your wife silly as well . . .

'*Don't* you?' he said, and shook her even harder.

She knew, dimly, that she must make an effort to reach him. 'Jeff,' she began, '*please* . . . I know it's frustrating . . .'

'Frustrating!' he screamed. 'You can say that again! With you and the kids hanging round my neck like bloody millstones!'

She looked down at little Midge cowering on the floor. Soft, gentle, three-year-old Midge with her wide grey eyes and honey-gold hair . . . a millstone?

'Then why don't you leave?' she heard herself say.

'*Leave?*' He began to laugh. It was an ugly sound. 'I might at that!' he said, still laughing. 'Except that you'd like that, wouldn't you?' And he hit her again.

She understood then, in a curious flash, that he would never leave her. He liked having someone to hit—and he liked having a reason for his anger and his grudges . . . She and the children were his excuse for violence—his escape from his own failures and shortcomings. He did not have to blame himself for anything. He only had to punish them.

Them? At this point, she realised all at once that her children were in danger. As she reached this brief glimpse of reality, Jeff lurched away and tripped over Midge's yellow lion which she had dropped in terror on the floor before crawling under the table. Now, he advanced on the child with a bunched fist. 'You bloody brat!'

'No!' said Laurie. 'No, Jeff! Not Midge!'

He had never yet hit the children. But now, Laurie was afraid. She stooped down and gathered the little girl into her arms. 'Jay!' she said sharply. 'Come on. It's past your bedtime. I'll put you both to bed.'

'You won't!' shouted Jeff. 'Leave them there!'

'No!' answered Laurie, and backed quickly away, keeping Jason behind her. Jeff overturned the table with a crash of crockery and came after her.

But one of the table legs caught him and sent him sprawling in a shower of broken glass and curses.

The wings were very strong in Laurie's head now. 'Fly, fly, fly!' they said . . . Somehow, without quite knowing how, she was out in the street with Midge in her arms and Jason by her side, and she was running—leaving Jeff and the cramped little house far behind . . . And with her, as she ran, the wings pulsed on.

WHEN THE STITCH in her side got too bad, she paused. They were in a part of London she did not know, but the streets seemed well lit, and there was an all-night coffee stall on the corner.

She looked down at the children. They still had their coats on, she also, she noticed vaguely, and her hand was clutching her handbag. Thank God for that, at least. There was a little money left in it, and Jason's school bus fare for tomorrow . . . Tomorrow? . . . She couldn't think that far ahead. Right now, they needed a hot drink and something to eat.

She approached the coffee stall warily. She did not know how she looked, of course, with her marked face and the cut below her eye still oozing blood, her hair dishevelled and her eyes dilated with shock.

The coffee stall owner took one look at her, poured out a steaming mug of tea, and slid it along the wooden counter towards her.

'What'd the kids like?' he asked.

'Tea,' said Jason promptly. 'Please.'

'And the little girl? Milk-and-a-dash? Warm her up a bit?'

Laurie nodded. She gulped down some hot tea. 'Could they have a hot dog?' she asked, trying to smile.

'Sure.' His alert brown eyes were watching her, but not unsympathetic. 'Had it rough tonight?' he asked gently. 'That cut wants seeing to. Needs a stitch, I'd say.'

She couldn't stop trembling. 'It doesn't matter . . .' she murmured.

'Going home, are you?' he asked.

'No,' she said, and shivered again. 'Never.'

He nodded, as if he understood the situation all too well. He had seen it all before. 'Where will you be going then?' he asked.

'I don't know . . .' she sighed. Then she leaned forward and said to him with great earnestness, 'It's the wings, you see. They won't let me think.' And she slid into a heap on the pavement, while Jason and Midge looked down at her in wonder.

SHE WOKE IN A STRANGE ROOM in a house full of strange sounds. She was lying on a camp bed, covered with a grey army blanket. There was another camp bed by one wall, and against the other were two bunk beds.

But there was no sign of her children. She started up in terror, but the sudden movement caused a violent pain in her head, and she leaned back, clutching her throbbing temples.

'It's all right,' said a voice, close by. 'Take it easy. I've brought you some tea.'

'My children—'

'They're fine. They're with the others. Penny's looking after them.'

Laurie opened her eyes. She found herself looking into the face of a woman with short grey hair, a straight, determined mouth and unexpectedly beautiful eyes of a curious golden colour.

'Where—? What is this place?'

'This is Hyde House—a refuge for women. They call it The Hide. And I'm its founder—Jane Everett.' She smiled at Laurie. 'There are a lot of women here in your predicament. We do our best to give them temporary shelter—and some kind of help and comfort, if we can . . .'

Laurie still looked confused. 'How did I—how did we get here?'

'Joe brought you in.
D'you remember Joe?
The coffee stall owner?
He often brings people in.
He's seen a lot of this—our
Joe. And he's a kind little man.'

Laurie sighed. 'Yes . . . I remember. He was very kind.'

Jane Everett sat down on Laurie's bed. 'Your sensible boy, Jason, told me your name—and Midge's. But there are one or two things I want to know. You see, I want you to go to hospital and get that head injury checked . . . and they will ask questions.'

'I don't need—'

'Oh, yes, you do.' She was silent for a moment, and then went on: 'And if, as I suspect, you have no intention of returning for another battering— at least for the moment—you may need the hospital's evidence of your injuries. Do you understand? Or—do you want to go back?'

'No,' said Laurie. 'No—I can't go back. It's the children, you see,' she explained, and was horrified to hear her own voice shake. 'They're not safe any more—they're not . . . safe . . .' And she began to weep.

Jane Everett put an arm round her shoulders. 'Don't worry now. They're quite safe here. I'll send them in with Penny, and you can see for yourself . . . But then I think I'd better take you down to the hospital myself. You needn't explain anything—I'll do all the talking, if you like.'

'Sorry!' Laurie murmured helplessly. 'Sorry . . . to be such a nuisance.'

Presently, Jason came in, carefully balancing a tray with some bread and jam and another cup of tea, and Midge brought a bright red geranium and climbed up onto the bed to watch Laurie eat. With them was a cheerful red-haired girl, pregnant and ringless.

'I'm Penny,' she said. 'Your two have taken to me OK, so it's all right to leave them while you go and get checked at the hospital.' She winked at Jason out of a blue, merry eye. 'Him and me's good friends, see?'

The room spun again, and Laurie lay back exhausted. Penny took a look at her and quietly beckoned to Jason, picked up Midge and went out of the room.

In a little while Jane Everett returned. She got Laurie to her feet, wrapped a blanket round her shoulders, and steered her out of the room, out through the front door to an ancient Ford van waiting at the kerb.

The hospital was brisk and efficient and unexpectedly kind. Jane gave a brief explanation of the situation, and Laurie fancied they were quite used to this. She then announced that she would be returning with a social worker and possibly a policewoman to hear the results of the examination.

Laurie was taken away for X-rays—and when they undressed her and stood looking at her bruised and battered body, even she was mildly surprised at the extent of her injuries. She seemed to be black and blue all over, her ribs hurt like fire when she breathed in, and her backbone where Jeff had rammed her against the rim of the sink was painfully stiff and sore, and had developed a deep, crippling ache . . .

They stitched up the cut in her cheek and X-rayed her head, her ribs and her spine. Then they took her to a ward and put her to bed. She was shaking badly by this time, and deathly cold, but they piled blankets on her and brought her some hot, sweet tea.

A young doctor appeared. 'How are you feeling now?'

'All right. Just c-cold . . .' She drew a shaky breath. 'Can I go soon? I've left my children—'

'They are being well looked after. Jane Everett promised me.' He smiled at her reassuringly. 'We want to keep you in for the night. After a bang on the head, we like to keep patients under observation for a little while. Just in case.'

274

She tried to answer his smile. 'Then—what's the damage?'

'You have a mild concussion, and a possible hairline fracture. You also have three cracked ribs, but they will heal in time. And a severely bruised spine which will be very painful for a while, but will also get better on its own.' He gave her arm a cheerful little pat. 'It sounds bad—but in fact they are all things that only require rest.'

Her smile was tired but relieved. At least she would be able to cope with the children . . . and finding somewhere to live . . . and all the rest of the difficult rearrangements she would have to make . . .

At that point, a voice behind the doctor said busily, 'Can we get her particulars now? Who is the next of kin? Shouldn't we send for her husband?'

'No!' exclaimed Laurie, and tried to leap out of bed.

'Don't be so stupid!' snapped Jane Everett's voice beside her. 'It's her husband that's put her here in this condition.'

'But,' persisted the voice, 'next of kin must always be informed.'

'Very well,' said Jane. 'Inform him. I have a policewoman here, and a social worker. They want to hear the doctor's report. When that has been done, you can inform her husband that if he attempts to come here and see her, or to make any disturbance, he will be arrested for common assault and causing grievous bodily harm.' She looked at the hapless official from the records office with grim dislike. 'You people,' she said, 'can't you use a little discretion?'

'Well, what about her mother?' insisted the bossy woman.

'My mother is in Sunderland,' said Laurie very distinctly. 'She is arthritic. She couldn't possibly come. Besides, she couldn't care less.'

There was a rather shocked silence at this. But young Dr Lang said firmly, 'I don't think this helps my patient. Leave the forms for now, and come to my office.' He signalled to the ward sister to prepare an injection, then he took Laurie's wrist in his hand and said, 'We're going to give you a shot to make you sleep. No one will come. Forget everything . . . You are quite safe.'

With the injection the pain and shock retreated into a warm haze . . . They waited till she was drowsy before they looked at her injuries and heard the doctor's report. Then they went away, grim-faced and silent, Jane Everett to set in motion the social services procedures that would help Laurie and her children to survive.

IN THE MORNING they let her have a bath, accompanied by a cheery young probationer to see that she didn't pass out. When she came back into the ward, wearing a hospital dressing gown, Penny was there with an armful of clean clothes.

'Thought you could do with 'em,' she grinned. 'Can't get into 'em now, meself . . . Not very posh, but we can wash yours when we get back . . .' She sat down on the end of Laurie's bed. 'OK if I wait here? Come to take you home, see?'

'Penny—' began Laurie unsteadily. 'It is Penny, isn't it?'

'That's me.'

'I don't understand what's happening . . .'

'I don't suppose you do.' Penny's grin was cheerful. 'With a bashing like that, you're bound to be a bit fazed. But Jane'll sort things out for you. She usually does.'

'Does she?' Laurie's head hurt when she tried to think. And those wings were still there . . .

At that moment, Dr Lang arrived. He looked at her eyes, studied her chart for a moment, and once more took her wrist in his firm, cool hand.

'You'll do,' he said, smiling. 'But I want you to take it easy for at least a week. And I want to see you again a week from now. If your headache gets much worse, or you start seeing double, come back at once.'

Laurie stared at him. How could she promise to return when she didn't even know where she would be in a week's time?

'Jane Everett has arranged for you and the children to stay at the Centre for a fortnight,' he said. 'After that, we shall see . . .'

'She said at *least* a fortnight,' interrupted Penny sturdily. 'And I can look after the kids . . . You'll be able to do just what the doc says! Come on, climb in!' She was holding out a clean pair of jeans. 'Doc says you can go.'

Laurie did as she was told. It seemed simpler.

When she was ready to go, the ward sister came over and handed her a packet of tablets and an appointment card. 'These are for your headache,' she said. 'The instructions are on the bottle. Don't take more than it says.'

'No,' agreed Laurie. Then, nervously, she asked the vital question: 'What—do you know what they did about . . . notifying anyone?'

The sister smiled. 'Dr Lang instructed the records office to notify your husband—but the letter was not to be posted until today.'

'Oh . . . *thank* you!' And Laurie moved away down the ward, with Penny's guiding arm round her shoulders. Outside the hospital Penny went up to an old green van parked on the corner and rapped on the window. 'This is Joe,' said Penny. 'Remember him? He runs a stall in the market. Get in.'

Laurie climbed in, and Penny got in the back with a load of cauliflowers and cabbages. Joe, Laurie discovered, was a squarish, brownish man with a sardonic twist to his mouth and very bright, very observant brown eyes—and she suddenly recognised him.

276

'I thought you ran an all-night coffee stall?'

'I do,' agreed Joe. 'Veggies, mornings. Coffee, nights.'

'You were the one who got me into Jane's refuge! Well—thanks!' breathed Laurie. 'You probably saved my life—and the kids' as well!'

'Think nothing of it, luv,' he said, and shot out into the traffic.

Joe turned into a road of tall, shabby houses in a long curving terrace. At the end of the row was one slightly larger semidetached house with a straggly back garden running along a side road. Here, he stopped and opened the back of the van to let Penny out. Then they both came round to help Laurie up the steps.

'I can manage,' she said. But her legs felt very wobbly and strange, and the steps seemed to weave up and down in front of her.

'Hold up!' said Penny cheerfully. 'Nearly there.'

Inside, the house was filled with the sound of children. It was also filled with the sound of women's voices talking.

There was a long, narrow hall stuffed with pushchairs, bundles of clothes, coats and shabby suitcases. On one side was a large, crowded day room with ancient armchairs set round in groups and a faded cord carpet on the floor. Various little knots of women and children were gathered here. Some were talking, others just sitting staring into space . . . Most of their faces showed signs of shock or exhaustion, and though some of them had clearly made an effort to look presentable there were others who looked unkempt and uncaring.

'Not in there,' said Penny. 'Jane says rest for you today.'

Laurie was occupied with trying to still the wings which were beating in her head again, trying to get out. The walls seemed to tilt inwards, forming a dark tunnel down which she was walking. And there was a light at the end of the tunnel, very bright and pure, if only she could reach it.

She stumbled a little, and Penny's strong young arms held her steady. 'In here,' she said. 'Where you were before. You can have the kids with you—and me as well, I'm afraid, but Jane thought you wouldn't mind. We're terribly short of beds.'

Laurie smiled vaguely. 'I'm glad . . .' she managed to say. 'Glad . . . you'll be here . . .' She fell onto the bed and seemed to float off at once towards that brilliant light at the end of the tunnel. While she was silently wrestling with this swimming darkness, there was a rush of small feet at the door, and Midge and Jason burst into the room.

'Mummy!' cried Midge, and hurled herself onto the bed and flung her arms round Laurie's neck.

Jason was quieter, but his eyes were full of relief and welcome. 'Are you better?'

'Much better,' lied Laurie. 'Quite all right, in fact,' and drew him close.

'Jane says we can bring you your dinner in here,' Jason explained, ' 'cos you've got to be quiet.'

'Come on,' said Penny. 'Let's go and see about that dinner. Give your mum a chance to rest a bit, see?' And she took them away; but even when they brought her a plate of stew, she could not eat it. She was still sitting there, staring at it, when Jane came in to see her.

'How are you feeling?' she asked, noting the plate of untouched food.

'I'm sorry,' began Laurie. 'I—I haven't touched it. Maybe—you could put it back?'

Jane knew then that Laurie understood poverty—and how every scrap of food had to be saved and used with infinite care.

'I've no money—' Laurie's voice was wavering again. 'Except two pounds for Jason's school bus fares. You could have that . . . he won't be needing it now.'

Jane smiled and patted her hand. 'You keep it . . . In any case, I've arranged something with Social Security for the moment—till you're fit to cope . . .' She was silent for a little while. 'Now,' she said at last, 'I'm only going to tell you enough to reassure you about the present. We can talk about the rest later. All right?'

'Yes,' agreed Laurie. 'But—'

'Just let go and accept things as they are,' said Jane smiling. 'I have a grant for running this place now. I get a subsistence allowance for you and your children while you're in my care. I've told the hospital you can stay at least a fortnight—and you can! I suggest you make use of that time to get well—and don't try to think too far ahead, or make any plans. Not yet. The time to make decisions is when you are rested and feeling strong.' She laid a friendly hand on Laurie's arm. 'Some of the women here are basically very weak, you know . . . and a bit—er—limited. But I don't think you are either! Just give yourself time. Time to heal and time to consider. We can talk again later. Now, I think you should sleep.'

'Yes,' agreed Laurie dutifully. 'I—I can't begin to—' she started to say.

Jane cut her short. 'Don't try. Just thank God Joe had the sense to bring you here.' She got up and gave Laurie's hand another a friendly pat. 'Sleep well!'

JEFF WAS CONFUSED. When Laurie ran out of the house with the children, he supposed she would come back, as usual. But she didn't. He surveyed the wreckage of the kitchen, and was a little ashamed of his violence. He wanted to blot it out, so he decided to go back to his mates in the pub. He could get a pie or something, and they would be sympathetic, and she would come back.

But when he got home, late, and even more belligerent with drink than

278

usual, there was no one to take it out on, no one at all. He fell into bed in a haze of alcohol and self-pity, and woke feeling sick. There was no one in the house, and its silence and emptiness seemed to mock him. Cursing, he looked at his pallid face and stubbly chin in the bathroom mirror—and winced. Was that him? That sagging, grey face with the bitter mouth and angry eyes? Where was the handsome, lively lad who had charmed all the girls from here to Bethnal Green? He should never have run off with Laurie, never have married her—an inexperienced child who couldn't cope with a man of the world like him . . . What he needed was someone stronger and more mature. No, what he needed was a drink.

He went downstairs, and once more stared at the kitchen with disgust. He went out, slamming the door, and staggered down to the workmen's café on the corner. The rest of the day passed in a haze of pubs and drinks and uneatable pies that stuck in his throat, and a sense of loss that he couldn't quite understand. When he got back to the house, there was still no one there.

He began to wonder in a muddled sort of way whether anything could have happened to Laurie. No, he thought. She's just paying me out—or trying to. She's probably staying with one of the neighbours. He cursed again, and kicked angrily at the overturned table on the kitchen floor. He only succeeded in stubbing his toe. Better clear up this mess, he thought. But he didn't. He left it where it was, and stumbled up to bed.

In the morning, he found the letter from the hospital. It was a printed form with bits filled in by hand. 'Mrs Laura Collins, wife of Jeffrey Collins of 14 Wetherby Terrace et cetera . . . admitted to Ward 10 of this hospital, suffering from fractured ribs, hairline fracture of the skull, concussion, severe spinal bruising and multiple contusions.' Nothing else. No word about how the injuries were acquired?

His stomach gave a heave of fear. Surely, all those injuries couldn't have been his fault? No, she must have been knocked down by a car, or mugged, or something.

He'd better go round there and see how she was, hadn't he? But supposing they accused him of . . . Maybe he ought to stay away, and wait for them to get in touch again, or send her home. Yes, better wait and see. Meanwhile he needed a drink . . . bit of a shock, news like that.

But after a morning at the pub he felt more courageous, and began to think maybe it would be better to go round after all, and seem concerned. Well, he *was* concerned. He wondered vaguely what had happened to the kids. She couldn't have them in the hospital with her, could she? Someone else must be looking after them.

It occurred to him then that if he was going to bring Laurie home, he'd better clear the place up a bit first. Clean himself up, too . . . He gulped down another drink, and as an afterthought bought a half-bottle of whisky with his last fiver. He might need it . . . things might get pretty hairy at the hospital. You never knew how people would take things.

Then he went back to the house to clear up, to sweep and clean and wash the dishes that were unbroken. He was a bit shaken to find blood on the walls. He looked round. It wasn't very good, but it was better than nothing. By this time, his courage was evaporating, so he poured out a stiff whisky . . . He needed it. He didn't like hospitals at the best of times, and this interview might be tricky . . .

After another drink, he felt quite jaunty. He changed into his one and only suit (a bit shiny at the edges but still quite respectable), picked up his salesman's briefcase to add to the professional image, and went off to get the tube. The hospital was in another part of London—a part he didn't know very well.

'I'VE COME TO SEE MY WIFE, Mrs Laura Collins,' he said. 'Ward Ten, I believe.'

The woman at the reception desk said automatically, 'Second floor. Take the lift at the end of the corridor.'

Jeff took the lift. He also, surreptitiously, took another swig from the bottle of whisky concealed in his pocket.

At the entrance to Ward 10, he met a pretty nurse. Smiling, he said, 'Are you going my way?'

'I shouldn't think so,' she replied tartly. 'Who did you want to see?'

'My wife. Laura Collins . . . This is Ward Ten, isn't it?'

The nurse looked at him. 'Did you say Mrs *Collins?*' She turned back towards the ward door. 'Wait there,' she said crisply. 'I'll make enquiries.'

Inside Sister's office there was a brief colloquy. 'What's he like?' asked Sister grimly.

'Drunk,' said the nurse. 'Or at least—the worse for wear.'

Sister reached for the phone. 'Bleep Dr Lang, will you? He's needed on Ward Ten.'

Outside, Jeff's courage was beginning to wane again. But he didn't dare take another swig. The nurse returned, with Sister, and said politely, 'If you would wait in here, Mr Collins? Dr Lang will be down to see you.'

The doctor? thought Jeff, with a slight lurch of alarm. 'Is she—can't I go in?' He tried to push past the two women.

'In here, if you please,' said Sister, adroitly steering him through a door into a small waiting room. 'The doctor won't be long.'

Defeated, Jeff sat down on a chair, next to someone else who was also waiting . . . Presently, the other waiting man was shepherded away. It gave Jeff just time to take another quick swig before a stern-faced young

280

doctor stood in the doorway. 'Are you Mr Collins?'

'Yes. That's me.' The jaunty tone rang false, and he stood up, not knowing quite what line he should take. 'I—came to see my wife.'

'I'm afraid you're too late. We discharged her this morning.'

'Discharged her? Where to?'

Dr Lang shrugged his shoulders. 'I've no idea. She said she had somewhere to go—where she would be looked after—so we let her go.'

'But—I want to know where she is! She's my wife!' He glared at the young doctor. 'Didn't she leave an address?'

'Only *your* address, Mr Collins—and that reluctantly.'

'What? Did she—did she say anything?'

'About what, Mr Collins? She was concussed. And in shock.'

'She must've fallen,' Jeff muttered. 'Been knocked down by a car or something . . . or mugged. Didn't she ask for me?'

'*Ask* for you?' The doctor sounded cold. 'No, Mr Collins. She did not. In fact, the only time you were mentioned, she got so frightened that she tried to get up and leave the hospital there and then.'

There was a pause. Finally, Jeff allowed fear and anger to get the better of him. 'It's ridiculous!' he raged. 'Refusing to tell me where she is! Making all these accusations!'

'No one has made any accusations, Mr Collins.'

'I demand to know where she is! She's my wife! And where are my children? She has no right to go off without leaving an address! And you've no right to let her—' He advanced on Dr Lang, pointing an accusing finger, but a hard, swift hand caught him by the wrist and forced his arm down.

'I wouldn't advise you to get rough, Mr Collins,' said Dr Lang pleasantly. 'I suggest you leave now, before I call a couple of porters to escort you.'

'I'm not leaving!' shouted Jeff. 'My wife's run off somewhere—and you tell me a cock-and-bull story about injuries—and—and shock or something!' His eyes focused on Dr Lang's quiet face. 'And you can stop looking so disapproving, too! What goes on between me and my wife is *my* bloody business—no one else's!'

'Indeed,' murmured Dr Lang. 'A bloody business is what it appears to be.'

Jeff tried to hit him. But this time Sister came in, followed by two burly porters who each took Jeff by an arm.

'I should go quietly if I were you,' said the doctor mildly. 'Or do you want me to call the police?'

'The *police?*' Jeff was startled. But the hard hands of the two porters gripping his arms made him mad. He flung them off. 'Let go of me! I've told you—I'm not leaving till I know where she is!'

The two porters grabbed him again, and a fight ensued. Sister went back into her office and called the police. They sent a man round right away, and by the time he got there, Jeff was beside himself with frustration and fright. He hit out at the porters, he hit out at Dr Lang, and he hit out at the police constable. They led him away, still struggling and shouting. It was a clear case of assault, drunk and disorderly behaviour, and public affray. They put him in a cell and wrote out a report.

'Well,' said young Dr Lang, looking at Sister grimly. 'There's not much doubt about where those injuries came from.'

'No,' agreed Sister. 'It seems fairly clear.'

IN THE BARE CELL, when the drunken rage wore off, Jeff sat and cried. He wanted to go home. He wanted his wife. He even wanted his children. He couldn't understand how life had suddenly gone so horribly wrong.

'Come on,' said the constable in charge, pulling him to his feet. 'No need for that. You can go home when you've made a statement. Desk sergeant's waiting.'

When that confusing ordeal was over, and he had been charged, the desk sergeant said. 'Court on Monday. Released on bail. Mind you're there! And you'd better stay sober till then—and keep out of trouble!'

THE NEXT DAY, Laurie got up, determined to be some use. But she found that her legs would scarcely hold her up, and she still shook badly whenever she tried to hold anything—even a cup.

She went in search of Jane and found her with a paintbrush and a pot of blue paint, explaining to one of the women residents how to paint a door.

'Can't I do that?' asked Laurie.

Jane looked at her pale, shadowed face. 'Not today you can't,' she said, smiling. 'Perhaps tomorrow . . . We're trying to brighten up the place.' She looked rather ruefully at the greyish-beige walls and dark brown paint of the long dark hall.

Laurie said in a choked voice, 'I must do *something!*'

Jane glanced at her again, and handed her paintbrush over to the waiting woman. 'There you are then, Molly—see what you can do.' She led Laurie away into the kitchen. 'You can help me with the vegetables,' she said, 'while we talk. I don't think you should tackle anything too strenuous at first, especially with three bust ribs.'

'All right,' Laurie said, and returned Jane's smile with a tentative one of her own. She looked like a small child not sure of her welcome, with her long fair hair and anxious blue eyes, and Jane felt moved to ask suddenly, 'How old are you, Laurie?'

282

'Twenty-seven.'

'And Jason is . . . ?'

'Eight. I married Jeff when I was eighteen.'

Jane picked up a bag of sprouts and a bowl and handed them to Laurie. 'You can do these. I'll do the potatoes.' She was wondering whether it would upset Laurie to talk, or if it was what she needed to do.

'How long has all this been going on, Laurie?' she asked in a gentle voice. 'I mean—this latest bust-up isn't the only occasion, is it?'

Laurie looked at her. 'No,' she said sadly. 'Oh no . . .' How to describe how it had been? How Jeff had changed from the jaunty, affectionate man he used to be. How she had changed too, she supposed, from the green girl who had loved him so much—she took a deep breath and tried to focus her flying thoughts. 'Well, I ran away with Jeff when I was eighteen. I'd just started a job in the bank, after my A-levels. But I threw it all up when Jeff asked me to go with him. That made my parents angry—or my mother, anyway. She—my mother—didn't like Jeff. He was a salesman for a software company—a good bit older than me, and very . . . very good-looking and full of charm . . .' She glanced at Jane, half sorrowfully. 'I was so young—so easily impressed!' A faint glimmer of a smile touched her—though it wasn't really funny. Not for her. 'He was all right till . . . till I was heavily pregnant with Jason. Up till then, he was quite loving and—and attentive—though he had moods, even then. But then—he seemed to go right off me. And when the baby came, he didn't want to know. He didn't even like it being a boy. I don't think he's a natural father.' She looked away from Jane, seeing the distaste in Jeff's eyes, his reluctance to help, his resentment at all those broken nights and dirty nappies. 'He didn't like the mess, and he didn't like having to stay in at night. He was used to having a good time, and he couldn't really understand why things had to change.' She sighed. 'So . . . he took to going out on his own . . . and found—er—other distractions.'

'Leaving you literally holding the baby?'

'Oh yes.' Her smile was bleak. 'It's a familiar pattern, isn't it? But I was very young—and silly enough to protest. That was . . . when it all started.'

Jane could see it. The small cramped rooms, the crying baby, the endless washing, and the tired, inexperienced young mother who had once been a pretty, adoring wife to take out and show off to his friends. And the smart-aleck young salesman who liked life to be bright and full of parties, and plenty of feminine admiration.

'What about your parents? Weren't they any help?'

Laurie sighed. 'They lived up north. And my father died of a heart attack not long after I ran away. My mother said it was my fault. She blamed me for everything—my father's death—the shortage of money—

having to sell the house—the lot. She wouldn't come to our wedding. She wouldn't have anything to do with us—not even when Jason was born.' She went on, more slowly, 'But I did go home once . . . when things got very bad . . . when Jason was about two. I had a miscarriage.'

'Was that Jeff's fault, too?' Jane's voice was grim.

'Yes. At least—partly. We had a row, and in the excitement he pushed me downstairs.'

'I wondered about the gap between Jason and Midge,' murmured Jane.

'I've never admitted it before . . .' Laurie said wonderingly, 'even to myself. But it wasn't *all* his fault. I must've provoked him.' She paused, and then continued in a flat voice, 'The doctors at the hospital said I'd twisted the womb or something—and I oughtn't to have another child.' She looked at Jane again, almost apologetically. 'I *was* careful . . . But Jeff—he was so unpredictable. He would go off me for weeks and then, suddenly—' But there she stalled, and shut her eyes and shuddered. Not even to Jane could she talk of the degradation that she had endured at his hands . . . of the violence that was almost rape, that left her bruised and abused.

'So—you did go home that time? What happened?'

'Oh, it was hopeless. My mother had moved into a flat when my father died. It's rather small, and my mother is obsessively neat and tidy—and her arthritis makes her extra crotchety. Jason was just at the age when he was into everything, and everything he did was wrong. She kept scolding and fussing, and in between telling me that Jeff was no good and it was only what she expected.'

'Didn't she tell you to leave him?'

'Oh no. She told me to go back.'

'You'd made your bed and you must lie on it?'

Laurie gave a helpless little laugh, and there was another small silence while Jane tried to imagine a woman who could send her daughter back to the kind of violence that she had clearly endured for so long.

'What did your father do?' she asked.

'He was assistant bank manager at the local bank. People liked him, and he was very—very respected in the town.' Her voice shook for a moment. She had loved her father. He had always been good to her, always fair-minded and kind. It was through him that she had got her own job in the bank. And she had rewarded him by throwing it all up and running away with Jeff.

'A respectable, quiet profession,' commented Jane.

Laurie gave her a rueful glance. 'Oh yes. Very respectable. That was part of the trouble, really. My mother thought Jeff wasn't good enough for me.'

284

'So she sent you back—to that?'

'I went back,' said Laurie, her small chin setting firmly. 'I made up my mind to try. It wasn't all bad, you know—at least at first. Sometimes things went all right, and Jeff was like he used to be—kind, I mean, and friendly, even generous.' Once more she glanced at Jane, almost pleadingly. 'I *did* try.'

'I'm sure you did.'

'But—' She pushed the long, limp hair out of her eyes. 'The trouble is, when all that's going on—rows and fights, and then reconciliations and attempts at patching things up, and then more rows—you get to a point where you can't think straight any more. You don't know what's happening . . . you can't see it clearly. And then Jeff lost his job. He couldn't get another—it's a bad time for unemployment, especially salesmen, and it was bad for him. I understood how he felt. He lost status. And he thought it was all my fault. He was convinced I had trapped him into marriage. And so—' Laurie looked at Jane painfully '—he began to drink a bit more, to boost his courage for interviews, and so on. He'd always been a bit on the heavy side about spirits. Part of his job, he used to say, oiling the works with clients . . . Only, it began to get out of hand.' Laurie shivered, remembering the drunken rows, the constant threat of violence erupting over trifles, the increasing shortage of money, the slow slide into poverty and debt and down-at-heel shabbiness . . .

'What finally made you go?' asked Jane.

'He started to go for Midge,' Laurie said. 'And I suddenly realised that the children weren't safe any more. My little Midge was reduced to crawling into the broom cupboard for safety, and Jay—he tried to get between Midge and his father—even between me and Jeff. He's absurdly brave for his age. And it wasn't fair on them. I can't think why I didn't see it sooner! I don't know what harm it may have done them already.'

'Had he ever hit them before, do you know?'

She looked at Jane with growing horror. 'I don't know. Never while I was there. But I—I used to leave them with him sometimes when I went to the shops. And—and sometimes they did have bruises I couldn't account for. I thought they were just childish tumbles . . . But now, I'm not so sure.'

'Did they ever complain?'

'No. Never. But sometimes . . . Jay's eyes looked . . .' Almost black with the thoughts he was trying to hide, she thought. My poor, brave Jason, hiding fear and hurt from his mother . . .

'But it was the swans, really . . .' she murmured.

'The swans?'

'Yes.' She kept her eyes shut. Far behind them, she could see those

285

dazzling white wings beating against the sun. 'So *beautiful,*' she whispered. 'Flying very high. They flew right over the house. I watched them go. The sound they made was like—like music—only wider . . . so strong and free . . . I listened a long time . . . until they were gone . . .' She opened her eyes and stared at Jane. 'I knew then that I must go. It all came clear to me. Somewhere—' She looked out of the window, to the clear sky beyond. 'Somewhere out there—is a world. I'd forgotten how beautiful it is. But I can't ignore it any longer—or let my children grow up without knowing it. I've got to get out and find it.'

'Yes!' agreed Jane. 'Yes! Of course you have.'

IT WAS LATE THAT AFTERNOON that the hospital telephoned Jane with the news of Jeff's arrest. She immediately rang the police and suggested that they should talk to the policewoman who had seen Laurie, and read the doctor's report. It seemed to her that there was enough evidence to bring a more serious charge of assault and grievous bodily harm, and also to get an injunction restraining the husband from molesting his wife further.

She knew from past experience that the police were reluctant to get involved in what they called 'domestic' disputes. However, for Laurie's sake she felt she had to try. And presently the young policewoman who had first seen Laurie in hospital came round to discuss the matter.

Laurie was quite calm about it. 'Yes, I'll see her. You'll be there, though, won't you?'

'Of course—if you want.'

Laurie thought for a moment. 'If they just convict Jeff on the first charge—what will happen?'

'He'll probably get a fine and be bound over.'

'To keep the peace?' Her smile was brittle. 'He won't, you know.' Laurie began to laugh. 'But if the second charge sticks—?'

'He'll get a month or two in jail—according to how lenient or how tough the magistrate is. Usually, in your kind of case, they're much too lenient!'

Laurie nodded wearily. 'So I've gathered. Not that I'm trying to make things worse for Jeff. I just want a bit of peace and safety . . . for me and the children.'

Jane agreed. 'An injunction would help. Also,' she went on carefully, 'a cooling-off period in jail might bring him to his senses a bit. Well, I'd better fetch the policewoman in, and you can tell her what you know.'

The policewoman was sympathetic and patient. She had seen Laurie in hospital, and she could see that she was still very shocked. She took careful notes and asked only relevant questions.

286

'Have you ever been to the police before?'

'Yes,' sighed Laurie. 'Twice. Once, I got frightened and locked him out, and he broke the door down. So I panicked and took the children round to the police station.'

'What did they do?'

'Nothing. They gave me a cup of tea and sent me home.'

The policewoman made no comment. 'And the second time?'

'He threw me through the window into the back yard. I was—I was afraid the children might get hurt by all the glass. So I went back to the police and asked them to come and—and speak to Jeff.'

'Did they?'

'Oh yes. A constable came back with me. But by this time Jeff had calmed down. He was very reasonable. He said it was an accident—and I was young and easily frightened. He more or less suggested I was hysterical and making it all up—or at least exaggerating. He can be very persuasive and charming when he likes . . . and I think the constable believed him.'

'Yes,' murmured the policewoman, busily scribbling. 'I see.' She glanced at Jane, and a look of grim understanding flashed between them. 'Well,' she added kindly, 'that'll be all, thanks, Mrs Collins. You've been most helpful. I hope we can get something sorted out.'

'One thing—' said Laurie. 'Will I—would I have to give evidence in court? Because I—I don't think I could face seeing him.'

'I would suggest,' said Jane crisply, 'that the doctor's report might be sufficient. You are clearly not fit to attend the court at present.' The policewoman agreed.

'And the—the injunction?' Laurie still sounded tense.

'That will go through, I'm sure,' said the policewoman. 'But if there was any doubt, you could take out a civil injunction yourself.' She turned to Jane. 'I'm sure Mrs Everett would arrange it for you.'

'Yes,' nodded Jane. 'I would.'

They left Laurie then, but as soon as they had gone she began to shake. The wings suddenly began their urgent beating in her head, seeming to swirl and grow until their mighty pinions blotted out the light. Before their powerful onslaught, Laurie went down without a cry.

IT WAS PENNY who picked her up and put her back to bed—Penny who brought her a hot bottle for the shakes and a cup of tea to warm her hands on, and Penny who perched on the bed and said with cheerful good sense, 'You oughtn't to let them get at you—I don't. Bugger the lot, I say!'

Laurie tried to laugh. 'You're such a comfort, Penny.' She looked at the friendly, easy-going girl and said suddenly, 'You haven't told me what you're doing here—among all us tired old battered women! You're much too young to be mixed up in all this, aren't you?'

Penny swung her foot to and fro as she sat on the edge of the bed. 'It depends what you mean by "too young",' she said.

Laurie was horrified. 'You? Battered?'

'Beaten up,' she agreed. 'Oh yes. But I wasn't exactly a *wife!*'

Laurie was puzzled. 'What, then?'

'A daughter.'

'You mean—your father beat you up?'

'Oh no. Well, not exactly . . .' She stared at Laurie. 'You don't understand a thing, do you? Well, I'll tell you.' The hard, flippant note was back in her voice. 'My ma married a man younger than her, see? A bit randy. Fancied little girls . . . So he—' She looked down at her bulging stomach.

'Oh, my God,' said Laurie. 'But—how old were you?'

'About—eight or nine, when it began. I couldn't tell my ma—or anyone, come to that. He threatened to beat me if I did. He said he'd deny it anyway, and no one would believe me. They'd think I was just a tart.' There was a small, rueful smile tugging at the corners of her mouth. 'And in the end that's just what they did think—my ma included.'

'*What?* When you—when he got you pregnant?'

'Why should they believe me? I told my ma what he was like. But she wouldn't believe me. She didn't *want* to believe me.' The blue-green eyes just touched Laurie's appalled gaze. 'So—my ma gave me the most godawful hiding I'd ever had, for being a liar and a trouble-maker, and having a sick mind, she said. And when my—when *he* came in, he gave me a beating, too, for telling my ma. I told him I was desperate—I was pregnant, and what was he going to do about it? And he said—nothing. How did he know the child was his? It was most unlikely, he said. . . and then my ma threw me out.'

'Just like that?'

'Just like that.'

'But—*Penny!* What on earth did you do?'

Penny sighed. 'Joe found me in the street—like he found you. And then Jane took over.' She grinned at Laurie, the old, perky cheerfulness coming to the surface again. 'Thank God for Jane, eh?'

'Yes, but—Penny, how old are you now? What will you do?'

'I'm nearly sixteen. And I shall manage! Jane says I can stay here till it's born, if I like. And if I kind of give her a hand with the kids, she can say I'm a helper and then I can stay longer than the others.'

'Do you want the baby? Could you have—'

'An abortion? They'd probably have given me one—seeing how young I was and all that. But I left it too late, see? They couldn't do it now.'

Laurie was silent for a moment. 'So . . . will you have it adopted?'

Penny hesitated. 'I dunno. Jane thinks I should. She says I'm too young to cope with being a single parent, and I oughtn't to have my life ruined before I start, and all that. But I'm not sure . . .' She looked at Laurie shyly. 'Thing is, I like kids. I'm good with 'em. I like *your* kids, Laurie. And I—I think I'd like looking after a baby. Not sure I'd want to part with it . . . Poor little bugger didn't ask to be born, after all—or to be foisted on someone else.' She looked through the window to the scruffy garden beyond, and added half to herself, 'And I'm not sure I'd want to keep it here, either. Not permanently, whatever Jane says.'

Laurie was also staring out of the window. 'Don't you like it here?'

'It's all right.' Penny was frowning a little. 'It's safe. I'm not saying I'm not grateful. Jane's been wonderful to me.' She glanced up at Laurie again, smiling a little. 'But . . . Oh, I dunno . . . I think a baby needs a more settled sort of place. Not with all these women and their problems. Not for ever!'

Laurie sighed. It was what she was already feeling about Jay and Midge—though she knew she couldn't change things for them yet. She simply wasn't strong enough.

'Anyway,' said Penny, suddenly cheerful again, 'this isn't doing you no good. I'm going to fetch some more tea. And then I'll bring the kids in.'

Laurie lay back against her pillows. She would have to pull herself together somehow. But she thought with longing of that clear blue sky, with the white swans flying . . .

JASON AND MIDGE had devised a way of avoiding trouble with the other kids. When squabbles broke out, they retreated round the other side of the shed where there was an old rubbish tip with a little hollow. It didn't take long to pile a few cardboard boxes together and make a kind of shelter, a small safe house of their own.

It was here that Penny found them next day, when Jane sent her to fetch them to see the social worker. But Penny was much too used to trouble herself—and too near childhood, perhaps—to blunder in upon their private sanctuary without asking.

'Jay?' she whispered loudly. 'It's me—Penny. You coming out?'

After a moment, Jason crawled out backwards.

'I won't tell,' said Penny quickly, and watched anxiety fade from the boy's eyes. They were like his mother's, Penny thought—grey and farseeing. In fact, he was very like his mother altogether, with that straight, thick honey-gold hair, and that determined-looking chin.

'There's a lady wants to see you,' she explained. 'Two of 'em, actually.'

She grinned at Jason. 'They might ask a few questions.'

Jason's face closed. 'Like what?'

'Like . . .' Penny paused, and then decided to be frank. It was always best with kids, to be honest. They saw through you too fast. 'Like . . . what happened at home? And whether your dad hit you or Midge, as well as your mum?'

Jason was silent.

After a moment, Penny said conversationally, 'My dad often hit me.'

'Did he?' Jason's eyes were fixed on her face, looking almost black with his secret thoughts. 'What do you want me to say?'

'The truth, of course.' Penny sounded quite definite. 'What really happened . . .'

He thought deeply. 'Not Midge?'

'No,' said Penny firmly. 'They'd like to see Midge—just to know she's OK. But they won't ask her anything. She's too small.'

'Good.' Jason bent down and called softly, 'Midge—it's all right. You can come out. We're going with Penny.'

LAURIE WAS FEELING AT BAY. They were in Jane's office. There was the social worker, Lois Brown, and a calm-looking woman solicitor called Madeleine Williamson, who seemed to be a friend of Jane's and well acquainted with the problems at the refuge. And there was Jane.

'If you have no objection . . .' Lois Brown was saying politely. But Laurie had.

'Aren't they—isn't Jason a bit young for questions?' she said.

'It might help,' said Lois carefully, 'for us to get the whole picture. We'll be very careful.'

Laurie looked helplessly at Jane, who said gently, 'We are very experienced here, Laurie. We would never browbeat a child.'

'Lois can ask all the questions,' said Madeleine pleasantly. 'I'll just listen. He won't be badgered, I promise you.'

At this point, Penny came in with the children. Midge ran straight to Laurie and climbed into her arms. But Jason stood still, looking from his mother to the others in mute enquiry.

'Jay—' Laurie drew him close. 'You can tell them what they want to know, I'm sure. Just answer them truthfully, won't you?'

'All right,' answered Jason, and kept his head high.

Jane got up. 'Then we'll go and make everyone some tea,' she said. 'Midge, are you going to stay with Jason?'

But Midge—for the first time since they came to The Hide—made a scene. She clung to Laurie, her arms tight round her neck, and screamed.

'Never mind.' Lois Brown spoke quickly. 'We'll just talk to Jason.'

'In any case,' remarked the solicitor in a cool, clear voice, 'I think Midge has told us what we want to know.'

Laurie turned rather desperately to Jane. 'Couldn't you stay?' After all, Jane was neutral. She would make Jason feel safer.

Jane looked at the other two enquiringly. They both nodded. 'Very well,' she said quietly. 'I'll stay.'

Penny, after a swift glance round, took Laurie and Midge away to make the tea.

So now it was Jason's turn to stand at bay.

'First of all,' began Lois Brown gently, 'do you want to go home?'

'No!' flashed Jason. And then, flatly, 'Not if *he's* there.'

'Then—' Lois Brown still sounded casual '—do you like being here?'

Jason considered. 'It's all right.' He looked at them, almost with contempt. They asked such obvious questions. 'It's safe,' he explained.

'Safe from what, Jason?' asked Lois, even more gently.

'From harm,' he said. And then he spelt it out for them. 'From my dad.'

Madeleine Williamson made a note.

'Did he often hit your mother, Jason?'

'Oh yes.' The contempt had come back. 'All the time.'

'And did he ever hit you—or Midge?'

His face seemed to close. He did not answer.

'Did he, Jason?' persisted the social worker.

'Yes,' he admitted. 'Sometimes.'

'When?'

'When Mum was out.'

'And Midge, too?'

A kind of darkness came into his eyes. 'Only when she cried . . . I tried to stop him . . .' He looked at them helplessly. 'But he was too strong . . . I did tell her not to cry,' he went on, with painful honesty. 'And she managed not to, mostly.'

There was a stunned silence. Then Lois Brown asked in a deceptively casual tone, 'I suppose your mother never hit you?'

He flared into anger then. 'My *mum?* She wouldn't hurt anyone!'

'Not even your dad?'

'No.' He spoke decisively. 'She used to tell us he was tired and it wasn't his fault. She used to say . . . people get cross when they're tired—and we mustn't hate him.' His face was suddenly as bleak as his cold young voice. 'But I *do* hate him, for hurting Mum and Midge!'

He stood there, taut and defensive, defying them all. But before they could ask any more, even if they had wanted to, Laurie came back into the room, with Midge running after her. She crossed swiftly to Jason and laid an arm round his shoulders.

'That's enough!' she said. 'Can't you see he's had enough?'

And Penny, behind her, added cheerfully, 'Look, Jay, we've brought you a cup of tea first—and a chocolate biscuit.'

Jason leaned against his mother and gave up trying to stand up straight and tall, like an adult.

Everyone relaxed then, and Madeleine Williamson said to Laurie, under cover of the general conversation, 'He's a brave boy, your son. You must be proud of him.' She added that she would be representing Laurie in court. 'You'll get legal aid, of course. For the rest, if you want to take other legal steps concerning your marriage or your maintenance and so on, I can come back here to discuss it with you. Or you can come to me at my office when you are feeling stronger.' She smiled. 'These sorts of decision need a clear head. I gather yours is still—er—?'

'Woolly,' said Laurie, smiling a little, too. 'Distinctly woolly. But—but thank you for coming here specially . . . and for your help.' Then, without waiting for anyone to reply, she took Jason and Midge out into the sooty garden to breathe. It was true, her head felt very woolly indeed. And the swans' wings were back inside it, beating and beating to get free . . .

'Is she all right?' asked Lois Brown anxiously.

'No,' said Jane. 'But she will be—given time.'

'Just leave her be!' exploded Penny. 'All this argy-bargy! What she needs is a bit of peace!' And she flounced out of the room.

The other three women looked at each other and sighed.

'Don't we all?' murmured Jane.

THAT NIGHT, LAURIE could not sleep. She lay in her narrow camp bed, tossing and turning, while her thoughts went round and round in her head, and every bruised bone and muscle seemed to ache more than ever. By morning she was in a high fever, tossing and muttering and crying out.

MEANWHILE, LIFE was not being very kind to Jeff. He got home to a cold, cluttered house, and nothing in the kitchen to eat.

He was angry about the mess, angry with the hospital and the police, angry with himself and, obscurely, even more angry with Laurie who had caused all this uproar by running off.

And the next day he was dragged down to the police station again, where he was told there was a second charge against him, and on top of that someone else came round to the door and served him with an injunction. He was astonished. Had Laurie done all this? He wouldn't have thought she had it in her. She must've found a pushy lawyer somewhere. And that reminded him—he'd better find one, too.

Down at The Dog and Bear, he asked his mates about lawyers, and someone recommended a bloke he knew who wasn't very expensive. He might have applied for legal aid but instead he swallowed a couple of drinks and went and hired his mate's seedy friend on the spot.

After this, he felt better. Things would be looked after for him now.

He went back to The Dog and Bear and leaned on the bar to talk to Brenda, the barmaid. She was large and plump, and usually jolly. Everyone liked her.

'Have one on me,' invited Jeff, waving a note in a reckless hand.

'Don't mind if I do,' agreed Brenda. 'Port and lemon, thanks. What's yours?'

'Whisky,' he ordered. 'Drowning my sorrows.'

'Oh yes? Why's that?'

'Lonely,' he sighed. 'Wife's gone off.'

'Sorry to hear that.'

'Got a court case coming up, too.'

'Bad luck.' She raised her glass. 'Cheers! Don't let it get you down.'

'No.' Jeff stared at his glass. He needed company. Well, he needed more than company. Let's face it, he needed sex. And Brenda wasn't half bad, when you came to think of it.

'What're you doing when you come off duty?' he asked.

'Nothing you'd be interested in,' replied Brenda.

'Are you sure?' asked Jeff, putting on all the charm he knew.

'Well . . . ' Brenda considered him with a fat jolly smile. 'We'll see.'

BY THE TIME the court case came up, he was feeling quite perky.

Brenda had let him come to her flat over the greengrocer's shop on the corner. She bestowed her favours cheerfully, but Jeff suspected she would throw him out quite forcibly if she got bored. In the meantime, she was solid and comforting to be with, and pretty good in bed. It made him feel ten foot tall again and brought back the swagger into his step.

All the same, in court he did not understand what was going on. When they asked him questions, he answered sullenly—and then tried to remember to be smooth and charming.

'I wanted to see my wife,' he said reasonably.

'When I understand you had put her in hospital with your brutality?'

That was the woman solicitor. ' . . . mistake . . . ' he muttered. 'A one-off thing . . . lost my temper—sorry . . .'

'I have here a statement that your wife had asked for police protection at least twice before, and had left home already once.'

There was a bit more talk, but the magistrate seemed indisposed to prolong things. 'Three months on the first count,' he rasped, 'and a further one month on the second. And you will be bound over to keep the peace—and not to approach or molest or harass your wife in any way—for one year.'

Jeff could not believe it. A prisoner? Him? *Three months?* No, *four!* What had he done to deserve it? It wasn't fair.

He suddenly stood up and shouted all this out loud. But it didn't do any good. They hustled him away, still shouting and trying to explain. And it was all Laurie's fault.

LAURIE WAS ILL for nearly a week. She missed her hospital checkup and missed Jeff's court case. In the end, though, she appeared in Jane's office and demanded to know what was going on.

Jane told her quietly.

'Four months?' said Laurie, wonderingly. 'Then—'

'That gives you a chance to get your life sorted out,' Jane intervened. 'By the time he comes out, you can be well out of reach, with everything settled. And I shouldn't waste any sympathy on him,' she added drily. 'I gather from Madeleine Williamson that he was having an affair with the local barmaid by way of consolation.'

Laurie sighed. Jane looked at her quite sternly. 'Laurie—you've made the break. Now you have to think of the future. You're still young. You have a whole life before you.'

'Yes,' agreed Laurie, still staring out of the window, 'a whole life. I'll—I'll go and see Madeleine Williamson tomorrow.'

'No need,' said Jane. 'She's here now, seeing someone else. I'll fetch her. In any case, you don't look fit yet to go anywhere. Sit down, I won't be long.'

Laurie almost fell into the nearest chair. It was true, she wasn't ready to go anywhere yet. Jane was right. It was time to plan for the future. She took a deep breath and tried to think ahead.

PART 2

TAKE-OFF

The morning after Madeleine Williamson's consultation, Penny came into the bedroom, smiling. 'You've got a visitor.'

Laurie's heart jumped. 'Who?'

Behind Penny, a square, brownish figure came forward. 'It's me. Joe. Remember me? How are you now, then?'

'Better.' Laurie smiled her relief. 'Much better, thanks.'

'We was wondering—Penny and me—if you'd like a trip to the

country? You and the kids, I mean? Gotta get some veggies, see? Thought maybe you could do with a breather?'

Radiance flooded her face. 'Oh Joe! What a lovely idea. Real country?'

'Real country.' He grinned. 'Green fields an' all!'

'Come on,' urged Penny. 'Don't waste time! I'll fetch the kids.' She turned to Joe. 'Shall I make some sandwiches?'

'No,' growled Joe. 'Fish and chips on me. Make a day of it.'

They all laughed. It was like a Sunday School treat already.

THE ANCIENT VAN RATTLED out into the sprawling suburbs. Before long, they turned off the Maidstone road into the rich Kentish countryside. Orchards and market gardens and hop fields spread out before them, until the old green van came to a farm gate leading into a sandy track with a farmhouse at the end.

On one side were fields of sprouts and cabbages, carrots and onions, and even rows of late strawberries. And on the other side were apple trees laden with fruit, while beyond them were the tall aisles of the hop gardens like a solid, leafy wall. There was a man with a tractor and trailer moving through the orchards, loading bushel baskets of fruit. And in the hop garden there were knots of people clustered round the hop bins, picking the green, spicy bobbles of the hops, while another tractor and trailer collected the filled sacks and took them off to the drying kilns.

At one end of the farmhouse buildings, as they drew up in the yard, Laurie saw a strange-looking barn with a beautiful circular roof of ancient reddish tiles with a tall cowl on top.

'What's that?' asked Jason, pointing.

'Oast-house,' Joe explained. 'Where they dries the hops.' He jerked a thumb at the tractor between the hop bines. 'They're picking the hops now, see? Most farms use the machines nowadays, but this one likes the old ways . . . Stan's old-fashioned.' He grinned sideways at Jason and Laurie. 'Used to use a lot of Londoners in the old days. A few of 'em still come down for casual labour—apples, sprout-picking, strawberries . . . the only holiday they ever get, some of 'em.'

He pulled up in the yard. 'Everybody out!' he said cheerfully, and went off to load up his van with produce.

Penny and the children scampered off down one of the green lanes of hops, Laurie following more slowly. It still hurt to walk fast, and her aching ribs still made breathing difficult. But it was wonderful to be out in the air, with these huge washed skies and argosies of bright clouds sailing above her.

One of the nearest group of women pickers looked up and smiled. A large, kindly-looking woman, she was busy stripping the hops from the

bines that the men had pulled down from the trellises of hop poles and wires above their heads, with the rest of her family working as a team round her. She was wearing a hessian apron wrapped round her cotton skirt, and her hands were stained green and gold with the hops as she dropped them into the hessian sack stretched on withies that made up each hop bin. All round them was the clean, spicy scent of the hops, and the laughter and chatter of the pickers and the children.

'Joining us?' the woman asked.

Laurie hesitated.

'Used to be more of us,' added the woman. 'But machines is quicker. They don't want us nowadays, most places.' She squinted up the hop garden. 'Tallyman's coming ... Competition today to see who's the fastest picker—prizes and all!' She winked at Laurie.

Laurie grinned. 'What's the prize?'

'Dunno. Bottle of beer, I expect! Or cider!' She laughed and glanced sideways at Laurie. 'You down for long?'

'No,' sighed Laurie. 'Wish I was ...' She suddenly thought, that's true. I do wish I was. She could see Jason and Midge dodging about, following a shrieking mob of children intent on some game of cops and robbers. It occurred to her that she hadn't seen them look so carefree and unafraid for a long time. Even Penny had shed some of her increasing heaviness. She was swerving and laughing, kicking up her heels like a young colt, and Laurie was absurdly touched by the sight.

'Why don't you stay?' said the woman. 'There's room in the huts. Some of 'em went home this week—and there's still a lot of hops to get in while the weather holds. Dessay the boss could do with you.'

Laurie stared at her. But she did not speak, as just then a knot of people headed by 'Spider', the tall tallyman, came down the hop ride towards them. He looked at the green mounds in the bins, and dipped his tally stick into them to measure the volume of picked hops. After a shrewd guess, he began to shovel the hops out into his bushel basket, counting as he went, and tipping them into the big sacks which would be loaded onto the tractor and taken away for drying. 'Three ... four ... five ...' his voice droned on. Then he totted them all up and wrote them down in his little black notebook.

'Most bushels so far, Dorrie!' he said to the woman. 'You're winning!' and he passed on to the next group of hop pickers.

Somewhere down at the far end a bell like an ice-cream van's carillon chimed. 'Grub's up,' said fat Dorrie. And from all over the hop field and the orchards and fields beyond, pickers and children streamed out in a cheerful, chattering crowd.

'Fish and chips,' said Joe's voice close behind Laurie. 'Promised you.'

They sat on a dusty bank near the end of the hop garden and ate fish and chips out of greasy newspaper. Then Joe went off to buy everyone an ice cream as an extra treat.

'Mum,' said Jason, with his mouth full, 'I like it here. Couldn't we stay?'

Midge agreed, and stuffed in another chip. Laurie looked from them to Penny.

'Well, why not?' said Penny sturdily. 'Do us good.'

Joe came back with the ice creams, and Laurie tried vainly to pay for them. 'I've got some money, Joe. The welfare people gave me an emergency grant, to tide me over. Jane fixed it for me.'

'I know,' growled Joe. 'She told me. But this is a present, see?'

Laurie looked at his face, and saw. She thanked him gravely. 'You're right, of course. I mustn't squander it. God knows where the next lot's coming from. But I was wondering—couldn't I earn some down here?'

'*Here?*' asked Joe, surprised. 'You mean—hop-picking?'

'Why not?' She glanced at the children's faces. 'They love it here, Joe—the space and the—the greenness. After London, it's so . . . *clean.*'

'You fit to work, then?' he asked. 'Only just out of bed an' all?' He looked at her severely. 'Another thing . . . Jane's very pushed for space, you know. If you stayed down here, she mightn't have room when you got back.'

Laurie nodded. 'I know . . . But in any case, I can't stay there for ever, Joe. I've got to move on somewhere.'

Joe thought for a bit. 'I s'pose—the Welfare'll house you?'

Laurie nodded again. 'Yes, a couple of rooms . . . or bed and breakfast, they said.' She pushed the hair out of her eyes in the familiar, anxious gesture. 'That's no good for the children, Joe. Not permanently, I mean.'

Joe agreed. 'What would you like, then?'

Laurie took a deep breath and looked up at the blue skies and the dazzling towers of cloud moving majestically across them. 'I'd like to go right away . . .' she murmured. 'Right away from London . . . to somewhere small and quiet—maybe by the sea or something—where it's empty and—and *clean* . . . and I could work.'

Joe said, half smiling, 'What can you do then—besides picking hops?'

Laurie sighed. 'Not much! I can cook a bit, and clean a house, I suppose. And dig a garden. I like gardens.' She sighed again. 'I used to help my father with the garden, when we got home from the bank.'

'The bank?' Joe's voice was sharper.

'Oh yes, I forgot . . . I can add up a cash balance.'

Joe laughed. 'Worth your weight in gold, girl!' He looked round at the sunny orchards and hop gardens. 'You really want to stay down here?'

'If there's any work—'

'What about me?' Penny demanded. 'I can pick. So could the kids.'

Joe shook his head, laughing. 'Bloody hell, kid—what've I let Stan in for?' He sighed. 'OK, I'll ask him.' He looked at Laurie's expressive face. 'You've got your green fields,' he said, smiling. 'Anything else you'd like?'

'Swans . . .' said Laurie suddenly.

Joe looked startled. 'Swans? Well, there's the River Medway just down the bottom. Why not go and see while I talk to Stan?'

Together, he and Laurie—with Penny and the two children dancing ahead—walked through the hop gardens and orchards until they came to the water meadows and the slow-moving river beyond. There he left them, and turned back towards the farm.

The banks were still flowery with balsam and loosestrife and meadow-sweet, and the brown stream flowed gently by, with cloud-shadow and tree reflected in its surface. A few moorhens and coots chugged busily about among the reed beds, and a pair of mallards sailed jauntily downstream on the twirling eddies.

'There!' breathed Jason, pointing. 'There they are!'

And there, drifting peacefully on the river's smooth flow, were two calm and graceful swans.

'Oh!' whispered Laurie. 'Aren't they *beautiful!*' And she sank down on the river bank to watch them, her eyes suddenly abrim with tears.

Penny looked at her, and then turned away and began to talk to Jason about mallard ducks, and swans, and boats on the river. Still talking, they wandered away along the river bank, with Midge held firmly by the hand in case she toppled into the water—she was so eager to see everything growing and green and new.

Laurie sat on in the sun, watching the quiet swans. She, too, seemed to be drifting into a world that was all green and gold, and white wings reflected in brown water . . . all stillness and peace, with no shadow of fear behind it . . .

Presently, the swans began to swim towards a small finger of land reaching out from the river bank. As they reached the reedy shallows, Laurie saw the figure of a man outlined against the sun. He too seemed all green and gold and brown—almost to merge with the landscape and to belong to it, he stood so still, planted on the river bank like a tree.

'*Men as trees walking*', thought Laurie vaguely. He lifted a hand to the swans and they came quite close so that he could lean out and stroke the beautiful curve of their heads and long white necks. He reached into a pocket and brought out food for them, and they took it from his hand. Then he gave them a final, loving stroke, and she caught the faint murmur of his voice as he turned away and came towards her. 'Grow strong,' she thought he said.

She sat watching him, and an extraordinary sense of release and gladness seemed to well up inside her—a feeling almost of recognition. Here was someone unafraid—someone untouched by the seeds of anger or spite—who walked through the dappled world of the water meadows not as if he owned it, but was part of it.

As he came close, she found herself looking into a brown, lean face with finely etched lines round eyes which were a deep cloud-shadow grey. There were two small wings of grey in his hair, which was brown and faintly curly. And his mouth curved gently like his hair, and was very kind.

He for his part saw a small pale girl with long fair hair and eyes too big and dark-shadowed. Her mouth was resolute, but seemed to tremble on the edge of tears.

'Are they yours?' she asked.

'What?'

'The swans.'

'Oh, no. They're wild swans—entirely wild and free.' He smiled at her.

'But—they knew you!'

'That's because they were injured, and I took them in. But they are well again now—and free to come and go as they please.'

'Free?' murmured Laurie, as if it was a strange word she didn't know.

'They only come back because they know I'm friendly, and it's safe.'

Because they know I'm friendly, and it's safe. Laurie shut her eyes for a moment, blinking back absurd tears. When she opened them again, he was sitting on the bank beside her.

'Do you—are there a lot of swans on the river?'

'Quite a few still. Not nearly so many as there used to be.'

'Why?'

'They get hurt . . . and they die.' His voice was grim. 'They get tangled up in fishing line—they get shot—they get fish-hooks embedded in their throats—they get attacked by people on the banks, people in boats.'

'*Attacked?* Swans?'

'Oh yes. Beaten with paddles. Tied to a tree and used as a dartboard. Dragged behind an outboard motor and chopped up by the propellor. Thrown on a bonfire and burnt. Their beaks cut off, their wings torn off. You name it, people have done it.'

Laurie's eyes were almost black with anger. '*Why?* What is it about us human beings? . . . *Why* are we so violent?'

The quiet man watching her knew she was talking of more than swans.

'It's a kind of despair,' he murmured. 'I think . . . yes. Despair. That life can be so ugly and disappointing.'

Laurie nodded. 'So they hit out?' She knew that pattern.

'At the nearest thing, yes.' He looked at her. 'Nothing has any right to be so beautiful and so pure. They hate it.' Once more he glanced fleetingly at Laurie. 'Innocence, they *have* to destroy it. It's like walking on new snow. It seems to mock them with its purity . . .' There was a strange edge to his tone. 'And it's the same with swans.'

Laurie sighed. So beautiful and so pure, she thought, watching the two wild swans still sailing on the river.

'It isn't, of course,' he added, his eyes also on the swans. 'Life isn't disappointing and ugly.'

'Isn't it?'

'No,' he said, not missing the wistful note in her voice. 'Not all the time.'

'Is it—a kind of sanctuary that you run?' she asked.

'Sort of . . .' His eyes crinkled with laughter. 'I had a caravan first, on the river bank. But now it's a small, rather derelict cottage on a backwater. It's just right for the birds—enclosed and quiet, with a stretch of safe water. But even so, I've had to dredge it for lead at the bottom. Fishermen's lead weights are lethal to swans . . . The injured ones stay in the house when they're really sick, and then they move out by stages.'

Laurie nodded. 'Not much room for you, by the sound of it!'

He laughed. 'I don't mind. I came to an arrangement with the Wildlife people. I've got a roof over my head—and a bed to lie on!'

A roof over my head, and a bed to lie on, thought Laurie. And I haven't. The children haven't, either—except the awful crowded chaos of Jane's hostel. *You've made your bed and you must lie on it!* . . . But I won't! she said to herself. I must pull myself together and find somewhere to live. I wonder if Joe will have persuaded the farmer, Stan, to let us stay?

Far down the bank, she heard the sound of Penny and the children returning, their clear young voices carrying across the quiet air.

'It will get better,' the man murmured, to no one in particular, and watched as Midge ran up to her mother, babbling happily of ducks and babies and water lilies. But Jason came up to her slowly, and held out a long white swan's feather which he had found on the river bank.

'Mum?' he said, and laid the feather in her lap.

Laurie smiled at him through tear-dazzled eyes. In the strangely adult gaze of her young son she saw reassurance and clear understanding. I know, he was saying. I know there's never been time to sit on a river bank and look at swans—not for ages and ages. I know when a thing is beautiful it makes you cry . . . But I'm here. And Midge is here. And Penny. And we're safe. There's nothing here to frighten us. Everything is all right.

Laurie picked up the feather. A sudden longing assailed her to plunge into the river beside the snowy swans, and dive down and down until her old life had been washed away—so that she could come to the surface all new and clean, like the swans sailing so proudly, healed and free.

But aloud she only said, 'One small piece of freedom, Jay!' and held up the feather in the late September sunlight.

The man at her side touched the feather with a gentle finger and smiled at her. 'There will be others,' he said softly, and got up and walked away into the sun.

AT THE END of the golden afternoon they wandered back towards the farm, and met Joe. With him came the farmer, a stocky, sandy-haired man with big, freckled hands and a steady stare.

'This is Stan,' said Joe. 'Might take you on for a week—if you think you're up to it.'

Stan looked at Laurie hard, and then at Penny and the children.

'*All* of you?' he enquired.

'All of us!' said Penny firmly. 'All or nothing, that's me.'

'Accommodation's rough.'

Laurie smiled. 'We're not fussy.' Then she looked at Joe and said, 'Jane?'

'You'd better talk to her,' Joe answered. 'Stan'll let you phone—if you're sure?'

'I'm sure,' murmured Laurie with her eyes on the children.

'Wages . . .' Stan was saying. 'Piece rates . . . tallyman will tot it up for you.' He looked at Laurie again and added kindly, 'Glad to have some extra pairs of hands this week. There's an empty hut, and the kitchen's at the end. The others'll show you. Fix yourself up with food and such tomorrow.'

'Tomorrow?' said Laurie, confused.

'Mobile shop comes up here most days. Keeps his prices down—I see that he does!' His mouth took on a grim but humorous quirk. 'Bring her up to the house, Joe. She can phone from there.' He stumped off.

Jane, when she heard the proposal, said at once, 'Yes, Laurie. Stay. Fresh air and sun will do you good. A week, you say? I may have to use your room.'

'Never mind. You've been wonderful to let us have it so long, anyway.' Laurie went back to Penny and the children, and found Joe with them, looking almost as anxious as they were.

'Well?' they all cried.

'Jane says make the most of it!' She stood there smiling, then she turned to Joe and hugged him. 'You're a crafty devil, Joe! I believe you planned this all along!'

'What, me?' Joe was all injured innocence. 'As if I would!'

302

FOR LAURIE—and for Penny and the children—there began a time of quite unexpected peace and freedom.

Accommodation was certainly 'rough'—but the old hoppers' huts were clean and newly whitewashed inside, and divided into separate rooms rather like loose boxes, with bunk beds along the sides. Each family was allocated one of these rooms, and a variety of blankets and rough coverlets. There was a communal kitchen at the end of the huts, but some families preferred to make their own cooking arrangements with camping gas, or open fires in the field outside.

Everyone was friendly, and someone lent Laurie a tin of baked beans and an old cooking pot until she could stock up at the mobile shop next day. Penny had also managed to get some eggs and milk from the farmer's wife, and someone else gave her a screw of tea and half a stale loaf of bread 'to be going on with'—so that the first night's meal seemed like a feast.

They got up early, when the others did, and after some smoky tea and a hunk of bread they all trooped out to the hop gardens for the day's work.

Jason and Midge scampered about, exploring everything in sight—and sometimes out of sight. But even so, Jason remembered that Laurie would be paid for the amount in her bin when the tallyman came round, so he came galloping back, with Midge, out of breath and happy, and began to strip off the bobbles from the bines like the rest of them.

All day they were out in the wind and sun, and in the evening they sat by the campfires and drowsed over more baked beans and sausages on sticks and baked potatoes in the embers.

The tallyman, Spider, had taken a fancy to Laurie. He often stopped by her bin for a chat, and in the evening he strolled up to her cooking fire and stood looking down at her. 'Mind if I join you?'

'Suit yourself,' said Laurie, ladling tinned Irish stew onto plastic plates for the children and Penny.

He glanced at her shrewdly before he sat down on the scuffed grass. Her long hair looked even fairer after the sun and wind, and her face had lost some of its pinched, weary look. But there were still shadows under those very blue eyes. Shadows—or were they bruises just beginning to fade?

'On your own, are you?' he said, with a mixture of friendliness and enquiry in his voice.

Laurie looked at him squarely. 'Yes,' she said, and heard her own voice continue—almost without conscious volition—'and I intend to keep it that way.' She poured some tea out of the old kettle someone had given her into a tin mug, and tipped some milk into it. 'Here,' she said. 'No sugar, I'm afraid.' She watched him for a moment as he sipped his tea. Then she added, 'And to tell you the truth, Spider, I've had my fill of men.'

Spider grinned, and emptied his mug. 'Message received and understood,' he said, and stood up.

Laurie felt a faint stirring of disappointment. Given the brush-off, he didn't want to know. Was ordinary friendship with a man impossible?

She was just reaching out to take his empty mug, when a fight broke out further down the line of fires. She had not really noticed till now that there were three distinct factions in the work force. There were the Cockneys, and the itinerant workers from East Kent, and there were the gypsies, who were touchy about their status, and belligerent, too.

Now, a largish gypsy lad had picked a fight with a Londoner. Blows were flying as fast as oaths, and the various factions had rallied to the assistance of their friends.

'Don't mind them,' said Dorrie, the woman who had been kind to Laurie when she first arrived. 'It don't mean nothing. They're always at it!' She snorted, and straightened her back to stand staring down the field at the group of heaving, struggling men. She turned sharply to Spider, who was also staring down the field. 'That's Slattery's boy—he's a mean one. Better get down there quick, Spider!'

He nodded and went off down the field, stopping to enlist a few burly bystanders on the way.

It was then that Laurie noticed the children had gone. 'Penny!' she said sharply. 'Where are the kids?'

Penny had been tending the fire. Now she looked up in dismay. 'Jay? Midge? I thought they were eating their stew.'

Laurie sprang to her feet. 'It's the fight,' she said. 'They're scared.'

'We'd better search,' said Penny, and went first to the long row of huts where they slept. The children weren't there.

They toured round all the campfires, except where the fight was now being quelled by a determined group of tough men headed by Spider. There was no sign of Jason and Midge, though. Not anywhere.

'Would they run off into the hop gardens?' asked Laurie doubtfully. 'Or the orchards?'

'They might. They could hide there and feel safe,' answered Penny.

Laurie turned desperately to Dorrie. 'Where can I borrow a torch?'

'Storm lantern,' said Dorrie. She waddled over to her sleeping quarters and returned with a paraffin lantern which she lit from the fire with a spill of paper. 'Kids gone off, have they?' She looked into Laurie's face for a moment, seeing the fear and dread in her eyes, and added, 'No good me coming. Too slow. But I'll get a few folk together. You go on . . .'

Laurie swung the lantern in front of her and ran into the dark lanes of hop bines. Penny followed her, calling. But though they stopped and listened at intervals, they heard nothing except the owls in the tall trees, and the distant shouts from the pickers' encampment.

'We'd better split up,' suggested Penny, when they came to a kind of crossroads in the line of hops.

Laurie stood irresolute. Behind her she heard voices, and another lantern swung into view, followed by several men and a woman with two teenage boys waving torches.

'You two go on,' instructed the lantern-swinger cheerfully. 'We can take the other lanes between us. And someone's checking the orchards. They can't have got far.'

Laurie and Penny plodded on, stopping to call and listen intently every few yards. Presently, Penny said, 'That little hut at the end, where they keep the baskets—it's like the back of the shed at Jane's where Jay and Midge used to hide. That's where they'll be. It's the way they'd think, if they were looking for somewhere safe.'

Somewhere safe? thought Laurie, filled with a sudden ache of grief and guilt. What had she done to her children, allowing them to see so much violence that they were afraid of any raised voice. 'Where is it?' she asked Penny sharply. 'Can you remember?'

'Right at the end of the hop garden—where the tractors turn round. I think it's this way . . .'

They hurried on, and soon came to the end of the row of hops and a long stretch of trodden ground and discarded hop bines. But there was no sign of the children, or of the hut they were looking for.

'It must be at the other flaming corner,' said Penny. 'This way!' And she set off again.

All at once there was a wild screech and clatter as a cock pheasant started up under their feet and flapped clumsily away into the darkness. Laurie felt her heart almost stop, she was so absurdly scared. And if she was scared in this country darkness, what must Jason and Midge be feeling?

'Here!' someone was shouting, from the other end of the hop row. 'Over here!'

Laurie ran, with Penny pounding after her. She reached the other clearing, and found a small knot of people waiting for her, standing by a heap of old bushel baskets stacked against the wall of a small shed. And there, curled up in a tight ball of misery and fear, was little Midge—with Jason standing protectively beside her.

Laurie knelt down and put her arms round Midge, and Midge buried her head against her mother's shoulder and burst into tears. Laurie looked at Jason over the top of Midge's golden head. 'Jay?'

'I'm sorry,' he said. 'It was the fight.' He looked at his mother anxiously. 'Midge ran off, and I couldn't make her come back, so I thought I'd better stay with her.' He added in a small, bleak voice, 'She's too little to be left alone in the dark.'

Too little—and too frightened—to be left alone in the dark. And her brave young son, Jason, stood guard . . .

'Never mind,' she said gently. 'You're both safe now. And you were quite right to stay with her. Only, you see, we didn't know where to look for you.'

'I did,' said Penny sturdily, smiling at them with relief. 'I guessed where you'd be, but I went the wrong way!'

Everyone laughed then—as filled with relief as Penny.

'Come on,' said one of the men, 'let's sing you home!' and he started up 'Roll out the Barrel' in a cheerful tenor. Soon they were all singing, and one of them hoisted Jason onto his shoulders and let him ride high among the green hops all the way home. But Midge clung tight to Laurie, and would not let anyone else carry her.

When they got back to the encampment, Dorrie had made a huge pot of soup, and everyone sat round her fire and went on singing. Some of the other groups were singing, too. Laurie saw then, with surprise, that Spider the tallyman had come back to join them, having quelled the fight.

'Glad you found 'em,' he said, and turned to put a piece of sticky chocolate in Midge's small clenched hand. 'You see, Little Miss Muffet, not *all* men are ogres,' he said softly.

But though Laurie smiled an astonished smile at his understanding, Midge was not impressed.

LATE THAT NIGHT, Laurie said to Penny as they lay side by side in the hop-scented darkness, 'Could you cut my hair?'

Penny was half asleep. 'Cut your hair? What—off, you mean?'

'Yes. Off. Quite short.' Her voice was crisp.

'I suppose so . . . given a pair of scissors. Why?' she asked.

Laurie laughed. 'I've decided I've got to be different from now on.'

Penny nodded. 'Yeah. You're the kind men can't keep their frigging hands off—one way and another!' Her voice was dry. 'Right! No more victim stuff. Not from you—or me, neither!'

'Exactly.' Laurie sounded equally matter-of-fact. 'Scissors tomorrow.'

Sleepily, Penny assented. The air and sun and the long day's picking were getting to her, and to Laurie, too. Soon they both slept—dreamlessly and deep.

WHEN THEY BORROWED Dorrie's scissors, and the long gold streamers of hair lay in swathes at Laurie's feet, Midge looked as if she might cry.

But Jason said stoutly, 'She looks smashing. Like a boy, only smarter!'

306

Laurie laughed. She did indeed look rather like a slender boy, with the jagged urchin cut Penny had given her, and the small sprinkling of freckles that the autumn sun was already dusting on her nose. She tried to see her reflection in the saucepan of water heating on the fire. A pale, glimmering image of a new, crisp stranger looked out at her ... New, she thought. All new. But aloud she said, 'I like it. Makes me feel quite tough!'

They went out to the hop fields that day cheerfully, like old hands. The sun shone out of a cloudless sky, though there had been a sharpness in the early morning air and a heavy silver dew on all the cobwebs. But the world was all green and gold. It was a lovely day.

AFTER PICKING, Laurie went up to the farm for eggs and milk. She passed the big oast-house with its load of drying hops (oil-fired drying, now, they told her—not slow-burning coke and sulphur fumes), and came to the farm office next to the dairy. Stan was sitting at his desk, going over the tallyman's figures and trying to assess the day's harvest. Spider was standing beside him.

He glanced up as Laurie came by, and his jaw dropped a little. 'Good grief !' he said. 'What have you done to yourself?'

Laurie grinned and tossed her fair cropped head. 'New me!' she said. 'Needed a change.' She walked on towards the dairy.

'Wait a minute,' called Stan, getting to his feet. 'Joe said something about you doing accounts—is that true?'

Laurie hesitated. 'I could add up money—and get a balance!'

The two men looked at one another and laughed. 'More than we can do!' said Spider.

Stan beckoned her over and showed her his lists and the crabbed, crossed-out entries in his books. 'Make any sense to you?' he asked.

Laurie looked at them cautiously. After a few moments, she nodded and said, 'Could do.'

Stan sighed with relief. 'Would you take them on? It'd be less like hard labour than picking.'

Laurie shook her head. 'No. Not by day. I have to be with the children—they'd fret otherwise.' She looked at him apologetically. 'Maybe I could come up for an hour in the evenings?' She glanced round the little farm office appraisingly. 'You've got electric light out here ... I could manage after dark.'

Stan's face split into a cheerful grin. 'Could you? Take a real weight off my mind!'

Laurie smiled. 'OK. Tomorrow.'

She went on to the dairy where Stan's wife handed over some eggs and a jug of milk.

On the way back, she called through the office door, 'By the way, I s'pose you'll pay me a bit extra?'

'Of course,' agreed Stan. 'Stands to reason.'

'Shall I see you back to the huts?' asked Spider.

'No,' said Laurie. 'No, thanks. I can manage on my own.' And she turned and left them, her bright head held high.

'Wow!' breathed Spider. 'Independent, that one!'

WHAT WITH THE HOP PICKING, and then cooking supper over a slow fire, and, on top of that, working on Stan's accounts in the late evening, it was some days before Laurie could get down to the river again to see the swans. But one afternoon it rained so they were laid off early. Penny and the children volunteered to cook the evening meal, so Laurie went off on her own to walk in the rain.

There were still times when thoughts of Jeff and the awful turmoil of her life with him besieged her—times when she felt racked with guilt because the poor wretch was in prison. But then those scenes of violence would come back into her mind, and she would give herself a mental shake and say, No, I will *not* be sorry for him. Not any more. I can't. I've got to think of the kids and the future now. I've got to build a new life of my own. Looking back is fatal!

She was walking along the river bank, pursued by these thoughts, when she almost cannoned into the man she had met before. He was crouched by the river's edge with a swan in his arms.

'Sorry—' she whispered, anxious not to frighten the injured bird. 'Can I help?' and she sank down onto the grass beside him.

'Fish-hook in her throat,' he said. 'No time to get her back to my place. She's suffocating . . .' He looked at Laurie assessingly. 'See if you can hold her still while I swaddle her wings.'

He brought out a long strip of cloth and swiftly bound it round the powerful wings, holding them close to the swan's body so that she could not struggle. 'One blow from those,' he said, 'can smash an arm or a leg just like that!'

Laurie held the limp bird still in her hands, feeling the frantic beating of its heart as it fought for breath. That's how I felt, she thought. Frantic and desperate . . . Poor bird, I know just how you feel.

The man reached for a pair of long, thin forceps from his medical bag which was on the grass beside him. Gently, delicately, he forced open the swan's beak and began probing. 'It's a long way down,' he muttered. 'I may not be able to reach it.' Laurie went on holding the bird steady, and instinctively began to croon to it and to stroke its smooth white feathers.

'That's good,' the man nodded, 'if you can keep her quiet. Sometimes

308

they just die of fright . . . Ah!' He seemed to twist his forceps a little and give them a small, sharp tug. 'There!' he exclaimed in triumph, and withdrew his hand. Between the blades of the forceps was a vicious steel fish-hook with a trail of nylon line attached to it, and after it came a mess of blood and clogging grit. The swan gave a convulsive heave and then began to breathe more normally.

'It's all right, my friend,' he said, stroking its long neck with a comforting hand. 'All over . . . You'll be fine after a little rest.'

The bird did not struggle. It lay passive in Laurie's hands, and leaned its head tiredly against the man's shoulder.

'She's a bit shocked,' he said. 'Usually I get them home first—but this was too urgent to wait.' He stood up. 'Maybe she'll let me take her home now,' he murmured. 'She'll need a week or two under my eye, and feeding up a bit . . .'

Now that the swan was out of immediate danger, the man seemed to see Laurie more clearly. She looked like a slim, shy boy sitting there, with her cropped golden head and her big anxious eyes. It occurred to him, with a lurch of surprise, that she was looking at him like the swan—with acceptance, almost with trust. The wariness of the other day was gone.

He reached out tentatively and touched a frond of the close-cut blonde hair. 'Another small piece of freedom?'

She smiled, and kept her hands round the swan till he stooped and tucked the drooping bird under his arm. 'Coming?' He stood looking down at her. 'You can help me put her to bed!'

'All right,' said Laurie. 'What do they call you?' she asked, as they walked together along the bank.

'Mostly they call me that batty swan man. But my friends call me Clem.'

She nodded. Clement means merciful, she thought. 'Clement?'

He laughed. 'A bit pretentious, that! Clem's short for always starving!' He cocked an eyebrow in her direction. 'What about you?'

'Me? I'm Laurie.'

He considered for a moment. 'Laura. Are you a fighter?'

It was her turn to consider. 'I am now,' she said.

He looked again at the bright tongues of hair curving round her head. 'Yes,' he agreed. 'That figures. Battle array!' He lengthened his stride a little. 'Come on! I'm starving—rescues always make me hungry!'

They came presently to a bend in the river and a small backwater with a rickety wooden bridge over it that led across to the other side. Here, on the edge of the next water meadow, stood an ancient caravan, propped up on brick stilts; and beyond it, half hidden in green willows, was a small cottage with a reddish tiled roof and a jumble of sheds and outbuildings at its side. There was a sizable pond carved out of the backwater close to the cottage, and here Laurie saw a number of swans and other waterfowl swimming about in peaceful seclusion.

The cottage was unlocked, and Clem shouldered his way in through the kitchen door and set his burden down in a wide, shallow basket filled with dried reeds and grasses, which stood near the old-fashioned kitchen range.

'Just a minute, my friend,' he said gently, and stroked the swan's languid head. 'A nice drink, and you'll feel better.'

He had a long workbench, neatly arrayed with a variety of medical supplies and instruments, and he busied himself mixing Complan, glucose and vitamins.

'Just hold her head up,' he instructed, and when Laurie held the small head still, he pushed open the swan's beak again and tipped the fluid down. 'Now you can rest . . .' he said. 'No one'll bother you any more. Just sit still and get strong,' and he gave the swan one last gentle pat and left her alone.

'Bread and cheese?' he asked. 'And tea?'

'Wonderful!' breathed Laurie. 'But not a lot. Penny and the kids are cooking supper.'

He slapped some cheese and a knob of butter onto a plate, added a slice of bread and handed it to her. Then he went over to the Aga—which Laurie now realised was alight and keeping the kitchen warm enough for Clem's injured birds—and tipped boiling water from the big black kettle into a brown teapot.

'Let's sit outside and watch the swans,' he said. 'The rain's stopped.'

They sat together on the kitchen step and ate hunks of bread and cheese and drank scalding tea. They did not talk much, but a sense of companionship was growing between them. Laurie felt years and years of tension and fear falling away from her.

At last she stirred and said, 'I must go now.'

He did not try to keep her. They stood side by side and gazed at the quiet water. 'I'll see you again,' he said.

Laurie looked into his face and answered, 'Yes. You will.'

BUT BY THE END of the week she had not seen Clem again, and Joe was due to come down for another load of vegetables and take Laurie's little party home. She was dreading it. She didn't want to go back to the crowded rooms of The Hide, or to her own problems of housing and maintenance, lawyers and divorce papers, social workers and prison officers. She wanted to stay here in the orchards and hop gardens of Kent, with the slow old Medway flowing by, and the swans . . . and Clem? Yes, she wanted to be like the swans who stayed near Clem 'because they know I'm friendly, and it's safe . . .'

310

But there was a life to be rebuilt—three lives, because Jay and Midge were as damaged as she was. And then there was Penny, Penny of the bright flame-red hair and sturdy common sense and ready laughter. Penny, who was due to have her own father's bastard child within the next three months. What was she to do with her?

'That's enough brooding for one day,' said Penny, standing over her with a mug of tea in her hand. 'Look, the sun's shining. And it's Sunday. No picking. Just lazing around.'

Laurie sighed and took the tea from her. 'No sign of Joe?'

'There is. And he's got a passenger. Look!'

Joe was strolling towards them, with Jane beside him.

Laurie got to her feet. 'How lovely!' she said, smiling. 'How did you manage to get away?'

'Joe said I needed a break.' Jane was smiling, too—and looking younger and less harassed out in the mild autumn air.

Laurie led them over to their smoky morning fire. 'Tea coming up,' sang out Penny. 'And then I'll go and round up the kids.'

It occurred to Laurie that this was all carefully orchestrated, and Penny knew quite well what she was doing. 'Tell me what's going on,' she demanded.

'First of all,' said Joe, 'Stan wants you to stay on another week. Picking isn't finished, and he says your bookkeeping is spot-on.'

'Really?' Laurie felt an absurd leap of pride. There was actually something she could do well and get paid for! And they could stay on—another week—in the green hop fields near the river . . . near the swans . . . near Clem?

'It would be lovely,' she sighed. 'But—there are so many things I need to do.' She looked at Jane, almost with appeal.

'Such as?' demanded Joe.

'Well—find somewhere to live—a job—a school for Jay—and . . .' She paused. There was Jeff. Something had to be done about Jeff.

'It's too soon,' murmured Jane, as if reading her thoughts.

'Is it?' She looked at Jane again, almost piteously. 'I'm stronger now. I ought to see him. He's got no one else.'

'What do you hope to achieve?' asked Jane.

'Nothing.' Laurie's glance was steady now. 'I know it won't change anything. But—but he *was* my husband for nine years. And he's in much worse trouble than I am.'

'He asked for it!' growled Joe.

'Yes. But that doesn't make it any better!' said Laurie. 'I just feel . . . I ought to see him—once more.'

Jane nodded. 'All right. It will be an ordeal. But it can be arranged.'

311

'As to the rest—' Joe cleared his throat, and looked from one to the other. 'Gotta proposition.'

Laurie's mind snapped to attention. 'Yes?'

'My dad,' said Joe, as if it solved everything. 'Gotta smallholding, see? In Cornwall. Grows veggies—and daffs in spring. By the sea.' His sharp brown eyes seemed to have a sudden warmth. 'You said you'd like to be by the sea . . .'

'Oh!' Laurie smiled at him. 'You remembered!'

'Course I remembered.' His own engaging smile flickered briefly out. 'Rang him up, didn't I?'

'So?' Laurie prompted him.

'Gotta cottage,' he explained. 'Empty in winter. Lets it for the holiday season.' His lively eyes were dancing now. 'If you can do his books—and, mind, he's worse than Stan at figures—and help with packing veggies and daffs—you can have it rent free, and get paid a wage on the side.'

Laurie gazed at him, open-mouthed. '*And* get paid? He must be bonkers.'

'No, he's not. Weight in gold, bookkeeping. I told you. It's kinda like a *tied* cottage.'

Laurie shook her head in disbelief. 'By the sea? . . . Are you sure?'

'Course I'm bloody well sure. Hundred yards down the cliff.'

'No, I mean . . .' She was laughing now. 'Are you sure he means it?'

'He's my dad,' said Joe, his mouth one straight, firm line. 'What he says, he means. Getting on a bit. Could do with some help. Sends his stuff up to me for the market by lorry—or by train—especially the daffs. Or some of it goes to the Penzance market and a coupla shops. Gets in a rare old mess with his books, see? All them different orders and prices. You'd be a godsend.' He looked at her sternly. 'Can't have my old Dad done in by his own books, can I?'

Laurie laid a hand on his arm. 'Joe—I think you're the kindest man I've ever known.'

'Rubbish!' said Joe crossly. 'Gotta think of me own, too! My dad's special, see?'

Laurie and Jane looked at one another and laughed.

'What do you think, Jane?' asked Laurie.

'I think Joe's right—it's a godsend,' said Jane. She glanced at Joe affectionately, and then turned back to Laurie. 'You know what the housing people suggested? That you go back to your old house.'

'*What?*'

'They'd pay the rent for you, and get another injunction to keep Jeff out.'

Laurie was appalled. 'But it wouldn't keep him out! I'd never have a moment's peace of mind.'

312

'Exactly.' Jane's mouth was as straight and hard as Joe's. 'So I suggest you accept Joe's offer—with alacrity!'

Laurie laughed again. Then she grew serious. 'Jane, what about Penny? She's kind of attached herself to us. The kids love her—and she loves them, I think. Well. Her baby's due in less than three months. What ought I to do about it?'

'What do you want to do about it?' asked Jane.

'I—I could take her with me. It would be a sort of home, at least. She could keep an eye on the kids while I worked, at first. And later on, maybe we could take it in turns or something . . . And the baby would fit in with my kids. Once it was born, Penny would be free to do what she liked.'

'You mean—you'd take the baby on?'

'Why not?' said Laurie, tossing her bright cap of hair in a defiant gesture. 'What's one more? We'd manage somehow—' She glanced at Jane. 'But she'd be more secure with you.'

'No. Not really.' Now Jane was regarding her with a straight, level gaze. 'Love makes security. Not a place.'

Yes, thought Laurie. Love, not a place . . . And a sudden vision of Clem's face bent lovingly over the swan's limp head, and his long, gentle fingers stroking its neck, came into her mind . . . She would have to leave Clem and his swans, Clem whom she was just beginning to trust . . . But Joe's offer was too good to refuse.

'Then,' she said slowly, 'you think Penny ought to come with me?'

'I should ask her,' said Jane.

PENNY, WHEN ASKED, went very pale—so pale that the freckles stood out on her face like a screen-printed pattern. She looked at Laurie with a kind of desperate candour and said, 'Do you really want me?'

Laurie realised suddenly that no one had ever told Penny she was wanted or loved in the whole of her young life—except perhaps her father, in a way that he had no right to use.

'Yes,' she said. 'And so do Jay and Midge.'

Penny's smile was like the sun coming out. 'Then I'll come!' she said.

'What do you think, Jay,' said Laurie, smiling, 'we're going to live in a cottage by the sea!'

'Our *own* cottage?' asked Jay, serious eyes fixed on his mother's face.

'Not our own exactly. It belongs to Joe's dad. But we can live in it on our own.'

'No dads,' said Midge suddenly. 'I don't want no dads.'

Laurie and Jane gave Joe a rueful glance. But Penny said sturdily, 'Don't be daft, Midge. Not all dads are bad, are they, Joe?'

'Course not!' growled Joe. 'Mine isn't anyways. The best—my old dad

313

is. You'll see!' He leaned forward and gave Midge a friendly pat. 'You don't mind me, do you, little 'un?'

'No,' said Midge. And, as an afterthought, 'You're nice.'

'Glad to hear it.' Joe looked inordinately pleased.

'You bought us an ice cream,' went on Midge, pursuing a thought.

'Did I, now?' Joe grinned, and got to his feet. 'Gotta load up my veggies now . . . Mind, if anyone was to help me, I might buy them another . . .'

Midge smiled seraphically and took his hand. 'I fought you might.'

PENNY AND JASON went with them, and left Jane and Laurie sitting by the fire. It was still quite warm in the sun, though the late September air was beginning to have a spicy chill to it at night and early morning, and there was a heavy dew on the orchard grass. Laurie had been obliged to buy some secondhand Wellingtons for the children from a family who were going home. It was the only way to keep their feet dry, and she would have to go back to the little house in London soon to collect all their clothes. It cost too much to buy new ones.

'I like your hair,' commented Jane, smiling. 'More positive!'

Laurie laughed. 'I know. I feel more positive, too. Though I still find it difficult to make decisions.'

'It'll take time.' Jane's voice was full of knowledge. 'It always does.'

That's what Clem said, thought Laurie. It takes time . . .

They saw Joe returning then, with Penny and the children beside him.

Jane said gently, 'Take this extra week, Laurie. You need it. You're not well yet. And there will be plenty to face when you come back.'

Jane would not stay longer. She had to get back to The Hide. So she gave little Midge a friendly tweak and ruffled Jason's hair in passing. 'Have a nice week, kids . . . I'll see you all next Sunday, providing Joe's van is still on its wheels!'

Joe grinned. 'Not on our last legs yet,' he said, and winked at Laurie. 'Grow strong, kid,' he added, unconsciously echoing Clem's words to his swans. Then he followed Jane across the dusty grass to his old van.

SO THERE WAS ANOTHER golden week to spend in the hop gardens. Laurie could scarcely believe her luck. And the next six months of winter solved, too. It was almost too good to be true.

She knew she must talk to Clem some time, and tell him she was going away. But something deep inside her still recoiled from any demand, any emotional tie, any feeling at all beyond a thankful acceptance of exhausted peace. Clem, with his deep, cloud-shadow grey eyes and slow smile of welcome, and his instant, unspoken understanding, was somehow more than she could bear. She wanted to run from him, away from the

314

beginnings of closeness stirring between them. It was too soon—she could not cope with it. Not yet . . .

And yet even so—something drew her to those dazzling swans on the tranquil river, and to the gentle, quiet man who watched over them.

It was, therefore, in a somewhat confused mood that she set out with Penny and the children, after Jane had gone, to walk by the river.

Penny had gone on ahead, with Jason and Midge, when Laurie heard her shout. Jason's voice, too, was raised, and Laurie thought she heard the shrill words, 'Let go!'

Panic-stricken, she began to run and, tearing round the curve of the river bank, she almost ran full tilt into a couple of leering louts who had Jason by both arms and were saying to each other, 'Shall we throw 'im in, then?'

Penny was hitting at them wildly with a stick she had picked up from the grass, but a third gangling youth was grabbing at her from behind. Little Midge, transfixed with horror, was slowly backing towards a clump of reeds right at the edge of the water.

'Stop that!' shouted Laurie, suddenly far too angry to be frightened. She also seized a stick from a broken piece of fencing and began to lay about her. 'Leave them alone!' she yelled. 'You stupid thugs! Why don't you try someone your own size!'

The three louts let out a few surprised oaths and the tallest one hit out wildly, catching Laurie a sharp blow on the side of her head. Then they turned and ran past Midge. She saw them coming, took one more terrified step backwards, and fell headlong into the river.

Their attackers gave one scared glance and went on running, making no attempt to rescue Midge. Jason, on the other hand, took a deep breath and plunged straight into the water after her.

'No, Penny!' snapped Laurie—seeing her also go towards the bank. 'You're too heavy. Stay there to pull us out!' and she too jumped into the oozy reed bed.

The water was deeper and colder than she expected, and the little girl had already gone under twice, but Jason had got hold of her hair and was gamely holding her head up. But he, too, was almost out of his depth, his feet sinking deeper into the river mud with every second. Laurie realised, with a flick of terror, that what had started out as a tiresome incident was fast turning into tragedy. She floundered out towards the children.

Penny, meanwhile, had wrenched a longer piece of paling from the fence and was reaching out with it, hanging dangerously over the water from the crumbling bank. But the stick was too short, and the children were being steadily pulled out into the slow current in midstream.

'Hang on!' called a voice from the river beyond them. 'I'm coming!'

Laurie found herself swimming frantically after the drifting children. She reached Jason just as Clem's ancient punt came across the river with a powerful thrust from his paddle.

'Hold on a minute,' he said calmly. 'I've got the little girl . . .' and he reached out and heaved Midge into the punt. 'Now you,' he said to Jason, who was gasping and spluttering. 'Take my hand.'

Then it was Laurie's turn, and she too landed in a sodden heap on the silvery planks of the old punt . . .

'Is the little girl all right?' asked Clem, manoeuvring the punt into the shallows.

Laurie had already picked Midge up and was instinctively holding her upside-down and shaking her. A whole lot of river water suddenly came out of her mouth and she began to splutter like Jason.

'Oh—thank God!' muttered Laurie, turning her right-side-up and cradling her in her arms. 'It's all right . . .' she murmured to the wet gold head against her shoulder. 'It's all right, Midge, you're safe now . . .' and she reached out her other hand to grasp Jason. 'Are you OK?'

He nodded, still too choked up to speak, but his colour was good.

Clem, meanwhile, was looking up at Penny on the river bank. 'Everyone safe . . .'

'Oh my God,' said Penny, and promptly sat down on the bank and burst into tears. 'I thought they were a goner!'

Clem laughed. 'Look at them! Nothing gone about them!' He turned to glance at his sodden cargo, and added, half to himself, 'Quicker by boat, I think.' Then he waved at Penny and said, 'Follow us downriver. My house is round the next bend . . .' and he turned the punt back into the stream with a skilful twist of his paddle.

Before long, they were safe inside Clem's house and he was filling his bath with hot water for them.

'Take everything off,' he commanded. 'And get into that bath before you all get a chill. I'll lend you some blankets to wrap round you when you come out. Hot tea all round, I think.' And he shut them all in his little bathroom and went off to brew the tea.

Meanwhile, Penny had arrived, breathless and anxious. But Clem just said, 'They're fine. Go and see for yourself. And bring out their clothes. We'll have to dry them over the stove.'

Penny found them immersed in hot water and clouds of steam, washing river mud out of their hair. 'Here,' she said, 'let me help.' And she rinsed off little Midge and picked her out of the bath and wrapped her in a towel. Jason got out next. He decided he was too old to be helped, but he submitted to a hug of relief from Penny when she wrapped the towel round him.

Presently they were all sitting round Clem's stove, draped in blankets, drinking tea. Midge was still tearful and clung to Laurie. Laurie herself was pale with fright, and her head was feeling strange again where the thug had hit it, but she looked from the children to Penny and then to Clem with thankfulness. Everyone was safe and warm.

'You seem to make a habit of rescuing things,' she said, smiling.

Clem laughed. 'Makes a change from swans!'

'How's the one with the fish-hook? Did she recover?'

'Oh yes.' He waved towards the door. 'She's out there with the others.'

'What others?' asked Jason, interested.

'Finish your tea, and I'll show you,' said Clem. He eyed Jason's blanket-covered form doubtfully and then added, 'I could fix you up with a T-shirt and some shorts. They'll be miles too big—but I dare say a belt would hold 'em up!'

He went off upstairs, and returned with an armload of clothes. 'You'll look absurd,' he said to Laurie, grinning. 'But at least they'll be dry!' He glanced at Penny and added with a gleam of mischief, 'Good thing I haven't got to fix you up, too!'

'It'd be the Battle of the Bulge,' agreed Penny, laughing.

'I'm going to feed my birds,' he announced, withdrawing with tact. 'See what you can do.' And he left Penny in charge of the pile of garments.

When they were all clothed, they looked at each other and fell about laughing. Jason's old T-shirt reached nearly to his knees, and he had tied Clem's navy shorts on with a piece of string, but as they were almost hidden under the T-shirt, it didn't matter how baggy they looked. Midge was wearing a towelling T-shirt like a nightdress; and Laurie had climbed into a faded pair of jeans, not so bad with the ends turned up, a belt holding the waistband in, another elongated T-shirt, and an old fawn cardigan over the top.

Clem, hearing the laughter, put his head round the door. 'That's better!' he said—though it was not clear whether he meant the clothes or the laughter. 'Who wants to come and help me feed the birds?'

They all trooped outside.

There were half a dozen swans swimming quietly on the little pond, several pairs of mallard, and some coots and moorhens. There was also a tall grey heron with a damaged bill, and a couple of seagulls who had been brought in with their feathers oiled. And there was one wet, sleek head that came swimming towards them.

'What's that?' asked Jason, pointing.

'That? Oh, that's Jaunty. He's an otter I found in an eel trap further downriver, near the estuary.'

'An *otter?* I've never seen a real live otter before.'

'Not many people have, these days,' replied Clem. 'They're getting rarer.'

'Why?'

'Oh, various reasons. People hunt them, and kill them.'

'What for?'

'Search me. They can't eat 'em . . . They don't use their fur . . . and the poor creatures don't do much harm to anyone—except take a few fish. And I reckon they're as much entitled to the fish in the river as men are. More so, really, because men can eat something else! And it's not only the hunters—the rivers get polluted, the reeds get cut down and the dredgers move in. All the wild, secret places where otters like to live are gradually disappearing . . . That's why Jaunty stays around. It's quiet here, and no one can cut down his reeds and willows.'

'Do you own it?'

Clem hesitated. 'Well, sort of. It's rather complicated . . . When I stopped being a town vet, my partner bought me out, so I had some money to spare. And then the Wildlife people and I got together, and between us we bought this cottage and as much land round it as we could afford. No one can cut anything down now. It's registered as a nature reserve and a bird sanctuary.'

Jason watched, fascinated, as Clem threw out some carefully balanced food for his convalescent swans, and delved into another blue plastic bucket to find a small fish which he tossed in the air for Jaunty.

'The thing is,' he said seriously to Jason, 'you mustn't feed them too much, or they'll never go away and forage for themselves . . . But some of these swans are still a bit weak, and they need a little extra help.'

'What about Jaunty?'

'He had an injured leg. It made swimming very difficult, and he was too slow to catch a fish. But now he's much better. Sometimes he stays away for several days. But he usually comes back for an extra titbit.' He smiled at Jason's round eyes. 'Would you like to throw him a fish?' He handed the boy a small, silvery minnow. 'The trouble is,' he went on, watching that alert, clever head in the water, 'otters get too friendly. They like company. They like feeling safe and secure . . . and then they find it hard to go away.' His eyes were still on the water, but Laurie felt sure he was not only talking about the friendly otter.

'Do they have to go away?' asked Jason wistfully.

The big, quiet man at his side glanced at him sympathetically. 'Yes,' he said firmly, 'they do. They have to learn to be independent—and free. That's what they were born to be.' His eyes strayed for a moment to Laurie's face, and he saw a curious look of recognition and resolve flash into it.

318

'But of course,' he went on softly, 'if they return now and then for a spot of comfort and reassurance, I'm only too pleased to see them. Only, it has to be up to them!'

Jason nodded wisely. 'I see,' he said.

'You know,' said Clem, looking up at the sun judiciously, 'unless you want to go back looking like Worzel Gummidge, you'll have to stay for lunch—or is it tea?'

'Oh but—' Laurie began to protest.

'No buts,' he said calmly. 'I've got some tins in my larder. I'm not a bad cook.'

'Nor am I,' volunteered Penny, smiling. 'Just show me where.'

Laurie was watching Penny's pale face. Clearly, she had been very frightened. 'Penny—are you sure you're all right?' she asked.

The girl's cheerful smile broke out again. 'Course I am. Takes more than a bit of a fight with some thugs to throw me!'

'What did they want?' asked Laurie mystified. 'Why pick on Penny and a couple of small kids?'

'They probably thought it was just a lark,' said Clem. 'These mindless hooligans do!' He paused, his face set into grim lines again. 'As a matter of fact, I think I know them. They're the same lot I caught tormenting a swan the other day.'

'What were they doing to it?' asked Jason.

'I'd rather not tell you.' Clem's face was stern. 'Yes, I think I know those nasty louts. I'll have a word with the village bobby.' He glanced at little Midge who was still clinging to Laurie's hand. 'What a good thing you have such a brave and resourceful brother!' he said gently, and saw a flush of pleasure rise in Jason's face.

It was at this point that Laurie suddenly passed out. Without warning, the river bank began to spin, the sky wheeled and went black, and she fell like a stone at Clem's feet.

Midge screamed. Jason came running. Penny stooped over her and tried to raise her head. But Clem simply picked her up in his arms, carried her indoors and laid her down on his lumpy old sofa in the corner. 'It's her head,' explained Penny, looking down at her anxiously. 'She's got a hairline fracture anyway—and I think one of them louts hit her.'

Clem nodded. 'She'll come round in a minute.' He turned to the children, his voice calm. 'There's an old sponge and a bowl in my sink. Bring a drop of water . . .' He knew that action of some kind would reduce panic. Already Midge had stopped crying and was following Jason. They returned, carefully carrying a bowlful of water, and he showed them how to bathe Laurie's forehead, which did indeed have a new angry red lump on it, and how to hold the cold sponge against her

320

pale temples. 'But don't swamp her,' he added, smiling. 'She's already been half drowned once today!'

In a few moments, Laurie's eyelids began to flutter and she opened her eyes to find a ring of anxious faces looking down at her. 'Sorry—' she muttered, struggling to sit up. 'What hit me?'

Clem smiled. 'A thug's fist, I should think. You rest there a while. Penny and I will see about some lunch, and Jason and Midge can lay the table—can't you?' He turned his reassuring smile on the children.

Thankfully, Laurie lay back and waited for the world to right itself.

Penny was good at whipping up scratch meals out of tins, and she soon had a savoury concoction of corned beef, baked beans, tinned tomatoes, spinach out of Clem's vegetable garden and fresh mushrooms from the fields. She set it down in triumph on the kitchen table. By this time Laurie had recovered sufficiently to sit down beside them all and to comment on the delicious smell—mostly thanks to Clem's herb patch outside the back door. It even made her feel quite hungry.

Before the meal was over, Midge's head began to droop. 'Put her down on the sofa,' said Clem.

Carefully, Laurie laid the sleepy child down and covered her with a blanket. Midge was soon fast asleep.

Penny, with her eyes on Laurie's pale face, said, 'I think Jay and I'll go and have a look round while you have a rest.'

Clem nodded. 'Just go quietly so that you don't disturb the birds.'

Laurie watched them go and thought in panic, I don't know what to say to this man. How can I explain what has been happening to me—or how I feel?

But Clem surprised her. 'When are you going away?' he asked.

Laurie gazed at him in wonder. 'Not till the end of the week.' Haltingly, she explained about Joe and the cottage that went with the job in Cornwall. 'I've got to take it,' she explained. 'It's a godsend, really. And just what they all need just now. And I—I wanted to be near the sea . . . to feel clean . . .'

He said suddenly, 'The children—can they swim?'

Laurie paled. 'N-no. As you saw today.'

'Bring them here,' he said. 'Every day. After work. The bit of backwater I've cleared is quite clean—and not too deep or muddy.'

'But—'

'Every day!' he said decisively. 'I can teach them in a week. At least I can make them safe in the water. I used to be a lifeguard once.' He smiled at her stunned expression. 'Listen,' he said, 'you know as well as I do that you nearly lost little Midge today. If it hadn't been for your young son, you probably would have. And he was none too safe, either!'

Laurie took a shaky breath. 'I know.'

'Well, then—it makes sense. We'll make them as safe as we can in the time. Penny, too—even in her condition she can learn to float!' He laughed, and added cheerfully, 'The water's fairly warm at this time of the year and swimming is quite good for pregnant ladies, I believe.'

'How do you know?' asked Laurie, laughing.

He laughed, too. 'Stands to reason. They are buoyant in the water—takes the weight off their feet!'

They were still laughing when Penny and Jason came back. Nothing serious had been said, but Laurie felt strangely comforted. Clem knew how she felt. He accepted her going. He even understood about the sea, and her longing to be scoured clean by the blowing sands and sharp fierce winds and the deep sea-swell of the Atlantic shore. Maybe, one day, she would feel clean again. Maybe, one day, she would return to this quiet backwater, like the swans—like Jaunty, the otter who knew where he would be welcome . . .

But in the meantime, there was this last golden week—and a swimming lesson every day!

'What's the joke?' asked Penny, smiling.

'You are,' grinned Laurie. 'You don't know it, but Clem's going to teach you to swim!'

'Me?' said Penny, with a hand on her swollen stomach. 'Are you sure?'

'All of you!' stated Clem. 'Starting tomorrow!'

'Smashing!' breathed Jason, his face aglow.

'No,' said Clem gravely. 'Not smashing, Jay. *Swimming!*'

CLEM WAS A QUIET MAN. Quiet, and slow to anger. But when he thought about it, he realised that he was very angry indeed. So angry that he couldn't keep still, so he set out to walk it off along the river bank.

He knew, when he considered it, that his anger was out of all proportion. Those mindless louts who tortured the swans, and bullied young Jason and frightened little Midge into the river, were not really monsters. They were ignorant and crass, yes—and probably a bit sadistic, too, like a lot of boys—but not monsters. And yet he wanted to kill them. They had hit Laurie and scared her children, when violence still cast far too real a shadow over them—when they were all just beginning to come out into the sun and smile. And he couldn't bear to see that new bright radiance quenched.

That told him something about himself that he had not known. Or had not quite admitted. Was it possible that in so short a space of time, another human being could come to mean so much to him?

For a long time now, Clem had walked alone. By choice. He found the

322

company of his wild creatures easier to deal with—and far more rewarding. He had sworn, when the final showdown came with Sylvia, that he would never again allow a human being to come close enough to shatter his life and destroy him. And here he was, caught inextricably like one of his own swans in a tangle of fishing twine, by a small, slender girl with bruised, shock-dilated eyes and a smile as fragile as glass.

Sylvia had not been fragile. She had been very sure of herself. Glossy and secure. And while he was out night after night on call, as a busy vet always was, she had her fun. He hadn't known about it at first, but when it turned out to be his own partner—his friend and colleague—it had been the last straw. It was also the last (almost the only) time he had allowed himself to get really angry. When Sylvia laughed, he had found himself trying to throttle her. And when his partner had intervened, he had knocked him down. Then he had fled, appalled at the rage within him.

Rage, he knew, was a killer. And he wanted no part of it. Not ever again. He had resigned from his practice, let his partner take over his share, and his wife as well. He had left the lot, and fled to this green and golden sanctuary behind the tangled willows. It was a long time ago now, and he had built a good, quiet life for himself here. There were always new crises, new challenges to be met, new battles to be won or lost. He felt reasonably useful and content. And when he saw a newly mended wing take flight, or a broken leg move comfortably in the water, he knew he was well rewarded. So why this sudden, searing anger? He knew why. And he knew what anger did to him. And he was afraid. So he went to The Bull, intending to get drunk. Somehow he found that he could not. He sat staring into his drink and seeing behind the smoky haze of the pub, Laurie's cropped golden head and pale, resolute face as she told him how she wanted to go to the sea and swim till she felt clean . . .

Damn it all, he thought, if I ever caught up with that husband of hers, I'd . . . He was surprised at the anger still burning inside him. Anger as deep and fierce as that was somehow very close to love.

JASON WAS A BIT WORRIED by that encounter with the thugs on the river bank. Not that he'd been frightened, of course. A boy his age ought not to be scared by three weedy louts who tried to twist his arm. He had met bullies at school, and he knew how to take care of himself. But since he was the man of the family now, he knew he ought to protect his mum and Midge. It was his job. And what kind of a help was he going to be to his mum if he couldn't even manage those boys on the river bank?

So he went to ask the only person he knew who was strong enough and kind enough to look after them all—his new friend, Clem.

He arrived, breathless from running down the towpath, and found

323

Clem feeding his birds. He watched him for a moment in silence, then he said obliquely, 'Does swimming make you strong?'

Clem smiled. 'It does. Strong, and independent.'

'How soon?'

Clem looked in surprise at the anxious little face. 'Well, not all at once. It takes time.' And then, seeing the boy's disappointment, 'Why?'

Jason hesitated. At last he said shyly, 'It's Mum. And Midge.' He paused, and then added as an afterthought, 'And Penny, too, really . . .'

'What about them?'

The boy looked up trustfully, sure that Clem would know the answer. 'How can I keep them safe?'

Clem's eyes grew so dark that Jason almost faltered. He thought he saw the glitter of tears behind them—but of course that couldn't be true.

Dear God, thought Clem. *How can I keep them safe?* He's only eight years old, and he asks me that!

'Jay,' he said at last, and laid a warm, comforting arm round his shoulders. 'You *have* kept them safe—all of them. But it shouldn't be nearly so bad from now on.'

Jason looked at him straight. 'It was bad by the river.'

'Yes, I know. But that won't happen again.'

'But—there'll be other times.' There was a world of flat knowledge in the young voice.

'Yes, Jay, there will,' Clem said gently. 'But they won't be important.' Clem pointed across the pond to where Jaunty, the little otter, was playing in the shallows.

'Remember him? When I first got him, life had been very bad for him. He was frightened of everything. He even bit me when I tried to help him. But now—' he glanced at Jason '—he can cope with anything that comes his way. I don't have to protect him any more.'

There was silence while Jason thought about this. He looked out over the little brown pond to where Jaunty was chasing his tail. 'I wish—' he began '—I wish I was bigger.'

Clem's smile was wide and loving. 'Do you? You seem pretty big for your age, one way and another.' He stooped down to his feeding buckets and found a fish. 'Here. Give Jaunty a treat. He might turn a somersault.'

Jason threw the fish high in the air and Jaunty leaped to catch it and did indeed turn a somersault. Then he came up in a swirl of brown water and laughed at them both in the sun.

'There!' said Clem. 'That's how life's going to be, Jay, from now on. All sunshine and somersaults.'

Jason looked at him seriously. 'I don't think Penny could turn a somersault just now.'

324

Clem began to laugh again. 'Not now, perhaps,' he said, still chuckling. 'But she will, Jay, she will!'

And there was such certainty in his voice that Jason almost believed it.

WHEN IT CAME TO IT, Clem was very clever with Midge. He had already worked out for himself that she would be scared of the water, after falling in so dramatically the day before. So he took her to see one of his patients, a mallard duck whose wing had been shattered by shot, but who was just about ready to go back on the water.

'She'll be scared at first,' he said, stroking the bird's iridescent head. 'But you're littler than me, so she won't mind you so much. Do you think you could hold her like this? With your hands round her wings so that she can't struggle? Very gently, mind . . .' Talking all the way, he led Midge down to the shallow reaches of the backwater. 'Now,' he said, 'take her out as far as you can into the water so that she's got plenty of room to move her legs . . . That's it . . . Walk on a bit . . .'

Gently, bit by bit, he coaxed Midge on until she was standing waist-deep in the water, with her small brown feet placed firmly on the sandy bottom.

'Now!' he said. 'Let her go . . . And watch what she does with her feet. She's a brave little bird . . . She'll soon get her balance . . .'

Midge took another step forward and opened her hands and let go. For a moment the bewildered mallard did not know where she was, but almost at once she felt the familiar buoyancy of the water under her, and she thrust out happily with her strong webbed feet and swam away.

'Oh!' cried Midge. 'Look at her go!'

Clem smiled. 'D'you see how she paddles with her feet? . . . One-two, one-two, like a little steam engine . . . If you lean forward on my hands, you can do it, too. Then you could follow her . . . Look, she's going to join her friends over there.'

'Won't we frighten her if we splash?' asked Jason, close beside them.

'No.' Clem shook his head. 'Good swimmers don't splash!'

Midge looked at the swans, and the cheerful mallards, and the cheeky moorhens. 'I'm not frightened,' she announced. And she leaned forward on Clem's arms and kicked her legs out behind her, trying to swim like a duck.

Clem's eyes met Laurie's. The first battle had been won.

SO EACH WARM EVENING, after a day in the hop fields, they all swam together in the little backwater. For the most part, the swans and mallards took little notice of them, and only came swimming up close to the bank when Clem stood with their evening meal ready for them.

Laurie felt the cool river water round her like balm. Scales and calluses, bruises and the grasp of hard, unloving hands—they all seemed to wash off in the river's quiet embrace. Each day she felt the sense of healing and newness grow within her.

Even Penny felt rested by the river. She floundered in it, rather like a fat and lazy seal, and Clem did not try to persuade her to do more than learn to keep afloat, and turn on her back and kick out vaguely with her legs. But the children were learning fast. Jason could already dog-paddle himself across the backwater from one side to the other, and Midge wasn't far behind.

Laurie had been a bit pushed to find them all swimsuits. Midge quite happily wore nothing, and Laurie had managed to buy Jason a pair of trunks in the village shop. But to waste money on swimsuits for herself and Penny seemed absurd. So she turned to the friendly Dorrie for advice.

'Penny can have mine,' said Dorrie, grinning. 'She's about my size—in front!' She rummaged in her battered old suitcase and brought out a crumpled black swimsuit of gigantic proportions. 'Always took a dip in the old Medway when it got hot,' she said. 'But I'm getting too old for it now. As for you—' She considered Laurie. 'I'll have to ask around.'

She waddled off, and returned, triumphantly waving another one-piece swimsuit of a shiny blue. 'All they could offer!' she apologised, grinning. 'At least it's your size. It won't fall off!'

Laurie was thankful it wasn't a bikini. Her bruises still showed too much for public display. But now she swam quietly and confidently about beside the children, and Clem, bronzed and powerful but always gentle, swam round them like a watchful shepherd, encouraging every stroke.

Afterwards, they would all sit round Clem's stove drinking hot tea, before they walked home again in the dusk. It was an enchanted time.

ON THE LAST EVENING, they invited Clem to come back with them for supper round their campfire. He hesitated a moment. 'Yes, I'd love to. But I must stay and see to the invalids first . . . I'll follow you on.'

Penny took Midge by the hand. 'We'll go and start the fire,' she said, with an imperious glance at Jason. 'Laurie can walk down with you.'

Laurie was not sure that she wanted to be left alone with Clem. But it seemed ungracious to walk off. So she turned back to help him with his sick birds. He put down food and water, dressed a knife-wound in a swan's breast, and one shattered wing that needed more antibiotics to stave off infection. He left some chopped-up food for the badger cub, and some more for the injured fox who kept leaping up and down in his cage like a welcoming little dog. And then he straightened up. 'They'll do,' he said. 'I'll have another look at them when I come back.'

326

He followed Laurie out into the westering sun. It was Saturday and there was no picking left to do. Some of the casual workers had gone home already, but there were a few families left and there was going to be a grand farewell party that night in the empty field. Now the stripped hop gardens and orchards lay silent, the hop poles in neat stacks on the ground beside the piles of bushel baskets and empty bins.

Laurie and Clem walked side by side and watched the shadows grow long on the river meadows. They did not talk much. But at last they paused, to look at the reflections on the river and the two white swans, drifting gently on its gleaming sunset surface.

Clem was very tempted then. He turned to her suddenly, and put his arms round her. But at once he felt her stiffen, and he said to himself despairingly, You fool! Too soon, too soon . . . So he slackened his embrace and smiled at her and murmured by way of apology, 'It's a magic time, sunset. Even the swans feel it . . .' And he bent his head and kissed her cheek, very gently.

Laurie knew she had hurt him, but her reaction had been instinctive. She could not help it. So she nodded quietly, and turned to look at the swans on the river.

As they watched, they suddenly took off in a long, slow glide, and flew away downriver in a wide arc, their wings glinting in the setting sun. Then, when they were almost out of sight, they turned and flew back upstream, landing in a shower of glittering spray almost at their feet . . . They seemed to look at Clem, as if satisfied that he was still there, and sailed placidly into the shallows, floating like white ghosts in the gathering shadows.

'Freedom,' said Clem softly, 'isn't only taking off . . . It's knowing where you want to land . . . and when it is time to come home.'

'Yes,' murmured Laurie, with her eyes on the swans. 'I know.'

THE SINGING WENT ON late that night. Everyone was packing up and leaving in the morning. Clem joined in the singing with his deep, musical baritone, and Jason sat beside him and piped up in a clear treble whenever he knew the song. And there was dancing, too—someone turned on a transistor and the young ones rocked and stamped and clapped in the flickering firelight. At one point, Spider caught Laurie round the waist and whirled her into the dance. It was the last night, so she let herself be pulled and twirled, breathless and laughing, through the fire-lit throng of dancers.

Clem, watching her, surprised himself with a sharp, unmistakable stab of jealousy, and after a moment got to his feet and pushed his way into the crowd till he came face to face with Spider.

'My turn, I think,' he said, smiling, and neatly twisted Laurie into his arms.

They did not speak, and Clem knew he must keep things cheerful. So he twirled and spun till she was dizzy with laughter and Kentish cider, and then led her back to their own campfire. There they sat peacefully side by side, listening to the singing.

Little Midge fell asleep in Laurie's arms amd was carried inside the hut and laid on one of the bunks, but Jason stayed wide awake till the end. But at last the singing died down and the fires burned low, and people began to drift away, some to the huts to sleep, and some to the green orchards and empty hop gardens.

Laurie had been watching the circle of faces round her fire in a kind of dream. She realised suddenly that she hadn't sat around like this, part of a cheery group of people enjoying themselves, for years and years—if ever. She had almost begun to believe that life was all grind and terror, and no one was to be trusted. It was good to be back among the human race.

Clem got to his feet, and stood looking down at her, smiling. 'Welcome back!' he said softly, and Laurie was not astonished that he understood her thoughts.

Jason was looking at his hero in the firelight. 'Will we ever—can we come to see you again?'

'Of course,' said Clem. 'Any time.'

'When?' asked Jason, his young voice sharp with anxiety.

'In the spring, I expect.'

'Will you still be here?'

'Sure. I'm always here.'

'And will you let me help with the swans again?'

'Why not?' Clem smiled his slow, comforting smile. 'You're a great little assistant! I can always do with another pair of hands—provided they're kind, that is.'

Jason looked down at his own hands, and then at Clem's brown ones. 'Kind?' he murmured, as if it was a new word he had only just discovered.

'Kindness,' repeated Clem gently. His eyes strayed now to Laurie's face. 'And letting them go when they're ready,' he said softly, 'and being there when they come back. That's all it takes.'

His smile rested on Laurie quietly. He did not seem to expect any reply. But her own smile flooded out to match his with sudden radiance.

Then Clem turned back to Jason. 'Don't worry,' he said gently, 'I'll be there.' And he strode away into the darkness without looking back.

Laurie, staring after him, suddenly understood that he meant exactly what he said. He would be there with her. Comforted, she took Jason by the hand. She would sleep now, in peace.

PART 3
FREE FLIGHT

Back in London, Laurie resolutely turned her mind to her immediate problems. She left Penny and the children at Jane's hostel and went back to the shabby little house to fetch some clothes.

The weather had changed, and a thin drizzle drifted out of a leaden sky. Laurie walked head down, hurrying to get the dreaded task out of the way.

She hated the cramped, squalid little house and all its grim memories. The rooms had a musty, unlived-in atmosphere. She did not go into the kitchen—she could not face it yet—but went straight upstairs to the bedroom. There were two old suitcases at the back of the cupboard, and she dragged these out and took one into the children's room. She crammed it with all the clothes she could find, including their shoes. Then she returned unwillingly to the dark bedroom she had shared with Jeff, and hastily flung some of her own clothes into the other case.

She carried the cases down the stairs and was standing irresolute in the hall when there came a sharp knock on the door. She froze. Could it be Jeff? Had they let him go early?

The knock came again. Laurie took a deep breath and went to the door.

Joe stood outside, his old green van parked by the kerb. Beside him was a woman with a clipboard in her hand.

'Thought you could do with a lift,' said Joe cheerfully. 'And this—er—this lady is from the housing. Met her on the step.'

'Oh.' Laurie hesitated, and then said quickly, 'I'll get the cases . . .' She left the woman standing on the steps till she returned. Then she slammed the door firmly behind her. 'Well?' she said, sounding a little belligerent.

'I—the authorities sent me round—' explained the woman, 'to ask if you had really considered their proposal.'

'What proposal?'

'Why, to come back to live here with your children.'

Laurie's stare grew cold. 'And leave them open to further attacks by my husband?'

The woman blinked. 'Surely, he wouldn't—'

'Oh yes, he would.' Laurie's face was bleak. 'He'd wait outside and accost the children. He'd get drunk and beat on the door, demanding to be let in. He'd climb in through the windows. I'd never have a moment's peace . . .' She looked at the woman with contempt. 'You want to subject us to that?'

'I—we could take out another injunction, if he got violent.'

'*If?*' Laurie's voice snapped with anger. 'It'd be a bit late then, wouldn't it?' She turned away. 'No thanks. I'd rather not take the risk.'

'But—you realise that by refusing to live here, you make yourself ineligible for other housing.' She consulted the lists on her clipboard. 'I mean—it is a roof over your head.'

'No!' said Laurie. 'I'd rather sleep out. It'd be safer in the streets.'

The woman looked shocked.

'In any case,' Laurie pointed out, 'this is a council house, let in his name, not mine. And since I have left him, he has more right to it than I have.'

'That's just the point,' explained the woman. 'It has been the marital home. If you and the children are already living in it, and you've got a separation order or a divorce pending, he can't come back.'

Laurie's gaze became incredulous. 'And can you imagine how he would feel about that? He'd have a real grudge against me then. He'd be more vindictive than ever.'

The woman put away her pen with a snap of her handbag. 'Very well,' she said. 'I will report back what you say. But I'm afraid the department will not feel that they are obliged to help you further.'

I'll bet they won't! Laurie thought. But Joe spoke up suddenly. 'You needn't bother. Not at the moment, anyways. She's got herself fixed up till the spring.'

The woman suddenly smiled and looked human. 'I'm glad to hear it.' She turned to go down the steps, then added, 'I don't make the rules, you know. In any case, we'd better keep your name on our lists. Things may look different in the spring.'

'I hope so,' said Laurie fervently.

Joe seized her cases and pushed her unceremoniously into his van, slammed the doors, and shot away into the traffic. 'Phew!' he said. 'Those housing berks give me the creeps!'

'Me too!' agreed Laurie. 'How did you know—?'

'Jane told me, didn't she? Can't have you lugging suitcases all over London. Besides—' he cocked a wary eye in her direction, not missing the signs of tension '—I thought that place might give you the shakes.'

'Yes,' admitted Laurie, with a pale grin, 'it did!'

Joe dropped her off at The Hide. He had arranged to take her and Penny with the children to the coach station in two days' time. In the meantime, Laurie had to see the solicitor, Madeleine Williamson—and also to make up her mind if she was going to visit Jeff or not.

Jane, when consulted, would not commit herself, she only said, 'I should ask Madeleine what she advises—and get her to come with you.'

330

That seemed a good idea. The prison authorities, when the situation was explained to them, agreed to let Laurie see Jeff, and also agreed to let the solicitor be present. Laurie put on her tidiest clothes and brushed her cropped hair smooth. She was very nervous.

Prison life did not agree with Jeff. To begin with, there was exercise, which he disliked, and 'slopping out' which he disliked even more. And then there were the inmates. Word had somehow got round on the prison grapevine that Jeff was a wife-beater. They didn't like that kind, and they let it show. And to make matters worse, there was no comforting drink to blot out the humiliations of the day.

The prison chaplain came round once or twice, and so did an earnest prison visitor who lectured him about the demon drink, but Jeff was not impressed. He felt sure he should not be here in this place. It was all Laurie's fault—she had no business to make such a fuss—gulling the hospital into believing all sorts of things about him—and taking the kids away, too . . . He'd see about that as well when he got out.

So he was brought out of his cell, angry and resentful, by a laconic warder who said simply, 'On your feet, Collins. Visitor.'

He went where he was told and found himself sitting with a window in front of him and Laurie's face on the other side.

But it was a different Laurie. Her hair was cut short, making her look older and somehow tougher.

'How are you, Jeff?' she said.

'How do you think? Shut up in here!' He glowered at her.

'It's not for long,' she said, almost kindly.

'Long enough,' he grumbled. 'I suppose you're crowing.'

'No,' said Laurie gravely. 'No. I'm not crowing, Jeff.'

'What did you come for then? Don't tell me you're having a change of heart?'

'No.' She spoke slowly. 'I simply wanted to see how you were.'

'Oh *thanks*. Since you put me here in the first place. A nice, condescending visit. That makes it all right, I suppose?'

She sighed. 'I didn't put you here, Jeff. You put yourself here. Just as you drove me away—and your children.'

'You bloody self-righteous cow!' he shouted suddenly, and banged his fist against the window. 'I'll get you when I come out!'

The warder in the corner came over. 'None of that!' he said.

Jeff subsided.

On the other side of the screen, Madeleine Williamson also came forward and laid a hand on Laurie's arm. Laurie looked up at her and smiled. 'It's all right,' she said. 'I'm not frightened.'

And oddly enough, it was true. Through the glass panel dividing them, she saw not the monster she had feared, but a bewildered, shrunken man, whose whole jaunty world of make-believe had crashed about his ears. She was sorry for him—not angry any more. 'I came to say goodbye, Jeff,' she told him. 'I'm going away.'

'Goodbye?' he snarled. 'You're not going anywhere, see? You're my wife—and they're my kids.'

'Not any more,' she answered. 'Don't you understand? It's over. The divorce is going through. And if you want to see the children, I'm afraid you'll have to wait till they're older. They're much too frightened of you now.'

'Frightened of me? Rubbish!' he growled. 'You've put them up to it.'

'You don't really want them, Jeff—you never did. Any more than you want me. We're only an encumbrance. Now you can go off anywhere you like and start again.' She watched that idea settle into his mind . . . a glimpse of a new, free life, with money to burn and girls to conquer.

But he still didn't like the idea of his wife and kids being on the loose.

'You can't just go like that,' he protested, trying to sound pathetic. 'I need you.'

Laurie got up from her chair. This was the Jeff she could not stand. 'It won't wash, Jeff. You can get in touch through my solicitor. Goodbye.'

Jeff could not believe it. She was really walking out on him. He let out a stream of furious obscenities. The warder hustled him away, none too gently. Madeleine Williamson steered Laurie out of the room and down the corridor, and out. 'Come on,' she said. 'What you need is a drink.'

She hailed a taxi and took Laurie to a friendly bar near her own office.

'Here,' she said, putting a brandy in front of Laurie. 'Get that down you. I told you it would do no good.'

'I know,' Laurie sighed. 'But I had to try.' She took a gulp of her drink and waited for the world to settle round her before she asked anxiously, 'About access . . . ?'

Madeleine shook her head. 'He won't get it. Not with that injunction still standing—and the magistrate's ruling about no molesting for a year.'

'That's only a year . . .'

'We can get it renewed.' Madeleine's voice was firm and kind. 'Leave it to me. Go away and make a fresh start. I'll see to all the chores.'

Laurie gave her a shaky smile. 'Well, I'm glad that's over!' she said.

THE PARTING WITH JANE was unexpectedly emotional. Laurie felt that a lifeline of sanity and rocklike support was being severed.

But Jane said steadily and kindly, 'We will keep in touch, Laurie. And you know you can always come back here if you're stuck.' Then she handed Laurie an envelope saying, 'This is the rest of your emergency

332

grant from Social Security. I've got the maximum out of them! And I've told them you will contact their Penzance office for your normal maintenance payments as soon as you arrive.'

Laurie flung her arms round Jane's neck and hugged her. 'I don't know what I'd have done without you!'

'Go on!' Jane's own voice was warm with affection. 'Have a good winter—and give my love to the sea.'

'How can we give your love to a lot of water?' asked Jason practically.

Jane looked down at him, smiling. 'You can get an old bottle and put a message in it,' she said. 'Write "Jane loves you" on it, and throw it in. Maybe it'll land up in the Thames estuary and come all the way to London. You never know!'

'All right,' agreed Jason, his eyes alight with resolve. 'I will.'

'On the other hand,' said Jane solemnly, 'it might just get washed back on shore at your feet. Then you can open the bottle again and read the message. It'll still be true.'

Laurie smiled. That was their farewell.

Joe and his van delivered them to Victoria coach station in the chill of early morning. Their cases were put in the luggage boot of the coach and they climbed on board. Laurie went on after Penny and the children, and at the last minute she put her arms round Joe's neck and said, 'Thanks for everything.'

Joe gave her a cheerful squeeze back and said to them all, 'Be happy, kids—' and turned back to his little green van.

We're away! thought Laurie. A new life is beginning! The wings in her head almost got out . . . She thought they might break free altogether when she got to the sea.

The coach made a left turn and started to run along the Embankment.

'Mum.' Jason leaned towards her. 'Could we put a message in a bottle for Clem as well?'

She turned her head, startled. 'I should think so, Jay. Why not?'

'Would it get there?'

'It might. The Medway is tidal. All rivers run to the sea . . .'

THE COACH RIDE seemed to take for ever. But at last they reached Penzance, bundled out with their luggage, and took a country bus which set them down at a crossroads beside an ancient Celtic cross, with the terse words, 'Tregarrow is that way,' from the bus driver. 'That way' seemed to point down the narrowest of the lanes before them, and they set out hopefully. They had not been walking for very long when a farm truck drew up beside them.

'Where you making for?' asked the driver.

'Tregarrow,' said Laurie. 'Mr Veryan's place.'

'Luke Veryan?' The weathered face broke into a smile. 'Passing that way meself. Hop in.'

They piled in with their luggage, and the truck went lurching on down the steep lane. Round one of the sharpest bends there was a gap in the hedge and they caught a glimpse of blue sea between two sloping headlands.

The farmer pointed. 'That's Tregarrow Head. Luke's place is up the valley a bit.' He lifted a bushy eyebrow in Laurie's direction. 'You like cliff walking?'

Laurie smiled. 'Yes. But I'm not here on holiday. I'm here to work.'

The farmer's brown face registered approval. 'Glad to hear it. Luke could do with a hand. Since his wife died, he's managed alone. But it's not been easy.'

He drew up at a grassy cart track and pointed to a cluster of roofs and barns. 'That's it, down there. You'll find Luke in the milking parlour about now, I should guess.'

'He's got cows as well?'

'Only a few. He supplies one or two hotels and guesthouses round about, and sends a churn or two to the depot—like I do.' He went round to help the others out, handed them their cases and climbed back into his truck. 'Button, that's me,' he said. 'My name. George Button. Bit of a joke round here, 'cos I'm six foot four!' He laughed, and shot off round the next bend in the lane.

The little party felt suddenly very alone. They picked up their luggage and trudged down the track until they came to a farm gate and a cattle grid across the track. Beyond they could see a muddy yard and a jumble of buildings, mostly of crumbling stone and flint-grey slate. A small farmhouse stood at one corner of the yard, and a clatter of churns and milking pails came from the open doors of the barn adjoining it.

Laurie approached the barn. Six red-brown Jersey cows stood patiently in their stalls, and a tall thin old man in a stained brown overall was pouring milk from a pail into a metal churn. He looked up when he saw Laurie, and a faint spark of acknowledgment crossed his bleak grey face, but he did not stop what he was doing till the pail was empty.

'Can I help?' asked Laurie, seeing the other full pails waiting to be poured.

'Why not?' said Luke Veryan in an abrupt, clipped voice. 'Save time, t'would.'

She came inside and carefully poured the frothy milk into the waiting churn. He did not speak again till the last pail was emptied. Then he straightened his back and looked at Laurie with a shade more warmth.

334

'You're Laurie Collins, I take it?' he said. 'Not much of a welcome, is it?' He smiled a craggy smile, and led the way out of the barn. 'Take you down to the cottage in a minute,' he said, eyeing Penny and the children speculatively. 'Getting late. Show you round tomorrow.' He scratched his head. 'Got to get the cows out first,' he muttered.

Jason came forward. 'I can help. Where do they have to go?'

Luke Veryan nodded. 'Mostly they knows the way. Just keep behind 'em, and walk on.'

He let his cows out into the yard. Automatically the leader made for the open gate into the field beyond, and slowly, ponderously, the others followed. Jason walked confidently behind them and only stepped out of line when one cow tried to go the other way.

'No!' he said, waving his arms. 'Not that way, silly! Come up, you old lazybones, come up! This way . . .' Laurie, watching him, thought he might have been herding cattle all his life.

When the cows were all in the field, Farmer Veryan turned to shut the gate and found the boy was before him. 'Good!' he said. 'You'll do!' A thin smile creaked out again, and Jason flushed with pleasure.

'Give me a couple of they,' he said, picking up two of their cases in large, competent hands. 'Follow I down,' and he led the way down a stony track along the side of the hill. The track widened and they came to a small, square cottage set with its back to the hillside. Below them lay a sloping cliff covered in late gorse and bracken, and beneath it, stretching out to a darkening horizon, lay the sea.

'Oh!' said a chorus of enthralled voices. 'The sea!'

Luke Veryan grunted noncommittally. 'Tregarrow is under the hill,' he said. 'Further up from the cove.' He jerked a thumb towards the narrow head of the valley where the two arms of the cliff met. 'Shop down there,' he added. 'But I stocked up for you, temporary like.'

He unlocked the cottage door. Inside there was one square room, whitewashed and clean, with a sofa and two small armchairs at one end, round an open fireplace. At the other end there was a small square dining table and four straight-backed chairs. Beyond this simple living room was a small kitchen with a new-looking electric cooker and a fridge and some cupboards set under white Formica working tops.

Luke Veryan was surveying this well-equipped little unit with a sardonic eye. 'Summer visitors,' he explained to Laurie. 'They likes everything quick and shiny . . . Me, I prefers an Aga, slow or no.'

Penny nodded. 'Cooks better, too.' She was rewarded by a slightly less creaky smile.

'Let you loose on it then, girl, shall I?' he said, and then on a note of caution, 'One of these days.'

Laurie went upstairs to have a look at the bedrooms. There were two—one with twin beds and one with two bunk beds and a single divan. Both of them had small windows looking out across the sloping hillside to the sea. It was wonderfully quiet.

'Leave it to you then—' she heard Luke Veryan say to Penny, and she hurried down to say to his retreating back, 'What time shall I start in the morning?'

The thin, spare figure turned back to look at her. 'No work tomorrow. Settling-in day. Come up after breakfast and I'll show you round.'

'All right,' agreed Laurie. 'And Mr Veryan—thanks!'

He nodded abruptly and stumped away up the hillside to his farm.

They sorted out their meagre possessions, and Penny firmly chose to share the children's bedroom. 'Give you a bit of peace,' she said. 'Besides, I like being with the kids.'

Laurie was looking out of the window at the slowly darkening sea. 'Is it too late to go down to the cove?' she wondered.

'Not if we hurry.' Penny was as eager as Jason and Midge.

They wasted no time. The narrow track wound downwards between gorse and bracken. Only once did it come near the edge of the cliff, and they looked over at a dizzying drop and a jumble of jagged rocks below, with a deep green sea-swell swirling round them.

Presently the path spread out into a little oasis of springy turf starred with pale autumn squills and clumps of late thrift. Below this the sand began, in a steep dune, and below that lay the cove—set in a curve of white sand, and guarded by two arms of curious gold-brown rocky cliff. The sea itself was green—green and calm and quiet.

'Oh!' cried the children, and threw off their shoes and went running.

Laurie ran after them across the firm white sand, and Penny followed.

'It's cold!' danced Jason, wriggling his toes in the water.

'Ooh, it is!' echoed Midge, prancing about at the edge.

Even Laurie waded in, and stood there surrounded by swirls of jade and emerald, ice-cold and clean and pure. Pure, she thought—tomorrow, I'll swim in it. There'll be time tomorrow. And then I might begin to feel clean and whole again . . .

Aloud, she said gently to the enchanted faces beside her, 'Tomorrow we'll swim. It's getting late now. It'll still be here tomorrow.'

They turned to leave, but Jason lingered. 'Mum?' he said. 'Could I earn some money?'

Laurie looked at him in surprise. 'I should think so, Jay—if you helped Mr Veryan. Or if you helped me, maybe I could pay you. Why? Is there something you want to buy?'

He hesitated, scuffing his bare feet in the sand. 'Only two bottles of pop.'

336

Penny laughed. 'That won't cost much! Even I could buy you those!'

'No,' said Jason, sounding obstinate. '*I've* got to buy them—myself.' He looked beseechingly at his mother. 'And two corks . . .'

'Oh,' said Laurie, smiling. 'Of course! To send a message to Jane.'

'And to Clem,' Jason insisted. 'Clem must have one as well.'

Laurie took his cold hand in hers. 'Tomorrow,' she agreed. 'We'll do all the things we promised . . . Now it's time to go in.'

Together they made their way back up the cliff path to the cottage on the hill.

IN THE MORNING, Jason went up to help Luke Veryan with the cows. He came back to breakfast glowing with sea air and achievement. 'He's waiting for you to come up,' he reported. 'And the farm is smashing!'

Laurie found Luke Veryan in the yard, hosing out the milking parlour. 'Show you the glasshouses first,' he said, leading the way to a long row of greenhouses behind the barns. 'Winter lettuce,' he explained, pointing to rows of seed boxes. 'And various. Late chrysanths and pot plants for the Christmas market.' Patiently, he explained about the winter market and the picking and packing. Then he took her out to his orderly market garden with its neat rows of vegetables and a glorious riot of late dahlias along one end of the field.

There was an old bent man hoeing between the rows. 'That's Bob,' said Luke. 'Comes up from the village most days—when his lumbago lets him! He'll be glad of an extra pair of hands.'

Laurie stood looking round her. Everywhere there were flowers waiting to be picked and bunched—late asters and outdoor chrysanthemums and gleaming rows of gladioli, besides the blaze of dahlias.

'Where are the daffodil fields?' she asked.

Luke Veryan's smile broke out. 'You come through them, girl . . . On the way up from the cottage. All them green spaces between here and the sea—they're full of daffs come spring. And there's more fields of 'em over there.' He chuckled. 'You was walking on 'em, girl, thousands of bulbs—under your feet!'

Laurie looked down at her own feet in their mud-caked Wellingtons and laughed. Thousands of bulbs, she thought. All that green and gold life under my feet . . . waiting for winter to be done, and spring to come.

Luke took her into the farmhouse, to the small room he used as an office. He showed her his order books and his accounts, his milk returns and his packing schedule, together with a whole lot of orders and bills. 'Chaos!' he admitted, waving a hand at them. 'Never catch up.' Then he pointed a stubby finger at another bookful of names. 'Take on pickers and packers come February,' he explained. 'Only trouble is, we has to pack

Sundays. To deliver to the Monday markets. Flowers isn't fresh enough, else. Or veggies. D'you mind?'

Laurie smiled. 'No. All days are much the same to me. Except—' and here she asked an important question. 'Jason, my boy, ought to go to school. Is there one within reach at all?'

Luke nodded. 'Right here in Tregarrow. One pub, one church, one school . . .' His voice was dry. 'We're the biggest village hereabouts, see? So we've kept our school. Kids come from miles around.' He paused, considering. 'I dessay it's not too full, though. Better ask Mrs Weelkes— head teacher.'

'And then,' Laurie pursued her next anxiety, 'there's Penny. Joe told you about Penny?'

He nodded noncommittally.

'Well, she ought to see the local doctor, shouldn't she? And get fixed up with a hospital bed. I mean—I wouldn't want the baby to arrive on your doorstep! I'm no midwife.'

'Neither am I!' growled Luke, but there was an unmistakable twinkle deep down. 'Dr Trevelyan,' he said then. 'Surgery in the village, three days a week. And there's Agnes Penwillis, she really *is* a midwife!'

Laurie nodded her relief.

Luke was saying something about wages and quoting a figure that made Laurie's eyes open wide.

'All that—as well as the cottage?' She felt almost outraged on his behalf. 'You'll never make a profit that way!'

Luke's sudden laughter was more like a bark. 'Are you refusing?'

She looked at him severely. 'No. I'm not that daft! But I think it should include a bit of help from the others. Penny can do packing—providing it's not too much stooping. And Jay loves helping with the cows.'

'So I've noticed.'

But Laurie had just thought of something. She told Luke about Jane and the message in the bottle. 'So you see, I'd be obliged if you'd knock a bit off my wages—just a little—and give it to Jason. He'd feel so much better if he thought he'd earned it.'

Luke stared at her thoughtfully. 'How much?'

'Oh . . . say fifty pence? He's not used to spending much.'

Luke considered. 'Make it a pound,' he said. 'And see he puts half in the post office. Good for him. Used to do it with Joe. And I won't knock it off yourn, neither.'

'Oh but—'

'No,' he said firmly. 'But I'll make him work for it, mind!'

Laurie grinned. 'You know,' she said conversationally, 'I told your Joe he was one of the kindest men I'd ever met. He must take after you.'

Luke made a growling noise in his throat and turned away to his littered desk. 'Well,' he said after a moment, 'all settled then? Take today for your own affairs. Get settled. Start tomorrow.'

LAURIE LEFT PENNY at Dr Trevelyan's surgery and went on up the village street to look for the school, with Jason and Midge running ahead. The road was steep and narrow, with the small flinty cottages crowding together with their backs to the rock-strewn hillside. The little school was at the far end, with its wide windows looking out over the sloping valley to the sea. There were quite a lot of children in the concrete playground, all rushing about and shouting, and a squarish, pleasant-looking woman with grey-flecked hair was standing watching them from the doorway.

Laurie thought, It's small, and not too tough—not nearly as tough as Jason's London school. I think Jay will be all right here . . . But aloud she said to Jason, 'What do you think, Jay? You don't *have* to go to school for a while, unless you want to.'

'Don't I?'

'No.'

His eyes strayed longingly back to the children.

Laurie knew then that Jason was lonely—that he needed the routine and companionship of school. It would reassure him that life was getting back to normal. Satisfied, she opened the gate and went towards the woman standing on the steps, with Midge clutching her hand very tight.

Emma Weelkes knew who Laurie was. The village grapevine had already spread the news of Luke Veryan's winter tenants. Tregarrow people were not unkindly. They were cautious, and slow to accept newcomers, but basically they were warm-hearted enough, and staunch allies in trouble. And already the word was out that Laurie could probably do with a helping hand. About the girl, Penny, they were not so sure. Pregnant? At that age? You could guess what sort of a girl *she* was—and what kind of a life she'd been living . . . And who was she, anyway? The young woman's kid sister? She was obviously too old to be her daughter.

So the village gossip went. Emma Weelkes heard most of it, but she kept her own counsel, and formed her own opinions.

Now, she welcomed Laurie with a smile and said, 'You must be Mrs Collins. Would you like to come in and have a look round?'

'If you're not too busy?' began Laurie, shyly.

She led them into a big sunny schoolroom, decorated with children's paintings and wall charts. 'We do most of our work in here,' she explained. 'The numbers are too small for separate classes—though we take small groups for special subjects in a couple of smaller rooms.' She took them into each room, and beyond them to a well-equipped kindergarten full of toys and small tables and chairs, with glass doors open to the side of the playground.

'How old is your little girl?' asked Emma Weelkes.

'Three . . . she'll be four at Christmas. Only, I think—we may have to wait a while before she's ready for kindergarten.' She felt Midge's grip tighten on her hand, and hoped that Emma Weelkes would not press the matter. The head teacher was no fool. She turned to Midge and said, 'Would you like to see our rabbit? He's called Maurice, and the children look after him themselves . . .' Talking all the time, she led them out through the glass doors to a couple of cages built close to the wall, with small wired-in runs on the grassy edge of the playground. Maurice was a large lop-eared buck with golden-brown fur and a bold look in his eye.

'Mrs Taggy lives in the next cage,' explained Emma. 'But she's going to have babies any day now, so she likes to be left in peace . . . I dare say when you next come, there'll be a whole lot of baby rabbits to see, too.'

Jason was enchanted. 'Can I stroke him?'

'I should think so. He's very tame. If you could find any dandelion leaves left, he loves those.' She showed Jason how to reach inside the cage. 'We've got a goat, too. She's out there, munching heather. Melanie, she's called, and she's got a kid that the children call "Buck's Fizz".'

Midge was watching Jason with the rabbit, fascinated. 'Can I feed him too?' she asked, and let go of Laurie's hand.

'Of course. If you hold that saucer steady, I'll put a little of his bran mash into it . . .'

After a few minutes, Emma and Laurie moved quietly away and left the children by the rabbit hutches.

'Would you have room for Jason?' asked Laurie, when they were sitting in Emma's small office.

Emma Weelkes smiled. 'I don't see why not. We're not overcrowded.'

'He's missed a few weeks . . .' She paused, and then added, 'And life has been a bit . . . difficult for him. But he's a good boy, and he's bright.'

The head teacher nodded. 'You needn't worry, I can see he needs a peaceful, trouble-free existence—just as much as our Mrs Taggy! And as for your little girl, I suggest you bring her each time you come to fetch Jason. Let her go to see the animals—she has to pass the kindergarten to get to them. I think she will soon want to stop and play with the others.'

Laurie smiled. 'You're very understanding.'

At this point, Jason appeared in the doorway, holding Midge by the hand. 'She wanted to know where you were,' he said apologetically.

'That's all right.' Emma smiled at him. 'We were just talking about you. Would you like to come to school here?'

340

'Yes, please,' said Jason.

Midge said nothing. But her eyes strayed to the window which looked out at the playground. The children were filing in now for lessons. And a small group of very young ones were gathered round a laughing girl who was teaching them how to skip.

'Tomorrow then?' said Emma Weelkes to Jason, getting to her feet.

'Magic!' said Jason.

PENNY MET THEM outside the village shop looking a bit pink, and Laurie fancied from the toss of her head in greeting that she was a little at bay.

'Come on.' Laurie glanced at her flushed face. 'We're going down to the cove for a breath of air. The shopping'll keep.' Laurie's voice was firm. 'Let's go and look at the sea.'

The sea was waiting for them—pearl and silver this morning, with a hint of mist on the horizon. A few gulls were sunning themselves on the sand, and took off as the children came running.

Laurie watched them chasing seagulls, and then turned abruptly to Penny. 'What did the doctor say?'

'Oh, he thinks everything is OK. But he's fixing a scan for me at the hospital.'

Laurie nodded. 'What about the district nurse?'

'She's coming up to see me at the house. And she'll fix the trip to the hospital in Penzance. There's a local ambulance bus, or something . . .'

'That's good.' So the nurse didn't upset her . . . then who had?

'Penny,' she said suddenly, 'do you want to wear a wedding ring? Would it make things easier?'

Penny tossed her red-gold mane. 'No thanks. Who would I say I was married to? My father?'

Laurie sighed. 'It was only a suggestion.'

Penny's indignation dissolved like the morning mist. 'I know . . . to save me trouble . . .' Her eyes softened as she looked at Laurie. 'But I don't need it. I'm OK.'

Laurie gave her a swift hug. 'Of course you are. I'm going to leave you here with the kids while I get the shopping. Then I'll bring our swimsuits down. We probably won't get many more warm days.'

She went back up to the village street, pondering what she should do about Penny . . . If they were going to stay here for six months, she couldn't let unfriendly gossip go on upsetting her.

As she went up the step to the little general store, the door opened and a woman came out. Behind her, another woman who was leaning on the counter said, 'No better than she should be, I shouldn't wonder . . . And at her age, too!'

341

A sudden hot anger surged up inside Laurie. She marched into the shop and plonked some money down on the counter with a sharp click. 'No one is any better than they should be,' she snapped. 'Especially a victim of rape. Or would you prefer the term "child abuse"?'

There was a horrified silence. The woman who had just been going turned back. 'We didn't mean—'

'Oh, I know—' said Laurie, pushing the hair out of her eyes in her familiar gesture of stress. 'It's not something one talks about to strangers, is it? But that child has suffered enough, believe me . . . And since I've taken her under my wing, I've got to protect her as best I can.' She looked at the three women appealingly. 'She needs all the help she can get—especially when the baby comes. It's no joke being a mother at sixteen!'

The women suddenly thawed. 'The poor girl!' said the one by the door.

'We'll do what we can,' said the one by the counter.

'This is a good sort of place to come to,' said the postmistress, smiling at them over the counter. 'We look after people in Tregarrow.'

Laurie smiled back—an enormous wash of relief flooding over her. She had been afraid of what might happen to Penny in this small place. But now it looked as if these women at least would be on her side. 'That's good to hear,' she said, and the sudden radiance in her face made the other women blink. 'Now I'd better buy some food. We can't let her starve, can we?'

After that, they couldn't do enough for her. They pointed out the cheapest brands of food, advised her where to find mushrooms in the morning fields, and when the fishermen came in with their catch and had fresh fish to sell. And finally, Annie Merrow—the postmistress—handed Laurie a small tin of Ovaltine, saying, 'Here. Have this on me. Good for expectant mothers!'

Laurie left the shop with a smile all round and a laden carrier bag. She had won Penny's first battle for her.

THE SEA, SHE THOUGHT—the cool, clean sea. It will wash it all away. In fact, it was more than cool. It was cold—breathtakingly cold and clear.

They all swam—though Laurie kept them near to the shore and privately blessed Clem for his foresight in teaching the children to be safe in the water. It still hurt her to swim, but the bruises on her body were healing. The ones in her mind would take longer, she knew.

'Come on,' she said. 'You'll get cold . . . time to come out.'

Golden October, she thought, looking up at the sun. Aren't we lucky? The bracken on the hillside had turned golden in the mild autumn air, and the gorse flamed yellow on the clifftops. It's so beautiful, thought Laurie, so calm and quiet, it almost makes me want to cry . . .

342

'We're lighting a fire!' called Jason, rushing past her with an armful of driftwood. 'Penny's got some matches.'

'Coming,' said Laurie, and stooped to pick up a silvery spar of wood lying on the sand.

THE NEXT DAY Laurie took Jason to school and then went on to her first day's work, leaving Midge with Penny. The first morning was a bit bewildering. But she began to make sense of Luke's books, and also went into the packing sheds and the greenhouses to help with the daily deliveries of vegetables and flowers. At lunchtime, when she was wondering if she ought to go and make Luke a cup of tea, she heard clatterings in his kitchen and went to investigate. Penny was there, encased in a large apron and clearly in charge, while Midge and Jason were putting knives and forks round the table.

Laurie hugged Jason, whose first morning had been 'smashing', then looked at Penny enquiringly. 'Does Luke Veryan know you're here?'

Penny nodded. 'Told 'im, didn't I? . . . Daft to cook Jay's dinner at the cottage, and leave you and Uncle Luke to go hungry.'

Laurie's eyes opened wide. 'Oh, so it's Uncle Luke now, is it?'

Penny's grin was wide and infectious. 'Easier for the kids,' she said briskly. 'Midge couldn't get her tongue round all that.' She tossed her red mane and gave the stew one more stir. 'Besides,' she added, 'I think he rather likes it. Gotta have some kinda family, hasn't he—with Joe so far away an' all?' She lifted the pot of stew off the stove and carried it over to the table.

'Jay,' she commanded, 'go and find Uncle Luke. And that old man, Bob. Could do with something hot—out there in the fields all day.'

So a routine was established. Luke Veryan never said he approved or disapproved—but he came in to Penny's meals, and so did old Bob, and both of them looked the better for it. Also, Luke's house mysteriously began to take on a more lived-in look. The rooms got cleaned and dusted, the windows got rid of their film of salt sea-spray, and the patch of earth round the kitchen door suddenly sprouted winter violet plants and tubs of geraniums.

Jason always brought the cows in before breakfast, and let them out again before he went to school, and usually ran all the way back in the afternoon to help again before it got dark. And even Midge had learned how to collect the eggs, and how to help old Bob pack the cut flowers for market.

Laurie had little time to herself. But she took to wandering down to the cove very early in the morning. It was peaceful then—cool and quiet. She did not stay long—one brisk swim across to the rocks and back was all the time she could spare. Then it was running across the sand to get warm, climbing the high dune and the cliff path to the cottage to get the breakfast with Penny, seeing Jason off to school, giving Midge an extra hug to make up for leaving her with Penny, and going on up the hill to Luke Veryan's farm and the day's work.

She was busy all day long, and sometimes the work was fairly backbreaking. But she did not mind. And putting Luke Veryan's accounts in order gave her an unexpected satisfaction . . . She even went to consult Farmer George Button about market prices and opportunities, and found that Luke's turnover could be improved in various ways.

The only thing that troubled her was her eyesight. She seemed to have recurrent attacks of double vision. But she decided that this would disappear in time and was just a hangover from the concussion and the hairline fracture. She didn't think it was worth mentioning to Dr Trevelyan.

Penny, though, was a different matter. She went with her to the hospital and was relieved to learn that the scan was satisfactory. The baby was due about the last week in December.

It had occurred to Laurie that Penny had made no provision for the child—no baby clothes, no cot, not even a packet of nappies—and certainly no garment for Penny herself to wear in the last few weeks.

'Come on,' she said, when they came out of the hospital with Midge between them, 'we're going shopping.'

'What with?' asked Penny, tossing her bright hair in the sun.

'Your maternity grant,' said Laurie grinning. 'And my wages.'

They were all happy that day, and they came home on the rattling country bus laden with parcels and full of cheerful chatter. Jason was home before them and had dutifully put the kettle on.

'We brung you a present,' stated Midge, and held out a crumpled-looking flat parcel.

Inside was a new pencil case for school, and a paperback about the Cornish coast and its wildlife, with a picture of a seal on the front.

Jason was delighted. 'There's seals in the cove sometimes,' he said. 'Mrs Weelkes told me.'

Midge held up her own small present. 'I've got a sea lion, 'stead of the lion I lost. And there's things for the baby, lots of them!'

'And I've got a new dress!' said Penny. 'Shall I put it on?'

Pleased at the brightness in her face, and the children's eager response, Laurie set about cooking the sausages for tea.

'Mum,' said Jason, leaning over her arm by the cooker, 'Mrs Taggy's had seven babies. But she sat on one.'

'Oh dear. Were the others all right?'

344

'Yes. They're a bit skinny though, at first . . . Will Penny have seven, do you think?'

'Good grief, no!' Penny exploded with laughter. 'Only one, Jay, I promise you!' And she twirled round the kitchen in her new green dress, giggling helplessly.

AT THE END OF THE WEEK, Jason got paid too.

'We'll go down to the post office,' decreed Laurie, 'and take you out a savings book right away . . . Mr Veryan says you're to put fifty pence away every week!'

'And then I can buy my bottles,' agreed Jason happily.

Laurie had not been working that Saturday morning, since they were going to be packing vegetables for the market on Sunday. So they all went down to the village post office together, and after Jason became the proud possessor of a savings book they bought some Cornish pasties and a bag of sticky buns from the baker, and two bottles of pop to go with them, and went down to the cove. The weather had changed in the night, and a heavy white mist had rolled in from the sea, blanketing the headlands and harbours. The foghorn on the clifftop had called its warning all night long to the ships out on the dark ocean.

But now, as Laurie and the children settled on the beach, an offshore wind got up, the mists rolled back, and there, out of the silvery swirls, came the fishing boats returning from their night's fishing.

'Oh!' breathed Jason. 'Don't they look super coming in! Now I can launch my bottles.'

He took a pencil and a scrap of paper out of his pocket, folded the paper in half and tore it in two. On one half he wrote, very carefully, *I love you, Jane*, and sat looking at it. 'Is that right?'

'Yes,' agreed Laurie, smiling.

He looked at her seriously. 'She said, "Jane loves you". But I thought this was truer. Because it means Jane loves the sea . . . and we love Jane.'

'Oh,' said Midge doubtfully. And then, 'Can I write on it, too?'

He hesitated. 'You can put a cross on it,' he said, and handed her the pencil. 'That means the same.'

Midge solemnly put a cross on the paper and watched, fascinated, while he rolled it up tight and shoved it into the bottle. Now he skilfully corked it, and turned to consider the one to Clem.

'Can I put the same? Is it *true?*' he asked, pencil poised.

'Yes,' said Laurie quietly. And felt strange echoes and certainties stir in her mind, like rings in a pool. 'It is true.'

Jason bent his head over the paper. *I love you, Clem*, he wrote. And Midge carefully put her mark there, too.

They all went down to the water's edge. 'Not near the rocks,' said Penny, sensibly. 'They might get smashed.'

Jason was already in his swimming trunks. He waded out until the water was up to his waist.

'Now!' called Laurie. 'No further . . . or you won't be able to throw them.'

He lifted his arm and threw Jane's first, and watched it bob and turn and ride the water and then drift out on a spent wave. A bigger swell was coming in now, and the careening bottle was suddenly swamped in a great sweep of jade-green water . . . When it had passed, the bottle was gone.

Then he took a deep breath and threw Clem's bottle. Like the first, it bobbed and lifted, heading away. And when he looked again, the second bottle was gone, too—taken by the sea.

He stood there a long time, gazing out across the waves. Presently, he felt a wet hand slide into his, and turned to find Laurie beside him, her jeans rolled up to her knees.

'They're safe now,' she said gently. 'The sea will look after them . . . Come and get warm. Penny's lit a fire.'

Together they waded back to the shore, to the driftwood fire, and Penny's welcoming smile.

'We're toasting buns,' she said. 'Don't they smell good?'

IN NOVEMBER, the first of the winter gales came tearing across the sea. The seas grew mountainous out in the bay, and the long Atlantic rollers raced into the cove and pushed the tide lines further up the beach.

Laurie was almost terrified by their power, and forbade the children to go anywhere near the water.

The fishing fleet from the next cove stayed inside its safe harbour wall, but there were always strange craft that did not know those waters.

Sure enough, late one evening the maroon went off for the lifeboat down at Newlyn or Mousehole, and a small knot of people—old retired fishermen and a few anxious women—gathered on Tregarrow Head to peer out to sea.

Luke Veryan and George Button passed Laurie, running, with a coil of rope and a life buoy in their hands, and a scatter of village boys after them.

'Ship on the rocks,' panted Luke. 'May be able to get some of 'em off . . .' and he went on running.

Laurie lit Luke's storm lantern and followed them down. At the cliff's end, where the jumble of rocks began, she stumbled into a small knot of people, among them Agnes Penwillis, the district nurse.

'What can I do?' asked Laurie.

346

'Nothing much any of us can do,' said the nurse, shaking her head. 'Ship's broken her back on the rocks . . . lifeboat's coming. We may get some of 'em off this way. They've got a line to her.' She looked at Laurie and added kindly, 'The lads are bringing down a couple of stretchers. There may be injuries. But blankets and a flask of tea—they might come in useful.'

Behind Laurie came Penny's cheerful voice in the dark. 'I've brought those, and a ground sheet to keep them dry.'

'Penny!' Laurie sounded almost angry. 'You shouldn't be out in this. You might slip on the rocks or something . . .'

'Safe as houses,' said Penny, grinning. 'And nearly as big!' Then, seeing Laurie's anxious face in the glimmer of the storm lantern, she added, 'Old Bob's staying with Midge at the cottage. Says he's too stiff to be any use. But Jay's coming down with the boys and the stretchers.'

There was a sudden flurry of movement and shouts from the rocks, and then a flare lit up the scene for a moment. In its glare, Laurie saw the bows of a ship jammed hard against the rocks on the spit of land enclosing the cove, and a line stretched taut from its shattered superstructure to some point closer in on the rocks . . . and a man dangling from the line.

'One!' muttered Agnes Penwillis, and got ready to receive her first casualty. Silently, efficiently, the villagers passed the injured man from one to the other until he was handed down to the nurse waiting on the shore. 'What's the damage?' she asked, lowering him gently onto the sand.

'Broken ankle, I think,' he said, speaking good but halting English. 'It's nothing much—there's others worse . . . She hit head-on . . . We couldn't save her.'

'Stretcher party's here,' said a dark shape in oilskins at her elbow. 'Ambulance coming to the top.'

'Better splint it first,' said Agnes. And she set about her work with swift decision. 'Here,' she snapped at Laurie, 'you look sensible. Hold this!'

When she had finished, Penny draped a blanket round the man's shoulders, and the stretcher-bearers carried him off to the clifftop.

Two more men were winched off uninjured, and passed on down to the waiting rescuers on the beach. Then came one more seriously hurt. Agnes did what she could for him, and sent him on to the waiting ambulance as fast as possible. Laurie seemed to have become her assistant, and handed bandages and scissors and swabs when required.

By this time the lifeboat had arrived and stood off the rocks, while overhead there was the thrum of a helicopter from Culdrose.

The rescue went on nearly all night, and between the three parties, on beach and sea, and in the sky, they got every man off, except one who had been lost overboard at the first impact.

Towards dawn the wind dropped a little and the lashing rain eased off, and the weary party of rescuers turned their backs on the sea and began the long walk home, drenched and tired.

Laurie walked back up the cliff path with Agnes Penwillis, and called in at the cottage on the way to reassure Midge and old Bob that everyone was safe. But she found the old man fast asleep in the chair by the fire, with little Midge curled up on his lap like a kitten, also fast asleep.

Smiling, Laurie left them undisturbed, following the nurse to Luke Veryan's kitchen, where warmth and light and hot drinks awaited everyone.

It was an exhausted party, but a cheerful one. They had done their best. Between them, twenty-one lives had been snatched from the sea. Even the captain was safe. But as soon as the soup and tea were demolished, they drifted off to their own homes, and all at once the big farmhouse kitchen was empty—save for Luke and the weary sea captain, and Penny and Laurie washing cups in the sink while Jason went round the room collecting more.

'Leave all that,' commanded Luke. 'It'll keep till morning . . . Get the boy home to bed. It's late.' He paused, straightening his back a little painfully, and added, 'Youm did a good job there, the three on you.' From Luke Veryan that was high praise.

So Penny and Laurie, with Jason between them, went stumbling back to their own cottage. We're safe, thought Laurie, before sleep engulfed her completely. Everyone's safe. The storm is over. We can sleep in peace.

LAURIE THOUGHT IT WAS from that night that the villagers of Tregarrow really began to accept her and the family. Even Penny noticed the difference, and met friendly faces in the village when she went shopping or took Midge to meet Jason from school. Midge herself met a small boy called Billy Tremain at the kindergarten who called out to her every time she came by, 'You comin', then? . . . You comin' soon?' And one day, Midge suddenly answered, 'Yes!'

She made no further comment. She marched on to see Maurice the rabbit and Mrs Taggy and her six fluffy babies, and then waited for Jason by the gate as usual. But the next morning, she announced calmly, 'I'm goin' to school today.'

Penny looked at her sternly. 'They may not let you stay—not without asking.'

'We'll ask,' stated Midge. And ask she did, as soon as she got to the door.

Jean, the kindergarten supervisor, smiled and said cheerfully, 'Of course you can stay. Where shall we put you, now?'

348

'Next to Billy,' said Midge, and walked over to where her dark-haired admirer was waiting for her.

'Hello,' he said, suddenly shy. 'You come, then . . .'

'Course,' agreed Midge. 'I said so, didn't I?' And she sat down beside him on the floor.

Above her head, Jean and Penny looked at one another and smiled.

When Penny reported this small triumph at lunchtime, Laurie picked Midge up and whirled her round. 'Aren't you clever! Staying at school all by yourself!'

'I wasn't by mineself,' pointed out Midge logically. 'I was with Billy.'

There was no answer to that, except laughter.

THAT WEEKEND THERE WAS a village jumble sale in the Methodist Hall, in aid of the Lifeboat Fund, and Penny bought a carrycot on wheels for two pounds. Laurie bought the children some winter jerseys and Penny a frilly nightie for going to hospital.

Laurie was standing beside one of the stalls, staring at pots of honey and homemade jam when suddenly she found herself looking at a double row of jam jars. She swayed a little, feeling dizzy.

'What's the matter?' said Penny's voice, close to her. 'Anything wrong?'

'No.' Laurie spoke vaguely. 'Hot in here . . . Get some air . . .' and she fought her way to the door. There was a wooden bench outside, and she sank down onto it, struggling to get the world back into focus.

Penny and the children came out after her. 'You all right?' asked Jason.

Laurie summoned a smile. 'Of course I am. You go on ahead with Penny and get the tea. I'll have a bit of a walk, clear my head.'

They looked at her for a moment, then Penny seized Midge by the hand and said cheerfully, 'Come on. You can help me push the new pram,' and they set off up the hill.

Laurie waited till they had gone, then got to her feet and made her way slowly down the street towards the cove. The sea, she thought, the sea will put me right.

She had just reached the little bay when seagulls scavenging on the high tide line flew up with a clatter of wings. And suddenly there were other wings in her head, beating frantically to get out, and she fell in a heap on the sand.

She came round, groggily, to feel a wet tongue licking her face, and to hear a man's voice saying, 'No, Corny. Leave her to me.'

At first she thought it was Clem's voice, but it couldn't be Clem . . . Clem was far away.

'Come on,' said the same kindly voice. 'Are you with us? Open your eyes.' Laurie did as she was told.

Beside her was the square, weatherworn face of Dr Trevelyan, and beyond him a beautiful creamy retriever sitting looking at her interestedly.

Laurie blinked, and tried to struggle up. 'I can't keep doing this!' she muttered crossly.

The doctor sat down on the sand beside her. 'Have you done it before?' he asked in a casual voice.

'Yes. But I thought I was over it.'

He was looking at her shrewdly. 'Headache?'

She shook her head faintly, and then realised it was a mistake and put up her hands to steady it. 'Not exactly. More like . . .'

'Yes?'

'Wings . . .' she murmured. 'Trying to get out.'

He grunted. 'Wings in the head? Don't think I've ever prescribed for them. Anything else?'

Laurie hesitated. 'No—o. Except that I see double sometimes still.'

'Double wings, eh?' He grinned encouragingly. Then he reached into the small haversack beside him and took out a Thermos, and briskly poured her out a cup of tea. 'Saturday,' he remarked, 'is my walking day. Corny waits all week for this moment. And so do I.' He looked round at the quiet cove and the empty sands. 'Cures everything . . . better than I can . . .' Then he looked at her sternly. 'Now, listen to me, young woman. Can't have you fainting all over the place. Come up and see me at the surgery—*tomorrow!*'

'Tomorrow's Sunday. And I'm packing for Mr Veryan.'

He glared. 'Well, Monday then. After work. We may need to get you X-rayed.'

Panic overcame her. 'I *can't*. I can't spare the time.'

'Nonsense!' Trevelyan spoke brusquely. 'Luke Veryan's not going to throw you out just because you take half a day off at the hospital.'

She was still looking distraught as he got to his feet and gave her a kindly pat. 'Sit there until you feel stronger,' he commanded. 'And then go home and have a rest. See you on Monday. No skiving, mind!' And he whistled to Corny and stumped off towards the cliff path round the bay.

Laurie closed her eyes for a moment. When she opened them again, Jason was coming down the dunes towards her.

'Thought you'd be here,' he said. 'Tea's ready. Penny sent me to fetch you.' And, like a true protective male, he put his arm through Laurie's and led her home.

DR TREVELYAN WAS AS GOOD as his word and insisted on Laurie having an X-ray. So she went down to Penzance on the country bus, leaving Penny behind with the children. Penny was getting too near her time for long and tedious journeys, and the bus was very bumpy.

The weather had suddenly changed too, from being mild and drizzly to furious gales and torrential rain. The bus churned on through clouds of spray and mud until it came in sight of Newlyn and Penzance, and a cold grey-black sea beaten flat by the rain.

Laurie had to wait a long time for her X-ray, and then a long time more before they decided the pictures were satisfactory and she could go home.

Once more the bus set off in driving rain and early darkness. Laurie could see nothing out of the windows, and the driver could see little beyond the swish of the windscreen wipers and the curtain of rain like a silver wall. But all at once there were lights and waving arms on the road ahead. 'Bridge down,' came the shout. 'Four feet of water on the road . . . turn back!'

The bus driver got out and consulted with the men in the road. Then he climbed in again, and called out to the passengers, 'We're returning to St Buryan. Can't get through this way. Sorry, folks.'

The bus set off back towards the little town it had left twenty minutes before. It pulled up in the main square and the driver and his passengers crowded into the nearest pub, where the driver made for the telephone. The bar was full of people sheltering from the storm, and the talk was all of trees down and roads blocked, rivers overflowing their banks and village streets becoming torrents of mud.

Laurie waited for the bus driver to get off the telephone. She wanted to ring Luke Veryan, and send a message down to Penny at the cottage. Finally, the driver returned and said to the passengers, 'Can't go no further tonight. Very sorry. I'm afraid you'll either have to stay here for the night, or come back with me to the bus station.'

Laurie went through to telephone. The phone rang for a long time and then a quavering voice said, 'Hello? Veryan's farm.'

'Who's that?' asked Laurie, surprised at the thin old voice. 'This is Laurie Collins here.'

'Oh, Laurie! It's Bob. There's trouble here, missus. Penny's started—'

'*What?*' But she's not due yet.'

'I know . . . Slipped on Mr Luke's floor, 'er did . . .'

'Have you sent for Doctor Trevelyan?'

'Missus, we'm tried . . . He's out on his rounds in his car, and he can't get back on account of the floods.'

'What about Nurse Penwillis?'

'She'm over to Poldurran, delivering another baby. We've tried to get a message through to the Shipwright's Arms and they've promised to tell her, if they can find her. But she'd have to walk over by the cliff path. No one can get here by road.'

Laurie went cold with fear. 'I'm stuck too, Bob. The bus had to turn round and go back to St Buryan. What are we going to do?'

Old Bob sighed. 'Mr Luke's gone down to look after her and the kids.' The reedy voice hesitated. 'He's used to birth, missus. Delivered a-many calves in his time, has Mr Luke. I dessay he'll know what to do.'

Laurie tried to picture Penny struggling to produce her baby with only the guidance of an old country farmer to help her. I must get through somehow, she thought. I simply *must*.

Aloud she said, 'You stay there, Bob. No sense trying to get back down to Tregarrow in this. But if you can get to the cottage a bit later, tell Mr Luke I'll get there somehow, and be sure to give Penny my love and tell her I'm coming.'

'I'll do that, missus.'

Laurie rang off, determined now to ask for help in the bar. Surely someone would have a Land-Rover or a truck able to get through.

She went back and spoke to the landlord. He nodded and rapped hard on his counter.

'Young lady here,' he said, 'wants a volunteer to get her as near Tregarrow as maybe. There's a baby on the way, doctor and nurse both out. Anyone feeling like braving the weather?'

There was silence for a moment, and then someone said, 'Where is it, exactly? You'll never get through to Tregarrow.'

'Luke Veryan's,' said Laurie. 'But I can walk, if anyone could get near the cliff path.'

A burly figure got up from a stool by the fire and said, 'I've got a Land-Rover here. If there's a baby coming, I reckon we'd best have a try.'

They went out into the rain and wind together. At the last moment, the landlord thrust a torch into Laurie's hand, and handed the driver a quarter-bottle of whisky.

The night seemed more black and tempestuous than ever, and the stocky man took Laurie's arm firmly and led her out to where his Land-Rover was parked in the main square. He helped her in, then climbed in himself, cursing amiably at the cascade of water that went down his neck as he opened the driver's door.

'We'd best try the top road and cut back,' he shouted at her over the sound of the engine and the roar of the wind outside.

Laurie willed herself not to start shouting, 'For God's sake hurry up!'

The Land-Rover churned steadily on into the night. There was a lot of water on the road. Once they had to swing over close to the hedge to avoid a fallen branch, and once they came to a heap of rubble in the road from a fallen wall, and a swirling mass of water round it. The way through seemed impassable. But the driver simply turned his vehicle into an open

352

gateway, drove across the top end of a field, and came out on the far side into a farm track and back onto the road again.

'Good thing I knows these parts!' he grinned. 'I'm Tom Tremayne from Tremayne's Farm.'

They had to make another detour round a fallen tree but at length they came to yet another crossroads and a signpost which said 'Tregarrow' on one arm and 'Poldurran' on the other.

'This is the one that's flooded,' said Tom. 'Don't think we'll get much further. It drops down too low.' He glanced at Laurie doubtfully. 'We'll go on as far as we can, but if I go right down, I may not be able to turn.'

They swerved again to avoid a broken wall and a fallen gatepost, and then the Land-Rover suddenly slid to a halt. Ahead of them was a steep drop in the road, and a gleaming expanse of black flood water—and two red paraffin lamps set across the road as a warning.

'No getting past that!' said Tom. 'We'll have to leave it and walk.' He got out and went round to help her down. 'Got the torch? Come on, then. I'll see you across the cliff path—tricky in this weather.'

He took no notice of Laurie's halfhearted protest, but took her firmly by the arm and leaned forward into the driving wind and rain.

They walked in silence. There were few lights to be seen, but at last they saw a couple of lighted windows in a cluster of long dark buildings on their right, and below it a smaller light in a smaller building that was unmistakably Luke Veryan's cottage.

'There you are!' said Tom. 'You'll be all right now.'

'Oh but—' Laurie spoke swiftly '—*please* just come in a minute. There might be a message you could take or something—and you could at least have some hot tea!'

'All right,' he said. They squelched on down the cliff path to the cottage and pushed their way inside.

Laurie went running upstairs, rushed into the bedroom and found Penny lying stretched out on the bed, clutching at the headrail with Luke Veryan in his shirtsleeves bending over her and saying, 'Take it easy, girl, take it easy . . .'

He looked up as Laurie came in, and his face broke into a grin of relief.

Laurie leaned over Penny and laid a cold, wet hand against her flushed face. 'I'm here now,' she said. 'Don't worry. Everything's going to be all right.' She didn't know how it was going to be all right. But after all, she'd had two children of her own—ought to know what to do . . .

Looking round at Luke's tired grey face, she said, 'Go down and talk to Tom Tremayne—and get yourself a cup of tea. He's been a tower of strength—and he may be able to get a message through to Poldurran for Agnes Penwillis.'

Luke nodded, and left the room.

Penny groaned and clenched her hands on the bedrail and arched her back against the pain. 'Waters broke . . . a while back . . .' she panted. 'Probably . . . won't be long . . . now . . . Oh God!' She gritted her teeth and groaned again, and then fell back exhausted as the pain left her.

Laurie stripped off her wet coat and sodden jeans, and padded round finding a dry skirt and jumper before the next pain attacked Penny. She was by her side holding her hands when the next more violent one came.

At this point Luke Veryan came back, carrying a jug of hot water and some clean sheets and towels.

'Tom Tremayne's going,' he reported. 'He'll do his best to get through to Agnes.'

'Oh!' yelled Penny. 'Oh God, let it hurry up and come!'

'Relax,' begged Laurie, holding on to her hand. 'Try to relax . . . and breathe . . . breathe deeply . . .'

Together Luke and Laurie worked over Penny, doing what they could to help her and keep her calm. They lost count of time and forgot to note the spaces between the contractions, but they all felt the inexorable rhythm of birth building up with each new contraction, gaining momentum and rising to its climax . . . And suddenly there was a final desperate heave and a short hoarse scream from Penny—and a small red creature lay squirming on the sheet between her legs, and a thin, fierce little cry of protest pierced the air.

Laurie remembered how to tie the cord before she snipped it. And it was Luke's old, steady hands that held the newborn infant while she washed it clean and wrapped it in a blanket.

'What is it?' murmured Penny, limp with exhaustion.

'It's a girl,' she said, smiling. 'And she's perfect. Look!'

She was just putting the baby in Penny's arms when there was a commotion downstairs, steps came pounding up, and Agnes Penwillis burst in, dripping rain from every angle.

'Sorry!' she gasped. 'Walked over by the cliff path. Weather's terrible . . .' Her eyes went to the bed, and her face broke into a cheerful grin. 'But I see you've managed very well without me!'

'Look!' said Penny, holding the baby up. 'Isn't she lovely?' And then her face contorted as another wave of pain brought on a new contraction to carry away the afterbirth.

Quickly Agnes Penwillis went into action. Laurie smiled at Luke, and said softly, 'Thank you—we couldn't have done it without you.'

He grunted noncommittally. 'Not all that different from calving,' he said, with a glimmer of mischief, 'except that cows is bigger!' Then he added, 'And more difficult to handle. Yon little lass was splendid!'

From Luke this was high praise, and Laurie glanced across at Penny. She looked terribly young and quenched lying there—a child in the grip of an experience too big to bear.

Sighing, Laurie turned away, and spoke gently to Luke. 'Come downstairs and have a rest by the fire. I expect Jay's kept it up. And I'll make some tea.'

'The kettle's boiling,' said Jason's voice from the doorway. 'I heard the baby cry . . . Can I see it?'

Laurie nodded, and drew him close to look at the tiny creature in her arms. Jason touched the baby's damp, downy head. 'So little!' he whispered. And then, drawing himself up straight, he added, 'I'll get the tea. Penny still needs you.'

So Laurie found the new baby's first clothes, and the pink frilly nightie she had bought for Penny, and brought them over. 'Here,' she said, smiling at Penny's tired young face, 'let's make you both beautiful.'

When Jason returned with Luke Veryan and a tray of tea, Penny was sitting up in bed in her new frills, her glorious hair brushed, and her eyes alight with triumph. And the new baby was lying peacefully against her arm, neatly wrapped in her new white shawl.

'What are you going to call her?' asked Jason.

'I dunno.' Penny looked down at her daughter. 'Should be a mixture of early-bird and storm-and-tempest . . . But I'll think of something.'

'Christmas Rose,' said Luke Veryan suddenly. 'They comes up sudden like, in early winter. They doesn't mind rain and wind—very sturdy, they be . . . and all white and pure like.'

There was an astonished silence in the room. None of them had expected such a poetic speech from the old Cornish farmer—though they knew he loved the flowers he grew.

Penny smiled with sudden radiance. 'Right then,' she said. 'Christmas Rose it is! But I 'spect we'll all call her Rose.'

'Rose!' And everyone lifted their mugs of tea in salute.

Little Rose just slept.

THE NEXT MORNING Dr Trevelyan stumped in, having also had to walk back over the cliffs, leaving his car behind. But he reported that the floods were going down, and the roads would be passable soon. An ambulance would be coming to take Penny and the baby to hospital. But here he met with a flat refusal. Penny's face went suddenly white and pinched, and she said in a tight voice, 'No. I don't want to. I'm all right as I am. I mean *we're* all right as we are.'

Laurie turned to Dr Trevelyan and said, 'Perhaps I could talk to her? I think Jay's got the kettle on again.'

Trevelyan was a wise man. Having completed his examination of mother and baby, he went off downstairs to have a chat with Jason.

Laurie sat down beside Penny. 'It's all right. No one's going to send you anywhere if you don't want to go.' She paused, watching the desperate pallor recede in Penny's face. 'What frightens you about hospital?' she asked gently.

Penny drew a quivering breath, and held little Rose tighter in her arms. 'They might try to take her away from me.'

Laurie was shocked. 'They wouldn't do that!'

'They might. The social worker might come. She was on at me again last time she came—about adoption.' She shot a fierce, defiant glance at Laurie. 'And I'm not letting them take her. She's *mine!*'

Laurie nodded. 'Of course she is. No one's going to take her from you.' She went on carefully, 'But they are thinking of you, too, you know—they probably think you're awfully young to tie yourself down to bringing up a child at this stage of your life. They think you might want to go off and do something else . . . take some exams, get some training . . . and meet other people—perhaps even find a nice boyfriend—or get married—instead of staying at home minding the baby!'

Penny snorted. 'I want to look after Rose,' she said obstinately. 'And Jay and Midge. That's what I'm good at.' But her face was still full of anxiety. 'You don't think . . . ? Would she have a better chance with—with someone else? Do *you* think I'm right to keep her?'

A lot hung on Laurie's answer, she knew. But looking into Penny's face, she could not ignore the passionate, protective love she saw there as the girl stared down at her sleeping baby.

'Yes,' she said slowly. 'I do . . . It's just that you're awfully young.'

Something flashed in Penny's face then. Not too young to be raped by my own father, it said. Not too young to have a baby. Doesn't that make me old enough to look after it, and give it a decent life of its own—with nothing ever happening to it like what happened to me?

After a small silence Laurie said tentatively, 'So—if we've dealt with what's worrying you—do you still not want to go to hospital?'

Penny looked away from Laurie. 'No.'

'Why not?' Laurie was nonplussed.

For a moment Penny did not answer—but then her face crumpled like a child's and she said in a strangled voice, 'I don't want . . . to go away from you.'

Laurie understood then that she was standing in for the mother who had rejected Penny when she most needed her, and must not fail her.

'Oh, my dear girl!' she said, and folded her in her arms, baby and all. 'Of course you needn't go away from me. We'll see this through together!'

356

And she rocked her to and fro, while Penny wept as she had not wept since she left home. When she was quiet, Laurie went downstairs to tell Dr Trevelyan that Penny would not be going to hospital.

He grunted his disapproval, and then smiled suddenly and called up the stairs, 'All right, young woman, you win! But mind you behave yourself. I'll be back in a day or two to make sure.'

Penny called back jubilantly, 'I'll be good as gold, I promise. And so will baby Rose.'

Laurie watched Trevelyan go, and turned back, wondering a little desperately how she was going to get through the next few days. But Jason came out into the hall with Midge and a cup of tea. 'Me and Midge'll look after Penny for a bit,' he said, and started up the stairs. 'Uncle Luke says not to come in today,' he added, pausing on the landing. 'The storm blew out some of the glass in the greenhouses. He and Bob will be all day mending them. He told me to tell you, when I went up for the cows.'

Laurie breathed a sigh of relief. Then another thought struck her. 'What about school?'

'Oh, stuff school!' replied Jason staunchly. 'Babies are more important.'

THE NEXT FORTNIGHT was hectic. The Christmas trade was building up, and Laurie found herself frantically picking and packing at all hours of the day. She had expected—and even ordered—Penny and the children to stay at home, but they took no notice. Penny pushed baby Rose up the hill in the pram and parked her in the warm greenhouses, and got on with helping the flower packers. Jason and Midge had already learned how to be useful, fetching boxes, holding string for tying bunches, and finding rubber bands.

Luke did not thank them—he was too busy himself. But he did occasionally stop and look into baby Rose's pram and smile. She was a good baby and did not cry a lot except when she was hungry, and Penny—to Laurie's secret relief—took to breastfeeding without the slightest difficulty.

On Christmas Eve Luke took the last load in early, and told everyone to stop clearing up by midday. He returned at lunchtime and stumped into the kitchen, where Penny and the children were just dishing up a hot meal.

'Something in the van for you,' he said to Jason.

Jason stopped stirring the stew. 'Come on, Midge,' he said. 'Let's go and see.'

When he opened the back door of the van, there inside was a large green Christmas tree. Together, he and Midge hauled it out and stood looking at it with awe. It was a beautiful tree.

They rushed into the kitchen. 'Mum, it's a Christmas tree. Where shall we put it?'

'It depends,' Laurie said, 'on Mr Veryan.'

'On me?' said Luke, surprised. 'Tree's yourn. Do what you like wi' it.'

'No. You don't understand. We want you and Bob to be with us—either at the cottage or here, we don't mind which. But we're going to cook you Christmas dinner somewhere!'

Old Bob was standing beside his chair, waiting for the stew to be ladled out. 'What?' he said, surprised. 'You wants I?'

Penny nodded. 'Course. All together. It's Christmas. Christmas Rose's first Christmas! Can't miss it, can you?'

The two men looked embarrassed. But at length Luke said—as gruffly as ever: 'Come down to you, then. Easier for Penny than lugging Rose up here.'

Laurie smiled. 'That's settled then.' She began ladling out the stew.

IN THE MORNING there were more surprises. First of all, there was a small pile of presents on the doorstep from the villagers of Tregarrow for the three children at Veryan's cottage. There was a small doll for Midge with a label attached, saying 'Love from Billy'; there was a red racing car for Jason from someone called 'Brandyball' who, Jason said, was a mate of his at school; there was a rattle with bells on for Rose from Agnes Penwillis; and a box of crackers from the shop.

But that was not the end of the morning's surprises. When the Christmas dinner was nearly ready, they heard steps on the path, and not two but three shadows passed the kitchen window.

Laurie went to the door—and there, beside Luke and old Bob, stood Joe.

'Joe!' she exclaimed, and called over her shoulder, 'Penny, look who's here!'

'Got enough to spare for an extra one?' he asked, sniffing the air appreciatively.

'Of course!' said Penny, smiling. 'Come on, Joe . . . Come and meet Christmas Rose!'

They drew Luke and old Bob in after them, and took them to admire the tree which stood shining in the corner of the living room. And it soon transpired that Joe had come laden with presents, too. There were secondhand clothes for the children, sorted out by Jane from her many donations, and even a special bundle for baby Rose. 'And then there's this for Jason, especially from Jane.' Joe handed over a strange-looking package.

When Jason unwrapped it, there was a beautiful little bottle garden,

358

gleaming with a wealth of tiny green plants and twining ivies inside.

'I gather,' said Joe solemnly, 'that you and Jane have something going about bottles.'

Jason went pale with joy. 'She—she must've got it, then...' he muttered.

Then there was a small music box for Midge that played 'Silent Night' when you wound the handle, and a woolly ball on a string to dangle from Rose's pram.

And last, Joe brought out another parcel for Jason, and said, 'This is from your friend Clem—and he says be careful. It's fragile.'

So Jason unwrapped it with fingers that trembled a little, and this time there was another small green bottle with a tiny ship inside.

'Oh!' breathed Jason, entranced. 'How did it get in there?' Then he looked at Laurie joyfully. 'He must've got mine, too! Magic!' he breathed.

In the package there were also some tiny carved wooden animals— whittled by Clem in the quiet dark hours at his cottage. There was a small model of an otter for Midge, and a fleet of little mallard ducks for Penny to float in Rose's bath. And last of all, Jason drew out one pure white swan's feather with a label tied to it which said 'For Laurie', and nothing else at all.

Laurie bent her head over it, ashamed of the tears in her eyes. One more token of freedom, the feather said ... Are you flying yet?

'Joe,' said Laurie at last, 'I think this is the happiest Christmas we've ever had. And it's all thanks to you!'

'Rubbish!' retorted Joe. 'Gotta come and see me old dad, haven't I?' He grinned, wilfully misunderstanding her. Then he demanded loudly, 'Where's this Christmas dinner then?'

While they were all laughingly occupied in bringing in dishes of sprouts and potatoes, and Laurie was getting the turkey out of the oven, old Bob shyly approached Jason. 'This is for all on you,' he said, and laid a package on Jason's knee. Inside was a black painted board with a whole series of beautifully tied sailors' knots in white string. There were several rows of them, intricate and delicate, and all neatly labelled. 'See—' he said, stooping beside the boy and pointing to them one by one with a gnarled finger. 'Tied 'em meself.. Used to be famous for 'em once—they'm got a set o' they in the museum.' He looked hopefully at Jason's interested face. 'I could teach you how to tie 'em, if you'd like?'

'Could you?' Jason touched the knots one by one with a tentative finger. 'That'd be brill.' He gave old Bob an admiring smile. 'You're a wizard at knots!'

Old Bob was enormously pleased.

And then the turkey came in, and the Christmas party began.

After the festivities were over, Joe and Laurie decided to walk down to the beach, leaving the two older men dozing by the fire and Penny occupied with the baby. Jason and Midge demanded to come too, and after a moment's hesitation Laurie agreed, provided they went off on their own along the sand for a bit. She wanted to talk to Joe.

'Well—' Joe was watching the children run on ahead '—you seem to be making a go of it here.'

Laurie nodded. 'Up to a point. I don't know how satisfied your father is.'

'Oh, he's as pleased as Punch with the whole set-up,' stated Joe.

'Is he?' She smiled a little. Then she grew serious. 'Well, it's about your father . . .' she began. 'He's been very good to us, and I think he's got quite fond of us all in his way, especially Penny and the baby. After all, he helped bring Rose into the world!'

Joe grinned. 'So I heard! So?'

'So . . . he's got used to Penny cooking for him—him and old Bob—and his house being cleaned occasionally and so on . . . What will he do when we go in the spring?'

'More important, what will *you* do when you go in the spring?' retorted Joe.

Laurie drew a long breath. 'I don't know yet, Joe. I—I can't plan very far ahead at present. But I'll think of something . . .' Not even to Joe—shrewd and experienced Joe—could she admit to the long wakeful hours of the night when worries about the future crowded in. 'But I've been thinking,' she went on shyly, 'I like this kind of outdoor work.'

'Even in winter when it's hard?'

'Yes. Even then. It's sort of—satisfying. And I'm not too bad at keeping people's books in order! So maybe I'd better aim at those kinds of jobs—on farms and such. And perhaps later on I could do a course in bookkeeping and management or something.'

Joe nodded again. 'Sounds sensible.'

'And what about your dad?'

He smiled and patted her arm. 'He'll be OK. Things is easier in the summer, anyways—you don't have to worry about him as well as everything else. Come on.' He gave her arm a friendly shake. 'It's Christmas Day. Can't have you getting broody. Let's go and look at the sea.'

Laughing, she began to run with Joe and the children to the sea.

JEFF WAS RELEASED from prison at the end of January. His first action was to get a drink. Someone from the prisoners' aid society had given him a little money 'to start him off'. Hunching his shoulders against the rain, he dodged into the nearest bar. After two whiskies, he felt better. After three, he looked at his dwindling money and decided to go home.

He let himself into a cold, empty house. There was a pile of bills on the floor, and a layer of grey dust over everything. Upstairs, he discovered that Laurie's things were gone. So were the children's. He didn't like it. Cursing, he kicked a chair out of the way and went out again.

He tried the local which he used to frequent, but no one seemed to want to know him, and Brenda the barmaid refused to serve him. The landlord gave him one whisky, and said, 'Better go elsewhere, Mr Collins. They know too much about you here.' There was no fight left in Jeff. Not at present. This cold silence unnerved him. Quickly, he swallowed his drink and left. He tried another pub down the road, where nobody knew him. But it wasn't the same without his mates. He drank alone, a solitary, morose figure, and wove his way home after closing time in a haze of self-pity.

THE NEXT MORNING he went down to the Social Security office and signed on—and asked for special supplementary benefit to help him on his way. They told him he couldn't have it: there was a maintenance order for his wife and children, and that had to be paid first. It would be deducted from his money accordingly, as ordered by the court. Was he staying on in his council house? If so, they would give him a rent allowance. There were arrears to pay, they understood. But it must be used on rent, so they would pay it for him.

Jeff was appalled. All these encumbrances round his neck, and not allowed to touch his own money! He asked them politely if they could give him his wife's address. The authorities said that they did not know it.

Jeff had an idea, and asked to see one of the social workers. Just someone he could talk to.

The girl in the outer office fetched a counsellor to talk to him, and Jeff stated his case. He was always a persuasive talker, and before long the woman opposite him had a picture of a conscientious, penitent husband, out of work and anxious to keep his young family together, who had once—just *once*—lost his temper, and never ceased to regret it. He wanted to see his wife, just to say he was sorry. He desperately wanted to persuade her to come back. He missed his children. A reconciliation would be so much better all round, wouldn't it? Could she help?

The counsellor considered. She did not know Laurie's case history, but she thought she knew a penitent man when she saw one, and after all, a reconciliation would be splendid, if she could arrange it. She went away to find out a few more details, and returned, having discovered what she needed from the Giro payment records. She had not managed to look up

362

Laurie's case history—those papers were somewhere else.

'Well, Mr Collins,' she said brightly, 'I'm very sympathetic to your story, of course. But I'm afraid I can't give you your wife's address—it's against the rules. In any case, her income-support payments are being handled by another office now, not in this area at all.' She saw his face take on the familiar despairing acceptance of the ex-prisoner who found the whole world against him, and added quite kindly, 'But if you were to write to us formally, requesting a meeting with your wife, I would see that your letter reached the right department.'

Stymied, thought Jeff. Now what? He looked across the desk and his glance fell on the papers in front of her. One of them seemed to be a notice of payment—with an address at the top from another office.

'Where should I send the letter to?' he asked humbly.

'Why, to me at this office. But of course, to effect any meeting with your wife you would have to be willing to travel.'

'Travel?' An eager light came into his eye. 'Where to?' He saw his mistake and added carefully, 'If it was a long distance, would I be able to get a travel allowance?'

'Yes. That could be arranged, I think.'

'Is there a form I could fill in?'

There was indeed a form, and the kindly woman counsellor went off to get it. Jeff leaned over and swiftly read the address on that top page on her desk. It was from the DHSS office in Penzance. *Penzance?*

The counsellor returned with a form. Jeff accepted it gratefully, thanked her for her time and patience, and escaped as quickly as he could. What the devil was Laurie doing in Penzance?

If he went down there and tried the other DHSS people, maybe they'd tell him something. It was worth a try.

But in the meantime he needed several drinks to boost his confidence. He also badly needed more money. After some thought, he went into a pawnbroker's and flogged his watch, a gold signet ring and his leather briefcase. By the time he made his way home, life looked a lot rosier but had shifted rather out of focus. He stopped outside his own front door to get his breath. That nosy old biddy, Mrs Banks from next door, was leaning on the fence looking at him.

'Gone for good then, has she?' she said loudly.

'Who?' said Jeff, taken unawares.

'Your wife. Took her bags and went off with a fella in a van. New boyfriend, I shouldn't wonder.' The voice was edged with malice.

A couple of the neighbourhood kids were playing on the pavement. One of them started hopping up and down and chanting: 'Laurie went off in a lorry. Laurie went off in a—'

'*What lorry?*' Jeff shouted, shaking the boy's arm.

'Joe's,' said the boy, wrenching his arm free. 'Said it on the van, see? *Joe's.*'

'Veggies,' added the other grinning urchin helpfully. 'Kite Street Market.'

'How do you know?' asked Jeff.

'Said-it-on-the-van-see?' they chanted, hopping up and down some more.

Jeff supposed that was as much as he could hope to get out of them, and went inside. He would have to think about it first—have another whisky to clarify his mind—go down to this market, wherever it was, tomorrow. Yes, tomorrow.

HE FOUND KITE STREET Market without much difficulty. It was tucked into the centre of a maze of grubby little side streets, and was full of stalls and people.

There was no sign of Joe, but the stallholders all knew him. Joe, they said, wasn't there Thursdays. Went down to Kent to collect his veggies, didn't he? He'd be there tomorrow, though, when the stuff came through from Penzance.

'*Penzance?*' said Jeff.

'His dad,' explained someone. 'Gotta smallholding somewheres. Sends stuff up regular.'

'Where?' asked Jeff. '*Where from?*'

A shrug. Somewhere in Cornwall. Silence.

'What's his name?' asked Jeff.

'Same as Joe's of course. Veryan.'

Veryan. Penzance. And Laurie had gone off in Joe's van. There must be some connection—and if there was, he'd find it. He'd go to Penzance tomorrow. My God, when he did catch up with Joe, whoever he was, he'd teach him to go off with his wife—he'd teach him a thing or two.

IN PENZANCE IT WAS WET and blowy, with a fine sea mist spread over the bay like a pall. It had taken Jeff all day to hitch down in a series of lorries, for he was rapidly running out of money—again. In the end he slept rough in a shelter on the seafront, with a newspaper and the rest of his bottle of whisky to keep out the cold. In the morning he was hungry, so he spent some money on breakfast in a seamen's café near the fish market, and shaved off his dark stubble in the men's washroom while he waited for the DHSS office to open.

The girl in the Social Security office knew nothing of Laurie's history. She listened to his polite enquiries indifferently, and then told him she could not disclose any information about Mrs Collins—if they had any.

Defeated, Jeff went into the first pub he found open and tried to think what to do next. After several boosts to his flagging confidence, he asked for the main post office. There, he took out the phone books and looked for the name Veryan. There were several—some in Penzance, some outside. He took out the Yellow Book and looked up Farmers. There were three Veryans—he would have to try them all.

He took a bus to the first address, wanting to confront Laurie in person rather than telephone. But the people there had never heard of Laura Collins. At the second, they were equally blank. That only left this place Tregarrow. But it was getting dark. He would go there tomorrow. In the meantime, the Penzance pubs were warm and anonymous. He drank till his money was running out. Then, once again, he slept in a shelter, wrapped in old newspapers and a comforting haze of whisky, and mercifully unnoticed by the patrolling police.

In the morning, he took a bus to Tregarrow.

At Tregarrow post office, it just happened that Annie Merrow was out at the back checking stock, and her niece, Donna, was serving in the shop. She did not have Annie's professional reticence about post office matters, nor her awareness of Laurie's situation ... She simply saw a reasonably well-dressed man enquiring politely about his friend Mrs Collins who he believed was staying nearby. Oh yes, she said, at Luke Veryan's, on Tregarrow Farm. Cliff Cottage, she thought Mr Veryan called it.

Jeff gave her a smile and asked if there was a pub in the village where he might get a sandwich?

Several drinks later, Jeff set off for Veryan's farm. As he climbed the hill, he came in sight of the village school, and a straggle of children just coming out. He looked at them more closely. Were Jason and Midge among them?

Yes, there they were—hand in hand, turning aside to a winding cliff path.

'Hey!' he called, lurching into a run. 'Jason! Midge! It's your dad!'

The two small figures stiffened—the two faces turned to him in frozen horror. Then, without a second's hesitation, they began to run.

'Wait!' called Jeff despairingly. 'I only want to talk to you!'

But they didn't wait. They went on running, streaking away up the narrow path till they were out of sight. Jason had two thoughts in his mind as he ran: I must get Midge home to the cottage—to Penny where she'll be safe. They can lock themselves in. And then I must go and warn Mum. I must get to the field before he does. Desperately, he went on running, with Midge's frightened little hand in his.

Jeff, meanwhile, had given up chasing them. His stamina wasn't very good nowadays and anyway, better see Laurie first. The children could wait.

But he was furious that his own kids had run away from him like that. What had Laurie been saying to them? It wasn't fair of her to make them afraid of him—and by God he'd tell her so when he saw her.

He had a small drop of whisky left in the bottle, and now he stopped and took another swig. It was the last.

LAURIE WAS PICKING DAFFODILS. Things had been slack on the farm for a bit after Christmas. The winter had stayed mild and very wet, and the fields of beet and swedes for the cattle were like seas of mud. But the daffodils were early. It was fairly backbreaking work, but Laurie loved it. She liked the feel of the sturdy stalks in her fingers and the fat green buds trying so passionately to burst into golden flower.

During the morning a lorryload of pickers had come in from St Buryan and were moving slowly down the daffodil fields. Laurie was used to seeing them out of the corner of her eye, so she did not look up when someone came and stood near her.

'Hello, Laurie,' said a voice close above her head.

Laurie froze. She looked up in dazed disbelief at Jeff, smiling at her.

A number of thoughts passed swiftly through her head. Uppermost was the realisation, He's drunk and angry. I must not take him near the cottage—Penny and the baby are there, and the children will be on their way back from school. I must lead him away from there—*and I must face up to him and make him see reason somehow.*

She got to her feet slowly, and laid down her bunches of daffodils. Her scalp was prickling with fear.

'Surprised to see me?' asked Jeff, his voice like the flick of a whip.

'Not very,' said Laurie truthfully. 'I thought you'd get round to it.' She glanced down the field to where old Bob was directing the pickers, and added, 'Wait there, will you? I must tell Bob I'm going.'

'Going where?' The question hung in the air like a threat.

'I suppose you want to talk?' Laurie spoke reasonably. 'We'd better walk along the cliff . . . it's more private.' She went quickly over to Bob. 'Bob . . . I've got to knock off early. Someone wants to see me.'

Bob looked up at her. 'OK, missus.'

Laurie walked back to where Jeff was standing. 'Shall we go?'

Jeff was a bit nonplussed by this cool, efficient Laurie.

'Well?' Laurie stopped walking when they were out of sight of the farm. 'What do you want?'

Jeff was amazed. '*What do I want?* I want you back where you belong—and the kids, too. You're my wife, and they're my kids!'

366

Laurie sighed. 'No, Jeff. Not any more. I explained all that before.'

'Explained, my arse!' shouted Jeff. 'You're coming back with me—*now!*' And he seized her by the arm and raised a hand—in an almost automatic gesture—to hit her across the face. But Laurie did not flinch this time. She said firmly, 'Don't be idiotic. If you hit me, you'll only land in prison again. There's an injunction out against you molesting me, remember? Why don't you calm down and be reasonable?'

'*Reasonable!*' Laurie's calm maddened him. 'How can you expect me to be reasonable when my wife and kids have walked out—my house is filthy and cold and there's nothing to eat!'

Laurie laughed. 'Ah! Now we're getting to it. You need a housekeeper, Jeff, not a wife. Only, of course, you couldn't knock *her* about. Or, alternatively, you could learn to cook.'

Jeff swore and lunged at her with flailing fists. One caught her a swinging blow to the side of the head, and Laurie stepped back a little, blinking.

My own fault, she thought. I must try to reason with him. But before she could say anything more, several things happened. Jeff lunged again, and she found herself wrestling wildly with him. Midge came running along the cliff path, calling, 'Mummy!' and just as Jeff turned his head, Jason came racing past her and launched himself straight at his father like a small tornado.

'Stop it!' he shouted. 'Stop hitting her! Go away!' and he pounded Jeff with his small fists in a blaze of protective anger.

'Jay!' called Laurie sharply.

But it was too late. Jeff let out a savage oath and felled Jason to the ground. Midge screamed, and backed away towards the edge of the cliff.

'No, Midge!' Laurie's voice rose desperately. '*Stay where you are!*'

But, as Jeff moved towards her, she screamed again and took another step backwards. Her foot slid and she disappeared over the edge of the cliff in a slither of stones and a wail of terror.

For a second, Laurie stood transfixed. Then she flung herself down on the edge and peered over . . . Midge was crouched on a ledge of rock, her skirts caught in a small gorse bush leaning out from the cliff face. She seemed unhurt, though almost beyond the limits of fear.

Jason was picking himself up by this time, shaken but not badly hurt. Laurie glanced round at him and said, 'Run, Jay! Run and get help!' and was relieved to see him take a deep, gulping breath and obey her.

But now Jeff was moving nearer—a strange, mad glitter in his eye.

'Jeff !' Laurie said. 'Think what you're doing! It's your daughter down there . . . your *daughter!* Do you want to kill her?'

Jeff stopped, weaving on his feet a little as the combination of drink and

367

anger and unexpected emotion surged round inside him. 'Midge?' he said
uncertainly. 'Midge?' and then he too looked over the edge. 'My God!'

He sounded suddenly stone-cold sober, and moved forward as if to
climb down after her. But Midge saw him, and screamed again, crouching
closer to the rock and clutching the gorse bush in small cold hands.

'No!' Laurie saw the danger. 'Not you, Jeff. She's terrified of you.'

She didn't notice the sudden flick in Jeff's face—the realisation that his
own small daughter was so frightened of him that she'd rather risk death
than have him come near her.

'I'll go down,' Laurie went on. 'In any case, I'm lighter, and you can
hold on to me and haul us up.'

She began cautiously lowering herself over the edge, a little to the right
of Midge in case she sent down a cascade of stones on top of her. There
were still tufts of heather and thrift growing in the rock crevices which
gave some sort of foothold. Slowly, inch by inch, she got nearer, until her
foot touched the ledge where Midge lay crouched. Here she paused. If she
tried to hold on to the same gorse bush, her added weight might pull it
from the rock . . . just as it might cause the little ledge itself to crumble
away.

So she edged her way down a little below Midge and anchored her feet
against a solid, jutting piece of rock. Only then did she reach up and fold
her arms round the terrified child above her.

'It's all right,' she murmured. 'It's all right. You're safe now.'

But Midge clung tightly to the bush, and would not move.

Gently, Laurie went on talking to her. If I could get her to stand, she
thought, with me holding her from behind, maybe Jeff could reach her.

Jeff, meantime, had taken off his jacket and was lying full length on the
clifftop, with the coat dangling over the edge. It was not long enough to
reach Midge. He took off his tie and tied it firmly to the end of a sleeve.
Then he dangled it down again. This time, Laurie could just reach it.

'Tie it to Midge somehow,' he called, 'and then I'll try to pull her up . . .
if you steady her from behind.'

Laurie did as she was told. But Midge took a lot of coaxing to move at
all. 'Try, darling,' begged Laurie. 'Try! Daddy's trying to help you . . .
Please try to climb up . . . That's it . . . Now the other foot . . . I'm right
behind you.'

Carefully, with awful slowness, Laurie coaxed the terrified little girl up
the treacherous cliff face. And slowly Jeff pulled and held her steady as
each small foot fumbled for a new hold and each frantic small hand
scrabbled for another grip. At last, Midge's head came up level with the
overhang, and swiftly Jeff reached down and hauled her to safety.

But as he did so, the overhang began to crumble under him in an

368

ominous rumble of stones. 'Get away, Midge! *Quick!'* he shouted, and shoved the child backwards before he began to topple in slow motion over the cliff.

Laurie was stranded on Midge's ledge as a shower of loose rock and pebbles began to pour down towards her—and with them, helplessly caught in the torrent of stone, came Jeff.

'Look out!' he screamed, as the rocks bounced down towards her.

Laurie shot out a hand to him as he spun past, and he reached out desperately and grasped it by the wrist. The shock of his weight pulled at her shoulder socket with such violence that Laurie fell to her knees and cried out. It's dislocated, she thought. I wonder if it'll hold? With her other arm she instinctively grasped the jutting rock that supported her.

She had shut her eyes at the initial jolt, but now she opened them again and found herself looking down directly into Jeff 's face. He was dangling in space, while the cascade of rocks went on falling round him, his grip on her wrist the only hold he had against certain death.

'Hold on!' she called faintly, sick with pain.

And Jeff held on. But the weight of his body was more than Laurie could withstand and she felt herself beginning to move very slightly downwards. Soon they would both be gone.

'Hold on!' she repeated. And she looked down, straight into Jeff 's terrified eyes.

But they weren't terrified any more. Somehow, as Laurie gazed down, they seemed to clear. In that look was the knowledge of everything Jeff had been, or might have been—and what his young wife had been when he first met her, young and pretty and believing in him . . . And what she might have been, if he had known how to love and cherish her—what she might be now, given half a chance. What his young children might have meant to him if he'd been good to them . . . the hopes and ambitions he had set out with, the dreams that mocked him and broke him with their false promises . . . And in that piercing look was the sudden awareness of Laurie's danger, how the dragging weight of his body was pulling them both to destruction . . .

'Laurie,' he said, quite clearly and calmly. 'I'm sorry . . .' and his fingers, grasping her wrist in their desperate, convulsive grip, slowly released themselves and let go.

Maybe his failing strength just suddenly gave out. Maybe his fingers just lost their grip and could not hold on any longer . . . No one would ever know the truth. But to Laurie, seeing the expression in his eyes, it was clear Jeff knew what he was doing. He had chosen. He let her go.

'Jeff !' screamed Laurie. 'Jeff ! *No!'*

For a second he seemed to hang in space, and then he was gone, hurtling down, wreathed in a cascade of stones, till he hit the rocks below and spread out in a sprawl of limbs . . .

Laurie could not see him. Mercifully, the cliff face bulged out a little before that final, sickening drop. She clung there, weeping, with her useless right arm swinging and her other hand gripping the only solid piece of rock she could find.

She wept painfully and with aching pity for the bright-haired young man with the engaging smile she had once loved so much.

They found her clinging there—still weeping—when the rescuers came running with ropes and clamps and stretchers, and with Jason racing at their head.

MIDGE WAS UNHURT except for a few bruises, and Jason only had one sizable bump on his head. But Laurie was not so lucky. Her arm was broken in two places, and she had to have it set and the dislocated shoulder pushed back into place. She didn't remember much about it, so she never saw the second stretcher party bring Jeff's body up from the rocks. But some time later she found herself lying in a hospital bed in a small side ward, with her plastered arm and strapped shoulder held securely in a sling and propped up on an extra pillow, and a friendly young nurse smiling at her from the open doorway into the general ward.

'The children?' she asked anxiously.

'They're fine,' said the nurse. 'They're here for a checkup—just to be on the safe side. They'll be in to see you, as soon as the doctor's been round. Oh—here he is now.'

The house doctor took her pulse. 'How are you feeling?'

'I'm fine,' Laurie lied. 'Can I go home?' she begged.

He shook his head firmly. 'I think we'll keep you in for the night. You've been through a very harrowing experience.' He smiled. 'Take it easy. I'll see you in the morning.'

As soon as he had gone, Midge rushed in, followed by Penny and Jason.

'All of you?' gasped Laurie, under the onslaught of Midge's embrace. 'I'm all right.' She drew Jason close. 'You fetched help so fast!'

'He ran all the way to the farm, and all the way back!' Penny told her. 'We all ran. But Jay ran fastest!'

Laurie gave him a silent hug.

'Now then,' ordered the young nurse, returning with a cup of tea. 'Time to go home.'

Jason looked at his mother for a moment, smiled at her with sudden radiance and followed the others out.

'Drink your tea,' said the nurse. 'You've got one more visitor.'

Luke Veryan looked quite grey with shock. 'Won't stay long,' he said gruffly. 'Came to say I'll keep an eye on young Penny and the children. Police want to see you—I said tomorrow.'

Laurie nodded. 'I suppose . . . Jeff ? No one's told me anything . . . '

'He was dead before we got to him. Must've been instantaneous.' He put out a gnarled hand and gripped hers hard. 'Don't grieve, girl. Better this way.'

THE NEXT DAY a sympathetic policewoman came to see Laurie and took down a careful statement. Laurie told her story as calmly as she could. She did not leave out the row with Jeff on the clifftop, but she went on to recount how Jeff had rescued little Midge, and had tried to save her, too. In fact, *had* saved her by letting go her wrist. 'I tried . . . I tried to make him hold on . . . but I couldn't.'

'Don't distress yourself,' said the kindly policewoman. 'It's all right. I've got all the facts now.' She got to her feet. 'Thank you for being so frank, Mrs Collins. We'll be in touch if we need to know anything more.' Then she left.

Laurie lay back with her eyes closed. So she did not see someone come and stand in the doorway of the little side ward—did not know anyone was there until a voice said, 'Laurie?'

I'm dreaming, she thought.

'Laurie?' said the voice again.

Her eyes flew open, incredulous and glad. 'Oh God . . . *Clem!*'

He was across the room with one stride and folding her close like a tired child. And suddenly the awful events of the day before caught up with her and she began to weep desperately. 'I tried . . .' she kept saying, 'I tried . . . but I couldn't hold him . . . Clem, *he let go!*'

'Yes,' said Clem calmly. 'Of course he did . . .' And he rocked her in his arms. If it occurred to him to have doubts about Jeff's intentions, he did not show it. It was clear to him that Laurie needed to believe it if she was to come to terms with his death. And anyway, Clem too was apt to believe the best of people, given half a chance.

At length Laurie was quiet, though looking so like a tearful child that Clem couldn't help smiling at her. He reached for a handful of tissues from her locker and gently mopped her face and brushed the hair out of her eyes with loving fingers.

'Come on,' he said, handing her a tissue. 'Blow!'

Laurie laughed and gulped and did as she was told. Then she said, still amazed at his presence, 'I don't understand why you're here.'

Clem took her hand in his and held it firmly. 'It's simple, really. I was coming to see you anyway. I had business in Exeter and Truro. I thought you might be glad of a visit. And I had something to suggest to you about the spring,' he added. 'But we can talk about that later.' He touched her face gently. 'Everything will be all right. Give yourself time.'

Laurie closed her eyes and drew another perilous breath.

'I rang Luke Veryan last night,' Clem was saying. 'He told me what had happened.' His firm fingers gripped her hand tightly. 'So I arranged with him to come and fetch you home today.'

'Now?' A sudden, enormous wave of relief engulfed her.

'As soon as they say you can go,' he told her. 'Rest a moment, I'll find out when you can leave.'

CLEM DID NOT IMMEDIATELY take her home. He stopped at a quiet pub and ordered her coffee and a small brandy, and took her over to a seat in the corner.

Then he said gently, 'I'm not going to talk about the future. It's only the present we need to think about now. So—first, I must warn you that the press may bother you.'

She looked startled. 'Oh God. I hadn't thought of that.'

Clem's face was a little grim. 'No. Well, I had. And so had old Luke Veryan. He gave them the bare details. And I routed 'em for you at the hospital. But I think you'd better see 'em and say something.'

'I don't know why they're so interested.'

'It was pretty spectacular, so I'm told. What did you tell the police?'

'The truth.' She spoke flatly. 'I mean, I couldn't leave out the—the violence. He knocked Jay down and bruised his face—and it showed. I—I didn't know what Jay might say . . .'

Clem nodded. 'Just as well. When he got to Luke, his first words were, "My dad's trying to kill my mum on the cliffs!" '

Laurie had tears in her eyes. 'I—I'd rather just say Midge went over the edge and Jeff got her back . . . and then he slipped.'

'Yes. That will do for now. But it depends on what comes out at the inquest.'

Laurie went pale. 'I suppose I'll have to attend?'

'I think so.' His eyes were full of reassurance. 'But I'll be there. And so will Luke, I'm sure. I'll stay till everything is settled.' His smile rested on her again, calm and loving. 'I just thought we'd better talk here, rather than at home. We needn't disturb the children any further.'

Laurie shuddered. 'They were just getting to feel happy again—and secure. And now it will all have to be done over again.'

Clem tightened his grip on her hand. 'No, it won't. I think Jeff's final action may have released you all from more than you know.'

Laurie looked at him gratefully. 'I think he knew that. I think he saw it all—the whole wretched mess. His eyes were somehow . . . filled with knowledge. He was like—like he might have been when he was older—and wiser. It was uncanny. He knew—and he *chose.*'

Clem did not contradict her. 'Yes, and that being the case, you mustn't undo his choice. You did your utmost—your absolute utmost. So no misplaced feelings of guilt, understand? You'll be defeating his purpose if you let it haunt you all your life.' He drew a long breath. 'You've got a lot of living to do yet, and a lot of happiness to look forward to—one way or another.' He smiled now directly into her eyes, making his meaning plain, and Laurie was shaken. She saw something flash deep down in those grey, cloud-flecked eyes that almost made her heart stop. But it was gone at once. 'I—I'll try . . .' she said.

He laughed. 'Enough lecturing. I'd better take you home.'

But something bothered Laurie. 'Clem—what about your swans? How can you leave them?'

He smiled. 'I have an assistant now. The Wildlife Trust gave me one, to help with the increasing work. They're talking of setting up another sanctuary or two, in other places. I was on official business down here.'

'Were you?' She was looking at him in a puzzled way.

'I was delivering a pair of swans to a man with a private lake.' Warmth came into his eyes. 'They were mended, and the water was unpolluted, so I knew they'd be safe and probably live happily ever after.' For a moment the new, unexplained warmth in his glance rested on her. 'They mate for life, you know—swans.' Then he continued more briskly, 'He was very pleased with them . . . So after that, I went on to arrange a couple of lectures in Exeter and Truro—just in case.'

'Just in case of what?'

'In case you were glad to see me.'

Laurie began to laugh.

'That's better,' approved Clem. 'Satisfied?'

'Not entirely,' admitted Laurie. 'I think you're up to something . . . And I still don't understand how you knew I needed you *just now.*'

The smile died in Clem's face. He looked at her with sudden piercing gravity. 'Nor do I,' he said softly. 'But thank God I did.'

THERE HAD TO BE A POST-MORTEM, and after it the police told Laurie as kindly as they could that it was death from multiple injuries, and would have been instantaneous . . . Then the press came and got their promised interview and asked a lot of impertinent questions. But Clem got rid of them for her when they became too tiresome.

He went with her to the inquest, where she gave evidence quietly and clearly—emphasising Jeff's rescue of Midge and his final attempt to save Laurie herself.

'Are you saying, Mrs Collins,' asked the coroner gently, 'that at the last moment, when he was hanging on to your wrist, your husband let go?'

'Yes,' said Laurie, her head held high. 'I think he realised I was being pulled down after him. He did it to save me.'

There was a silence round her in the little courtroom. If the coroner had any doubts about that final gesture of Jeff's, he did not say so. It did not seem to him relevant now. And clearly it mattered to this young woman to believe what she did.

'Thank you, Mrs Collins,' he said quietly. 'You have been very brave and helpful. I'm sorry to have distressed you.'

Clem came forward then and took her out of the courtroom, out of the town altogether, and drove away up onto the moors where there was nothing to see but moving cloud-shadows on wide hillsides, and splashes of sunshine on golden outcrops of rock.

They walked a long time that day, and only returned to the cottage when it grew dark. And there were the children and Penny waiting for them in the firelight, and they drew the curtains against the night and sat round the table together to demolish the meal Penny had got ready for them. Even Laurie ate something that evening, for the long walk had made her hungry.

Clem watched her and said nothing. But seeing her there in the firelight with her children round her put a darkness into his eyes that he could not hide. Only Penny saw it. Laurie was too tired to notice, and for that he was thankful. But he kept very still in his chair.

THE FUNERAL WAS SMALL and quiet. After the bleak little service at the crematorium, when it was time to go, Laurie turned a little blindly, and found herself looking down at a surprisingly beautiful heap of flowers lying at her feet.

'Old Bob put them together,' said Luke Veryan's gruff voice beside her. 'He said you'd think it was right.'

Laurie felt tears prick her eyes. So much shy kindness lay in that simple statement. So Jeff was gone—and there was nothing left now but a few ashes and a bunch of bright spring flowers . . .

CLEM WAITED THREE more days before he went home. By that time, he decided, Laurie was over the worst and had no more ordeals to face. She had talked to her solicitor, Madeleine, on the phone, and arranged to go up to London later on to sort out her affairs. Jeff hadn't had much to leave—only the furniture in the house, and a life insurance which would mostly be swallowed up in paying off his debts. But at least Laurie would be clear, with a little extra left at the end.

She also spoke briefly to Jane on the phone, and she was firm and kind and told her to take a deep breath and get on with living.

After all these things were settled, Clem took her out onto the hills again, and sat her down on a rock in the pale spring sunshine and prepared to talk.

'I miss the swans,' said Laurie suddenly. 'There's everything else down here—sea and hills and sky . . . and sea birds, but no swans.'

It was the opening Clem was waiting for. He took something small out of his pocket and laid it in her hand.

'This is the key to my caravan,' he said. 'Do you remember it? Quite old, but watertight. There are four bunks and room for a baby's cot. A little kitchen area, not smart but practical. Water and light laid on . . . You'd be all right for the summer.'

Laurie was gazing at him, speechless.

He laughed a little at her expression, and laid an arm round her shoulders and gave her a loving shake. 'Don't look so startled. It seems obvious to me. Or do you want to stay on at Luke Veryan's? I'm sure he'd let you.'

'No,' said Laurie swiftly. 'I couldn't—not after all that's happened.'

'That's what I thought.' He nodded. 'As to the practical details—there's quite a good little primary school in the village—rather like Tregarrow's, small and friendly. I think Jay and Midge would like it. And as to jobs, I'm sure Stan would welcome you back—not to mention several of his farmer friends who are all hopeless bookkeepers—'

'Stop it!' said Laurie. 'Oh Clem!' She touched his face with a shaking hand. 'What am I to say to you? I'm not—I don't know if I—'

'It's all right,' he said quickly. 'No strings attached. I know you have a long way to go yet—but one day . . . ?'

'That's just it. I don't know if I'll ever—if I'm capable of—'

He laughed suddenly, and without any warning kissed her. It was meant to be a light kiss, but it became something else entirely, long and strong and passionate . . . and Laurie felt her own longing rise into vivid response . . .

After a strange moment out of time, Clem withdrew and looked down at her, smiling. 'You were going to say you didn't know if you were capable of loving anyone, weren't you?' She nodded. 'Well, you know now.'

Yes, she thought, panic-stricken, I know now, and I'm terrified. I know what passion can do to people.

'No,' said Clem gently, to all those thoughts, 'it needn't be like that, my dearest child. It could never be like that with us.'

'Couldn't it?' Laurie's gaze was piercing. 'Why not?'

'Because,' Clem's voice was gentler and slower than ever, 'we already care more about each other than ourselves.'

Laurie's expression changed. 'You do, Clem. You've already—already almost killed me with kindness.' Her tremulous smile was still laced with tears. 'But I—I seem to have done nothing so far but take—it isn't fair,' she whispered. 'As things are—it's not fair to you.'

'That's for me to decide,' said Clem, and his smile was full of quiet certainty. 'My swans have taught me not to expect too much too soon.'

Laurie looked at him despairingly. 'But it may take—for ever.'

'Never mind.' He was still smiling a little. 'I can watch you learn to fly.'

She suddenly beat at his arm with her clenched fist. 'Don't you see? I'm *using* you. I've leaned on you shamefully these last few days . . . I ought not to do this to you!'

'Yes, you ought.' He captured her beating hand. 'I *need* to be leaned on. I love you, dammit!'

Laurie was silent. She did not know how to answer him.

'You don't have to decide anything now,' he told her. 'You have the key. You can come when you want. I must go back to my swans tomorrow—but you don't have to leave the cottage till April, do you?'

'No.'

'Then—I shall expect you when you're ready.'

'Oh *Clem!* You haven't heard a word I said.'

'Yes, I have. You are as free to come and go as the wildest swan in the world! But I am also free to hope! And I hope you *will* come soon, and be glad to come!' He folded her fingers over the key, and kissed her again—this time very gently and softly.

Both of them knew that it was a promise given.

AFTER CLEM LEFT, the world seemed curiously empty and cold to Laurie. She did her best to fill her days with work—in so far as her one-armed state allowed—and spent rather more time than usual in the greenhouses, or with Luke Veryan's books. She also spent more time with baby Rose, as Penny cheerfully took on most of the work outside in the daffodil fields. Laurie came out there too, though—and found a strange kind of healing in the clean, flower-scented winds of March and the great sweeps of burgeoning flower heads all round her. It was mild weather, and old Bob said them plaguey daffs was coming on too soon.

She hadn't been near the cliffs since the day of Jeff's death—nor even down to the little cove. But she knew she must face it some time. She also spent a lot of time trying to build up Midge's confidence again, and comforting Jason. For, to her surprise and dismay, the boy was heart-broken at Clem's departure.

376

'Jay,' she said suddenly one day when he had come up to the daffodil fields after school to fetch her home to tea, 'do you miss Clem a lot?'

The boy looked at her out of blue honest eyes. 'Yes. Don't you?'

She nodded, hardly daring to admit how much, even to herself.

'Will we see him again soon, then?' asked Jay.

'Yes,' agreed Laurie, sighing. 'Soon.'

It was then that old Bob came running. His wispy hair was on end, and his eyes were wide with fright. 'Come quick, missus! Come quick! It's the boss!'

Laurie put down her flowers and went running after him. Penny turned to Jason and said urgently, 'Take Midge and the baby up to the farm, Jay, and wait for us there . . .' then she followed Laurie to the end of the field where a small knot of people had gathered.

Luke Veryan lay on his face among a tangle of broken daffodils. His hands were clenched into claws of agony, grasping at the red stony earth.

Laurie bent over him and tried to turn him over. Someone helped her to lift him a little so that she could support his head. He was still breathing, but each breath was harsh and laboured, and his face was grey with pain.

It's a heart attack, she thought. What ought I to do? 'Get Doctor Trevelyan,' she said. 'Fast.' She loosened Luke's collar and tried to help him to breathe.

Presently some of the workers came with a wattle windbreak and laid him on it and carried him into the house.

The rest was stark nightmare. Dr Trevelyan was out, Nurse Penwillis was over at a remote farm, the ambulance from Penzance would take at least half an hour. And meanwhile, Luke Veryan's face got greyer with every breath.

At last they heard the ambulance siren ringing as it came down the hill to the farm—and at the same time, Dr Trevelyan's car arrived from the other direction.

Between them, they got Luke fixed up with an injection and an oxygen mask, and lifted him into the ambulance. Laurie had thought he was unconscious by now, but he opened his eyes and looked at her as he was being carried out, and seemed to be trying to say something to her.

She came close and stooped over him. He pushed the oxygen mask away and whispered, 'Good girl . . . thanks . . .'

Then the ambulance man clamped the mask back on, the doors were shut and he was driven away.

Joe, thought Laurie. Joe must be told. She got through to Jane at the hostel and left an urgent message. But by the time Jane reported back that Joe was on his way, the hospital had rung Laurie to say that Luke Veryan had died in the ambulance before reaching them.

Laurie was stunned. Luke had seemed as well and sturdy as usual, stumping about his fields, directing his pickers and looking after his cows . . . his cows! Had they been milked yet? At this point, old Bob himself came into the office where she was sitting and said, awkwardly twisting his old seaman's cap in his brown hands, 'I can see to the cows, missus—and get a boy up from the village to help—and your boy, Jason, he'll help too—till Mr Joe says what's to do.'

Laurie nodded, and patted his arm kindly. 'Thanks, Bob. I know you're as upset as I am. We'll keep things going till Joe arrives. I should go home now and get some rest. We'll all be busy tomorrow.'

Bob gave a brief nod and turned to go. 'One of the best, the boss was,' he muttered as he went out. 'They doesn't come like that no more.'

Laurie was left alone in the farmhouse. It felt very empty and cold. Sighing, she closed the farm books, and went methodically round, tidying the rooms and closing doors and windows. It seemed strange and rather terrifying that she should have to cope with death and its endless difficulties and arrangements twice in a month . . .

When she had done all she could, she left some cold food on the table and a note for Joe, and went sadly away down the path to the cottage.

WHEN JOE CAME, he was crisp and efficient. He got on with all the arrangements, dealt with the hospital and the undertakers, the solicitors and the farm, and came down to Laurie and Penny at the cottage for a hot meal and a bit of warmth and comfort.

The funeral was very unlike Jeff's bleak little ceremony at the crematorium. Luke was buried on the windy hillside, in sight of the sea, and his grave was heaped high with daffodils and jonquils and all the spring flowers he loved. There was one small wreath specially made by Penny and the children and it contained a few Christmas roses in its centre.

The whole village was there. They all wanted to say farewell to the tough old man. So Laurie and Penny laid on a spread at the farmhouse. 'He'd have wanted to do right by his mates,' said Joe. And everyone climbed the hill path from the little village church and its flowery churchyard full of the graves of dead sailors and farmers from Tregarrow's long history of toil and struggle against the elements.

Farmer George Button was there, and so were Dr Trevelyan and Nurse Agnes Penwillis, and Annie the postmistress. They all greeted Laurie with much kindness, and George Button went so far as to say gruffly, 'Bad time you've been havin'. Very sorry!'

Laurie had not been in the village since Jeff's death. She had left the shopping to Penny, for in truth she had been afraid of the bright, knowing

378

glances and gossiping tongues of the villagers. It had been all over the local paper—her private life with Jeff, his prison sentence, the injunction and her flight to Cornwall, and the final tragedy on the cliffs. She did not know how they would take all this melodrama. And now, this—though it was not of her making this time. Or was it? Did Luke's collapse stem from his efforts over the cliff rescue? That frantic run from the house, carrying ropes and grappling irons?

'Running out of tea,' said Joe in her ear. 'Better make another pot . . .' He looked at her shrewdly. 'No good brooding. Here, sit down and have a cuppa yourself.' And he pushed her onto a chair at the kitchen table.

'Joe,' she said sorrowfully, 'did I—add to it?'

'You did not,' he retorted. 'Massive heart attack. No previous trouble. Happens that way with men like my dad. They told me at the hospital.' He was still looking at her. 'You did a lot for Dad—made him very happy, you and Penny and the kids, especially baby Rose. He told me.' He gave her a cheerful push. 'Go on! You know he'd rather go out with a bang like this. Stands to reason!'

He stumped off, looking rather like his dad.

Obediently, Laurie drank her tea and was surprised to find Agnes Penwillis at her side saying in her comfortable voice, 'Bear up, my dear, they'll soon be gone.'

Laurie smiled at her and protested, but it seemed to go on a long time before the final stragglers had departed, and Penny and Laurie were left to do the clearing up. Joe helped them, and then strolled with them down to the cottage. 'Want to talk to you,' he said. 'Are you tired?'

'No.' Laurie took him in and Penny deftly got the fire going. Finally they all sat down together to watch the flames leap up the chimney.

'My dad,' said Joe, without preamble, 'knew what he was about. So I'd better tell you where we all stand. The farm goes to me—debts and all. I can sell it, or try to run it, or put in a manager—though it would scarcely pay for that. But this cottage—' he looked from Laurie to Penny with a curious half-smile '—he left to baby Rose.'

'*What?*' Penny sat up straight, and baby Rose, asleep in her arms, uttered a sleepy protest.

'Yep.' Joe nodded. 'Lock, stock and barrel. Baby Rose's.' He laughed at Penny's stunned expression. 'With me as trustee.'

Penny was looking at him in disbelief. 'But—what does that mean?'

'It means you can live in it, or you can let it and bring in an income, but you can't sell it. Not till Rose is eighteen and can make the choice herself. It means you've got a roof over your head if you want it. Or you and Rose can have money to spend on her upbringing . . . Whatever you decide, at least she won't need to starve!'

Tears spilled onto Penny's flushed cheeks. Joe was smiling at her with the same bluff kindness as his father's. 'After all,' he added, 'he did help to bring her into the world. I guess he felt kinda responsible!'

Then he looked at Laurie. Joe was shrewd enough to see that this made life more complicated for her. 'Now, about the farm,' he said briskly, 'I don't want to run it meself. Got my own patch in London. And I like helping out with Jane's work at the refuge and all. Well—' Joe was still looking at Laurie in an enquiring kind of way. 'I don't know how you feel about it all? I reckon you could manage it yourself, if you wanted to. You know the set-up, you've done the books and you know the turnover. But you'd need another man, younger and more active than old Bob. It'd be a long, hard grind—more or less for ever. It's not a big enough holding really to make a decent profit. But you could all live in the farmhouse, and let the cottage.'

Laurie nodded.

'Or—' Joe went on, now looking away into the fire '—I could sell up. And in that case, I'd have to ask you to hang on with Bob and give him some help until things were settled.'

'What do you want to do, Joe?'

He sighed. 'I don't know, girl. I think it depends on you. I don't want to saddle you with it if you've got other plans?'

Other plans, thought Laurie desperately. Clem. How can I ever leave now? I can't leave Penny here on her own. 'I—I'll have to think about it,' she said.

Joe nodded. 'There's no hurry.' He looked directly at Laurie now. ' 'Tisn't much of a living, you know. Mostly hard grind and damn-all return. And as for you, Penny . . .' His gaze moved to the younger girl's face. 'Not sure it's a good idea to bury yourself here for ever. Other things to do and learn. Other people to meet!'

Penny was staring down at the baby's downy head. 'I want what's best for Rose,' she said slowly. 'And I'm not sure what that is—not yet!'

Joe got to his feet and touched the baby's head with one blunt finger. 'She's got the right idea. Sleep on it!' He grinned at them both and went away into the quiet night.

LAURIE SPENT THE NEXT few days in a state of tired confusion. Thoughts went round and round in her head—endless questions, and never any answers.

Could she manage the farm on her own? Would the children be happy there? Would it be right for Penny? Or could she leave Penny and Rose behind, and go to be near Clem? Of course she couldn't. Penny depended on her. But then how could she take her away, now that she had got

380

somewhere of her own to live? It was impossible to know what to do.

Penny watched her trying to sort out her thoughts, and forbore to say anything at first. But at last she could stand it no longer, and said, late one evening after the children were asleep: 'Hadn't we better get things straight?'

Laurie sighed. 'Oh Penny—I wish I could!'

'As I see it, you need Clem. And so do the kids.'

'Yes, but—you and Rose need me here. And so does the farm.'

'Not important.' Penny shook her head. 'Not like Clem's important.'

'Don't be idiotic!' snapped Laurie. 'Of course you're important—both of you, especially to me.'

Penny's tough young face softened a little. 'Well, that's nice to know, but it doesn't solve anything, does it?'

'Do you want to stay in the cottage?'

Penny looked round thoughtfully. 'I like it here . . . but it'd bring in good money, let.'

'What about the farm? Would you like living there?'

'It'd be OK.' She sounded offhand.

'Or you could come with us to Clem's caravan . . . ?'

'Or I could stay here on my own.'

Laurie looked at her in astonishment. 'Do you want to stay here on your own?'

Penny stared at Laurie defiantly for a moment and then her face crumpled. 'Of *course* I don't. You're my family. But I—I thought . . .'

'You thought I'd want to run off to Clem and leave you?' Her voice was gentle now. 'Then you've got another think coming!'

'But—do you really want to run the farm? It'll be bloody hard!'

'I know it will.' Laurie pushed the hair out of her eyes with a nervous hand. 'But you'll all help. I dare say we shall manage . . .'

Penny looked unconvinced. 'And what about Clem?'

Laurie tried to sound calm. 'He'd understand.'

'Jay wouldn't,' said Penny starkly.

Laurie closed her eyes. Clem and Jay, she thought. They love each other already like father and son. What am I to do?

'You know what I think?' sniffed Penny, gulping back tears and trying to be reasonable. 'I think you should go and ask Clem.'

'*Ask Clem?*'

'Yes. Why not? He'd know what to do. He's fair, Clem is. He'd listen, and he'd know what's right. You go and ask him, you'll see!'

Laurie was silent. At last she said, 'Are you serious?'

'Yes. I am. Go while Joe's still here, and leave the kids with me. Joe'll look after us till you get back.'

Laurie was staring at her. 'Penny . . . What's got into you?'

'Oh God!' said Penny, with sudden violence. 'I can't stand seeing you torn to pieces! And I don't go much for broken hearts, either. For God's sake, go and see Clem!'

PART 4
LANDFALL

It was April now, and a scented spring evening with blackbirds singing in the orchards as Laurie walked down the river. The old Medway looked calm and placid. She went on along the bank, following the curve of the river towards Clem's cottage, her feet slow with doubt. Ought she to have come—with nothing settled? How could he possibly answer her, feeling as he did? It simply wasn't fair to ask him.

As she reached the next bend, two swans came out of the shadows under the willows and sailed towards her. She thought she recognised them—they were the same pair she had seen on that first occasion when Clem had come to sit beside her on the bank.

'Hello,' she said. 'Do you remember me?'

It seemed that they did, for they swam confidently towards her, and trod water as if waiting for something. She remembered how Clem had reached into his pocket for something to give them. 'In the end,' he had said, '*they eat out of my hand . . . .*'

I've got the rest of my sandwiches, she thought. I wonder if they'll accept them from me? She brought out a crumbly piece of bread and held it out. The swans looked at her questioningly for a moment, and then both beautiful slender necks bent towards her outstretched hand. They ate all she had to offer, and when she held out her empty hand to them and murmured, 'It's all gone now,' they turned quietly away and sailed out again into the centre of the river.

Sighing with pleasure at the quietness and peace of the spring evening, she walked on. There was no sign of Clem. She began to wonder if he might be out—or away. She had sent no message to him—it suddenly seemed to her monstrously arrogant to come strolling in and expect him to be waiting.

Round the corner she found herself looking at his old caravan, standing on its little isthmus of reeds. It had been given a new coat of paint and was gleaming with polish and care—awaiting her arrival.

What was she to say to him? Filled with aching doubt, she went on across the dyke and along the mossy track to the back of the cottage. The

382

back door stood open, but though dusk was falling, there was no yellow lamplight inside. Puzzled, she stepped over the threshold and looked into the kitchen. A soft exclamation escaped her. For there lay Clem, stretched out on the lumpy old sofa, a two-day growth of beard on his chin, his eyes shut, his face grey with exhaustion, and one stiff plastered leg stuck out before him on a cushion.

'Clem!' she said, going swiftly to him. 'What have you done?'

He opened his eyes incredulously and for a moment his piercing gaze looked straight into hers. 'You came!' he murmured. And then he began to laugh. 'Look at us!' he grinned, waving a hand at Laurie's plastered arm and his own propped-up leg. 'Between us, we'd just about make a whole person!' And then, as if he suddenly understood what he had said, the laughter died and he looked at Laurie again with the same gravity.

'Yes,' agreed Laurie softly, 'I think we would.' For, seeing him there, vulnerable and in pain, she felt all her doubts dissolve before his need of her. This was where she ought to be—beside Clem. Nothing else had any significance.

'Be careful,' said Clem, smiling a little. 'I always knew you had too soft a heart! And an injured animal always brings out your protective instincts!'

Laurie laughed. 'Who's talking?' But then she grew grave. 'Clem—' she began, and reached blindly for his hand, 'I didn't—I haven't come . . . to stay . . .'

'I know,' he said calmly. 'My dearest girl, you didn't look like a radiant bride coming to meet her lover, standing there!'

His choice of words made her blink. 'How—how did I look?'

'Scared to death! And worn out. What's been happening to you?'

'What's been happening to you, more likely!' she countered. 'Tell me!'

He sighed and shifted his leg a little. 'It's only a simple fracture. I was out in the boat, trying to rescue a swan. It had got its feet entangled in some plastic netting. The poor creature was trapped and terrified—the more it struggled and flapped its wings, trying to break free, the tighter the tangle became. I was reaching down to cut it free with my knife, when one of its wings caught me off balance. They're very powerful, you know, swans' wings. Snapped my leg like a twig, and I fell overboard. Nearly drowned me, the poor demented creature!'

'Did you manage to save it?'

'Oh yes. I cut the netting under water, before I went under again! And then I held on to the boat and pushed myself ashore with my good leg.'

'Well, go on,' said Laurie. 'How did you get home—with a broken leg?'

He grinned. 'Crawled—mostly. But that was ridiculously painful. So I managed to get hold of a branch of something to use as a crutch, and hopped the rest of the way . . . and then I passed out, I think.'

Laurie shivered. 'How did you get help then?'

'Telephone.' Clem waved a cheerful hand. 'Had it installed not long ago. The Wildlife Trust people insisted—for emergency calls, they said!' He laughed. And then, seeing Laurie's expression, he touched her face gently and said, 'Don't look like that. It's all right now. All it has to do is mend—like your arm!'

Laurie shut her eyes. 'You might have died!' she whispered.

'Yes, but I didn't. I'm very much alive. And now hadn't you better tell me what's on your mind?'

She looked into his face, knowing that a crisis of decision awaited them. Then she told him all that had happened, and all that Luke Veryan's death and his gift of the cottage to Rose implied.

Clem heard her out without interruption. When she had finished, he sat looking at her intently for a moment, and then said, 'Laurie, before I—before we decide what must be done, I want to ask one question.'

'Yes?' Laurie knew what the question would be—and everything seemed to fall into place in her mind as she faced the truth.

'Do you love me?'

'Yes.' Her voice was calm and clear. 'Of course I do.'

He nodded. 'Not afraid of it any more?'

'No.' Her smile matched his. Then she went on with desperate candour, 'But I can't leave Penny and Rose.'

'Of course you can't.'

'And—and there are the children . . .'

'Don't be absurd. They already seem like my own—especially Jason.'

'But—'

He stooped suddenly and stopped her with a kiss. It was a quiet movement—gentle and consoling—but there was a hint of hidden fire beneath it. 'Stop fretting,' he said. 'We can work something out. As a matter of fact, I've been doing a bit of quiet spadework already. Do you remember that man I took the swans to? And the possibility of starting up other wildlife sanctuaries elsewhere?'

'Yes.'

'As I say, I've been working on it.' He was smiling. 'I thought it was about time I took a hand in my own future for a change.'

She was looking at him expectantly. 'Well?'

'Have a look on my desk . . . There's a letter there somewhere from the Wildlife Trust. Read it,' he commanded.

'Dear Clem,' it said. 'You'll be pleased to hear that Lord St Curnow is very happy with his swans, and has come up with a suggestion that ties in with what we were discussing the other day. He is willing to let his three lakes be used as a permanent safe haven for recovered swans—from any area. And he would also like to share the expense of setting up new sanctuaries elsewhere—initially in Devon and Cornwall as they are within his area, but later on even further afield, if you can find suitable sites for them.

'You say you are pleased with Alec. Could he be left in charge in the Medway sanctuary while you set up a couple of places elsewhere and find people to run them? I don't suppose it will be that easy—good wildlife handlers are hard to find—but, as I see it, the work needs to be spread around the whole of the country—given time and money!

'This offer of financial support from Lord C: is probably too good to waste. It would mean a lot of travelling, but I can't think of anyone else experienced enough to tackle it.

'Let me know what you think. I shall be at headquarters during April. Then I am off to Iceland.

Yours ever, John (Montrose).'

Laurie read the letter through slowly. Then she looked at the date. It was written soon after Clem's return from Cornwall. He must have had it lying on his desk for at least three weeks.

'Clem—have you answered it?'

'No. I was waiting for you.'

'But I might not have come.'

'You'd have come,' he said tranquilly. 'You are much too kind and honest to leave me in suspense for ever. Though of course I didn't know what you might say.'

'Nor did I—till now.'

He drew her close. 'You see? Nothing is insuperable. It'll take time to set up of course . . . I'll have to wander about a bit. But we've got time, haven't we? All the time in the world . . .'

She looked at him curiously. 'You think very far ahead, don't you?'

'Very,' he said, smiling, and kissed her again.

She emerged, rosy and laughing, but still serious underneath. 'What would you have done if—?'

'If you'd turned me down?' He grew grave again, but there was still a hint of a smile lurking somewhere. 'I'd have agreed anyway. It's my job, after all, and I think it's important. But I dare say I'd have found every excuse I could to come and make sure you were all right.'

She laughed, but it was rather a broken sound.

'You know something?' Clem's smile had grown very tender. 'You're scared of happiness.'

She nodded, unable to speak.

'Too much has happened to you,' he murmured, holding her cradled against his arm. 'But I'll make you believe in it, if it kills me!'

'That'd be a lot of help!' Her laughter was still more like a gasp.

'Sunshine and somersaults,' he said obscurely, with a reminiscent grin. 'And that reminds me, we'd better do the rounds before it gets dark.'

Laurie was a bit alarmed. 'Can you? Are you safe?'

'Oh yes. I'm a dab hand on crutches. Especially with you to guide me.' He reached out for the crutches that lay beside him, and heaved himself to his feet. For a moment he stood there, weaving slightly till he got his balance, and Laurie saw how thin and tired he looked.

'You're thinner,' she said, standing beside him.

'Pining,' he agreed, with mischief in his glance. 'The only drawback with crutches is,' he complained, 'I can't kiss you without falling over.'

Laurie laughed. 'I can wait.'

'Ah!' said Clem darkly. 'But can I?'

Together, they went out into the spring evening. A pale sky was deepening into sapphire night. One star winked through the tangled arms of the willows, and a thin silver moon climbed behind the tall elms in the water meadows. A late blackbird still sang of love and ecstasy on the topmost branch of Clem's favourite chestnut tree.

'He's got the right idea,' said Clem, looking up. 'Shouting it to the housetops!' And there was such a thrill of joy in his voice that Laurie was dazzled.

As they stood there side by side, gazing out towards the quiet river, there was a sudden thrum of wings across the water, and the two swans—Clem's special ones—came swinging down the river in a long, pulsing flight above their heads. And Laurie was reminded of Clem's voice long ago, when she first said goodbye to him among the silent hop fields and empty orchards: *'Freedom isn't only taking off—it's knowing where you want to land—and when it is time to come home.'*

The great white birds swung on across the sky, seeming to head straight for the pale golden light in the west.

'Where are they going?' wondered Laurie, feeling a strange sense of loss as the sound of their flight grew fainter on the wind.

Clem watched them with an experienced eye as they turned in the darkening sky, their wings still pulsing with that unearthly sound.

'They aren't going anywhere,' he said, and there was a world of love and reassurance in his voice. 'They're coming home.'

ELIZABETH WEBSTER

Elizabeth Webster has always been a storyteller—first making up tales for her own children, then plays and operas for the Young Arts Centre in Cheltenham which she founded and directed for twenty-two years. But she was sixty-five years old before she published her first book, a novel exploring the perils of 'boat children' leaving war-torn Vietnam.

Like all Mrs Webster's subsequent novels (which include previous Condensed Books selections *Bracken*, *Johnnie Alone* and *Chico the Small One*), its purpose is to educate as well as entertain. 'In fiction I feel that you can reach a much bigger public, and get them more sympathetic, more interested in a subject,' she says. And *The Flight of the Swan* is no exception. 'People are only just coming round to the view that the battered wife needs to be taken seriously,' Mrs Webster explains. 'It's a subject that very badly needs airing.' She speaks from experience: after the Second World War she organised a residential nursery school for children of families with problems, and before writing *The Flight of the Swan*, she visited a number of shelters that are in operation today.

Mrs Webster also knows how the power of nature can heal troubled spirits, a constant theme in her work. Her home is in the beautiful Gloucestershire countryside, where there are quite a few quiet, solid people like Clem Harper who look after swans and other wildlife. 'Living close to nature makes you calmer,' she says. 'You begin to learn about the real values of life.'

One of those values is definitely family. In the summer of 1989, as *The Flight of the Swan* was going to press, Elizabeth Webster and her husband Neil cut their Golden Wedding cake with their three children and ten grandchildren.

TIEBREAKER

A CONDENSATION OF THE BOOK BY

JACK M. BICKHAM

ILLUSTRATED BY HODGES SOILEAU

Brad Smith, tennis star and part-time CIA operative, is persuaded to take just one more assignment. All he has to do is meet Danisa Lechova, a beautiful young Yugoslav tennis player who wants to defect to the West. And at Belgrade's first international tournament, he may even get to play some tennis.

But Danisa is more important than she knows. Caught up in a ruthless power play between East and West, her chances for escape are slim. While Brad, her last hope, is more than a little confused by his feelings for her . . .

Set during the last days of the Iron Curtain, this taut thriller crackles with nonstop excitement.

1

The last thing I had on my mind was somebody breaking into my flat and dragging me into the past.

What I was worried about right now was a heart attack.

I could imagine the headlines the next day: FORMER WIMBLEDON CHAMP DIES ON COURT. And the subhead: HEART ATTACK FELLS SMITH IN CHARITY MATCH. What they wouldn't add was the obvious: 40-YEAR-OLD IDIOTS SHOULD NOT TRY TO BEAT HOTSHOT KIDS.

It was early July in Richardson, Texas, my home, just north of Dallas. Ten thirty at night, when old folks should be home with their feet propped up, ready to watch Johnny Carson. I had been on the court with the hotshot Texas Christian University varsity player for three and a half hours, which was at least two hours too long.

Hotshot, whose real name was Randy Ferrell, looked like he wanted to kill me.

It was just a little community tournament, ostensibly held to raise money for the Heart Fund, but in reality a promotion for the tennis club. The men's field was open to anyone with a racket and the fifty-dollar fee. Hotshot took out our best paying member in the quarter finals and then humiliated Jack Stephensen, our club pro and manager, in the semis. I had come up through the easier half of the draw, with the result that I had walked onto the club's floodlit centre court a little before seven this evening for my turn facing the lion who had eaten everybody else.

It was still ninety degrees, despite the hour. Almost everyone had gone from the stands and my legs were just about gone too. I had long since pushed myself well beyond the limits of sanity, for no good reason except my dislike of Hotshot.

Across the net, he bounced a ball on the line, getting ready to serve with that machinelike motion that most young players are taught now. His white shorts and shirt were as sweat-soaked as mine, and his blond hair looked pasted to his forehead. But he was only twenty, a beautiful athlete, and he almost surely had me at last. He was ahead 8-10, 6-4, 11-10, and 40-love, triple match point; and we might have been safely home an hour ago if I hadn't had the brilliant idea of making this tournament follow the old-time scoring rules, as in the Davis Cup—no tiebreakers—to give the players their money's worth.

He served. Somehow I got my racket to the yellow blur and bounced it down the line, hitting the back corner, close. How nice, I thought. My point.

Hotshot slammed his racket onto the ground and turned and yelled at the middle-aged woman calling the back line. She looked scared but stubborn. He strode across the court to glare up at Dr Hugh Olafson, our volunteer in the chair.

'That ball was out a foot!' Hotshot screamed.

Dr Olafson, a grey-haired man of sixty with bottle-bottom spectacles, leaned forward. 'The ball was called good.'

'It was out! Couldn't you see it was out?' Hotshot's face was very red. 'Can you see *anything* through those glasses?'

'The call was good,' Dr Olafson told him. 'Continue play.'

'No! Change that call! This is the worst thing I've ever seen!'

He kept raving and hurling insults, his voice getting louder and shriller. Dr Olafson listened with an eerie calm.

'Play,' he said firmly. 'Now.'

'I'm not playing till you change that call.'

'Undue delay,' the doctor said. 'Forfeit one point.'

'*What?*'

'The score is now forty-thirty. Play.'

I thought the kid might explode. He stormed back to his racket, picked it up, bashed it on the ground, wiped his forehead, gave the good doctor a killing look, and signalled for the ball boy to toss him balls. I waited, doing a little shuffle to prove I wasn't comatose. Come on, legs.

The ball went up and the racket came down and the yellow blur went wide to my forehand. I got it back down the line. Hotshot blasted a backhand to the other corner, a clear winner. Nobody in his right mind, especially a forty-year-old magazine writer not in the best of shape, would have gone after it.

So naturally I went over there and scooped up a lob that looked like it was going nice and deep. I staggered up to the net behind my lob. Which was a mistake. The ball fell shorter than I had expected. I saw Hotshot cock his arm for an overhead. His glance betrayed where he planned to hit it: right between my eyes.

Self-defence is a wonderful thing. I got my racket in front of my face just in time. The ball hit it, and by a freak of fate the resulting drop shot plinked over and fell for a winner.

The kid, with dead eyes, walked halfway in to the net. 'Old man,' he said softly, 'why don't you just give up?'

I grinned at him. So now we were at deuce.

It would be wonderful to report that I pulled it off after that. God knows I tried. We went to deuce another eleven times, and I had two break points. But finally he put away the winner.

At the net he gave me a wet-fish handshake, then gathered up his gear and headed for the lockers. I sat on the courtside bench and started setting a new world record for liquid intake while the last onlookers filed out of the stands. Then I managed to limp to the clubhouse before the muscle spasms started. An hour later I drove home.

As I APPROACHED my flat I saw a faint light moving against the curtains of the living room. I hadn't left any lights on, and I lived alone, so no one was supposed to be inside. It was just past midnight.

Rather than pulling into the driveway, I went on to the next corner, turned right, and right again, up a narrow alley behind the apartment block. I parked out of sight.

Going soundlessly to the side door of my garage, I unlocked it and slipped in. I didn't need a light to find the camping gear, or the .38 revolver tucked inside a sleeping-bag.

My key opened the back door noiselessly. Everything black in the kitchen but a thin bead of grey under the closed door that led to the living room. I could hear the faintest of sounds beyond it.

It was a sliding-pocket door. Made a racket when I slid it hard into the wall, hitting the light switch in the same motion.

The faint light I had spotted was from the television set, which had a Western on. He was sitting comfortably in my recliner chair, his stockinged feet stretched out and one of my beers in his hand. My Smith & Wesson didn't seem to startle him at all.

'BRAD,' HE SAID, unmoving. 'Good morning.'

'You idiot!' I said.

Collie Davis grinned at me and my weapon. 'This is great. This is really dramatic.'

He was not as lanky as I remembered him from our last meeting, almost five years previously. In those days he had looked like a kid, but now he had lost a little of his sandy hair, and his face had been roughened by unacceptable losses. Under some circumstances I might have been happy to see him again.

I put the revolver on the TV set with an angry *thunk*. 'You were really stupid to come in here this way, you know. I might have shot your head off.'

'Are you kidding? I've seen you shoot.'

'What do you want, Collie?'

He uncoiled himself from my chair, turned the TV off, and sat down again. 'It was really pretty important to see you as soon as possible, but not in the public eye.'

So he had picked the lock on one of my doors and come in like a second-rate burglar. It didn't strike me as all that smart. But there had always been things about the Company that didn't make a lot of sense to me, so I chose not to argue about it.

I repeated, 'What do you *want*, Collie?'

'We've got a little contract job. In Belgrade. Shall I start at the beginning?'

'You can start,' I told him, 'by getting out of here.'

'We need a tennis player—tennis journalist.'

'What for?'

'To go to Belgrade for their new tournament, in two weeks' time. Do some journalism, play in the celebrity matches, handle something routine for us on the side.'

'Why me?'

'You fit the job description. There aren't many who do.'

'Get Ted Sherman,' I said, naming another former tennis pro who, like me, had done some work for them in earlier years, while earning his real money on the players circuit.

'We prefer you.' He paused to light a cigarette. 'Besides, he's in hospital with back trouble.'

'So I'm the best man for the job because I'm the only man?'

He ignored that. 'Do you know Danisa Lechova?'

'The Yugoslav player? Sure, I know who she is. We've never met.'

'She's twenty-one now,' Collie told me, 'and most people think she'll be the number one women's player in the world by next year. They've brought her along slowly, evidently guarding against burnout. But many people think she'll be better than Navratilova, Mandlikova or Graf. May be already.'

I had seen Lechova play on television. She was tall, slender, blonde, beautiful, and absolutely unflappable, combining the cool of a Chrissie Evert with the dynamite attack of a Martina Navratilova. 'She's great,' I conceded. 'So what?'

'So she didn't play in the Wimbledon that just finished.'

'Strained knee, I heard.'

'Wrong. The Yugoslav government kept her out. Now they've set up this invitation tournament in Belgrade to showcase her and her sister.'

'Are you telling me she wasn't injured? They kept her from travelling to England for the biggest tournament in the world?'

'Precisely. They pulled her passport. Her sister Hannah's too. They can't leave Yugoslavia.'

'But why?'

'Who knows for sure?' He shrugged. 'The point is, she's had enough of it. She wants to defect to the US.'

'Why doesn't she just wait until the US Open in September and walk out of the locker room and ask for asylum? Surely her passport thing will be cleared up by then.'

'Don't bet on it.'

I thought about it. 'Collie,' I said, 'a lot of people over there would like to come to the West. She may be great, but she's just a tennis player. Why is she of such interest to us?'

Collie's jaw set. 'There's no need for you to know.'

I sighed. Somehow I had known he would say that. They were very dramatic sometimes, these guys. 'All right,' I said. 'Danisa Lechova wants out, you think you can get her out during the Belgrade International, and I can help. How?'

'All you have to do is go over there, play in the celebrity matches, interview her a couple of times, and facilitate communication between her and our people, who will do the work.'

'A go-between.'

'Yes. We can't talk direct. They keep a close eye on her.'

' "They" being the UDBA?'

He looked uncomfortable. 'And possibly the KGB.'

'The Yugoslavs have never let the Russians meddle in their internal affairs. And you're telling me their secret police and the KGB are *cooperating* in watching Danisa Lechova?'

'It's an unusual case, Brad,' he said lamely. 'But your part is relatively straightforward.'

'Just dodge the UDBA and the KGB. Right.'

'Well, there's also a minor problem with her coach.'

'Fjbk? Is Fjbk still coaching her?'

'Yes. Miloslav Fjbk. A Serb. Not a bad player once. Great coach. Fjbk sees Lechova as his greatest production. Also, although he's old—over forty—it appears he's interested in a lot more than the lovely Danisa's backhand.'

'So the man who makes contact with her will have a jealous lover glowering nearby.'

'He's not her lover. We're told she isn't even aware of his crush. But our informants say he watches her like a sheepdog and goes crazy if she so much as smiles at a man her own age.'

'Well, that's good,' I said. 'Fjbk shouldn't worry about me. I'm almost as old as he is.'

Collie missed my irony. 'You'll go, then?'

'I don't know. This all sounds fishy to me.'

He gave me his sincere look. 'Brad, would we lie to you?'

'Yes.'

'It's routine.'

'Collie, I've done enough for you guys to know that these last-minute assignments are never quite routine.'

'Well, we realise that it's inconvenient for you. So I can offer more than the usual hundred and sixty dollars a day.'

My suspicions deepened, but only enough to resemble the Grand Canyon. How much more?'

'Whatever you think is fair,' he told me, with opaque eyes. The highest authority wants her out of there as soon as possible, and the Belgrade International gives us our chance. You're the only man who can get close enough to her to work well as our go-between. You can make a small fortune.'

'I'm not rich,' I cut in, really angry, 'but I never did *anything* for you people for the money.'

'Calm down, Brad. I was just trying to show you that it's a vital assignment.'

I said, 'If I do it, I'll take the usual rate. Nothing more.'

'Fine.' Collie grinned, confident again. 'We'll provide you with background information tomorrow, and precisely what we want done. You'll have to meet me in Dallas to read it. None of it leaves the Federal Building. So what do you say?'

'I just have a few thousand questions to clear up first. How do I get an invitation to play in the celebrity matches over there?'

'We can take care of that.'

'I don't have an assignment. No freelance flies to Belgrade to cover a new tournament on spec.'

'Assignments from tennis magazines can be arranged.'

I asked more questions. He was evasive. There was far too much that I

396

didn't know. That was one of the reasons I was interested. It was clear the Company was ready to mount an extraordinary effort to get this girl out. I was very curious as to why. And, I thought, they must really need me, or they wouldn't ask.

Finally it became clear that I was going to accept or reject this job on the basis of vastly incomplete information. I gave up trying. 'OK,' I said wearily, 'I'll read the background.'

'Tomorrow. Two o'clock. I'll meet you in the Federal Building.' He got up to leave. It was almost one am.

Browning, Montana

It was morning, but already hot in Browning. A stiff wind out of the south blew yellow clouds of grit across the highway. Dominic Partek had not expected this kind of discomfort when he chose Montana as a place to hide.

A big RV camper lumbered off US 89 and into the Shell station, kicking up a tiny cloud of dust of its own. Partek, the lone attendant on duty, detached himself from his penny-pitch game with three ragged Indian boys. 'Work to do. I'll be right back.'

'You better!' one boy cracked. 'You owe me thirteen cents.'

Partek went out to greet the people in the RV. The chubby middle-aged driver rhapsodised about the scenery while Partek was pumping in the gas.

'We've never been in the Rockies. We've got a treat, huh?'

Partek smiled as he finished the fuel and started on the windshield. 'They're very beautiful.'

'You a native?'

'Yes,' Partek lied.

'You must get to the mountains often.'

'Every chance I get.' He had never been in them.

The man paid him. The camper pulled away, nosing west onto the highway. Partek walked back to the kids.

'Your turn, Johnny,' the one named Jerry told him, 'if you feel like living dangerously.'

Partek wiped his hands on a red towel. He wondered how many people really understood what it felt like to live dangerously.

He had done it almost all his life, but never as dangerously as now. He wondered if ordinary people ever experienced the constant dread of discovery, the painful constriction of breathing that he lived with daily. He knew he wasn't really sick. The breathing problem was his body's protest against his iron control of the fear and anxiety battering at the doors of his mind.

He pitched his penny, purposely making a bad toss. The kids loved beating a grown-up. He liked kids. And they were the only companionship he could risk right now.

'Ouch. I'd better drop out awhile, guys.'

'Yeah, just when we were getting to you!'

He went into the station and watched traffic churn along the highway. It's safe here, he told himself.

But he knew better. Nowhere was entirely safe. They might come at any time.

Dominic Partek was thirty-nine, but felt much older. Dark-haired, with a pug nose and square chin, he had the stubby legs of his peasant ancestors and the slender torso he had got from his mother. He was five foot ten inches tall, a hundred and sixty pounds, in moderately good physical condition. He spoke flawless idiomatic English and wore his jeans and denim shirt like a native.

His driver's licence said he was from Missouri. He was not. That was just the licence that the counterfeiter had had on hand when Partek needed a new ID fast.

Partek was not even an American.

I'm not any nationality now, he thought with sudden anguish. Then he thought about his sister, whom he had never known. And I will never see you now.

Unless they can do as they promised.

His eyes felt hot—tears. He felt almost overwhelmed by his dilemma. Whatever he did, he seemed sure to lose. His pursuers might be anywhere, ready to run him to ground like a scared little rabbit. He, who had been so often the instigator, the unafraid one.

The little boys drifted away, waving goodbyes. A few more customers came. One of the other attendants arrived at noon, freeing him to go to lunch.

Partek climbed into his pick-up and drove up the street to where he always had his sandwich. In the small low-ceilinged room he nodded to other workers he had come to recognise during his month in Browning. He sat at the counter alone.

Molly Walkingstick, the owner, put a glass of ice water in front of him. 'Afternoon, Johnny. Usual?'

'Yes. That would be fine.'

'Did your two friends find you at the station?'

'Friends?' The chill in his gut deepened. 'When?'

'Two, three hours ago. David and Steve, their names were.'

'Oh, yes. David and Steve.' Partek had never in his life known any David or Steve.

Molly Walkingstick shrugged. 'Maybe they're waiting at the motel. Shucks, me and my big mouth! They said they wanted to surprise you.'

The chill was overpowering. 'They're great jokers, Molly. It's OK, believe me.'

Molly sighed and returned to the kitchen.

Partek slipped off the stool and went into the hall, as if going towards the men's room. He let himself out by the side door and hurried to his truck.

He did not go to his room in the Warbonnet Motel. He drove straight out of town, heading east for a hundred miles before he so much as stopped for gasoline. His stomach was killing him.

Until he learned whether the Americans could deliver on their promises in Belgrade, he had no option.

This time, he thought, he would hide deeper. And wait.

2

It had been a while since I had done any kind of assignment for the Company, and I had figured I was off the hook. Collie's visit was an unpleasant reminder that maybe you're never off the hook, unless you choose to resign from living.

Tired as I was, I lost a little sleep that night. But by morning my curiosity, and an archaic sense of duty, overcame my doubts. They wouldn't be this interested in Danisa Lechova for her tennis. The stakes had to be a lot higher. Which fascinated me.

And, I told myself, it would be a good working vacation, returning to big-time tennis for a week, seeing old friends.

That people sometimes got killed on little junkets like this did enter my mind, but perhaps it really would be a routine job. I devoutly hoped so. I was concentrating hard on that hope when I walked into the Federal Building and met Collie.

He took me on a stroll through narrow corridors and finally into a room behind a sign that said it was the office of something called the Agricultural Stabilization Service. He locked the door.

The room contained a lot of computer equipment and a tall woman with a face like a hatchet. Collie sat me down at a keyboard console facing a fourteen-inch screen. Then he unlocked the combination on a thin metal attaché case and removed a computer disk. The woman sat at a nearby keyboard and typed in some security commands that allowed the disk to boot up. Collie patted me on the shoulder and withdrew.

What came up first on my screen was condensed data about LECHOVA,

399

DANISA, born 11 November 1965, in Belgrade, Yugoslavia. The parents were listed as Leon and Geneta Lechova, both citizens of Yugoslavia, both instructors in physical education. They were both in their forties.

Danisa, the computer report said, had attended state schools. Various newspaper and magazine articles were quoted next. In 1975, at the age of ten, she won her first tournament, against girls whose ages ranged up to sixteen. Her athletic parents had introduced her and her older sister, Hannah, to numerous sports at a very early age. Danisa quickly showed a precocious talent for tennis.

Reading between the lines, I decided her parents drove her hard. There was a long list of academic awards that she had won, starting in the earliest grades. Her sister excelled too.

In 1981 Danisa got to the quarterfinals of the German Open. Tennis journalists rhapsodised about her talents. In 1981 also, the Lechovas first used Miloslav Fjbk to coach their daughters, a relationship that would later become his full-time occupation. Fjbk came with a reputation as a dour perfectionist. The Lechova girls dropped out of the sports news for three years, except for an occasional note about some local tournament appearance. Fjbk and their father were keeping them in school.

In 1983 both Lechova sisters graduated. Hannah went into a women's unit of the army, but with a public relations job that kept her near home and free to work on her tennis. Danisa won a scholarship to the academy, where she started work in history.

In 1984, after Danisa lost to Chris Evert in Rome—all three sets going to tiebreakers—tournament appearances became more regular for both sisters. Danisa won the Monte Carlo that April, playing on clay, her favourite surface. The sisters lost in the French Open women's doubles the following month, when Hannah twisted an ankle and was forced to scratch from the semifinals.

Then some personality profiles appeared. The general impression of Danisa was of a bright, energetic, frighteningly talented young athlete. Her sister was also very good, but by no means a star like Danisa. There was no evidence of serious stress between the girls because of Danisa's stardom. Hannah, however, was into state politics and had turned in a friend for 'disloyal speeches against the government' in 1985. If Danisa wanted to defect, she was probably at odds with a sister who seemed well on the road to becoming a Yugoslav superpatriot.

The girls' father, Leon Lechova, was a former middle-distance runner who had once won a bronze at the Olympics. He had begun teaching in 1965, the year of Danisa's birth. Danisa's mother, the former Geneta Trencek, had been on state gymnastics teams. She sounded a formidable woman, both demanding and fiercely protective of her daughters.

The remaining screens of data on the family were routine. They lived in a cramped three-room apartment and had been trying for ever to get better quarters. If there was any bitterness about this among the Lechovas, however, it was buried far beneath the surface. These people were loyal.

Except that Danisa wanted out . . . for no reason that the files explained.

The screen files on Fjbk were interesting, but I yearned for more. Born in 1934, Fjbk was a Serb of peasant stock, with a background that included a few years in the Yugoslav army and a career as a minor tennis player. His reputation came as a coach. He had worked with Borg, Lendl and Graf. None of the relationships had been of long standing, probably because Fjbk was never satisfied; he wanted every player he worked with to become the world's greatest, and if the player achieved that, Fjbk drove him even harder.

The file went on to point out that the Lechova girls had won quite a bit of money in the last few years and that Fjbk had received a share. With his tangled black hair, straggly beard and squat physique, he had become a recognisable figure on TV tennis coverage. He had bargained his newfound visibility into advertising contracts, and seemed to be working on making himself more visible yet: his latest acquisitions included a Mercedes and a big red Harley motorcycle.

The last section outlined my mission: go to Belgrade, cover the matches, establish interview contact with Danisa Lechova, and facilitate communication between her and our local people, who would actually do the hard part.

All very neat.

And most of what I wanted to know left out.

I finished reading the file, called Collie, and watched him lock the disk away. 'No problem,' he said, turning to me. 'Right?'

I took a slow breath, aware that this was my last chance to back out gracefully. Then I said, 'OK, Collie. Fine.'

THAT SAME NIGHT there came the inevitable problem with June.

I should have foreseen it. But sometimes I think I have an infinite capacity for deceiving myself. When I picked her up for dinner, it was with pleasant anticipation and a real joy in simply being with her. I didn't think the job in Belgrade would matter.

The first part of the evening was fine. She looked wonderful, as she always did: bright, slim, buoyant, filled with energy despite what had been a long day on behalf of a client in district court in Fort Worth. She had won. June liked winning.

She bubbled about it all through drinks and dinner.

'And how was your day?' she asked finally, over coffee. 'Recovered from the match with that awful little creep last night?'

'My body, almost. My pride, maybe not quite yet.'

'I really wanted to be there. But that damned hearing in Oklahama City—'

'I was creaky at the end. Best you didn't watch.'

She mugged. 'I'm feeling a little creaky, too.'

'Wait till you're as old as I am.'

'Thirty-three is no spring chicken, Mr Smith.' She lit one of the cigarettes I wished she didn't smoke. 'So. Anything else that's new or different?'

It was then I realised I didn't feel very good about broaching the subject. I made my voice casual. 'Actually, yes. I had a nice call from New York today. Interesting freelance assignment coming up next week.'

Her gaze sharpened, and I thought her antennae went up. 'Oh?'

'Yeah. *International Tennis* wants special coverage on a couple of events in Europe. Nice piece of change and some really good exposure for my byline in both their magazines. I'll have all expenses paid, of course, and I'll get to play in a couple of celebrity doubles events and have a lot of fun.'

I stopped. I seldom made long speeches. I had just made one. I had blown it.

'So where are you going?' she asked.

'Europe. Three or four places.'

Her lips thinned. 'I hope your itinerary gets more specific before you climb on the first airplane, Brad.'

I tried lamely to salvage it. 'I'm sure my editor will have a plan drawn up to run me ragged interviewing everybody in sight.'

She just looked at me and didn't say anything. The bloom was off the evening, and when she said she wanted to get home early, I drove her there.

At the kerbside she turned in the front seat to nail me with those eyes, which were now bright with anger. 'I thought you weren't going to do any more work for them.'

There was no sense pretending. It's just a little routine job, June. I'm going to cover some tennis.'

'And do something else.'

'OK. Yes. But it isn't dangerous and it's no big deal.'

'Where? No need for me to know, right?'

'It's no big deal.'

There was silence as she stared ahead through the windscreen. Finally she said in a different voice, 'I don't want you to go. I'm very serious, Brad.'

I met her angry eyes. 'So am I. You can't expect to control my life.'

'Meaning that you're going whether I like it or not.'

'Do you have to put it that way, June?'

'That's the way it is!' She made a little groaning sound of frustration. 'You met Elizabeth more than twenty years ago, Brad. Then in she divorced you, in nineteen sixty-eight. When was it that you started working for the CIA part-time, playing *I Spy* while you were on the tennis circuit? Nineteen seventy?'

'What are you getting at, June?'

'You've never gotten over your divorce, what Elizabeth did to you with all her affairs. I know how terrified you are of loving a woman again and risking another betrayal. I can live with that. But you're still playing *I Spy* too. And I don't think I can abide that any more.'

'June!'

She faced me, her eyes bright with angry tears. 'I can live with the ghosts. For three years I've been patient, haven't pushed you. You can't help the ghosts. But I can't accept the CIA thing as well, Brad. It's too much.'

'It's my country, dammit. If I can help them with some little deal—'

'It's not just that I don't know what you're doing, or why. I think a lot of the time you don't know either. Someone issues an order, and you go and do something—you never know what it's all about, whether it's worthwhile, or whether it was even necessary, or just some damned bureaucrat's idea of cops and robbers.'

Suddenly I felt tired and a little defeated. We had been over this ground many times before. 'You trust. You do what they ask, if you can, because it's your country and you owe it. If it works out or doesn't, it's not your concern. You have to accept the uncertainty. You do what you can and hope it makes sense to somebody, somewhere—does some good.'

'That's all?'

'What the hell is there for anybody besides doing your best?'

With a little moan, she began to get out of the car. I started to open my door to walk her in.

'No,' she said.

'I'll call you tomorrow.'

'No.'

'In a day or two, then.'

'No, Brad. This is it. I'm through.'

I looked at her and didn't know what to say. I knew I should say I loved her, but I just couldn't.

Instead I tried to make a joke. 'Hey, I'll send you a postcard.'

She got out of the car. 'Don't bother.' Shhe walked, pretty heels clicking sharply, up to her apartment entrance, and went inside.

THE NEXT DAY I told the people at the tennis club about my writing assignment for *International Tennis*. They swallowed it whole, said they could fill in for me while I was gone. I thought a lot about calling June, but I knew it was pointless. And part of me was relieved.

The day after that I got my letter from the tennis magazine, giving me the assignment. Sometimes the Company worked fast.

In the days remaining, I reviewed the things I had learned about the Lechova family and Miloslav Fjbk. Collie came by again and talked for an hour, telling me who I was to meet and how, and what I was supposed to do. I memorised names and photographs of faces, procedures and verbal bona fides.

I wondered a lot more about why we were so fired up over helping one pretty girl—even a potential tennis star—to flee from her country. But I didn't ask, because I knew Collie would either tell me nothing, or lie.

Langley, Virginia

The meeting started very early. Three men sat round a small conference table: Kinkaid, Exerblein and Dwight.

'So we've lost him again,' Dwight said glumly. 'We blew the job in Browning.'

'Maybe we overlooked something,' Kinkaid said, dogged. 'Some clue to where he might have headed next.'

'Our guys out there say no such luck.'

'It was a mistake to wait at his motel,' Kinkaid said. 'They should have gone straight to the gas station and taken him there.'

'Take him for what?' Dwight's eyes were flat and cold.

'Phony ID, if nothing else!'

'No, no,' Exerblein put in. 'He came to us. We're supposed to be his *friends*. Your friends don't arrest you.'

Kinkaid looked at Exerblein a moment, clearly struggling with an impulse to tell him off. Instead, Kinkaid said, 'Protective custody?'

'Not,' Exerblein retorted, 'if he didn't request same.'

'So now he's lost again, and the KGB may be right on his tail, and the next time we find him we may find him making fish food in the bottom of a lake, wearing concrete boots.'

'Let's review, just for a minute,' Dwight said, ticking off the points on blunt fingertips. 'He came to us talking defection and asylum. We checked everything and it looked legitimate—a real change of loyalty, not a trick.

404

by the other side to put him in where he can get information from us for them.'

He paused, then went on, 'We can't know what happened after our initial contacts. We can only assume that they made threats about his family. Hearing that, he could hardly stay with the Soviet delegation in New York. But he couldn't come over to our side either, or they might institute reprisals. So he bugged out to think about it.'

'And to wait,' Exerblein intoned, 'to see if we could make good our promises.'

'Or,' Dwight countered, 'just to deal with the shock. Up until a few days ago he didn't know if he *had* a family any more, remember?'

Kinkaid said, 'None of that is going to help us if the KGB finds him before we do.'

'I suppose we can only hope the Russians have lost him too,' Exerblein said, maddeningly cool.

'If they haven't,' said Kinkaid, 'we've lost one of the most valuable people we've ever had a chance at. When you think of the places he's worked, the KGB operations he probably took part in, the agents he could finger!'

'I've talked to Daniels at the FBI,' Dwight told the others. 'With a good chance that Partek might have gone over the border into Canada, I thought it wise to share info.'

'And what now?' Kinkaid asked.

Dwight leaned back in his chair. 'Brad Smith is all set up?'

'Yes.'

'Well, once he gets over there we'll be able to get things moving. Assuming Partek is still alive, we've got a chance to salvage this whole business.'

Exerblein stirred. 'Does Smith know what's at stake here?'

'No,' Dwight said. 'Let him think it's a simple defection. He'll function better if he doesn't feel that much pressure.'

Kinkaid said, 'Sure, unless he gets killed.'

Browning, Montana
Shortly after dawn a man who looked like a tourist placed a call from a telephone booth at a truck stop. Trucks thudded by, and the ground trembled slightly beneath the man's feet.

'Yes?' a voice answered.

'Sir, I have a collect call from Sylvester. Will you accept the charge?'

'Yes. . . . Hello, Sylvester?'

Sylvester—as good a name as any—plugged one ear with his fingertip. 'Our information was correct,' he said.

'They were about to take the merchandise?'

'Yes. Clearly they had it ready to be picked up. However, they delayed. The merchandise has been shipped elsewhere.'

'You are to remain in place. When we have new information, we will contact you.' The connection was broken.

Sylvester left the booth. The day was already warm, and he was sweating. He thought about Dominic Partek. He had always liked him—brilliant, a professional, loyal. Now this.

Sylvester was a killing machine. But he had never carried out an assignment against a fellow countryman, much less a man he had worked beside and had liked. It was very unfortunate.

None of that mattered much now, of course. When Partek was spotted again, Sylvester would move to reach him before the Americans tried once more to take him captive. If Sylvester reached him, there would be nothing left for the Yanks to take into custody.

New Belgrade, Yugoslavia

Late-day sun gilded the underside of the great translucent dome that covered the People's Sports Arena. Seated in the first row of the nearly empty stands coach Miloslav Fjbk watched, as Danisa Lechova tossed a ball high, and put every ounce of her strength into the serve. For just an instant there was nothing in the world for the dour Serb except Danisa's movement, the meeting of racket against ball.

For Fjbk it was a moment of timeless love.

The serve, overstruck very slightly, sizzled over the net towards another young woman, as tall as Danisa, nearly as blonde, and nearly as pretty. Hannah Lechova sidestepped the ball.

'Back!' Hannah's sharp cry echoed through the dome.

Fjbk raised his eyes. Across the arena a lone figure sat unmoving. Fjbk had noticed him earlier: Maleeva, perhaps the most powerful UDBA officer in Belgrade. He had been here yesterday, too. What did he want?

Danisa served another ball. It went long, like the one before it. Fjbk felt a pulse of puzzled irritation. Danisa's concentration was terrible today. He watched her closely and saw her glance up over his head to some point in the stands.

Fjbk turned abruptly to find the spot her eyes had sought.

Near the topmost row a boy was sitting with his lanky legs over the seats in front of him. Fjbk had seen him around before. He attended the academy and had become a persistent hanger-on. He sent Danisa notes pleading for dates. She laughed and ignored him. Or had ignored him in the past. The angry discomfort that stabbed through Fjbk was only partly professional concern.

Below him Danisa had served another fault. Now her eyes wandered briefly over her shoulder, again picking out the boy.

Fjbk decided. 'Time!'

Danisa stopped serving as Fjbk strode across the gritty black clay towards her. She was sweat-soaked, the overhead lights making her sleek arms and legs glisten. Her hair, tied in a single long plait down her back, gleamed wet. Fatigue was clear in her face.

'You are not paying attention,' Fjbk snapped at her. 'You are not giving a good effort.'

Danisa's beautiful eyes narrowed under his attack. 'I'm trying, Milo.'

'The toss is too far forward. You cannot reach the ball to turn the racket over the top. The spin becomes too flat.'

Danisa looked dubious, but she turned to the service line, carefully bounced the ball four times, tensed, tossed. The *thwack!* of gut against ball hammered Fjbk's eardrums.

Net. And again her eyes swept for an instant towards the boy.

'No, no, no!' In a frenzy of anger Fjbk twisted the racket out of her hand. 'You turn the racket and your hip comes round too early! Do you get nothing right? Look!' He demonstrated, exaggerating every movement, blasting a sharp, flat serve over Hannah's head. 'You see?' he demanded.

Danisa's fatigue vanished as she erupted into gales of girlish laughter.

'What is it?' Fjbk yelled, torn between rage and astonishment. 'What is so *funny?*'

'Oh, Milo,' Danisa gasped, holding her sides. 'If you could only see yourself, your exaggeration.' Quicksilver, she grabbed the racket back from him and tossed an imagined ball. She jerked her head to one side, cocked her elbow wrong, swung her hip like a belly dancer. Across the net Hannah's laughter pealed.

Fjbk's rage vanished. How could any man be angry at this girl? She was the most beautiful and talented and unpredictable woman in the world. His lip curled in a smile.

'You see how funny you looked?' Danisa cried with glee. 'Oh, Milo, we have worked so long today, and we so need to rest!'

Fjbk fought to control himself. He had to be cruel now. 'Then perhaps you should sleep,' he snarled.

Danisa's grin started to fade. 'What?'

'Perhaps you should sleep for a month, right through the tournament. Fail me, fail your parents, fail Yugoslavia's honour.'

The grin was gone. Danisa's face went ivory. 'You have no right—'

'No right? You tell me I have no right? I have given you years of the best coaching. And God has given you this body, this talent. You play games out here. You serve carelessly, like a cow! Maybe you should take a long nap.'

Danisa grabbed a ball, faced the line, tossed it, and brought her racket through with vicious, controlled accuracy. The toss was perfect, and the ball hammered across the net, deep to the back corner. A startled Hannah lunged and missed the clean ace.

Danisa turned and glared at Fjbk. He shrugged, spat, walked back to his seat in the stands.

Danisa Lechova, her nervous system re-energised by anger, began to serve like a demon, or an angel. Fjbk watched, fascinated. She was his creation. She was his song.

He adored her.

Across the broad floor of the sportsdome there was a slight movement in the stands. Fjbk saw that Maleeva, the UDBA man, was leaving. Fjbk momentarily forgot the practice match. He thought, Why do you watch us, swine? Why do you spy on Danisa? You did not let her play at Wimbledon. You have made her a prisoner in her native land. Why is this? You will not harm her, swine. I will die before you or anyone else harms her. She is the best. I love her.

Below, on the court, Danisa slid into a backhand. Her timing was fractionally off and the ball went wide. She turned, and once more her eyes flashed upwards, to the seats behind Fjbk.

It was the last straw. Fjbk signalled for another point. As Danisa served he left his chair and trotted up the steps.

The boy saw him coming and climbed over the back railing to the mezzanine. Boiling, Fjbk rushed after him and caught him by the arm, spinning him against a concrete wall.

'What do you want?' the boy asked.

'Damn you! Leave her alone, you got me?' Fjbk's right fist slammed into the boy's face, knocking him backwards. Red appeared in a gush on his chin.

'You're crazy!' the boy gasped, scrambling to escape. 'I haven't—'

Fjbk pounced on him and pinned him to the ground. He slammed his right fist into the boy's face again. He used his left and his right again, and there was blood everywhere. Sobbing and choking, the boy lay half unconscious, terrified.

Someone grabbed Fjbk's long hair. Something cold and hard pressed against the back of his neck. 'Idiot!' the voice said with soft fury. 'Move and your brains will decorate the wall.'

Fjbk went cold, did not move.

The gun muzzle in his neck jabbed harder. 'Get up.'

Fjbk climbed to his feet. The boy scuttled out of his reach, mopping at his broken face with his sleeve. Maleeva moved round to confront Fjbk, his .38 automatic levelled on the coach's chest. He was glacier white with rage.

'You are a madman. You should be institutionalised. Another trick like this and you will never see the outside world again.'

Fjbk stared. The boy got unsteadily to his feet. Maleeva glanced at him. 'Can you walk to the car?'

'Yes, sir,' he said thickly.

'Then go. Report for medical aid at once.'

'What?' Fjbk blustered. 'You help malingerers who—'

'He is part of our security detail, pig-brain,' Maleeva bit off.

'I thought—'

'You thought nothing. You never think. You boast. You posture. You go crazy. You make our work twice as hard, Fjbk. I swear to you, this evil temper of yours will be your death.'

Fjbk wiped his face and broke into a radiant grin. In an instant he seemed a totally different personality. 'Hey, it was only a joke, right? I just wanted to scare him. I will take the kid for a ride on my Harley and make up for everything, OK?'

Grinning as if nothing at all had happened, Fjbk rushed down to the arena again. Maleeva heard the crazy Serb calling, 'Ten more serves for each of you, my pets. Then we will call it a day, eh?'

Maleeva looked down with disgust at the blood on the ground. As if it was not hard enough, with all the pressure from headquarters and Moscow, he also had to be saddled with the world's biggest fool—and potentially one of its most dangerous madmen.

For he had no doubt that Fjbk was fiendishly clever, wholly unpredictable, and capable of anything. If it were not for his fame, Maleeva would have arrested him.

But he could not do that. Not yet. He could only hope that Fjbk would hold on to his thin thread of sanity through this tournament.

3

The Yugoslav Air Transport 747 descended bumpily out of rain-swollen clouds and began its approach into Belgrade-Surčin Airport. I looked out from my seat at my first view of Yugoslavia.

I saw tree-stubbled hills, the grey expanse of the Sava River, and out ahead the tight cluster of the old city at the place where the Sava conjoined with the Danube. There was a·hazy view of twisting streets and orange-tiled roofs and church steeples, and beyond them the concrete blocks of New Belgrade sticking up like giant tombstones. So it begins, I thought.

Local time was five pm. After an all-night flight my biological clock said ten in the morning. I hadn't slept much and was having difficulty functioning mentally.

I needed to be alert. I had no knowledge of the native language. My country-and-customs briefing had been kept sketchy to make sure I would not blow my own cover by inadvertently revealing knowledge that a travelling tennis journalist shouldn't have. I had read a little on my own, as any visitor might.

Nominally, Yugoslavia remained a Communist country. But even its buses and taxis were privately owned, and there were few countries in Europe with more freelance small entrepreneurs. Education, health care and housing, however, were under the total control of an often corrupt state, and only the press and television appeared to be uncontrolled.

In some ways the country proved to the world that Tito had been right when he fought Soviet domination after World War II. Superficially it was more prosperous than its Iron Curtain neighbours. Inflation, however, was out of control, and housing in urban areas had been a disaster for decades. The big projects in New Belgrade had eased the pressure, but not enough.

There was slight but growing political dissent. The UDBA—*Uprava Drzavne Bezbednosti*, local equivalent of the KGB—was nowhere near as efficient as its Russian counterpart. But it had plain-clothes members everywhere, and informing to the secret police out of patriotism, fear or hope of favours was a way of life. I did not delude myself: anyone might betray me if they guessed my real mission.

My 747 swept in over the airport fence, hammered onto the runway, braked, and rolled to the terminal. I retrieved my rackets, attaché case and portable computer from the overhead compartment.

In the terminal, I followed the crowd down a broad hallway and into a large barren room, for the checking of visas. Stood in a queue.

Finally it was my turn. The sour woman behind the window stared at my passport, then at me. 'Occupation, sir?'

'Writer of sports news. Here to cover the tennis tournament.'

'Duration of stay?'

'Ten days.'

'Local address?'

'Hotel Metropol.'

She took my passport into a back room, where presumably she checked my name against lists of suspect people. She came back, returned the passport, and said, 'Enjoy your stay in our country, sir.' She said it like someone who had seldom enjoyed anything in her life.

In the baggage room, I picked up my suitcase and went through customs. I was feeling tight inside. Militia were everywhere, in their blue uniforms, busy looking friendly for the unaccustomed throngs of tourists coming in for the tournament.

The Belgrade International format was going to be a little weird. Sandwiched in between Wimbledon and Davis Cup zone matches, it was to have a limited invitational field. Elimination play for a handful of qualifying slots would be restricted to two days, at a killing pace. Even the top pros would have to play two matches a day in the first two rounds. Nobody would have put up with it if the government hadn't put up such an ungodly amount of prize money. As it was, everybody would be here, and the whole thing would be run off in nine days.

No one was to meet me at the airport, so I was surprised when, as I walked out into the main lobby, someone touched my elbow. 'Mr Smith? Mr Brad Smith?'

I turned to face a little man not more than twenty-five years old, pink and cherubic, with blond hair already getting thin, and thick eyeglasses. He was wearing a rumpled suit and a red tie about three inches wide.

'Hello,' he said, sticking out a moist, soft hand. 'I'm Michael Nariv. With the tournament committee. Welcome to Belgrade. I shall help you to your hotel and answer any questions.'

'I wasn't expecting anyone.'

Nariv grabbed my bag, staggering slightly under its weight. 'We were pleased to know of your arrival, Mr Smith. Having a journalist with your past tennis triumphs—winner of the US Open, Wimbledon, doubles champion in the French, and so on—is feathers in our hat. Please follow me. I have a car.'

It didn't feel quite right to me. The unexpected never set well on a job. But I went along.

Outside the terminal dense humidity greeted us. The sun was well into the west and there was impatient traffic everywhere. Nariv wrestled the bag and the computer onto the back seat of a Fiat saloon car, awkwardly held the door for me, then drove into the terminal-area traffic like a mad stock-car driver.

'The air trip was OK?' he asked. 'We have many extra flights coming in now for the tournament. It will be a great success.'

'I hope so,' I said.

'The tournament starts next Monday, as you know,' he chattered on, cutting in on a Volkswagen and almost sideswiping a truck. 'But tomorrow morning, Friday, the qualifying playing begins, and on Saturday also is the celebrity playing. Many notables have already arrived. Becker is here. Connors and McEnroe from your own country, and Wilander, Lendl, Mecir, Garcia—many others. This is wonderful. Martina Navratilova and Pam Shriver arrive today. Steffi Graf and Chris Evert and your wonderful young player Karyn Wechsting are already here, practising. And many, many great tennis journalists such as yourself. Tomorrow night there is the giant reception and party for all participants. The excitement has standed the city on its skull!'

Feeling exhaustion tug at my mind, I said something noncommittal, and he launched into another enthusiastic monologue. We screamed into the city at a speed that would not have been safe in twice the car. I got fleeting impressions: an ancient Coptic church, a junkyard, and a ruin that had to date back to the Turks.

Michael Nariv chattered happily on. He said he would be my official guide through the tournament, and it was a great honour, et cetera. I half listened. He seemed incompetent and harmless.

Which kept a small alarm ticking in my mind.

This seemingly inept young PR man had spotted me unerringly in an airport teeming with visitors. How? And why would the tournament assign an employee to a relatively minor magazine writer? I paid closer attention. It was an awfully good act. But I felt pretty sure it was an act. Nariv might work for the committee, but he had another employer, too. I would have bet on that.

Which meant—maybe—that my cover had already been blown, and I hadn't even started yet.

Which meant I had to deviate from the plan at once, in order to make a contact. But I had to wait for an opportunity.

When we walked into the Hotel Metropol lobby, we found it crowded with sports writers and TV people. George Plimpton was there, talking with Dick Enberg. I recognised Bud Collins behind his bushy beard. He grinned and waved.

Nariv insisted on accompanying me to my room. As we crossed towards the lift a tall man of about fifty intercepted us.

'My good friend Michael,' he said, with a smile which had no warmth in it.

Nariv suddenly looked slightly pale and very nervous. 'Major Maleeva! Good afternoon, sir.'

Maleeva had a beefy face, with a five-o'clock shadow and wide eyes in deep, tired sockets. The smile had a gold front tooth in it. His hair was dense, black, wavy. In his black summerweight suit and white shirt and grey tie, he looked heavy, muscular, military.

He said to me, 'Please take no notice of Michael's use of a title.' His ball-bearing eyes swivelled to Nariv. 'I am off duty, merely familiarising

412

myself with some of those for whom we will provide the maximum in security and safety.'

'Yes.' Nariv choked, still uptight. 'I—'

Maleeva turned back to me, extending a big paw. 'Allow me the honour. I am Ladislav Maleeva.'

He reeked of UDBA. I shook his hand and gave him my name.

'Of course. Mr Brad Smith,' he said. 'Another American journalist. I hope you are one of the truthful ones.'

'I try to be.'

'It is unfortunate that more of your colleagues in the press do not share your interest in writing the truth.'

'Well, they're at a disadvantage, Major. They don't have a government telling them what the truth is, the way you do.'

For a fraction of a second startled anger heated his eyes. But he was good; the neat, meaningless smile never faltered. He replied smoothly, 'I hope your stay in Belgrade is a pleasant one,' then excused himself. Nariv and I finally got into the lift.

After we had got out on my floor, I said, 'Maleeva is UDBA?'

Nariv patted his face with a handkerchief. 'Yes. A very important man.'

I didn't reply. Was Nariv acting? Maybe the meeting with Maleeva hadn't been accidental, but set up so Nariv's boss could look me over for himself. I badly needed to make a contact.

'You will wish to have a tour of the city later tonight?' Nariv chirped as I unlocked the door to my room. 'Dinner, perhaps?' He smirked. 'It could be arranged for a very beautiful young lady to accompany you and provide . . . answers to all your questions, and friendship away from home.'

'I just want some sleep right now, Michael,' I told him.

'In the morning you wish to see the tennis facility? Perhaps to meet Danisa Lechova and her sister, Hannah?'

'I would like that very much. Yes.'

'Excellent. The committee recognises the importance of your magazine and an article written by a personage of your illustriousness. I will see what can be arranged.'

'Fine.' I put my bag inside and turned quickly, or he would have followed me. 'See you later, Michael. Thanks.'

'I will call you from the lobby in the morning at nine hundred hours, sharply, my good Mr Smith. You will find our hospitality beyond recall. Anything. Ask anything!' He was still talking when I closed the door.

It was a nice room: small, contemporary, with white walls, chocolate-coloured carpet, a draped window looking out over a six-inch decorative balcony. Beyond was a wooded park.

413

I opened my bag and found the bright red T-shirt. I put it on a hanger and hung it next to the window glass, as if put there to dry. I checked my watch and finished unpacking.

I gave them an hour. Then I wrote my note: 'Trouble? Met at airport by Michael Nariv. Says he is part official welcoming committee. Is this true???'

Pocketing that, I went down to the vast lobby and found some postcards. I sat and filled out one to the club back home.

When I walked to the main post office there was still a lot of traffic on the Boulevard of the Revolution and many tourists with cameras. My man, Mitchell, was standing on the corner studying a street map. The photos of him had been excellent. He was young, dark-haired, casually dressed, blending nicely with the other visitors.

Our eyes met for an instant as I approached. Then he folded his map and stepped to the kerb, ready to cross. As I moved beside him in the crowd, he dropped the map. I bent to retrieve it and slid my palmed note inside as I handed it back. He thanked me. The light changed. We crossed. He turned right, and I walked on towards the imposing grey stone bulk of the post office.

I mailed my card and returned to the Metropol. Fatigue was really crashing in on me. I showered, set my travel alarm for an early wake-up and climbed into bed. Almost instantly I was asleep. Then came the telephone call.

For a second or two I had no idea where I was. I got my eyes open and found the telephone—a chunk of white plastic. I picked it up. 'Brad Smith speaking.'

'Brad?' It was a woman's voice, husky and warm. 'Do you remember me? I think we met in London two years ago. It was an experience—'

I slammed the instrument back into its cradle.

Sleep was scalded out of me now, and in its place was incredulous anger. How clumsy could someone be, to call me on the hotel phone! And then she had—without any masking preamble—simply started to dump the first of her verbal bona fides.

Almost certainly the hotel lines were bugged. Even the dullest militia bureaucrat, wearily reviewing hundreds of calls off the tapes every day, would notice this weird opening.

I had hoped for a prompt return contact in response to my query about Michael Nariv. But *this* was like hanging a SPY sign round my neck and lighting it with neon.

Going to the windows, I shot the draperies open. Night was almost upon the city, the sun a red ball behind lavender and blue clouds. I could see the last sunlight on the domes and roofs of huge public buildings. I

414

could even see the glitter of a river, the Sava, far off. Beyond glowed the lights of New Belgrade.

I wished I had someone to ring up and curse. The woman obviously had been another contact. But she had almost surely compromised me, plain and simple. If this first gambit was any indication of how well the operation was laid out, we were dead.

I looked out at the big, darkening foreign city. First Nariv, then Maleeva. Now this. Sleep was not going to come back easily.

BY MORNING—after five hours' sleep—I had made a decision. Until someone gave me definite word that my cover had been blown, I would assume I was still operational and press on.

I hadn't got any further than that when I went down to the hotel coffee shop and ordered my breakfast. Michael Nariv arrived ten minutes early, as I had known he would.

We headed for the new arena, where the tournament would be held. It was a fine day, the sun warm as it moved between puffy white clouds. At the sports complex we found players of all rankings working out on the outdoor courts. Danisa and a few others, Nariv informed me, were on the courts inside, where the major matches would be played. The arena seated twenty-two thousand, and Danisa would play all her matches inside.

The interior still smelled of fresh paint and plaster. I spotted Martina rallying with Chrissie under the watchful eye of Renée Richards. On an adjacent court Lisa Bonder was working out with Karyn Wechsting. A few members of the press were scattered around the stands.

All of that, however, was a fleeting impression. My attention went at once to the number three court, where two blonde young women were hitting back and forth with silent, ferocious intensity. Beside the court stood a squat, powerfully-built man with a mane of black hair, a towel over his shoulder—Miloslav Fjbk.

The Lechova women looked almost like twins at a distance, and their carbon-copy style of play enhanced the eerie impression that Danisa Lechova was shadowboxing with a mirror. Both of them moved with a steady, powerful grace. Their long golden hair and brief tennis dresses increased the confusion. I knew that Danisa was prettier, up close, with finer features, and of course her trademark pigtail identified her further; but at any distance they might have been confused for one another. Danisa wore blue, Hannah pale lavender. As Nariv and I settled in the lowest row to watch, however, it quickly became apparent that the similarities stopped short of their game. Danisa Lechova had it all over her sister, Hannah.

Just as we sat down, Hannah hit a backhand down the line. Danisa was

415

far out of position. She started after the shot, and somehow as the ball skidded off the line she was *there*, sliding into the shot and extending her slim body to its maximum length. Her racket preparation, especially under the circumstances, was marvellous. She blasted back a fireball forehand.

Fascinated, I watched as Danisa hit phenomenal shot after phenomenal shot. Her sister was game, hanging in on every point and winning a lot of them. In other company all eyes would have been on her. That she was hanging on by her fingernails was not a disparagement of her play; it was just that Danisa was fabulous.

After a while Fjbk called a halt. As the sisters towelled their faces Nariv opened the gate to the arena floor, motioning to me. 'We will meet them now. It is arranged. Come!'

I followed him. He greeted Fjbk with his usual enthusiasm, and the Serb gave me a glower that would have frozen a bonfire. When the Lechova sisters came over, I had an overwhelming impression of pretty bare arms and long legs, blonde hair and beautiful eyes—Danisa's blue, Hannah's brown.

'Danisa,' Nariv gushed. 'Hannah. Allow me to present the former United States Open champion, Wimbledon champion, three-time Davis Cup team member—'

'Tennis writer and six-time quitter of smoking,' I cut in, extending my right hand. 'Brad Smith. Hello.'

Danisa shook my hand. Her vivid, happy smile blew me away. Up close she was simply stunning. No small girl she, and her features were not delicate or weak. Her mouth was wide and what they used to describe as generous, her eyes large.

'I am happy to meet you, Mr Brad Smith,' she told me. 'It is said we are to have interviews.'

Hannah cut in almost violently. 'Hey, I hope we have interviews too.' She pumped my hand. 'Gosh, Brad Smith, you are—let me think of the right word—you are *gorgeous!*' She rolled roguish eyes.

'Hannah,' Fjbk rumbled reprovingly.

'But look at him!' Hannah cried. 'Brad Smith, here to do interviews. I can't stand it!'

Danisa's calm eyes watched my reaction. She was amused. It was the first of many times I would get the impression that she was far older and wiser than her years.

She said, 'It has been arranged that we will play together in the celebrity mixed doubles.'

Someone had moved fast. 'I look forward to that.'

Hannah broke in. 'You still like to play, right?'

'Of course.' The question surprised me. 'Don't you?'

'I love it. I love all of it. Sometimes I get so excited. Ooh!' She wriggled from head to foot, with interesting results.

'Time for showers,' Fjbk interrupted. He was not amused.

'I have shocked Milo,' Hannah said. 'You have to forgive me. We Yugoslavs are very excitable.'

Danisa smiled at Hannah, then turned to me. 'You will be at the reception and ball tonight? We might have time to start our talks.'

'That would be fine.'

Our eyes met. Hers questioned me. She knew, I thought, that I was here to help her get out. I wondered—

Hannah broke into my wondering. 'We will dance tonight,' she said, stroking my arm. 'You will see, I dance as beautifully as I play this game!'

Danisa's smile became a radiant grin. 'Hannah, you will not be allowed to monopolise Mr Smith.'

It was a cute thing to say. But as she said it Fjbk's mouth tightened almost imperceptibly, and there was a faint narrowing of his dark eyes. It was as if a galvanic current had surged through him, and only by the application of tremendous control had he been able to mask its effect.

Miloslav Fjbk was crazy in love with Danisa.

'Come,' he rumbled. He put a hand on Danisa's shoulder, gentle and tentative on her skin. 'Shower now,' he ordered.

They hurried off, two laughing girls and a squat middle-aged man scowling out at the world.

'So,' Michael Nariv said, 'this is perhaps the time to ask you. Did we not meet in London two years ago?'

Looking at Nariv's crooked little grin and the sudden crafty slant to his eyes, I felt new surprise, like icy sludge, creep through my bloodstream. Getting blown away by surprises was starting to get old.

Like a good boy I went ahead with it. 'It must have been three years ago if it was London.'

Nariv said, 'On the bridge?'

'Under the clock.'

His shoulders slumped slightly. 'So.'

'Who the hell,' I asked, 'called my hotel room last night?'

'Paula Bansky.' His smile widened. 'She wished to assure you that I am trustworthy.'

'She was reckless. I don't like that a bit. She started the verbal bona fides right on the damned telephone.'

'But the telephones are not monitored regularly.'

'You don't *know* that. You—oh, just take care, and make sure there are no repetitions.'

'If you had allowed me to supply you with a female companion, Paula would have been the one who came to you.'

'And how would that have looked, you jerk?'

He couldn't be flapped. 'Normal. Paula is very beautiful, and she works for one of the city's busiest escort services. She will, as a matter of fact, be your companion at the reception tonight.'

He looked round. We were alone in an acre of empty blue seats. 'You are to tell Danisa Lechova that the thing will be done at the earliest Tuesday night and at the latest Thursday.'

'What is she supposed to do?'

'I have been told there will be more instructions. She must understand that when the time comes it will be quick. She will not be able to take anything with her.'

'Is that all?'

'I have been told you will have a role in getting her out of the arena and to a point where she will be met.'

'I was told I would be a go-between and nothing more.'

He shrugged. 'Hey, I do not know a lot. I am . . . little potato.'

I sighed. 'So what are my instructions?'

'It is imperative that you spend a lot of time with Danisa. You will interview her in width. This is to establish your right to be close to her at the proper time. One more thing—you are to win the confidence of Miloslav Fjbk and the family.'

'How am I supposed to do that?'

'Fjbk,' he said, as if I hadn't spoken, 'watches the young women with the eyes of a falcon. Fjbk is a jealous man and can cause grave difficulties for us.'

'I noticed.'

'You are to be aware that Hannah Lechova has strong ties to the army. She is known to have informed on friends she suspected of political deviation. She is to be handled with kid shoes.'

Something told me Hannah might be my biggest immediate problem. The look in her eyes when she smiled at me had not had anything to do with political deviationism.

Nariv took my silence for the conclusion of our discussion. 'You wish now to watch other warming-ups?' he asked.

At the far end of the arena I could see Pat Cash, Paul Annacone, Yannick Noah and several other familiar faces getting ready to work out. 'I'd better do some journalist work, yes.'

'Good.' Nariv beamed. 'Then, I will take you to your hotel, and you will be joined by Paula Bansky this evening.'

'What's Paula's role in all this?'

'I do not know, my good friend Brad Smith.'

'Seems to me there's a lot we don't know, as little as four days away from carrying the operation to its conclusion.'

'Yes,' Nariv said, and giggled nervously. 'Suspense. Intrigue. Is wonderful, right?'

Ministry of Culture, Belgrade

In the office building just off Marshal Tito Street, Major Ladislav Maleeva fought his anger as he faced M. Y. Altunyan, ostensibly an attaché for cultural affairs at the Soviet embassy, but in reality the KGB's chief resident in Belgrade.

'This is an internal matter of my country,' Maleeva insisted.

'There is no intention of interfering in Yugoslavia's internal affairs.' Altunyan, mountains of fat rumpling his expensive suit, reached inside his jacket and took out one of the long black cigars that Maleeva despised. 'We wish only to cooperate,' the Russian added heavily.

Maleeva did not miss the condescension. He was trapped, and the KGB resident knew it. Maleeva hated all Russians. He hated Altunyan more, because of his power.

Ordinarily, the KGB was only tolerated in Belgrade. But a month ago the orders had come from the highest authority: the UDBA would cooperate with the KGB on this case.

Maleeva bitterly resented it. But he was a good soldier and he would obey. He told Altunyan, 'We will keep you informed of our surveillance.'

'Insufficient,' Altunyan responded, lighting his cigar. 'Routine reports will not satisfy our needs. This man Nariv—'

'He is being watched day and night.'

'Insufficient. We must know his role and mission. Now.'

'I told you! We are watching. What more can we do?'

Altunyan leaned forward through the acrid smoke. 'I will tell you.'

Swift Current, Saskatchewan

Standing in front of his motel unit, Dominic Partek looked out over the low sprawl of the town of Swift Current. He stared at the Saskatchewan prairie, letting the sadness move through him.

The sadness was unrelated to the danger that choked him. This barren country reminded him of the flatlands of his homeland, Serbia.

Partek had driven hard and slept a long time. Now he had to decide his next step. He faced the cruellest kind of dilemma. If he went back, the punishment would possibly be death. But if he reverted to his decision to defect to the West, others would pay.

Whatever I do, he thought, there will be suffering. He was sick of suffering, of dilemmas, of uncertainty ... sick of himself.

He remembered his childhood in Surčin. His ailing father, when drunk, had beaten Dominic with cold fury. The boy had grown up in terror. Usually his mother had been able to intervene, but sometimes Alexi Partek beat her too, for intervening.

Dominic's mother had always loved him, had held him and smiled at him when he did well, protected him as best she could. And Dominic had adored her, would have done anything for her. So in school he worked very hard and led his class.

Dominic was good in athletics too, which his mother told him should be no surprise: his father, long ago, before his tragic injuries at Stalingrad, had been an athlete. His father had been a great hero at Stalingrad, and this was why he limped so, experienced such constant pain.

Alexi Partek was from the Ukraine, she told Dominic, and should have been compensated by the Russians for his heroism. That the Russians had discarded him was proof that the Russians were evil men. Alexi told his son that it had been an honour to give up his health for the USSR, and if he fell into fits of violent melancholy, it was because circumstances forced him to live here, in Yugoslavia, Martina Partek's homeland. Disagreements of this sort were part of the fabric of Dominic's childhood.

After graduating from high school, Dominic had entered the Yugoslav army by conscription. At almost the same time, something wonderful and something disastrous happened in the family. His mother, astonishingly, told him that she was pregnant. And his father, after a ghastly scene, ran away.

Sending her son off to the army, Martina Partek was pale but resolute. 'I will manage,' she told him.

'Father will come back,' Dominic told her.

'No.' She was like ice-covered stone. 'He will not come back. But if he tries, he can never stay here again.'

'Mother!'

'You are a man now,' she told him with an eerie calm. 'I will tell you this. Alexi has gone away because of this child in my belly. You heard the shouting, the threats. We cannot feed another child, he says. But I tell you this, my son—I will not lose this child. Alexi is gone because I have chosen this child before him.'

It had been a grim home-leaving, but once in the army, Dominic had put it behind him as best he could. He did what he always had done: fought to excel. Almost all of his pitiful monthly cheque was mailed back to Surčin. He finished basic training and was selected for special code-and-cipher school near Sarajevo.

While he was in that school, word came that his father had died in

Moscow. Dominic was granted leave, to attend to final arrangements. His father's 'estate' amounted to a cheap watch, a few items of clothing, and unpaid rent at a cheap rooming house.

Dominic returned to his post. He wrote a long letter to his mother, in Surčin. Two weeks later this envelope was returned, stamped UNKNOWN. Badly alarmed, he sought emergency leave. He was told he had just had an emergency leave.

For three weeks he stewed and waited for the leave that would come automatically at the end of the first phase of his intelligence training. When he finally got to Surčin, he went at once to the tiny wooden shack where he had grown up. He found another family there. They knew nothing about his mother. Neighbours said Martina Partek had simply vanished, taking her few possessions with her.

Frantic, Dominic called on the militia. But they pointed out that his mother had taken her things with her, so foul play seemed unlikely. Dominic spent his last day of leave walking up and down streets in Belgrade, the nearest city, thinking that somehow he would just look up and there by magic she would be.

All that year a haunted Dominic Partek wrote letters, filled out enquiry forms. His mother would not have deserted him. What had happened to her? And to the child she had been carrying?

His letters and tracer forms came back stamped NO RECORD. FOR-WARDED. RETURNED. UNKNOWN. Twice he got short leaves and rushed to Surčin, but no one knew anything. Old friends shook their heads sadly. These things happened.

After two years, Dominic's hopes had gone. He completed intelligence school and was assigned as an attaché in the Yugoslav embassy in Moscow. There he met a man named Kudirka, a Lithuanian who worked in the Soviet government. One evening, walking near the Kremlin, Kudirka bluntly asked Dominic if he had ever considered a career with the KGB.

'Your files could be transferred to our offices on a permanent basis,' Kudirka said. 'We have a great need for men of your loyalty, intelligence and integrity. We would provide additional training. Within two years' time you could be an attaché at a Soviet embassy in another part of the world.'

'But my government would never agree,' Dominic replied.

'It is not impossible,' Kudirka told him.

Kudirka spoke of advancement, world opportunities. They were magic words. Partek had already begun to see the parochialism of the UDBA. He was a good Communist and, despite his suspicion of things Russian, considered the KGB a valiant and praiseworthy operation. Here was his chance to become part of it. He had no family to hold him back.

The decision was made. With amazing alacrity the Yugoslav bureaucracy spat out the necessary paperwork. Before Christmas Partek reported to the KGB's great old stone headquarters on Dzerzhinsky Square. How far I have come, he thought in wonderment. And how far I will go.

His real life's work began on that day.

So long ago, Partek thought now, standing on the breezy, sunny pavement outside his motel in Canada. He wondered what he would have done if he could have foreseen what he knew now, could have guessed the disillusionment and treachery.

He had thought he was being clever enough in the way he contacted one of his counterparts in the CIA in New York. He had only needed to know at that point how he might turn himself over and live out his life in the West. He had not even been sure he could take such a step, despite the disillusionment with his Soviet masters. He was only gathering information for a contingency.

And he was so careful, so circumspect.

But not careful enough. Somehow his KGB masters got wind of his change of perspective—possibly a difference in his disposition at work, possibly something of more substance. That was when they had allowed him to learn about his family, after all these years. So he would know what he had to lose if his loyalty ever faltered. But their ploy had backfired. Rather than frightening Partek, it had enraged him. They knew and never told me, he thought. It was my right to know!

His American contacts pressed him for a final decision.

He agonised and delayed.

'They suspect you, Dominic. Better to come over now.'

'I cannot defect now. They will retaliate in Belgrade.'

'What if we could get her out, so there could never be any reprisals?'

'You could do that?'

'We can try.'

So Partek had fled, buying time. But now, by his actions, he stood convicted by his KGB masters. He knew they were looking for him. To make matters worse, the CIA was also chasing him 'for his own protection'.

So that now all he could do was keep hiding, see if the CIA's promises would be fulfilled. If they were, there was hope.

A truck horn sounded on the highway by the motel. The sound jarred Partek out of his reverie, reminding him of the danger and the need to move. He climbed into his truck.

He had to keep moving—do the unexpected.

New Belgrade

Late afternoon sun baked Michael Nariv's face as he strolled through the grounds of the Sava Center, waiting for the meeting with his contact. It was nice here on the vast green lawns, cars purring along the wide streets, tourists walking idly.

Then Nariv realised he was being followed.

He was not deeply trained, but the surveillance would have been obvious to almost anyone. The two men behind him were not making any real attempt to be subtle. He immediately panicked.

Hurrying to the kerbside taxi stand, he hopped into a cab, slamming the door behind him. He blurted the first thing that came into his mind. 'United States embassy! Hurry!'

The driver nodded and put the car in gear. Outside the taxi Nariv's two pursuers hurried into the cab behind him. Nariv felt sweat burst from every pore on his body. They are after me, he thought, there can be no doubt. And they must be UDBA.

His driver turned out of the Sava Center roadway and approached the Gazela Bridge, over the Sava. Nariv twisted around to peer through the rear window and saw his pursuers' cab behind him. His panic intensified. He had to think!

The taxi swept over a crossroads. Then they were on the bridge, speeding. The other car was still close behind.

Nariv thought about the embassy. He realised he could not get inside before the UDBA seized him. His only hope was to escape them somehow, then seek asylum.

Frantically he looked up and down the river. He saw, away to his left, the trees and ancient walls of the Kalemegdan. He poked the driver's shoulder. 'I have changed my destination. The Kalemegdan—the Stambol Gate. Please hurry!'

The driver changed lanes for an exit. Nariv leaned back, fighting to concentrate. He had to have a plan.

The Kalemegdan—the ancient fortifications and parkland dominating the conjunction of the Sava and the Danube—had been a fortress throughout history. Old Roman ruins were there, and walls and towers dating to the Middle Ages. It was an area Nariv had explored in childhood. Surely, if he could get inside the Stambol Gate he could hide himself, perhaps in the maze of streets of the lower town near Nebojša Tower.

The following car had dropped back almost a block. Nariv began to get his hopes up. I can do this, and they said I could go to America one day. What a story I will tell my children, the ones I shall have with a beautiful blonde American girl.

The traffic became worse. The park appeared on the right, the pavement choked with people strolling alongside a great medieval grey wall.

The taxi came to a complete halt. 'The way is blocked,' the driver said, pointing to a solid jam of cars ahead.

Nariv pulled money from his pocket, tossed it onto the front seat, and vaulted onto the sidewalk. Startled tourists got out of his way as he ran for the great maw of the gateway through the stone battlements. Behind him he heard brakes squeal.

Through the blackness of the gate Nariv ran, and came out in blinding sunlight. Ahead was the garden area round the old Roman baths, and beyond were walks, trees, heavy shrubbery.

Within a minute or two he came to crumbling stone steps leading down into a moss-green grotto, where stood a statue to war dead. A squirrel ran, frightened, as Nariv rushed round the statue and plunged through a slit in another fortification. He could hear water running not far away—the Amber Fountain.

There was no sign of pursuit. He began to believe he had made it. Slightly slowing his pace, he proceeded along a small creek and down stone steps towards the lower town. Soon he emerged onto an outcropping that looked down upon walls and willows and the Nebojša Tower well beyond, against the blue haze of the confluence of the rivers.

Nariv started down more steps.

A bulky man stepped out of a niche in the wall. One of the men who had been chasing him. Nariv made an involuntary gagging sound and turned, every nerve screaming with fear.

The other man stepped out also.

Sobbing, Nariv tried to rush past. The first man caught him and spun him round like a doll. Then the other man also had Nariv, pinioning him against the rock wall. The second man took something out of his coat pocket. A needle. A syringe.

'No!'

The needle plunged into Nariv's left shoulder, and he felt the hot squirt go in. Then reality melted.

4

That evening, waiting for Paula Bansky in the lobby of the Metropol for the ride to the tournament ball, I expected to meet a dull-eyed idiot. What appeared was Miss World.

'Mr Smith?' she said with a vivacious smile. 'I'm Paula.' She was

424

diminutive, curvy and dark, with smashing emerald eyes. She was wearing a wine-coloured cocktail dress that bared her arms and shoulders, and nicely displayed her marvellous legs.

We left the lobby and crossed the tiled entryway to her waiting Cortina. She drove briskly and well. She talked about the crowds coming into the city for the tournament.

'You're very quiet,' she observed after a while. 'You aren't ill, are you?'

'No. If your telephone call, with the bona fides right out in the open, doesn't result in my getting killed, I'll be just fine.'

She flushed. 'I'm sorry. That was a stupid mistake.'

'Yes, it was,' I agreed, and dropped it. The harm was done, and I felt sure she had already been chewed out elsewhere.

At the old hotel that was the site of the ball, the huge ballroom was already crowded. To one side, under flag-festooned arches, a dance orchestra played. Tables surrounded the dance floor, and the room opened through an elaborate archway into an adjacent room almost as large, where crystal chandeliers blazed with light. I saw people of all ages and in all manner of dress. Many older men wore tuxedos, their ladies elaborate ball gowns. The tennis people generally wore light shifts or slacks.

Paula and I made for a tiny table and sat down. One waiter brought champagne and another plied us with hors d'oeuvres. A man from the tournament committee dragged up a chair and talked endlessly about how wonderful the tournament was going to be. I tried to discourage him by not taking notes.

Paula was tapping feline fingertips in time with the music.

'Dance?' I asked.

'Yes,' she said eagerly.

She was a great dancer. I decided this was fun. 'How long,' I wondered aloud, 'before Michael shows up and spoils this?'

'He isn't to come tonight,' she replied. 'It was thought he shouldn't be seen with you except when he is presumably discharging official tournament duties on your behalf.'

'So you're my contact.'

'For the moment.'

'So do you have any news for me?' I asked.

'As I understand it, the celebrity draw places you with Danisa Lechova tomorrow in the mixed doubles, against Ted Treacher and Karyn Wechsting. It is suggested that you use the remainder of tomorrow and Sunday to interview Danisa, to cement the impression of a major in-depth article in preparation.' She paused to follow me through a promenade, then added, 'And on Monday there will be further instructions.'

'It's about time.'

We danced a little more, and then the orchestra took a break. 'I think,' I told Paula, 'it's time to try to run into the Lechovas.'

'Yes,' she said, and we began a slow, aimless circuit of the rooms. Five minutes later we ran straight into Hannah.

'Oh, no!' Hannah cried, a vision in far too much lace and too little bodice. 'The man of my dreams!' She seized my arm and pleaded with Paula. 'Oh, let me steal him for a few minutes, will you? I am *so* hungry for conversation with a real man.'

Paula smiled. 'I'll be around, Brad.' She moved off.

Hannah leaned conspiratorially close to me. 'She's gorgeous, darling. Do you mind that I took you away? Come on! I want champagne.' She dragged me to the nearest serving tables.

After we had been served, we drifted through the crowd. A young man in army uniform came over to say hello to Hannah. He seemed drawn and tense, but eager to please her. She went cold, unapproachable as a cemetery statue, and after a couple of minutes he went away.

'Seemed like a nice guy,' I said, puzzled.

'He is an enemy of the state,' she snapped.

'What? In army uniform?'

'I have heard him speak against the state. He said openly that there is corruption, at all levels.'

I tried a lame joke. 'Sounds like a death penalty offence.'

'No. But he is now in the army, where he can be watched.'

A small chill went down my back. 'You turned him in.'

Her eyes glowed hotly with vindictive pride. 'I did my duty as a citizen.'

I had been warned about her chameleon personality, the fanatic-patriot side of her. We had been having fun, I thought, with the repartee. But Hannah's radicalism had fixed all that. This was no casual flirtation, and Hannah was no sweet young thing. Quite possibly Hannah could be lethal. In seconds, however, she recovered her sunny side. Grasping my arm, she said, 'Come! For dancing.'

I resisted. 'Is your family here? I'd like to meet them.'

Her eyes flared again just for a second. 'And switch me for Danisa?'

I slipped my arm round her waist. 'There will *never* be anyone else for me.'

She laughed and wriggled out of my grasp. 'Hey, watch your step! Maybe I can get *you* in the army too.'

We soon found the Lechova family at a table well back from the major hubbub: Danisa, wearing a simple white dress with her hair tied back and no make-up, looked about fifteen; her father in a black suit and tie, tall, a grey-haired man nearing fifty; her mother a surprisingly youthful redhead with freckles and green eyes and a guarded, austere expression.

'Momma! Poppa!' Hannah gushed. 'Here is the man of my dreams for you to approve.'

'Hannah,' Leon Lechova growled. He stood up and held out his hand with all the welcome of a border guard, his vivid blue eyes crackling with hostility. 'I recognise you, Mr Smith, from photographs. Allow me to present my wife.'

Geneta Lechova studied me coolly. She seemed drawn with tension despite the fact that she looked younger than I had expected, pretty, tanned, athlete-slim. 'Welcome to our country.'

Lechova pulled up an extra chair, and I sat down. Hannah sat close to me and made some silly remark. I exchanged looks with Danisa; there was a wary quality to her gaze, worried. Lechova said I would play with Danisa in the celebrity doubles.

'Danisa understands she is not to exert herself in the celebrity playing,' he added. 'Hannah and Danisa must be fresh for the singles play. They have been placed in opposite brackets for the championships. They must meet in the finals.'

It was a shocking thing to say. Danisa, except for a slight, pained narrowing of her pretty eyes, showed no reaction. I saw a deeper flicker of anguish in Hannah's expression, there and gone instantly. No wonder Hannah acted a little crazy, I thought. Dear old Dad. How long had he played them against each other?

Geneta Lechova spoke into the widening silence. 'Mr Smith, you are to write an article about our daughters?'

'Yes,' I said.

Lechova cut in. 'About Danisa. But when Hannah meets Danni in the finals, that plan will have to be changed. The article will celebrate *both* our daughters.'

His wife stiffened almost imperceptibly. 'Leon,' she said softly, 'we have no guarantees.'

'We have groomed them. The time for greatness has come.'

Mrs Lechova stared at her husband, her eyes filled with disappointment. I asked Danisa a dumb journalistic question designed to reduce the tension, and she seemed to recognise that. While she was giving me a stock answer the orchestra came back. A boy with a sunburned nose asked Hannah to dance, and they went off.

Lechova seemed to cock his ear towards the music—an old Glenn Miller song. His face actually warmed in a smile as he turned to his wife. 'Geneta. Come.' With a little flush of nervous pleasure she left the table with him.

Danisa looked so pretty and vulnerable it made me ache for her. 'That leaves us,' I told her. 'Will you dance with me?'

She stood up. 'Of course.'

I had enjoyed dancing with Paula Bansky, but Danisa was different, a dream. She was so airy and graceful that it took a few turns for me to lighten up and really begin to enjoy her.

I said, 'Your father is excited about the tournament.'

'You must not hold it against him that he pushes us so hard. He and Mother have given us everything. We owe it to them to be as good as we can be.'

She was so serene. I sensed that in earlier times the pressure must have been agony for her. She had come to terms with it all on her own. I had the first inkling of the extraordinary personality that lay behind the marvellous tennis machine.

'Will there really be an article?' she asked.

'Yes. Whatever else happens, I'm going to do the article.'

She stiffened in my arms, although she kept moving. 'I know this is necessary. There is no other way for me to leave my country now, and time is everything. I'm scared. I wish—' She stopped dancing and looked at me. She was on the brink of tears.

I took her by the arm and hurried her unobtrusively off the dance floor. Through tall French doors I led her onto a brick terrace overlooking a dimly lit fountain and rose garden.

'I'm sorry,' she said huskily. She was crying now.

Feeling awkward, I gave her my handkerchief. 'No need to apologise. I know this is hard.'

'I wanted to come to the West. I love your country. But I would never have abandoned my family and Yugoslavia like this—abruptly, with trickery. My poor mother. It will kill my father.'

'It will hurt. But your father is tough as a boot.'

'Why,' she demanded in a soft burst of pain, 'did they *do* this? All these years? Why didn't they tell me? Why did they hide it from him? My own brother. What kind of beasts are the Russians? And my own people? To do this to us!'

I had no idea what she was talking about. 'I guess we'll get answers later.'

'I hoped,' she said, 'to be free. Travel the world, play in all the tournaments, but visit Yugoslavia often. But I can never have good feelings about my country again, that they could do this!'

She shook her head impatiently. 'I'm sorry. I'm better now.' She wiped her eyes and handed back my handkerchief, now damp with her tears. 'What do we do next?'

'We wait. We do the interviews. When they tell me, I tell you and help with the arrangements. It happens next week.'

She shuddered slightly. 'Do you do this work a lot?'

'No.'

She was watching me in the half-light. Her voice changed. 'You are a nice man, I think, Brad Smith. I understand why my sister is already in love with you.'

'I get the impression she falls in love every fifteen minutes.'

'But of course, and so do I!'

'Lucky guys.'

'Shall I fall in love with you?'

I studied her incredible face. 'Maybe you'd better not.'

'Would you break my heart?'

'No. But you might break mine.'

She smiled and moved away a few inches. 'You're a gentleman. You're very nice.'

I just looked at her. In this light she was older, mysterious, wonderful-looking. My heart flip-flopped.

She said, 'Is this very dangerous for you? It must be.'

'Well, your country wouldn't like it a lot if they knew what was up. But I don't think I'm in great danger. You're the one with more to lose. If you try, and fail, you may *never* get out again.'

'But I have no choice. I've seen that you can't fulfil yourself as an athlete in Yugoslavia. There are always barriers, controls.'

'Like when they kept you from playing at Wimbledon?'

Her jaw tightened, and I got a glimpse of the iron inside her. 'It was the last revelation,' she said grimly, 'about freedom in my country. It made me face the facts. And after our passports had been picked up, your people came to me and told me about the lies that had been told to me ever since I was born.'

'I don't know about all the lies, Danisa.'

Her eyes glistened with tears again. 'We can talk later about that.' Her effort to shake herself mentally was visible. 'Not now. Now is a party, and for joy. Is that OK with you, Brad Smith?'

'That's fine.'

We stood there for a while in silence. I wondered about the pain she had suffered and how she had come finally to this decision to leave her family and country.

The old-fashioned dance music sounded fine, coming out of the ballroom. The garden smelled of lilacs. It was really very nice, and we turned to look at each other, sharing the moment. Then she turned away. Neither of us said anything, we just stood there—she looking out at the garden and I watching her.

I don't know how to explain it, but there are times like that, very rarely, between a man and a woman. There was no rationality to it. She, standing there, quiet and vulnerable and young and lovely, said nothing aloud; but everything was being said to me without words. And I guess my own messages were going back, because after a while she turned to me and smiled.

'Oh my, Brad Smith,' she said wonderingly. And her breath caught in her throat.

'We'd better go in,' I said. My voice sounded funny.

'Yes,' she said softly, the wonder still in her eyes.

SATURDAY MORNING I FOUND no surprises in the results of the tournament qualifying rounds held Friday. The surprise came when Michael Nariv didn't show up at the crack of dawn. Instead, after eight, I was confronted in the hotel lobby by a short, rotund, nervously sweaty little man with no hair on top.

'Mr Smith? I am Victor Lobanov. I am assigned to escort you and other players to the stadium for the celebrity matches.'

'Where's Michael today?'

'He is reported ill. I have a limousine outside with a driver. Please tell me, what time do you and your associates wish to go?'

He was so earnest and nervous that I couldn't doubt his authenticity as a tournament flunky. I wondered if Michael had been pulled off as a precaution of some kind. There was nothing for me to do but follow the programme and see what developed.

I told Lobanov, 'I haven't seen Karyn Wechsting or Ted Treacher yet. They will be playing in the doubles with me. It's early. Why don't you relax for an hour?'

Lobanov's jaw set with painful tension. 'Yes, sir.' He walked to a chair and sat down, looking thoroughly miserable.

After exchanging a few friendly words with Bud Collins, I went in to breakfast. I spied Karyn Wechsting sitting at a table halfway down the room. As I approached her, two unmistakably American tourists had just abandoned a table near the back. The man was tall, overweight, bald and fiftyish, wearing Bermuda shorts and a straw hat. The woman was shorter and broader, with copper-wire hair. Her dress resembled what they used to call a muumuu.

'Mr Smith?' the man boomed, turning heads. 'Surely you're Brad Smith, aren't you? Wow, great! Hey, we're fellow Americans.' He started pumping my hand. 'Henry Beamer, and this is my wife, Muriel. Hays, Kansas. That's our hometown. Hey, Brad, would you sign our tournament programme for us?'

430

Muriel Beamer chimed in. 'Not for us, actually. For our daughter.'

'We've got Lendl and Mecir already,' Beamer said as I scrawled my signature on the programme. 'Hey, Brad, thanks a million, that's great, I really do appreciate it—'

His wife nudged him and pointed to Karyn Wechsting.

'Oh, wow!' Beamer cried. 'Miss Wechsting? Hey, this could make our day.'

I took a detour past the breakfast bar, and by the time I got to Karyn's table, the Beamers were departing. 'Gee, we sure wish you the best in the tournament, Karyn! I hope you just beat the pants off everybody. And thanks a million for the autograph.'

'It's for our daughter, not for us,' Muriel Beamer added. 'She's such a sweet little thing.'

The couple scurried off on some other mission outside the breakfast room. They seemed nice enough, but I felt vaguely embarrassed for them.

'Join you?' I asked Karyn.

'Great.' She gave me a kilowatt smile.

Karyn was young, freckled, sandy-haired, a California girl in the best sense, and a really sweet young woman, one of the few bright young stars of an American tennis establishment that badly needed some. At twenty-four, she had come along late as a big-time player. She wasn't even number one on the UCLA women's team when she was a student. After graduation she went to dental school and played only a few tournaments, but then she decided to give it a whirl for a year on the pro tour before putting up her plate. She promptly beat Chrissie in a Virginia Slims event and realised for the first time that she could be *very good* at this.

So here she was, America's number two, looking tanned and whip-slender and vibrant, a tall girl with pale blue eyes and a face and figure that writers might call wholesome.

'So it's Ted Treacher and me against you and Danisa Lechova this morning,' she said. 'Do you want to surrender now, or play it out?'

Treacher was an old party, like me, now shuttling round the world making publicity for a racket company. He still played enough to be ranked about hundred and sixtieth in the world on some computers. He and Karyn made a good team.

I told her, 'Play it out, I guess. Maybe Danisa can carry me.'

'Isn't she great?' Karyn asked with her customary sunny enthusiasm. 'I just love to watch her play! Martina and Steffi better watch out.'

'She'll have to get by Sabatini and Evert first.'

'Yeah, I expect some great matches. But I think Danni is just coming into her game. And she's such a nice person. Just as unassuming as she can be.'

'Maybe,' I suggested, '*you* want to surrender.'

Karyn's grin broadened. 'Cowboy, you'd better protect yourself up at that net today. I intend to make you eat those words.'

We talked about other personalities in Belgrade for the tournament and what was likely to happen at Flushing Meadow in the Open in September. After a while, as I put away my third cup of great, creamy Turkish coffee so strong you could almost chew it, Karyn said she would go and find Treacher. I dawdled, then went out to the lobby and Victor Lobanov.

When Karyn came back with Ted in tow, we went to our limousine for the ride to the stadium. On the way they talked tennis and tourism, and I thought about Danisa.

'What will our interviews be about?' she had asked late last night. 'You will ask me what kinds of things?'

'About tennis. About your career. Like, Are you happy, making big money on the tour? Do you feel excited?'

She had frowned, then shrugged and changed the subject. 'I look forward to partnering you tomorrow. You were a wonderful player in your time, and I bet you're still good.'

'I'll try not to fall down or anything.'

'You Americans! You either boast or you show this false modesty. I saw you on television at Wimbledon, the time you played Borg. You almost had him.'

I had nodded, remembering. I didn't have to tell her that almost in tennis is nowhere at all. She was a pro.

Now, approaching the stadium, I gave myself a small lecture about my station in life, hers, my real mission in Belgrade.

I dressed for the doubles, walked through the tunnel to the brilliant lights of the floor, and saw her already warming up with Fjbk. She was gliding from one side of the court to the other, braided ponytail flapping. I told myself to calm down.

'There you are!' she called. 'Milo, Brad will warm up with me now.'

Fjbk turned his side of the court over to me with bad grace, and I took a couple of balls from the nearest ball boy and patted one over the net to her. Danisa popped it back gently to my backhand, and I stroked a return. The seats flanking our court began to fill up, with another notable clustering of spectators off to our right, where, three courts away, Hannah was on court. There was some cheering when Lendl and Becker showed up at the other end of the arena, but the Lechova women were obviously the big draw.

Seeing Danisa from the stands had not prepared me for the experience of being on court with her. After a while we began to rally a little more intensely. Testing her, I hit one deep to her backhand with some angle on it, and she glided over and slid three feet into the shot, conserving energy, then hit it back down the line. When I went crosscourt on her, she went after it like a beautiful soaring bird and hit a huge forehand behind me for a winner.

'Nice shot!' she called happily. 'Hard to get.'

Soon Karyn and Ted strolled out to join us. We had fun even with the warm-ups. The crowd continued to come in, and the public-address system came on, the officials came out, a band played the Yugoslav national anthem, and we were ready.

Danisa and I won the toss and said we would serve. Ted went back to receive first, with Karyn at the net. Danisa walked back onto our court with me. 'You serve first,' she said. 'Get us off to a good start.'

It was a nice compliment.

The best-of-three match went more than two hours, much to Miloslav Fjbk's glowering displeasure. He wanted to conserve Danisa's energy, but Karyn and Ted were great to play with, and our competitive juices got flowing. After winning my serve, Danisa and I went down 1-3, mainly due to some flubbed net play on my part and some neat tricks by Karyn. Then, however, we rallied and took five in a row to win the first set.

They won the second set, 6-3, and we won the third, 6-2. The crowd was having a great time, applauding every good shot, but on the last point of the match the whole thing got spoiled. Going all out to return Danisa's crosscourt drop shot, Karyn slipped and took a nasty fall, her left ankle twisting under her.

By the time I got round the net, Ted was helping her up, her face white with pain. 'We'd better get you to the locker room right now,' he said, and

Karyn, limping badly, didn't argue, heading off to concerned applause from the stands.

Danisa got held up momentarily by the local press. I hung back, gathering my equipment along with Karyn's. After a while Ted hurried out to report Karyn thought she would be OK, and Danisa and I exchanged looks of relief.

She said, 'You will come to our house tomorrow, and we will start our interviews. After church. Two o'clock?'

I nodded. She walked to the tunnel that led to the women's dressing rooms. I watched her go.

Ted Treacher put a sweaty hand on my shoulder. 'Hey, friend, be careful. There are photographers around.'

I looked sharply at him, a pulse of paranoia thumping.

He chuckled. 'If they caught your expression, there's only one caption they'd use: "Old Gent Gets Hit by Cupid's Forehand." '

I started for the lockers. 'You're full of bull, Treacher.'

'Sure I am,' he chortled. 'Sure I am!'

I hurried through my shower and change of clothes. Outside, an attendant reported that Miss Wechsting had been in pain, and had been driven back to the hotel. Ordinarily I would have gone to the stands to watch some of the other fun. But, concerned about Karyn, I went back to the hotel myself, arriving far earlier than anyone could have anticipated.

At the desk they said someone had taken Miss Wechsting to the medics. As I turned away I was confronted by the couple from Kansas who had been in the coffee shop earlier. The Beamers, I remembered—Henry and Muriel.

'My gosh,' Henry groaned. 'We just heard about poor Karyn! Do you think she's going to be all right?'

'Too early to say,' I told them, fighting my impatience. 'I suppose we'll know—'

'Do you think there's anything we should do?' Muriel demanded anxiously. 'Henry, we should order flowers.'

He frowned. 'Well, we're on a tight budget here, honey. No sense going overboard.'

I left them there, debating flowers, and went back to the desk to ask that I be notified when Karyn returned.

Went up to my room.

Found the door standing slightly ajar.

Never suspecting—thinking it was the maid—I rapped lightly and swung the door open and took a step inside.

Whoever it was, he was quick. I got only a surprised glimpse of a dark

435

suit—a very large dark suit—before he finished crossing the room and hit me in the breadbasket. I doubled over and he hit me with something behind the ear, and that was all I knew.

New Belgrade
Michael Nariv swam up out of the ocean of pain and felt his heart lurch with a great thud as it resumed its beat.

Michael did not know his name any more. He did not know anything but the pain and a red glare and what he must not tell.

The voice came from a great distance. 'Do you hear me now?'

'I hurt,' Michael whined.

'Who do you work for at the American embassy?'

Panic blew through Michael. 'No. No.'

'You work for the CIA.'

'No.'

'Tell me the name of your CIA officer.'

The great engine of his heart shuddering, Michael only knew he must fight on. 'No!'

There was silence. Waves of new pain washed into his consciousness. I am doing so well, he thought. I will not tell. You will be proud of me, Mother. Then he saw the beautiful blonde girl in his mind, the girl he would meet after he got to America . . .

The voice came again. 'Give him more.'

Another voice said something.

'I don't care. Give him more. Now!'

The pain increased and increased and increased.

Missoula, Montana
On the theory that no one would predict such a move, Dominic Partek had doubled back. In Missoula he rented a room near the University of Montana campus. He used the name John Todd and told the landlady that he was a visiting professor. She gave him the address of a friend who had a garage for rent.

Ordering a late breakfast in a fast-food restaurant, he drank coffee that hit his stomach like battery acid. He looked at the cars parked outside. A young couple drove up, the man heavyset and bearded, the girl willowy, blonde. The pang of loneliness that hit Partek was devastating.

Since his earliest days at the Military Diplomatic Academy he had been a loner. The occasional woman only intensified his awareness that he was entering a life in which he could scarcely afford close ties. During all the years past he had told himself continually that his isolation was necessary for his work.

436

Since the profound shock of learning the story of his mother's death, and the fact that he had a sister he had never known, his perception of himself had changed. He saw now that he had spent his life alone because the only thing he had ever been able to trust was his belief in Communism—his work. It had provided an escape from the self-hatred planted by his father. You are alone, Dominic had thought, because you are worthless—your father always proved that. Without your patriotism you are a cipher.

He had gone to Paris and London and later to the United Nations. But the years in the KGB—life in America—had begun to erode his blind faith in the political creed that had sustained him. He had been so sick of all the secrecy, politics and suspicion. He longed for real freedom.

It was clear, however, that his associates suspected something. Otherwise his personnel file would never have been left out 'accidentally', for him to study. The facts about his family leaped out at him. Shocked, he confronted his superior.

Mikynian, the KGB resident in New York, had been icily controlled. 'Yes, Dominic. All true.' Partek's father, Mikynian said dispassionately, had not died of natural causes in Moscow. He had been shot while attempting a burglary. Nearly to term with her child, deserted, and now disgraced by her husband's fate, Martina Partek had moved to one of the poorest sections of Belgrade, assuming her maiden name of Naracic. She planned to write to her son when she was resettled. But she had had her baby prematurely, in a state hospital. She developed sepsis and died, never having written to her son. Her infant daughter was placed in an orphanage and later adopted.

Somewhere in the course of all this an investigative officer had found papers giving the real married name of Martina Naracic. The report was discovered years later during a routine rescreening of Partek's past. At that time the KGB had decided no benefit would come from telling Partek that he had a sister in Belgrade. The sister, of course, also knew nothing. But the information had slept in the files like a little time bomb, and when doubts about Partek surfaced, the complete dossier had been forwarded to New York, his place of assignment, for review.

'You are of great value, Comrade Partek,' Mikynian had told him. 'If you desire, we can arrange that you meet your sister, and have the reunion you have earned.'

'I . . . don't know. Her life would be disrupted.'

The resident had added as if as an afterthought, 'Your loyalty and devotion assure that she will always have safety and the friendship of the Soviet people.'

Remembering now, Partek relived the scalding bitterness he had felt then. They had betrayed him. Without a feeling of loyalty, Partek could no longer serve his KGB masters. But his sister was an unknowing hostage. If he defected, reprisals would be taken against her and her adopted family.

The persons from the CIA with whom he had been in contact were puzzled by his sudden remoteness. They applied pressure, asked questions. Partek told them part of it. They offered to try to get his sister out.

But it was too much. Partek felt he belonged with neither faction. He had to think. He had to have some time.

So he had run away. And was still running.

He was more confused and bitter than ever. He knew how valuable he could be to the Americans. If he chose to give them information, the Soviet espionage apparatus inside the US military would be set back ten years. But even knowing what he knew now, could he so betray the system that had reared him? He was torn by old loyalties, new hates.

He sat in the coffee shop, his hand around a cooling cup. The questions pounded. If she wanted to flee, could the CIA really help her?

He finished his meal, drove to the address given him by his landlady, and rented the garage. He hid the pick-up truck in it and walked back to his temporary home.

Belgrade

Thin rain streaked the windows of the American embassy. In the office of the attaché for cultural affairs, hiking his feet onto his desk, David Booth stared across the clutter of paperwork at his chief aide, Joe Mitchell. 'Then they've got him,' Booth, a thin, greying man, concluded.

Mitchell, younger, with close-cropped black hair, wearing the immaculate uniform of a marine major, nodded grimly. 'Nariv wouldn't just vanish like this otherwise. Poor Michael. The little guy really enjoyed the work.'

'I've sent a report,' Booth said, 'but I assume we press on.'

'Who maintains contact with Brad Smith?'

'The easy part is over. They may be watching him round the clock. Pull Paula. Let him cool until we get new instructions.'

'But surely the basic plan stays in place?'

'Oh, I think so. This has the highest priority. The boys at Langley haven't left any doubt of that.'

Mitchell stood. 'We'll need to contact him soon. Damn! I didn't think they would pull poor Michael like this.'

Booth's eyes were frosty. 'What's done is done. Nariv knew the risk. As for Smith, he won't even begin to tumble to what's really going on until the day after tomorrow, earliest, and by then it will be too late.'

New Belgrade

'Wechsting is out of the tournament,' Miloslav Fjbk said. 'And it could have been Danisa.'

'Or Hannah,' Geneta Lechova added quickly.

'Oh, Mother.' Hannah winced. 'Everyone knows it is Danisa who is the star. I am so much extra baggage.'

'No!' Fjbk growled, stricken by his error. 'You are important also, Hannah. You can win many matches. People love you.'

Hannah's eyes sparked. 'It is Danisa who is the shining star. I am a dismal little satellite, an orbiting cinder. Mother does not have to pretend otherwise. If I had hurt my ankle, as Karyn did today, it would be a sadness. But for Danisa—a catastrophe!'

'Hannah,' Leon Lechova said reprovingly.

They were in the tiny kitchen of the Lechova apartment, high in a six-storey building facing a tiny park in New Belgrade. It was stuffy, and Fjbk was sweating profusely, torn between his angry worry about an injury to Danisa and regret over his gaffe.

'The point,' he said heavily, 'is that both of you must be careful. Anything could happen. Karyn Wechsting is finished. I have it on the best authority. She will leave early in the week to return to the United States.' He scowled at Hannah. 'What if you or your sister had to retire from this tournament?'

'I would go to America on a holiday!' Hannah shot back.

'You could not,' the literal-minded Serb replied. 'Your passport is being reviewed, as is Danisa's.'

'And we will miss the US Open,' Hannah cut in. 'Why is that, Milo? I am as loyal as any Yugoslav citizen. I have never criticised the state in any way. Danisa also is totally loyal. Why have our passports been taken from us?'

'*I* should know?' Fjbk asked, at a loss.

'Is it possible that you have had this done to keep us in this country, to make us slave even harder on the practice court?'

'The idea is crazy! I know nothing. I swear it.'

'You are a cruel, mean, torturing man!' Hannah screamed.

'I only want what is best for you.'

'You only want my sister's body, you old liar!'

'Hannah!' Geneta Lechova cried.

'Apologise at once,' Leon Lechova ordered angrily. 'You will apologise, or you will not play in this tournament.'

Hannah went pale. The anger drained out of her. Her shoulders slumped. She looked at the floor. 'I'm sorry, Milo.'

'Leave the apartment,' her father said. 'We will talk later.'

Hannah rushed out of the kitchen. In seconds the hall door slammed, and she was gone.

Leon Lechova sighed. 'I am sorry, my friend.'

'It is good,' Fjbk told him. 'It is the competitive fire burning bright. I have pushed them both hard. Hannah is on edge. So is Danisa. They will go through the women's field like wildfire.'

'But for her to say something vile like she did! To say you . . . desire . . . Danisa. You, who are older than I am. Even to suggest such a thing is obscene.'

Geneta Lechova saw the flicker of deep pain before Fjbk made his dark face impassive again. So it's true. She felt icy foreboding in her veins. She had denied this possibility for what seemed for ever. She could not deny it any longer. My poor Danisa.

Fjbk gathered his practice notes and schedules and prepared to leave. 'We have centre court at seven hundred hours tomorrow morning. Each girl will warm up lightly for forty-five minutes. They will be brought directly back here in time for church.'

'It will be as you say,' Lechova said.

The two men, so different in appearance and stature, stared at one another, then shook hands. You are alike, Geneta Lechova thought with a pang. You would both destroy the girls to win your dream of number one ranking in the world.

But you are worse, she thought, again studying Fjbk's black expression as he lumbered to the door. You would inflict that gross, hairy body on my Danisa.

For an instant Geneta Lechova almost retched. My God, what am I to do?

HANNAH FOUND DANISA where she had expected, in the little café across the road from the park. Alone at a corner table, Danisa was having a salad with Turkish coffee.

'You won't tell?' Danisa said when her sister sat down.

'Never,' Hannah snapped. 'Waiter! Slivovitz. And a chocolate torte.'

Danisa bent double with giggles. 'Plum brandy and a torte? If Milo saw us now, he would kill us both.'

'Forget Milo. Hey! Are you looking forward to seeing this Brad Smith tomorrow?'

Danisa's face turned pink.

'Ha!' Hannah cried. 'Maybe you walk in the park, go talk somewhere nice . . . alone. Then maybe some kiss-kiss.'

'I couldn't do that!'

'Then how about turning him over to your sister, eh? Oh my!'

440

'Oh, Hannah,' Danisa gasped, fighting to control her laughter. 'How do we love each other the way we do, with the way Poppa and Milo try to make us compete all the time?'

'Because we are sisters,' Hannah said staunchly. 'Because *nobody* comes between us.'

Danisa looked at Hannah and started to cry.

'Hey! *Now* what?'

'Nothing,' Danisa lied, wiping her eyes on her napkin. 'I'm just tired. And the tournament—'

'Nobody is ever going to spoil our sisterhood, you hear me? Hey, we have always been special. Nobody changes that. I get mad at you, sure. Sometimes on the court I would like to tear your hair out.'

Danisa started laughing again, through the tears.

'How do you like that?' Hannah grinned, pleased. 'But listen. Let's enjoy this tournament, right? Let's defeat everybody. Then let's *both* get this Brad Smith to do some kiss-kiss. How would that be, fine?'

Sometimes, Danisa thought, she felt they were almost twins. And yet Hannah suspected nothing of the planned escape. Danisa wondered how this could ever work, leaving this woman who was so unlike her, yet so bound up in her spirit and soul. She was filled with sadness.

Not to be able to trust your own sister. It was almost the worst thing of this whole plan. But all of it had pain as a component. She was misleading her mother, her father. Her father was not a bad man. He was only an obsessed one.

Danisa wondered if she would ever have considered renouncing her homeland if she had not learned about her brother. That had come on top of other disillusionments and restless yearnings to make the decision possible.

Disgust with the excesses of the government would not have motivated her to leave permanently; hate for the bureaucrats and bunglers who kept her family in their tiny apartment while sycophants moved to better quarters—not even rage at that unfairness would have done it. Even the fire inside herself—the drive to travel the world and face the best, to *be* the best in women's tennis—might not have made her ready to slip away.

But all together they had been enough. She was ready and committed, despite the sadness.

MICHAEL NARIV LAY stripped naked on the bare metal table, intravenous tubing feeding silvery fluid into a vein in his left arm. Thin rivulets of blood drained from his nostrils, and his pain-shocked eyes stared unblinking into the brilliant overhead light.

'He is dead,' the lab technician said.

Major Ladislav Maleeva wiped sweat from his forehead. He hated work like this. Why couldn't they provide him with new and better drugs, which were faster-acting and less likely to kill the subject before you were through with him?

The technician looked stricken. 'I am sorry,' she said.

Maleeva forced himself to be charitable. 'It is of little consequence.' He walked out of the room.

And now, he thought, he faced the task of reporting everything he had learned to M. Y. Altunyan. The idea of reporting the disloyalty of one of his own countrymen to the sneering resident revolted him. In this case, however, the KGB was calling the shots.

Maleeva again wondered why, and had no theory.

He walked into an office where there was a secure telephone and dialled the number Altunyan had given him.

5

'Brad, let me call for a doctor.'

'Damn it, Karyn, I said no!'

Karyn Wechsting, leaning on the frame of the bathroom door to take the weight off her twisted ankle, surveyed me with an uncomprehending look. 'That lump over your ear is as big as an egg.'

I looked in the mirror and used a cool cloth to touch the spot where somebody had slugged me. 'I noticed.'

Struggling against my dizziness, I gently but firmly led Karyn back into the hotel bedroom. Hearing that I was looking for her, she had come to my room when she returned from having her ankle looked after. My door was ajar, and she had found me on the floor. Thank the Lord for a professional athlete's nerves: she hadn't screamed, but had knelt to examine me, and when she touched me I had staggered back to consciousness.

I sat Karyn on the couch and hung on to her hands, which were icy. 'So what's the verdict on the ankle?' I asked.

She moaned. 'Here I find you almost killed by somebody, and you ask about my ankle.'

I managed a dishonest grin. 'I'm feeling fine, and I don't have to play in the tournament.'

'Well, I'm not playing either. There might be a hairline compression fracture. Stay off it all I can for a week, they said. Then new X-rays back home.'

'You're out of the tournament? That's terrible.'

'Brad, I had Martina in the second round, and she would probably have whacked me.' But then Karyn's vivid eyes showed her competitiveness. 'I sure wanted a shot at her, though.'

'When do you go home?'

'Thursday. Ted is flying back with me in case I need help.'

'You can't get out any sooner?'

She shrugged. 'I'm here. I might as well watch part of the tournament. Assuming Danisa gets by Sabatini on Tuesday, she'll almost certainly meet Chrissie on Wednesday. I'd like to see that. But you're trying to avoid discussing this attack on you.'

'I must have walked in on a thief.'

'Then we'll call the authorities.'

'No. Look, I'm a journalist. I don't want any trouble. The chance to interview Danisa is the biggest break I've ever had as a tennis writer. I'm not doing anything that might mess it up.'

'How could reporting a robbery mess anything up?'

'I don't know. The militia might nag me with questions, cut into my time with the Lechovas.' I took her by the shoulders. 'Trust me. We'll talk later, OK?'

It took some doing. She didn't want to leave—she was afraid I would lapse into a coma or something if left alone. I finally talked her into giving me time to clean up and change my clothes, promising to meet her in the bar downstairs in an hour.

The dizziness was still with me, but I was functioning mentally. I searched the room, with the knowledge that electronic eavesdropping devices these days are so tiny they can be hidden anywhere. I didn't find any, but that didn't mean they weren't there.

The sealing wax hidden in the compartments of my miniature cassette recorder popped reassuringly when I opened them, so I felt reasonably sure it hadn't been compromised. As to finding bugs in my clothing, forget it; I knew all about buttons that transmitted over several hundred yards, and cloth tape stuck inside coat linings. I had to assume I was now wired for sound.

The fact someone had searched my room was sufficient proof that I was—at best—under general suspicion. My feeling grew that I had about as much chance as a germ under a microscope.

I washed my face, examined my bump again, took three Tylenol tablets, and went downstairs to the lobby. I examined my options. The boys needed to know about the break-in right away. I didn't feel quite spry enough to do the walk-past at the old cathedral as a signal, and there wasn't time to wait for Paula Bansky to contact me. So that put me back to the third option.

Using a public telephone in the lobby, I dialled the embassy. The girl who answered sounded Midwestern, which was reassuring. I told her, 'This is Bob Green calling for Mr Booth.'

'Sir, Mr Booth is in conference. May I take a message?'

'Yes. Please tell him I called. My name is Bob Green. *Green*. And the bridge game is at six o'clock tonight. Did you get that?'

'I'll give Mr Booth your message, sir.'

I hoped I wasn't panicking, giving them the green signal indicating a serious problem. 'Bridge game' was true enough: almost certainly I was under surveillance, and the meeting would have to be to all outward appearances not a meeting at all. The meeting site was obvious, since I hadn't specified, and we were operating on the rule of minus two, which meant we would meet at four.

It was a short walk to a nice little clothing store. I had intended to buy some Yugoslav slacks and shirts anyway. When I went back to the hotel, I was also the proud owner of locally produced underwear, socks and canvas shoes.

Karyn met me in the bar. She tried again to wrestle information out of me, but I played dumb. Her ankle started hurting a little worse, and she limped off, feeling out of sorts with me. I stayed for a time and reflected on how much I liked her. I thought of June and wished I hadn't. Then I drifted mentally for a while. I beat up on myself, telling myself how ridiculous it was to be entertaining vague fantasies about someone like Danisa Lechova. Then I went up to my room, changed into the new clothes that I knew didn't have any listening devices in them, and strolled out again, avoiding my friends from Kansas who seemed to live in the lobby.

By the time I was approaching Republic Square, it was exactly four o'clock. Before I was halfway round the plaza, gawking up at the equestrian statue of Prince Mihajlo, I spotted my man. It was Mitchell, dressed like a tourist, with sunglasses. He saw me and paused to open his Nikon and snap a couple of shots of the statue.

I walked near him, studied my guidebook. 'Somebody broke into my room, bashed me on the head. I think I must be blown.'

He nodded, pulled out a cigarette, lit it. 'Nariv got pulled in.'

'On what charge?'

'Don't know. Keep on with what you're doing. More instructions to follow.' He turned and walked off.

I walked round the statue in the opposite direction, then sat on a bench for a few minutes. When I got up to start back, I noticed a man standing on the far side of the plaza, leaning against a lamppost. The guy was thin and nondescript, but he had been watching me. When he looked away, he looked away too fast. I could only hope my contact had not been recognised.

I went back to the hotel. New effects of the blow to the head: I felt slightly nauseated and totally worn out. I sat in the café with Jimmy Connors for a while and wished I could see Danisa before tomorrow. My headache got worse. I went to my room, where I went to bed but didn't sleep. I worried about Michael Nariv and about tomorrow. I hoped my feelings of impending disaster were inaccurate. If we failed Danisa Lechova after setting her up, every important aspect of her life could be wrecked.

ON SUNDAY MORNING the time finally rolled around for my appointment at the Lechova home. I carted my microcassette recorder across the Sava into New Belgrade, to the apartment building where the family lived. They had just got back from church.

Hannah, wearing what I had learned was her trademark, hot pink, descended on me like a lost lover. 'Here he is! Oh, I thought you were never coming. We're having coffee and cake. You will join us. Then, do you *have* to interview my sister? Wouldn't you rather have an assignation with me in the woods?'

'Hannah.' Geneta Lechova, pretty in an ivory silk summer suit, was quietly disapproving. 'Some day a man will take you seriously. Then the trouble will be serious too.'

'Oh, I *hope* so.'

Leon Lechova walked into the tiny living room from the room next door. He coolly shook hands and offered me a seat. Danisa came out of another room. Her dress was *her* trademark colour, the pale blue that so accented her eyes. Unlike Hannah, who always wore her hair flowing loosely down her back, Danisa's was tied in her customary braid.

'Aha!' Hannah cried. 'You have kept on your church clothes to impress our guest.'

Clothes had nothing to do with how impressed I was. Hannah was pretty and fun. But when Danisa walked in, she made things go flip-flop in my chest. It was, I lectured myself, ridiculous.

Mrs Lechova went into the closet-sized kitchen, and soon the aroma of brewing coffee filled the apartment. She came back with baklava on a tray, and then with the coffee. As we ate, Hannah prattled and flirted outrageously. I tried to respond good-naturedly, but could not keep my eyes off Danisa. Hannah noticed and began to get irritated.

I tried to take control, telling Lechova, 'You have a nice place here. Convenient for a sports hall too.'

He nodded stiffly. 'We are comfortable.'

'Yes,' Hannah burst in. 'But after Danisa and I are world champions, the housing committee will move us to Dedinje.'

'Hannah,' Lechova growled.

'What is Dedinje?' I asked.

'It is where the very rich once lived.'

Hannah put in, 'Before the revolution did away with classes in our society.'

'Now, high Party officials and other very important people live there,' Danisa added.

'The old privileged go, the new privileged move in,' I said before I could catch myself. And instantly knew my mistake.

Hannah's eyes blazed with anger. 'There is no comparison,' she snapped. 'The people in Dedinje now have *earned* their privileges, through service to the state. The people who used to live there had done nothing—only inherited wealth from corrupt ancestors who stole from the peasants.'

I tried to recoup. 'I don't know your country very well. I'm sure you're right.'

But she didn't take criticism of Yugoslavia well, and she had already been teed off at my obvious preference for Danisa. She threw down her napkin, got up abruptly, and left the room, closing the bedroom door none too gently.

'I apologise,' Geneta Lechova said quickly.

'I should be the one to apologise.'

'Why?' Danisa asked softly. 'Because you spoke the truth?'

Lechova said, 'There will be none of that talk here.'

'But Hannah will be the first to wallow in the luxury of the rich if we are successful enough and the committee does assign us housing in Dedinje,' Danisa insisted.

'If we have earned such an honour—'

'Yes. We all will accept it. But Poppa, will we really have *earned* a great house because we can strike a ball across a net? Is that so deserving of high honour when compared with a man who has worked forty years in a steel mill or a mine, so that his eyes are seared nearly blind and his lungs are filled with dust?'

'That,' Lechova snapped, 'will be enough.'

Danisa flushed angrily, but lowered her gaze. In the silence Mrs Lechova extended a dish. 'Another cake, Mr Smith?'

I took one. I felt a little like Alice in Wonderland at the tea party.

After more coffee Hannah came back. She acted as if nothing had happened, then sailed out of the apartment to go and watch the qualifying matches. While Danisa was changing her clothes, and her mother was in

446

the kitchen, Lechova faced me in the living room.

'The slight disagreements in our family are of no importance,' he told me with his grim bulldog look. 'They will not be included in your story. My daughters are devoted and loyal. They compete in tennis, but they stand together as a family.'

'They're remarkable,' I agreed. 'Mr Lechova, I have no desire to drive a wedge between your daughters.'

He nodded. 'They are as loving as real blood sisters.'

The implication of that startled me. I showed it.

He said, 'Hannah and Danisa are adopted, Mr Smith. Hannah in nineteen sixty-five, Danisa a year later.'

'They look alike enough to be real sisters.'

'The state matches children to the parents whenever possible.'

'I see.'

'Nothing will ever divide our family,' he went on. 'We are loyal to each other, and nothing can change that.'

It was heartfelt. I didn't reply. If my mission succeeded, I thought, he would never get over the pain.

Danisa came back, wearing slacks and a sleeveless sweater. She had got over the tense scene with her sister and had that serene grace about her again. She perched on the edge of a chair. 'You said we would conduct the interview in another location?'

'I thought it might be easier in the park,' I said.

'I'm ready.'

We left the apartment, me carrying the recording gear again, and rode the elevator to street level. A lot of people were out strolling. There was an old-fashioned neighbourhood feel about it that I liked. In the park across the street children were everywhere, and the yelps and laughter would have ruined any recording. Danisa said there was a quieter park nearby, and we walked down a concrete canyon of apartment buildings towards it.

'Once we get to the park,' I told her, 'nothing gets said that might compromise our real business in any way.'

She looked puzzled. 'But if we find an isolated spot in the trees, who could overhear?'

I gave her the Reader's Digest condensed version of finding someone in my room, getting creamed, and suspecting electronic surveillance. 'There are a few things we have to talk about before the interview. Once we're settled, somebody could have a listening bazooka trained on us from a couple of hundred yards.'

She was pale, but she nodded gamely. 'We will take this turning and walk an extra two blocks to the park.'

'Danisa. Are you sure you want to defect?'

She didn't hesitate. 'Yes.'

'It's going to hurt your father a lot. And it might get very dangerous.'

'I love my parents . . . and Hannah. But now there is no choice. No choice at all. You know that.'

'Because they've restricted your travel to play tennis?'

She stopped and stared at me in disbelief. 'They send you here to help me, and you don't know the true story?'

'I'm a contact man. What I don't need to know—'

'I had thought much about the West, as I told you before. But I think, probably, I would never have left this way, permanently. But my *real* family—my real brother—is in America!'

Surprised, I stared at her. It began to make sense. 'You have a brother?'

'I knew none of it. Oh, my parents told Hannah and me we were adopted. Both orphans, they said, with no living family. I know they believed that. But someone knew otherwise.'

People were looking at us. I started walking again, and she fell in beside me. 'You'd better tell me all you know,' I said.

'I know now that my mother had a son, many years older than I.' Her voice was faint with emotion. 'My brother was already in the army when I was born. My father died. There was some . . . great disgrace. My mother came here, went back to her maiden name. I was born, and she died. I was adopted. My brother, far away, lost me. But someone, searching my real mother's things, found some document that said her married name— Partek.'

I chilled. 'Partek?'

She cut into my racing thoughts. 'A report was filed somewhere. And it must have lain buried and forgotten for a long, long time. But my brother became important. He was recruited by the Soviet KGB. I think he did much work for Russia as a spy.'

'Dominic Partek,' I said. 'Good Lord.'

'Lately, he wanted to defect to the West,' Danisa went on. 'It was then that the KGB let him learn about me. They hinted, I think, that if he showed disloyalty, I would never leave this country again and would be in disgrace. Unless I can get to the West, they can control him for ever by using me as a hostage.'

It all made sense now—why a Yugoslav tennis player rated all this attention. 'So,' I said, 'if we get you out, it makes it safe for Partek to come over to our side.'

'It will save his life,' she said.

The sprawling park was just ahead. I had to ask one more question, even though I knew the answer and didn't want to hear it.

448

'Who told you all this?'

'A man from your embassy.'

Ah, we were such wonderful guys.

Danisa was a pawn for us as much as for the KGB. They would use her to keep Dominic Partek in line. We would use her so that his treasure trove of KGB information could be ours.

But it wasn't quite that simple, despite my feelings of angry dismay. If Partek wanted to defect, I told myself, he had the right. If Danisa wanted to go to the United States and see him at last, what was wrong with that? On balance, we were in the right.

And then it occurred to me that right or wrong didn't make any difference: Danisa wanted out; I was here to help her; and I would have helped her now, regardless.

We reached the park, passed a flower seller, and moved under the shade of a maple tree, to a park bench with no one near it.

Danisa asked, 'What else must we talk about before we sit down?'

I forced my still aching head into the proper track. 'I don't know what procedure we'll use to get you out. I don't have instructions yet. I need a detailed timetable of your likely match times, other engagements, everything, for planning purposes.'

'Yes. I will write it tonight.'

I dusted off the bench, for her to sit down. 'That's it, then.'

She faced me, her eyes narrowed with determination. 'One more thing, Brad Smith.'

'Yes?'

'It is my decision. I trust you. I will do what you order. You are never to feel that I am being used. I am not. I am a free woman.' Her eyes shone with sudden tears.

Before I quite knew what I was doing, I pulled her close in a hug that ached because it felt so right. She caught her breath, and for a second she responded, electric in my arms.

We pulled apart awkwardly. I sat down, started my recorder. 'We'll begin at the beginning,' I said, brisk and businesslike. But my voice, even to me, sounded hoarse.

THAT DAY I USED ALL of one microcassette and most of another. Danisa was a wonderful subject—candid, bright, informed. She gave me some quotes about her father and her early tennis training that would have curled any Svengali's hair. It seemed a complicated family—Leon Lechova driving the girls with his version of perfection, Geneta Lechova quietly trying to protect and nurture them. We talked about Hannah, and the relationship between the two of them. She thought Hannah was funny. I thought Hannah was warm, volatile, loving, generous, suspicious, watchful, vengeful, cold. Take your pick.

We filled almost an entire tape with observations about tennis, other world-class players, Danisa's experiences and hopes for the future. After we had got well into it, I caught her asking *me* questions, turning my interview technique back on myself. It became an exchange, a mutual learning. She was one of the most caring and understanding people I had ever met. And through all of it there was the physical side: the pale glow of sunlight on her hair through the trees; the way she tossed her foot, moving one long leg; her hands, and the way she used them when she got excited about what she was saying; her eyes and her mouth.

Finally we stopped talking, and I turned the recorder off. 'Thank you,' I said.

We stood and walked out of the park. She turned and smiled at me and impulsively reached for my hand. We walked through the shade, holding hands like kids. Then I let her go.

I had no clear idea of how she felt. But the hours with her that day, and then the way she reached out to me, without artifice, changed me. Once before I had felt something like it, with Elizabeth. But I had been a kid then, and hadn't understood about pain. This time, I could stand back just a little and guess the likely outcome.

No matter about the likely outcome. It was too late to question my feelings, or control them. I would do anything for her.

We crossed the street and started back towards her home.

I forgot to check for surveillance.

COLONEL V. N. UBEZHKO, chief of the UDBA for the Belgrade-Surčin district, folded beefy hands over his desk blotter. 'Other than that Nariv was employed by the CIA, we know nothing.'

Facing his superior, Major Ladislav Maleeva felt deeper foreboding. First the pressure to cooperate with the KGB. Now this attack on his investigation. 'Who could have known Nariv would fight the drug so tenaciously?'

Ubezhko's fist hammered the desk. '*You* should have known!'

Maleeva bit his lip and fought for calm.

'Well'—Ubezhko sighed heavily—'it is done. What is your recommendation, if any, to maintain control of the situation?'

'We do not know what may actually be planned.'

'Maleeva! Kindly stop reviewing our state of ignorance and make recommendations!'

'Altunyan says this Brad Smith should be expelled at once.'

'Altunyan does not operate this office, or our government.'

'But our orders are to cooperate—'

'Those orders do not mean we let the KGB issue orders to us! This tennis tournament is a major event designed to encourage tourist visits and place the healthy, open nature of our society on display for the world to see. We will *not* smear ourselves in the eyes of the world by expelling Western journalists.'

'But,' Maleeva pointed out cautiously, 'if Nariv was CIA, and his assignment was as contact with Smith, then Smith—'

'Obviously is CIA, also. Yes.' Ubezhko sighed again. 'It appears he is in Yugoslavia to assist in the defection of Danisa Lechova. But we have no proof.'

'But if we can't expel Smith, Danisa Lechova must be placed in protective custody immediately.'

'We can't do that, you fool. We *fear* she plans to defect. But we cannot arrest her. She is in this tournament. The eyes of the world are on her . . . and us. She is a national heroine.'

'Then what?'

'Round-the-clock surveillance of Smith and anyone he contacts.'

'And what of Altunyan? He is persistent.'

'I,' Ubezhko said, 'will deal with Altunyan. He will not interfere. There will be no problem.'

THAT NIGHT HANNAH and Danisa went to bed at ten o'clock. It was routine on the night before tournament play: a light supper, early to bed. As was also routine, neither sister could sleep.

'Was he wonderful?' Hannah whispered across the narrow gap separating the twin beds.

Danisa smiled in the dark. 'He is a very nice man.'

Hannah chuckled throatily. 'He is a *man*.'

Danisa didn't answer. She thought of how she had felt in his arms that day. She felt warm and excited, just remembering it. The excitement mixed with her sadness and apprehension.

'Hannah?'

'Yes?'

Danisa felt driven. 'If you knew of someone who . . . was thinking about some disloyal act, what would you do?'

'Inform the authorities, of course,' Hannah said at once. Then, more sharply, 'Do you know of someone?'

'No. I was just thinking. During a tournament like this, there must be so many temptations for our younger players, the ones hypnotised by Western music, Western styles. It was idle speculation.'

Hannah was silent for a while. Then she said, 'If you have suspicions and lack the will to contact the UDBA, you will tell me. I will report anyone, Danisa. You will remember that?'

'I'll remember,' Danisa said, her throat dry.

'Good.' Hannah sounded relaxed again. 'Now tell me everything that was said today of a personal nature. Tell me if he tried to kiss you. I must know! Oh, if I have an opportunity like you had, I will throw myself all over him.'

Alexandria, Virginia
The telephone rang at Kinkaid's home. He answered it, immediately recognising Dwight's voice.

'We think he's in Missoula, Montana,' Dwight said. 'So get up there. We're telling Belgrade to move everything up.'

'On my way,' Kinkaid at once said.

#

The first Belgrade International moved into top gear early on Monday morning. Danisa and Hannah teamed up in the women's doubles at ten am. Sunlight filtered through the great dome of the stadium as four thousand people watched them take on an Italian pair.

The sisters started fast, going 4-0 up in the first set. They looked good. Miloslav Fjbk, sitting next to me in the first row of stands, put on his own show for the reporters.

'How do they look to you today?' an American asked him.

Fjbk made two fists. 'Hey, rush and crush, right? The officials ought to call out—what do you call it in your country?—the Humane Society, right? Is cruelty, put ordinary players in with my rush-and-crush girls.'

Pencils scribbled. Fjbk saw he was making a hit.

'My coaching genius is pay off,' he went on. 'Sometimes I think how tennis would be if the game had not had me. I taught them everything they know. No wonder I am now a celebrity, eh?'

Someone asked, 'Will the Lechovas meet in the women's finals?'

'Sure! No problem! Let me tell you something. Today we start a new era in history of the world. I, Miloslav Fjbk, unleash my rush-and-crush girls. Get that down.'

Danisa and Hannah won the first set, 6-1, and Fjbk's repartee became even more outrageous. In the second set, however, Hannah started hitting some shots long, and Danisa's serve faltered. The Italians, with nothing to lose, began hitting harder. It went to a long tiebreaker before Danisa hit a winning crosscourt volley between her opponents for a 10-8 victory.

452

The players headed for the tunnel to the locker rooms. Fjbk, whose good humour had faltered late in the match, hurried to meet them at the tunnel. I went with him.

We found that Danisa and Hannah had already gone inside the locker room. We waited with a few press people. I went to the water fountain against the far wall, and Fjbk followed me.

'Damn you,' he rumbled, blocking my way as I turned from the water. His eyes were smoky, and he looked a different man from the one who had clowned for the press upstairs.

'What's the problem?' I demanded.

'You saw how they played in the second set! They lost concentration. They would not have done that if you had not been with them yesterday, distracting them, filling them full of nonsense.'

I found it interesting, how his English improved when he was not performing for someone. 'Fjbk, don't lay their poor play on me. I'm just doing a job.'

He punched a finger into my chest. 'Stay away from them for rest of tournament. I must refocus their attention. Danisa's timing is bad. She must improve before tonight.'

'Fjbk, you can't keep her in a bottle all her life.'

'I have waited all my life for this one. She is my chance.' He punched me again. '*Nobody* is going to take her from me. I have my champion, who will stay with me always.'

'What happens when she meets a man and falls in love?'

'Don't talk about that! I control her. She is mine. You hear?'

His eyes were crazy. I would be glad when we were out of here.

THAT AFTERNOON DANISA was edgy too.

She sat with me in the stands while Hannah played Bettina Fulco, of Argentina. In the first set Hannah struggled a little, making several unforced errors. But in the tiebreaker she got herself together and won it, 9-7. Danisa leaned back to talk.

'You have given them my schedule?' she asked.

'It was passed to my contact person an hour ago.'

'When will it happen?'

'That isn't certain yet.'

'Why are we waiting? Why do we just *wait?*' The tension made her voice crack slightly.

'As soon as I know something, you'll know something, Danisa. These things have to be orchestrated very, very carefully. Everything is being arranged. It's going to be all right.'

She sighed, said nothing.

I wished I felt half as confident as I had just sounded.

I was still brooding about Michael Nariv's disappearance. It meant arrest. Which meant interrogation. I harboured no illusions about the UDBA: if they had him, they would break him. Then they would know—at least—that I was here under false colours.

One had to assume I'd been blown. Yet whoever was calling shots at the US embassy seemed intent on pressing on. It was almost as if they wanted the operation to go down the tubes.

I needed something to happen.

It was about to.

THAT NIGHT DANISA and Hannah both had singles matches. Danisa went on first, at seven pm, against the Czech, Zrubakova. The stadium was packed with Belgrade sports nuts anxious to see their heroine take her first step towards the championship. I sat with Ted Treacher and Karyn Wechsting.

Danisa cruised to a 6-0 victory in the first set. She served an ace to open the second. It was simply no contest. Her opponent was a fine player, and she worked hellishly hard to win the second game, but Danisa took the third to love and broke her again in the fourth.

'When she's like this,' Karyn murmured, 'I wouldn't want to play her.'

'Nobody should have to play her,' Treacher added.

The rest of the set was a slaughter. Some players might have extended things by trying impossible angle shots, but Danisa was kinder. Dropping a game or two by trying the impossible is insulting, really, and she knew that. She was relentless. Her game was fluid, graceful, powerful, with impeccable court tactics.

There is a beauty in tennis that comes to you sometimes when you're playing. Movement and countermovement become part of an unfolding dance that can even envelop the knowing spectator. Serve becomes the opening lead in the duet. And the ball comes back, and your body and spirit are one with it and even with the movement of your opponent across the net. Body, mind, ball, racket, court, opponent, angles, lights, all become part of something very difficult to define. You can hate your opponent and want to whip him, yet love him at the same time for being part of this with you, making it possible. Danisa's concentration was so total, her movements so right, that she wove that kind of spell.

The match was over in fifty-five minutes. Danisa walked off with her arm over her opponent's shoulders. She looked up at us in the stands—her parents were just behind us—and sent a joyous smile that would have melted an iceberg.

There was time to move along a few courts to see Hannah's match.

Hannah walked over after her practice serves.

'Hi, lover.' She grinned, towelling her face. 'Hey, if I win in straight sets, we will have time to go park in your car, huh?'

I nodded towards the far tunnel entrance, where Fjbk was re-emerging after walking Danisa to the showers. 'Not with Dick Tracy around.'

She grimaced. 'And here come Momma and Poppa down the stairs behind you. Oh, boy, our romance hasn't got a chance!' She turned and strode to the sidelines, where the referee was waiting to give the contestants a final word before play. The Lechovas slid into two seats across the aisle. Fjbk joined them.

My two biggest problems relating to Danisa's escape were her sister and her coach. One or the other was with her almost all the time. I wondered how my pals at the embassy were going to get round these two.

Hannah won the toss and elected to serve. She was not as smooth, not as overpowering as Danisa. But the Fjbk style was there, and she won in straight sets in less than an hour.

I expected Danisa to join the family to watch her sister. I think the Lechovas did too, because I saw them turn and look expectantly up the steps a number of times. But Danisa didn't show up. Even Hannah glanced up hopefully after the match, and her face fell a little when she saw Danisa wasn't there.

When Hannah headed for the lockers, her parents and Fjbk trailed after her. I went along too, stopping to loiter in the concrete tunnel with friends and relatives of several of the women players.

Hannah finally came out. She hadn't showered or changed yet. She walked over to her waiting parents, who had been talking with Fjbk. I joined them.

'Danisa's not inside,' Hannah told us. 'She told an attendant that she had a headache and was going to walk home to get some fresh air.'

'Home without us?' Lechova said, his face darkening with worry. 'But she has never done such a thing!'

That was when I started to worry.

'But,' Hannah said, 'the attendant walked her to the players' gate, gate sixty-four. He saw her leave.'

Both parents looked stunned. Fjbk muttered something about questioning the guard and pushed into the crowd in front of the locker room doors.

Leon Lechova said, 'Geneta, you will start home. I will wait here for Hannah. We will join you as soon as possible.'

I left them there and headed for the players' gate, feeling badly scared. Maybe somebody had seen where Danisa was heading for when she left, whether anyone intercepted her.

Unfortunately, gate 64 was not normally manned. It was at the end of a long, poorly lighted concrete tunnel, well off the beaten path. When I got there, the tunnel and gate were deserted.

I looked around, thinking that I might find a clue. Just inside the gate were two cabinets, one containing a house telephone, the other a fire alarm box and fire axe. Except for a poster advertising the tournament, there was nothing else around.

I opened the gate a crack and peered outside. The doors opened onto a ramp leading up to a dark corner of a parking lot. I propped the gate open with my tournament programme and climbed the ramp. I saw nothing helpful: cars gleaming under sodium-vapour lights, some screening trees.

Danisa had not planned a getaway. She would have told me if anything was afoot. She could not have played so flawlessly if she had known anything out of the ordinary was imminent.

Then somebody must have nabbed her.

Deep in worried thought, I descended the concrete ramp, swung the gate door open, and reentered the tunnel.

Standing there waiting for me, breathing fire, was Fjbk.

'What have you done to her?' he rasped. 'Tell me!'

'Oh, swell,' I muttered. I thought I had seen him looking crazy before, but at the moment he looked like a total maniac. His eyes were wild, without focus. He crossed the distance between us with a squat, powerful grace that said bad things to me at the instinctive level. I tried to back away, but the tunnel wall stopped me.

'What have you done with her?'

'Fjbk, I don't know anything about this!'

'She never did such a thing before. You must be responsible.'

'Fjbk!'

He swung at me. I half blocked the blow with my left arm, but his fist crashed into my throat with a force that knocked me sideways, seeing stars.

I did not go all the way down. The wall propped me up.

He charged right after me. His fist hammered into my midsection, doubling me over, and he simply grabbed me by the shoulders and threw me about six feet up the tunnel, where I hit the floor with shocking impact.

Scrambling, I managed to get to my knees, when he hit me in the face, and red stuff sprayed in all directions. He bear-hugged me and, muttering hoarse Serbian obscenities, started hammering my skull against the wall. He was completely out of his head.

Panic gave me strength. I got a knee into his groin and twisted free. I was one step away from him, when he slammed his right arm down onto my shoulder, buckling me again.

456

'You will die,' he said, panting.

I managed to get in a weak left hand. It made him crazier. He knocked me back against the wall, hammering with both hands. And for the first time I began to feel primitive fear. He meant it when he said I would die. He was going to beat me to death.

'Fjbk,' I managed through a mouthful of blood, 'I don't know anything about this—'

A paralysing right hand crashed into my head, knocking me to my knees. I felt him pick me up bodily. He threw me again.

This time I hit the wall near the entrance. Right beside the cabinet with the fire axe. I broke the axe out of its bracket. Almost dropped it because my hands were slippery from my own blood. Fjbk skidded to a stop, his eyes suddenly wide with fear.

That look in his eyes gave me a jolt of strength I didn't know I had in me. And I went a little crazy myself. I swung the axe.

I missed by a mile. The axe powdered the concrete wall, sending chunks and dust everywhere. But I was trying. So help me, I would have taken his head off. Everything inside me was yelling for revenge. Every once in a while something happens to us to let us know we aren't all that far out of the cave. Part of me was insanely exultant, seeing the idiot back off.

The next swing of the axe almost winged him. I was yelling something, but I didn't know what. Next I took out one of the low roof lights, and shards of glass popped from the exploding bulb.

I swung again. He danced back another step. Then, as I kept coming, he turned and ran.

I stood there, axe over my shoulder, staring at the suddenly empty tunnel. What do you know? I thought. Amazing.

Which was when my burst of adrenalin began to run low. I dropped to my knees with my head down, bleeding all over everything. A minute or two passed.

I heard running footsteps approaching.

The maniac was coming back.

IN THE DARK BACK SEAT of the dirty Volkswagen, Danisa Lechova tried breathing deeply, but her heart was crashing about in her chest. She wriggled around, trying to get more comfortable in the clutter, which included her leather racket case and blue duffel bag, along with suitcases that didn't belong to her.

This was the moment she had dreamed of and dreaded, and she would leave her country with nothing but her rackets and duffel.

In the front seat the heads of Henry and Muriel Beamer were outlined against the lights of an oncoming car. The car passed with an instant's brightness that made Danisa flinch. Then the dimness of streetlights again.

Danisa's shocked feeling of unreadiness had been intensified by the fact that it was these two—the silly American tourists who had been bothering everybody for autographs—who were to take her out. But there wasn't any doubt.

She had thought they wanted another autograph when they met her at the door of the dressing room. Beamer had chattered about that for a minute or two, so that even the bored security guard drifted out of hearing. Then Beamer had said softly and distinctly, 'Your best effort was a star-spangled success.'

For an instant Danisa stared at him in mute surprise.

Muriel Beamer's smile was soft and seemingly brainless, as usual, but her eyes were flint. 'We're the ones, Danisa. This is the all-American sweepstakes. Now.'

Both statements contained what the man from the embassy had called—what?—verbal bona fides. The Beamers had just repeated them to perfection.

'I thought . . . Brad Smith . . .' Danisa fumbled.

Beamer took her arm in what looked like a casual gesture. His fingers bit painfully. 'The folks with the camera are right outside,' he said loudly enough for the guard to hear. 'We'll just go get the picture took, by golly, and you can get right back.'

The guard ignored them. They went down the tunnel and out to the edge of a parking lot. There was no one else there.

'Where is the car?' Danisa asked, confused.

Beamer said briskly, 'You're to go back inside, be seen again by the guards, use the back security tunnel, walk two blocks east, to the lighted statue of the partisan fighter.' He studied her keenly. 'You know where that is?'

His voice and demeanour were so different, so chilly and efficient. Danisa stared. 'Yes. Yes!'

'Get inside. Be seen again. The security tunnel. Walk. We'll be in a dirty yellow Volkswagen.'

Danisa started to turn towards the gate.

'Nothing more than you usually take home after a match,' Muriel Beamer said.

Danisa was still in a daze. 'Yes,' she mumbled, and hurried back into the arena.

It had taken only minutes to leave the complex. She walked to gate 64 as if leaving routinely. Then, after the guard had gone, she had doubled back in the direction she really wanted to go.

The security tunnel was for use by militia in case of trouble ana was presumably sealed off. But somebody had neatly broken the lock bars at both ends; Danisa went through. Once in the street, she had hurried, and the Beamers, as in a dream, had been there.

Now they had been driving for a while—she was too wrought up to know how long—and they were on a bumpy side street, with the yellowish lights of the road to Surčin just ahead.

Henry Beamer pulled onto the highway and headed south. Muriel looked over the seat back at Danisa. 'Are you all right?'

'Yes. I'm just confused. I didn't expect it so soon.'

The older woman nodded. 'If you need something for your nerves, I have something.'

'No!' The idea scared Danisa. They might give me anything, she thought. 'I'm fine.'

'We've got a long drive tonight,' Henry Beamer told her. 'If you're hungry, there are sandwiches under my seat.'

'No. Nothing.' Danisa was still struggling to get orientated. 'I thought Brad Smith was to make the arrangements.'

'That's what you were supposed to think,' Beamer said.

'He deceived me? It was all a trick?'

'Don't worry about him.'

Danisa reeled inwardly. Brad had lied to her, she thought. She had trusted him. She had thought he was so wonderful. But now everything had changed. It was just a job, deluding the stupid little peasant girl. And I thought he really, really liked me.

'We'll be turning west in a few miles,' Beamer told her. He was driving at a steady speed. 'We cross the border at Trieste.'

'They'll have missed me long before we can reach Trieste,' Danisa said, worried. 'And if they search this car—'

'We cross in the car. You don't.'

'I don't understand.'

'There's a farmer near the border who has a dairy. Every morning he takes his cartload of big milk cans across to sell. *Big* cans. It'll be a squeeze, but you'll fit inside one nicely.'

Danisa felt her panic rise. 'How will I breathe?'

Muriel Beamer said, 'There are air holes. You won't be in the can very long. We'll give you a pill to help you relax.'

'And we'll be raising hell with the guards at the same time,' Beamer added cheerfully. 'They don't let you take Yugoslav money back out, and we've got a pile of it.'

Muriel Beamer studied Danisa's expression. 'Not very elegant, dear. But it will work. And you'll be on your way.'

They had neared the outskirts of the city. Up ahead were flashing yellow lights. Beamer slowed abruptly.

'What is it?' the woman asked tautly.

'Some kind of roadblock,' he muttered, braking.

'They must be checking licences, permits,' Danisa said. 'They do that a lot around the city.'

Beamer got the VW onto the shoulder and cranked the wheel sharply, making a U-turn and heading back the way they had come. 'Can't risk it. Let me think.'

They drove a mile or two in silence. Headlights of a car behind them shone faintly into the passenger compartment.

'We'll try the other highway,' Beamer said. He sounded grim. 'Once in the country, we'll just have to drive faster.' He glanced back at Danisa. 'No sweat. It's just an added irritation.'

'Have you done this often?' Danisa demanded. 'Are you vastly experienced?'

Both the Beamers chuckled at that. Muriel said, 'Bless your heart, honey, yes. Look at us. We're old folks. You don't get these wrinkles without a few memories.'

'That's what we call it,' Beamer said. 'Building memories. Lots of fun.' Then, before Danisa could react, he added, 'We're being followed.'

Muriel twisted in her seat to look. 'That van back there?'

'He isn't gaining and he isn't falling back.' Beamer's voice had a cutting edge. He removed his foot from the accelerator. The following headlights got nearer for a moment, then fell back.

Beamer increased speed steadily until the engine began to whine. The lights behind them remained at the same distance.

'That tears it,' he said. His face was heavily lined by worry. 'Danisa, listen. I'm going to take the highway straight back into Belgrade. Once we get there, I'll drive around, take a couple of corners. When I stop, you have to hop out fast. You understand?'

'Do you pick me up later?'

'Not tonight. I stop. You jump out and take your stuff. I'll pick a spot where you can duck into a doorway or something. Which you do the instant you're out of this car. Got it?'

'Yes. I think so . . .'

'You'll be contacted. Once you're clear of this tail, you get yourself home, say you were strung out and wanted a nice long walk to relax. OK?'

'OK,' Danisa echoed, dismayed.

'You got money for a cab home?'

'No. Hardly any.'

Muriel dug a wad of bills from her purse. 'Honey, I'm sure sorry we

didn't get this dance after all. But you be ready. We'll be back in touch.'
She smiled brightly. 'Right?'

'Yes,' Danisa managed. Her mouth was desert-dry. Brad Smith, she
thought, had known of this all along. He had lied all the time. And to set
up this flimsy plan, so easily thwarted. Nothing had gone right. Her
chance for freedom had gone.

Beamer pressed the accelerator, driving as fast as he dared. Ahead was
the Sava, with the city sprawl growing bright around them. They sped
across the bridge.

A light was changing as they approached an intersection, and people
moved out onto the pedestrian crossing. Beamer slapped the horn,
changed down, and scooted through a right turn. People scattered, yelling
angrily.

At the next corner they turned left and at the next right again. Danisa
was getting dizzy. She saw they had moved into a decrepit
neighbourhood—old secondhand shops and deserted office buildings and
several taverns, with shadowy figures on the dark pavements.

'Get ready, Danisa,' Beamer said tightly.

He turned again. There were warehouses, an old church, a building site.
Beamer sawed the Volkswagen round another corner and pulled up in
front of a drinking club.

'Out,' he snapped.

Danisa grabbed her rackets and duffel bag and climbed out onto the
pavement. Muriel Beamer hauled the door shut, and the VW leaped from
the kerb.

Danisa scurried for the doorway. As she reached it the VW went round
a corner half a block away, and a van bounced round the corner to her
left.

It shot past, and she had a glimpse of blue uniforms inside.

She leaned back against the rough stone wall of the building, hearing
her heartbeat in her ears. The sidewalk was deserted, and she didn't think
anyone had seen her leave the car. But everything had failed. She was
shaken, scared, and filled with rage at Brad Smith. He had tricked her.
Then he had abandoned her. How he must have laughed at her! She hated
him.

She didn't want to walk far lugging her tennis gear. She would be
recognised, and there would be hard questions to answer. She saw a
cabstand across the street and a cab parked at it.

She crossed the street briskly. If the cab driver recognised her, he gave
no evidence of it. She told him an address that was three blocks from her
parents' apartment, and sank back into the dark rear seat. Then the silent
tears came.

Browning, Montana

In the motel room the telephone rang for the first time in days.

'Yes?'

'Sylvester?'

'Yes.'

'Instructions. Missoula. Call on arrival.'

'Yes,' the man called Sylvester said, and hung up.

Twenty minutes later he was on the road, driving fast.

So, my old friend, he thought dispassionately, it was a good trick, turning back west. But we have you.

Missoula, Montana

Dominic Partek had made a mistake. It was a very slight one, involving his truck. But bad luck magnified the error.

He knew there was every chance that his pursuers had had time to observe his lifestyle in Browning, including the description and licence of his pick-up truck. That was why he had replaced the number plates and rented a garage.

Unfortunately for Partek the divorcée who rented the garage to him was dating a Missoula policeman.

'Yeah, I rented it, finally,' she told him the same night. 'This weird guy wanted it for his beat-up Chevy pick-up.'

'Why do you say he's weird?' the policeman asked casually.

'His accent's the slightest shade off, somehow. And he told me he's a visiting professor at the university. I know that's a lie. His fingernails were all black round the cuticle. Like you get when you're a car mechanic or something.'

'That is interesting. You got an extra key to the garage?'

'Sure. Why? Do you think the truck's stolen?'

'It never hurts to check.'

The garage was opened, and the registration number of the truck, along with serial number and description, was run through the police computer. The truck did not check stolen, but the computer crosschecked against other information and gave the duty captain a number to call. When Washington responded, the information was noted with interest by a close department observer who reported regularly to a friend in Detroit. This was how the man called Sylvester was notified within hours of the computer check.

The divorcée, however, was a great talker. When Partek visited the garage later to check his battery and add a quart of oil, she sailed out of the house and chatted with him.

'Nice truck,' she told him, rubbing a finger through the grime on the

462

rear mudguard. 'Dirty, though. My boyfriend said you could still have salt up under there from last winter.'

'When did he see the truck?' Partek asked casually.

The lady looked blank. 'I guess I just mentioned it was dirty.'

Good try, but Partek knew better. She had already boasted about her boyfriend being a cop.

Several hours before the Continental flight with Kinkaid on board landed at Missoula, Partek left town on a bus.

Belgrade

In the room at the Metropol adjacent to the one occupied by Brad Smith, Major Ladislav Maleeva chain-smoked cigarettes and awaited reports. The two UDBA technicians manning the eavesdropping equipment sat silent, bored, nothing to do. In the room next door it was quiet, nobody at home.

Except for the heavy smoking, Maleeva showed no sign of his inner turmoil. He had no idea what had happened. Danisa Lechova was missing. Did this mean her defection scheme was in motion? If it was, then Maleeva's career was finished, because he had guessed wrong on everything, and his lavish attention to the American, Brad Smith, had been a disastrous waste of time.

Feverishly he reviewed the things he knew: the authorities were certain the Lechova girl would defect if given a chance. Brad Smith had been contacted—clumsily—on arrival, by not one but two agents of the CIA. Altunyan, using information probably from the highest echelons of the KGB, felt certain Smith constituted the major threat of Danisa Lechova's escape.

So it had to be Smith. But Danisa Lechova was missing, and Smith had been seen since her disappearance.

Maleeva sighed. He felt driven to prove to Altunyan how efficient he and the UDBA really were. So he had been working night and day, and now perhaps he had been proved a fool.

Danisa Lechova had to be found. This had to be a mistake— perhaps the temperamental erratic behaviour of a high-strung athlete. Danisa had never been known for such flights, but the Belgrade tournament had put more pressure on both Lechova women than they had ever known. So there was still hope.

There had to be hope. Maleeva could not have failed. His record was perfect: no mistakes, no failures of loyalty or devotion. And this case was to mark him as a man ready for even greater responsibility, perhaps work as a supervisor in headquarters.

Assuming he succeeded.

464

7

Luckily for me the person I heard pounding down the corridor from gate 64 was not Fjbk coming back for round two.

It was Ted Treacher, who had heard what was going on and guessed that I might have headed for the gate where Danisa had last been seen. Partway down he had encountered Fjbk, boiling up the tunnel in the opposite direction with blood on his shirt. From that point Ted had come running.

'Brad!' he said, squatting beside me. 'What the hell happened to you?'

'A truck?' I muttered through my handkerchief as I tried to slow down some of the bleeding.

He didn't get the joke. 'I'll get help.'

I grabbed him. 'No!'

'No! *No?* You need a doctor, man.'

'Help me to the nearest men's room, Ted. Just give me a hand, OK? Do what I ask.'

Leaning on him, I limped to a rest room and did what fixing up I could do at a basin in front of the mirrors. Once I got the bleeding stopped and some mopping-up done, the evidence was not as bad as it should have been. Some of my teeth felt loose. My nose made an unhappy crunching sound when I moved it with my fingers. I was going to have a black eye and a lot of swelling round my mouth. But overall I was reasonably intact.

'Do you want me to call the security guards now?' Ted demanded as I turned from the basin.

'No, thanks. I want a ride to the hotel in your courtesy car.'

'But you've been beaten up. Why not call the cops? Did Fjbk do this?'

'I fell down.'

'You're lying.'

His concern was touching, but I just didn't have time. 'Ted, one of these days I'll explain. But if you want to help me right now, just drop me at the back door of the hotel and forget this happened.'

He gave me a hard sideways look, almost protested again, then he capitulated. He drove out to the Metropol in silence and, looking deeply frustrated, left me at the rear entrance.

Inside the hotel, I did some further patchwork on my face and changed my clothes. Some talcum masked the darkening facial bruises. Nothing short of a false face would hide the swelling. Feeling like something that had been shot out of a cannon, I found a taxi and rode to the Lechova family's address.

465

There were two UDBA operatives stationed at the doorway to the apartment building when I arrived. They looked as worried as I was. The fact that they were here was good indication the UDBA had no more idea of Danisa's whereabouts than the rest of us.

Which, I thought, probably meant that the most likely explanation for Danisa's disappearance was *us.*

Right now she was almost certainly on her way out of the country. The boys had swung into action without bothering to tell me about it. Which shouldn't have surprised me, really. I had already begun to suspect that I had been set up to act as a diversion. They had wanted the UDBA to suspect me.

At least she was getting out, I lectured myself. And I had done my part. Nobody had promised to let me in on everything.

Anyway, the UDBA folk let me go up to the apartment. Leon Lechova, his wife and Hannah were in the small living room, along with Fjbk. Fjbk stiffened visibly as I joined them.

'What happened to you?' Lechova demanded.

'I fell,' I said. 'What news of Danisa?'

Lechova shook his head and resumed pacing in front of the window. 'Geneta came home. There was no sign Danisa had been here. The authorities have been notified. We know nothing.'

I glanced at Fjbk. 'I wish I knew something,' I said.

His sullen eyes showed his disbelief. But there were both uncertainty and worry there too. He was smart enough to see that I probably wouldn't have been here if I knew anything about Danisa's disappearance. He also had to be wondering why I hadn't turned him in for assault. Fine, I thought. Let him stew.

No one spoke for a while. Traffic sounds and voices came in from outside. My ears began to ring. My body hurt all over. I figured my only remaining job on the mission was to act dumb until Danisa was out safe.

Hannah left the room. She came back with a cup of tea and put it down with a clatter. 'Where *is* she?' she cried.

Geneta Lechova patted her daughter's arm. 'We must try to stay calm, Hannah.'

'Calm! How can we stay calm when—'

'They said Danisa left the stadium alone, of her own free will. There may be some explanation for all this. We must not start thinking the worst. It may be well.'

It was a nice speech, and a brave one. But the haunted look in Geneta Lechova's eyes said it was a lie.

Conversation lapsed again. The situation seemed unreal. Part of that came from my headache and my proximity to Fjbk. I picked up an

466

English-language magazine and tried to read it.

An hour passed. Then there was a commotion downstairs. Lechova leaned far out of the living-room window and turned back with fierce elation.

'It's Danisa!'

Fbjk sprang to his feet. Hannah whooped and clapped her hands. Geneta Lechova hugged herself. Lechova rushed out and in a moment was back.

Danisa was behind him. She had her racket bag and duffel as if nothing had happened and she had just strolled out of the locker room. But her shocking pallor told a different story.

My relief was so intense my knees got weak. Whatever had happened, she was safe.

'Danisa!' Hannah screeched, and then did her hysterical number, grabbing Danisa, twirling her round, and making her drop her duffel and racket bag. 'Where have you been? We have all been insane with worry. Oh, Danisa, if something had happened to you, I would have killed myself!'

Danisa gave her father and mother a half-frightened, contrite look, and me a glance I couldn't read. 'I'm sorry. I was upset tonight. I decided to take a walk to calm my nerves. And then I walked much too far. I had no money for a cab and had to walk all the way home. I'm fine.'

'But why didn't you tell someone?' Hannah demanded. 'I thought everything! I thought, Some terrible mugger, with yellow teeth and a knife, has taken her into a park and slashed her body. I thought, A car driven by a crazy man has run over her in the street and—'

'You just . . . walked?' Danisa's mother cut in, her face the colour of flour. 'But you never do things like this, Danisa.'

'I was overwrought,' Danisa said. She seemed deeply contrite. 'If I had just thought ⸴. . . But the pressure made me break.'

'You're all right?' her father demanded. His eyes burned with bleak, bewildered anger. 'Nothing more happened?'

Danisa dropped into a rocking chair near the kitchen door. 'What can I say except how sorry I am?'

All of this had been in English—they made it a point of etiquette to speak English when I was in the room. Now, however, Leon Lechova said something long, strained and angry in his native tongue. Danisa reacted by flushing with mortification, and said something I couldn't begin to follow.

Lechova snapped back, bitter. Fjbk rumbled a few words that sounded like an attempt to calm things. Lechova turned fiery eyes on him and let loose a string of language that could only be an order to mind his own blankety business. Fjbk flinched as if he had been slapped, and headed for the front door.

'Milo!' Danisa called huskily.

Already in the doorway, Fjbk glowered back at her.

'I am sorry, Milo, to have worried you too.'

Fjbk locked glances with Lechova, then was gone.

Danisa said, 'I wish you had not attacked him, Poppa. He was afraid for me.'

'We were all afraid for you. You must never do anything like this again!'

Her words were almost inaudible. 'I won't, Poppa.'

She had given me only the briefest glance.

Lechova got to his feet, still glaring daggers at her. Then her stricken expression got to him. He crossed the room and took her in his arms, hugging her convulsively. 'You girls,' he groaned. 'You two girls!'

Hannah started crying with relief. Danisa, her face wet, disengaged from her father and put an arm round Hannah. The two of them trooped out of the room and through the door of their shared bedroom. It closed behind them.

Mrs Lechova looked at me. 'You have been kind to stay with us through our worry.'

'I thank you for letting me be with the family at a time like this,' I told her.

'Will this . . . be in your story?'

'This is private. I wasn't here for any story.'

She studied me, motherlike. 'I did not think you were here as a journalist tonight,' she said, and went into the kitchen.

I hesitated. Surely Danisa was going to come back out and say something to me?

Lechova stood by the door, obviously waiting for my departure. At that moment Danisa came out again. Without looking at us, she snatched up her gear and started back to the bedroom.

'Danisa?' I said.

She turned on me with eyes that brimmed with rage. 'I have no quotations for you!' she snapped, and went out of sight.

I went down alone in the elevator. I still had no idea what had happened.

Had I been wrong in guessing that there had been an attempt to get Danisa out? Obviously, if a try had been made, it had failed. What did that mean? And why was Danisa blaming me?

Downstairs, I met the UDBA man, Maleeva. He spoke stiffly and went into the elevator I had just vacated. So now his interest was overt.

468

Everything seemed to be getting harder and harder.

I caught a taxi back to the Metropol. I hurt all over. I wondered what else could go wrong.

We never guess bad enough.

THE MAN WHO FLEW in to Belgrade from Moscow early on Tuesday morning was named Sislinsky. He was tall and gaunt, with a perpetual stubble on his cheeks. He and M. Y. Altunyan conferred in the quiet room on the second floor, the one with lead screening and a white-noise generator to thwart electronic eavesdropping.

'I have every reason to believe that a defection attempt was aborted for unknown reasons last night,' Altunyan said. 'I believe Smith arranged a departure with other case officers, but bad luck or timing intervened. I believe he will make another attempt.'

'I note your concern. However, I have brought additional case information that may alter your perceptions.' Sislinsky related Moscow's suspicion that Smith was a decoy to divert attention from some other plan to get Danisa Lechova out of Yugoslavia.

'If this is true, it changes everything,' Altunyan said.

'The turning back of the couple identified as Beamer is additional evidence,' Sislinsky told him.

'And my instructions?'

'The subject must remain in Belgrade. Your orders are to ensure that she cannot make good on her defection schemes.'

Altunyan thought about it. 'By whatever means I find appropriate?'

'She is to remain alive.'

'Of course. But beyond that proviso?'

'Use your best judgment. And do whatever is necessary.'

Langley, Virginia

It was before six am when Dwight and Exerblein reported to Simon Bixby's office and found they had walked into a buzz saw.

Bixby was a fleshy man of fifty, a close adviser and aide to Director Jeremy Malcomber. He was a quiet, controlled administrator. But when Dwight and Exerblein walked in to respond to his emergency summons, Bixby was in a towering rage.

'What the hell is going on?' he rasped.

'About what?' Dwight asked. He figured he knew, but it never hurt to ask.

'In Belgrade! In Montana! Last night I get a call—Partek has vanished again, this time in Missoula. So I come into the office to try to assess the damage. In the Partek file I notice a cross-reference number. I dig it out.

It's a Belgrade embassy file. I see a message in it saying one of our agents there'—fuming, Bixby stirred his papers—'Nariv, Michael Nariv, got picked up by the UDBA and then showed up at the state morgue with a rigged-up death certificate. Then comes another message, saying our agents had to abort their operation last night and asking are there any further instructions.'

Bixby paused, an angry facial tic leaping under his eye. Dwight stood still and said nothing. This was bad enough already.

Bixby resumed. 'And I don't know what's been coming down. I haven't been informed. We've got a serious operation in motion over there, the Russians are messed up in it, and a couple of supervisors here are playing Cowboys and Indians and not bothering to tell anybody what's going on.'

'Every decision and action has been memoed,' Dwight said.

'Yes,' Bixby exploded, 'and buried in a damn file and put into this ocean of paperwork. You could report the Second Coming and nobody would pick up on it for six weeks!'

Dwight kept quiet. Beside him, Exerblein was like a statue.

'What were you guys thinking of?' Bixby went on. 'You can't mount an operation like this in a closet. You should have kept us informed. The days of this kind of freelance stuff are gone!'

'I thought you knew,' Dwight said, with absolute honesty. He was amazed. He had forgotten—again—what a labyrinth this place could be. He had really fouled up.

'And what's this report from Collie Davis?' Bixby asked.'What's all this about Brad Smith? What was in your mind? You can't just set up a trusted employee—a US citizen—this way!'

Exerblein stirred. In his colourless voice he said, 'Smith volunteered to work on contract.'

'I don't care how he came on board! You're fixing to have him killed or imprisoned, and you're liable to have an international incident, when we're trying to improve relations with those people. The plan won't work anyway. It's ridiculous.'

'What do you want us to do?' Dwight asked.

'Stop playing Wyatt Earp. Get Kinkaid back from Missoula. Cancel your little adventure in Belgrade.'

'What happens to Danisa Lechova?'

'As far as we're concerned right now, she's had it. She stays put. If that changes, I'll let you know.'

Dwight had a bad taste in his mouth. 'And Partek?'

'Unlike you, Dwight, I think I'll go higher up with what I know and let my superiors make that decision. Of course, at the moment we've lost him again, anyhow. Maybe the KGB hasn't. We'll see.'

'And Smith?'

Bixby's eyes became opaque. 'Smith? I don't know anybody named Smith. I don't think you do, either.'

8

Thanks to Fjbk's brutal artistry I didn't get much sleep Monday night. The application of a lot of ice kept the facial swelling within manageable limits. But worry kept me awake as much as the pain did. I badly needed to know exactly what had happened to Danisa. And why she was angry with me.

Good boy that I was, I did not use any of my emergency telephone numbers during the night. I couldn't call the situation a life-threatening crisis. On Tuesday morning, however, I was awake and pacing at dawn. I put a small potted plant out on my ledge and waited. Nobody showed up across the street, and no one called my room with a wrong number. So I would have to fume a while longer before they acknowledged my request for a contact.

At five past eight Karyn Wechsting knocked on my door, took one look at my face and came in like an avenging angel.

'You look like hell,' she said. 'Ted told me about it this morning. Have you called the police?'

'No.'

'It has to be reported. Fjbk could have killed you!'

'Well, he didn't. And having him arrested would just cause nasty publicity.'

'Have you seen a doctor?'

'No. I'm OK.'

Karyn's eyes narrowed. 'All right. What's going on here?'

'Nothing. Forget it.'

'You mean he attacked you for no reason?'

'No. Of course not. He's jealous.'

'Of *you?*'

I felt my face flush. 'Silly, right?'

'I didn't mean . . .' Karyn began quickly. 'Brad—'

'Look,' I cut in, tired of it. 'I've spent some time with both Hannah and Danisa. Then Danisa pulled a vanishing act last night and took a long walk alone. Fjbk was upset when no one knew where she was. Somehow he blamed me. So he had a go at me.'

'Long speech for you,' she said. 'Only other time I heard you make a speech like that, you were lying through your teeth.'

'Karyn, I never lie, and that's the truth.'

She sighed bitterly and headed for the door. 'I'm not through with you yet.'

'Come back often,' I replied cheerfully.

She left. I fretted. I hoped she wasn't going to create new problems for me.

Thirty minutes later still no signal in response to my flowerpot. I reverted to plan two, and walked to the Church of the Assumption, but there was no one to meet me. I waited an hour. When I went back to my room, I walked in to a ringing phone.

'Brad Smith speaking.'

'Brad? Is that you?' It was a voice I had never heard before. 'Brad, this is your Uncle Carl.'

My pulse rose so much that I felt it. 'Uncle Carl,' I said, 'how are you? How are Aunt Margaret and the family?'

'Brad, I have bad news. Aunt Margaret is very, very sick. As a matter of fact, the doctors have abandoned all hope for her recovery. They say there is nothing more to be done.'

'They have really abandoned all hope?' I said.

'Yes, I'm sorry to say that is correct.'

I stayed on the line another minute, inanely ad-libbing sad remarks about my nonexistent Aunt Margaret to my nonexistent Uncle Carl. I told him I would be home soon, and then I hung up.

And stood there, looking out of the window, absolutely stunned by surprise and disappointment.

THERE WAS NO OPPORTUNITY to speak to Danisa before her early match with Gabriela Sabatini. I sat in the stands with Karyn Wechsting and pretended to jot a few notes, primarily to keep myself from having to maintain a running conversation.

I didn't expect Danisa to play very well after whatever had happened to her the night before. Right.

The match started with Danisa double-faulting. That set the tone for the early play. She moved round the court like a pretty blue robot, ponytail bobbing as she continually got just out of position or failed to anticipate. The only thing that kept her in the first set at all was that Sabatini, for some reason, was also having a bad day. Sabatini won the first set, 6-4.

'She isn't playing well,' Karyn observed.

'She hasn't gotten into it yet.'

'You're not much into it, either.'

'Thinking about the story,' I told her.

472

Karyn studied me, and her questions were clear in her pretty, vivid eyes. 'You absolutely refuse to talk about it?'

'Talk about what?'

'OK, Brad. You get mysteriously mugged in your hotel room and won't call the police. Then you get mugged by Fjbk and won't report that, either. There's obviously something weird going on, but you play dumb. Fine, Brad! I'd like to be your friend. But if you say no, then it's no.'

I felt uncomfortable, wishing I could open up with her. 'Karyn, I appreciate it. Better we just let things stand.'

'Sure?'

'Sure.'

'OK.' She didn't like it a bit.

We returned our attention to the match, more or less. But my thoughts were miles away.

THERE WERE ALWAYS prearranged signals to order an abort. For a meeting at a café, for example, you might find your contact fiddling with an unlit cigarette, which could mean, Keep going, don't approach. A magazine, or lack of one, could abort a drop. A chalk mark on the side of a certain utility pole or a spilled drink in a crowded bar might signal possible surveillance. In the case of Belgrade, the Uncle Carl signal meant simply that whatever I had been doing, forget it: my part in the operation was scrubbed. As of now, I could finish up whatever I needed to do for the writing assignment and head home.

In some circumstances I would have accepted the order and thought little about it. This time it hit me hard.

First—let's be honest—was the way I now felt about the lady in blue out there on the court in front of me. I have not done a good job of defining the feelings that seemed to flow between us every time we were close. Maybe those feelings can't be defined. But there they were. Her strength and intelligence were part of it. She responded to me with quickness and sensitivity. And there was a sense of reliability, of straightforward openness, that was unique to her. I felt crazy every time I looked at her too—her hair, her eyes, the liquid movements of her body. There just wasn't a lot more to be said about it.

I didn't hold out hope that the personal thing would ever get beyond its present stage. I knew that the gulf between our backgrounds, and the age difference, logically made my feelings absurd. That was all right. I had intended to help get her out and enjoy the good feelings that left me. As for the rest of my feelings, disappointment was something I had learned to handle. But helping her had become very important to me, and I hated to be robbed of that satisfaction.

Another reason my abort order rankled was that I had the unpleasant feeling that it meant the whole operation had been cancelled. And that, quite aside from my personal involvement, was simply a gross injustice.

Karyn's squeal of pleasure brought my mind back to the match, where Danisa had just hit a rifle shot down the line. 'She's paying attention now. She's really something!'

Danisa had a frown of concentration now, and her movements had become smooth and purposeful. Whatever had been bothering her was out of her mind, and she was in the zone, playing the match, not knowing much else. She won the second set.

There are people who show some aspects of their character in their play. Connors used to be like that when he was down in a match and suddenly began playing with a controlled ferocity, as if he were saying, Win or die, this is my game, so here I come at you. And did anyone ever watch Chrissie prepare to serve, late in an exhausting match—see that total determination—and fail to realise that this was a lady to contend with in any situation?

Danisa's character was overwhelming in the third and deciding set. She was everywhere. Every forehand smoked. There was no wasted movement, no error. Sabatini did not go quietly. But she went.

I told Karyn, 'I'm going below decks and see if I can get a few words with her.'

Karyn eyed me. 'Tell me something, Smith,' she said bluntly. 'Have you got something going with that girl?'

'You must be out of your mind. I'm a news hack, that's all.'

'I wish you trusted me, Brad. I really do.'

I stood up. 'Karyn, I certainly wish your suspicions were accurate. Nothing has happened between Danisa and me, although I'm not above trying to seduce beautiful young women—something to keep in mind, incidentally, for your own protection.'

She coloured, just a little, around all her freckles. 'Promises, promises,' she said wryly, and I grinned and left the stands.

Down below, the usual collection of onlookers, press people and guards jammed the tunnel. Danisa came down from the arena with Fjbk. In the crowded shoving, with people calling questions and applauding in the background, she started past me.

'Danisa,' I said. 'When can we talk?'

The look she gave me was quick, spiteful. 'You are a liar.'

'What?'

'I know now,' she bit off. 'You were never going to help me. It was a lie. All a lie.' Then, before I could respond, she whirled away through the doors of the locker room.

I took an involuntary step after her. Fjbk shoved me back. A security guard grabbed my arm and made sure I didn't go any further. Fjbk hadn't missed the bitterness of our exchange. His expression was fiercely triumphant. I felt like I had been shot.

ON TUESDAY I SAW part of Pat Cash's match between trips to the Church of St Mark. Nobody showed up to meet me there, either. I was getting desperate. Finally, a few minutes before five o'clock, I called the embassy from a payphone and gave the woman a seemingly innocuous message that told Booth I needed to see him *now* in the designated pastry shop off Slavija Square: emergency.

Again nobody.

They had dropped me. Period.

One of the endless press-celebrity parties was on for six pm at the Hotel Yugoslavia. I went, on the theory that I might see Hannah there. Her second match of the day was over, and tournament officials were pressuring the athletes to grace as many social functions as possible. I hoped she might shed some light on why Danisa suddenly seemed to think I had rabies or something.

Reebok, the party's sponsor, had supplied a spicy apple punch along with champagne, spritzers and slivovitz. Everybody seemed pretty happy but me. I talked a bit with Tony Trabert, and then Hannah came in, her mother at her side.

Hannah looked freshly scrubbed and gorgeous, wearing a hot-pink pantsuit. I approached confidently, expecting, I guess, her usual effusive flirtatiousness.

'Hello, Hannah,' I said. 'Congratulations on a fine match.'

'Swine!' she spat, her eyes ablaze and her entire body coiling as if she were about to strike. 'Never speak to me again.'

A few people nearby heard her outburst and turned in surprise. I didn't know what was going on. 'Hannah—'

'My sister was happy, just fine, until you came along. I don't know what you do, Mr So-called Journalism Man, but Danisa is now sad. She won't tell me nothing. You have taken advantage of her and broken her heart, and I think you are nothing but a pig.'

She turned to flounce away through the crowd, hips swaying in angry rhythm. I looked at Mrs Lechova. My face was hot.

Geneta Lechova was very pale and solemn, but the eyes with which she studied me were neither angry nor full of hate. In her simple grey dress she looked almost as young as her daughters, and austerely handsome. 'I am sorry for Hannah's outburst,' she said quietly. 'We can get punch, do you think? Then perhaps we can find a quiet place to talk.'

'Yes.' At least she didn't seem ready to kill me, like everybody else in the family.

We got the punch, then in the hotel corridor found a small abandoned alcove with two red velvet chairs. I was strung tight. 'Mrs Lechova, I know Danisa is outraged at me, and so now is Hannah. I need you to know I didn't do anything.'

She nodded and said calmly, 'I understand. However—I am guessing—Danisa must be very disappointed and shocked. Does her disappearance and return last night mean you will not be able to help her to leave our country?'

My surprise must have been clear on my face. Before I could think of something to say, she added, 'Mr Smith, I know my daughters. I know Danisa has been unhappy. Tennis is her life, and she has not been allowed a passport to play out of our country since New South Wales, last February. Now . . . this matter out of the past.'

I didn't reply. I instinctively liked this woman. Trust was another matter.

She said, 'You must get her out, Mr Smith.'

'What?'

'Do not pretend. I am not a fool. You are here to arrange it.'

I gave up on pretence. Maybe she could even help. 'My role was very small. I didn't know any of the details.'

'Was?' she repeated. 'You are no longer involved?'

'I don't know what happened last night, but it changed everything. My instructions seem to be to go home and forget it.'

She remained calm, in control. Behind the scenes Geneta Lechova was perhaps a greater force than anyone else.

She said, 'My heart breaks to think of her leaving. I think it may be a very great mistake. But we talked. She told me everything. About her brother. Which neither my husband nor I knew anything about. Everything.'

Again I didn't know how to respond. Instead of panicking, this amazing woman was ready to help Danisa go. I owed her honesty in return. 'Mrs Lechova, it may be that the idea of helping her escape at this time has been abandoned.'

'She must go. She will never be free here. Knowing what she knows now, her heart will break. And there is the added problem of Milo.'

I misunderstood. 'He can be kept in the dark.'

'No, no. I mean that he is a problem for Danisa now. He wants her. My husband does not see this. He does not want to see it, because Milo is a great coach. I see it and my blood runs cold.'

'Your husband thinks a lot of him.'

Her face became stone. 'Leon is a good man. He loves us very much.'

It was one of those statements that didn't seem to be finished. I said nothing, just waiting.

'But he does not understand about Milo. He does not understand that a young woman must live her own life—must grow up and leave. And her parents must do the hardest thing they ever did, out of love for her—let her go.'

'If he gets wind of any of this—'

'He will stop you, of course. Notify the militia. And as much as she loves her sister, so might Hannah. She is hard, my Hannah. Very patriotic. And that is good. But is the state supposed to stand in the way of a citizen's happiness? I think not.'

'I wish I could promise to do something,' I said. 'But Danisa won't even see me.'

'She will. I have convinced her. Tonight is the match against Zina Garrison. But tomorrow there is only the one quarterfinal match, against your Chris Evert, in the evening. In the morning I will say I am taking Danisa to look at a dress, to take her mind away from worry over tennis. Leon will like that.'

'And we can meet?'

'Yes. At your hotel. Between ten am and eleven.'

'I'll be in the coffee shop.'

She nodded, close to tears. 'I must find my headstrong Hannah now.' She stood and walked briskly towards the ballroom.

As I started back to the party I saw Paula Bansky, dressed to the nines, ahead of me. Her eyes met mine for just an instant. She turned back the way she had come.

Startled and angry, I hurried after her. She half ran through the lobby, swaying on her high heels.

'Paula!' I caught her by the arm just as she was about to rush out through the revolving doors.

'Release me!' she hissed.

'I need to know what's going on,' I told her.

She pulled free. She looked angry and badly scared. 'I know nothing. Get away from me. I'm to have nothing to do with you.'

'I have to see them. Tell them to react to my signals.'

'Do you want me arrested?' she demanded, and bolted through the glass doors, which revolved wildly in her wake.

I went to the stadium. It was impossible to keep my mind on my alleged job as a journalist. Paula's reactions left no doubt. I had been cancelled out. The sensible thing was to accept it and go home like a good little boy.

I knew I wasn't going to do that.

ZINA GARRISON'S MORNING MATCH had been a killer, and that night she came out looking stiff and tired. Danisa, on the other hand, looked grim, but fresh as a daisy. I watched her put Zina away, 6-3, 6-1, in a match that required only fifty-four minutes.

I left the arena and took a cab back to the hotel. I went straight upstairs, headed for my room. As I turned down the corridor I saw the briefest flash of a blue police uniform just beyond my door. It was a militiaman, carrying a tray of sandwiches into the next room.

It was obvious I was still being bugged, and the electronics boys had moved into the room right next to mine. It struck me almost as funny. Spying on me at this point was like placing a bet on a horse after it had dropped dead at the far turn.

I went straight to bed, but my damaged ribs hurt and I slept badly again. I was glad when daylight came. I showered and dressed.

Downstairs, at ten twenty, they arrived, Geneta Lechova in a coffee-coloured dress and Danisa in a brief sundress of her trademark blue. She looked tired and tense, but marvellous.

They sat down, and Danisa gave me a wan, cautious smile. 'My mother says you do not know anything of what happened the other night with the American couple.'

'I don't even know what couple you're talking about.'

'They have been everywhere, asking for autographs, mingling with everyone. The man slightly loud, foolish, the woman with frilly dresses—'

Light dawned. 'The Beamers?'

'Yes. They met me in the arena. They knew the code words. I left with them in a Volkswagen for the border, but there was a roadblock; then we were followed and ran fast, and Mr Beamer stopped the car. I jumped out, they went on, a police van went by, I made my way home.'

The Beamers! But it made sense. They had been too touristy to be true in the first place.

I said, 'No wonder you were scared. Did anyone see you?'

'No. I am sure of that.'

I reached across the table and took her hand. 'Danisa, I didn't know an attempt was going to be made. I've been completely in the dark. Uninformed.'

She frowned. 'But I thought you were here to help me. The interviews . . . to cover it up for you to be of assistance.'

'I was to be a contact man, as I told you. Nothing more.'

Her lip trembled. 'I thought you had—what is it called?—set me up.'

'You weren't the one who was set up, Danisa. My people haven't been straight with me.'

Her eyes were alive again. 'I am glad you did not abandon me.'

478

'I would never do that.'

'What, then, are your instructions for me now?'

'We're going to get it straightened out,' I told her. 'Hang in there. Just give me a little more time.'

Her expression changed in a way that cut to my heart. She said, 'I will do what you say.'

New York City

Dominic Partek's flight landed shortly after dawn. The bus had taken him from Missoula to Helena. He had caught a flight to Denver, another to New York. Now he was back where he knew the territory, where they would never expect him to hide.

Partek took a taxi to Park Avenue South, had breakfast at a cafeteria, and walked to his bank. He was getting low on funds.

Skin prickling with the sense that someone was watching, he walked out with two thousand dollars in his pocket. He started south on foot. A block or two later the feeling of surveillance became so intense that sweat ran out of his pores.

It cannot be.

Partek waited at a traffic light. He looked up the street in the direction he had come. In a second he burned everyone into his memory. The light changed. He crossed the intersection, walked the next block, turned right, went through a wooden tunnel round a construction site, turned left. At the next corner he looked back again.

And felt his blood chill.

There were two of them. A thickset man his own age, wearing a dark suit, a quarter of the way down the block. On the other side of the street, almost opposite him, a younger man, blond, dressed in a delivery uniform and carrying a small parcel.

There were five branches of Partek's bank in Manhattan. So they had gone so far as to watch all of them.

Partek walked faster, weaving through thick pedestrian traffic. He had to assume the worst, that they were KGB. He had to shake them off now, before they had people on all sides of him.

Partek turned into a shabby-looking store whose windows were filled with cameras. It was long and narrow, with a back partition and a doorway. A swarthy man behind the counter asked, 'Can I help you?'

His fear dancing, Partek ignored the question, walked towards the back door and pulled it open. It led to a narrow hallway. 'Hey!' the man called. 'You can't go back there!'

Partek rushed down the hallway to a steel rear door. He pulled the security bar out of its cradle on the door and pushed hard. He stepped out into a trash-littered alley. A truck driver was carrying a box inside another building.

Partek ran.

The driver was just coming out as Partek went into the building. Partek pushed past him into a corridor. He ran through to the front door and out onto the street: street vendors with scarves and watches. Partek stepped off the kerb, looking for a break in the traffic.

A quick movement at the next corner, north, caught his eye: the blond man, skidding on the sidewalk as he looked up and down—his head coming up as he spied Partek.

Partek took a step into the street. Three of the lanes coming at him were yellow cabs. He raised his hand and waved frantically.

The centre-lane taxi braked, swerved to a halt. Partek got in. The driver pulled away and Partek looked back. The blond man was standing on the kerb, angry, hands on his hips.

Partek leaned back against the grimy seat. His heart lurched in his chest like a wild thing.

Belgrade

M. Y. Altunyan was ready to take decisive action.

Recent activities by the American, Brad Smith—trips about the city and calls that had to be in code—had refortified his fear that Smith could yet be the major player, and that a new and complex scheme to slip Danisa Lechova out of Yugoslavia was in motion. For the next few days the only safety lay in making sure Danisa could not travel anywhere. But she could not simply be abducted. Strong-arm tactics might be revealed, poisoning Soviet-Yugoslav relations.

Subtlety, then.

Altunyan's first stop was a store that sold chemical products. He purchased an organic phosphate insecticide that the owner assured him would control pests in his garden.

The owner sternly reminded him of the dangers of applying the material close to food products near harvest time. 'Please remember, phosphate products are very powerful.'

'Yes. Thank you. I will remember. Goodbye.'

Altunyan's next stop was the large hospital nearest the sports arena. The young doctor met him in the cafeteria.

'You will be on emergency duty this evening?' Altunyan verified.

'Yes,' said the doctor, whose name was Bulganik. He was pale and very frightened. He had many relatives in the Soviet Union. 'I can arrange the schedule.'

'Good. And you understand exactly what is to happen and what you are to do. There must be no slip-ups of any kind. You remember what you are to say?'

'Yes. Yes, I remember everything.'

The doctor was pitiful in his eagerness to please. Altunyan gave the wretch a sombre look designed to intimidate him further, got up without another word, and left the hospital.

New York City

In his new rented room in a shabby residential section of Queens, Dominic Partek read a story in the *Times* about the first annual Belgrade International. The story led with Danisa Lechova, 'headed for a show-down with America's Chris Evert'.

There was a blurred laser photo of Danisa. Partek studied it. His sister was so young. And despite the quality of the photo he could tell she was beautiful. His heart ached, seeing her.

He wanted more than anything to see her in person, to put his arms round her. She was a gift from the God he had always pretended he did not believe in. He had lived his adult life thinking he had no family anywhere. Now, here she was, in his beloved Belgrade, destined for greatness, according to all accounts.

He was shockingly tired. But the near miss this morning, coupled with this story of Danisa, made sleep impossible. He had to know if the Americans were any closer to getting her out. He could not run much longer. Someone would spot him again.

If the KGB located him now, he thought, they would have him murdered. But if he sought CIA protection, the KGB would know. And Danisa would suffer. First would come news that she had decided to 'retire' from competition. Next, that she had accepted an appointment at some remote gymnasium. Her passport would be permanently revoked. She would never be heard of again.

Partek tried to tell himself that such a fate was not so bad. The life of a professional athlete was very short anyway. She would probably do good work in some little town, meet a nice young man, settle down, accept her lot in life, have babies . . .

Coward! a voice screamed inside Partek's head. Liar!

He was disgusted by his own weakness. Had he sunk so low that he would sacrifice his young sister for a few years of freedom—in hiding, under an assumed identity—for himself?

He told himself there was more than his own life involved. The network he had organised to penetrate missile defence secrets of the United States was among the most powerful espionage operations of the century. He knew it was still fully functioning, with an efficiency and breadth that would shock American counterintelligence. If he defected, more than forty crucially placed spies would instantly be rounded up. A hole in American security as serious as the Rosenberg case would stand revealed.

Partek knew that to defect was the correct moral choice. His disillusionment had been growing for years. The KGB's cruelty in exploiting his innocent, long-lost sister was just the final blow.

He reverted again to the American promises. Could they deliver? He had to know.

He thought about it for another hour or so, pacing his room.

HE SIMPLY HAD TO TAKE a chance and find out where things stood.

Leaving the rooming house, he walked down the street to a public telephone. He dialled a Manhattan number.

A woman's voice answered after the first ring. She gave the number. 'May I know who is calling, please?'

'This is Mr East. I must speak to Mr Martin at once.'

There was the slightest pause, during which the woman might have held back her gasp of surprise. 'Please hold.'

The line clicked to music for what seemed an eternity. Then Martin's familiar voice came on. 'Hello? Can I help you?'

'This is East. And every hound must have its day.'

Martin's tone changed. 'Where are you? Are you all right?'

'I am nearby. We must meet. I must know what has happened about my acquaintance across the ocean.'

'I understand. Let me think. . . .' Martin seemed to fade out for a few seconds. 'OK, you want to meet here in Manhattan?'

'No, no!'

'Uh . . . all right, how about this? There is an inn in Chappaqua. You know where that is? Upstate?'

'That sounds better. I can find it.'

'The inn is called Darlington House. Check in there. Use the name Archibald. We'll meet you tonight.'

'Not tonight,' Partek corrected. Desperately as he wanted the meeting at once, he had to find a secondhand store and get some clothes no one could recognise. He had to rent a car. And his brain was dying for lack of sleep.

'Tomorrow night,' he said.

'OK, friend. That's fine. You're all right?'

'Yes. But I *must* know about the things we have discussed. Perhaps then I can . . . come over.'

'I understand. We will have an update for you.'

'Please.' Partek hung up.

IN HIS BEEKMAN PLACE QUARTERS, Charles Martin placed an immediate high-security call to Dwight at Langley.

Dwight was excited.

So was Constance Hazeltine, the divorced mother of two who had answered Partek's call to Martin. But she waited until after work to call her friend.

His name was Bill Adwan. He was a member of the permanent United States diplomatic staff at the UN, a translator. He had been Constance's lover for almost two years. She worshipped him. It would not have occurred to her to question his 'other duties', involving investigation of security risks. She told him about the telephone call from Mr East, and what she had heard—at hair-raising personal risk—about the meeting to be held in Chappaqua.

Adwan told her she was the most wonderful person in the world, and this information would be of great interest at the highest levels of US government. Adwan immediately made a call of his own to his contact. But that person was about as far away from any branch of the US government as it was possible to go.

9

'I suppose,' Karyn Wechsting said on Wednesday afternoon, 'you still haven't reported Fjbk's attack on you.'

'That's over with,' I told her.

She gave me a disgusted look. 'When do you go home?'

'My flight is Sunday night.'

'Well, Ted and I are reconfirmed for tomorrow. I think I'm more than ready. This ankle isn't getting any better, and if Fjbk has another go at you, I'd just as soon not be around to see the results.'

'Karyn, there's no problem.'

But of course there was a problem.

They had ignored another meeting signal in the morning, and my Jack Black telephone call to the embassy—the ultimate escalation—was not answered either. So after the visit with Karyn I took the most circuitous route imaginable to the embassy.

The marine guard viewed me suspiciously, the receptionist was cold, and when I finally got to see David Booth, he was livid.

'Can't you understand the message?' he asked hotly. 'You have been pulled out. It's over.'

'Fine work,' I told him. 'You meant all along to blow my cover and set me up.'

483

'Nobody set you up. Just get out of here.'

'Drop dead. Even slow learners finally see the pattern: the phone call on a bugged line, tipping the bona fides; Michael Nariv being so obvious. You intended me to be picked up by the UDBA security system from the time I got off the plane.'

'Not true,' Booth said stiffly, without conviction.

'The idea,' I went on heatedly, 'was for the Beamer couple to do the deed while I had everybody looking the wrong way.'

Booth sat down again behind his big walnut desk. His eyes sagged with something between contempt and fatigue. 'The Beamers' attempt failed because of a fluke. That can't be tried again. You're blown—and if you weren't before, you probably dragged half the UDBA down the street behind you just now. We're out of bullets, friend. When the bullets run out, you quit.'

'Does that mean Danisa Lechova is being abandoned?'

Booth just stared at me.

'You can't abandon her,' I said. 'She'll never get out after this. You told her about her brother. She made a tough decision. You got her hopes up. Now you just say, "Hey, forget it"?'

Booth's mouth tightened. 'I'm sorry, Smith, but the best course now is to prevent further losses. Maybe something will be done at a later time.'

'And that's that?' I said bitterly.

'That,' he said, 'is that.'

So I felt like hell when I walked into the stadium for the Evert match. Nobody was going to help, and after tonight's match I was going to have to tell Danisa that I was powerless.

It didn't make me feel any better, sitting in the stands with Karyn and Ted Treacher, when Danisa came out for the warm-ups, obviously searched for me with her eyes, and lit up when she saw me. Her wave—despite all the pressures—was pure joy.

'Oh my,' Karyn murmured ironically.

The capacity crowd, after the hot day, had made the domed interior stifling. Both Danisa and Evert began to perspire heavily. I expected a hard and taxing match. The soft clay was ideal for Evert's patient, backcourt game, and everybody in the press knew how much she wanted another crack at Martina or Steffi.

After the warm-up both players towelled down. My mind shunted to what I was now defining as The Problem: how was I going to live with myself after abandoning her? Letting her down was what rankled. Thinking I would never be with her again after the next day or two was what hurt.

Karyn Wechsting nudged me. 'Are you paying attention?'

'Absolutely,' I lied.

The players had gone back on the court, Evert to serve. She waited for the crowd to quiet. She looked across the net at Danisa, blue skirt swaying as she shifted from foot to foot in anticipation. Then she tossed the ball up, and the match was on.

From the outset it was close. Evert held serve at love, and Danisa returned the favour. In the third game Danisa worked the score to deuce, but Evert held through two long seesaw rallies.

Danisa held the fourth game, hitting her first ace. As she went to her bench to towel off during the court change she stumbled ever so slightly. I tensed, noticing it, and below me Fjbk sat up like he had been stabbed.

Danisa seemed to think nothing of it. She wiped the sweat from her hands and racket handle and returned to the court.

Twice in the next game Danisa seemed to start crosscourt a second late. 'She looks leg-weary,' Ted observed.

Karyn frowned. 'What d'you think, Brad? Does Danisa look off-form to you?'

'She looks groggy,' I admitted.

'Maybe she'll get going,' Karyn said, ever the optimist.

In the sixth game Danisa held again. The rallies had lengthened. In one the ball crossed the net thirty-one times.

In the seventh game Danisa staggered slightly again on the change of court. She rubbed her hand across her forehead as if she were dazed. Her colour seemed to go in a twinkling. All at once concern hit me deep. Was she sick?

Game eight. The second point. I leaned forward, watching with everything in me. Danisa's left knee seemed to buckle as she started forward to hit a short ball. She stopped, and the shot passed her. She turned and looked after it. And then she simply went down in a heap.

People cried out in alarm. One of the linesmen ran forward, and Evert hurried around the net. Below us the Lechovas were on their feet, and Fjbk jumped the railing to run onto the court.

'What the—' Karyn gasped. We were standing too. Everyone was. Danisa, sprawled on the clay, now stared up at Fjbk and the others with eyes that looked vacant and on the edge of shock.

There was a hurried consultation. A doctor and a couple of locker room assistants came out with a stretcher and carried Danisa to the exit tunnel. The applause was scattered, shocked.

I turned to my companions. 'I've got to go see.' I climbed to the top row and fought the milling crowds. When I finally got to the locker rooms, it was pandemonium.

Blue and white lights rotated, flashing blindingly. Medical technicians

were just loading a stretcher into an ambulance. Danisa, apparently unconscious, was on it. I tried to work my way through, but the attendants jumped in and closed the doors. The ambulance pulled away, its siren beginning to wail.

THE HOSPITAL WAS AN UGLY concrete monolith surrounded by car parks. I found the emergency area, and there, in a waiting room, were the rest of the Lechova family, a couple of militia, and of course Fjbk. In a treatment room two nurses, a lab technician and a doctor were all working over somebody. Danisa?

The Lechovas turned anxiously to me as I entered. Fjbk, standing at a window, was so worried he forgot to glower.

'You are here, Mr Smith,' Mrs Lechova said with great solemnity. 'Good.' She was pale, and her eyes looked haunted.

Before I could respond, Hannah seized both my arms. 'Oh, Brad Smith. Did you see what happened? Poor Danisa! What if she is dying? I could not live a day with such tragedy.'

'It might be something simple, Hannah. The heat—'

'Or food poisoning,' Leon Lechova said. He fixed me with eyes that were pinpoints of shock. 'She said she started having a headache in the third game. And then she felt weak, and some of the balls seemed blurred. You saw how she was sweating.'

'It was awfully hot.'

'But then she was dizzy. She stumbled . . .'

'What does the doctor say?'

Lechova shook his head. 'The doctor knows nothing yet. They will test. I watched until they put me out. They washed her hands and arms repeatedly and gave her some kind of injection.'

I looked at Mrs Lechova. 'That sounds like they've got some idea what's wrong.'

There was an interruption. Chris Evert, still in the dress she had worn on court, hurried in with two companions.

She told the Lechovas how sorry she was, and what a wonderful competitor Danisa was. Lechova was stiff, proud. Geneta Lechova let a tear slide down her face, and Hannah impulsively gave Chrissie a hug. Through all of it Fjbk remained at the window; he acted like a man in a trance.

During Chris's visit I managed to slip closer to the treatment room. I could see Danisa's feet sticking out from a white cloth. The doctor was gaunt and intent. As I watched he injected a tiny amount of fluid into the IV connector attached to Danisa's arm. One of the nurses was sponging her hands.

Danisa appeared to be conscious. She looked flushed and was breathing hard. One of the nurses gave her a drink of water.

Evert and her friends left as I turned back.

'It was wonderful of her to come,' Hannah said.

'Danisa would have beaten her,' Lechova said hollowly. He looked hard at Hannah. 'Now you will play her.'

'I can't think about that now. I am so worried!'

'But you must think about it,' Lechova snapped. 'Danisa is out of the tournament. It is all up to you now, Hannah.'

Hannah's gasp was audible.

'You have a responsibility to your sister, to us, to Yugoslavia!'

Hannah looked stricken, like a child given an impossible task. 'I will do my best, Poppa.'

Mrs Lechova put a hand on his arm. 'Leon, not now.'

He flushed, looked at the floor, and then walked across to say something to Fjbk. Hannah stared at her mother, then at me. I felt sorry for her. In this unguarded moment all the breezy flamboyance was gone. She left the room, scared half out of her wits.

In a minute or two, one of the attendants came out of the treatment area. He glanced round and spied Danisa's bag and rackets, which had been tossed into the ambulance and brought to the waiting room. The attendant picked up the gear and carried it down a narrow corridor to a doorway at the far end.

A suspicion dawned. 'What was that all about?' I asked.

'They wish to examine those things,' Lechova said. He was matter-of-fact, preoccupied.

'I must go and see if Hannah is all right,' Mrs Lechova said, and walked out of the room in the direction Hannah had gone.

I shifted my weight from foot to foot. The police stood outside in the hall, smoking. Lechova and Fjbk were in deep, quiet conversation. No one was paying any attention to me. I slipped to the end of the corridor.

In a utility washroom the attendant was bent over a deep sink of sudsy water. Danisa's rackets were beside him—all but the one he had in his hands. He was scrubbing the handle.

That told me enough to make an educated guess.

I turned back the way I had come, so angry I began to shake.

Over the next two hours the doctor, whose name was Bulganik, came out several times to say Danisa was doing fine. He said he had no idea yet what had caused her collapse, but her fever and other symptoms were abating. He was not a good liar, but no one else seemed to notice the evasive shifting of his eyes.

More time passed. Finally attendants wheeled Danisa out. She still looked flushed, and her pupils were widely dilated.

'Oh, Danisa. We were so worried!' Hannah exploded.

'We love you,' her mother said, squeezing her hand.

Danisa's dazed eyes found me. 'Brad?' Tears came.

I bent over her and soothed my hand through her hair. I kissed her forehead. 'You're OK, babe. It's OK.'

She clutched my hand for an instant. Her father and Fjbk stood mute, at a loss for a reaction.

The attendants wheeled her out of the area. Dr Bulganik faced us. Out of deference to me, he spoke English.

'We wish to keep her here through the night to assure there is no more trouble. But I think she can be released in morning.'

'What caused the sickness?' Leon Lechova demanded.

'More studies must be done. But we think food poisoning. She is ÓK. That is biggest thing, eh?'

He hurried away. The family conferred. Respecting their privacy, I drifted into the hall.

Which was when I saw him.

Standing at the end of the long hall, smoking a cigarette.

The KGB man, Altunyan.

I took a step in his direction, but got no farther because Fjbk came out of the emergency room behind me and caught my arm. 'She will be of no more use to you now,' he said blackly. 'You will leave her alone so she can get well.'

'You idiot,' I said hotly. 'Are you so hung up on your jealousy you haven't figured out what probably happened to her?'

He went blank and let go of my arm. 'You know?'

'Not for sure.' I pointed. 'You see him down there? Our friendly neighbourhood KGB man? Ask *him* what happened.'

'What would he know?' He seized my arm again. 'Tell me!'

'Ask him,' I said, angling my head in Altunyan's direction.

Fjbk stared. 'He is gone.'

I glanced down there. He was right.

'You tell me,' Fjbk rumbled threateningly.

'No. Ask yourself why they scrubbed her racket handles.'

'You think he made my Danisa sick?'

'Ask him, Fjbk.' I walked away from him and left the hospital and found a cab.

On the way back to the hotel I reviewed what had happened. This time they had gone too far. They had hurt her, might have ended her life. Was there the slimmest chance that I could get her out of this madhouse country without help from anybody?

One idea was forming in my mind. It was a long shot, but if Danisa was released in the morning—and if she could walk a few hundred yards—it might just be crazy enough to work.

After what had happened, I was ready to try anything.

New York City and Suburbs
The flight with the man named Sylvester on board landed at La Guardia shortly after six o'clock on Wednesday evening. Sylvester retrieved his suitcase and went directly to the Hertz counter. By seven thirty he was driving his rented car through hectic traffic.

Sylvester had not eaten for hours, but food was the last thing on his mind. When he stopped in White Plains, it was to unlock his suitcase and feel through the clothing to assure himself that his foil- and towel-wrapped Makarov pistol had not been disturbed. The automatic and its package of 9-mm ammunition were just as he had packed them. The syringe and puff device were fine too.

He drove on sedately to Chappaqua. There was no hurry now.

Virginia
At almost the same time as Sylvester began his drive north, Kinkaid and Exerblein met Dwight at his home. He had coffee ready, and they took their cups into the panelled office in his basement. It was quiet there and virtually soundproof.

'This time everything has been cleared and recleared,' Dwight told them. 'You take the shuttle in the morning. You drive up there, check into this motel'—he held up a matchbook with advertising on it—'under your travelling names. Your contact from the FBI, Joe Darby, will call you no later than six o'clock. You will tell Partek his sister is safe. We are still working on getting her out. We urge him to seek immediate asylum.

'We are now playing by all the rules. The surrender itself—assuming he agrees—will be an FBI operation. The FBI guys will take him straight back to New York in an armoured limousine, and our interviews will be started in a safe house.'

'How many people will they have there?' Kinkaid asked.

'Not more than three, under cover. Partek will be checked in at the inn, and you and the FBI man will make a simple, direct contact. Once he has been reassured, we think he'll go for our offer. You walk him out to the limo. Exerblein, you're outside in your car. You'll be armed for this one.'

Exerblein nodded. He looked almost sleepy. 'Why do we wait until tomorrow evening?'

'He seemed to think he needed the time. We had no choice.'

'It gives the other side more time to catch on.'

490

'Not if we keep the operation small and quiet.' The three men looked at each other. 'Other questions?' Dwight asked.

It was Kinkaid who broached the matter. 'What's the truth about his sister in Belgrade?'

Dwight's eyes turned bleak. 'At this time no opportunities exist for a viable attempt to remove Danisa Lechova from Belgrade. The matter will be reviewed on a regular basis. Let's just not mess up the defection. Convince him to come over now.'

Exerblein stirred. 'Yes,' he said, with no emotion. 'After all, once we have Partek, the Lechova woman doesn't matter.'

Dwight's distaste was obvious, but he said nothing.

New Belgrade

The hour was now far past midnight. Miloslav Fjbk stood in the deepest shadows of the hospital's parking lot. Upstairs, his beloved Danisa slept, a pale statue. The doctor had said she would recover totally. But Fjbk's senses still reeled under the knowledge that she had seemed on the brink of death itself.

Fjbk had surreptitiously examined Danisa's racket case after it was placed in the locker in her ward. Smith had not lied about that: the handles of all five rackets were soaked from washing.

Smith had pointed to Altunyan, who, Fjbk knew, was a secret operative, surely KGB. Altunyan had vanished. But Fjbk had to know if Altunyan knew what had happened to his Danisa.

Altunyan, Fjbk thought, would be back tonight if he was suspicious that Danisa had been purposely harmed. Fjbk would ask him directly.

Her shocking collapse during the match with Chris Evert had been a vast disappointment to Fjbk. He had felt in his bones that Danisa was ready for the start of a march to world dominance in women's tennis—her glory as well as his. The disappointment, however, was nothing compared to Fjbk's pain for Danisa herself. The thought that someone might harm this beautiful, graceful, compelling woman filled him with miserable rage.

He would wait all night, if necessary, to see if Altunyan came back, if he could shed any light. He owed it to Danisa. He would never rest until the mystery had been solved.

His wristwatch showed a few minutes past one thirty am, when a dark Mercedes pulled into the car park near the emergency-room doors. In the feeble light from the entrance Fjbk saw Altunyan get out and hurry inside. Fjbk waited, blood thumping in his ears. His worry and anger made him feel almost sick.

After twenty minutes Altunyan came back, walking briskly. Fjbk hurried across the pavement, intercepting the Russian beside his car.

'Comrade. A word, please,' he said.

Altunyan spun round, recognised him, and relaxed slightly. 'You startled me, my friend.'

'What of Danisa?'

'I have just enquired of the doctors. She will be released in the morning, but will be very weak for several days. All is well.'

'What was done to her?'

'I have no idea. My concern is that of a sports enthusiast—'

'No lies!' Fjbk rasped. 'I think you are of the KGB. Danisa is my ward, my pupil. I must know what happened to her.' In his fervour he grabbed the lapels of Altunyan's jacket.

The Russian, though considerably taller, was pushed off-balance against the car. 'Release me!'

'They washed the racket handles. She was poisoned!'

The Russian's face twisted with surprise and alarm. 'Who told you such a thing?'

'Tell me what you know. I will find out who did this!'

Now it was Altunyan who grabbed Fjbk, clutching his thick bare arms. 'Fjbk, I know your background. Your loyalty has never been in question. You must listen. There are factors here beyond your knowledge. What I did to the Lechova girl was for her own safety, for her country as well as mine.'

Fjbk staggered back a half step. It felt as though he had been hit in the chest with a sledgehammer. 'You did this?'

'Silence! Listen to me. The insecticide did not seriously harm her. Painted on her rackets, it penetrated when she sweated. But the treatment is reliable, and all was in readiness.'

'She could have died!'

'Lower your voice! No. She was never in danger.'

Fjbk reeled mentally. Altunyan and everything else had become blurry, red-tinged. The horror and anger were out of all bounds, like nothing Fjbk had ever experienced.

'You swine! You hurt my Danisa. You will pay for it.'

Altunyan moved, and a small automatic appeared in his hand. 'Get back, you fool.'

Fjbk's rage burst out of control. With speed far greater than the Russian anticipated, Fjbk knocked the gun out of his hand and went for his throat, closing both powerful hands round his windpipe.

Altunyan lurched sideways, trying to fight. But the Serb was far too strong in his crazy rage. Altunyan twisted his body too far, wrenching his neck just as Fjbk squeezed convulsively.

There was a crunching sound. Altunyan gasped and went limp. His collapse almost pulled Fjbk down on top of him.

Sobbing for air, Fjbk looked down at what he had done. He dropped to one knee and probed the lolling, shattered neck. There was no pulse.

Fjbk panicked. He looked around.

Only a few feet away stood a large trash container, heavy steel. With strength born of desperation Fjbk heaved the body over the high lip of the container and out of sight. Looking round again, he saw no one. He turned and ran.

10

It was after nine am when the doctor signed authorisation for Danisa to be discharged. Geneta Lechova waited with me. She had a small bag with Danisa's going-home clothes.

'My husband has taken Hannah for a light workout,' she told me. Her expression was that flinty kind people sometimes get when they are hiding everything.

'Fjbk is with them?'

She countered, 'Are you going to help her?'

'I'm going to try. But maybe the less you know the better.'

She accepted that with grave silence.

In a little while we were allowed upstairs. We found Danisa in a medium-sized ward, pale sunlight spilling from high, soot-streaked windows. She looked totally wrung out and colourless, but her smile beamed when she saw us. Her mother embraced her. I did too.

'How do you feel?' her mother asked.

Danisa brushed a wisp of hair out of her eyes. 'A little fuzzy. I don't remember a lot after the match started, Momma.'

'Have you eaten this morning?'

'Oat cereal.' Danisa made a face. 'I left it.'

Mrs Lechova laughed. 'Once you are dressed, we can go home. There are fresh rolls and cakes.'

I said I would wait for them outside the ward.

There had been no problem last night in tracking down Ted Treacher and Karyn Wechsting. I asked the two of them to go for a stroll with me, and both read my expression and agreed, puzzled.

The Belgrade streets were vast and vacant. I didn't see any sign of being followed. After they had asked about Danisa's condition, I told them I could explain a lot of things.

Except for the part about Danisa's brother in America, I gave it to them fairly straight.

'I *knew* that business about a burglar was bull,' Karyn said triumphantly. 'And that's why you wouldn't notify the police.'

'So what happens now?' Treacher demanded. 'You really think somebody poisoned her to keep her here?'

'I think so,' I said. 'But there still may be a chance to get her out. It's a long shot, but it might be tried.'

'Can we help?' Karyn asked. 'Tell us.'

I did.

'We'll do our part,' Treacher said. 'So go for it.'

Maybe it was crazy. But I intended to try. Right now, I was aware of the pressure starting to build up.

DANISA AND HER MOTHER walked out of the ward. Danisa moved slowly and cautiously, as if she might lose her balance and fall. That didn't bode well for my plan.

'I will sign the papers at the desk,' Mrs Lechova said.

Danisa looked towards the elevators. 'Brad and I will go on downstairs, wait for you out in the fresh air.'

Once out in front of the great monolith, under a thin sun and with a humid breeze stirring her hair, she seemed better. 'I think I'm hungry,' she said with a smile.

'Danisa, we don't have much time. If we go, it's right away.'

'There is some chance?' she asked, surprised.

'There's one possible way. But it isn't authorised, and the chances of its working may be less than fifty-fifty.'

She studied my face, and her expression made butterflies in my midsection. Finally she said, 'Will you take me?'

'Yes.'

'Then I am ready.'

Militia Headquarters, Belgrade

At ten am Ladislav Maleeva's emergency meeting was interrupted by the insistent chirping of his beeper.

'Continue,' he told the other investigators in the room. He went to a private office nearby and called Lieutenant Rodor, in charge of surveillance on the street.

Rodor told him, 'The Smith man appeared at the hospital. Danisa Lechova was released. Smith went with her and her mother to the Lechova apartment. He then returned to the Metropol.'

'How did Danisa Lechova look to you?' Maleeva asked.

'Very weak, like someone after a long illness. We believe, however, she will leave the family apartment shortly.'

'On what basis?'

'Our telephone tap intercepted a message from Smith. He wishes one more interview before his Sunday departure. Danisa Lechova stated that she would meet him as soon as possible, at his hotel room to assure no interruption of their final talk.'

'All right,' Maleeva said after a moment's thought. 'Continue electronic surveillance of Smith's room from next door and make sure the interview is recorded for analysis.'

'Do we also post a man in the hall and in the lobby?'

'No. We need our manpower on the Altunyan investigation. You stay in the room. The equipment will warn us when the interview is concluded and one or both are about to leave. I will join you within the hour.'

Maleeva was irritated and worried. The Altunyan disaster had complicated everything a thousandfold.

The body of the KGB man had been found by a hospital orderly in the predawn hours. Shock waves had already rippled all the way to Moscow. Maleeva hadn't liked Altunyan. But having a senior operative of the KGB murdered in your jurisdiction was not the kind of thing that looked good on your record. Maleeva had to pull out all the stops to solve this one.

The earlier mystery—Danisa Lechova's collapse last night— was now partly explained. Maleeva's man inside the hospital had reported promptly. Danisa had been treated with repeated two-milligram doses of atropine sulfate. Her collapse had been caused by skin absorption of a powerful insecticide. The doctor's instructions for cleansing her rackets pointed to the fact that the poison had been painted on the handles. The doctor was being questioned and so far was pretending ignorance, but he would be broken eventually; his diagnosis had been too swift for guesswork.

Maleeva suspected Brad Smith, although the logic of such an escapade eluded him. Perhaps a plan to spirit her away in a bogus ambulance? Whatever the scheme, it had backfired.

The Americans, Henry and Muriel Beamer, had been watched closely. They had departed Yugoslavia and were now in Vienna. This proved that they were no longer involved in any plan to take Danisa out. Which sharpened the focus on Smith.

Despite these conclusions the pressure resulting from the Altunyan murder had forced Maleeva to accommodate to political realities. Officers maintaining surveillance on Smith had been transferred to the Altunyan investigation.

The information that Danisa was going to meet Smith in his hotel room for a final interview did nothing to change Maleeva's plans. The electronic equipment would keep an eye on them. He went back into the meeting discussing Altunyan's death.

New Belgrade
'Momma! Where is Danisa?'

After morning warm-up Hannah had left her father at the stadium and returned home buoyant, expecting to see her sister safe and recovering. But when she breezed into their shared bedroom, she found Danisa nowhere to be seen.

Now Hannah rushed into the kitchen, where her mother was peeling fruit for a salad. 'Momma, Danisa is not here.'

'I know,' Geneta Lechova said, calm and stoical.

Hannah noticed her mother's pallor. 'But what happened? Was she not released from the hospital? Oh, my God, has there been a setback? Tell me!'

Her mother carefully dried her hands on her apron and came to sit at the tiny dining table. 'There's no need for alarm, Hannah. She needed to go for a final interview with Mr Smith.'

Hannah could scarcely believe her ears. 'How could you let her go, in her condition? She should be in bed.'

'The doctor said she could do as much as she felt able.'

'Why the sudden rush? And why did Smith not come here?'

'He is leaving on Sunday. It was Danisa's idea to meet at once, to have the talk behind her. And she suggested his hotel. She wanted no interruptions, so that it could be done as quickly as possible.'

Hannah's vivid imagination saw X-rated pictures. 'In his hotel? In his *room?* Oh! How could you let her do such a thing, Momma? Where was your sanity?' She started out of the kitchen. 'I will go there. She is not well, and I do not trust that man.'

'Hannah!' her mother called very sharply.

Surprised at the tone of her mother's voice, Hannah stopped and looked back. Her mother was sitting at the tiny table, her hands folded in front of her.

'No,' Geneta Lechova said.

'But Momma, I do not understand. I am going! You cannot stop me. When Poppa hears of this, he will—'

'Hannah,' her mother said very firmly. 'Sit down.' Geneta Lechova's voice had quiet steel in it.

Baffled, Hannah obeyed, facing her mother across the table where the family had eaten a thousand meals. 'What is it?' she asked hoarsely. 'What has happened?'

'I know your patriotism, your loyalty to Yugoslavia. But I know also how much you love Danisa, and us. I could lie to you, but I will trust your love for your family above all things.'

Hannah waited, silent for once, holding her breath.

'Danisa is fleeing from this country,' her mother began sombrely. 'No, no. You may not interrupt. For once you are going to listen.'

Geneta Lechova stared at her hands. 'It is Danisa's wish to leave Yugoslavia. She has asked the United States to help her. At this hour Brad Smith is trying to get her out of the country.'

'But that's . . . that's mad. That is treason to our nation. Oh! This is worse than I had imagined! My poor sister, her head and heart turned by an imperialist—'

'Hannah, Danisa asked the Americans. They did not ask her. Look at what has been done to her! The authorities knew she wished for freedom in the West. That is why your passports were withdrawn. And your father has known nothing, because he would side with the state. Milo may even have been in the conspiracy. Hannah, are you fully aware of Milo's unhealthy fascination with your sister?'

It was too much too fast. Hannah reeled. But the part about Fjbk hit home. She thought, Danisa can be safe from him now! And then was shocked at herself.

She tried to think straight. 'It is my duty to report this at once. They cannot yet be out of the country.'

'What of your duty to your sister?'

'But she is wrong. Misguided.'

'And you know better than Danisa what is best for Danisa? Who does that sound like, Hannah?'

Hannah saw. She hung her head. 'Poppa.'

'Yes, Poppa. Will you try to run lives the way he has always run yours?'

'But I have my duty . . .' Hannah said miserably, wavering.

'If you betray Danisa, Hannah, never again imagine that I will consider you my daughter.'

'Momma!'

'I love you more than you know. You will do the right thing because you are a good person and your family is more important to you than the state. I know this. I trust you.'

Geneta Lechova stood up and went to the sink. Hannah stared at her back. Her emotions swirled: shock, rage, fear, even jealousy. Yes, jealousy. She realised that Danisa must love Brad Smith. Hannah had been almost in love with him herself. And I must report them, have them arrested.

But she would be happy in the West. I know of her misery here, and she would never have to fear Milo again.

Or Poppa.

Hannah went to the bedroom and stared at Danisa's unrumpled bed. She remembered all the times they had giggled in the night, told each other outrageous lies and even more astounding truths.

Weeping, without a sound, she sat on her bed. Where were her sister and Brad Smith going? How could they hope to get out? She thought feverishly. Of course, it had to be the airport.

But Danisa was so well known. She would be recognised in an instant, merely by her trademark blue and her pigtail. They were sure to catch her. The plan was doomed. Unless Danisa went in disguise.

She imagined her sister, sick and frightened, trying to slip past sharp-eyed passport inspectors. Fear wrenched her gut.

Which was when her imagination made another leap. She realised she was no longer thinking at all about duty to the state. Danisa was in peril. And if she really wanted to leave, why should she not leave?

The pain welled up in Hannah's throat. It was going to be so hard, so lonely. But if it was what Danisa wanted . . .

Hannah thought, She has the right.

Then she thought, Is there any way I can help my sister?

WITH HIS MEETING CONCLUDED, Major Maleeva drove to the Hotel Metropol. He went to the room next to Brad Smith's.

Lieutenant Rodor was there, with a technician operating the equipment. 'They are conducting the interview,' Rodor said.

'You are dismissed. Return to headquarters.'

Lieutenant Rodor silently left the room. Maleeva put on a set of headphones. The voices from the next room were distinct, unmistakable—Smith's baritone, Danisa Lechova's soft alto.

'Danisa, do you consider your win in New South Wales your best performance to date?'

'Grass is not my best surface, and I was pleased to do so well.'

'You consider clay your best surface?'

'At this time, yes. But I am working hard on clay, and I think that will speed my game on all kinds of courts.'

There was a slight flaw in the equipment, a mildly irritating hiss in the headphones. Maleeva removed them, satisfied that everything was being recorded accurately.

His plan was to stay here until the interview was over. Then, he had decided, he would ask Danisa some questions about the attempt last night to make her ill. In her weakened condition she might give away something about Smith.

Maleeva lit a cigarette and sat back to wait.

11

Danisa, wearing shapeless overalls, a shawl that hid her hair and big sunglasses, got out of a taxi to meet me at the car rental agency. She had her racket bag and a cosmetic case hidden in plastic shopping bags. She looked pale and shaky.

'You OK?' I asked as we waited.

'A little hazy, but yes, fine,' she said. She didn't look at all fine, but she was dead game. We were going to need that.

Except for the garage driver who brought our car, and the woman behind the counter, no one was around. Neither gave us a second look. I tossed Danisa's things into the back seat with my suitcase and racket bag, and we drove off immediately.

'How much time do we have?' she asked nervously, looking at everyone on the street as if they might be UDBA.

'Plenty.' I turned left.

'You're going in the wrong direction!'

'I want to make sure no one is following us.' I did the cops-and-robbers thing through four more turns. There was no sign of a familiar car in the mirror. Finally I headed for the highway.

'You brought the other clothes?' she asked.

'Yes.' I pointed to the bag in the back.

'Where are your camera and recorder?'

'That stuff says "reporter", and they can have it. Ted is going to bring my credit cards and personal stuff out with him. And I've got everything else I want or need right here in this car with me.'

It was an almost unconscious remark; I was referring—mostly—to our borrowed IDs, a wad of money in my pocket, and my real passport stuffed in the bottom of my shoe. But her little intake of breath told me she took it as meaning *her*.

I glanced at her. She had momentarily removed her sunglasses, and the look in her eyes was so open and so vulnerable that I almost forgot to watch where I was going. My heart began pounding faster.

'It's true,' I said. I kept my eyes on the traffic. 'But you needn't worry. I don't expect any kind of payback, Danisa.'

'Oh, Brad.' She sighed. 'Sometimes you can be a little stuffy, you know.'

I risked a startled glance and saw she was smiling. 'What?'

'Stuffy,' she said. 'Don't you know how much I like you?'

'You don't know me!'

'Stuffy,' she repeated. 'Sometimes you remind me just a bit of Poppa. But you didn't kiss me like Poppa. You don't look at me like Poppa.' She giggled nervously. I realised that fear and excitement had made her hyper. 'It'll be OK,' I told her. 'We'll make it, babe.' I reached across the seat with my free hand to grasp hers. She squeezed mine hard with fingers that were icy from nervousness.

'I guess I'd better get ready,' she said. She crawled into the back seat and rummaged around. I checked my watch and recalculated our plans. Talking over my shoulder, I repeated everything. Danisa said she understood. When she crawled back in her bright California clothes and began brushing out her hair, she looked like a different person.

When we reached the airport, we had more than thirty minutes to kill. I parked in short-term parking and unloaded our few things: my mostly empty suitcase and racket bag, Danisa's rackets and cosmetic case. She put on a wide-brimmed straw sunhat, and I put on Ted's cap. We both wore sunglasses. When we checked each other over, it was quite amazing. The girl who stood there with me, in lime-coloured slacks and a pink sleeveless top, with white loafers and dramatic sunhat, didn't look at all like Danisa Lechova.

'Well, Ted?' she asked tautly.

'Perfect, Karyn,' I told her.

WE WALKED INTO THE AIRPORT to find it crowded, with militia everywhere, as usual. In the departure area we checked schedules. Flight 608 for Frankfurt, with an intermediate stop in Munich, was listed as on time, departing at one pm.

'Do we go now to the gate area?' Danisa asked.

I looked over at the militia, knowing that UDBA plain-clothes men were also in the crowd. 'We'll get a snack,' I replied.

'I couldn't eat anything.'

'Danisa, we don't want to get to customs any sooner than we have to. The later we are, the faster they may shoo us through. But we shouldn't just stand here inviting attention.'

'I can have tea,' she said.

We went looking for a place. Danisa walked slowly, and not in a perfectly straight line. In the tearoom, strangers swirled round us. The PA system announced flights. I was coiled as a spring. We were so close now, so far. I took her hand and squeezed it. What am I doing, making her take this risk? I asked myself.

After a while I checked my watch. 'It's time.'

She heaved a deep breath. 'I'm ready.'

We started towards the international gate area and the people who would examine our passports. Danisa seemed rested, a little stronger. But her mood changed again.

'Will I ever come back?' she asked softly.

'Yes, you will. Of course you will.'

'I love them.'

'I know.'

'I'm really scared, Brad.'

'It's going to be all right.'

We neared the gate for our flight. There was a hellish queue backed up from passport inspection. I could see three clerks checking passports, and four or five militia standing nearby, eyeing every passenger. I didn't like the look of it. And the length of the queue made it impossible to estimate just when we should approach, to rush through at the last moment. I slowed down a bit.

'Are we too early?' Danisa asked.

Suddenly I got tired of feeling like a mouse. 'No. Let's go.'

We went through the metal detectors and filed in at the end of the line waiting to have exit papers stamped. There was a pair of militiamen at this end, with several photographs glued to a card. I got a look as we moved by, and my guts went icy. One picture was of Danisa.

One of the militiamen looked us over with idle curiosity. The sleek lines of Danisa's legs, in Karyn Wechsting's pants, drew a second look. He studied Danisa and I tightened, not sure what I was going to do when he pulled us out of the line.

He did no such thing. He simply liked what he saw. His eyes moved over her, and then he caught himself and looked away.

I glanced at Danisa. She had missed the by-play entirely. My brief inspection of her was reassuring. Without her trademark blue, without her plait, wearing uncharacteristic clothes, she *wasn't* Danisa Lechova. Not to a casual glance. Now, if the passport checkers would just please be casual too . . .

The line edged forward slowly. We still had about a dozen people between us and the checkpoints. Departure time was only twenty minutes away. The airline people at the boarding pass counter were looking irritated. Clearly the checkers were holding things up. I saw the woman handling our line glare at the next passenger's passport and face, comparing several times. No airline would hurry *her*, she was saying.

She was being careful. Too careful.

At that moment I became aware of a commotion in the corridor just outside our lounge. People were turning to stare. Two of the militia hurried out to see what was going on. My first thought was that somebody was coming after us. But whatever was happening out there was staying out there. With Danisa craning her neck beside me, I located the commotion. A young woman surrounded by uniformed militia.

Shock travelled through me. It was Danisa. Danisa in every way, except that the woman out there couldn't be Danisa.

But the woman was wearing Danisa's shade of blue. She had the pigtail down her back. She even had a tennis racket. She was arguing heatedly with a militia lieutenant and his men.

Our line moved up a clump. The woman out there was drawing the attention of everybody within a hundred yards. Even the checkers looked a little distracted. Then Danisa stiffened convulsively beside me. She turned, her face slack with shock. 'Hannah!' she said softly.

It *was* Hannah. Couldn't be anyone else.

In her blue dress and pigtail she could have fooled anyone who didn't know both Lechova women. She gestured angrily and started to walk away from the guards. One moved, blocking her way. Another restrained her on the other side.

Danisa took a half step out of line. I caught her arm, and she tried to pull free. 'I have to help her,' she whispered.

'No! Don't you get it? She's doing this on purpose.'

'But she's in trouble.'

'We don't have time to argue. Look.'

The people in line ahead of us were through, and the airline people gestured at us to have our passports checked.

'Come on. And don't forget your ankle. *Now!*'

She hesitated, agonising. Hannah argued more heatedly, drawing even more attention. Everyone was watching.

'Now!' I repeated.

Danisa gave a last despairing glance, then moved forward. She remembered to limp. My heart in my throat, I stayed close to her. She was really pale now and shaking visibly. The woman at the checkpoint tore her eyes away from the confusion outside long enough to take the passport from Danisa and glance at the picture inside. She said, 'We were sorry to hear of your injury, Miss Wechsting.'

'Thank you,' Danisa murmured.

'We hope you will visit us again.' The rubber exit stamp came down on the passport page. She took the passport I offered. 'Mr Treacher. I hope you enjoyed your visit to our country.'

'Very much,' I told her.

The rubber stamp came down again. The woman was already trying to make out what was happening with Hannah.

We went to the boarding gate, down the tunnel, and into the plane. I managed to cram our gear into an overhead compartment, and we slid into our seats. Danisa leaned against me, still shaking.

'Hang on,' I soothed. I found her hand and held it.

The last handful of passengers came on board. The door closed, and the lights flickered for an instant as engines were started. The cabin attendants went through the safety rules.

Come on, come on!

The plane backed out, taxied to the runway. It seemed like for ever. The pilot ran up the engines. We rolled.

Moments later we were airborne. I breathed.

Belgrade

Major Ladislav Maleeva was still in the electronic-surveillance room, watching recorder lights flicker, when his beeper sounded. He returned the call at once.

'Major Maleeva,' Lieutenant Rodor said, sounding excited, 'Danisa Lechova has been apprehended at the airport.'

Maleeva couldn't believe his ears. 'Lechova? It cannot be!'

'Sir, the officers recognised her at once. She attempted to escape. They are holding her pending your instructions.'

Maleeva grabbed the headphones. He heard the ongoing murmur of voices next door. He did not understand. And then he did.

'Hold,' he snapped into the telephone.

He rushed to the elevators and down to the lobby. The startled desk clerk produced a duplicate key at once. Maleeva was breathing hard by the time he threw open Smith's door.

On the coffee table sat a cassette recorder, its dial light showing ON. From its speaker came voices and the telltale tape hiss Maleeva had not identified through the wall. With an angry motion, he cut the machine off and ran back next door.

He grabbed the telephone. 'I am on the way immediately.'

Hudson River Valley, New York

Dominic Partek drove north towards Chappaqua. He told himself that the news at this meeting would be good. He was going to see his sister, and both of them were going to have a new life.

Partek wondered if Danisa would share some of her new life with him. Then he realised with a pang of sadness that their meetings might always be clandestine. The KGB would not molest her. But their desire for revenge on Partek would be never-ending. For the rest of his life he would live in hiding. And every precaution would have to be taken to prevent the KGB's following Danisa as a way of locating him.

Well, so be it. It could be that Partek would see her soon. It would be joyous. And there would be other meetings.

As to his own future, Partek thought, the cash he had hidden against the eventuality of defection, while not an enormous amount, might be enough to buy a piece of property in the mountains somewhere. He had a dream about a small cabin, an A-frame, on perhaps an acre. He could find work in town as a mechanic or a repairman. His knowledge of computers might bring in spending money. Conceivably he might write a book.

Driving up the Hudson River Valley, Partek dictated an hour's notes into his small recorder. He would play the recording for the FBI when he was in a safe house somewhere. It would save time. He laid out the major operations he had taken part in, including names, dates and places.

When he drove into the picturesque outskirts of Chappaqua, he slipped the recorder back into his bag. He found the inn and drove twice round its environs, the old habit of caution prompting the search for suspicious persons and reconnaissance of quick escape routes. Satisfied, he pulled into the parking lot and went inside.

His reservation under the name of Archibald was in order. He took the room key and climbed the staircase to the second floor, where he found his room. It was high-ceilinged, airy, with a big canopied bed.

Partek went into the bathroom and sponged his face and arms with a cool, wet towel. He went back to the corridor door, heading for the parking lot so that he could bring in his bag.

Humming softly, he swung the door open.

Somebody was standing there. Partek recognised him. Sylvester.

The man had a small cylindrical object in his hand, and the cylinder made a spiteful little puffing sound. A cloud of gas shot into Partek's face, and he felt a very sharp, very astonishing pain.

Belgrade

All morning Miloslav Fjbk had expected the militia. When he had gone to the arena for the early workout with Hannah, he had been sure he would be arrested. But no one had shown up.

Now he was home again, and he was still unmolested. Fjbk began to feel hope: he might get away with what he had done.

Nervously he reviewed for the hundredth time everything that had happened: no one had seen him in the hospital car park with Altunyan. He had been miles away, surely, before Altunyan's body was found. There was nothing he could think of to link him with the KGB resident. Unless he gave himself away by his nervousness, he was not likely to be suspected in any way.

It was too soon to relax entirely. But Fjbk had begun to feel much better. He decided to shower, trim his beard, and visit the Lechova home. He was eager to see Danisa this morning.

He hummed an old Serbian folk tune in his shower.

MAJOR MALEEVA HURRIED into the airport security office. Three officers were there, and the Lechova woman was sitting on a couch against a side wall. Her large, frightened eyes swept up to meet his, and Maleeva experienced a shock greater than any he had had previously on this blighted day.

'*You?*'

'Major Maleeva!' Hannah Lechova cried, jumping to her feet. 'Tell them who I am, please. Why have I been held?'

'You cretins,' Maleeva snarled. 'This is not Danisa Lechova. This is her sister.' He grabbed Hannah's arm. 'Where is she?'

'At home. You're hurting me! Please. I only came to the airport to see off my friends, and these swine accosted me—'

'Major,' one of the officers said hoarsely, 'she said nothing to indicate she was not Danisa Lechova. Her clothing, her hair, all match the description—'

'You thought I was Danisa?' Hannah cried in a very good semblance of surprise. 'But all you had to do was ask my name!'

'Take her to headquarters,' Maleeva snapped. 'We will sort this out later. Right now I have other things to do.'

Maleeva ordered an immediate visit to the Lechova apartment. Danisa Lechova had to be located at once. Fuming, he drove back to the city at maniacal speed. He was almost there when he got back-to-back calls on his radio. Danisa Lechova was nowhere to be found. And two American tennis players at the Metropol had reported a burglary. Maleeva nearly ran a bread truck off the road as he changed course.

Hurrying into the hotel manager's office, he found Karyn Wechsting and Ted Treacher apparently in a state of outrage.

'Someone broke into our rooms,' Treacher told him. 'Our passports have been stolen.'

'When did you discover this?' Maleeva demanded.

'Just a while ago,' Karyn told him. 'We were getting ready to go to the airport, and now we've missed our flight!'

'*What flight?*' Maleeva's voice thundered.

'The one leaving for Frankfurt. The—'

Maleeva rushed to the telephone. He went straight through to state security headquarters. In stunned tones his commander asked two key questions, then said he would ring right back.

Maleeva turned to the two Americans. 'It is possible,' he said with acid sarcasm, 'that a Yugoslav national and a renegade of the American CIA have used your credentials to flee our country. You would not know anything about that, would you?'

'I don't know, old man,' Treacher said, 'and I don't care. I demand to see someone from the United States embassy.'

'And,' Karyn said, 'I demand to know what you intend to do about this abominable theft.'

Maleeva lit a cigarette. He was beginning to feel sick.

The telephone rang. His commander talked excitedly. Maleeva listened to the sound of his future going down the sewer.

The flight could not be called back. It had already landed in Munich and disgorged some of its passengers.

Chappaqua, New York

Kinkaid and his associate from the FBI, Joe Darby, parked in the inn car park and went inside. The other security people were on station, and all seemed well. Kinkaid led the way to the head of the stairs, then down the hallway to Mr Archibald's room. The door swung open at his knock. He groped for a light switch, started to enter, and looked down.

'Oh, hell,' Kinkaid said. 'Oh, damn.'

Darby pushed past him to stare. Then, after bending to make the briefest, really unnecessary, examination, he pulled his walkie-talkie from his jacket and spoke into it very quietly.

Kinkaid went to the window and looked out. When the others arrived, he just stayed at the window, staring into the dark.

12

It was a beautiful Sunday morning in Westchester County. In Belgrade, half a world away, they were staging the ceremonies that closed Yugoslavia's first big venture into international tennis. Pam Shriver had shocked everyone by winning the women's title, beating Martina in three sets. Martina had beaten Hannah in the semis. Lendl was the men's champion.

But none of that seemed to matter much.

'Are you OK?' I asked Danisa as I pulled into the parking lot of the building where her brother's body was being held.

'Yes,' she said tonelessly. 'OK.' She was wearing a pale tan sundress she had bought, without much sense of pleasure, the previous day. She had got most of her colour back and was regaining strength after her poisoning. But the death of Dominic Partek had hit her very hard.

'I must see him,' she told me, for the fifth or sixth time.

Collie Davis, who had shown up at Kennedy Airport and stayed with us ever since, got out of the back seat to open Danisa's door for her. The three of us went inside.

After getting directions from a policeman at the desk, we found an office with double glass doors. In it were a couple more guys from Langley, named Kinkaid and Dwight, and an FBI agent whose name was Darby. I introduced Danisa, and they all seemed genuinely sorry about what had happened.

Kinkaid told her, 'If there had been any way to prevent what happened, Miss Lechova, we would have done it.'

Danisa studied him with dignity. 'But it was all for nothing.'

'No,' Dwight said. 'Not for nothing, Miss Lechova. Maybe it's small consolation, but we found a tape in his car. It contained information that's going to help the free world.'

Danisa's throat worked. 'Where is he? I want to see him.'

Dwight nodded. He turned to Darby. 'If you could take Miss Lechova into the other office for a cup of coffee, we'll take just a couple of minutes with Brad here, first.'

Danisa looked questioningly at me, then went with Darby.

Dwight said, 'Brad, that tape is dynamite. The FBI is rounding up a dozen people, and putting surveillance on many more. The s.o.b.s may have gotten Partek, but he got them too.'

'What's happened to Karyn and Ted?'

'They flew out of Belgrade a couple of hours ago. The Yugoslavs couldn't make anything stick. I mean, Wechsting and Treacher were victims of a burglary, right?'

'How about Danisa's family?'

'It's too early to say. Her father is torn up, we hear. But Hannah played well in that tournament. She's got the world press watching her. With Danisa gone, the Yugoslavs already seem to be making Hannah their new heroine. So we think she's safe, protected by her new role.'

'They know she tricked them to help us get out.'

'Yes.' Dwight smiled. 'Are they going to prosecute her for that and admit they were fooled by a girl?'

'Or,' Kinkaid added, 'admit they were trying to keep Danisa a prisoner?'

The answer to the latter was obvious. The Yugoslav government hadn't made a peep about Danisa's departure. They were saving face by pretending nothing had happened.

'There's something else you have to know,' Kinkaid said. 'The Russians are alleging we murdered Partek. They're sending some embassy goons this morning to claim his body.'

'Forget it,' I said instantly.

Dwight shrugged. 'We're on uncertain ground. He was a Russian national.'

'You can't let them murder him and then take the body. That's crazy!'

507

'We've got calls in to check it out.' Dwight studied me. 'You disobeyed orders, but you did do a hell of a job, Brad.'

Collie said, 'They'll probably never want to use you again.'

'I weep,' I said. 'So can she see her brother's body now?'

Dwight signalled Kinkaid, who went out and came back with the FBI man and Danisa. She looked ashen.

'Are you ready, Miss Lechova?'

'Yes.' Almost inaudibly.

We went into a chill, barren room with a gleaming tile floor. On a trolley was a body covered by a white cloth.

'Death was caused by inhalation of a chemical which caused heart failure,' Kinkaid said. His voice echoed. He paused and looked at Danisa. 'It was quick,' he added softly.

Danisa started across the room. I stayed close to her. Kinkaid drew the sheet to reveal Dominic Partek's head and shoulders. He lay peacefully, his face calm. He looked younger than I would have imagined, handsome. Danisa leaned over, intensely studying her brother's face. It was as if she wanted to memorise every detail. Tenderly she touched his hair, his eyebrows.

It was tomb-silent in the lab.

She bent over and kissed his forehead. Then her grief broke through, and she started to sob. I let her get some of it out, and then I couldn't stand it any more. I put my arms round her. 'Come on, Danisa,' I said.

I led her away from the trolley. She stumbled slightly as I went into the office with her, somewhat supporting her weight. We got her some fresh coffee. Nobody knew what to say. After a few minutes she began to get hold of herself, and that was when the Russians arrived.

There were five of them: bulky, wool-suited diplomat types with briefcases. The boss was perhaps sixty, steel grey, with a face that belonged on a Soviet Mount Rushmore.

'I,' he announced, 'am Anatoli Gulgradnik, first officer for cultural affairs of the embassy of the Soviet Union. We have come to claim the body of an employee of our delegation, one Dominic Partek. Where is he?'

Danisa looked up at them, tears fading.

Dwight spoke formally. 'The question of custody of the body is being discussed at the highest level. You will be informed of the decision of the United States government.'

Gulgradnik drew himself up to his full height, probably five inches over six feet. 'We demand *now* the body of Dominic Partek. We have an ambulance to take him at once.'

Dwight started to reply, but Danisa sprang to her feet. 'No!'

The Russian turned to her. 'What right do you have to interfere?' He looked at Dwight. 'Who is this—'

'I am Danisa Lechova!' Danisa shot back. 'His sister.'

Gulgradnik must have anticipated it. He was not flustered. 'You have no rights here. You are a criminal in your own country and have no status in the United States.'

'You'll never have him!' Danisa's eyes were alight with combat. 'I am his only living relative, and *I* will say where his body stays. I say he will be buried here, in America.'

The Russian's face darkened with anger. He swung around to Dwight. 'Are you going to allow this affront to the delegation of the Union of Soviet—'

'I think so, yes,' Dwight cut in.

'You will regret this. We will seek legal orders. This woman has—what do you call it?—no leg to stand on.'

'I doubt it, sir.' Dwight was grinning now. 'The question of custody would be difficult only if next of kin did not step forward. Miss Lechova, you are making a request for custody?'

'Yes.'

'Then,' Dwight told Gulgradnik, 'Miss Lechova has every leg to stand on, and you don't have doodley. Was there anything else you gentlemen wished to discuss before you leave?'

The Russian's lips worked. With a muffled oath he turned to his entourage. 'Come! We are getting nowhere here.'

They filed out. Danisa, defiant, watched them go.

She turned. I held out my arms, and she fled into them.

'Oh, Brad, I was scared. But they made me so mad!'

'You, lady,' I told her, 'are so wonderful.'

She rolled her eyes. 'I have to go to the bathroom.'

Smiling, Kinkaid led her out. Darby went to a telephone to make a report. A building security man came in to see what was happening, and Dwight took him over into a corner for a discussion.

Which left Collie and me.

'Collie,' I said, 'is she the world's greatest, or what?'

'You, sir, have a serious problem,' he replied. He put an arm over my shoulder. 'I got you into this. I feel responsible. So let me ask you. What are you going to do about her?'

'What do you mean, do about her?'

'Brad, I admit she's dynamite. Great-looking, courageous, loyal. She's *great*. And any idiot could watch her with you for five minutes and know she's crazy about you.'

'Any idiot would know that?'

'Of course. But what are you going to do? You can't just'—he gestured aimlessly—'take advantage of her.'

'What do you think I should do, Collie?'

'Brad.' He squeezed my shoulder big-brother fashion, always a bad sign with Collie. 'She's far too young for you. She's infatuated with you, sure. But later that will wear off. Then where would you be? You'll end up getting dumped.' He paused.

I was still chewing on the delightful morsel of information that she was obviously crazy about me. I had been afraid to believe the evidence. 'So your advice is?'

'Cut your losses, man. Don't set yourself up for disappointment. Be nice. Be friendly. But end it before things get messy.'

Through the glass doors I could see Danisa coming back. She looked young, beautiful, strong, full of fight and the rage to live.

Then she saw me watching her, and her whole demeanour changed. Her smile came, filled with love.

'So?' Collie goaded with another brotherly squeeze.

'Collie, I'll tell you what. Right now she does love me. I'm just going to go with that, as long as it lasts, and to hell with later on.'

'Brad, you'll be sorry.'

Danisa came into the room, ponytail swishing.

'Collie,' I said, 'you've got to be insane.'

WHEN DANISA AND I returned to the car, she sat in the front seat and wept again, softly, from fatigue and hurt and relief.

'He will be buried here,' she told me again. 'In America.'

'Yes,' I said. 'He will. And what about you, now that he's dead?'

She thought a minute or two, and it was very quiet in the car. Then her chin came up. 'I will not go back. I will bury my brother here, and I will stay in America. I will play tennis and make my new country proud of me.'

My eyes felt hot. 'I'll help you all I can, if you want.'

'Yes,' she said softly.

'I have to go back to Texas in a few days. I've got a job there.'

She watched me with those great, vulnerable, trusting eyes.

It was dragged out of me. 'Would you think about going to Texas with me?'

'I will go anywhere in the world with you.'

I took her face between my palms. 'You know what you're saying?'

Now even my idiot eyes could see her love. 'Oh, yes,' Danisa said. 'I know what I am saying. Now hold me, Brad. Please hold me.'

And I did.

510